Mollie
P9-DNY-667

#1 *NEW YORK TIMES*
BESTSELLING AUTHOR
MARY HIGGINS CLARK

"Not to be read alone at night. . . ." —*Cosmopolitan*

"Truly a mistress of high tension." —*The New Yorker*

"Mary Higgins Clark really knows how to tell a story. . . . She'll keep you up past sandman-time reading through the pages." —*Associated Press*

"Suspenseful . . . thrilling!" —*UPI*

MORE PRAISE FOR
MARY HIGGINS CLARK
AND HER BESTSELLING NOVELS

WHILE MY PRETTY ONE SLEEPS

"A flashlight-under-the-covers book for grownups."
—People

"Great fun to read. . . . You won't be able to stop."
—Cosmopolitan

LOVES MUSIC, LOVES TO DANCE

"The throat-clutching denouement is pure Clark—
inevitable . . . and, ultimately, irresistible."
—People

"Clark grabs you from the git-go. . . . Brilliant."
—USA Today

ALL AROUND THE TOWN

"*All Around the Town* is perfectly orchestrated from
the intriguing beginning to the resounding finish. It's a glittering
addition to a treasure trove of Mary Higgins Clark mysteries."
—Boston Sunday Herald

"Mary Higgins Clark knows how to deliver."
—Philadelphia Inquirer

MARY HIGGINS CLARK

Three *New York Times* Bestselling Novels

Enjoy these suspense-filled collections
from MARY HIGGINS CLARK and WINGS BOOKS

Mary Higgins Clark: Three Complete Novels
Where Are The Children?
A Stranger Is Watching
The Cradle Will Fall

Mary Higgins Clark: Three Complete Novels
Weep No More, My Lady
Stillwatch
A Cry in the Night

MARY HIGGINS CLARK

THREE *NEW YORK TIMES* BESTSELLING NOVELS

WHILE MY PRETTY ONE SLEEPS

LOVES MUSIC, LOVES TO DANCE

ALL AROUND THE TOWN

WINGS BOOKS
NEW YORK

This omnibus was originally published in separate volumes under the titles:

This edition contains the complete and unabridged texts of the original editions. They have been completely reset for this volume.

This 1996 edition is published by Wings Books,
a division of Random House Value Publishing, Inc.,
201 East 50th Street, New York, New York 10022,
by arrangement with Simon & Schuster, Inc.

Random House
New York • Toronto • London • Sydney • Auckland
http://www.randomhouse.com/

Printed and bound in the United States of America

Library of Congress Cataloging-in-Publication Data

Clark, Mary Higgins.
[Novels. Selections]
Mary Higgins Clark, three *New York Times* bestselling novels.
p. cm.
Contents: While my pretty one sleeps — Loves music, loves to dance — All around the town.
ISBN 0-517-18368-4
1. Detective and mystery stories, American. I. Title.
PS3553.L287A6 1996
813′.54—dc20

96-28364
CIP

8 7

CONTENTS

INTRODUCTION
by
MARY HIGGINS CLARK

Perhaps the most common question any writer hears is a very simple one: "Where do you get your ideas?"

In my case the answer is *everywhere*. I used to go regularly to criminal trials and take notes. Sometimes the testimony of a witness would be especially poignant and become an important element in a future book.

It was the testimony of a witness that became the seed of my first novel in this collection, *While My Pretty One Sleeps*. A few years before I wrote it, I was at a trial and observed a prosecution witness, the coworker of a murdered young woman, identify the dress her friend had been wearing on the last day of her life.

The garment was now crumpled and stained. When asked how she could be sure it was the dress the victim had been wearing only hours before she died, the witness said, "It was the first time she wore it. She came over to my desk to show it to me and twirled around in it. She looked so pretty."

That poignant testimony stayed with me. Sometime later when I was chairman of the Third International Crime Congress, I was scurrying around from seminar to seminar making sure that the mikes were working properly, that there were enough chairs, that the speakers had the necessary props. For the most part, I glanced in and ran onto the next room. But then I heard Robert Ressler, Associate Director of Forensic Behavioral Sciences (FBI), lecturing and I stayed.

What he said that day rounded out the plot of *While My Pretty One Sleeps* and inspired *Loves Music, Loves to Dance*.

When discussing homicide investigations, Ressler said, "Every killer leaves his calling card. It's our job to find out what the calling card is."

I was just starting to plot *Pretty One*. I knew I wanted it to be set in New York's fashion world. My mind raced back to the testimony about the dress. A thought flashed through my mind. *Suppose the victim is wearing the clue to the killer?* The story line fell into place that day.

Ressler then went on to discuss serial killers. One of them, a particularly vicious murderer, had found his victims through the personal ads. Ressler concluded his lecture by saying, "Yes, nice people may meet nice people through those ads. They are also a mecca for the losers, the loners, the psychopaths and the serial killers, so be careful."

Five words jumped into my head: *Loves Music, Loves to Dance*. And I knew that book was just waiting to be written, a story about two friends who answer personal ads for a lark. One of them is murdered and the other, seeking the killer, dates the men her friend had seen.

Finally, *All Around the Town*. As I travel across the country on publicity trips for my publisher, I always read local newspapers because often I learn about an interesting case that did not receive national attention. I was fascinated to see that in the northeast, in the south, and in the midwest, there were trials in which a person suffering multiple personality disorder was claiming as a defense that he or she could not be held responsible for the actions of a persona beyond his or her control. I thought: *Suppose a young woman who is a multiple personality is accused of murder, the evidence is overwhelming, and she has no recollection of committing the crime?* That was the seminal moment for *All Around the Town*.

I enjoyed writing these novels. I do hope you enjoy reading them. The people whose stories I tell are nice people whose lives are invaded, the kind of people you might enjoy having as friends.

A last thought. You'll find there's a love interest in each novel. I'm a romantic. That's why after many years of widowhood I'm remarrying. His name is John Conheeney. Several of his friends have asked if he was the model for Myles Kearny, a main character in *While My Pretty One Sleeps*. The answer is no. I didn't know John when I was writing that book. But the physical description suits him. And, like Myles, he's a stand-up guy.

WHILE MY PRETTY ONE SLEEPS

FOR MY NEWEST GRANDCHILDREN,
COURTNEY MARILYN CLARK
AND
DAVID FREDERICK CLARK,
WITH CONTINUING LOVE,
AMUSEMENT AND DELIGHT

1

He drove cautiously up the Thruway toward Morrison State Park. The thirty-five-mile trip from Manhattan to Rockland County had been a nightmare. Even though it was six o'clock, there was no sense of approaching dawn. The snow that had begun during the night had steadily increased until now it was beating relentlessly against the windshield. The overhead clouds, heavy and gray, were like enormous balloons pumped to the breaking point. The forecast had been for two inches, with "precipitation tapering off after midnight." As usual the weatherman had been wrong.

But he was near the entrance to the park, and, with the storm, there probably wouldn't be anyone hiking or jogging. He'd passed a State Trooper ten miles back, but the car had rushed past him, lights flashing, probably on the way to an accident somewhere. Certainly the cops had no reason to even think about the contents of his trunk, no reason to suspect that under a pile of luggage a plastic bag containing the body of a prominent sixty-one-year-old writer, Ethel Lambston, was wedged in a space-defying squeeze against the spare tire.

He turned off the Thruway and drove the short distance to the parking lot. As he had hoped, it was nearly empty. Only a few cars were scattered around and they were coated with snow. Some damn fools camping out, he supposed. The trick was not to bump into them.

He glanced around carefully as he left the car. No one. The snow was piling in drifts. It would cover the tracks when he left, cover any signs of where he was going to put her. With any luck, by the time she was discovered there wouldn't be much left to find.

First he made his way to the spot alone. His hearing was keen. Now he tried to maximize it, to force it to filter past the sighing of the wind and the creaking of the already heavy branches. Down this way there was a steep path. Past it and on a sharp incline was a pile of rocks layered by heavy loose stones. Very few people bothered to climb there. It was off-limits for riders—the stable didn't want the suburban housewives who were its main customers breaking their necks.

A year ago he had happened to be curious enough to make that climb, and had rested on a boulder-sized rock. His hand had slid across the rock and he'd felt the opening behind it. Not a cave entrance, but a natural formation like the mouth of a cave. Even then, the thought had passed his mind that it would be a great place to hide something.

It was exhausting to reach with the snow turning icy, but, slipping and sliding, he made the climb. The space was still there, a little smaller than he remembered, but he could force the body in. The next step was the worst. Going back to the car, he would have to take infinite caution to avoid any chance of being observed. He'd parked at an angle so that no one who happened to drive in would have a direct view of what he was removing from the trunk, and anyhow a black plastic bag in itself wasn't suspicious.

In life Ethel had been deceptively slim. But as he picked up the plastic-shrouded body he reflected that those expensive outfits had concealed a heavy-boned frame. He tried to heave the bag over his shoulder, but, perverse in death as she had been in life, Ethel must have begun the process of rigor mortis. Her body refused to slide into manageable lines. In the end, he half carried, half dragged the bag as far as the incline, then sheer adrenaline gave him the strength to haul her up the sloping, slippery rocks to the spot.

His original plan had been to leave her in the bag. But at the last minute he changed his mind. Forensics units were getting too damn smart. They could find evidence on anything, fibers from clothes or carpets or human hair that no eye would notice.

Ignoring the cold as the gusting wind seared his forehead and the pellets of snow turned his cheeks and chin into a chunk of ice, he placed the bag in position over the cave and began to rip. It would not give. Two-ply, he thought grimly, remembering all the commercials. Savagely he tugged at it and then grimaced as the bag gave and Ethel's body came into view.

The white wool suit was stained with blood. The collar of her blouse was caught in the gaping hole in her throat. One eye was slightly open. In the gathering dawn it seemed less sightless than contemplative. The mouth that never knew repose in Ethel's life was pursed as though about to start another one of her interminable sentences. The last one she ever got to spit out had been her fatal mistake, he told himself with grim satisfaction.

Even with gloves on, he hated touching her. She'd been dead nearly fourteen hours. It seemed to him there was a faint, sweet odor coming from her body. With sudden disgust he shoved her corpse down and began wedging stones on top of it. The opening was deeper than he'd realized, and the stones dropped neatly in place over her. A casual climber wouldn't dislodge them.

The job was finished. The blowing snow had already covered up his footsteps. Ten minutes after he got out of here, all trace of him and the presence of the car would be obliterated.

He crushed the shredded plastic into a wadded ball and began hurrying toward the car. Now he was frantic to leave, to be far from this exposure to discovery. At the border of the parking lot, he waited. The same cars were there, still untouched. There were no fresh tracks in the lot.

Five minutes later, he was back on the Thruway, the bloodied, torn bag that had been Ethel's shroud jammed under the spare tire. Now there was plenty of room for her suitcases and carry-on and purse.

The roadway was icy now, the commuter traffic beginning, but in a few hours he'd be back in New York, back to sanity and reality. He made his final stop, a lake he remembered not far from the Thruway, that was too polluted now for fishing. It was a good place to dump Ethel's purse and luggage. All four pieces were heavy. The lake was deep, and he knew they'd sink and get caught in the mass of junk that rested on the bottom. People even dumped old cars here.

He tossed Ethel's belongings as far as he could heave them and watched as they disappeared under the dark-gray water. Now the only thing left to do was to get rid of the torn, bloodstained wad of plastic. He decided to stop at a garbage bin when he got off the West Side Highway. It would be lost in the mountain of trash carted off tomorrow morning.

It took three hours to get back into the city. The driving became more treacherous and he tried to keep his distance from other cars. He didn't need a fender bender. Months from now no one would have any reason to know that he'd been out of the city today.

It worked according to plan. He stopped for a split second on Ninth Avenue and got rid of the plastic bag.

At eight o'clock he was delivering the car back to the gas station on Tenth Avenue that rented old cars as a sideline. Cash only. He knew they didn't keep records.

At ten o'clock, freshly showered and changed, he was in his place, gulping straight bourbon and trying to shake the sudden chilling attack of nerves. His mind went over every instant of the time that had elapsed since he'd stood in Ethel's apartment yesterday and listened to her sarcasm, her ridicule, her threats.

Then she'd known. The antique dagger from her desk in his hand. Her face filled with fear and she'd started to back away.

The exhilaration of slashing that throat, of watching her stumble backward through the archway to the kitchen and collapse onto the ceramic-tile floor.

He still was amazed at how calm he'd been. He'd bolted the door so that by some crazy trick of fate the superintendent or a friend with a key couldn't walk in. Everyone knew how eccentric Ethel could be. If someone with a key found that the door was bolted, they'd assume she didn't want to be bothered answering.

Then he had stripped his clothes off down to his underwear and put on his gloves. Ethel had been planning to go away to write a book. If he could get her out of here, people would think she'd left on her own. She wouldn't be missed for weeks, even months.

Now, gulping a mouthful of bourbon, he thought about how he had selected clothes from her closet, changing her from the blood-soaked caftan, pulling her pantyhose on, slipping her arms into the blouse and the jacket, buttoning the skirt, taking off her jewelry, forcing her feet into pumps. He winced as he remembered the way he'd held her up so that blood spurted over the blouse and the suit. But it was necessary. When she was found, if she *was* found, they had to think she'd died in that outfit.

He had remembered to cut out the labels that would have meant immediate identification. He had found the long plastic bag in the closet, probably returned by a cleaner on an evening gown. He had forced her into it, then cleaned the bloodstains that had spattered on the Oriental throw rug, washed the kitchen tile with Clorox, packed the suitcases with clothes and accessories, all the while working frantically against time. . . .

He refilled the glass to the brim with bourbon, remembering when the phone had rung. The answering machine had come on and the sound of Ethel's rapid speech pattern. "Leave a message. I'll get back when and if I feel like it." It had made his nerves scream. The caller broke the connection and he'd turned off the machine. He didn't want a record of people calling, and perhaps remembering broken appointments later.

Ethel had the ground-floor apartment of a four-story brownstone. Her private entrance was to the left of the stoop that led to the main entry. In effect her door was shielded from the view of anyone walking along the street. The only period of vulnerability was the dozen steps from her door to the curb.

In the apartment, he'd felt relatively safe. The hardest part had come when, after he hid Ethel's tightly wrapped body and luggage under her bed, he opened the front door. The air had been raw and damp, the snow obviously about to begin falling. The wind had cut a sharp path into the apartment. He'd closed the door immediately. It was only a few minutes past six. The streets were busy with people coming home from work. He'd waited nearly two hours more, then slipped out, double-locked the door and gone to the cheap car rental. He'd driven back to Ethel's apartment. Luck was with him. He was able to park almost directly in front of the brownstone. It was dark and the street was deserted.

In two trips he had the luggage in the trunk. The third trip was the worst. He'd pulled his coat collar up, put on an old cap he'd found on the floor of the rented car and carried the plastic bag with Ethel's body out of the apartment. The moment when he slammed the trunk down had brought the first sense that he'd surely make it to safety.

It had been hell to go back into the apartment, to make certain that there was no trace of blood, no sign that he'd been there. Every nerve shrieked at him to get to the state park, to dump the body, but he knew that was crazy. The police might notice someone trying to get into the park at night. Instead he left the car on the street six blocks away, followed his normal routine and at 5 A.M. set out with the very early commuters. . . .

It was all right now, he told himself. He was *safe!*

It was just as he was draining the last warming sip of bourbon that he realized the one ghastly mistake he had made, and knew exactly who would almost inevitably detect it.

Neeve Kearny.

2

The radio went on at six-thirty. Neeve reached out her right hand, groping for the button to tune out the insistently cheery voice of the newscaster, then stopped as the import of what he was saying sifted into her consciousness. Eight inches of snow had fallen on the city during the night. Do not drive unless absolutely necessary. Alternate-side-of-the-street parking suspended. School closings to be announced. Forecast was for the snow to continue until late afternoon.

Terrific, Neeve thought as she leaned back and pulled the comforter around her face. She hated missing her usual morning jog. Then she winced, thinking of the alterations that had to be completed today. Two of the seamstresses lived in New Jersey and might not get in. Which meant she'd better get to the shop early and see how she could juggle the schedule of Betty, the only other fitter. Betty lived at Eighty-second and Second and would walk the six blocks to the shop no matter how bad the weather.

Hating the moment she abandoned the cozy warmth of the bed, she threw back the covers, hurried across the room and reached into her closet for the ancient terrycloth robe that her father, Myles, insisted was a relic of the Crusades. "If any of the women who spent those fancy prices buying your dresses could see you in that rag, they'd go back to shopping in Klein's."

"Klein's closed twenty years ago, and anyhow if they saw me in this rag they'd think I'm eccentric," she'd told him. "That would add to the mystique."

She tied the belt around her waist, experiencing the usual fleeting wish that she had inherited her mother's pencil-thin frame instead of the square-shouldered, rangy body of her Celtic forebears, then brushed back the curly coal-black hair that was a trademark of the Rossetti family. She also had the Rossetti eyes, sherry-colored irises, darker at the edges so they blazed against the whites, wide and questioning under sooty lashes. But her skin tone was the milk white of the Celts, with a dotting of freckles against the straight nose. The generous mouth and strong teeth were those of Myles Kearny.

Six years ago when she graduated from college and persuaded Myles that she had no intention of moving out, he'd insisted she redo her bedroom. By haunting Sotheby's and Christie's, she'd assembled an eclectic assortment of a brass bed, an antique armoire and a Bombay chest, a Victorian chaise and an old Persian rug that glowed like Joseph's coat. Now the quilt and the pillows and the dust ruffle were stark white; the reupholstered chaise was covered in turquoise velvet, the same turquoise tone that ribboned through the rug; the stark-white walls were a background for the fine paintings and prints that had come from her mother's family. *Women's Wear Daily* had photographed her in the room, calling it cheerfully elegant, with the peerless Neeve Kearny touch.

Neeve wiggled her feet into the padded slippers Myles called her booties and yanked up the shade. She decided that the weatherman didn't have to be a genius to say this was an important snowstorm. The view from her room in Schwab House at Seventy-fourth Street and Riverside Drive was directly over the Hudson, but now she could barely make out the buildings across the river in New Jersey. The Henry Hudson Parkway was snow-covered and already filled with cautiously moving traffic. The long-suffering commuters had undoubtedly started into town early.

Myles was already in the kitchen and had the coffeepot on. Neeve kissed him on the cheek, willing herself not to remark on how tired he looked. That meant he hadn't slept well again. If only he'd break down and take an occasional sleeping pill, she thought. "How's the Legend?" she asked him. Since his retirement last year, the newspapers constantly referred to him as "New York's legendary Police Commissioner." He hated it.

He ignored the question, glanced at her and assumed an expression of amazement. "Don't tell me you're not all set to run around Central Park?" he exclaimed. "What's a foot of snow to dauntless Neeve?"

For years they had jogged together. Now that he could no longer run, he worried about her early-morning sprints. But then, she suspected, he never *wasn't* worrying about her.

She reached into the refrigerator for the pitcher of orange juice. Without asking she poured out a tall glass for him, a short one for herself, and began to make toast. Myles used to enjoy a hearty breakfast, but now bacon and eggs were off his diet. So were cheese and beef and, as he put it, "half the food that makes you look forward to a meal." His massive heart attack had restricted his diet as well as ending his career.

They sat in companionable silence, by unspoken consent splitting the morning *Times*. But when she glanced up, Neeve realized that Myles wasn't reading. He was staring at the paper without seeing it. The toast and the juice were untouched in front of him. Only the coffee showed any sign of having been tasted. Neeve put section two of the paper down.

"All right," she said. "Let me have it. Is it that you feel rotten? For heaven's sake, I hope you know enough by now not to play the silent sufferer."

"No, I'm all right," Myles said. "Or at least if you mean have I been having chest pains, the answer is no." He tossed the paper onto the floor and reached for his coffee. "Nicky Sepetti gets out of jail today."

Neeve gasped. "But I thought they refused him parole last year?"

"Last year was the fourth time he came up. He's served every day of his sentence, less time for good behavior. He'll be back in New York tonight." Cold hatred hardened Myles's face.

"Dad, take a look at yourself in the mirror. Keep it up and you'll bring on another heart attack." Neeve realized her hands were trembling. She gripped the table, hoping Myles would not notice and think she was afraid. "I don't care whether or not Sepetti made that threat when he was sentenced. You spent years trying to connect him to . . ." Her voice trailed off, then continued, "And not one shred of evidence has ever come up to tie him to it. And for God's sake don't you dare start worrying about me because he's back on the street."

Her father had been the U.S. Attorney who put the head of the Sepetti Mafia family, Nicky Sepetti, behind bars. At the sentencing, Nicky had been asked if he had anything to say. He'd pointed at Myles. "I hear they think you done such a good job on me, they made you Police Commissioner. Congratulations. That was a nice article in the *Post* about you and your family. Take good care of your wife and kid. They might need a little protection."

Two weeks later, Myles was sworn in as Police Commissioner. A month later, the body of his young wife, Neeve's mother, thirty-four-year-old Renata Rossetti Kearny, was found in Central Park with her throat cut. The crime was never solved.

Neeve did not argue when Myles insisted that he call for a cab to take her to work. "You can't walk in that snow," he told her.

"It isn't the snow, and we both know it," she retorted. As she kissed him goodbye, she put her arms around his neck and hugged him. "Myles, the only thing that we both have to worry about is your health. Nicky Sepetti isn't going to want to go back to prison. I bet if he knows how to pray he's hoping that nothing happens to me for a long, long time. There isn't another person in New York besides you who doesn't think some petty crook attacked Mother and killed her when she wouldn't give up her purse. She probably started screaming at him in Italian and he panicked. So please forget Nicky Sepetti and leave to heaven whoever took Mother from us. Okay? Promise?"

She was only slightly reassured by his nod. "Now get out of here," he said. "The cab meter's ticking and my game shows will be starting any minute."

The snowplows had made what Myles would call a lick-and-a-promise attempt to partially clear the accumulated snow from West End Avenue. As the car crawled and slid along the slippery streets and turned onto the west-to-east transverse road through the park at Eighty-first Street, Neeve found herself wishing the fruitless "if only." If only her mother's murderer had been found. Perhaps in time the loss would have healed for Myles as it had for her. Instead for him it was an open wound, always festering. He was always blaming himself for somehow failing Renata. All these years he had agonized that he should have taken the threat seriously. He could not bear the knowledge that with the immense resources of the New York City Police Department at his command, he had been unable to learn the identity of the thug who had carried out what he was convinced had been Sepetti's order. It was the one unfulfilled need in his life—to find that killer, to make him and Sepetti pay for Renata's death.

Neeve shivered. The cab was cold. The driver must have been glancing in the rearview mirror, because he said, "Sorry, lady, the heater don't work so good."

"It's all right." She turned her head to avoid getting into a conversation. The "if onlys" would not stop running through her mind. If only the killer had been found and convicted years ago, Myles might have been able to get on with his life. At sixty-eight he was still an attractive man, and over the years there had been plenty of women who had a special smile for the lean, broad-shouldered Commissioner with his thick head of prematurely white hair, his intense blue eyes and his unexpectedly warm smile.

She was so deep in thought she did not even notice when the cab stopped in front of the shop. "Neeve's Place" was written in scroll on the ivory-and-blue awning. The display windows that faced both Madison Avenue and Eighty-fourth Street were wet with snowdrops, giving a shimmering look to the flawlessly cut silk spring dresses on the languidly posed mannequins. It had been her idea to order umbrellas that looked like parasols. Sheer raincoats that picked up one color in the print were draped over the mannequins' shoulders. Neeve joked that it was her "don't-be-plain-in-the-rain" look, but it had proved wildly successful.

"You work here?" the cabby asked as she paid him. "Looks expensive."

Neeve nodded noncommittally as she thought, I own this place, my friend. It was a realization that still thrilled her. Six years ago the previous shop at this location had gone bankrupt. It was her father's old friend the famous designer Anthony della Salva who had bullied her into taking it over. "So you're young," he'd said, dropping the heavy Italian accent that was now part of his persona. "That's a plus. You've been working in fashion since you got your first after-school job. Better yet, you've got the know-how, the flair. I'll lend you the money to get started. If it doesn't work, I can use the write-off, but it'll work. You've got what it takes to make a go of it. Besides, I need another place to sell my clothes." That was the last thing Sal needed, and they both knew it, but she was grateful.

Myles had been dead set against her borrowing from Sal. But she had jumped at the chance. Something she had inherited from Renata besides her hair and eyes was a highly developed fashion sense. Last year she had paid back Sal's loan, insisting on adding interest at money-market rates.

She was not surprised to find Betty already at work in the sewing room. Betty's head was bent down, her frown of concentration now a permanent set of lines on her forehead and between her brows. Her hands, slender and wrinkled, handled a needle and thread with the skill of a surgeon. She was hemming an intricately beaded blouse. Her blatantly dyed copper-colored hair accentuated the parchment-thin skin on her face. Neeve hated to realize that Betty was past seventy. She didn't want to visualize the day when she decided to retire.

"Figured I'd better get a jump on things," Betty announced. "We've got an awful lot of pickups today."

Neeve pulled off her gloves and unwound her scarf. "Don't I know it. And Ethel Lambston insists she has to have everything by this afternoon."

"I know. I've got her stuff ready to do when I finish this. It wouldn't be worth listening to her jabbering if every rag she bought isn't ready to go."

"Everybody should be such a good customer," Neeve observed mildly.

Betty nodded. "I suppose so. And, by the way, I'm glad you talked Mrs. Yates into this outfit. That other one she tried on made her look like a grazing cow."

"It also was fifteen hundred dollars more, but I couldn't let her have it. Sooner or later she'd have taken a good look at herself in the mirror. The sequin top is enough. She needs a soft, full skirt."

A surprising number of shoppers braved the snow and slippery sidewalks to come into the store. Two of the saleswomen hadn't made it, so Neeve spent the day on the sales floor. It was the part she enjoyed most about the business, but in the past year she'd been forced to limit herself to handling only a few personal clients.

At noon she went into her office at the back of the shop for a deli sandwich and coffee and dialed home.

Myles sounded more like himself. "I would have won fourteen

thousand dollars and a Champion pickup truck on *Wheel of Fortune*," he announced. "I won so much I might even have had to take that six-hundred-dollar plaster-of-paris Dalmatian they have the gall to call a prize."

"Well, you certainly sound better," Neeve observed.

"I've been talking to the boys downtown. They've got good people keeping tabs on Sepetti. They say he's pretty sick and hasn't much fight left." There was satisfaction in Myles's voice.

"And they also probably reminded you that they don't think he had anything to do with Mother's death." She did not wait for an answer. "It's a good night for pasta. There's plenty of sauce in the freezer. Yank it out, okay?"

Neeve hung up feeling somewhat reassured. She swallowed the last bite of the turkey sandwich, gulped down the rest of the coffee and went back to the sales floor. Three of the six dressing rooms were occupied. With a practiced eye, she took in every detail of the shop.

The Madison Avenue entrance opened into the accessory area. She knew that one of the key reasons for her success was the availability of jewelry, purses, shoes, hats and scarves so that a woman purchasing a dress or a suit didn't have to hunt elsewhere for accessories. The interior of the shop was in shadings of ivory, with accents of blush pink on the upholstered sofas and chairs. Sportswear and separates were contained in roomy alcoves two steps up from the showcases. Except for the exquisitely gowned display mannequins there was no clothing in sight. A potential customer was escorted to a chair, and the sales clerk brought out dresses and gowns and suits for her selection.

It had been Sal who advised Neeve to go that way. "Otherwise you'll have klutzes yanking clothes off the racks. Start exclusive, honey, and stay exclusive," he had said, and as usual he was right.

The ivory and blush had been Neeve's decision. "When a woman looks in the mirror, I don't want the background fighting what I'm trying to sell," she'd told the interior designer who wanted her to go into great splashes of color.

As the afternoon wore on, fewer clients came in. At three o'clock Betty emerged from the sewing room. "Lambston's stuff is ready," she told Neeve.

Neeve assembled Ethel Lambston's order herself. All spring clothes. Ethel was a sixtyish free-lance writer with one best-seller to her credit. "I write on every subject under the sun," she had breathlessly confided to Neeve on the opening day of the shop. "I take the fresh approach, the inquiring look. I'm every woman seeing something for the first time or from a new angle. I write about sex and relationships and animals and nursing homes and organizations and real estate and how to be a volunteer and political parties and . . ." She had run out of breath, her navy-blue eyes snapping, her white-blond hair flying around her face. "The trouble is that I work so hard at what I do, I don't have a minute for myself. If I buy a black dress, I end up wearing brown shoes with it. Say, you have everything here. What a good idea. Put me together."

In the last six years, Ethel Lambston had become a valuable customer. She insisted Neeve pick out every stitch she bought as well as choose accessories and compile lists to tell her what went with what. She lived on the ground floor of a brownstone on West Eighty-second Street, and Neeve stopped there occasionally to help Ethel decide what clothes to keep from year to year and what to give away.

The last time Neeve had gone over Ethel's wardrobe was three weeks ago. The next day Ethel came in and ordered the new outfits. "I've almost finished that fashion article I interviewed you about," she'd told Neeve. "A lot of people are going to be mad at me when it comes out, but you'll love it. I gave you lots of free publicity."

When she made her selections she and Neeve had differed on only one suit. Neeve had started to take it away. "I don't want to sell you that. It's a Gordon Steuber. I refuse to handle anything of his. This one should have gone back. I cannot stand that man."

Ethel had burst out laughing. "Wait till you read what I wrote about him. I crucified him. But I want the suit. His clothes look good on me."

Now, as Neeve carefully placed the garments in heavy protective bags, she felt her lips narrow at the sight of the Steuber outfit. Six weeks ago, the daily maid at the shop had asked her to speak to a friend who was in trouble. The friend, a Mexican, told Neeve about working in an illegal sweatshop in the South Bronx that was owned by Gordon Steuber. "We don't have green cards. He threatens to turn us in. Last week I was sick. He fired me and my daughter and won't pay what he owes us."

The young woman didn't look to be more than in her late twenties. "Your daughter!" Neeve had exclaimed. "How old is she?"

"Fourteen."

Neeve had canceled the order she'd placed with Gordon Steuber and sent him a copy of the Elizabeth Barrett Browning poem which had helped change the child-labor laws in England. She underlined the stanza "But the young, young children, oh my brothers, they are weeping bitterly."

Someone in Steuber's office had tipped off *Women's Wear Daily.* The editors printed the poem on the front page next to Neeve's scathing letter to Steuber and called on other retailers to boycott manufacturers who were breaking the law.

Anthony della Salva had been upset. "Neeve, the word is that Steuber has a lot more than sweatshops to hide. Thanks to what you stirred up, the Feds are nosing around his income-tax returns."

"Wonderful," Neeve had retorted. "If he's cheating at that too, I hope they catch him."

Well, she decided as she straightened the Steuber suit on the hanger, this will be the last thing of his that goes out of my shop. She found herself anxious to read Ethel's fashion article. She knew it was due to come out soon in *Contemporary Woman,* the magazine where Ethel was a contributing editor.

Finally, Neeve made up the lists for Ethel. Blue silk evening suit; wear white silk blouse; jewelry in box A. Pink-and-gray ensemble; gray pumps, matching purse; jewelry in box B. Black cocktail dress . . . There were eight outfits in all. With the accessories they came to nearly seven thousand dollars. Ethel spent that amount three or four times a year. She'd confided to Neeve that when she was divorced twenty-two years before, she'd gotten a big settlement and invested it wisely. "And I collect a thousand bucks a month alimony from him for life," she'd laughed. "At the time we broke up, he was riding high. He told his lawyers it was worth every cent to get rid of me. In court, he said that if I ever marry again the guy should be stone deaf. Maybe I'd have given him a break if it weren't for that crack. He's remarried and has three kids, and ever since Columbus Avenue got classy his bar's been in trouble. Every once in a while he phones and begs me to let him off the hook, but I tell him I still haven't found anyone who's stone deaf."

At that moment Neeve had been prepared to dislike Ethel. Then Ethel had added wistfully, "I always wanted a family. We separated when I was thirty-seven. The five years we were married, he wouldn't give me a child."

Neeve had made it her business to read Ethel's articles and had quickly realized that even though Ethel might be a talkative, seemingly scatterbrained woman, she was also an excellent writer. No matter what subject she tackled, it was obvious her research was massive.

With the help of the receptionist, Neeve stapled the bottoms of the garment bags. The jewelry and the shoes were packed in individual boxes and then gathered in ivory-and-pink cartons with "Neeve's Place" scrolled along the sides. With a sigh of relief, she dialed Ethel's apartment.

There was no answer. Nor had Ethel left her answering machine on. Neeve decided that Ethel would probably arrive any minute, breathless and with a taxi waiting outside.

At four o'clock there were no customers in the shop and Neeve sent everyone home. Darn Ethel, she thought. She would have liked to go home as well. The snow was still falling steadily. At this rate, she'd never get a cab herself later. She tried Ethel at four-thirty, at five, at five-thirty. Now what? she wondered. Then she had an idea. She'd wait until six-thirty, the usual closing time, then deliver Ethel's things on her way home. Surely she could leave them with the superintendent. That way if Ethel had imminent travel plans, she'd have her new wardrobe.

The taxicab-company starter was reluctant to accept her call. "We're telling all our cars to come in, lady. Driving's a mess. But gimme your name and phone number." When he heard her name, the starter's tone changed. "Neeve Kearny! Why didn't you tell me you're the Commissioner's daughter? You bet we'll get you home."

The cab arrived at twenty of seven. They inched through the now almost impassable streets. The driver was not pleased to make an additional stop. "Lady, I can't wait to pack it in."

There was no answer at Ethel's apartment. Neeve rang in vain for the superintendent. There were four other apartments in the brownstone, but she had no idea who lived in them and couldn't risk leaving the clothes with strangers. Finally she tore a check out of her book and on the back of it wrote a note to slip under Ethel's door: "I have your purchases. Call me when you get in." She put her home phone number under her signature. Then, struggling under the weight of the boxes and bags, she got back into the cab.

Inside Ethel Lambston's apartment, a hand reached for the note Neeve had pushed under the door, read it, tossed it aside and resumed his periodic search for the hundred-dollar bills that Ethel regularly squirreled away under the carpets or between the cushions of the couch, the money she gleefully referred to as "Seamus the wimp's alimony."

* * *

Myles Kearny could not shake off the nagging worry that had been growing in him for weeks. His grandmother used to have a kind of sixth sense. "I have a feeling," she would say. "There's trouble coming." Myles could vividly remember when he was ten and his grandmother had received a picture of his cousin in Ireland. She had cried, "He has death in his eyes." Two hours later the phone had rung. His cousin had been killed in an accident.

Seventeen years ago, Myles had shrugged off Nicky Sepetti's threat. The Mafia had its own code. They never went after the wives or children of its enemies. And then Renata had died. At three o'clock in the afternoon, walking through Central Park to pick up Neeve at Sacred Heart Academy, she'd been murdered. It had been a cold, windy November day. The park was deserted. There were no witnesses to tell who had lured or forced Renata off the path and into the area behind the museum.

He'd been in his office when the principal of Sacred Heart phoned at four-thirty. Mrs. Kearny had not come to pick up Neeve. They'd phoned, but she was not at home. Was anything wrong? When he hung up the phone, Myles had known with sickening certainty that something terrible had happened to Renata. Ten minutes later the police were searching Central Park. His car was on the way uptown when the call came in that her body had been found.

When he reached the park, a cordon of policemen was holding back the curious and the sensation seekers. The media were already there. He remembered how the flashbulbs had blinded him as he walked toward the spot where her body was lying. Herb Schwartz, his deputy commissioner, was there. "Don't look at her now, Myles," he begged.

He'd shaken Herb's arm off, knelt on the frozen ground and pulled back the blanket they'd put over her. She might have been sleeping. Her face still lovely in that final repose, none of the expression of terror that he'd seen stamped on so many victims' faces. Her eyes were closed. Had she closed them in that final moment or had Herb closed them? At first he thought she was wearing a red scarf. Denial. He was a seasoned viewer of victims, but at that moment his professionalism abandoned him. He didn't want to see that someone had slashed down the length of her jugular vein, then slit her throat. The collar of the white ski jacket she'd been wearing had turned crimson from her blood. The hood had slipped back, and her face was framed by those masses of jet-black hair. Her red ski pants, the red of her blood, the white jacket and the hardened snow under her body—even in death she'd looked like a fashion photograph.

He'd wanted to hold her against him, to breathe life into her, but he knew he should not move her. He'd contented himself with kissing the cheeks and the eyes and the lips. His hand grazed her neck and came away bloodstained, and he'd thought, We met in blood, we part in blood.

He'd been a twenty-one-year-old rookie cop on Pearl Harbor Day, and the next morning he'd enlisted in the Army. Three years later he was with Mark Clark's Fifth Army in the battle for Italy. They'd taken it town by town. In Pontici he'd gone into a church that seemed to be deserted. The next moment he'd heard an explosion, and blood had gushed from his forehead. He'd spun around and seen a German soldier crouched behind the altar in the sacristy. He managed to shoot him before he passed out.

He came to, feeling a small hand shaking him. "Come with me," a voice whispered in his ear in heavily accented English. He could barely think through the waves of pain in his head. His eyes were crusted with dried blood. Outside it was pitch black. The sounds of gunfire were far away, to the left. The child—he realized somehow it was a child—led him down deserted alleys. He remembered wondering where she was taking him, why she was alone. He heard the scraping of his combat boots against the stone steps, the sound of a rusty gate opening, then an intense, rapidly speaking whisper, the child's explanation. Now she was speaking Italian. He couldn't understand what she was saying. Then he felt an arm supporting him, the feeling of being lowered onto a bed. He passed out and awoke intermittently, aware of gentle hands bathing and bandaging his head. His first clear recollection was of an army doctor examining him. "You don't know how lucky you were," he was told. "They drove us back yesterday. It wasn't good for the ones who didn't make it out."

After the war, Myles had taken advantage of the GI Bill of Rights and gone to college. The Fordham Rose Hill campus was only a few miles from where he'd grown up in the Bronx. His father, a police captain, had been skeptical. "It was all we could do to get *you* through high school," he'd observed. "Not that you weren't blessed with a brain, but you never chose to place your nose between the covers of a book."

Four years later, after graduating magna cum laude, Myles went on to law school. His father had been delighted but warned, "You've still got a cop in you. Don't forget that cop when you get all your fancy degrees."

Law school. The DA's office. Private practice. It was then he'd realized it was too easy for a good lawyer to get a guilty defendant off. He didn't have the stomach for it. He'd jumped at the chance to become a U.S. Attorney.

That was 1958. He'd been thirty-seven. Over the years he'd dated plenty of girls and watched them marry off, one by one. But somehow anytime he'd come close, a voice had whispered in his ear, "There is more. Wait a bit."

The notion of going back to Italy was a gradual one. "Being shot at through Europe is not the equivalent of the grand tour," his mother told him when, at a dinner home, he tentatively mentioned his plans. And then she'd asked, "Why don't you look up that family that hid you in Pontici? I doubt you were in any condition to thank them at that time."

He still blessed his mother for that advice. Because when he knocked at their door, Renata had opened it. Renata who was now twenty-three, not ten. Renata tall and slender, so that he was barely half a head over her. Renata who incredibly said, "I know who you are. I brought you home that night."

"How could you have remembered?" he asked.

"My father took my picture with you before they took you away. I've always kept it on my dresser."

They were married three weeks later. The next eleven years were the happiest of his life.

Myles walked over to the window and looked out. Technically, spring had arrived a week ago, but nobody had bothered to pass on the word to Mother Nature. He tried not to remember how much Renata had loved to walk in the snow.

He rinsed the coffee cup and the salad plate and put them into the dishwasher. If all the tunas in the world suddenly vanished, what would people on a diet have for lunch? he wondered. Maybe they'd go back to good, thick hamburgers. The notion made his mouth water. But it did remind him that he was supposed to defrost the pasta sauce.

At six o'clock he began to prepare dinner. He brought out the makings for a salad from the refrigerator and with skillful hands broke lettuce, chopped scallions, sliced green peppers into razor-thin bands of green. Unconsciously he smiled to himself, remembering how, growing up, he'd thought a salad was tomato and lettuce globbed with mayonnaise. His mother had been a wonderful woman, but her calling in life was clearly not as a chef. She'd also cooked meat until "all the germs were killed," so that a pork chop or a steak was dry and hard enough to be karated instead of cut.

It was Renata who had introduced him to the delights of subtle flavors, the joys of pasta, the delicacy of salmon, tangy salads that hinted of garlic. Neeve had inherited her mother's culinary skills, but Myles acknowledged to himself that along the way he'd learned to make a damn good salad.

At ten of seven he began to worry actively about Neeve. Probably few taxis on the road. Dear God, don't let her walk through the park on a night like this. He tried calling the shop, but there was no answer. By the time she struggled in with the bundles of clothes over her arm and dragging the boxes, he'd been ready to call headquarters and ask the police to check the park for her. He clamped his lips together before he admitted that.

Instead as he took the boxes from her arms he succeeded in looking surprised. "Is it Christmas again?" he asked. "From Neeve to Neeve with love? Have you used up today's profits on yourself?"

"Don't be such a wise guy, Myles," Neeve said crossly. "I tell you, Ethel Lambston may be a good customer, but she's also a royal pain in the neck." As she dropped the boxes onto the couch she skimmed through the tale of her attempt to deliver Ethel's clothing.

Myles looked alarmed. "Ethel Lambston! Isn't she the ditsy you had at the Christmas party?"

"You've got it." On impulse, Neeve had invited Ethel to the annual Christmas party she and Myles gave in the apartment. After pinning Bishop Stanton to the wall and explaining why the Catholic Church was no longer relevant in the twentieth century, Ethel had realized Myles was a widower and hadn't left his side all evening.

"I don't care if you have to camp outside her door for the next two years," Myles warned. "Don't let that woman set foot in this place again."

3

It was not Denny Adler's idea of a good time to be breaking his neck for minimum wages plus tips at the deli on East Eighty-third Street and Lexington. But Denny had a problem. He was on probation. His probation officer, Mike Toohey, was a swine who loved the authority vested in him by the State of New York. Denny knew that if he didn't have a job, he couldn't spend a dime without Toohey asking him what he was living on, so he worked and hated every minute of it.

He rented a dingy room in a fleabag on First Avenue and One Hundred and Fifth Street. What the parole officer *didn't* know was that most of Denny's time away from the job was spent panhandling on the street. He changed both the locations and his disguises every few days. Sometimes he'd dress like a bum, put on filthy clothes and shabby sneakers, smear dirt on his face and hair. He'd prop up against a building and hold a torn piece of cardboard which read, "HELP, I'M HUNGRY."

That was one of the better sucker baits.

Other times he'd put on faded khakis and a gray wig. He'd wear dark glasses, carry a cane, pin a sign to his coat, "HOMELESS VET." At his feet a bowl quickly filled with quarters and dimes.

Denny picked up a lot of loose pocket change that way. Nothing like the thrill of planning a real job, but it was something to keep his hand in. Only once or twice, when he'd come across a wino with a few bucks, had he succumbed to the need to waste someone. But the cops didn't give a damn when a wino or a bum was beaten or stabbed, so it was practically risk-free.

His probation would be finished in three months, then he'd be able to drop out of sight and decide where the best action was to be found. Even the parole officer was relaxing. On Saturday morning, Toohey phoned him at the deli. Denny could just picture Mike, his puny frame hunched over the desk in his sloppy office. "I've been talking to your boss, Denny. He tells me you're one of his most dependable workers."

"Thank you, sir." If Denny had been standing in front of Toohey's desk he would have twisted his hands in an attitude of nervous gratitude. He'd have forced moisture into his pale-hazel eyes and manipulated his narrow lips to an eager grin. Instead he silently mouthed an obscenity into the phone.

"Denny, you can skip reporting to me on Monday. I've got a heavy schedule and you're one of the men I know I can trust. I'll see you next week."

"Yes, sir." Denny hung up the phone. A caricature of a smile slashed creases below his prominent cheekbones. Half of his thirty-seven years had been spent in custody, beginning with his first break-in when he was twelve. A permanent grayish prison pallor was ground into his skin.

He glanced around the deli, at the sickeningly cute ice-cream tables and wire chairs, the white Formica counter, the luncheon-special signs, the well-dressed regulars deep in their newspapers over French toast or corn flakes. He was interrupted in his dream of what he'd like to do to this place and to Mike Toohey, by the manager shouting, "Hey, Adler, get it moving! Those orders won't deliver themselves."

"Yes, sir!" Countdown on *yes sir!* Denny thought, as he grabbed his jacket and the carton of paper bags.

When he got back to the deli, the manager was just answering the phone. He looked at Denny with his usual sour expression. "I told you no personal calls during business hours." He slammed the receiver into Denny's hand.

The only one who ever called him here was Mike Toohey. Denny snarled his name and heard a muffled "Hello, Denny." He recognized the voice immediately. Big Charley Santino. Ten years ago Denny had shared a cell in Attica with Big Charley, and from time to time he had done a couple of jobs for him. He knew that Charley had important mob connections.

Denny ignored the "Get on with it" expression on the manager's face. There were only a couple of people at the counter now. The tables were empty. He had the pleasurable glow of knowing that whatever Charley wanted would be interesting. Automatically he turned to the wall and cupped his hand over the speaker. "Yeah?"

"Tomorrow. Eleven o'clock. Bryant Park behind the library. Watch for an '84 black Chevy."

Denny did not realize that he was smiling broadly when the click indicated the connection was broken.

Over the snowy weekend, Seamus Lambston huddled alone in the family apartment on Seventy-first Street and West End Avenue. On Friday afternoon, he called his bartender. "I'm sick. Get Matty to fill in till Monday." He'd slept soundly Friday night, the sleep of the emotionally spent, but he woke up on Saturday with a sense of ultimate dread.

Ruth had driven up to Boston on Thursday and stayed until Sunday. Jeannie, their youngest daughter, was a freshman at the University of Massachusetts. The check Seamus sent for spring semester had bounced. Ruth had gotten an emergency loan from her office and rushed up with the replacement. After Jeannie's distraught call, they'd had a row that must have been heard five blocks away.

"Damn it, Ruth, I'm doing my best," he'd shouted. "Business is lousy. With three kids in college, is it my fault we're scraping the bottom of the barrel? Do you think I can pull money out of the thin air?"

They'd confronted each other, frightened, exhausted, hopeless. He'd been shamed by the look of distaste in her eyes. He knew he hadn't aged well. Sixty-two years old. He'd built up his five-foot-ten frame with sit-ups and barbells. But now he had a potbelly that wouldn't go away, his once thick sandy hair was thinning and dirty yellow, his reading glasses accentuated the puffiness of his face. He sometimes looked in the mirror, then at the picture of Ruth and himself on their wedding day. Both in handsome suits, both pushing forty, second marriages for both of them, happy, eager for each other. The bar had been going great, and even though he'd mortgaged the hell out of it, he'd been sure he'd be able to recoup in a couple of years. Ruth's quiet, tidy ways were like sanctuary after putting up with Ethel. "Peace is worth every nickel it will cost," he'd told the lawyer who didn't want him to agree to lifetime alimony.

He'd been delighted when Marcy was born. Unexpectedly Linda had followed two years later. They'd been shocked when Jeannie came along as he and Ruth were turning forty-five.

Ruth's slender body had grown stocky. As the rent for the bar doubled and tripled and the old customers moved away, her serene face had taken on a look of perpetual worry. She wanted so much to give things to the girls, things they couldn't afford. Frequently he snapped at her, "Why not give them a happy home instead of a lot of junk?"

These last years with the college expenses had been excruciating. There just wasn't enough money. And that thousand dollars a month to Ethel until she married or died had become a bone of contention, a bone that Ruth gnawed at incessantly. "Go back into court, for God's sake," she'd nag him. "Tell the judge you can't afford to educate your children and that parasite is making a fortune. She doesn't *need* your money. She's got more than she can spend."

The latest outburst, last week, had been the worst. Ruth read in the *Post* that Ethel had just signed a book contract for a half-million-dollar advance. Ethel was quoted as saying the tell-all book would be a "stick of dynamite thrown into the fashion world."

For Ruth that was the last straw. That and the bounced check. "You go see that, that . . ." Ruth never swore. But the unspoken word might have been shouted. "You tell her that I'm going to go to the columnists and tell *them* she's bleeding you dry. Twelve thousand dollars a year, for over twenty years!" Ruth's voice got shriller with every syllable. "I want to quit working. I'm sixty-two years old. The next thing you know it will be weddings. We'll go to our graves with a choke collar around our necks. You tell her that she'll make news all right! Don't you think her fancy magazines might take exception to one of their feminist editors blackmailing her ex-husband?"

"It's not blackmail. It's alimony." Seamus had tried to sound reasonable. "But yes, I'll see her."

Ruth was due back late Sunday afternoon. At noon on Sunday, Seamus stirred himself from his lethargy and began to clean the apartment. They'd given up the once-a-week cleaning woman two years ago. Now they shared the chores, with Ruth's complaints a running part of the process. "Just what I need after being crushed on the Seventh Avenue subway to spend weekends pushing a vacuum." Last week she'd suddenly burst into tears. "I'm so damn tired."

At four o'clock the apartment was in decent shape. It needed painting. The linoleum in the kitchen was worn. The building had gone co-op, but they hadn't been able to afford to buy the place. Twenty years and nothing to show for it but rent receipts.

Seamus laid out cheese and wine on the cocktail table in the living room. The furniture was faded and shabby, but in the soft light of the late afternoon it didn't look bad. In three years more Jeannie would be finished school. Marcy was a senior this year. Linda a junior. Wishing your life away, he thought.

The closer it came time for Ruth to arrive, the more his hands trembled. Would she notice anything different about *him?*

She got home at five-fifteen. "The traffic was terrible," she announced, her voice querulous.

"Did you give them the certified check and explain about the other one?" he asked, trying to ignore the tone in her voice. It was her let's-have-this-out tone.

"I certainly did. And let me tell you, the bursar was shocked when I told him about Ethel Lambston collecting alimony from you all these years. They had Ethel on a panel at college six months ago, blasting off on women getting equal pay." Ruth accepted the glass of wine he handed her and took a long swallow.

With a shock he realized that somewhere along the way she'd

picked up Ethel's habit of licking her lips after she finished an angry sentence. Was it true that you kept marrying the same person? The thought made him want to burst into hysterical laughter.

"Well, let's have it. Did you see her?" Ruth snapped.

A great weariness came over Seamus. The memory of that final scene. "Yes, I saw her."

"And . . ."

He chose his words carefully. "You were right. She doesn't want it to leak out that she's been collecting alimony from me all these years. She's going to let me off the hook."

Ruth set down the wineglass, her face transfigured. "I don't believe it. How did you talk her into it?"

Ethel's taunting, derisive laugh at his threatening and begging words. The jolt of primitive anger that had gone through him, the look of terror in her eyes . . . Her final threat . . . Oh God . . .

"Now when Ethel buys her precious Neeve Kearny clothes and eats high on the hog, *you* won't be paying." Ruth's triumphant laugh pounded against his eardrums as her words sank into his consciousness.

Seamus put down his wineglass. "What made you say that?" he asked his wife quietly.

On Saturday morning the snow was over and the streets were somewhat passable. Neeve brought all Ethel's clothes back to the shop.

Betty rushed to help her. "Don't tell me, she doesn't like *anything?*"

"How would I know?" Neeve asked. "There wasn't hide nor hair of her at her apartment. Honest to God, Betty, when I think of the way we rushed, I could wrap every stitch around her neck."

It was a busy day. They'd run a small ad in the *Times* showing the print dresses and the raincoats, and the response was enthusiastic. Neeve's eyes sparkled as she watched her clerks write up formidable sales slips. Once again, she silently blessed Sal for staking her six years ago.

At two o'clock, Eugenia, a black former fashion model who was now Neeve's second-in-command, reminded Neeve that she hadn't stopped for lunch. "I have some yogurt in the fridge," she offered.

Neeve had just finished helping one of her personal clients select a four-thousand-dollar mother-of-the-bride gown. She smiled quickly. "You know I hate yogurt. Send for a tuna-salad sandwich and a diet Coke, okay?"

Ten minutes later, when the order was delivered to her office, she realized she was starving. "The best tuna salad in New York, Denny," she told the delivery man.

"If you say so, Miss Kearny." His pale face creased into an ingratiating smile.

While she hurried through lunch, Neeve dialed Ethel's number. Once again, Ethel did not answer. Throughout the afternoon the receptionist continued to try to reach her. At the end of the day Neeve told Betty, "I'll take this stuff home once more. I sure don't want to waste my Sunday having to come back here because Ethel suddenly decides she's got a plane to catch and needs everything in ten minutes."

"Knowing her, she'd have the plane make a special trip to the gate if she'd missed it," Betty snapped.

They both laughed, but then Betty said quietly, "You know those crazy feelings you get sometimes, Neeve. I swear they're catching. Pain in the neck that Ethel is, she never pulled anything like this before."

Saturday night, Neeve and Myles went to the Met to hear Pavarotti. "You should be out on a date," Myles complained as the waiter at the Ginger Man handed them after-theater supper menus.

Neeve glanced at him. "Look, Myles, I go out a lot. You know that. When someone important comes along, I'll know it, just the way you and Mother did. Now why don't you order me some shrimp scampi?"

Myles usually attended early Mass on Sunday. Neeve enjoyed sleeping late and going to the Pontifical Mass at the cathedral. She was surprised to find Myles in the kitchen in his bathrobe when she got up. "Giving up the faith?" she asked.

"No. I thought I'd go with you today." He tried to sound casual.

"Would that have anything to do with Nicky Sepetti's release from prison?" Neeve sighed. "Don't bother to answer."

After church they decided on brunch at Café des Artistes, then caught a movie in the neighborhood theater. When they got back to the apartment, Neeve again dialed Ethel Lambston's number, let the phone ring a half-dozen times, shrugged and raced Myles in their weekly contest to finish the *Times* puzzle first.

"A lovely, unraveling day," Neeve commented as she bent over Myles's chair to kiss the top of his head after the eleven-o'clock news. She caught the look on his face. "Don't say it," she warned.

Myles pressed his lips together. He knew she was right. He'd been about to say, "Even if it's clear tomorrow, I wish you wouldn't jog alone."

The persistent ringing of the phone in Ethel Lambston's apartment did not go unnoticed.

Douglas Brown, Ethel's twenty-eight-year-old nephew, had moved into the apartment on Friday afternoon. He'd hesitated about taking the risk, but knew he could prove he'd been forced that day out of his illegal sublet.

"I just needed a place to stay while I found a new apartment." That would be his explanation.

He figured it would be better not to answer the phone. The frequent calls irritated him, but he did not want to advertise his presence. Ethel never wanted him to answer her phone. "None of your business who calls me," she'd told him. Other people might have been told the same thing.

He was sure it had been a wise decision not to answer the doorbell on Friday evening. The note slipped under the door into the foyer was about the clothes Ethel had ordered.

Doug smiled unpleasantly. That must have been the errand Ethel had scheduled for him.

Sunday morning Denny Adler waited impatiently in the sharp, gusty wind. Precisely at eleven o'clock, he saw a black Chevy approaching. With long strides, he hurried from the comparative shelter of Bryant Park onto the street. The car pulled over. He opened the passenger door and slid in. The car was moving even as he yanked the door closed.

In the years since Attica, Big Charley had gotten a lot grayer and put on more weight. The steering wheel was burrowed between the folds of his stomach. Denny said, "Hi," not expecting an answer. Big Charley nodded.

The car moved swiftly up the Henry Hudson Parkway and over the George Washington Bridge. Charley turned onto the Palisades Interstate Parkway. Denny noted that while the remaining snow in New York was slushy and soot-filled, the snow on the sides of the parkway was still white. New Jersey, the Garden State, he thought sarcastically.

Past Exit 3 there was a lookout point for people who, as Denny sometimes observed, had nothing better to do than stare at the New

York landscape across the Hudson River. Denny was not surprised when Charley pulled into the deserted parking area there. This was where they'd discussed other jobs.

Charley turned off the ignition and reached back over the seat, groaning with the effort of stretching. He pulled up a paper bag containing a couple of cans of beer and dropped it between them. "Your brand."

Denny felt pleased. "Nice of you to remember, Charley." He opened the can of Coors.

Charley swallowed deeply from his own can before he replied, "I forget nothing." He drew an envelope from his inside pocket. "Ten thousand," he told Denny. "The same when the job is finished."

Denny accepted the envelope, taking sensual pleasure in its bulk. "Who?"

"You deliver lunch to her coupla times a week. She lives in Schwab House, that big place on Seventy-fourth between West End and Riverside Drive. Usually walks to and from work coupla times a week. Cuts through Central Park. Grab her handbag and waste her. Clean out the wallet and dump the bag so it looks like a junkie cut her. If you can't nail her in the park, the garment center might be it. She goes there every Monday afternoon. Those streets are packed. Everybody in a rush. Trucks double-parked. Brush by her, shove her in front of a truck. Take your time. It gotta look like an accident or a mugging. Follow her around in one of those panhandler outfits of yours." Big Charley's voice was thick and guttural, as though the rolls of fat around his neck were choking his vocal cords.

For Charley it had been a long speech. He took another deep draught from the beer can.

Denny began to feel uneasy. "*Who?*"

"Neeve Kearny."

Denny shoved the envelope toward Charley as though it contained a ticking bomb. "The Police Commissioner's daughter? Are you nuts?"

"The *ex*-Commissioner's daughter."

Denny could feel the perspiration on his brow. "Kearny was in office for sixteen years. Not a cop in the city who wouldn't risk his life for him. When his wife died they put the heat on everyone who ever stole an apple off a cart. No way."

There was an almost imperceptible change in Big Charley's expression, but his voice was the same guttural monotone. "Denny, I told you I never forget. Remember all those nights in Attica when you used to brag about the jobs you got away with and how you did it? All I need to do is make a no-name-given call to the cops and you won't get to deliver another baloney sandwich. Don't make me a crime-stopper, Denny."

Denny considered and, remembering, cursed his own big mouth. Again he fingered the envelope and thought of Neeve Kearny. He'd been delivering to her shop for nearly a year now. It used to be that the receptionist would tell him to leave the bag with her, but now he went right back to the private office. Even if Kearny was on the phone, she'd wave and smile, a real smile, not that tight-lipped snobby nod that most of his customers gave him. She always told him how great everything tasted.

And she sure was a good-looking babe.

Denny shrugged off the moment of sentiment. It was a job he had to do. Charley wouldn't turn him in to the cops, and they both knew it. His knowledge of the contract had made him too dangerous. To refuse it meant that he'd never make it back to the George Washington Bridge.

He pocketed the money.

"That's better," Charley said. "What are your hours at the deli?"

"Nine to six. Mondays off."

"She leaves for work between eight-thirty and nine. Start hanging around her apartment building. The shop closes at six-thirty. Remember, take your time. *It can't look like a deliberate hit.*"

Big Charley started up the engine for the return trip to New York. Once again he fell into his customary silence, broken only by the grunting sound of his breathing. An overwhelming curiosity was consuming Denny. As Charley turned off the West Side Highway and drove across Fifty-seventh Street, Denny asked, "Charley, got any idea who ordered the job? She don't seem like the kind to get in anyone's way. Sepetti got sprung. Sounds like he's got a memory."

He felt the angry eyes flash in his direction. The guttural voice was now clear, and the words fell with the impact of a rock slide. "You're getting careless, Denny. I don't know who wants her wasted. The guy who contacted me don't know. The guy who contacted *him* don't know. That's how it works, and no questions asked. You're a small-time, small-mind bum, Denny, and some things are none of your business. Now *get out.*"

The car stopped abruptly at the corner of Eighth Avenue and Fifty-seventh Street.

Uncertainly, Denny opened the door. "Charley, I'm sorry," he said. "It was just . . ."

The wind was whipping through the car. "Just shut up and make sure that job gets done right."

An instant later, Denny was staring at the back of Charley's Chevy as it disappeared down Fifty-seventh Street. He walked toward Columbus Circle, stopped at a street vendor for a hot dog and a Coke. When he had finished, he wiped his mouth with the back of his hand. His nerves began to settle. His fingers caressed the bulky envelope inside the pocket of his jacket.

"Might as well start earning my keep," he muttered to himself, and began to head up Broadway toward Seventy-fourth Street and West End Avenue.

At Schwab House, he sauntered casually around the block, noting the Riverside Drive entrance to the building. No chance she'd use that. The West End Avenue one was much more convenient.

Satisfied, he crossed the street and leaned against the building directly opposite Schwab House. It would make a great observation point, he decided. The door opened near him, and a cluster of residents came out. He didn't want to be observed, so he casually moved on, reflecting that his wino outfit would make him blend into the background while he stalked Neeve Kearny.

At two-thirty, as he crossed town toward the East Side, he passed a line of people waiting to buy tickets for the movie. His narrow eyes widened. Halfway along the queue Neeve Kearny was standing next to a white-haired man whose face Denny recognized. Her father. Denny hurried by, his head buried in his neck. And I wasn't even looking for her, he thought. This is going to be the easiest hit I ever made.

4

On Monday morning, Neeve was in the lobby, her arms once again filled with Ethel's clothes, when Tse-Tse, a twenty-three-year-old actress, emerged breathlessly from the elevator. Her curly blond hair was early Phyllis Diller. Her eye makeup was violent shades of purple. Her small, pretty mouth had been painted into a Kewpie-doll bow. Tse-Tse, born Mary Margaret McBride, "After guess who?" as she'd explained to Neeve, was always appearing in off-off-Broadway productions, most of which lasted less than a week.

Neeve had gone to see her several times and had been astonished at how really good Tse-Tse was. Tse-Tse could move a shoulder, droop a lip, change her posture and literally become someone else. She had an excellent ear for accents and could range her voice from a Butterfly McQueen high pitch to a Lauren Bacall throaty drawl. She shared a studio apartment in Schwab House with another aspiring actress and filled out her family's grudgingly small allowance with odd jobs. She'd given up waitressing and dog-walking in favor of cleaning. "Fifty bucks for four hours and you don't have to drag along a pooper-scooper," as she'd explained to Neeve.

Neeve had suggested Tse-Tse to Ethel Lambston, and she knew Tse-Tse cleaned for Ethel several times a month. Now she regarded her as a messenger from heaven. As the cab arrived, she explained her dilemma.

"I'm supposed to go there tomorrow," Tse-Tse explained breathlessly. "Honest to God, Neeve, that place is enough to drive me back to walking pit bulls. No matter how tidy I leave it, the next time it's always in shambles."

"I've seen it." Neeve considered. "Look, if Ethel doesn't pick up this stuff today, I'll take you there in a cab tomorrow morning and leave everything in her closet. You have a key, I guess."

"She gave me one about six months ago. Let me know. See you." Tse-Tse blew Neeve a kiss and started jogging down the street, a flamingo with her permed golden hair, her crazy makeup, her bright purple wooly jacket, red tights and yellow sneakers.

At the shop, Betty helped Neeve again hang Ethel's purchases on the Will Call rack in the sewing room. "This has gone beyond Ethel's rattlebrain behavior," she said quietly, a worried frown creasing the permanent furrows in her forehead. "Do you think she's been in an accident? Maybe we should report her missing."

Neeve piled the accessory boxes next to the rack. "I can ask Myles to check about accident reports," she said, "but it's too soon to report her missing."

Betty grinned suddenly. "Maybe she's found a boyfriend at last and is off somewhere on an ecstatic weekend."

Neeve glanced through the open door onto the sales floor. The first customer had arrived, and a new saleswoman was showing her gowns that were absolutely unsuitable for her. Neeve bit her lip. She knew she had something of Renata's fiery temperament and had to watch her tongue. "For Ethel's sake, I hope so," she commented, then with a welcoming smile went over to the customer and the saleswoman. "Marian, why don't you bring the green chiffon Della Rosa gown?" she suggested.

It was a briskly busy morning. The receptionist kept trying Ethel's number. The last time she reported no response, Neeve had the fleeting thought that if Ethel had met a man and ended up eloping, no one would cheer louder than Ethel's former husband, who after twenty-two years was still sending alimony checks every month.

Monday was Denny Adler's day off. He had planned to spend it following Neeve Kearny, but on Sunday evening there was a call for him at the public phone in the hallway of the rooming house.

The manager of the deli told Denny he'd have to come in to work the next day. The counterman had been fired. "I was figuring out the books and the sonofabitch had his hand in the till. I need you."

Denny swore silently. But it would be stupid to refuse. "I'll be there," he said sullenly. As he hung up, he thought of Neeve Kearny, the smile she'd given him the day before when he delivered lunch, the way that coal-black hair framed her face, the way her breasts filled out the fancy sweater she'd been wearing. Big Charley said that she went to Seventh Avenue on Monday afternoons. That meant there'd be no point trying to catch up with her after work. Maybe just as well. He'd made plans for Monday evening with the waitress at the bar across the street and hadn't wanted to break them.

As he turned to walk the dank, urine-smelling hallway back to his room, he thought, You won't get to be another Monday's child, Kearny.

Monday's child was fair of face. But not after a few weeks in the cemetery.

Monday afternoon was Neeve's usual time to spend on Seventh Avenue. She loved the bizarre bedlam of the Garment District, the crowded sidewalks, the delivery trucks double-parked on the narrow streets, the agile delivery boys manipulating racks of clothes through the traffic, the sense of everyone rushing, no time to spare.

She'd begun coming here with Renata when she was about eight years old. Over Myles's amused objections, Renata had taken a part-time job in a dress shop on Seventy-second Street, just two blocks from their apartment. Before long, the aging owner turned over to her the job of buying for the shop. Neeve could still visualize Renata shaking her head no as an overeager designer tried to persuade her to change her mind about an outfit.

"When a woman sits down in that dress, it will crawl up her back," Renata would say. Whenever she felt strongly, her Italian accent would leap into her voice. "A woman should get dressed, look in the mirror to make sure she doesn't have a run in her stocking, a drooping hem, and then she should forget what she is wearing. Her clothes should fit like a second skin." Renata had pronounced it "skeen."

But she also had an eye for new designers. Neeve still had the cameo pin one of them had presented to Renata. She had been the first to introduce his line. "Your mama, she gave me my first break," Jacob Gold would remind Neeve. "A beautiful lady, and she knew fashion. Like you." It was his highest compliment.

Today as Neeve wended her way from Seventh Avenue through the West Thirties, she realized she was vaguely distressed. There was a throbbing pain somewhere in her psyche, like an emotional sore tooth. She grumbled to herself, Before long, I'll really be one of those superstitious Irish, always getting a "feeling" about trouble around the corner.

At Artless Sportswear, she ordered linen blazers with matching Bermuda shorts. "I like the pastels," she murmured, "but they need a dynamite something."

"We're suggesting this blouse." The clerk, order pad in hand, pointed to a rack of pale nylon blouses with white buttons.

"Uh-uh. They belong under a school jumper." Neeve wandered through the showrooms, then spotted a multicolored silk T shirt. "That's what I mean." She picked up several of the T shirts in different color patterns and brought them over to the suits. "This with the peach; that one with the mauve. Now we've got something going."

At Victor Costa, she chose romantic boat-necked chiffons that floated on the hangers. And once again Renata drifted into her mind. Renata in a black velvet Victor Costa, going to a New Year's Eve party with Myles. Around her throat she'd worn her Christmas present, a pearl necklace with a cluster of small diamonds.

"You look like a princess, Mommy," Neeve had told her. That moment had been imprinted on her memory. She'd been so proud of them. Myles, straight and elegant with his then prematurely white hair; Renata, so slender, her jet-black hair piled in a chignon.

The next New Year's Eve, a few people came to the apartment. Father Devin Stanton, who was now a bishop, and Uncle Sal, who was still struggling to make his mark as a designer. Herb Schwartz, Myles's deputy commissioner, and his wife. Renata had been dead seven weeks . . .

Neeve realized that the clerk was waiting patiently at her elbow. "I'm woolgathering," she apologized, "and it isn't the season for that, is it?"

She placed her order, went quickly to the next three houses on her list and then, as darkness began to fall, headed for her usual visit to Uncle Sal.

The showrooms of Anthony della Salva were now spread throughout the Garment District. His sportswear line was on West Thirty-seventh Street. His accessories on West Thirty-fifth. His licensing on Sixth Avenue. But Neeve knew she would find him in his main office on West Thirty-sixth. He had started there in a tiny two-room hole-in-the-wall. Now he occupied three sumptuously equipped floors. Anthony della Salva, *né* Salvatore Esposito from the Bronx, was a designer on a par with Bill Blass, Calvin Klein and Oscar de la Renta.

To Neeve's dismay, as she crossed Thirty-seventh Street she came face to face with Gordon Steuber. Meticulously dressed in a tan cashmere jacket over a brown-and-beige Scottish pullover, dark-brown slacks and Gucci loafers, with his blaze of curly brown hair, slender, even-featured face, powerful shoulders and narrow waist, Gordon Steuber could easily have had a successful career as a model. Instead, in his early forties, he was a shrewd businessman with an uncanny knack of hiring unknown young designers and exploiting them until they could afford to leave him.

Thanks to his young designers, his line of women's dresses and suits was exciting and provocative. He makes plenty without having to cheat illegal workers, Neeve thought as she stared coldly at him. And if, as Sal hinted, he was in income-tax trouble, good!

They passed each other without speaking, but it seemed to Neeve that anger emanated from his persona. She thought of hearing that people emitted an aura. I don't want to know the color of that aura right now, she thought as she hurried into Sal's office.

When the receptionist spotted Neeve, she rang through immediately to the private office. An instant later, Anthony della Salva, "Uncle Sal," came bounding through the door. His cherubic face beamed as he hurried to embrace her.

Neeve smiled as she took in Sal's outfit. He was his own best ad for his spring line of menswear. His version of a safari outfit was a cross between a paratrooper's jumpsuit and Jungle Jim at his best. "I love it. It will be all over East Hampton next month," she said approvingly as she kissed him.

"It already is, darling. It's even the rage of Iowa City. That frightens me a little. I must be slipping. Come. Let's get out of this." On the way to his office, he stopped to greet some out-of-town buyers. "Are you being helped? Is Susan taking good care of you? Wonderful. Susan, show the lazy-time line. It will walk out of the store, I promise you."

"Uncle Sal, do you want to take care of those people?" Neeve asked as they cut through the showroom.

"Absolutely not. They'll waste two hours of Susan's time and end up buying three or four of the cheapest pieces in the place." With a sigh of relief he closed the door of his private rooms. "It's been a crazy day. Where does everyone get the money? I raised my prices again. They're outrageous and people are fighting to put in rush orders."

His smile was beatific. His round face had become puffy in the last years, and now his eyes crinkled till they were lost under his heavy lids. He and Myles and the Bishop had grown up in the same Bronx neighborhood, played stickball together, gone to Christopher Columbus High School together. It was hard to believe that he too was sixty-eight years old.

There was a jumble of swatches on his desk. "Can you beat this? We have an order to design interiors for scale-model Mercedes for three-year-olds. When I was three I had a secondhand red wagon, and one of the wheels kept falling off. Every time it did, my father beat me up for not taking care of my good toys."

Neeve felt her spirits lift. "Uncle Sal, honest to God I wish I had you on tape. I could make a fortune blackmailing you."

"You're too good-hearted. Sit down. Have a cup of coffee. It's fresh, I promise."

"I know you're busy, Uncle Sal. Five minutes only." Neeve unbuttoned her jacket.

"Will you drop the 'uncle' business? I'm getting too old to be treated with respect." Sal eyed her critically. "You look good, as usual. How's business?"

"Great."

"How's Myles? I see Nicky Sepetti got sprung Friday. I suppose that's tearing his guts out."

"He was upset Friday and pretty good over the weekend. Now I'm not sure."

"Invite me up to dinner this week. I haven't seen him for a month."

"You're on." Neeve watched as Sal poured coffee from the Silex on a tray beside his desk. She glanced around. "I love this room."

The wall covering behind the desk was executed in a mural of the Pacific Reef motif, the design that had made Sal famous.

Sal often told her about his inspiration for that line. "Neeve, I was in the Aquarium in Chicago. It was 1972. Fashion was a mess that year. Everyone sick of the miniskirt. Everyone afraid to try something new. The top designers were showing men-tailored suits, Bermuda shorts, skinny unlined suits. Pale colors. Dark colors. Ruffled blouses that belonged in boarding school. Nothing that makes a woman say, 'I want to look like that.' I was just wandering around the Aquarium and went up to the floor with the Pacific Reef exhibit. Neeve, it was like walking underwater. Tanks from floor to ceiling were filled with hundreds of exotic fish and plants and coral trees and shells. The colors on everything—you'd think Michelangelo painted them! The patterns and designs—dozens and dozens, every one unique. Silver blending into blue; coral and red entwined. One fish was yellow, bright as the morning sun, with black markings. And the flow, the grace of movement. I thought, If I can only do this with fabric! I started sketching right on the spot. I knew it was great. I won the Coty Award that year. I turned the fashion industry around. Couturier sales were fantastic. Licenses for the mass market and accessories. And all because I was smart enough to copy Mother Nature."

Now he followed her gaze. "That design. Wonderful. Cheerful. Elegant. Graceful. Flattering. It's still the best thing I ever did. But don't tell anyone. They haven't caught up with me yet. Next week I'll give you a preview of my fall line. The second-best thing I've ever done. Sensational. How's your love life?"

"It isn't."

"What about that guy you had to dinner a couple of months ago? He was crazy about you."

"The fact you can't remember his name says it all. He still makes a pile of money on Wall Street. Just bought a Cessna and a co-op in Vail. Forget it. He had the personality of a wet noodle. I keep telling Myles and I'll tell you: When Mr. Right comes along, I'll know it."

"Don't wait too long, Neeve. You've been raised on the fairy-tale romance of your mother and father." Sal swallowed the last of his coffee with a great gulp. "For most of us, it don't work like that."

Neeve had a fleeting moment of amusement reflecting that when Sal was with close friends or ready to wax eloquent, the suave Italian accent disappeared and his native jargon took over.

Sal continued. "Most of us meet. We get a little interested. Then not so interested. But we keep seeing each other and gradually something happens. Not magic. Maybe just friendship. We accommodate. We may not like opera, but we go to the opera. We may hate exercise but start playing tennis or jogging. Then love takes over. That's ninety percent of the people in the world, Neeve. Believe me."

"Was that the way it happened for you?" Neeve asked sweetly.

"Four times." Sal beamed. "Don't be so fresh. I'm an optimist."

Neeve finished the coffee and got up feeling immensely cheered. "I think I am, too, but you help bring it out. How's Thursday for dinner?"

"Fine. And remember, I'm not on Myles's diet and don't say I should be."

Neeve kissed him goodbye, left him in his office and hurried through the showroom. With a practiced eye, she studied the fashions on his mannequins. Not brilliant but good. Subtle use of color, clean lines, innovative without being too daring. They'd sell well enough. She wondered about Sal's fall line. Was it as good as he claimed?

She was back in Neeve's Place in time to discuss the next window display with the decorator. At six-thirty, when she closed the shop, she began the now familiar job of carrying home Ethel Lambston's purchases. Once again there had been no message from Ethel; no response to the half-dozen phone calls. But at least there was an end in sight. Tomorrow morning she'd accompany Tse-Tse to Ethel's apartment and leave everything there.

That thought made her mind jump to a line from the poignant Eugene Field poem "Little Boy Blue": "He kissed them and put them there."

As she tightened her hold on the armful of slippery garment bags, Neeve remembered that Little Boy Blue had never returned to his pretty toys.

5

The next morning, Tse-Tse met her in the lobby promptly at eight-thirty. Tse-Tse was wearing her hair in braided coils pinned over her ears. A black velvet cape hung loosely from her shoulders to her ankles. Under it she was attired in a black uniform with a white apron. "I just got a part as a parlor-floor servant in a new play," she confided as she took boxes from Neeve's hands. "I thought I'd practice. If Ethel's there she gets a kick out of it when I'm in costume." Her Swedish accent was excellent.

Vigorous bell-ringing did not elicit a response at Ethel's apartment. Tse-Tse fumbled in her purse for the key. When she opened the door, she stepped aside and let Neeve precede her. With a sigh of relief, Neeve dropped the armful of clothes on the couch and started to straighten up. "There is a God," she murmured, then her voice trailed off.

A muscular young man was standing in the entrance of the foyer that led to the bedroom and bath. Obviously in the process of dressing, he was holding a tie in one hand. His crisp white shirt was not yet fully buttoned. His pale-green eyes, set in a face that with a different expression might have been attractive, were narrowed by an annoyed frown. His as yet uncombed hair fell over his forehead in a mass of curls. Neeve's startled response to his presence was replaced by the immediate sense that his tangled hair was the product of a body wave. From behind her, she heard Tse-Tse draw in her breath sharply.

"Who are you?" Neeve asked. "And why didn't you answer the door?"

"I think the first question is mine." The tone was sarcastic. "And I answer the door when I choose to answer it."

Tse-Tse took over. "You are Miss Lambston's nephew," she said. "I have seen your picture." The Swedish accent rose and fell from her tongue. "You are Douglas Brown."

"I know who I am. Would you mind telling me who *you* are?" The sarcastic tone did not abate.

Neeve felt her temper rising. "I'm Neeve Kearny," she said. "And this is Tse-Tse. She does the apartment for Miss Lambston. Do you mind telling me where Miss Lambston is? She claimed she needed these clothes on Friday and I've been carrying them back and forth ever since."

"So you're Neeve Kearny." Now the smile became insolent. "Number-three shoes go with beige suit. Carry number-three purse and wear box-A jewelry. Do you do that for everyone?"

Neeve felt her jaw harden. "Miss Lambston is a very good customer and a very busy woman. And *I'm* a very busy woman. Is she here, and if not, when is she coming back?"

Douglas Brown shrugged. Something of the animosity left him. "I have no idea where my aunt is. She asked me to meet her here Friday afternoon. She had an errand for me."

"Friday afternoon?" Neeve asked quickly.

"Yes. I got here and she wasn't around. I have a key and let myself in. She never came back. I made up the couch and stayed. I just lost my sublet, and the Y isn't my speed."

There was something too glib about the explanation. Neeve looked around the room. The couch on which she'd laid the clothes had a blanket and a pillow piled together at one end. Piles of papers were thrown on the floor in front of the couch. Whenever she'd been here before, the cushions were so covered with files and magazines it was impossible to see the upholstery. Stapled clippings from newspapers were jumbled on the dinette table. Because the apartment was street level, the windows were barred, and even the bars had been used as makeshift files. At the opposite end of the room, she could see into the kitchen. As usual, the countertops looked cluttered. The walls were haphazardly covered with carelessly framed pictures of Ethel, pictures that had been cut from newspapers and magazines. Ethel receiving the Magazine Award of the Year from the American Society of Journalists and Authors. That had been for her scathing article on welfare hotels and abandoned tenements. Ethel at the side of Lyndon and Lady Bird Johnson. She'd worked on his 1964 campaign. Ethel on the dais at the Waldorf with the Mayor the night *Contemporary Woman* had honored him.

Neeve was struck by a thought. "I was here early Friday evening," she said. "What time did you say you arrived?"

"About three. I never pick up the phone. Ethel has a thing about anyone answering it when she's not here."

"That's true," Tse-Tse said. For a moment she forgot her Swedish accent. Then it came back. "Yah, yah, it's true."

Douglas Brown slipped his tie over his neck. "I've got to get to work. Just leave Ethel's clothes, Miss Kearny." He turned to Tse-Tse. "And if you can find some way to clean this place up, that's fine, too. I'll pile my stuff together just in case Ethel decides to favor us with her presence."

Now he seemed in a hurry to get away. He turned and started for the bedroom.

"Just a minute," Neeve said. She waited until he stopped and looked over his shoulder. "You say you came around three o'clock on Friday. Then you must have been here when I was trying to deliver these clothes. Would you mind explaining why you wouldn't answer the door that night? It could have been Ethel forgetting her key. Right?"

"What time did you get here?"

"Around seven."

"I'd gone out for something to eat. Sorry." He disappeared into the bedroom and pushed the door closed.

Neeve and Tse-Tse looked at each other. Tse-Tse shrugged. "I might as well get busy." Her voice was a singsong. "Yumpin' Yimminy, you could clean Stockholm faster than this place with all the junk around." She dropped the accent. "You don't suppose anything happened to Ethel, do you?"

"I've thought about having Myles call for accident reports," Neeve said. "Although I must say the loving nephew doesn't seem frantic with worry. When he gets out, I'll hang these things in Ethel's closet for her."

Douglas Brown emerged from the bedroom a moment later. Fully dressed in a dark-blue suit, a raincoat over his arm, his hair brushed into a thick, wavy coiffure, he looked sullenly attractive. He seemed surprised and not pleased that Neeve was still there.

"I thought you were so busy," he told her. "Are you planning to help clean?"

Neeve's lips narrowed ominously. "I'm planning to hang these clothes in your aunt's closet, so she'll be able to put her hands on them when she needs them, and then I intend to leave." She tossed her card at him. "You will let me know if you hear from her. I, for one, am getting concerned."

Douglas Brown glanced at the card and pocketed it. "I don't see why. In the two years I've lived in New York, she's pulled the disappearing act at least three times and usually managed to keep me cooling my heels in a restaurant or this place. I'm beginning to think she's certifiably nuts."

"Are you planning to stay until she returns?"

"I don't see that is any of your business, Miss Kearny, but probably yes."

"Do you have a card where I can reach you during business hours?" Neeve felt her temper rising.

"Unfortunately, at the Cosmic Oil Building, they don't have cards made for receptionists. You see, like my dear aunt, I'm a writer. Unfortunately, unlike her, I have not yet been discovered by the publishing world, so I keep body and soul together by sitting at a desk in Cosmic's lobby and confirming the appointments of visitors. It's not the job for a mental giant, but then Herman Melville worked as a clerk on Ellis Island, I believe."

"Do you consider yourself a Herman Melville?" Neeve did not try to conceal the sarcasm in her voice.

"No. I write a different sort of book. My latest is called *The Spiritual Life of Hugh Hefner.* So far no editor has seen the joke in it."

He was gone. Neeve and Tse-Tse looked at each other. "What a creep," Tse-Tse said. "And to think he's poor Ethel's only relative."

Neeve searched her memory. "I don't think she ever mentioned him to me."

"Two weeks ago when I was here, she was on the phone with him and real upset. Ethel squirrels money around the apartment, and she thought some of it was missing. She practically accused him of stealing it."

The dusty, crowded apartment suddenly made Neeve feel claustrophobic. She wanted out of this place. "Let's get these clothes put away."

If Douglas Brown had slept on the couch the first night, it was clear he had been using Ethel's bedroom since then. There was an ashtray full of cigarettes on the night table. Ethel didn't smoke. The antique-white provincial furniture was, like everything else in the apartment, expensive but lost in clutter. Perfumes and a tarnished silver brush, comb and mirror set were scattered on the dresser. Ethel had notes to herself jammed into the large gold-framed mirror. Several men's suits, sports jackets and slacks were draped over a rose damask chaise longue. A man's suitcase was on the floor, shoved under the chaise.

"Even he didn't have the nerve to disturb Ethel's closet," Neeve observed. The back wall of the fairly large bedroom consisted of an elaborate closet that ran the length of the room. Four years ago when Ethel first asked Neeve to go through her closet, Neeve had told her that it was no wonder she never could put any outfits together. She needed more space. Three weeks later Ethel had invited Neeve back. She had led her to the bedroom and proudly displayed her new acquisition, a custom-built closet that had cost her ten thousand dollars. It had short poles for blouses, high poles for evening gowns. It was sectioned off so that coats hung in one area, suits in another, daytime dresses in another. There were shelves for sweaters and purses; racks for shoes; a jewelry unit with brass extensions shaped like branches of a tree, to hold necklaces and bracelets. A pair of ghoulishly real plaster hands were upraised as though in prayer, the fingers separated.

Ethel had pointed to them. "Don't they look as though they could strangle you?" she'd asked gleefully. "They're for rings. I told the guy from the closet place that I keep everything in marked boxes, but he said I should have this anyhow. Someday I'd be sorry if I didn't take it, he told me."

In contrast to the rest of the apartment, the closet was exquisitely neat. The clothes were hung precisely on the satin hangers. Zippers were fastened up to the top. Jackets were buttoned. "Ever since you started dressing her, people keep commenting on Ethel's clothes," Tse-Tse observed. "Ethel loves it." On the inside of the doors, Ethel had pasted the lists Neeve had given her, which accessories to wear with which outfits.

"I went through everything with Ethel last month," Neeve murmured. "We made room for the new stuff." She laid the clothes on the bed and began to peel the plastic bags from them. "Well, I'll just do what I'd have done if she were standing here. Get this load in place and tack up the list."

As she sorted and hung the new garments, she skimmed the contents of the closet. Ethel's sable coat. Her stone marten jacket. The red cashmere coachman coat. The Burberry. The herringbone cape. The white wraparound with caracul collar. The belted leather. Next came the suits. The Donna Karans, the Beenes, the Ultrasuedes, the—Neeve paused, the hangers with the two new suits still in her hand.

"Wait a minute," she said. She peered up at the top shelf. She knew that Ethel's Vuitton luggage consisted of four matching pieces in a tapestry motif. They were a garment-bag carryall with zippered pockets, a carry-on oversized tote, a large and a medium-sized suitcase. The garment bag, the tote and one suitcase were missing. "Good old Ethel," Neeve said as she hung the new suits in the closet. "She did take off. That beige ensemble with the mink collar is gone." She began poking through the racks. The white wool suit, the green knit, the black-and-white print. "So help me, she just packed up and took off. I swear I could choke her myself." She pushed her hair back from her forehead. "Look," she said, pointing at the list on the door and then the bare spots on the shelves. "She took everything she needed to get all gussied up. I guess the weather was so lousy, she decided she didn't need light spring things. Well, wherever she is, I hope it hits ninety degrees. *Che noiosa spera che muore di caldo*—"

"Easy, Neeve," Tse-Tse said. "Whenever you start lapsing into Italian, you're getting mad."

Neeve shrugged. "The blazes with it. I'll send my bill to her accountant. At least *he* has his head screwed on tight. He doesn't forget to pay on time." She looked at Tse-Tse. "What about *you?* Were you counting on getting paid today?"

Tse-Tse shook her head. "Last time she paid me in advance. I'm okay."

At the shop, Neeve related to Betty what had happened.

"You should charge her your cab fare and for personal-shopper assistance," Betty said. "That woman is the limit."

At noon when Neeve spoke to Myles, she told him what had happened. "And I was about to have you check the accident reports," she said.

"Listen, if a train saw that woman in its path, it would jump the track to duck her," Myles replied.

But, for some reason, Neeve's irritation did not last. Instead, the nagging, persistent feeling that something was wrong about Ethel's sudden departure stayed with her. It accompanied her when she closed up at six-thirty and rushed to the cocktail party in the St. Regis given by *Women's Wear Daily.* In the glitter of the fashionably dressed crowd, she spotted Toni Mendell, the elegant editor in chief of *Contemporary Woman,* and hurried over to her.

"Do you know how long Ethel will be gone?" she managed to ask over the din.

"I'm surprised she isn't here," Toni told her. "She said she was coming, but we all know Ethel."

"When is her fashion article due?"

"She turned it in Thursday morning. I had to have the lawyers go over it to make sure we don't get sued. They made us cut out a few things, but it's still wonderful. You heard about the big contract she has with Givvons and Marks?"

"No."

A waiter offered canapés, smoked salmon and caviar on toast points. Neeve helped herself to one. Toni mournfully shook her head. "Now that waists are back in, I can't afford even an olive." Toni was a size six. "Anyhow, the article is about the great looks of the last fifty years and the designers behind them. Let's face it, the subject has been done and done, but you know Ethel. She makes everything gossipy and fun. Then two weeks ago she got terribly mysterious. I gather the next day she charged into Jack Campbell's office and talked him into a contract for a book on fashion with a six-figure advance. She's probably holed up somewhere writing it."

"Darling, you look divine!" The voice came from somewhere behind Neeve.

Toni's smile revealed every one of her faultlessly capped teeth. "Carmen, I've left a dozen messages for you. Where have you been hiding yourself?"

Neeve began to edge away, but Toni stopped her. "Neeve, Jack Campbell just came in. He's that tall guy in the gray suit. Maybe he knows where you can reach Ethel."

By the time Neeve had made her way across the room, Jack Campbell was already surrounded. She waited, listening to the congratulations he was accepting. From the gist of the conversation, she gathered that he had just been made president and publisher of Givvons and Marks, that he had bought an apartment on East Fifty-second Street, and that he was sure he'd thoroughly enjoy living in New York.

She judged him to be in his late thirties, young for the job. His hair was dark brown and cut short. She suspected that if longer, it would have been quite curly. His body had the lean, taut look of a runner. His face was thin; his eyes were the same dark brown as his hair. His smile seemed genuine. It caused small crinkles to form at the corner of his eyes. She liked the way he bent his head forward to listen to the elderly editor who was speaking to him and then turned to someone else without seeming abrupt.

A real art, Neeve thought, the kind of thing politicians did naturally, but not many businessmen.

It was possible to keep observing him without being obvious. What was there about Jack Campbell that seemed familiar? Something. She'd met him before. But where?

A waiter passed and she accepted another glass of wine. Her second and last, but at least sipping it made her look busy.

"It's Neeve, isn't it?"

In the moment she'd turned her back to him, Jack Campbell had come over to her. He introduced himself. "Chicago, six years ago. You were on your way back from skiing and I'd been on a sales trip. We started talking five minutes before the plane landed. You were all excited about opening a dress shop. How did it work out?"

"Fine." Neeve vaguely remembered the exchange. She'd bolted out of the plane to make her connecting flight. Jobs. That was it. "Weren't you just starting work for a new publisher?"

"Yes."

"Obviously, it was a good move."

"Jack, there are some people I'd like you to meet." The editor in chief of *W* was plucking his sleeve.

"I don't want to keep you," Neeve said quickly. "But just one question. I understand Ethel Lambston is writing a book for you. Do you know where I can reach her?"

"I have her home number. Will that help?"

"Thanks, but I have it, too." Neeve lifted her hand in a quick, self-deprecating gesture. "I mustn't hold you up."

She turned and slipped through the crowd, suddenly weary of the babble of voices and conscious that it had been a long day.

The usual cluster of people waiting for cabs crowded the sidewalk in front of the St. Regis. Neeve shrugged, walked to Fifth Avenue and started uptown. It was a pleasant enough evening. Maybe she'd cut through the park. A walk home would clear her head. But at Central Park South a cab deposited a fare directly in front of her. She hesitated, then held the door and got in. The idea of walking another mile in high heels was suddenly distinctly unattractive.

She did not see the frustrated expression on Denny's face. He had waited patiently outside the St. Regis and followed her up Fifth Avenue. When she began to head for the park he thought that his opportunity was at hand.

* * *

At two o'clock that morning, Neeve awakened from a sound sleep. She had been dreaming. She was standing in front of Ethel's closet, making a list.

A list.

"I hope she melts, wherever she is."

That was it. Coats. The sable. The jacket. The cape. The Burberry. The wraparound. The coachman. They were all there.

Ethel had turned in her article on Thursday. No one had seen her on Friday. Both days had been windy and miserably cold. There'd been a snowstorm on Friday. But every one of Ethel's winter coats was still in place, in her closet. . . .

Nicky Sepetti shivered in the cable-knit cardigan his wife had made for him the year he went to prison. It still fit at the shoulders, but now it hung loosely over his middle. He'd lost thirty pounds in prison.

It was only a block from his home to the boardwalk. Shaking his head impatiently at his wife's fussing—"Put on a scarf, Nicky, you've forgotten how strong the wind is from the ocean"—he pushed open the front door and closed it behind him. The tang of the salty air tickled his nostrils, and he breathed it appreciatively. When he was a kid growing up in Brooklyn, his mother used to take him down on the bus for a swim at Rockaway Beach. Thirty years ago he'd bought the house in Belle Harbor for a summer place for Marie and the kids. She'd moved here for good after his sentencing.

Seventeen years that ended last Friday! His first deep breath outside prison walls brought on waves of chest pain. "Avoid the cold," the doctors had cautioned him.

Marie had had a big dinner cooked, a sign, "Welcome Home, Nicky." He'd been so bushed that halfway through the meal he'd gone to bed. The kids had phoned, Nick Junior and Tessa. "Poppa, we love you," they said.

He hadn't let them visit him in prison. Tessa was just starting college when he went to jail. Now she was thirty-five, had two kids, lived in Arizona. Her husband called her Theresa. Nick Junior had changed his name to Damiano. That was Marie's maiden name. Nicholas Damiano, a CPA who lived in Connecticut.

"Don't come now," Nicky cautioned them. "Wait till the press isn't hanging around."

All weekend, he and Marie stayed in the house, two silent strangers, while the television cameras waited for him to come out.

But this morning they'd been gone. Stale news. That's all he was. A sick ex-con. Nicky breathed in the salt air and felt it fill his lungs.

A baldheaded guy in one of those crazy sweatsuits was jogging toward him, stopped. "Great to see you, Mr. Sepetti. You're looking great."

Nicky frowned. He didn't want to listen to that stuff. He *knew* how he looked. After he had showered, only half an hour ago, he'd studied himself fully and deliberately in the mirror on the bathroom door. Hair completely gone on top, but still thick around the fringes. When he started serving time, it had been black shot with silver: pepper and salt, the barber used to say. Now what was left of it was a faded gray or a dirty white, take your choice. The rest of the self-examination hadn't cheered him any. Protruding eyes that had always annoyed him, even when he was a pretty good-looking younger guy. Now they stuck out like marbles. A faint scar on his cheek that flamed against the pallor of his skin. The weight loss hadn't made him trim. Instead he looked saggy, like a pillow that had lost half its feathers. A man pushing sixty. He'd been forty-two when he went to jail.

"Yeah, I look great," he said. "Thanks." He knew that the guy who was blocking the sidewalk, beaming at him with a nervous, big-toothed smile, lived two or three houses up, but he couldn't remember his name.

He must have sounded annoyed. The jogger looked uncomfortable. "Anyhow. Glad you're back." His smile was forced now. "Terrific day, isn't it? Pretty cool, but you can tell spring is here."

If I want a weather report, I'll turn on the radio, Nicky thought, then raised his hand in a salute. "Yeah, yeah," he muttered. He walked quickly on until he reached the boardwalk.

The wind had whipped the ocean into a mass of churning foam. Nicky leaned on the guardrail remembering how when he was a kid he used to love to ride the waves. His mother was always hollering at him, "Don't go out so far. You'll drown. You'll see."

Restlessly he swung his body around and began walking down toward Beach Ninety-eighth Street. He'd go until he could see the roller coaster and then start back. The guys were coming to pick him up. They'd go to the club first and then have a celebration lunch on Mulberry Street. A sign of respect for him, but he didn't kid himself. Seventeen years was too long to be away. They'd gotten into stuff he never would have let them touch. The word was out that he was sick. They'd complete what they'd started in these last years. Ease him out. Take it or else.

Joey had been sentenced with him. Same amount of time. But Joey got out in six years. Joey was in charge now.

Myles Kearny. He could thank Kearny for those extra eleven years.

Nicky bent his head against the wind, still trying to cope with two bitter pills. His kids might claim they loved him, but they were embarrassed by him. When Marie went to visit them, she told their friends she was a widow.

Tessa. God, she'd been crazy about him when she was a little kid. Maybe he'd been wrong not to let her visit him all these years. Marie went to see her regularly. Out there, and in Connecticut, Marie called herself Mrs. Damiano. He wanted to see Tessa's kids. But her husband thought he should wait.

Marie. Nicky could feel the resentment in her for all the years she'd waited. It was worse than resentment. She tried to act glad to see him, but her eyes were cold and veiled. He could read her mind: "For what you did, Nicky, even among our friends we were outcasts." Marie was only fifty-four and looked ten years older. She worked in the personnel office of the hospital. She didn't have to, but when she took the job she'd told him, "I can't just sit in the house and look at four walls."

Marie. Nick Junior, no, *Nicholas,* Tessa, *no,* Theresa. Would they have been really sorry if he'd had a heart attack in prison? Maybe if he'd gotten out in six years like Joey it wouldn't have been too late. Too late for everything. The extra years he'd served because of Myles Kearny, and he'd still be there if they'd been able to figure a way to keep him in.

Nicky had passed Ninety-eighth Street before he realized he hadn't noticed the lumbering structure that was the ancient roller coaster, then was startled to see it had been torn down. He turned and began retracing his steps, shoving his chilled hands into his pockets, hunching his shoulders against the wind. The taste of bile was in his mouth, blotting out the fresh, salty tang of the sea on his lips. . . .

The car was waiting for him when he got home. Louie was behind the wheel. Louie, the one guy he could always turn his back to. Louie who didn't forget favors. "Any time you're ready, Don Sepetti," Louie said. "It's good to say that to you again." Louie meant it.

Nicky saw the hint of sullen resignation in Marie's eyes when he went into the house and changed his sweater for a suit jacket. He thought of the time in high school when he'd had to do a short-story report. He'd chosen a story about a guy who disappears and his wife thinks he's dead and "she comfortably settled herself into her life as a widow." Marie had comfortably settled herself into a life without him.

Face it. She didn't want him back. His children would be relieved if he vanished, Jimmy Hoffa style. Better yet, they'd like a nice, clean, natural death, one that didn't need explanations for their kids later on. If only they knew how close they were to having it all work out for them.

"Will you want supper when you come home?" Marie asked. "I mean, I'm on the noon-to-nine shift. Should I fix something and leave it in the refrigerator?"

"Forget it."

He was silent on the trip down the Fort Hamilton Parkway, through the Brooklyn–Battery Tunnel, into lower Manhattan. At the club, nothing had changed. Still a shabby storefront exterior. Inside, the card table with chairs grouped ready for the next game; the oversized, tarnished espresso machine; the pay telephone that everyone knew was tapped.

The only difference was in the attitude of the family. Oh sure, they clustered around him, paid their respects, smiled, phony welcoming smiles. But he knew.

He was glad when it was time to go to Mulberry Street. Mario, the restaurant owner, at least seemed glad to see him. The private room was ready for them. The pastas and the entrees were his favorites from the years before jail. Nicky felt himself start to relax, felt some of the old power flow into his body. He waited until dessert was served, cannoli with rich, black espresso coffee, before he looked from face to face of the ten men who were sitting like two identical rows of tin soldiers. He nodded, acknowledging those on his right side, then those on his left. Two of the faces were new to him. The one was okay. The other was introduced to him as "Carmen Machado."

Nicky studied him carefully. About thirty, dark thick hair and eyebrows, blunt nose, scrawny, but tough. He'd been around three, four years. Been in the slammer for auto theft when Alfie got to know him, they said. Instinctively Nicky did not trust him. He'd button Joey down on how much they really knew about him.

His eyes came to rest on Joey. Joey who had gotten out in six years, who had taken over control while he, Nicky, was locked up. Joey's round face was creased in lines that passed for a smile. Joey looked like the cat who swallowed the canary.

Nicky realized his chest was burning. Suddenly the dinner was lying heavy in his stomach. "Okay, so tell me," he ordered Joey. "What's on your mind?"

Joey continued to smile. "With respect, I got great news for you. We all know how you feel about sonofabitch Kearny. Wait till you hear this. There's a contract out on his daughter. *And it's not ours.* Steuber is gonna waste her. It's almost like a gift to you."

Nicky jumped up and slammed his fist on the table. Awash with rage, he hammered the heavy oak. "You stupid bastards!" he shouted. "You stinking, stupid bastards! Get it called off." He had a momentary impression of Carmen Machado, and suddenly knew he was looking into the face of a cop. "Get it called off. I tell you to get it called off, understand?"

Joey's expression turned from fear to concern to pity. "Nicky, you have to know that's impossible. Nobody can cancel a contract. It's too late."

Fifteen minutes later, beside a silent Louie at the driver's wheel, Nicky was on his way home to Belle Harbor. His chest was aflame with waves of pain. The nitroglycerin under his tongue was useless. When Kearny's kid got hit, the cops wouldn't stop till they hung it on him, and Joey knew it.

Drearily he realized he'd been a fool to warn Joey about Machado. "No way that guy worked in Florida for the Palino family," he'd told Joey. "You were too dumb to check him out, right? You stupid bastard, every time you open your mouth you're spilling your guts to a cop."

On Tuesday morning Seamus Lambston woke after four hours of sleep that had been plagued with troubled dreams. He'd closed up the place at two-thirty, read the paper for a while and silently crept into bed trying not to disturb Ruth.

When the girls were young, he'd been able to sleep later, get to the bar at noon, come home for an early dinner with the family and then go back till closing. But in the last years as business fell off in a relentlessly unchanging pattern and the rent doubled and doubled again, he'd let bartenders and waiters go and cut down on the food until now he had only a sandwich menu. He did all the buying himself, got to the place by eight or eight-thirty and, except for a rushed dinner, stayed until closing. And he still couldn't keep his head above water.

Ethel's face had haunted his dreams. The way her eyes bulged when she was angry. The sardonic smile that he'd eradicated from her face.

When he'd arrived at her place on Thursday afternoon, he'd pulled out a snapshot of the girls. "Ethel," he'd pleaded, "look at them. They need the money I'm paying you. Give me a break."

She had taken the picture and studied it carefully. "They should have been mine," she said as she handed it back to him.

Now his stomach squeezed in apprehension. His alimony payment was due on the fifth. Tomorrow. Did he dare not write the check?

It was seven-thirty. Ruth was already up. He could hear the splashing of the shower. He got out of bed and walked into the room that served as den and office. It was already harshly bright from the rays of the early-morning sun. He sat at the rolltop desk that had been in his family for three generations. Ruth hated it. She wanted to be able to replace all their old heavy furniture with modern pieces in light, airy colors. "In all these years, I've never bought so much as a new chair," she liked to remind him. "You left Ethel all your good furniture when you broke up, and I've had to live with the junk from your mother. The only new furniture I ever had were the cribs and beds for the girls and nothing like what I wanted for them."

Seamus put off the agony of decision about Ethel's check by writing some of the others. The gas and electric, the rent, the telephone. They'd canceled cable TV six months ago. That saved twenty-two dollars a month.

From the kitchen he heard the sound of the coffeepot being put on the stove. A few minutes later Ruth came into the den, with a glass of orange juice and a cup of steaming hot coffee on a small tray. She was smiling and for an instant reminded him of the quietly pretty woman he'd married three months after his divorce. Ruth was not given to affectionate gestures, but when she set the tray on the desk she bent down and kissed the top of his head.

"Seeing you write the monthly checks makes it really sink in," she said. "No more money to Ethel. Oh God, Seamus, we can finally begin to breathe. Let's celebrate tonight. Get someone to cover for you. We haven't gone out to dinner in months."

Seamus felt the muscles in his stomach twist. The rich smell of the coffee suddenly made him nauseous. "Honey, I just hope she doesn't change her mind," he faltered. "I mean I haven't got anything in writing. Do you think I should just send the check as usual and let her return it? I really think that would be best. Because then we'd have something legal, I mean, proof that she said it was okay to stop paying."

His voice choked to a gasp as a stinging slap snapped his head over his left shoulder. He looked up and winced at the murderous outrage on Ruth's face. He had seen that look on another face only a few days ago.

Then Ruth's expression dissolved into bright-red spots on her cheekbones and weary tears that welled in her eyes. "Seamus, I'm sorry. I just snapped." Her voice broke. She bit her lip and straightened her shoulders. "But *no more checks.* Let her try to go back on her word. I'll kill her myself rather than let you pay her another dime."

6

On Wednesday morning, Neeve told Myles about her concern over Ethel. Frowning as she spread cream cheese on a toasted bagel, she voiced the thoughts that had kept her awake half the night. "Ethel is rattlebrained enough to fly off without her new clothes, but she had made a date with her nephew for Friday."

"Or so he claims," Myles interjected.

"Exactly. I do know that on Thursday she turned in the article she was writing. Thursday was freezing cold, and it started to snow late in the day. Friday was like the middle of winter."

"You're turning into a meteorologist," Myles observed.

"Come on, Myles. I think something might be wrong. All of Ethel's warm coats were in her closet."

"Neeve, that woman will live forever. I can just see God and the Devil telling each other, 'Take her, she's yours.' " Myles smiled, enjoying his joke.

Neeve made a face at him, exasperated that he was not taking her concern seriously, but grateful for the bantering tone. The kitchen window was open a few inches, bringing in a breeze from the Hudson, a hint of salt that managed to camouflage the inevitable exhaust fumes of the thousands of cars that traveled the Henry Hudson Parkway. The snow was vanishing in the same abrupt manner it had arrived. Spring was in the air and maybe that fact had helped Myles's spirits. Or was there something else?

Neeve got up, went over to the stove, reached for the coffeepot and freshened both their cups. "You seem pretty chipper today," she commented. "Does that mean you've stopped worrying about Nicky Sepetti?"

"Let's just say I spoke to Herb and I'm satisfied that Nicky won't be able to brush his teeth without one of our boys gazing at his cavities."

"I see." Neeve knew better than to ask Myles any more about that. "Well, as long as you stop fussing over me." She looked at her watch. "I've got to get moving." At the door, she hesitated. "Myles, I know Ethel's wardrobe like the back of my hand. She vanished on Thursday or Friday in bitterly cold weather without a coat. How would you explain that?"

Myles had started to read the *Times.* Now he put it down, his expression patient. "Let's play the pretend game," he suggested. "Let's pretend that Ethel may have seen a coat in someone else's show window and decided it was just what she wanted."

The pretend game had started when Neeve was four and had helped herself to a forbidden can of soda. She'd looked up from the open refrigerator door, where she was blissfully draining the last drop, to see Myles eying her sternly. "I've got a good idea, Daddy," she'd said hurriedly. "Let's play the pretend game. Let's pretend the Coke is apple juice."

Neeve suddenly felt foolish. "That's why you're the cop and I run a dress shop," she said.

But by the time she had showered and dressed, in a boxy cocoa-brown cashmere jacket with bracelet sleeves and turned-back cuffs and a softly gathered black wool midcalf skirt, she had located the fallacy in Myles's thinking. Long ago the Coke hadn't been apple juice, and right now she'd stake everything she had that Ethel hadn't purchased a coat from anyone else.

On Wednesday morning, Douglas Brown awakened early and began to expand his domination over Ethel's apartment. It had been a pleasant surprise on returning from work last night to find it sparkling clean and as reasonably tidy as any human being could make it, given Ethel's massive piles of papers. He'd found some frozen meals in the freezer, selected a lasagna and sipped a cold beer while it heated. Ethel's television set was one of the new massive forty-inch units, and he'd set up a tray in the living room, eating while he watched.

Now, from the luxury of her silk-sheeted four-poster bed, he eyed the contents of the bedroom. His suitcase was still on the chaise, his suits draped over the back on hangers. Screw it. It wouldn't be smart to start using that precious closet of hers, but no reason he couldn't settle into the other one.

The front closet was clearly a catchall. He managed to arrange the photo albums and stacks of catalogues and piles of magazines so that he could use the clothes pole for his suits.

While coffee perked, he showered, appreciating the sparkling white tile, the fact that Ethel's rubble of perfume bottles and lotions was now neatly arranged on the glass tray to the right of the door. Even the towels were folded in the bathroom linen closet. That thought brought on a frown. The money. Had that Swedish kid who cleaned for Ethel found the money?

The thought made Doug jump from the shower, rub his lean body vigorously, wrap the towel around his middle and rush to the living room. He'd left a single hundred-dollar bill under the carpet near the wing chair. It was still there. So either the Swedish kid was honest or she hadn't noticed it.

Ethel was such a dope, he reflected. When that check came in every month from her ex, she had it cashed into one-hundred-dollar bills. "My mad money," she told Doug. That was the money she used when she took him out to dinner in an expensive restaurant. "They're eating beans and we're dining on caviar," she'd say. "Sometimes I go through it all in a month. Sometimes it piles up. Every so often I look around and send the leftover bucks to my accountant toward clothes. Restaurants and clothes. That's what the stupid worm has kept me in all these years."

Doug had laughed with her, clicking glasses as they toasted Seamus the worm. But that night he'd realized that Ethel never kept track of how much cash she had hidden around and so would never miss a couple of hundred bucks a month. Which was what he'd helped himself to these last two years. A couple of times she'd half suspected, but the minute she said anything he'd acted indignant, and she'd always backed right off. "If you'd just write down when you spend that money, you'd *see* where it goes," he'd shouted.

"I'm sorry, Doug," Ethel had apologized. "You know me. I get a bee in my bonnet and start shooting off my mouth." He blotted out the memory of that last conversation when she'd demanded that he run an errand for her on Friday and told him not to expect a tip. "I took your advice," she said, "and kept track of what I spent."

He'd rushed over here, sure of his ability to sweet-talk her, knowing that if she dumped him she'd have nobody she could order around. . . .

When the coffee was ready, Doug poured a cup, went back into the bedroom and dressed. As he knotted his tie, he surveyed himself critically in the mirror. He looked good. The facials he'd started having with the money he pilfered from Ethel had cleared up his skin. He'd also found a decent barber. The two suits he'd bought recently fitted him the way clothes were supposed to fit. The new receptionist at Cosmic had big eyes for him. He had let her know that he was only doing this crummy desk job because he was writing a play. She knew Ethel's name. "And you're a writer, too," she'd breathed in awe. He wouldn't mind bringing Linda here. But he had to be careful, for a while at least. . . .

Over a second cup of coffee, Doug methodically went through the papers in Ethel's desk. There was one cardboard expansion folder marked "Important." As he flipped through it, his face drained of color. That old windbag Ethel had blue-chip stocks! She had property in Florida! She had a million-dollar insurance policy!

There was a copy of her will in the last section of the folder. He couldn't believe his eyes when he read it.

Everything. Every single dime she had had been left to him. And she was worth a bundle.

He'd be late for work, but it didn't matter. Doug restored his clothes to the back of the chaise, made the bed carefully, got rid of the ashtray, folded a quilt, a pillow and sheets on the couch to suggest he'd slept there, and wrote a note: "Dear Aunt Ethel. Guess you're on one of your unexpected trips. Knew you wouldn't mind if I continue to bunk on the couch until my new place is ready. Hope you've been having fun. Your loving nephew, Doug."

And that establishes the nature of our relationship, he thought as he saluted Ethel's picture on the wall by the front door of the apartment.

At three o'clock on Wednesday afternoon, Neeve left a message at Tse-Tse's answering service. An hour later, Tse-Tse phoned. "Neeve, we just had a dress rehearsal. I think the play is great," she exulted. "All I do is pass the turkey and say, 'Yah,' but you never know. Joseph Papp might be in the audience."

"You'll be a star yet," Neeve said, meaning it. "I can't wait to brag 'I knew her when.' Tse-Tse, I have to get back into Ethel's apartment. Do you still have her key?"

"Nobody's heard from her?" Tse-Tse's voice lost its lilt. "Neeve, there's something weird going on. That nutty nephew of hers. He's sleeping in her bed and smoking in her room. Either he doesn't expect her back or he doesn't care if she tosses him out on his ear."

Neeve stood up. Suddenly she felt cramped behind her desk, and the samples of gowns and purses and jewelry and shoes strewn about her office seemed terribly unimportant. She'd changed to a two-piece dress from one of her newest designers. It was a pale-gray wool with a silver belt that rested on her hips. The tulip skirt barely skimmed her knees. A silk scarf in tones of gray, silver and peach was knotted at her neck. Two customers had ordered the outfit when they saw her wearing it on the sales floor.

"Tse-Tse," she asked, "would it be possible for you to go to Ethel's apartment again tomorrow morning? If she's there, fine. Admit you were worried about her. If the nephew is around, could you say that Ethel wanted you to do some extra work, clean out the kitchen cabinets or whatever?"

"Sure," Tse-Tse agreed. "I'd love to. This is off-off-Broadway, don't forget. No salary, just prestige. But I have to tell you, Ethel isn't worried about the state of her kitchen cabinets."

"If she turns up and doesn't want to pay you, I will," Neeve said. "I want to go with you. I know she has an appointment book in her desk. I'd just like to have some kind of idea about what plans she may have made before she disappeared."

They agreed to meet at eight-thirty the next morning in the lobby. At closing time, Neeve turned the lock on the Madison Avenue entrance to the store. She went back into her office for a quiet time over desk work. At seven she phoned the Cardinal's residence on Madison Avenue and was put through to Bishop Devin Stanton.

"I got your message," he told her. "I'll be delighted to come up to dinner tomorrow night, Neeve. Sal's coming? Good. The Three Musketeers from the Bronx don't get together enough these days. Haven't seen Sal since Christmas. Has he gotten married again, by any chance?"

Just before he said goodbye the Bishop reminded Neeve that his favorite dish was her pasta al pesto. "The only one who could make it better was your mother, God rest her," he said gently.

Devin Stanton did not usually refer to Renata in a casual phone call. Neeve had a sudden suspicion that he'd been chatting with Myles about Nicky Sepetti's release. He rang off before she could pin him down about that. You'll get your pesto, Uncle Dev, she thought—but you'll also get a flea in your ear. I can't have Myles hovering over me for the rest of my life.

Just before she left, she phoned Sal's apartment. As usual, he was in bubbling good humor. "Of course I haven't forgotten tomorrow night. What are you having? I'll bring the wine. Your father only thinks he knows about wine."

Laughing with him, Neeve replaced the receiver, turned off the lights and went outside. The capricious April weather had turned cool again, but even so she felt the absolute need for a long walk. To appease Myles, she hadn't jogged in nearly a week, and her entire body felt stiff.

She walked rapidly from Madison to Fifth Avenue and decided to cut through the park at Seventy-ninth Street. She always tried to avoid the area behind the museum where Renata's body had been found.

Madison Avenue had still been busy with cars and pedestrians. On Fifth, the taxis and limousines and shiny town cars whizzed by quickly, but on the west side of the street, bordering the park, there were few people. Tossing her head as she approached Seventy-ninth Street, Neeve refused to be deterred.

She was just turning into the park when a squad car pulled up. "Miss Kearny." A smiling sergeant rolled down the window. "How's the Commissioner doing?"

She recognized the sergeant. At one point he had been Myles's driver. She went over to chat with him.

A few paces behind her, Denny stopped abruptly. He was wearing a long, nondescript overcoat with the collar turned up and a stocking cap. His face was almost concealed. Even so he could feel the eyes of the cop at the passenger window of the squad car boring into him. Cops had long memories about faces, could recognize ones they knew even from glimpses of their profiles. Denny knew that. Now he resumed walking, ignoring Neeve, ignoring the cops, but he could still feel eyes following him. There was a bus stand directly ahead. As a bus pulled up, he joined the cluster of waiting people and got on it. When he paid his fare, he could feel the perspiration forming on his forehead. Another second and that cop might have recognized him.

Sullenly Denny took a seat. This job was worth more than he was being paid. When Neeve Kearny went down, forty thousand New York cops would be on a manhunt.

As Neeve entered the park, she wondered whether it was just coincidence that Sergeant Collins had happened to spot her. Or, she speculated as she walked rapidly along the path, has Myles got New York's finest playing guardian angel to me?

There were plentiful joggers, few bicyclers, some pedestrians, a tragic number of homeless resting under layers of newspapers or ragged blankets. They could die there and no one would notice, Neeve thought as her soft Italian boots moved soundlessly along the paths. To her annoyance she found herself glancing over her shoulder. In her teens she had gone to the library and looked up the pictures in the tabloids of her mother's body. Now, as she hurried with increasingly rapid steps, she had the eerie feeling that she was seeing the pictures again. But this time it was her facc, not Renata's, that covered the front page of the *Daily News* above the caption "Murdered."

Kitty Conway had joined the riding class at Morrison State Park for only one reason. She needed to fill time. She was a pretty woman of fifty-eight, with strawberry blonde hair and gray eyes that were enhanced by the fine lines that edged and framed them. There was a time those eyes had always seemed to dance with an amused and impish glow. When she turned fifty, Kitty had protested to Michael, "How come I still feel twenty-two?"

"Because you *are* twenty-two."

Michael had been gone for nearly three years. As Kitty gingerly hoisted herself up on the chestnut mare, she thought of all the activities she'd become involved in during these three years. She now had a real-estate license and was a pretty darn good saleswoman. She'd redecorated the house in Ridgewood, New Jersey, which she and Michael had bought only the year before she lost him. She was active in the Literacy Volunteers. She volunteered one day a week at the museum. She'd made two trips to Japan, where Mike Junior, her only child, a career army officer, was stationed, and had delighted in spending time with her half-Japanese granddaughter. She'd also resumed piano lessons without enthusiasm. Twice a month she drove disabled patients to doctor appointments, and now the latest activity was horseback riding. But no matter what she did, no matter how many friends she enjoyed, she was always haunted by the feeling of aloneness. Even now, as she gamely fell in with the dozen other student riders behind the instructor, she found only profound sadness in observing the aura around the trees, the reddish glow that was a promise of spring. "Oh, Michael," she whispcred, "I wish it would get better. I'm really trying."

"How are you making out, Kitty?" the instructor yelled.

"Fine," she shouted.

"If you want to be fine, keep your reins short. Show her you're boss. And keep those heels down."

"Gotcha." Go to hell, Kitty thought. This damn nag is the worst of the lot. I was supposed to have Charley, but of course you assigned him to that sexy-looking new girl.

It was a steep climb up the trail. Her horse stopped to eat every piece of green along the way. One by one, the others in the group passed her. She didn't want to get separated from them. "Come on, damn you," she murmured. She kicked her heels against the horse's flanks.

In a sudden, violent movement, the mare threw back her head, then reared. Startled, Kitty pulled at the reins as the animal swerved down a side path. Frantically she tried to remember not to lean forward. Sit *back* when you're in trouble! She felt the loose stones slide under the hoofs. The uneven canter changed to a full gallop, downhill, over the uneven ground. Dear God, if the horse fell, it would crush her! She tried to slide her boots so that only the tips were still in the stirrups, so as not to get hung up if she fell.

From behind, she heard the instructor yelling, "Don't pull on the reins!" She felt the horse stumble as a rock gave way under its hind leg. It started to pitch forward, then regained its balance. A piece of black plastic flew up and grazed Kitty's cheek. She looked down, and an impression of a hand framed by a bright-blue cuff darted through her mind and was gone.

The horse reached the bottom of the rocky incline and, taking the bit between its teeth, galloped flat out toward the stable. Kitty managed to hang on till the last moment, when she went flying from the saddle as the mare came to an abrupt stop at the watering trough. She felt every bone in her body bounce as she hit the ground, but she was able to pull herself to her feet, shake her arms and legs and move her head from side to side. Nothing seemed to be badly strained or broken, thank God.

The instructor galloped up. "I told you, you gotta *control* her. You're the boss. You okay?"

"Never better," Kitty said. She started for her car. "I'll see you in the next millennium."

A half hour later, gratefully reclining in her steaming, churning bathtub Jacuzzi, she began to laugh. So an equestrian I'm not, she decided. That's it for the sport of kings. I'll just jog like a sensible human being from now on. Mentally she relived the harrowing experience. It probably hadn't lasted more than two minutes, she thought. The worst part was when that miserable nag slipped. . . . The image of the plastic flying past her face returned. And then, that impression of a hand in a sleeve. How ridiculous. But still, she *had* seen it, had she not?

She closed her eyes, enjoying the soothing, whirling water, the scent and feel of the bath oil.

Forget it, she told herself.

The sharply cool evening caused the heat to go on in the apartment. Even so, Seamus felt chilled to the soul. After pushing a hamburger and French fries around on his plate, he gave up the pretense of eating. He was aware of Ruth's eyes boring into him across the table. "Did you do it?" she asked finally.

"No."

"Why not?"

"Because it might just be better to let it go."

"I told you to put it in writing. Thank her for agreeing that you need the money and she doesn't." Ruth's voice began to rise. "Tell her that in these twenty-two years you've paid her nearly a quarter of a million dollars on top of a big settlement and it's obscene to want more for a marriage that lasted less than six years. Congratulate her on the big contract she has for her new book and say that you're glad she doesn't need the money but your kids sure do. Then sign the letter, and drop it in her mailbox. We'll keep a copy of it. And if she squawks, there won't be a person alive who doesn't know what a greedy phony she is. I'd like to see how many colleges drape her with honorary degrees if she reneges."

"Ethel thrives on threats," Seamus whispered. "She'd turn a letter like that around. She'd make the alimony payments sound like a triumph for womankind. It's a mistake."

Ruth shoved the plate aside. "Write it!"

They had an old Xerox machine in the den. It took three attempts before they had a clear copy of the letter. Ruth handed Seamus his coat. "Now march yourself over and stick that in her mailbox."

He elected to walk the nine blocks. His head sunk in misery, his hands jammed into his pockets, he fingered the two envelopes he was carrying. One held a check. He had taken it from the back of the checkbook and written it without Ruth's knowledge. The letter was in the other envelope. Which one should he put into Ethel's box? As though she were standing before him, he could see her reaction to the note. With equal clarity, he could visualize what Ruth would do if he left the check.

He turned the corner of West End Avenue onto Eighty-second Street. There were still plenty of people out. Young couples, shopping on the way home from work, their arms filled with groceries.

Well-dressed middle-agers, flagging cabs, off to expensive dinners and the theater. Derelicts huddled against brownstones.

Seamus shivered as he reached Ethel's building. The mailboxes were in the vestibule inside the locked main door at the top of the steps. Whenever he was down to the wire with the check, he'd ring the bell for the superintendent, who'd let him in to drop the check into Ethel's mailbox. But today that wasn't necessary. A kid he recognized as living on the fourth floor brushed past him and started up the steps. On impulse he grabbed her arm. She turned, looking scared. She was a bony-looking kid, thin face, sharp features. Maybe about fourteen years old. Not like his girls, Seamus thought. From somewhere in their genes, they'd received pretty faces, warm, loving smiles. A moment of profound regret washed over him as he pulled out one of the envelopes. "Would you mind if I went into the vestibule with you? I have to put something in Miss Lambston's mailbox."

The cautious expression faded. "Oh sure. I know who you are. You're her ex. It must be the fifth of the month. That's when she always says you deliver the ransom." The girl laughed, showing gaping spaces between her teeth.

Wordlessly, Seamus fumbled in his pocket for the envelope and waited as she unlocked the door. The murderous rage washed over him again. So he was the laughingstock of the building!

The mailboxes were directly inside the outer door. Ethel's was fairly full. He still didn't know what to do. Should he leave the check or the letter? The girl waited by the inner door, watching him. "You're just on time," she said. "Ethel told my mother she yanks you right into court when you're late with her check."

Panic swept over Seamus. It would have to be the check. He grabbed the envelope from his pocket and tried to force it down the narrow slit in the mailbox.

When he arrived home, he nodded yes to Ruth's fiercely angry question. He could not at this moment stand the explosion that would occur when he admitted he'd dropped off the alimony. After she stalked out of the room, he hung up his coat and took the second envelope from his pocket. He glanced into it. It was empty.

Seamus sank into a chair, his body trembling, bile rising in his throat, his head in his hands. He had managed to fumble again. He had put the check and the letter into the same envelope, and now they were in Ethel's mailbox.

Nicky Sepetti spent Wednesday morning in bed. The burning in his chest was even worse than last night. Marie was in and out of the bedroom. She brought in a tray with orange juice, coffee, fresh Italian bread spread thick with marmalade. She pestered him to let her call a doctor.

Louie arrived at noon, shortly after Marie went to work. "With respect, Don Nicky, you look real sick," he said.

Nicky told him to watch television downstairs. When he was ready to go to New York, he'd let him know.

Louie whispered, "You were right about Machado. They got him." He smiled and winked.

In early evening, Nicky got up and began to dress. He'd be better off on Mulberry Street, and it wouldn't be good for anyone to guess how sick he really was. As he reached for his jacket, his skin became damp with perspiration. Holding on to the poster of the bed, he eased himself down, loosened his tie and shirt collar and lay back on the bed. For hours, the chest pain kept swelling and receding like a giant wave. Under his tongue, his mouth began to burn from the nitroglycerin tablets he kept swallowing. They did nothing to ease the pain, only gave him the familiar sharp, brief headache as they melted.

Faces began drifting past his vision. His mother's face: "Nicky, don't hang around with those guys. Nicky, you're a good boy. Don't get into trouble." Proving himself to the mob. No job too big or too small. But never women. That dumb remark he'd made in the courtroom. Tessa. He'd really like to see Tessa once more. Nicky Junior. No, *Nicholas. Theresa and Nicholas.* They'd be glad he'd died in bed like a gentleman.

From far away he heard the front door open and close. Marie must have come in. Then the doorbell ringing, a hard and demanding sound. Marie's angry voice. "I don't know if he's home. What do you want?"

I'm home, Nicky thought. Yeah. I'm home. The bedroom door swung fully open. Through glazed eyes, he saw the shock on Marie's face, heard her shriek, "Get a doctor." Other faces. Cops. They didn't have to be in uniform. He could smell them even when he was dying. Then he knew why they were there. That undercover guy, the one they'd wasted. Right away the cops had come to him, of course!

"Marie," he said. It came out a whisper.

She bent over, put her ear to his lips, smoothed his forehead. "Nicky!" She was crying.

"On . . . my . . . mother's . . . grave . . . I . . . didn't . . . order . . . Kearny's wife killed." He wanted to say that he'd intended to try to get the contract on Kearny's kid stopped. But all he managed to cry was "Mama" before a last blinding, tearing pain ripped through his chest, and his eyes went out of focus. His head slumped over on the pillow as his agonized breathing filled the house, and abruptly stopped.

How many people had Bigmouth Ethel told that she thought he was helping himself to the money she hid around the apartment? It was a question that haunted Doug Wednesday morning after he arrived at his desk in the lobby of the Cosmic Oil Building. Automatically he verified appointments, wrote names, doled out plastic visitors' cards and collected them back again as people departed. Several times, Linda, the seventh-floor receptionist, stopped by to chat with him. Today he was a little cool to her, which she seemed to find intriguing. What would she think if she knew that he was going to inherit a bundle of money? Where had Ethel *made* all that loot?

There was only one answer. Ethel had told him that she'd taken Seamus for his eyeteeth when he wanted out of the marriage. Besides the alimony, she'd come off with a hefty settlement and had probably been smart enough to invest it. Then that book she wrote five or six years ago had sold well. Ethel, for all her scatterbrained act, had always been pretty shrewd. It was that thought that caused Doug to feel queasy with apprehension. She had known that he was helping himself to money. *How many people had she told?*

After wrestling with the problem until noon, he made his decision. There were just about enough supercheck funds available in his checking account to take out four hundred dollars. Impatiently he waited on the interminable line at the bank and got the money in hundred-dollar bills. He'd stash them in some of Ethel's hiding places, the ones she didn't use most of the time. That way, if anybody searched, the money would be there. Somewhat reassured, he stopped for a hot dog at a food cart and went back to work.

At six-thirty, as Doug was rounding the corner from Broadway to Eighty-second Street, he saw Seamus hurrying down the steps from Ethel's building. He almost laughed out loud. Of course! It was the fifth of the month, and Seamus the wimp was there, right on the button with his alimony check. What a sad sack he was in that shabby coat! Regretfully, Doug realized that it would be a while before he himself could buy any more new clothes. He'd have to be very, very careful from now on.

He'd been collecting the mail every day with the key Ethel kept in a box on top of her desk. The envelope from Seamus was jammed into the box, still sticking out a little. Other than that there was mostly junk mail. Ethel's bills went directly to her accountant. He flipped through the envelopes, then dropped them on the desk. All except the unstamped one, the contribution from Seamus. It hadn't been sealed properly. There was a note inside, and the outline of the check was clearly visible.

It would be easy to open and reseal it. Doug's hand lingered on the flap, then, taking care not to cause a tear, he opened the envelope. The check fell out. Boy, he'd like to have the handwriting on it analyzed. If ever stress showed like a road map, it was in the slanted squiggle that was Seamus' penmanship.

Doug laid the check down, opened the note, read it, reread it and felt his mouth drop in amazement. What the hell . . . Carefully he reinserted the note and the check in the envelope, licked the glued area and pressed the flap firmly down. An image of Seamus with his hands hunched in his pockets, almost running as he crossed the street, loomed like a freeze-time in Doug's mind. Seamus was up to something. What kind of game was he playing, writing to say that Ethel had agreed not to take any more alimony and then including the check?

In a pig's eye she let you off the hook, Doug thought. A chill came over him. Had that note been intended for *his* eyes, not Ethel's?

When Neeve arrived home, she found to her delight that Myles had done a massive grocery shopping. "You even went to Zabar's," she said happily. "I was trying to figure how early I could leave the shop tomorrow. Now I can get everything started tonight." She had warned him that she'd be doing paperwork in the shop after closing hours. She uttered a silent prayer of gratitude that he did not think to ask her how she had gotten across town.

Myles had cooked a small leg of lamb, steamed fresh green beans and made a tomato-and-onion vinaigrette salad. He'd set the small table in the den and had a bottle of burgundy open nearby. Neeve rushed to change into slacks and a sweater, then with a sigh of relief settled into a chair and reached for the wine. "This is very kind of you, Commish," she said.

"Well, since you're feeding the aging Musketeers from the Bronx tomorrow night, I figured one good turn deserves another." Myles began to carve the roast.

Neeve observed him silently. His skin tone was good. His eyes no longer had that sick, heavy look. "I hate to compliment you, but you do realize you look darn healthy," she told him.

"I feel okay." Myles placed the perfectly done slices of lamb on Neeve's plate. "I hope I didn't use too much garlic."

Neeve sampled the first bite. "Great. You have to be feeling better to cook this well."

Myles sipped the burgundy. "Good wine, if I say so myself." His eyes clouded.

Some depression, the doctor had told her. "The heart attack, giving up his job, the bypass . . ."

"And always worrying about me," Neeve had injected.

"Always worrying about you because he can't forgive himself for not worrying about your mother."

"How do I make him stop?"

"Keep Nicky Sepetti in jail. If that's not possible, by spring urge your father to get busy on some project. Right now his guts are torn, Neeve. He'd be lost without you, but he hates himself for depending on you emotionally. He's a proud guy. And something else. Stop babying him."

That had been six months ago. It was spring now. Neeve knew she had made a real attempt to treat Myles in their old way. They used to have vigorous debates about everything from Neeve's acceptance of the loan from Sal to politics on every level. "You're the first Kearny in ninety years to vote Republican," Myles had exploded.

"It's not quite the same as losing the faith."

"It's getting warm."

And now just when he's on the right track, he's all upset about Nicky Sepetti, she thought, and that could go on forever.

Unconsciously shaking her head, she glanced around, deciding as always that the den was her favorite room in the apartment. The worn Oriental carpeting was in shades of red and blue; the leather couch and the matching chairs were handsome and inviting. Pictures covered the wall. Myles receiving innumerable plaques and honors. Myles with the Mayor, the Governor, the *Republican* President. The windows overlooking the Hudson. The tieback draperies were the ones Renata had hung. Victorian-era, they were a deep warm blue and crimson, a subtle stripe that shimmered in the reflection of the crystal sconces on the wall. Between the sconces were Renata's pictures. The very first one her own father had taken when she was the ten-year-old child who had saved Myles and now looked at him adoringly as he lay, his head bandaged, propped on pillows. Renata with Neeve as a baby, with Neeve as a toddler. Renata and Neeve and Myles snorkeling off Maui. That was the year before Renata died.

Myles asked about the menu for the next night's dinner. "I didn't know what you'd want, so I bought everything," he said.

"Sal told me he doesn't want to eat your diet. The Bishop wants pesto."

Myles grunted. "I can remember when Sal thought a hero sandwich was a rare treat and when Devin's mother sent him to the deli for nickel fish cakes and a can of Heinz spaghetti."

Neeve had coffee in the kitchen as she began to organize the dinner party. Renata's cookbooks were on the shelf over the sink. She reached for her favorite, an old family relic with northern-Italian recipes.

After Renata's death, Myles had sent Neeve to a private tutor to keep up her conversational Italian. Every summer growing up she'd spent a month in Venice with her grandparents, and she'd taken her junior year in college in Perugia. For years she'd avoided the cookbooks, unwilling to see the notations in Renata's bold, curlicued hand. "More pepper. Bake only twenty minutes. Hold the oil." She could see Renata singing to herself as she cooked, letting Neeve stir or mix or measure, exploding, *"Cara,* this is either a misprint or the chef was drunk. Who could put so much oil in this dressing? Better to drink the Dead Sea."

Sometimes Renata had drawn quick sketches of Neeve on the margins of the pages, sketches that were charming, beautifully drawn miniatures: Neeve dressed as a princess sitting at the table, Neeve hovering over a large mixing bowl, Neeve in a Gibson Girl dress sampling a cookie. Dozens of sketches, each one evoking a sense of profound loss. Even now Neeve could not allow herself to do more than skim her eyes over the sketches. The memories they recalled were too painful. She felt sudden moisture in her eyes.

"I used to tell her she should take art lessons," Myles said.

She had not realized he was looking over her shoulder. "Mother liked what she did."

"Selling clothes to bored women."

Neeve bit her tongue. "Exactly how you'd classify me, I guess."

Myles looked conciliatory. "Oh, Neeve, I'm sorry. I'm on edge. I admit it."

"You're on edge, but you also meant it. Now get out of my kitchen."

Deliberately she slammed pots as she measured, poured, cut, sautéed, simmered and baked. Face it. Myles was the world's leading male chauvinist. If Renata had pursued art, if she'd developed into a mediocre painter of watercolors, he would have considered it a ladylike hobby. He simply couldn't understand that helping women select becoming clothing could make a big difference for those women in their social and business lives.

I've been written up in *Vogue, Town and Country, The New York Times* and God knows where else, Neeve thought, but that doesn't cut any ice with him. It's as though I'm stealing from people when I charge them for expensive clothes.

She remembered how annoyed Myles had been when, during their Christmas party, he found Ethel Lambston in the kitchen browsing through Renata's cookbooks. "Are you interested in cooking?" he'd asked her icily.

Naturally Ethel hadn't noticed his annoyance. "Not at all," she'd told him airily. "I read Italian and happened to notice the books. *Queste desegni sono stupendi."*

She'd been holding the book with the sketches. Myles had taken it from her hand. "My wife was Italian. I don't speak the language."

That was the point at which Ethel realized Myles was an unattached widower and latched onto him for the evening.

Finally everything was prepared. Neeve put the dishes into the refrigerator, tidied up and set the table in the dining room. She studiously ignored Myles, who was watching television in the den. As she finished placing the serving dishes on the sideboard, the eleven-o'clock news came on.

Myles held out a snifter of brandy to her. "Your mother used to bang the pots and pans when she was mad at me, too." His smile was boyish. It was his apology.

Neeve accepted the brandy. "Too bad she didn't throw them at you."

They laughed together as the phone rang. Myles picked it up. His genial "Hello" was quickly replaced by rapid-fire questions. Neeve watched as his mouth tightened. When he replaced the receiver, he said tonelessly, "That was Herb Schwartz. One of our guys had been planted in Nicky Sepetti's inner circle. He was just found in a garbage dump. Still alive, and there's a chance he'll make it."

Neeve listened, her mouth going dry. Myles's face was contorted, but she didn't know what she was seeing in it. "His name is Tony Vitale," Myles said. "He's thirty-one years old. They knew him as Carmen Machado. They shot him four times. He should be dead, but somehow he hung on. There was something he wanted us to know."

"What was it?" Neeve whispered.

"Herb was there in the emergency room. Tony told him, 'No contract, Nicky, Neeve Kearny.' " Myles put his hand over his face as though trying to hide the expression on it.

Neeve stared at his anguished face. "You didn't seriously think there would be one?"

"Oh yes I did." Myles's voice rose. "Oh yes I did. And now for the first time in seventeen years, I can sleep at night." He put his hands on her shoulders. "Neeve, they went to question Nicky. Our guys.

And they got there just in time to watch him die. The stinking sonofabitch had a heart attack. He's dead. Neeve, Nicky Sepetti is dead!"

He put his arms around her. She could feel the wild beating of his heart.

"Then let his death free you, Dad," she begged. Unconsciously she cupped his face in her palms, and remembered that that was Renata's familiar caress. Deliberately she imitated Renata's accent. "*Caro* Milo, leesten to me."

They both managed shaky smiles as Myles said, "I'll try. I promise."

Undercover detective Anthony Vitale, known to the Sepetti crime family as Carmen Machado, lay in the intensive-care unit of St. Vincent's Hospital. The bullets had lodged in his lung, split the ribs protecting his chest cavity and shattered his left shoulder. Miraculously he was still alive. Tubes invaded his body, dripping antibiotics and glucose into his veins. A respirator had taken over the function of breathing.

In the moments of consciousness that came to him from time to time, Tony could perceive the distraught faces of his parents. I'm tough. I'll try to make it, he wanted to reassure them.

If only he could talk. Had he been able to say anything when they found him? He had tried to tell them about the contract, but it hadn't come out the way he meant it.

Nicky Sepetti and his gang hadn't put a contract on Neeve Kearny. Someone else had. Tony knew he'd been shot on Tuesday night. How long had he been in the hospital? Dimly he remembered fragments of what they'd told Nicky about the contract: You can't call off a contract. The ex-Commissioner will be planning another funeral.

Tony tried to pull himself up. He had to warn them.

"Easy does it," a soft voice murmured.

He felt a prick in his arm and a few moments later slid into a quiet, dreamless sleep.

7

Thursday morning at eight o'clock, Neeve and Tse-Tse were in a taxi across the street from Ethel Lambston's apartment. On Tuesday, Ethel's nephew had left for work at eight-twenty. Today they wanted to be certain to avoid him. The cabdriver's protest, "I don't get rich on waiting time," was mollified by Neeve's promise of a ten-dollar tip.

It was Tse-Tse who at eight-fifteen spotted Doug. "Look."

Neeve watched as he locked the door of the apartment, glanced around and headed for Broadway. The morning was cool, and he wore a belted trench coat. "That's a real Burberry," she said. "He must get paid awfully well for a receptionist."

The apartment was surprisingly tidy. Sheets and a quilt were stacked under a pillow at the end of the couch. The pillow sham was wrinkled. Clearly it had been slept on. There was no sign of a used ashtray, but Neeve was sure she detected the faint odor of cigarette smoke in the air. "He's been smoking but doesn't want to be caught at it," she observed. "I wonder why."

The bedroom was a model of neatness. The bed was made. Doug's suitcase was on the chaise; hangers with suits, slacks and jackets were laid across it. His note to Ethel was propped against the mirror on the dressing table.

"Who's kidding who?" Tse-Tse asked. "What made him write that and stop using her bedroom?"

Neeve knew that Tse-Tse had an excellent eye for detail. "All right," she said. "Let's start with that note. Has he ever left one for her before?"

Tse-Tse was wearing her Swedish-maid outfit. The coil of braids shook vigorously as she said, "Never."

Neeve walked to the closet and opened the door. Hanger by hanger, she examined Ethel's wardrobe to see whether she had missed any of her coats. But they were all there: the sable, the stone marten, the cashmere, the wraparound, the Burberry, the leather, the cape. At Tse-Tse's puzzled expression, she explained what she was doing.

Tse-Tse reinforced her suspicions. "Ethel always tells me that she's given up being an impulse buyer since you took over dressing her. You're right. There's no other coat."

Neeve closed the closet door. "I'm not happy snooping around like this, but I have to. Ethel always carries a daily calendar in her purse, but I'm pretty sure she has a ledger-sized one as well."

"Yes she does," Tse-Tse said. "It's on her desk."

The appointment book was lying next to a pile of mail. Neeve opened it. It consisted of a full eleven-by-fourteen page for each day of the month, including December of the previous year. She flipped the pages until she reached March 31. In a bold scrawl, Ethel had written: "Have Doug pick up clothes at Neeve's Place." The slot for three o'clock was circled. The notation next to it was "Doug at the apartment."

Tse-Tse was looking over Neeve's shoulder. "So he's not lying about that," Tse-Tse said. The morning sun had started to pour brightly into the room. Suddenly it vanished behind a cloud. Tse-Tse shivered. "Honest to God, Neeve, this place is starting to spook me."

Without answering, Neeve flipped through the month of April. There were scattered appointments, cocktail parties, lunches. All the pages had a line drawn through. On April first, Ethel had written, "Research/Writing Book."

"She canceled everything. She was planning to go away or at least hole up somewhere and write," Neeve murmured.

"Then maybe she left a day early?" Tse-Tse suggested.

"It's possible." Neeve began to turn the pages backward. The last week of March was crammed with the names of prominent designers: Nina Cochran, Gordon Steuber, Victor Costa, Ronald Altern, Regina Mavis, Anthony della Salva, Kara Potter. "She can't have seen all these people," Neeve said. "I think that she phones to verify quotes just before she turns an article in." She pointed to an entry on Thursday, March 30: "Deadline for *Contemporary Woman* article."

Quickly she skimmed through the first three months of the year, noticing that next to her appointments Ethel had scrawled in the cost of cabs and tips, memos about lunches, dinners and meetings: "Good interview but annoyed if you keep him waiting. . . . Carlos new headwaiter at Le Cygne. . . . Don't use Valet Limo—car smelled like Airwick factory. . . ."

The notes were erratic jottings, the figures often crossed out and changed. Besides that, Ethel was obviously a doodler. Triangles, hearts, swirls and drawings covered every inch of the pages.

On impulse Neeve turned to December 22, the day of the Christmas party she and Myles had given. Ethel had obviously considered the event important. The address of Schwab House and Neeve's name were in block letters and underscored. Swirls and twirls accompanied Ethel's comment: "Neeve's father, single and fascinating."

On the side of the page Ethel had drawn a crude imitation of a sketch from Renata's cookbook.

"Myles would have an ulcer if he saw this," Neeve commented. "I had to tell her that he was still too sick to plan any social events. She wanted to invite him to some formal dinner for New Year's. I thought he'd choke."

She turned the pages back to the last week in March and began to copy the names Ethel had listed there. "At least it's a starting place," she said. Two names jumped out at her. Toni Mendell, the editor of *Contemporary Woman*. The cocktail party hadn't been the place to ask her to search her memory for any comment Ethel might have made about a possible writing retreat. The other name was Jack Campbell. Obviously the book contract had been all-important to Ethel. Maybe she had told Campbell more about her plans than he'd realized.

Neeve snapped her notebook shut and zipped up the case. "I'd better get out of here." She reknotted the red-and-blue scarf at her throat. The collar of her coat was high, and her mass of black hair was pulled back in a chignon.

"You look great," Tse-Tse observed. "This morning on the elevator, I heard the guy in Eleven C ask who you were."

Neeve pulled on her gloves. "A Prince Valiant type, I trust."

Tse-Tse giggled. "Somewhere between forty and death. A bad rug. Looks like black feathers on a field of cotton."

"He's yours. Okay, if Ethel pops up or her loving nephew comes home early, you have your story. Do some work on the kitchen cabinets, wash the glasses on the top shelves. Make it look as though you've been busy, but keep your eyes open." Neeve glanced at the mail. "Take a look through that. Maybe Ethel received a letter that made her change her mind. God, I feel like a Peeping Tom, but this is something we have to do. We both know something's strange, still we can't be marching in and out of here indefinitely."

As she started for the door, Neeve glanced around. "You do manage to make this place look positively livable," she said. "In a way, it reminds me of Ethel. All you usually notice around here is the surface clutter, and it turns you off. Ethel always acts so dizzy you forget she's a very sharp lady."

The wall with Ethel's myriad of publicity pictures was by the door. Her hand on the knob, Neeve studied them carefully. In most of her pictures, Ethel looked as though she'd been photographed in the middle of a sentence. Her mouth was usually slightly open, her eyes blazing with energy, the muscles of her face visibly in motion.

One snapshot caught Neeve's eye. The expression was tranquil, the mouth quiet, the eyes sad. What was it Ethel had once confided? "I was born on Valentine's Day. Easy to remember, huh? But do you know how many years it's been since anyone sent me a card or bothered to phone me? I end up singing 'Happy Birthday' to myself."

Neeve had made a mental note to send Ethel flowers and invite her out to lunch the past Valentine's Day, but she'd been away that week skiing in Vail. I'm sorry, Ethel, she thought. I'm really sorry.

It seemed to her that the mournful eyes in the snapshot were unforgiving.

After his bypass surgery, Myles had begun the habit of taking long afternoon walks. What Neeve did not know was that for the last four months he had also been seeing a psychiatrist on East Seventy-fifth Street. "You're suffering from depression," his cardiologist had told him bluntly. "Most people do, after this kind of operation. It goes with the territory. But I suspect yours had other roots." He'd bullied Myles into making the first appointment with Dr. Adam Felton.

Thursday at two was his regular time. He hated the idea of lying on a couch and instead sat in a deep leather chair. Adam Felton was not the stereotypical psychiatrist Myles had expected. In his midforties, he had a crew cut, somewhat rakish-looking glasses and a slender, wiry body. By the third or fourth visit, he had won Myles's trust. Myles no longer felt he was baring his soul. Instead he had the feeling that when he spoke to Felton it compared with being back in the squad room, laying out all the aspects of an investigation to his men.

Funny, he thought now as he watched Felton twirl a pencil between his fingers, it never occurred to me to talk to Dev instead. But this was not a matter for the confessional. "I didn't think that shrinks were supposed to have nervous habits," he observed dryly.

Adam Felton laughed and gave the pencil he was twirling another deft spin. "I have every right to a nervous habit when I'm giving up smoking. You seem pretty upbeat today." The remark could have been made casually to an acquaintance at a cocktail party.

Myles told him about Nicky Sepetti's death and at Felton's probing questions exclaimed, "We've been through this territory. I've had seventeen years of feeling as though something would happen to Neeve the minute Sepetti got out. I failed Renata. How many damn times do I have to tell you that? I *didn't take Nicky's threat seriously.* He's a cold-blooded killer. He wasn't out three days before our guy was shot. Nicky probably fingered him. He always said he could smell a cop."

"And now you feel your daughter is safe?"

"I *know* she's safe. Our guy was able to tell us there's no contract on her. It must have been discussed. I know the rest of them wouldn't try. They were going to ease Nicky out anyhow. They'll be happy to drape him in a casket blanket."

Adam Felton began to twirl the pencil again, hesitated and dropped it decisively into the wastebasket. "You're telling me that Sepetti's death has released you from a fear that has haunted you for seventeen years. What does that mean to you? How will it change your life?"

Forty minutes later when Myles left the office and resumed his walk, his step was reminiscent of the brisk pace that at one time was typical of him. He knew that he was almost fully recovered physically. Now that he didn't have to worry about Neeve, he'd take a job. He hadn't told Neeve that he'd had inquiries about his availability to head up the President's Drug Enforcement Agency in Washington. It would mean spending a lot of time there, getting an apartment. But it would be good for Neeve to be on her own. She'd quit spending so much time home and get involved with young people. Before he got sick she used to spend summer weekends in the Hamptons and do a lot more skiing in Vail. In the last year he'd had to force her to go away even for a few days. He wanted her to get married. He wouldn't be around forever. Now, thanks to Nicky's timely heart attack, he could be in Washington with a free mind.

Myles could still remember the awesome pain of his own massive heart attack. It was as though a steamroller with spikes had rolled across his chest. "I hope that's what you felt on the way out, Buster," he thought. Then it was as though he could see his mother's face, sternly fixed on him. *Wish evil to someone else and evil will come to you. What goes around comes around.*

He crossed York Avenue and passed Bella Vita restaurant. The faint delicious aroma of Italian cooking tantalized his nostrils, and he thought with pleasure of the dinner Neeve had prepared for tonight. It would be good to get together with Dev and Sal again. God, how long ago it seemed since they were kids growing up on Tenbroeck Avenue. The way people knocked the Bronx these days! It had been a great place to live in. Only seven houses on the entire block, woods that were thick with birch and oak. They'd made tree houses in them. Sal's parents' truck garden on what was now industrial Williams-bridge Road. The fields where he and Sal and Devin had gone sleigh-riding—the Einstein Medical Center covered those fields now. . . . But there were still plenty of good residential areas.

On Park Avenue, Myles walked around a small mound of slushy melting snow. He remembered the time Sal had lost control of his sled and run over Myles's arm, breaking it in three places. Sal had started to cry, "My father will kill me." Dev jumped in to take the blame. Dev's father had come to apologize. "He meant no harm, but he's a clumsy oaf." Devin Stanton. His Grace the Bishop. Rumor was, the Vatican had its eye on Dev for the next archdiocese opening, and that could mean a cardinal's hat.

When he reached Fifth Avenue, Myles glanced to the right. His eye took in the roof of the massive white structure that was the Metropolitan Museum of Art. He'd always meant to get a better look at the Temple of Dendur. On impulse he walked the six blocks and spent the next hour absorbed in the exquisite remnants of a lost civilization.

It was only when he consulted his watch and decided it was high time to get home and set up the bar that he realized that his real intention in coming to the museum was to visit the site of Renata's death. Forget it, he told himself fiercely. But when he was outside, he could not keep his footsteps from leading him around the back of the museum and to the spot where her body had been found. It was a pilgrimage he made every four or five months.

A reddish haze around the trees in Central Park was the first promise of the greening that would soon take place. There were a fair number of people in the park. Joggers. Nurses pushing baby strollers. Young mothers with energetic three-year-olds. The homeless, pathetic men and women hunched on benches. A steady stream of traffic. Horse-drawn carriages.

Myles stopped at the clearing where Renata had been found. Funny, he thought, she's buried in Gate of Heaven Cemetery, but for me it's as though her body is always here. He stood with his head bowed, his hands in the pockets of his suede jacket. If it had been a day like this, there would have been people in the park. Someone might have seen what was happening. A line from a Tennyson poem ran through his mind: *Dear as remember'd kisses after death . . . Deep as first love, and wild with all regret; O Death in Life, the days that are no more.*

But today, for the first time in this place, Myles experienced a tentative sense of healing. "No thanks to me, but at least our girl is safe, *carissima mia*," he whispered. "And I hope that when Nicky Sepetti stood before the Judgment Seat, you were there to point his way to hell."

Myles turned and walked briskly through the park. Adam Felton's final words echoed in his ears: "All right. You don't have to worry about Nicky Sepetti anymore. You experienced a terrible tragedy seventeen years ago. The point is, are you finally ready to get on with your life?"

Myles whispered again the answer he had snapped decisively at Adam. "Yes."

When Neeve arrived at the shop from Ethel's apartment, most of the staff were already in. Besides Eugenia, her assistant manager, she employed seven regular saleswomen and three seamstresses.

Eugenia was dressing the showroom mannequins. "I'm glad ensembles are in again," she said as she expertly adjusted the jacket of a cinnamon silk outfit. "Which purse?"

Neeve stood back. "Hold them up again. The smaller one, I think. The other has too much amber for the dress."

When Eugenia retired from modeling, she'd happily gone from a size four to a size twelve, but she still retained the graceful movements that had made her a favorite with the designers. She hung the purse on the mannequin's arm. "You're right as usual," she said cheerfully. "It's going to be a busy day. I can feel it in my bones."

"Keep feeling it." Neeve tried to sound casual, but the effort failed.

"Neeve, what about Ethel Lambston? She still hasn't shown up?"

"Not a trace." Neeve glanced around the shop. "Look, I'm going to hole up in the office and make phone calls. Unless it's absolutely necessary, don't let on that I'm here. I don't want to be bothered with salesmen today."

Her first call was to Toni Mendell at *Contemporary Woman.* Toni was at an all-day seminar of magazine editors. She tried Jack Campbell. He was in a meeting. She left word for him to return her call. "It's rather urgent," she told his secretary. She went down the list of the designers whose names had been scribbled in Ethel's book. The first three she reached hadn't seen Ethel last week. She'd simply called to confirm the direct quotes she was attributing to them. Sportswear designer Elke Pearson summed up the irritation Neeve caught in all their voices. "Why I let that woman interview me I'll never know. She kept hammering questions at me till I was dizzy. I practically had to throw her out, and I have a hunch I'm not going to like her damn article."

Anthony della Salva was the next name. Neeve didn't worry when she couldn't reach him. She'd see him tonight for dinner. Gordon

Steuber. Ethel had confided that she'd crucified him in her article. But when was the last time she saw him? Reluctantly, Neeve dialed Steuber's office and was put through immediately to him.

He did not waste his time on amenities. "What do you want?" he asked stiffly.

She could picture him, leaning back in the ornate leather chair with its elaborate brass nailheads. She made her voice as cold as his. "I've been asked to try to locate Ethel Lambston. It's quite urgent." On a hunch she added, "I know from her appointment book that she met with you last week. Did she give you any indication of where she might be planning to go?"

Long seconds passed in total silence. He's trying to decide what to say, she thought. When Steuber spoke, his tone was detached and even. "Ethel Lambston tried to interview me weeks ago about an article she was writing. I did not see her. I have no time for busybodies. She phoned last week, but I did not accept her call."

Neeve heard a click in her ear.

She was about to dial the next designer on the list when her phone rang. It was Jack Campbell. He sounded concerned. "My secretary said your call was urgent. Is there any problem, Neeve?"

She suddenly felt ridiculous trying to explain to him on the phone that she was worried about Ethel Lambston because Ethel hadn't picked up her new clothes.

Instead she said, "You've got to be awfully busy, but is there any chance I could talk to you for about half an hour very soon?"

"I have a lunch date with one of my authors," he said. "How about three o'clock in my office?"

Givvons and Marks occupied the top six floors of the building on the southwest corner of Park Avenue and Forty-first Street. Jack Campbell's personal office was a huge corner room of the forty-seventh floor with dazzling views of downtown Manhattan. His oversized desk was finished in black lacquer. The bookshelves on the wall behind the desk were filled with manuscripts. A black leather couch and matching chairs were grouped around a glass cocktail table. Neeve was surprised to see that the room was devoid of personal touches.

It was as though Jack Campbell could read her mind. "My apartment isn't ready yet, so I'm staying at the Hampshire House. Everything I own is still in storage, which is why this place looks like a dentist's waiting room."

His suit jacket was on the back of his desk chair. He was wearing an argyle sweater in tones of green and brown. It suited him, Neeve decided. Autumn colors. His face was too thin and his features were too irregular to be deemed handsome, but were infinitely attractive in their quiet strength. There was good-humored warmth in his eyes when he smiled, and Neeve found herself glad she had changed to one of her new spring ensembles, a turquoise wool dress and matching stroller-length jacket.

"How about coffee?" Jack offered. "I drink too much of it, but I'm still going to have some."

Neeve realized she had skipped lunch and her head was vaguely aching. "I'd love it. Black, please."

While they waited, she commented on the view. "Don't you feel like the king of New York at least?"

"In the month I've been here, I've had to fight to keep my mind on work," he told her. "I became a would-be native New Yorker when I was ten. That was twenty-six years ago and it took all this time to make the Big Apple."

When the coffee came, they sat around the glass table. Jack Campbell lounged on the couch. Neeve perched on the edge of one of the chairs. She knew he had to have pushed off other appointments to see her so quickly. She took a deep breath and told him about Ethel. "My father thinks I'm crazy," she said. "But I've got a weird feeling that something happened to her. The thing is, did she give you any indication that she might be going off by herself? I understand that the book she's writing for you is scheduled for fall release."

Jack Campbell had listened to her with the same attentive posture she had observed at the cocktail party. "No, it isn't," he said.

Neeve felt her eyes widen. "Then how . . . ?"

Campbell sipped the last drops in his coffee cup. "I met Ethel a couple of years ago at the ABA when she was promoting her first book for Givvons and Marks, the one about women in politics. It was darn good. Funny. Gossipy. Sold well. That's why when she wanted to see me, I was interested. She gave me a rundown on the article she was doing and said she might have stumbled across a story that would rock the fashion world and if she wrote a book about it, would I buy it and what kind of advance could she expect?

"I told her I obviously had to know more about it, but, based on the success of the last book, if this one was as explosive as she claimed, we'd buy it and we'd probably be talking a mid-six-figure advance. Last week I read on Page Six in the *Post* that she had a contract with me for a half-million dollars and the book would be on the fall list. The phone's been ringing off the hook. All the softcover houses want to have a chance to bid on it. I called Ethel's agent. She never even talked to him about it. I've tried phoning her without success. I've neither confirmed nor denied the terms. She's a real publicity hound, but if she writes the book and if it's good, all the advance interest is just fine with me."

"And you don't have any idea what she considered a story that would rock the industry?"

"Not a clue."

Neeve sighed and stood up. "I've taken enough of your time. I suppose that I should be reassured. It would be just like Ethel to get hot on a project like this and go hole up in a cabin somewhere. I'd better start minding my own business." She held out her hand to him. "Thank you."

He did not release her hand immediately. His smile was quick and warm. "Do you always make such fast getaways?" he asked. "Six years ago you darted out of the plane like an arrow. The other night when I turned around you'd disappeared."

Neeve withdrew her hand. "Occasionally, I slow down to a jog," she said, "but now I'd better run and pay attention to my own business."

He walked with her to the door. "I hear Neeve's Place is one of the most fashionable shops in New York. Can I get to see it?"

"Sure. You don't even have to buy anything."

"My mother lives in Nebraska and wears sensible clothes."

On her way down in the elevator Neeve wondered whether that was Jack Campbell's way of telling her that there was no special lady in his life. She found that she was humming softly as she stepped out into the now warm April afternoon and hailed a cab.

When she reached the shop, she found a message to call Tse-Tse at Ethel's apartment immediately. Tse-Tse answered on the first ring. "Neeve, thank God you called. I want to get out of here before that jerky nephew comes home. Neeve, something is really queer. Ethel has a habit of stashing hundred-dollar bills around the apartment. That's how she happened to pay me in advance last time. When I was here Tuesday, I saw one bill under the carpet. This morning I found one in the dish closet and three others hidden in the furniture. *Neeve, they absolutely weren't here on Tuesday.*"

Seamus left the bar at four-thirty. Oblivious of the jostling pedestrians, he darted along the crowded sidewalk up Columbus Avenue. He had to go to Ethel's apartment, and he didn't want Ruth to know he'd been there. Since his discovery last evening that he'd put the check and the note into the same envelope, he'd felt like a trapped animal, leaping wildly, trying to find a way to escape.

There was just one hope. He hadn't stuffed the envelope deep into the mailbox. He could visualize the way the edge of it had been sticking out of the slot. He might be able to retrieve it. It was a one-in-a-million chance. Common sense told him that if the postman had brought more mail, he probably shoved that envelope down. But the possibility still allured him, offering the only course of action.

He turned up Ethel's block, his eyes skimming the passersby, hoping he would not encounter the familiar faces of any of Ethel's neighbors. As he reached her building, his sense of hopeless misery swelled to the point of despair. He couldn't even try to steal a letter without bungling it. You needed a key to get into the vestibule where the mailboxes were located. Last night that obnoxious kid had opened the door for him. Now he'd have to ring for the superintendent, and the super certainly wouldn't let him fool with Ethel's mailbox.

He was in front of the brownstone. Ethel's apartment was the walk-in entrance on the left. There were a dozen steps up to the main entrance. As he stood, uncertain what to do, the fourth-floor window opened. A woman leaned out. Over her shoulder, he could see the face of the kid he'd talked to yesterday.

"She hasn't been around all week," a strident voice told him. "And listen, I almost called the cops last Thursday when I heard you shouting at her."

Seamus turned and fled. His breath came in harsh gasps as he ran unseeingly down West End Avenue. He did not stop until he was safely inside his own apartment and had bolted the door. Only then was he aware of the pounding of his heart, the shuddering sound of his struggle for oxygen. To his dismay, he heard footsteps in the hallway coming from the bedroom. Ruth was home already. Urgently he wiped his face with his hand, tried to pull himself together.

Ruth did not seem to notice his agitation. She was holding his brown suit over her arm. "I was going to drop this at the cleaners," she told him. "Will you kindly tell me why in the name of God you have a one-hundred-dollar bill in the pocket?"

Jack Campbell stayed in his office for nearly two hours after Neeve left him. But the manuscript which had been messengered to him with an enthusiastic note from an agent he trusted simply could not hold his attention. After valiant efforts to become involved in the story line, he finally shoved it aside with rare irritability. The anger was directed at himself. It wasn't fair to judge someone's hard work when your mind was ninety-nine percent preoccupied.

Neeve Kearny. Funny how six years ago he'd had that moment of regret that he hadn't managed to get her phone number. He'd even looked it up in the Manhattan directory when he was in New York some months later. There were pages of Kearnys in the book. None of them Neeve. She'd said something about a dress shop. He'd looked under Kearny. Nothing.

And then he'd shrugged and put it in the back of his mind. For all he knew she had a live-in boyfriend. But for some reason he'd never quite forgotten her. At the cocktail party, when she approached him, he'd recognized her immediately. She wasn't a twenty-one-year-old kid in a ski sweater anymore. She was a sophisticated, fashionably dressed young woman. But that coal-black hair, the milk-white skin, the enormous brown eyes, the dotting of freckles across the bridge of her nose—all these were the same.

Now Jack found himself wondering whether she had a serious involvement. If not . . .

At six o'clock his assistant poked her head in. "I've had it," she announced. "Is it okay if I warn you that you'll wreck it for everyone else if you keep late hours?"

Jack shoved aside the unread manuscript and got up. "I'm on my way," he said. "Just one question, Ginny? What do you know about Neeve Kearny?"

He mulled over the answer on the walk uptown to his rental apartment on Central Park South. Neeve Kearny had a sensationally successful boutique. Ginny bought her special outfits there. Neeve was well liked, well respected. Neeve had caused an uproar a few months ago when she pulled the plug on a designer who had kids sewing in sweatshops. Neeve could be a fighter.

He'd also asked about Ethel Lambston. Ginny had rolled her eyes. "Don't get me started."

Jack stopped in his apartment long enough to be sure that he didn't feel like fixing his own dinner. Instead he decided that pasta at Nicola's was the right way to go. Nicola's was on Eighty-fourth Street between Lexington and Third.

It was a good decision. As always, there was a line for tables, but after one drink at the bar his favorite waiter, Lou, tapped his shoulder. "All set, Mr. Campbell." Jack found himself relaxing at last over a half bottle of Valpolicella, a watercress-and-endive salad and linguine with frutti di mare. When he ordered a double espresso he also asked for his check.

As he left the restaurant, he shrugged. He had known all evening that he was going to walk over to Madison Avenue and see Neeve's Place. A few minutes later, as a now cooling breeze made him aware that it was still April and that early-spring weather could be capricious, he studied the elegantly dressed windows. He liked what he saw. The delicately feminine soft print dresses and matching umbrellas. The assured poses of the mannequins, the almost arrogant tilt of their heads. Somehow he was sure that Neeve was making a statement with this combination of strength and softness.

But carefully studying the window display made him aware of the elusive thought that had evaded him when he was trying to tell Neeve exactly what Ethel had pitched to him. "There's gossip; there's excitement; there's universality in fashion," Ethel had told him in that hurried, breathless way of hers. "That's what my article is about. But just suppose I can give you a lot more than that. A bombshell. TNT."

He'd been late for an appointment. He'd cut her off. "Send me an outline."

Ethel's insistent, persistent refusal to be dismissed. "How much is a blockbuster scandal worth?"

His almost joking "If it's sensational enough, mid–six figures."

Jack stared at the mannequins holding their parasollike umbrellas. His eyes shifted to the ivory-and-blue canopy with the scrolled letters, "Neeve's Place." Tomorrow he could call Neeve and tell her exactly what Ethel had said.

As he turned down Madison Avenue, once again finding it necessary to walk off the vague, undefined restlessness, he thought, I'm really reaching for an excuse. Why not just ask her out?

At that moment, he was able to define the cause of the restlessness. He absolutely did not want to hear that Neeve was involved with someone else.

Thursday was a busy day for Kitty Conway. From nine in the morning till noon she drove elderly people to doctors' appointments. In the afternoon she worked as a volunteer in the small sales shop of the Garden State Museum. Both activities gave her a sense of doing something useful.

Long ago in college she had studied anthropology with some vague idea of becoming a second Margaret Mead. Then she'd met Mike. Now as she helped a sixteen-year-old select a replica of an

Egyptian necklace, she thought that maybe in the summer she'd sign up for an anthropology tour.

The prospect was intriguing. As she drove home in the April evening, Kitty realized that she was getting impatient with herself. It was time to get on with the business of living. She turned off Lincoln Avenue and smiled as she saw her house perched high at the bend of Grand View Circle, an impressive white colonial with black shutters.

Inside she walked through the downstairs rooms turning on lights, then lit the gas-fueled fireplace in the den. When Michael was alive, he'd made satisfying, glowing fires, expertly piling logs over the kindling and feeding the flames regularly so that the hickory scent of the wood filled the room. No matter how she tried, Kitty couldn't get a fire started properly, and with apologies to Michael's memory she had had the gas jet installed.

She went upstairs to the master bedroom that she'd redone in apricot and pale green, a pattern copied from a museum tapestry. Peeling off her two-piece gray wool dress, she debated about showering now and getting comfortable in pajamas and a robe. Bad habit, she told herself. It's only six o'clock.

Instead she pulled a teal-blue sweatsuit from the closet and reached for sneakers. "I'm back to jogging as of right now," she told herself.

She followed her usual path. Grand View to Lincoln Avenue, a mile into town, circle the bus station and back home. Feeling pleasantly virtuous, she dropped her sweatsuit and underwear into the bathroom hamper, showered, slipped on lounging pajamas and studied herself in the mirror. She'd always been slim and was holding her shape reasonably well. The lines around her eyes weren't deep. Her hair looked pretty natural. The colorist in the beauty parlor had managed to match her own shade of red. Not bad, Kitty told her reflection, but ye gods, in two years I'll be *sixty*.

It was time for the seven-o'clock news and obviously time for a sherry. Kitty walked across the bedroom toward the hallway and realized she'd left the bathroom lights blazing. Waste not, want not, and anyhow you should conserve electricity. She hurried back and reached for the bathroom light switch. Her fingers turned numb. The sleeve of her blue sweatsuit was dangling from the hamper. Fear, like a cold blade of steel, made Kitty's throat constrict. Her lips went dry. She could feel the hairs on her neck bristle and tighten. That sleeve. There should be a hand on it. Yesterday. When the horse bolted. That scrap of plastic that had hit her face. That blurred image of blue cloth and a hand. She hadn't been crazy. *She had seen a hand.*

Kitty did not remember to turn on the seven-o'clock news. Instead, she sat in front of the fire, hunched forward on the couch, sipping the sherry. Neither the fire nor the sherry could ease the chill that was engulfing her body. Should she call the police? Suppose she was wrong. She'd look like a fool.

I'm *not* wrong, she told herself, but I'll wait until tomorrow. I'll drive back to the park and walk down that embankment. That was a hand I saw, but whoever it belongs to is beyond help now.

"You say Ethel's nephew is in the apartment?" Myles asked as he filled the ice bucket. "So he borrowed some money and then put it back. It's been known to happen."

Once again, Myles's reasonable explanation of the circumstances surrounding Ethel's absence, her winter coats and now the hundred-dollar bills made Neeve feel slightly foolish. She was glad she hadn't yet told Myles about her meeting with Jack Campbell. When she arrived home, she'd changed into blue silk slacks and a matching long-sleeved blouse. She'd expected Myles to say, "Pretty fancy for slinging hash." Instead his eyes had softened when she came into the kitchen, and he'd remarked, "Your mother always looked lovely in blue. You grow more like her as you get older."

Neeve reached for Renata's cookbook. She was serving thinly sliced ham with melon, pasta with pesto, sole stuffed with shrimp, a mélange of baby vegetables, an arugula-and-endive salad, cheese and a tulip pastry. She flipped through the book until she reached the page with the sketches. Again she avoided looking at them. Instead she concentrated on the handwritten instructions Renata had scrawled over the baking time for the sole.

Deciding she was fully organized, she went over to the refrigerator and took out a jar of caviar. Myles watched as she put toast points on a platter. "I never developed a taste for that stuff," he said. "Very plebeian of me, I know."

"You're hardly plebeian." Neeve scooped caviar onto a sliver of toast point. "But you're missing a lot." She studied him. He was wearing a navy jacket, gray slacks, a light-blue shirt and a handsome red-and-blue tie she had given him for Christmas. A good-looking guy, she thought, and best of all, you'd never dream he'd been so sick. She told him that.

Myles reached over and gingerly popped a caviar toast point into his mouth. "I still don't like it," he commented, then added, "I do feel well, and inactivity is getting on my nerves. I had some feelers about heading up the Drug Enforcement Agency in Washington. It would mean spending most of my time there. What do you think?"

Neeve gasped and threw her arms around him. "That's wonderful. Go for it. You could really get your teeth into that job."

She hummed as she brought the caviar and a platter of Brie into the living room. Now if only Ethel Lambston could be tracked down. She was just in the process of wondering how long it would be before Jack Campbell phoned her when the doorbell rang. Their two guests had arrived together.

Bishop Devin Stanton was one of the few prelates who at private functions still seemed more comfortable in a Roman collar than a sports jacket. Traces of now subdued copper-color hair mingled with gray. Behind silver-rimmed glasses, his mild blue eyes radiated warmth and intelligence. His tall, thin body gave an impression of quicksilver when he moved. Neeve always had the uncomfortable impression that Dev could read her mind and the comfortable reaction that he liked what he read. She kissed him warmly.

Once again, Anthony della Salva was resplendent in one of his own creations. He was wearing a charcoal-gray suit of Italian silk. The elegant lines masked the additional weight that had begun creeping onto his always rotund body. Neeve remembered Myles's observation that Sal reminded him of a well-fed cat. It was a description that suited him. His black hair untouched by gray glistened, matching the gloss of his Gucci loafers. It was second nature for Neeve to calculate the cost of clothes. She decided that Sal's suit would retail for about fifteen hundred dollars.

As usual, Sal was bursting with good humor. "Dev, Myles, Neeve, my three favorite people, not counting my present girlfriend but certainly counting my ex-wives. Dev, do you think Mother Church will take me back in when I get old?"

"The prodigal son is supposed to return repentant and in rags," the Bishop observed dryly.

Myles laughed and put his arms around the shoulders of both his friends. "God, it's good to get together with you two. I feel as though we're back in the Bronx. Are you still drinking Absolut vodka or have you found something more trendy?"

The evening began in the usual pleasantly comfortable fashion that had become a ritual. A debate about a second martini, a shrug, and "Why not, we're not together that much" from the Bishop, "I'd better stop" from Myles, a nonchalant "Of course" from Sal. The conversation veered from present-day politics, "Could the Mayor win again?" to problems of the Church, "You can't educate a kid in a parochial school for less than sixteen hundred dollars a year. God, remember when we were at St. Francis Xavier and our parents paid a buck a month? The parish carried the school on Bingo games," to

Sal's laments about the foreign imports, "Sure, we should use the union label, but we can get the clothes made in Korea and Hong Kong for a third of the price. If we don't farm some of it out, we outprice ourselves. If we do, we're union busters," to Myles's dry comment, "I still think we don't know the half of how much mob money is on Seventh Avenue."

Inevitably it turned to Nicky Sepetti's death.

"It was too easy for him, dying in bed," Sal commented, the jovial expression gone from his face. "After what he did to your pretty one."

Neeve watched as Myles's lips tightened. Long ago Sal had heard Myles teasingly call Renata "my pretty one" and, to Myles's annoyance, had picked it up. "How's the pretty one?" he would greet Renata. Neeve could still remember the moment at Renata's wake when Sal had knelt at the casket, his eyes flowing with tears, then gotten up, embraced Myles and said, "Try to think your pretty one is sleeping."

Myles had said flatly, "She's not sleeping. She's dead. And, Sal, don't call her that again ever. That was my name for her."

Till now he never had. There was a moment of awkward silence, then Sal gulped the rest of his martini and stood up. "Be right back," he said, beaming, and headed down the hallway to the guest bathroom.

Devin sighed. "He may be a genius designer, but he still has more spit than polish."

"He also gave me my start," Neeve reminded them. "If it weren't for Sal, I'd probably be an assistant buyer in Bloomingdale's right now."

She saw the look on Myles's face and warned, "Don't tell me I'd be better off."

"That never crossed my mind."

When she served dinner, Neeve lit the candles and muted the overhead chandelier. The room was softly shadowed. Each course was pronounced excellent. Myles and the Bishop had seconds of everything. Sal had thirds. "So forget the diet," he said. "This is the best kitchen in Manhattan."

Over dessert inevitably the talk turned to Renata. "This is one of her recipes," Neeve told them. "Prepared especially for you two. I've really just started getting into her cookbooks, and it's fun."

Myles told them about the possibility of heading up the Drug Enforcement Agency.

"I may be keeping you company in the Washington area," Devin said with a smile, then added, "strictly off the record."

Sal insisted on helping Neeve clear the table and volunteered to prepare the espresso. As he busied himself with the espresso machine, Neeve took from the breakfront the exquisite gold-and-green demitasse cups that had been in the Rossetti family for generations.

The sound of a thud and a cry of pain made them rush to the kitchen. The espresso pot had toppled over, flooding the counter and soaking Renata's cookbook. Sal was running his fiery-red hand under cold water. His face was ghastly white. "The handle on that damn pot came off." He tried to sound nonchalant. "Myles, I think you're trying to get back at me for breaking your arm when we were kids."

It was obvious the burn was nasty and painful.

Neeve scrambled for the eucalyptus leaves Myles always kept for burn emergencies. She patted Sal's hand dry and covered it with the leaves, then wrapped it in a soft linen napkin. The Bishop righted the demitasse pot and began mopping up. Myles was drying the cookbook: Neeve saw the expression in his eyes as he studied Renata's sketches, which were now thoroughly soaked and stained.

Sal noticed as well. He pulled his hand from Neeve's ministrations. "Myles, for God's sake, I'm sorry."

Myles held the book over the sink, drained the puddles of coffee from it and, covering it with a towel, laid it carefully on top of the refrigerator. "What the hell have you got to be sorry about? Neeve, I never saw that damn coffeemaker before. When did you get it?"

Neeve began to make fresh espresso in the old pot. "It was a gift," she said reluctantly. "Ethel Lambston sent it to you for Christmas after she was here for the party."

Devin Stanton looked bewildered as Myles, Neeve and Sal burst into wry laughter.

"I'll explain it when we get settled, Your Grace," Neeve said. "My God, no matter what I do, I can't lose Ethel even for the space of a dinner."

Over espresso and Sambuca, she told about Ethel's apparent disappearance. Myles's comment was, "As long as she *stays* out of sight."

Trying not to wince at the pain in his rapidly blistering hand, Sal poured a second Sambuca and said, "There isn't a designer on Seventh Avenue she hasn't bugged about that article. To answer your question, Neeve, she phoned me last week and insisted on being put through. We were in the middle of a meeting. She had a couple of questions like 'Was it true you had the school record for playing hookey at Christopher Columbus High School?' "

Neeve stared at him. "You've got to be joking."

"No joke at all. My guess is Ethel's article is to debunk all the stories we designers pay publicists to grind out about us. That may be hot stuff for an article, but tell me it's worth half a million bucks for a book! It boggles my mind."

Neeve was about to volunteer that Ethel wasn't actually offered the advance, then bit her tongue. Jack Campbell had obviously not meant that to get around.

"By the way," Sal added, "the word is that your tip about Steuber's sweatshops is really turning up a lot of dirt. Neeve, stay away from that guy."

"What's that supposed to mean?" Myles asked sharply.

Neeve had not told Myles about the rumor that, because of her, Gordon Steuber might be indicted. She shook her head at Sal as she said, "He's a designer I stopped buying from because of the way he does business." She appealed to Sal, "I still say there's something wrong about the way Ethel dropped out of sight. You know she bought all her clothes from me, and every single one of her winter coats is in the closet."

Sal shrugged. "Neeve, I'll be honest, Ethel's such a flake she probably ran out without a coat and never noticed it. Watch and see. She'll show up in something she bought off the rack at J. C. Penney's."

Myles laughed. Neeve shook her head. "You're a big help."

Before they left the table, Devin Stanton offered grace. "We thank Thee, Lord, for good friendship, for the delicious meal, for the beautiful young woman who prepared it, and we ask you to bless the memory of Renata whom we all loved."

"Thank you, Dev." Myles touched the Bishop's hand. Then he laughed. "And if she were here, she'd be telling you to clean up her kitchen, Sal, because you made the mess."

When the Bishop and Sal had left, Neeve and Myles stacked the dishwasher and washed the pots and pans in companionable silence. Neeve picked up the offending espresso pot. "Might as well ditch this before somebody else is scalded," she observed.

"No, leave it alone," Myles told her. "It looks expensive enough, and I can fix it someday when I'm watching *Jeopardy*."

Jeopardy. To Neeve the word seemed to hang in the air. Shaking her head impatiently at the thought, she turned off the kitchen light and kissed Myles good night. She glanced around to be sure everything was in order. The light from the foyer shone faintly into the den, and Neeve winced as she watched it fall on the blistered, smeared pages of Renata's cookbook, which Myles had placed on the top of his desk.

8

On Friday morning, Ruth Lambston left the apartment while Seamus was shaving. She did not say goodbye to him. The memory of the way his face had convulsed in anger when she held out the hundred-dollar bill to him was imprinted on her mind. In these last years, the monthly alimony check had choked off every emotion she felt for him except resentment. Now a new emotion had been added. She was afraid. Of him? For him? She didn't know.

Ruth made twenty-six thousand dollars a year as a secretary. With taxes and Social Security taken out and her expenses for carfare and clothes and lunches, she estimated that her net earnings three days a week just about made up Ethel's alimony. "I'm slaving for that harridan" was a sentence that she regularly threw at Seamus.

Usually Seamus tried to soothe her. But last night his face had convulsed in rage. He'd raised his fist and for a moment she'd flinched, sure he was going to hit her. But he'd snatched the hundred-dollar bill and torn it in half. "You want to know where I got it?" he'd shouted. "That bitch gave it to me. When I asked her to let me off the hook, she told me that she'd be glad to help me. She'd been too busy to eat out much, so this was left over from last month."

"Then she didn't tell you to stop sending the checks?" Ruth cried.

The anger on his face had turned to hatred. "Maybe I convinced her that any human being can take just so much. Maybe it's something you ought to learn, too."

The answer had left Ruth in a temper that still made her breath come in sharp, harsh gasps. "Don't you dare threaten me," she'd shouted and then watched horrified as Seamus burst into tears. Sobbing, he told her how he'd put the check with the letter, how the kid who lived upstairs from Ethel had talked about his delivering the ransom. "Her whole building thinks I'm a joke."

All night Ruth had lain awake in one of the girls' bedrooms, so filled with contempt for Seamus that she could not endure the thought of being near him. Toward morning she realized that the contempt was for herself as well. That woman has turned me into a shrew, she thought. It's got to end.

Now her mouth was set in a harsh, straight line as, instead of turning right toward Broadway and the subway station, she walked straight up West End Avenue. There was a sharp early-morning breeze, but her low-heeled shoes made it possible to move quickly.

She was going to confront Ethel. She should have done it years ago. She'd read enough of Ethel's articles to know that Ethel postured herself as a feminist. But now that she'd signed a big book contract, she really was vulnerable. Page Six of the *Post* would love to print that she was gouging one thousand dollars a month from a man with three daughters in college. Ruth permitted herself a grim smile. If Ethel didn't surrender her alimony rights, Ruth would go for her throat. First the *Post*. Then court.

She'd gone to the personnel office of her company for an emergency loan to cover the tuition check. The personnel director had been shocked to learn about the alimony. "I've got a friend who's a good matrimonial lawyer," she'd said. "She can afford to do pro-bono work and she'd love to have a case like this. The way I understand it, you can't break an irrevocable alimony agreement, but it might be about time to test the law. If you get public outrage going, things might happen."

Ruth had hesitated. "I don't want to embarrass the girls. It would mean admitting the bar is barely making enough money to keep the doors open. Let me think about it."

As she crossed Seventy-third Street, Ruth thought, Either she gives up the alimony or I see that lawyer.

A young woman with a child in a stroller was bearing down on her. Ruth stepped to one side to avoid her and collided with a thin-faced man in a cap that almost covered his face and a filthy overcoat that smelled of stale wine. Wrinkling her nose in disgust, she clutched her pocketbook and scurried to the opposite curb. The sidewalks were so crowded, she thought. Kids rushing with schoolbooks, old-timers making an outing of the daily walk to the newsstand, people on the way to work trying to flag down cabs.

Ruth had never forgotten the house they'd almost bought in Westchester twenty years ago. Thirty-five thousand dollars then and must be worth ten times that now. When the bank saw the alimony payments, the mortgage hadn't been approved.

She turned east on Eighty-second Street, Ethel's block. Squaring her shoulders, Ruth adjusted her rimless glasses, unconsciously preparing herself like a fighter about to enter the ring. Seamus had told her that Ethel had the ground-floor apartment with its own entrance. The name over the bell, "E. Lambston," confirmed that fact.

From inside she could hear the faint sounds of a radio playing. She pressed her index finger firmly on the bell. But there was no response to her first or second ring. Ruth was not to be dissuaded. The third time she rang the bell, she pressed relentlessly.

The loud ringing went on for fully a minute before she was rewarded by the click of the lock turning. The door was yanked open. A young man, his hair tousled, his shirt still unbuttoned, glared at her. "What the hell do you want?" he asked. Then he made a visible attempt to calm down. "I'm sorry. Are you a friend of Aunt Ethel's?"

"Yes, and I must see her." Ruth moved forward, forcing the young man to block her way or let her pass. He stepped back, and she was in the living room. Quickly she glanced around. Seamus always talked about Ethel's messy housekeeping, but this place was spotless. Too many papers around, but they were stacked in neat piles. Fine antique furniture. Seamus had told her about the pieces he had bought for Ethel. And I live with those overstuffed horrors, Ruth thought.

"I'm Douglas Brown." Doug felt clammy apprehension. There was something about this woman, about the way she was sizing up the apartment, that made him nervous. "I'm Ethel's nephew," he said. "Do you have an appointment with her?"

"No. But I insist on seeing her immediately." Ruth introduced herself. "I'm Seamus Lambston's wife and I'm here to collect the last check he gave your aunt. As of now there's no more alimony being paid."

There was a stack of mail on the desk. Near the top of the pile, she saw a white envelope with maroon edging, the stationery the girls had given Seamus for his birthday. "I'll take that," she said.

Before Doug could stop her, the envelope was in her hand. She ripped it open and pulled out the contents. Scanning them, she shredded the check and returned the note to the envelope.

As Doug Brown stared, too startled to protest, she reached into her purse and extracted the pieces of the hundred-dollar bill Seamus had torn. "She isn't here, I gather," she said.

"You have a hell of a nerve," Doug snapped. "I could have you arrested for this."

"I wouldn't try," Ruth told him. "Here." She shoved the torn pieces of the bill into his hand. "You tell that parasite to tape this together and have her final fancy dinner on my husband. Tell her she's not getting another nickel from us and if she tries she'll regret it with every breath she draws for the rest of her life."

Ruth did not give Doug a chance to answer. Instead she walked over to the wall where Ethel's pictures were displayed and studied them. "She postures herself as doing good for all kinds of vague, undefined causes and goes around accepting her damn awards, and yet the one person who ever tried to treat her as a woman, as a human being, she's hounding to his grave." Ruth turned to face Doug. "I think she's despicable. I know what she thinks of you. You eat the food at fancy restaurants that my husband and I and our children are paying for, and, not satisfied with that, you steal from that woman. Ethel told my husband about you. I can only say, you deserve each other."

She was gone. His lips ashen, Doug collapsed onto the couch. Whom else had Ethel, with her big mouth, told about his habit of helping himself to her alimony loot?

When Ruth stepped onto the sidewalk she was hailed by a woman standing on the stoop of the brownstone. She looked to be in her early forties. Ruth observed that her blond hair was fashionably messy, that her pullover sweater and narrow slacks were trendy, and that her expression could only be described as one of unrestrained curiosity.

"I'm sorry to bother you," the woman said, "but I'm Georgette Wells, Ethel's neighbor, and I'm worried about her."

A thin teenager pushed open the house door, clattered down the steps and stood beside Wells. Her sharp eyes looked over Ruth and took in the fact that she was standing in front of Ethel's apartment. "You a friend of Ms. Lambston?" she asked.

Ruth was sure that this was the girl who had taunted Seamus. Intense dislike combined with cold, sinking dread to congeal her stomach muscles. Why was this woman worried about Ethel? She thought of the murderous fury on Seamus' face when he talked about Ethel's thrusting the hundred-dollar bill into his pocket. She thought of the tidy apartment she had just left. How many times over the years had Seamus told her that all Ethel had to do was walk into a room and it was as though the nuclear bomb hit it? Ethel had *not* been in that apartment recently.

"Yes," Ruth said, trying to sound pleasant. "I'm surprised Ethel isn't in, but is there any reason to worry?"

"Dana, get to school," her mother ordered. "You'll be late again."

Dana pouted. "I want to hear."

"All right, all right," Wells said impatiently, and turned back to Ruth. "There's something funny going on. Last week Ethel had a visit from her ex. Usually he only comes on the fifth of the month if he hasn't mailed the alimony. So when I saw him sneaking around last Thursday afternoon, I thought something was funny. I mean it was only the thirtieth, so why should he pay her early? Well, let me tell you, they had a battle royal! I could hear them shouting at each other like I was in the room."

Ruth managed to keep her voice steady. "What were they saying?"

"Well, what I mean is I could hear shouting sounds. I couldn't hear what they were saying. I started to come downstairs just in case Ethel might be in trouble . . ."

No, you wanted to hear better, Ruth thought.

". . . but then my phone rang and it was my mother calling from Cleveland about my sister's divorce, and it was an hour before Ma stopped for breath. By then the fight was over. I phoned Ethel. She's really funny about her ex. Her imitation of him is priceless, you know? But she didn't answer, so I figured she'd gone out. You know the kind of person Ethel is—always rushing somewhere. But she usually tells me if she's going to be away for more than a couple of days, and she didn't say a word. Now her nephew is staying at the apartment and that's funny, too."

Georgette Wells folded her arms. "Kind of cold, isn't it? Crazy weather. All that hair spray in the ozone, I guess. Anyhow," she continued as Ruth stared at her and Dana hung on every word, "I have a *very funny feeling* that something happened to Ethel, and that wimp of an ex-husband of hers had something to do with it."

"And don't forget, Mama," Dana interrupted, "he came back on Wednesday and he acted real scared about something."

"I was going to get to that. You saw him Wednesday. That was the fifth, so that means he was probably delivering the check. Then I saw him yesterday. Will you tell me why he came back? But nobody's seen Ethel. Now, the way I figure it, he might have done something to her and maybe left a clue that's worrying him." Georgette Wells smiled triumphantly, her story completed. "As a good friend of Ethel's," she asked Ruth, "help me decide. Should I call the police and tell them I think my neighbor may have been murdered?"

On Friday morning, Kitty Conway received a call from the hospital. One of the volunteer drivers was sick. Could she possibly fill in?

It was late afternoon before she was able to go home, change to a jogging suit and sneakers and head her car in the direction of Morrison State Park. The shadows were getting longer, and on the way she debated with herself about waiting until morning, then resolutely kept driving until she reached the park. The sunshine of the past few days had dried the macadam surface of the parking lot and the footpaths that arteried from it, but the heavily wooded areas were still damp underfoot.

Kitty walked to the perimeter of the stable, attempting to follow the trail that would retrace the route from which the horse had bolted forty-eight hours ago. But, to her chagrin, she realized that she was totally unsure which trail to follow. "Absolutely no sense of direction," she muttered as a branch slapped her face. She remembered that Mike used to draw painstaking sketches showing crossroads and landmarks whenever she drove alone to an unfamiliar place.

After forty wasted minutes, her sneakers were muddy and soaked, her legs were aching and she had accomplished nothing. She stopped to rest at a clearing where the riding classes from the stable would pause and regroup. There were no other hikers around and she could not hear any sounds of riders on the trails. The sun was almost completely gone. I must be crazy, she thought. This is no place to be alone. I'll come back tomorrow.

She got up and began to retrace her steps. Wait a minute, she thought, it was just past here. We took the fork on the right and went up that incline. Somewhere along there is where that damn nag decided to take off.

She knew she was right. A sense of anticipation combined with mounting dread made her heart pound furiously. During the sleepless night, her mind had been an out-of-control pendulum. She *had* seen a hand . . . She *should* call the police . . . Ridiculous. It was all her imagination. She'd look like a fool. She should make an anonymous call and stay out of it. No. Suppose she was right and they traced the call somehow. In the end she returned to the original plan. Look for herself.

It took twenty minutes to cover the ground the horses had made in five minutes. "This is where the stupid thing started eating all the junk-food weeds," she remembered. "I tugged the reins and it turned and went straight down here."

"Here" was a steep rocky incline. In the gathering darkness, Kitty began to make her way down it. The rocks slid out from under her sneakers. Once she lost her balance and fell, scraping her hand. I really need this, she thought. Even though it was very cool, beads of perspiration were forming on her forehead. She wiped them away with a hand now soiled from the loose dirt between the rocks. There was no sign of a blue sleeve.

Halfway down she came to a large rock and paused to rest on it. I was crazy, she decided. Thank God I didn't make a perfect fool of myself by calling the police. She'd catch her breath and get home to a hot shower. "Why anybody thinks hiking is fun is beyond me," she said aloud. When her breathing became even, she wiped her hands on her light-green jogging suit. She grasped the side of the rock with her right hand as she prepared to hoist herself up. And felt something.

Kitty looked down. She tried to scream, but no sound came, only a low, disbelieving moan. Her fingers were touching other fingers, manicured, with deep-red polish, held upward by the rocks that had slid around them, framed by the blue cuff that had intruded upon her subconscious, a scrap of black plastic, like a mourning band, embracing the slender inert wrist.

Denny Adler, in the guise of a wino, settled at seven o'clock on Friday morning against an apartment building directly across from Schwab House. It was still raw and breezy and he realized the odds were against Neeve Kearny walking to work. But long ago when he was tracking someone he had learned to be patient. Big Charley had said that Kearny usually left for her shop pretty early, somewhere between seven-thirty and eight.

At about quarter of eight, the exodus started. Kids being picked up by a bus, headed for one of those fancy private schools. I went to a private school, too, Denny thought. Brownsville Reformatory in New Jersey.

Yuppies began to pour out. All in identical raincoats—no, *Burberrys,* Denny thought. Get it straight. Then the gray-haired executives, men and women. All sleek and prosperous-looking. From where he was positioned, he was able to observe them clearly.

At twenty of nine, Denny knew this wasn't his day. The one thing he couldn't risk was the deli manager getting mad at him. He was sure that with his record, he'd be pulled in for questioning when he completed the job. But he knew that even his parole officer would go to bat for him. "One of my best men," Toohey would say. "Never even late for work. He's clean."

Reluctantly Denny stood up, brushed his hands together and glanced down. He was wearing a filthy loose overcoat that smelled of cheap wine, an oversized cap with earmuffs that practically covered his face, and sneakers with holes in the sides. What didn't show was that under the coat he was neatly dressed in his work clothes, a faded denim zip-up jacket and matching jeans. He was carrying a shopping bag. It contained his everyday sneakers, a wet washcloth and a towel. A switchblade knife was in the right-hand pocket of the overcoat.

His plan was to go to the subway station at Seventy-second and

Broadway, make his way to the end of the platform, drop the coat and cap into the shopping bag, change the filthy sneakers for the others, and sponge off his face and hands.

If only Kearny hadn't stepped into a cab last night! He could have sworn she was going to walk home. It would have been a great chance to hit her in the park. . . .

Patience born of the absolute certainty that his goal would be achieved, if not this morning, maybe this evening, if not today, maybe tomorrow, sent Denny on his way. He was careful to walk unevenly, to dangle the shopping bag as though he was hardly aware he was carrying it. The few people who bothered to glance at him edged away, the expression on their faces either disgusted or pitying.

As he crossed Seventy-second Street and West End, he collided with an old broad who was walking with her head down, her arm clamped around her pocketbook, her mouth mean and small. It would have been fun to give her a shove and grab that bag, Denny thought, then dismissed the idea. He hurried past her, turned onto Seventy-second Street and headed for the subway station.

A few minutes later he emerged, his face and hands clean, his hair slicked down, his faded denim jacket zipped neatly to his neck, the shopping bag containing the coat, cap, towel and washcloth tied into a neat bundle.

At ten-thirty he was delivering coffee to Neeve's office.

"Hi, Denny," she said when he went in. "I overslept this morning and now I can't get going. And I don't care what everybody else in this place says. Your coffee beats the stuff they brew in the coffeemaker."

"We all gotta oversleep once in a while, Miss Kearny," Denny said as he pulled the container from the bag and solicitously opened it for her.

Friday morning when Neeve awakened, she'd been startled to see that it was quarter to nine. Good Lord, she thought as she tossed back the covers and jumped out of bed, there's nothing like staying up half the night with the kids from the Bronx. She pulled on her robe and hurried into the kitchen. Myles had the coffee perking, juice poured and English muffins ready to be toasted. "You should have called me, Commish," she accused.

"It won't hurt the fashion industry to wait on you for half an hour." He was deep in the *Daily News*.

Neeve leaned over his shoulder. "Anything exciting?"

"A front-page account of the life and times of Nicky Sepetti. He's being buried tomorrow, escorted into eternity from a High Mass at St. Camilla's to interment in Calvary."

"Did you expect them to kick him around until they lost him?"

"No. I was hoping he'd be cremated and I could bid for the pleasure of sliding the coffin into the furnace."

"Oh, Myles, be quiet." Neeve tried to change the subject. "Last night was fun, wasn't it?"

"It *was* fun. Wonder how Sal's hand is. I'll bet he wasn't making love with his latest fiancée last night. Did you hear him say he's thinking of getting married again?"

Neeve downed the orange juice with an all-in-one vitamin. "You're kidding. Who's the lucky lady?"

"I'm not convinced 'lucky' is the word," Myles commented. "He's certainly had a variety of them. Never married till he made it big, and then runs the gamut from a lingerie model to a ballerina to a socialite to a health nut. Moves from Westchester to New Jersey to Connecticut to Sneden's Landing, and leaves them all behind in a fancy house. God knows what it's cost him over the years."

"Will he ever settle down?" Neeve asked.

"Who knows? No matter how many bucks he makes, Sal Esposito is always going to be an insecure kid trying to prove himself."

Neeve popped an English muffin into the toaster. "What else did I miss while I was fussing over a hot stove?"

"Dev's been summoned to the Vatican. That's just between us. He told me as they were leaving, when Sal went to pee—excuse me, your mother forbade me to say that. When Sal went in to wash his hands."

"I heard him say something about Baltimore. The archdiocese there?"

"He thinks it's coming."

"That could mean a red hat."

"It's possible."

"I must say you Bronx boys have been achievers. Must be something in the air."

The toaster popped. Neeve buttered the English muffin, generously spread it with marmalade and bit into it. Even though the day was obviously going to stay gloomy, the kitchen was cheerful with its white-stained oak cabinets and ceramic-tile floor in tones of blue, white and green. The place mats on the narrow butcher-block-top table were mint-green linen squares with matching napkins. The cups and saucers and plates and pitcher and creamer were legacies from Myles's boyhood. The English blue willow pattern. Neeve couldn't conceive of starting the day at home without that familiar china.

She studied Myles carefully. He really looked like himself again. It wasn't just Nicky Sepetti. It was the prospect of getting to work, of doing a job that was needed. She knew how Myles deplored the drug traffic and the carnage it was causing. And who knows? In Washington he might meet someone. He should marry again, and God knows he was a good-looking guy. She told him that.

"You mentioned the same thing last night," Myles told her. "I'm thinking of volunteering to pose for the centerfold of *Playgirl*. Do you think they'll take me?"

"If they do, bimbos will be lining up to seduce you," Neeve told him as she took her coffee back to her room, deciding it was high time to get a move on and go to work.

When he came out from shaving, Seamus realized that Ruth had left the apartment. For a moment he stood irresolute, then lumbered across the foyer into the bedroom, untied the cord of the maroon terry-cloth bathrobe the girls had given him for Christmas, and sank down on the bed. The sense of fatigue was so overwhelming that he could barely keep his eyes open. All he wanted to do was get back into bed, pull the covers over his head and sleep and sleep and sleep.

In all these years with all the problems, Ruth had never *not* slept with him. Sometimes they'd go for weeks, even months on end without touching each other, so strained with the money worries that their guts were torn out, but even so, by mutual unspoken consent they had lain together, both of them bound by the tradition that a woman slept at her husband's side.

Seamus looked around the room, seeing it through Ruth's eyes. The bedroom furniture that his mother had bought when he was ten. Not antique, just old—mahogany veneer, the mirror veering crazily on the supporting posts over the dresser. He could remember how his mother polished that piece of furniture, fussing over it, rejoicing in it. For her the matching set, the bed, dresser and chest, had been an accomplishment, the realized goal of a "nice home."

Ruth used to cut pictures from *House Beautiful* of the kind of rooms she'd like to have. Modern furniture. Pastel shades. Airy open look. Money worries had squeezed hope and brightness from her face, had made her too strict with the girls. He remembered the time she'd shrieked at Marcy, "What do you mean you tore your dress? I *saved* for that dress."

All because of Ethel.

Seamus leaned his head on his hands. The phone call he had made lay on his conscience. No way out. That had been the title of a movie a couple of years ago. *No Way Out.*

Last night he'd almost hit Ruth. The memory of those last few minutes with Ethel, the exact moment when he'd lost all control, when he'd . . .

He slumped back on the pillow. What was the point of going to the bar, of trying to keep up a front? He'd taken a step he wouldn't have believed possible. It was too late to call it off. He knew that. And it wouldn't do any good. He knew that too. He closed his eyes.

He wasn't aware that he'd dozed off, but suddenly Ruth was there. She was sitting on the edge of the bed. The anger seemed to have drained from her face. She looked haunted and panic-stricken, like someone facing a firing squad.

"Seamus," she said, "you've got to tell me everything. What did you do to her?"

Gordon Steuber arrived at his office on West Thirty-seventh Street at ten o'clock on Friday morning. He had come up in the elevator with three conservatively dressed men whom he instantly recognized as government auditors returning to pore over his books. His staff had only to see the scowl that made his eyebrows meet, the angry stride, to have the word begin to spread. "Watch out!"

He cut through the showroom, ignoring both clients and employees, walked rapidly past his secretary's desk, not deigning to respond to May's timid "Good morning, sir," and entered his private office, slamming the door behind him.

When he sat at his desk and leaned back in the ornate morocco leather chair that always inspired admiring comments, the scowl disappeared and was replaced by a worried frown.

He looked around the office, drinking in the atmosphere he had created for himself: the tooled-leather couches and chairs; the paintings that had cost a king's ransom; the sculptures that his art consultant assured him were of museum quality . . . Thanks to Neeve Kearny, there was a damn good chance he'd be spending more time in court than in his office. Or prison, he reflected, if he wasn't careful.

Steuber got up and walked over to the window. Thirty-seventh Street. The frantic atmosphere of the street peddler. It still had that quality. He remembered how as a kid he'd come directly from school to work for his father, a furrier. Cheap furs. The kind that made I. J. Fox creations look like sables. His father declared bankruptcy every couple of years like clockwork. By the time he was fifteen, Gordon knew he wasn't going to spend his life sneezing over rabbit hairs, talking dopes into thinking they looked good in mangy animal skins.

Linings. He'd figured it out before he was old enough to shave. The one constant. Whether you sold a jacket, a full-length, a finger-tip, a stole or a cape, it had to be lined.

That simple realization together with a grudging loan from his father had been the beginning of Steuber Enterprises. The kids he'd hired fresh from FIT or Rhode Island School of Design had imagination and flair. His linings with their exciting patterns had caught on.

But linings didn't make you a byword in a business that hungered for recognition. That was when he started looking for kids who knew how to design suits. He made it his ambition to be the new Chanel.

Once again he'd succeeded. His suits were in the best stores. But he was one of a dozen, two dozen, all competing for the same up-scale customer. Not enough money there.

Steuber reached for a cigarette. His gold lighter with his initials blazoned in rubies was on his desk. For an instant after he lit the cigarette, he held the lighter, turning it over and over in his hand. All the Feds had to do was add up how much the contents of this room and this lighter had cost and they'd keep digging till they had enough to indict him on income-tax evasion.

It was the damn unions that kept you from making a real profit, he told himself. Everyone knew that. Every time Steuber saw the ILGWU commercial he wanted to throw something at the television set. All they wanted was more money. Stop all the importing. Hire us.

It was only three years ago that he'd started doing what the rest of them did, set up off-the-books places for immigrants without green cards. Why not? The Mexicans were good seamstresses.

And then he'd found where the real money lay. He'd been all set to close out the sweatshops when Neeve Kearny blew the whistle on him. Then that crazy Ethel Lambston had started snooping around. He could still see that bitch bursting in here last week, last Wednesday evening. May was still outside. Otherwise right then . . .

He'd thrown her out, literally taken her shoulders and shoved her across the showroom to the main door, pushed her so she stumbled against the elevator. Even that hadn't fazed her. As he slammed the door, she'd shouted, "In case you haven't found out yet, they're going to get you on income tax as well as sweatshops. And that's just for starters. I know how you've been lining your pockets."

He'd known then that he couldn't let her keep digging into his affairs. She had to be stopped.

The phone rang, a soft purring sound. Annoyed, Gordon picked it up. "What is it, May?"

His secretary sounded apologetic. "I knew you wouldn't want to bc disturbed, sir, but the agents from the United States Attorney's office insist on seeing you."

"Send them in." Steuber smoothed the jacket of his light-beige Italian silk suit, flicked a handkerchief over a smudge on his square-cut diamond cufflinks and settled himself in his desk chair.

As the three agents came in, professional and businesslike in their attitude, he remembered for the tenth time in the last hour that all this had begun because Neeve Kearny had blown the whistle on his illegal factories.

At eleven o'clock on Friday morning, Jack Campbell returned from a staff meeting and again attacked the manuscript he had meant to read the night before. This time he forced himself to concentrate on the spicy adventures of a prominent thirty-three-year-old psychiatrist who falls in love with her client, an over-the-hill film idol. They go off to St. Martin's together on a clandestine vacation. The film idol because of his long and lusty experience with women breaks down the barriers the psychiatrist has built around her femininity. In turn, after three weeks of unending coupling under starry skies, she rebuilds his confidence in himself. He goes back to Los Angeles to accept the role as grandfather in a new situation comedy. She returns to her practice knowing that someday she'll meet a man suitable for a life with her. The book ends as she admits her new client, a handsome thirty-eight-year-old stockbroker who tells her, "I'm too rich, too scared, too lost."

Oh my God, Jack thought as he skimmed through the final pages. He tossed the manuscript on his desk just as Ginny came into the office, a pile of letters in her hand. She nodded in the direction of the manuscript. "How was it?"

"Frightful but it will sell big. Funny, in all those sex scenes in the garden, I kept wondering about love bites from the mosquitos. Is that a sign I'm getting old?"

Ginny grinned. "I doubt it. You know you have a lunch date?"

"I marked it down." Jack stood up and stretched.

Ginny looked at him approvingly. "Do you realize that all the junior editors are twittering about you? They keep asking me if I'm sure you're not involved with someone."

"Tell them you and I are an item."

"I wish. If I were twenty years younger, maybe."

Jack's smile turned to a frown. "Ginny, I just thought of something. How far ahead is the lead time of *Contemporary Woman?*"

"I'm not sure. Why?"

"I'm wondering if I can get a copy of the article Ethel Lambston did for them, the one on fashion? I know Toni usually won't show anything before the magazine's put to bed, but see what you can do, okay?"

"Sure."

An hour later when Jack left for lunch, Ginny called to him. "The article comes out in next week's issue. Toni said as a favor she'll let you see it. She's also going to send Xeroxes of Ethel's notes."

"That's great of her."

"She volunteered them," Ginny said. "She told me the outtakes of Ethel's articles usually make hotter reading than what the lawyers let them print in the magazine. Toni's getting worried about Ethel, too. She says since you're publishing Ethel's fashion book, she doesn't feel as though she's breaking confidentiality."

As Jack went down in the elevator on his way to his lunch date, he realized that he was very, very anxious to get a look at the outtakes in Ethel's file that were too hot to print.

Neither Seamus nor Ruth went to work on Friday. They sat in the apartment staring at each other like people caught together in quicksand, sinking, unable to reverse the inevitable. At noon, Ruth made strong coffee and grilled-cheese sandwiches. She insisted Seamus get up and dress. "Eat," she told him, "and tell me again exactly what happened."

As she listened, she could only imagine what it would do to the girls. Her hopes for them. The colleges she'd scrimped and sacrificed for. The dancing lessons and singing lessons, the clothes so carefully bought at sales. What good if their father was in prison?

Again Seamus blurted out the story. His round face glistening with perspiration, his hands thick and helpless in his lap, he recounted how he had begged Ethel to let him off the hook, how she'd toyed with him. "Maybe I will and maybe I won't," she'd said. Then she'd searched down behind the cushions of the couch. "Let me see if I can find some of the money my nephew forgot to steal," she told him, laughing, and, finding a hundred-dollar bill, she stuck it into his pocket with the remark that she hadn't had much time to eat out this month.

"I punched her," Seamus said tonelessly. "I never knew I was gonna do it. Her head lobbed to one side. She fell backwards. I didn't know if I'd killed her. She got up and she was scared. I told her if she looked for another dime, I would kill her. She knew I meant it. She said, 'All right, no more alimony.' "

Seamus gulped the rest of his coffee. They were sitting in the den. The day had started gray and cold, and now it was like early evening. Gray and cold. Just the way it had been last Thursday, at Ethel's apartment. The next day the storm broke. The storm would break again. He was sure of it.

"And then you left?" Ruth prompted.

Seamus hesitated. "And then I left."

There was a sense of something unfinished. Ruth looked around the room, at the heavy oak furniture she had despised for twenty years, at the faded machine-made Oriental that she had been forced to live with, and knew that Seamus had not told her the whole truth. She looked down at her hands. Too small. Square. Stubby fingers. All three girls had long, tapering fingers. Genes from whom? Seamus? Probably. Her family pictures showed small, square people. But they were strong. And Seamus was weak. A weak, frightened man who had turned desperate. *How* desperate? "You have not told me everything," she said. "I want to know. I have to know. It's the only way I can help you."

His head burrowed in his hands, he told her the rest. "Oh, my God," Ruth cried. "Oh, my God."

At one o'clock Denny returned to Neeve's Place carrying a cardboard tray containing two tuna-fish sandwiches and coffee. Again the receptionist waved him toward Neeve's office. Neeve was deep in conversation with her assistant, that good-looking black gal. Denny did not give either of them time to dismiss him. He opened the bag, removed the sandwiches and said, "You gonna eat here?"

"Denny, you're spoiling us. This is beginning to feel like room service," Neeve told him.

Denny froze, realizing his mistake. He was getting too visible. But he wanted to hear any plans she might have.

As though in answer to his unspoken request, Neeve told Eugenia, "I'll have to wait until late afternoon to go to Seventh Avenue on Monday. Mrs. Poth is coming in at one-thirty and wants me to help her select some gowns."

"That'll pay the rent for the next three months," Eugenia said briskly.

Denny folded the napkins. *Late afternoon on Monday.* That was good to know. He glanced around the room. Small office. No window. Too bad. If there'd been a window in the outside wall he'd have a direct shot at her back. But Charley had told him it couldn't look like a hit. His eyes swept over Neeve. Really good-looking. Really classy. With all the dogs out there, it was a real shame to have to waste this one. He muttered goodbye and departed, their thanks ringing in his ears. The receptionist paid him, adding the usual generous tip. But two bucks a delivery takes a long time before it adds up to twenty thousand, Denny thought as he opened the heavy glass door and stepped into the street.

While she was nibbling at the sandwich, Neeve dialed Toni Mendell at *Contemporary Woman.* When she heard Neeve's request, Mendell exclaimed, "Ye gods, what is this all about? Jack Campbell's secretary phoned asking for the same thing. I told her I'm worried about Ethel, too. I'll be honest. I let Jack see a copy of Ethel's notes because he's her publisher. Those I can't give you, but you can have the article." She cut through Neeve's attempt to thank her. "But for Pete's sake don't show it around. There'll be enough people in the rag game unhappy as it is when they see it."

An hour later, Neeve and Eugenia were poring over the copy of Ethel's article. It was entitled "The Masters and the Masterful Phonies of Fashion," and even for Ethel it was bitingly sarcastic. She began by naming the three most important fashions of the past fifty years: the New Look by Christian Dior in 1947, the Miniskirt by Mary Quant in the early sixties, and the Pacific Reef Look by Anthony della Salva in 1972.

About Dior, Ethel had written:

> In 1947 fashion was in the doldrums, still hung over with the military fashions of the war. Skimpy material; boxy shoulders; brass buttons. Dior, a shy young designer, said that we want to forget all about the war. He dismissed short skirts as a fashion of restriction. Showing what a real genius he was, he had the guts to tell a disbelieving world that the gown of the future for daytime wear would extend to twelve and a half inches from the ground.
>
> It wasn't easy for him. A California klutz tripped over her long skirt getting off the bus and helped fan a national revolt against the New Look. But Dior stuck to his guns, or his scissors, and, season after season, introduced graceful, beautiful clothes—drapery below the décolletage, molded midriffs with unpressed pleats that merged onto slender skirts. And his long-ago prediction was proven in the latest miniskirt disaster. Maybe someday all designers will learn that mystique is an important guideline to fashion.

By the early sixties the times were changing. We can't blame it all on Vietnam or Vatican II, but the wave of change was in the air and an English designer, young and perky, swept onto the scene. She was Mary Quant, the little girl who didn't want to grow up and never, never wanted to wear grown-up clothes. Enter the Miniskirt, the shift, colored stockings, high boots. Enter the premise that the young must *never* on any account look old. When Mary Quant was asked to explain the point of fashion, where it was leading, she brightly answered, "Sex."

In 1972 it was all over for the Miniskirt. Women, tired of being confused by the hemline game, gave up the struggle and switched to menswear.

Enter Anthony della Salva and the Pacific Reef Look. Della Salva began life not in a palace on one of the seven hills of Rome, as his publicist would have you believe, but as Sal Esposito, in a farm on Williamsbridge Road in the Bronx. His sense of color may have been cultivated by helping his father arrange the fruits and vegetables on the truck from which they peddled their wares throughout the neighborhood. His mother, Angelina, not *Countess* Angelina, was famous for her cant-like greeting, "God bless youra momma. God bless youra papa. How about some nicea grapefruit?"

Sal was a mediocre student at Christopher Columbus High School (that's in the Bronx, not Italy), a very mildly talented student at F.I.T. Just one of the crowd, but as fate would have it, eventually one of the blessed. He came up with the collection that put him over the top: the Pacific Reef Look, his one and only original idea.

But what an idea. Della Salva, in a single, magnificent stroke, put fashion back on the track. Anyone who attended that first fashion show in 1972 still remembers the impact of those graceful clothes that seemed to float from the models: the tunic with the drifting shoulder panel, the wool afternoon dresses cut so that they draped and shaped the body, the use of pleated sleeves in tones that shimmered and changed with the light. And his colors. He took the colors of the tropical Pacific ocean life, the coral trees and plants and underwater creatures, and borrowed the patterns nature gave them to create his own exotic designs, some brilliantly bold, some muted like the blues into silvers. The designer of the Pacific Reef Look deserves all the honors the fashion industry can bestow.

At that point, Neeve laughed reluctantly. "Sal will love what Ethel wrote about the Pacific Reef," she said, "but I don't know about the rest. He's lied so much, he's convinced himself he was born in Rome and his mother was a papal countess. On the other hand, from what he said the other night, he's expecting something like it. Everyone's hollering about how tough their parents had it these days. He'll probably find out what ship his folks were on when they sailed to Ellis Island and have a replica made of it."

Having covered the giant fashion looks as she saw them, Ethel proceeded in the article to name the society designers who couldn't tell "a button from a buttonhole" and hired talented young people to plan and execute their lines; to expose the conspiracy among designers to take the easy way out and try to turn fashion upside down every few years, even when it meant dressing aging dowagers like cancan girls; to mock the cowlike followers who plunked down three or four thousand dollars for a suit with barely two yards of gabardine.

Then Ethel turned her guns on Gordon Steuber:

> The Triangle Shirtwaist Company fire of 1911 alerted the public to the horrendous working conditions of garment workers. Thanks to the International Ladies Garment Workers Union, the ILGWU, the fashion industry has become a field where talented people can make decent incomes. But some manufacturers have found a way to increase their profits at the expense of the helpless. The new sweatshops are in the South Bronx and Long Island City. Illegal immigrants, many of them hardly more than children, work for pitiful wages because they don't have green cards and are afraid to protest. The king of these cheating manufacturers is Gordon Steuber. Much, much more about Steuber in a future article, but just remember, folks. Every time you put one of his suits on your back, give a thought to the kid who sewed it. She probably can't afford a decent meal.

The article concluded with a paean of praise for Neeve Kearny of Neeve's Place, who started the investigation of Gordon Steuber and who banned his clothes from her shop.

Neeve skimmed the rest of the text about her, then put down the papers. "She's drawn a bead on every major designer in the field! Maybe she scared herself and decided to get away until the heat dies down. I'm beginning to wonder."

"Can't Steuber sue her and the magazine?" Eugenia asked.

"Truth is the best defense. They obviously have all the proof they need. What *really* kills me is that despite all this, Ethel bought one of his suits last time she was here—the one we slipped up on returning."

The phone rang. A moment later the receptionist buzzed on the intercom. "Mr. Campbell for you, Neeve."

Eugenia's eyes raised. "You should see the look on your face." She gathered the remains of the sandwiches with the paper wrappings and the coffee containers and swept them into the wastebasket.

Neeve waited until the door closed before she picked up the phone. She tried to make her voice casual when she said, "Neeve Kearny." Dismayed, she realized she sounded breathless.

Jack came right to the point. "Neeve, can you have dinner with me tonight?" He didn't wait for her answer. "I was planning to tell you that I have some of Ethel Lambston's notes and maybe we could go over them together, but the real fact is I want to see you."

Neeve was embarrassed to realize how her heart was pounding. They agreed to meet at the Carlyle at seven o'clock.

The rest of the afternoon became unexpectedly busy. At four, Neeve went out on the showroom floor and began to take customers. They were all new faces. One young girl who couldn't have been more than nineteen bought a fourteen-hundred-dollar evening gown and a nine-hundred-dollar cocktail dress. She was very insistent that Neeve help her choose. "You know," she confided, "one of my girlfriends works at *Contemporary Woman* and she saw an article that's coming out next week. It says you have more fashion in your little finger than most of the designers on Seventh Avenue and that you never steer people wrong. When I told my mother she sent me over here."

Two other new customers had the same story. Someone knew someone who had told them about the article. At six-thirty, Neeve gratefully put a "CLOSED" sign on the door. "I'm beginning to think we'd better stop knocking poor Ethel," she said. "She's probably hyped business more than if I'd taken ads on every page of *W*."

After work Doug Brown stopped at the local superette on his way to Ethel's apartment. It was six-thirty when, as he was turning the key in the lock, he heard the persistent ringing of the phone.

At first he decided to ignore it as he had done all week. But when it relentlessly continued to peal, he debated. It was one thing that Ethel didn't like anyone to answer her phone. But after a week, wouldn't it seem logical that she might be trying to reach him?

He placed the grocery bag in the kitchen. The harsh ringing continued. Finally he picked up the receiver. "Hello."

The voice at the other end was slurred and guttural. "I have to talk to Ethel Lambston."

"She isn't here. I'm her nephew. Do you want to leave a message?"

"You bet I do. Tell Ethel her ex owes a lot of money to the wrong people and can't pay it while he's paying her. If she don't let Seamus off the hook, they're going to teach her a lesson. Tell her she might have a hard time typing with broken fingers."

There was a click and the line went dead.

Doug dropped the receiver onto the cradle and sank onto the couch. He could feel the perspiration on his forehead, in his armpits. He folded his hands to keep them from trembling.

What should he do? Was the call a real threat or a trick? He couldn't ignore it. He didn't want to call the police. They might start asking questions.

Neeve Kearny.

She was the one who was worried about Ethel. He'd tell her about the call. He'd be the scared, concerned relative asking for advice. That way, no matter whether it was a trick or for real, he'd have covered himself.

Eugenia was locking the cases with the fine costume jewelry when the phone rang in the shop. She picked up the receiver. "It's for you, Neeve. Someone sounds terribly upset."

Myles! Another heart attack? Neeve rushed to the phone. "Yes."

But it was Douglas Brown, Ethel Lambston's nephew. There was none of the usual sarcastic insolence in his voice. "Miss Kearny, have you *any* idea where I can try to reach my aunt? I just got back to her place and the phone was ringing. Some guy told me to warn her that Seamus, that's her ex-husband, owes a lot of money and can't pay it while he's paying her. If she doesn't let Seamus off the hook they're going to teach her a lesson. *She might have a hard time typing with broken fingers,* the guy said."

Douglas Brown sounded almost tearful. "Miss Kearny, we have to warn Ethel."

When Doug hung up, he knew he had made the right decision. At the advice of the ex–Police Commissioner's daughter, he would now phone the police and report the threat. In the eyes of the cops, he'd be viewed as a friend of the Kearny family.

He was reaching for the phone when it rang again. This time he picked it up without hesitation.

The police were calling *him.*

Myles Kearny believed in getting out of the way on Friday whenever it was possible. Lupe, their longtime cleaning woman, was there all day, washing and polishing, vacuuming and scrubbing.

When Lupe arrived, the morning mail in her hand, Myles retreated to the den. There was another letter from Washington, urging him to accept the post as head of the Drug Enforcement Agency.

Myles felt the old adrenaline flowing through his veins. Sixty-eight. It wasn't that old. And to get his teeth into a job that needed doing. Neeve. I fed her too much of love at first sight, he told himself. For most people it just doesn't work like that. Without me around all the time, she'll join the real world.

He leaned back in the desk chair, the old, comfortable leather chair that had been in his office the sixteen years he'd been Police Commissioner. It fits my butt, he thought. If I go to Washington, I'll ship it down.

In the foyer he could hear the sound of the vacuum. I don't want to listen to that all day, he thought. On impulse he phoned his old number, the office of the Commissioner, identified himself to Herb Schwartz's secretary, and a moment later was on the phone with Herb.

"Myles, what are you up to?"

"My question first," Myles responded. "How is Tony Vitale?" He could envision Herb, small stature, small frame, wise and penetrating eyes, tremendous intellect, incredible ability to see the whole picture. And, best of all, true-blue friend.

"We're still not sure. They left him for dead and, believe me, they had a right to think they knew what they were doing. But the kid's tremendous. Against all odds, the doctors think he'll make it. I'm going to see him later. Want to come?"

They agreed to meet for lunch.

Over turkey sandwiches in a bar near St. Vincent's Hospital, Herb briefed Myles on the upcoming Nicky Sepetti funeral. "We've got it covered. The FBI has it covered. The U.S. Attorney's office has it covered. But I don't know, Myles. My guess is that with or without the celestial summons, Nicky was old news. Seventeen years is too long to be out of circulation. The whole world's changed. In the old days the mob wouldn't have touched drugs. Now they're swimming in them. Nicky's world doesn't exist anymore. If he'd stayed, they'd have had him hit."

After lunch they went to the ICU at St. Vincent's. Undercover detective Anthony Vitale was swathed in bandages. Intravenous fluid dripped into his veins. Machines registered his blood pressure, his heartbeats. His parents were in the waiting room.

"They let us see him for a few minutes every hour," his father said. "He's going to make it." There was quiet confidence in his voice.

"You can't kill a tough cop," Myles told him as he gripped his hand.

Tony's mother spoke up. "Commissioner." She was speaking to Myles. He started to indicate Herb, but was stopped by the slight negative movement Herb made. "Commissioner, I think Tony is trying to tell us something."

"He told us what we needed to hear. That Nicky Sepetti didn't put a contract out on my daughter."

Rosa Vitale shook her head. "Commissioner, I've been with Tony every hour for the last two days. That's not enough. There's something else he wants us to know."

There was a round-the-clock guard on Tony. Herb Schwartz beckoned to the young detective who was sitting in the nurses' station of the ICU. "Listen," he told him.

Myles and Herb went down in the elevator together. "What do you think?" Herb asked.

Myles shrugged. "If there's anything I've learned to trust, it's a mother's instinct." He thought of that long-ago day when his mother had told him to look up the nice family who had sheltered him during the war. "There's plenty Tony could have learned that night. They must have been going over everything to make Nicky feel up-to-date." A thought struck him. "Oh, Herb, by the way, Neeve has been pestering me because some writer she knows has dropped out of sight. Tell the guys to keep an eye out for her, will you? About sixty. Five five and a half or six. Dresses well. Dyed silver blonde. Weighs about one-thirty-five. Name is Ethel Lambston. She's probably making someone's life miserable interviewing them for her column, but . . ."

The elevator stopped. They stepped into the lobby, and Schwartz pulled out a pad. "I've met Lambston at Gracie Mansion. She's been giving the Mayor a lot of plugs and he has her there all the time now. Something of an airhead, isn't she?"

"You've got it."

They both laughed.

"Why is Neeve worried about her?"

"Because she swears Lambston left home last Thursday or Friday without a winter coat. She buys all her clothes from Neeve."

"Maybe she was going to Florida or the Caribbean and didn't want to drag one along," Herb suggested.

"That was one of the many possibilities I pointed out to Neeve, but she claims all the clothes missing from Ethel's closet are for winter wear, and Neeve would know."

Herb frowned. "Maybe Neeve is onto something. Go over the description again."

Myles went home to the peace and quiet of the shiningly clean apartment. Neeve's phone call at six-thirty both pleased and disturbed him. "You're going out to dinner. Good. I hope he's interesting."

Then she told him about her call from Ethel's nephew. "You told him to report the threat to the police. That was the right thing to do. Maybe she did get nervous and take off. I spoke to Herb about her today. I'll let him know about this."

Myles settled for fruit and crackers and a glass of Perrier for his own dinner. As he ate and tried to concentrate on *Time* magazine, he found himself increasingly concerned that he had so casually brushed off Neeve's instinct that Ethel Lambston was in serious trouble.

He poured a second Perrier and got to the center of his discomfort. The threatening phone call, as reported by the nephew, did *not* have the ring of truth.

Neeve and Jack Campbell sat on a banquette in the dining room of the Carlyle. On impulse, she had changed from the sweater dress she'd worn to work to a soft multicolored print. Jack had ordered drinks, a vodka martini straight up with olives for himself, a glass of champagne for Neeve. "You remind me of the song 'A Pretty Girl Is Like a Melody,' " he said. "Or is it all right to call anyone a pretty girl these days? Would you rather be a handsome person?"

"I'll settle for the song."

"Isn't that one of the dresses the mannequins are wearing in your show windows?"

"You're very observant. When did you see them?"

"Last night. And I didn't just happen by. I was overwhelmingly curious." Jack Campbell did not seem uncomfortable disclosing that fact.

Neeve studied him. Tonight he was wearing a dark-blue suit with a faint chalk stripe. Unconsciously she nodded approval at the overall effect, the Hermès tie that exactly picked up the blue, the custom-made shirt, the plain gold cufflinks.

"Will I pass?" he asked.

Neeve grinned. "Very few men manage to wear a tie that really goes with the suit. I've been laying out my father's ties for years."

The waiter arrived with the drinks. Jack waited until he'd left before he spoke. "I wish you'd fill me in a little. Starting with where did you get the name Neeve?"

"It's Celtic. Actually it's spelled N-I-A-M-H and pronounced 'Neeve.' Long ago I gave up trying to explain it, so when I opened the shop I just used the phonetic spelling. You'd be amazed at how much time I've saved myself, to say nothing of the aggravation of being called Nim-ah."

"And who was the original Neeve?"

"A goddess. Some say the exact translation is 'star of the morning.' My favorite legend about her is that she swooped down to earth to pick up the fellow she wanted. They were happy for a long time, then he wanted to visit earth again. It was understood that if his feet touched the ground he would become his real age. You can guess the rest. He slipped from the horse, and poor Niamh left him a bag of bones and returned to the skies."

"Is that what you do to your admirers?"

They laughed together. It seemed to Neeve that it was by mutual consent they were putting off talking about Ethel. She had told Eugenia about the phone call, and, oddly, Eugenia found it reassuring. "If Ethel got a call like that, it says to me that she decided to take off until things cool down. You told her nephew to report it to the police. Your father's on top of it. You can't do anything else. My bet is that good old Ethel is holed up in a spa."

Neeve wanted to believe it. She put Ethel out of her mind as she sipped the champagne and smiled across the table at Jack Campbell.

Over celery rémoulade, they talked about growing up. Jack's father was a pediatrician. Jack had been raised in a suburb of Omaha. He had one older sister, who still lived near his parents. "Tina has five kids. The nights get cold in Nebraska." He had worked in a bookstore summers during high school and become fascinated with publishing. "So after Northwestern, I went to work in Chicago selling college textbooks. That's enough to prove your manliness. Part of the job is to see if any of the professors you're peddling books to may be *writing* a book. One of them haunted me with her autobiography. Finally I said, 'Madam, let's face it. You've had a very boring life.' She complained to my boss."

"Did you lose your job?" Neeve asked.

"No. They made me an editor."

Neeve glanced around the room. The soft elegance of the ambience; the delicate china, handsome silver and fine damask tablecloths; the flower arrangements; the pleasant murmur of voices from other tables. She felt remarkably, absurdly happy. Over rack of lamb, she told Jack about herself. "My father fought tooth and nail to send me away to college, but I liked being home. I went to Mount St. Vincent and spent one term in England at Oxford, then a year at the University of Perugia. Summers and after school I worked in dress shops. I always knew what I wanted to do. My idea of a good time was to go to a fashion show. Uncle Sal was great. From the time my mother died, he'd send a car to take me when a collection was being unveiled."

"What do you do for fun?" Jack asked.

The question was too casual. Neeve smiled, knowing why he'd asked it. "For four or five summers I had a share in a house in the Hamptons," she told him. "That was great. I skipped last year because Myles was so sick. In the winter, I ski in Vail for at least a couple of weeks. I was there in February."

"Who do you go with?"

"Always my best friend, Julie. The other faces change."

He asked it straight out. "How about men?"

Neeve laughed. "You sound like Myles. I swear he won't be happy till he's playing father of the bride. Sure I've dated a lot. I went with the same guy practically through college."

"What happened?"

"He went to Harvard for an MBA and I got involved with the dress shop. We just drifted into our own worlds. His name was Jeff. Then there was Richard. A really nice person. But he took a job in Wisconsin and I knew there was no way I could leave the Big Apple forever, so it couldn't be true love." She began to laugh. "The nearest I came to getting engaged was a couple of years ago. That was Gene. We broke up at a charity do on the *Intrepid*."

"The ship?"

"Uh-huh. It's docked on the Hudson at West Fifty-sixth. Anyhow, the party's held on Labor Day weekend: black tie, tons of people. I swear I know ninety percent of the regulars at it. Gene and I got separated in the crowd. I didn't worry. I figured we'd catch up eventually. But when we did, he was furious. Thought I should have tried harder to find him. I saw a side of him I knew I didn't want to live with." Neeve shrugged. "The simple truth is I don't think anyone has been right for me."

"So far," Jack smiled. "I'm beginning to think you *are* the legendary Neeve who leaves her admirers behind as she rides away. You haven't been exactly pounding me with questions about myself, but I'll tell you anyhow. I'm a good skier, too. I went to Arosa the past couple of Christmas holidays. I'm planning to look for a summer place where I can have a sailboat. Maybe you'd better show me around the Hamptons. Like you, I came close to settling down a couple of times. In fact, I actually got engaged about four years ago."

"My turn to ask: What happened?" Neeve said.

Jack shrugged. "Once the diamond was on her finger, she became a very possessive young lady. I realized I'd run out of breathing room pretty fast. I'm a great believer in Kahlil Gibran's advice on marriage."

"Something about 'the pillars of the temple stand apart'?" Neeve asked.

She was rewarded by his expression of amused respect. "You've got it."

They waited until they'd finished their raspberries and were sipping espresso before they discussed Ethel. Neeve told Jack about the phone call from Ethel's nephew and the possibility that Ethel was hiding out. "My father is in touch with his department. He'll get them to run down who's making the threats. And, frankly, I have to say I do think Ethel should let that poor guy off the hook. It's disgusting to be collecting from him all these years. She needs that alimony like a hole in the head."

Jack pulled the folded copy of the article from his pocket. Neeve told him she'd already seen it. "Would you call this scandalous?" Jack asked her.

"No. I'd call it funny and bitchy and sarcastic and readable and potentially libelous. There isn't a thing in it that everyone in the business doesn't know already. I'm not sure how Uncle Sal will react, but knowing him I swear he'll turn it into a virtue that his mother peddled fruit. Gordon Steuber I'd worry about. I have a hunch he could be vicious. The other designers Ethel drew a bead on? What can you say? Everyone knows that except for one or two, the society designers can't draw straight. They just love the excitement of playing at working."

Jack nodded. "Next question. Do you think anything in this article would make an explosive book?"

"No. Even Ethel couldn't pull that off."

"I have a file of all the outtakes from the article. I haven't had a chance to study them yet." Jack signaled for the check.

Across the street from the Carlyle, Denny was waiting. It was a long shot. He knew that. He'd followed Neeve when she walked along Madison Avenue to the hotel, but there'd been absolutely no chance to get near her. Too many people. Big guys on their way home from work. Even if he'd been able to waste her, the chances that someone would deck him were too strong. His only hope was that Neeve might come out alone, maybe walk to the crosstown bus, or even walk home. But when she came out, she was with some guy and they got into a cab together.

A sense of frustration made Denny's face turn ugly under the smears of dirt that made him blend in with the other winos in the area. If this weather kept up, she'd always be in cabs. He had to work over the weekend. There was no way he was going to risk drawing attention to himself at the job. So that meant he could only hang around her apartment building early in the morning in case she went to the store or jogged, or after six o'clock.

That left Monday. And the Garment District. Somehow Denny felt in his bones that that was where he'd end up. He slipped into a doorway, shrugged off the ragged overcoat, wiped his face and hands with a grimy towel, shoved coat and towel into a shopping bag and headed for a bar on Third Avenue. His gut was burning for a boilermaker.

It was ten o'clock when the cab pulled up to Schwab House. "My father will be having a nightcap," Neeve told Jack. "Are you interested?"

Ten minutes later they were in the study, sipping brandy. Neeve knew that something was wrong. There was a look of concern in Myles's expression even while he chatted easily with Jack. She sensed he had something to tell her that he would not discuss now.

Jack was telling Myles about meeting Neeve on the plane. "She ran so fast I couldn't get her number. And she tells me she'd missed her connection."

"I can vouch for that," Myles said. "I waited for her at the airport for four hours."

"I must say I was delighted when she came up to me at the cocktail party the other day and asked about Ethel Lambston. I gather from what Neeve tells me Ethel isn't one of your favorite people, Mr. Kearny."

Neeve gasped at the change in Myles's face. "Jack," he said, "someday I'll learn to listen to Neeve's intuition." He turned to Neeve. "Herb phoned a couple of hours ago. A body was found in Morrison State Park in Rockland County. It answered Ethel's description. They brought Ethel's nephew out and he identified her."

"What happened to her?" Neeve whispered.

"Her throat was cut."

Neeve closed her eyes. "I *knew* something was wrong. I *knew* it!"

"You were right. They already have a hot suspect, it seems. When the upstairs neighbor saw the squad car she came running down. Seems Ethel had a colossal fight with her ex-husband last Thursday afternoon. Apparently no one has seen her since then. On Friday she broke her appointments with you and with her nephew."

Myles swallowed the last of the brandy and got up to refill his glass. "I don't usually have a second brandy, but tomorrow morning the homicide guys from the Twentieth Precinct want to talk to you. And the DA's office in Rockland County has asked if you'd go out and look at the clothing Ethel was wearing. The point is they know the body was moved after death. I told Herb that you spotted the fact that none of her coats was missing and that she bought all her stuff from you. The labels were ripped out of the suit she was wearing. They want to see if you can identify it as one of yours. God *damn* it, Neeve," Myles exclaimed. "I don't like the idea of you being a witness in a murder case."

Jack Campbell reached out his glass for a refill. "Neither do I," he said quietly.

9

Sometime during the night the wind had shifted, and the low-hanging clouds were blown out over the Atlantic. Saturday dawned with a welcoming golden sun. But the air was still unseasonably cold, and the CBS weatherman warned that the clouds would be back and there might even be snow flurries in the afternoon. Neeve bounded out of bed. She had a date to go jogging with Jack at seven-thirty.

She pulled on a sweatsuit, her Reeboks, and tied her hair back into a ponytail. Myles was already in the kitchen. He frowned.

"I just don't like you jogging alone this early."

"Not alone."

Myles raised his eyes. "I see. Moving fast, aren't we? I like him, Neeve."

She poured orange juice. "Now, don't get your hopes up. You liked the stockbroker too."

"I didn't say I liked that one. I said he seemed respectable. There's a difference." Myles dropped the bantering. "Neeve, I've been thinking. It makes more sense for you to go to Rockland County and talk to those detectives before you sit down with our guys. If you're right, the clothes Ethel Lambston was wearing came from your shop. So that's the first thing we establish. My guess is that after that you should go through her closet with a fine-tooth comb and see exactly what else is missing. We know homicide is going to zero in on the ex-husband, but you can't assume anything."

The intercom rang. Neeve picked up the receiver. It was Jack. "I'll be right down," she told him.

"What time do you want to go to Rockland County?" she asked Myles. "I really have to go to work for a while."

"Midafternoon will be fine." At her surprised expression, Myles added, "Channel Eleven is covering Nicky Sepetti's funeral live. I want a front-row seat."

Denny had taken up his position at seven o'clock. At seven-twenty-nine he saw a tall guy in a running suit go into Schwab House. A few minutes later, Neeve Kearny emerged with him. They started jogging toward the park. Denny swore silently under his breath. If she'd only been alone. He had cut through the park on the way over. It was almost deserted. He could have wasted her anywhere. He felt for the pistol in his pocket. Last night when he'd gone back to his room Big Charley had been parked across the street waiting for him. Charley had rolled down the car window and handed out a brown paper bag. Denny had taken it, and his fingers had felt the outline of the gun.

"Kearny is starting to cause real trouble," Big Charley told him. "It don't matter no more if it looks like an accident. Get her any way you can."

Now he was tempted to follow them into the park, to hit the two of them. But Big Charley might not like that.

Denny began to walk in the opposite direction. Today he was wrapped in a bulky sweater that hung to his knees, torn chinos, leather sandals, a stocking cap that had once been bright yellow. Under it he was wearing a gray wig; bits of greasy gray hair were plastered on his forehead. He looked like a mainliner with scrambled brains. In the other getup he looked like a wino. But this way no one would remember that any one guy had been hanging around Neeve Kearny's building.

As Denny put a token into the turnstile at the Seventy-second Street subway, he thought, I oughtta charge Big Charley the money it cost me to change my clothes.

Neeve and Jack entered the park at Seventy-ninth Street and began jogging east, then north. As they approached the Metropolitan Museum, Neeve instinctively began to cut west again. She did not want to pass the place where her mother had died. But at Jack's puzzled glance she said, "Sorry, you lead."

She tried to keep her eyes resolutely forward but could not resist glancing at the area past the still bare trees. *The day Mother hadn't arrived to pick her up at school. The principal, Sister Maria, had her wait in the office and suggested she begin her homework. It was nearly five o'clock before Myles came for her. By then she'd been sure something was wrong. Mother was never late.*

The moment when she'd looked up and seen Myles standing over her, his eyes red-rimmed, his expression a mixture of anguish and pity, she'd known. She'd reached up her arms to him. "Is my mother dead?"

"You poor little kid," Myles had said as he picked her up and hugged her against him. "You poor little kid."

Neeve felt tears glisten in her eyes. In a burst of speed she ran past the quiet lane, past the extension of the Met that held the Egyptian collection. She was almost to the reservoir before she slowed down.

Jack had kept pace with her. Now he took her arm. "Neeve." It was a question. As they turned west and then south, now gradually reducing their pace to a fast walk, she told him about Renata.

They left the park at Seventy-ninth Street. The last few blocks to Schwab House they walked side by side, their fingers linked.

When she turned on the radio at seven o'clock on Saturday morning, Ruth heard the news of Ethel's death. She had taken a sleeping pill at midnight and for the next hours slept a heavy, drugged sleep that was filled with vaguely remembered nightmares. Seamus was arrested. Seamus on trial. That she-devil, Ethel, testifying against him.

Years ago Ruth had worked in a law office, and she had a fair knowledge of the kind of charges that could be leveled against Seamus.

But as she listened to the newscast and lowered the teacup from her trembling fingers, she realized that she could add one more count: *murder*.

She shoved her chair back from the table and ran into the bedroom. Seamus was just waking up. Shaking his head, he ran his hand over his face, a characteristic gesture that had always annoyed her.

"You *killed* her!" she screamed. "How can I help you if you won't tell me the truth!"

"What are you talking about?"

She snapped on the radio. The newscaster was describing how and where Ethel had been found. "You took the girls picnicking to Morrison State Park for years," she cried. "You know the place like the back of your hand. *Now tell me the truth! Did you stab her?*"

An hour later, paralyzed with fright, Seamus made his way to the pub. Ethel's body had been found. He knew the police would come for him.

Yesterday, Brian, the day bartender, had worked a double shift. To show his displeasure, he'd left the bar sticky and untidy. The Vietnamese kid who handled the kitchen was already there. At least *he* was a willing worker. "Are you sure you should have come in, Mr. Lambston?" he asked. "You still look real sick."

Seamus tried to remember what Ruth had told him. *"Say you have a touch of flu. You never miss work. They've got to believe you were really sick yesterday, that you were sick last weekend. They've got to believe you never left the apartment last weekend. Did you talk to anyone? Did anyone see you? That neighbor is bound to tell them you were there a couple of times last week."*

"Darn bugs keep coming back on me," he mumbled. "Yesterday was bad, but over the weekend I was *sick*."

Ruth phoned at ten o'clock. Childlike, he listened and repeated word for word what she told him.

He opened the pub at eleven. At noon the old-timers who were still around started drifting in. "Seamus," one of them boomed, his jovial face creased in smiles, "sad news about poor Ethel, but grand that you're off the hook for the alimony. Drinks on the house?"

At two o'clock, shortly after the reasonably busy lunch service was winding down, two men entered the bar. One was in his early fifties, with a beefy build and ruddy complexion, a man who might as well have had a sign on him reading "COP." His partner was a slim Hispanic, in his late twenties. They identified themselves as Detectives O'Brien and Gomez from the Twentieth Precinct.

"Mr. Lambston," O'Brien asked quietly. "Are you aware that your former wife, Ethel Lambston, has been found in Morrison State Park, that she has been the victim of a homicide?"

Seamus gripped the edge of the bar with knuckles that turned white. He nodded, unable to speak.

"Would you mind stepping over to headquarters?" Detective O'Brien asked. He cleared his throat. "We'd like to go over a few things with you."

After Seamus left for the pub, Ruth dialed Ethel Lambston's apartment. The phone was picked up, but no one spoke. Finally she said, "I would like to speak with Ethel Lambston's nephew, Douglas Brown. This is Ruth Lambston."

"What do you want?" It was the nephew's voice. Ruth recognized it.

"I must see you. I'll be right there."

Ten minutes later a cab was dropping her in front of Ethel's apartment. As she stepped out and handed the fare to the driver, Ruth looked up. A curtain moved on the fourth floor. The upstairs neighbor who missed nothing.

Douglas Brown had been watching for her. He opened the door and stepped back to allow her to come into the apartment. It was still inordinately tidy, although Ruth noticed a fine layer of dust on the table. New York apartments needed daily dusting.

Not believing that the thought could even cross her mind at a time like this, she stood directly in front of Douglas, noticing the expensive bathrobe, the silk pajamas that peered out from the hem of the robe. Douglas looked heavy-eyed, as though he'd been drinking. His even features would have been handsome if they were strong. Instead they reminded Ruth of sculptures children made in sand, sculptures that washed away with wind and the tide.

"What do you want?" he demanded.

"I won't waste your time or mine saying I'm sorry Ethel is dead. I want the letter Seamus wrote her, and I want you to put this in its place." She extended her hand. The envelope was unsealed. Douglas opened it. It contained an alimony check dated April 5.

"What are you trying to pull?"

"I'm not pulling anything. I'm making an even exchange. Give me back the letter Seamus wrote Ethel, and get something straight. The reason Seamus came here on Wednesday was to deliver the alimony. Ethel wasn't home and he came back on Thursday because he was worried that he hadn't been able to force the envelope into her mailbox. He knew she'd haul him into court if it wasn't there."

"Why would I do that?"

"Because last year Seamus asked Ethel to whom she was going to leave all her money, that's why. She told him she had no choice—you were her only relative. But last week Ethel told Seamus you were stealing from her and she was planning to change her will."

Ruth watched as Douglas turned a chalky white. "You're lying."

"Am I?" Ruth asked. "I'm giving *you* a break. You give Seamus a break. We'll keep our mouths shut about your being a thief, and you keep your mouth shut about the letter."

Douglas felt grudging admiration for the determined woman who was standing in front of him, handbag clutched under her arm, sensible all-weather coat, sensible shoes, frameless glasses that magnified her pale-blue eyes, thin, rigid mouth. He knew she wasn't bluffing.

He raised his eyes to the ceiling. "You seem to forget that the blabbermouth upstairs is telling everyone who'll listen that Seamus and Ethel had a big fight the day before she didn't show up for her appointments."

"I talked to that woman. She can't quote one single word. Just claims she heard loud voices. Seamus naturally talks loud. Ethel shrieked every time she opened her mouth."

"You seem to have thought of everything," Doug told her. "I'll get the letter." He went into the bedroom.

Ruth moved noiselessly to the desk. Beside the pile of mail, she could see the edge of the red-and-gold-handled dagger Seamus had described to her. In an instant it was in her purse. Was it only her imagination that it felt sticky?

When Douglas Brown emerged from the bedroom carrying Seamus' letter, Ruth glanced at it and shoved it deep into the side pocket of her purse. Before she left, she extended her hand to him. "I am very sorry about the death of your aunt, Mr. Brown," she said. "Seamus has asked me to convey his sympathy. No matter what troubles they had, there was a time when they enjoyed and loved each other. That is the time he will remember."

"In other words," Douglas said coldly, "when the police ask, this is the official reason for the visit."

"That's right," Ruth said. "The unofficial reason is that if you keep your bargain, neither Seamus nor I will even hint to the police that your aunt was planning to disinherit you."

* * *

Ruth went home, and in an almost religious fervor began to clean the apartment. Walls were scrubbed, curtains ripped down and left soaking in the bathtub. The twenty-year-old vacuum whined its ineffectual path along the threadbare carpet.

As she worked, Ruth was obsessed with the realization that she had to get rid of the dagger.

She discarded all the obvious places. The incinerator? Suppose the police checked the building trash. She didn't want to drop it into a waste bin on the street. Maybe she was being followed and some cop would retrieve it.

At ten o'clock she phoned Seamus and rehearsed him on what he must say if he was questioned.

She could not delay any longer. She had to decide what to do with the dagger. She took it from her purse, ran it under boiling water and rubbed it with brass polish. Even so it seemed to her that it felt sticky—sticky from Ethel's blood.

She was beyond even a pang of pity for Ethel. All that mattered was to preserve an untainted future for the girls.

She stared with loathing at the dagger. Now it looked brand-new. One of those crazy Indian things, blade sharp as a razor, with an ornate handle, decorated in an intricate pattern of red and gold. Probably expensive.

Brand-new.

Of course. So simple. So easy. She knew exactly where to hide it.

At twelve o'clock, Ruth made her way to Prahm and Singh, an Indian artifacts store on Sixth Avenue. She moseyed from display to display, pausing at counters and poring over baskets of trinkets. Finally she found what she was looking for, a large basket of letter openers. The handles were cheap copies of the ornate design of Ethel's antique. Idly, she picked one up. As she'd remembered, in a shabby way it did resemble the one she was carrying.

From her handbag, she extracted Ethel's dagger and dropped it into the basket, then pushed all the contents around until she was sure Ethel's murder weapon was at the bottom of the pile.

"Can I help you?" a clerk asked.

Startled, Ruth looked up. "Oh . . . yes. I was just . . . I mean I'd like to see some coasters."

"They're in aisle three. I'll show you."

At one o'clock Ruth was back in the apartment, making a cup of tea and waiting for her heart to stop pounding. No one will find it there, she promised herself. Never, ever . . .

* * *

After Neeve left for her shop, Myles had a second cup of coffee and contemplated the fact that Jack Campbell was going to drive with them to Rockland County. Instinctively he liked Jack very much and wryly acknowledged that for years he'd been urging Neeve not to get hung up on the myth of love at first sight. My God, he thought, is it possible that lightning does strike twice after all?

At quarter of ten, he settled himself in his deep leather chair and watched as television cameras relayed the pageantry of Nicky Sepetti's funeral. Flower cars, three of them overflowing with expensive arrangements, preceded the hearse to St. Camilla's Church. A fleet of hired limousines carried mourners and those who pretended to mourn. Myles knew that the FBI and the U.S. Attorney's office as well as the Police Department racket squad were there, taking down the license numbers of private cars, photographing the faces of the people filing into the church.

Nicky's widow was escorted by a stocky fortyish man and a younger woman who was swathed in a black hooded cape that concealed much of her face. All three were wearing dark glasses. The son and daughter don't want to be recognized, Myles decided. He knew that both had distanced themselves from Nicky's associates. Smart kids.

The coverage continued inside the church. Myles lowered the volume and, keeping one eye on the set, went to the phone. Herb was in his office.

"Have you seen the *News* and the *Post?*" Herb asked. "They're really playing up the Ethel Lambston murder."

"I saw them."

"We're still concentrating on the ex-husband. We'll see what the search of her apartment turns up. That argument the neighbor heard last Thursday might have ended in the stabbing. On the other hand, he may have scared her enough to make her decide to get out of town and then followed her. Myles, you taught me that every murderer leaves a calling card. We'll find this one."

They agreed that Neeve would meet the homicide detectives from the Twentieth Precinct at Ethel's apartment on Sunday afternoon. "Call me if you pick up anything of interest in Rockland County," Herb said. "The Mayor wants to announce that this case is solved."

"What else is new about the Mayor?" Myles asked dryly. "Talk to you, Herb."

Myles turned up the volume of the set and watched as Nicky Sepetti's remains were blessed by the priest. The casket was wheeled out of church as the choir sang "Be Not Afraid." Myles listened to the words, "Be not afraid, I am with you always." *You've* been with me day and night for seventeen years, you sonofabitch, he thought as the pallbearers folded the casket blanket and hoisted the heavy mahogany coffin onto their shoulders. Maybe when I'm sure you're rotting in the ground, I'll be free of you.

Nicky's widow reached the bottom of the church steps, then abruptly turned and walked from her son and daughter to the nearest television commentator. As her face loomed into the camera, a face weary and resigned, she said, "I want to make a statement. A lot of people did not approve of my husband's business dealings, may he rest in peace. He was *sent* to prison for those dealings. But he was *kept* in prison, for many extra years, for a crime he did *not* commit. On his deathbed, Nicky swore to me that he had nothing to do with the murder of Police Commissioner Kearny's wife. Think what you want of him, but don't think of him as the person responsible for that death."

A barrage of unanswered questions followed her as she walked back to stand with her children. Myles snapped off the set. A liar to the end, he thought. But as he pulled on his tie and with quick, deft movements knotted it, he realized that for the first time a seedling of doubt was sprouting in his mind.

After learning that Ethel Lambston's body had been found, Gordon Steuber went into a frenzy of activity. He ordered his last illegal warehouse in Long Island City vacated and the illegal workers warned of the consequences of talking to the police. He then phoned Korea to cancel the expected shipment from one of his factories there. On learning that the shipment was already being loaded at the airport, he threw the phone at the wall in a savage gesture of frustration. Then, forcing himself to think rationally, he tried to assess the damage. How much proof did Lambston have and how much had been bluff? And how could he disentangle himself from her article?

Although it was Saturday, May Evans, his longtime secretary, had come in to catch up on filing. May had a drunk for a husband and a teenage kid who was always in trouble. At least half a dozen times Gordon had bought him out of an indictment. He could count on her discretion. Now he asked May to come into his office.

His calm restored, he studied her, the parchment skin that was already falling into wrinkles, the anxious, downcast eyes, the nervous, eager-to-please manner. "May," he said, "you've probably heard about Ethel Lambston's tragic death?"

May nodded.

"May, was Ethel in here one evening about ten days ago?"

May looked at him for a clue. "There was a night I worked a little late. Everyone was gone except you. I thought I saw Ethel come in and you make her leave. Am I wrong?"

Gordon smiled. "Ethel didn't come in, May."

She nodded. "I understand," she said. "Did you take her call last week? I mean I thought I put her through, and that you were terribly angry and hung up on her."

"I never took her call." Gordon took May's blue-veined hand in his and squeezed it lightly. "My recollection is that I refused to speak to her, refused to see her, and had no idea what she might have written about me in her forthcoming article."

May withdrew her hand from his grip and backed away from the desk. Her faded brown hair was frizzy around her face. "I understand, sir," she said quietly.

"Good. Close the door on your way out."

Like Myles, Anthony della Salva watched the Nicky Sepetti funeral on television. Sal lived in a penthouse on Central Park South, in Trump Parc, the luxurious apartment building that had been renovated for the very rich by Donald Trump. His penthouse, furnished by the hottest new interior designer, in the Pacific Reef motif, had a breathtaking view of Central Park. Since his divorce from his last wife, Sal had decided to stick to Manhattan. No more boring homes in Westchester or Connecticut or the Island or on the Palisades. He liked the freedom of being able to go out at any hour of the night and find a good restaurant open. He liked first night at the theater and chic parties and being recognized by the people who mattered. "Leave the suburbs to the hicks" had become his motto.

Sal was wearing one of his latest designs, tan doeskin slacks with a matching Eisenhower jacket. Dark-green cuffs and a dark-green collar completed the sportsman look. The fashion critics had not been kind to his last two important collections, but had grudgingly praised his menswear. Of course, the real stardom in the rag game was reserved for the couturiers who revolutionized women's fashion. And no matter what they said or didn't say about any of his collections, they still referred to him as one of the master trendsetters of the twentieth century, the creator of the Pacific Reef look.

Sal thought about the day two months ago when Ethel Lambston had come to his office. That nervous flapping mouth; her habit of speaking so quickly. Listening to her was like trying to follow the numbers on a ticker tape. She had pointed to the Pacific Reef mural on the wall and pronounced, "That is genius."

"Even a nosey journalist like you recognizes truth, Ethel," he had retorted, and they both laughed.

"Come on," she had urged him, "break down and forget the villa-in-Rome crap. What you guys don't understand is that phony nobility is out of style. It's a Burger King world. The man from humble beginnings is hot. I'm doing you a favor when I let people know you came from the Bronx."

"There are a lot of people on Seventh Avenue with more to sweep under the rug than being born in the Bronx, Ethel. I'm not ashamed."

Sal watched Nicky Sepetti's coffin carried down the steps of St. Camilla's. Enough of that, he thought, and was about to turn off the set when Sepetti's widow grabbed the mike and pleaded that Nicky had nothing to do with Renata's murder.

For a while Sal sat with his hands folded. He was sure Myles had been watching. He knew how Myles must be feeling, and decided to phone him. He was relieved to hear Myles sound fairly matter-of-fact. Yes, he'd seen the sideshow, he said.

"My guess is, he hoped his kids would believe him," Sal suggested. "They both married pretty well and won't want the grandchildren to know that Nicky's portrait has a number under it in the police files."

"That's the obvious answer," Myles said. "Although to tell you the truth, my gut says a deathbed confession to save his soul was more Nicky's style." His voice trailed off. "Gotta go. Neeve will be along soon. She has the unpleasant job of seeing if the clothing Ethel was wearing came from her shop."

"I hope not, for her sake," Sal said. "She doesn't need that kind of publicity. Tell Neeve that if she's not careful people will start saying they wouldn't be caught dead in her clothes. And that's all it will take to break the mystique of Neeve's Place."

At three o'clock, Jack Campbell was at the door of apartment 16B in Schwab House. When Neeve returned from the shop, she'd changed from her Adele Simpson navy suit to a red-and-black hip-length ribbed sweater and slacks. The harlequin effect was accentuated by the earrings she had designed for the outfit: the masks of comedy and tragedy in onyx and garnets.

"Her nibs, the checkerboard," Myles said dryly as he shook hands with Jack.

Neeve shrugged. "Myles, you know something? I don't relish what we've got to do. But I have a feeling that Ethel would be pleased if I arrived in a new outfit to talk about the clothes she was wearing when she died. You just can't understand how much pleasure she got from fashion."

The den was brightened by the last of the waning sunshine. The weather forecaster had been on target. Clouds were gathering over the Hudson River. Jack glanced around, appreciating some of the things he had missed the night before. The fine painting of the Tuscany hills that was on the wall to the left of the fireplace. The framed sepia photograph of a toddler in the arms of a dark-haired young woman with a hauntingly beautiful face. He was sure it was Neeve with her mother. He wondered what it would be like to lose the woman you loved to a murderer. Intolerable.

He noticed that Neeve and her father were glaring at each other with exactly the same expression. The similarity was so great he wanted to smile. He sensed that this fashion debate was a running issue between them and had no intention of being caught in the middle. He walked over to the window, where a book that had obviously been damaged was exposed to the sunlight.

Myles had made a fresh pot of coffee and was pouring it into handsome Tiffany china mugs. "Neeve, let me tell you something," he said. "Your friend Ethel is beyond spending a king's ransom on extravagant clothes. Right now she's in her birthday suit, on a slab in the morgue with an ID tag on her big toe."

"Was that the way Mother ended up?" Neeve asked, her voice low and furious. Then she gasped and ran to him, putting her hands on his shoulders. "Oh, Myles, I'm sorry. That was a cheap, rotten thing to say."

Myles stood statue still, the coffeepot in his hand. A long twenty seconds passed. "Yes," he said, "that was exactly the way your mother ended up. And it was a rotten thing for both of us to say."

He turned to Jack. "Forgive the domestic upheaval. My daughter is either blessed or cursed with the combination of a Roman temperament and Irish thin skin. For my part, I have never found it possible to understand how women can make such a fuss over clothes. My own mother, God rest her soul, did all her shopping in Alexander's on Fordham Road, wore housedresses every day and a flowered print, also from Alexander's, for Sunday Mass and banquets of the Policemen's Glee Club. Neeve and I, like her mother before her, have interesting discussions on the subject."

"I gathered that." Jack lifted a mug from the tray Myles offered to him. "I'm glad somebody else drinks too much coffee," he observed.

"A whiskey or a glass of wine would probably go down better," Myles observed. "But we'll save that for later. I've got an excellent bottle of burgundy that will offer an appropriate warmth at a suitable hour, despite what the doctor told me." He walked over to the wine rack in the bottom section of the bookcase and pulled out a bottle.

"In the old days, I didn't know one from the other," Myles told Jack. "My wife's father had a truly fine wine cellar, and so Renata grew up in a connoisseur's home. She taught me about it. She taught me about many things I'd missed along the way." He pointed to the book on the windowsill. "That was hers. It got drenched the other night. Is there any way of restoring it?"

Jack picked up the book. "What a shame," he said. "These sketches must have been charming. Do you have a magnifying glass?"

"Somewhere."

Neeve scouted through Myles's desk and came up with one. She and Myles watched as Jack studied the stained and crumbled pages. "The sketches really didn't blur," he said. "Tell you what. I'll check with a couple of people on my staff and see if I can come up with the name of a good restorer." He handed the magnifying glass back to Myles. "And, by the way, I don't think it's a great idea to let the sun get at them."

Myles took the book and the magnifying glass and laid them on his desk. "I'd be grateful for anything you can do. Now we'd better get started."

All three sat in the front seat of Myles's six-year-old Lincoln Town Car. Myles drove. Jack Campbell casually threw his arm across the back of the seat. Neeve tried not to be aware of its presence, not to lean against him when the car circled the ramp from the Henry Hudson Parkway to the George Washington Bridge.

Jack touched her shoulder. "Relax," he said. "I don't bite."

The District Attorney's office in Rockland County was typical of district attorneys' offices all over the country. Crowded. Old uncomfortable furniture. Files piled high on cabinets and desks. Overheated rooms except where windows had been opened, and then blasts of chilly air became an unpleasant alternative.

Two detectives from the homicide squad were waiting for them. Neeve noticed how the moment he entered the building, something changed about Myles. His jawline firmed. He walked taller. His eyes took on a hue of flinty blue. "He's in his element," she murmured to Jack Campbell. "I don't know how he's managed the inactivity this past year."

"The District Attorney would like you to drop by, sir." It was clear the detectives were aware they were in the presence of New York City's longest-serving and most highly respected Commissioner.

The District Attorney, Myra Bradley, was an attractive young woman who could not have been more than thirty-six or -seven. Neeve relished the look of astonishment on Myles's face. God, you're a chauvinist, she thought. You have to have known Myra Bradley was elected last year and you chose to block it out.

She and Jack were introduced. Myra Bradley waved them to seats and got to the point. "As you are aware," she said, "there is a matter of jurisdiction. We know the body was moved, but we don't know from where it was moved. She could have been murdered in the park five feet from where she was found. In which case, we take charge."

Bradley indicated the file on her desk. "According to the M.E., death was caused by a violent slash with a sharp instrument which cut her jugular vein and sliced her windpipe. She may have put up a struggle. Her jaw was black and blue and there was a cut on her chin. I might add, it was a miracle the animals didn't get to her. Probably because she was pretty well covered by the rocks. She wasn't supposed to be discovered. Burying her there took careful planning."

"Meaning you're looking for someone who knows the area," Myles said.

"Exactly. There's no way to pinpoint the exact time of death, but from what her nephew told us she failed to meet him last Friday, eight days ago. The body was pretty well preserved, and when we check the weather we see that the cold spell started nine days ago, on Thursday. So if Ethel Lambston died on Thursday or Friday and was buried shortly thereafter, it would account for the lack of decomposition."

Neeve was sitting to the right of the District Attorney's desk. Jack was in the chair beside her. She felt herself flinch, and his arm went over the back of her chair. *If only I had remembered her birthday*. She tried to push away the thought and concentrate on what Bradley was saying.

". . . Ethel Lambston could easily have gone undetected for months, even to the point where identification would have been extremely difficult. She wasn't meant to be found. She wasn't meant to be identified. She was wearing no jewelry; there was no handbag or wallet near her." Bradley turned to Neeve. "Do the clothes you sell always have your labels sewn in them?"

"Of course."

"The labels in Ms. Lambston's clothing had all been removed."

The District Attorney got up. "If you don't mind, Miss Kearny, would you look over the clothing now?"

They went into an adjoining room. One of the detectives brought in plastic bags filled with rumpled and stained clothing. Neeve watched as the bags were emptied. One of them contained lingerie, a matching bra and panties, both edged with lace, the bra spattered with blood; pantyhose with a wide run up the front of the right leg. Medium-heel pumps of a soft periwinkle-blue leather were held together by a rubber band. Neeve thought of the racks of shoe trees Ethel had been so proud to display in her state-of-the-art closet.

The second bag held a three-piece suit: winter-white wool with periwinkle-blue cuffs and collar, a white skirt and a striped blue-and-white blouse. All three were soaked in blood and smeared with dirt. Neeve felt Myles's hand on her shoulder. Resolutely she studied the garments. Something was wrong, something that went beyond the gruesome end to which these garments and the woman who wore them had come.

She heard the District Attorney ask, "Is this one of the outfits that was missing from Ethel Lambston's closet?"

"Yes."

"Did you sell her this outfit?"

"Yes, around the holidays." Neeve looked up at Myles. "She wore it at the party, remember?"

"No."

Neeve spoke slowly. She felt as though time had dissolved. She was in the apartment and it had been decorated for their annual Christmas cocktail buffet. Ethel had looked particularly attractive. The white-and-blue suit was handsome and very becoming with her dark blue eyes and silver-blond hair. A number of people complimented her on it. Then, of course, Ethel zeroed in on Myles, talking his ear off, and he spent the rest of the party trying to avoid her. . . .

There was something wrong with the memory. What was it? "She bought that suit with some other clothes in early December. That's a Renardo original. Renardo is a subsidiary of Gordon Steuber Textiles." What was eluding her? She simply didn't know. "Was she wearing a coat?"

"No." The District Attorney nodded to the detectives, who began to fold the clothing and replace it in the plastic bags. "Commissioner Schwartz told me that the reason you began worrying about Ethel was that all her warm coats were in her closet. But isn't it a fact that she could easily have bought a coat from someone other than you?"

Neeve got up. The room seemed to smell faintly of antiseptic. She was not about to make a fool of herself by insisting that Ethel simply didn't shop anywhere except from her. "I'll be glad to do an inventory of Ethel's closet," she said. "I have all the receipts from her purchases in a file. I can tell you exactly what's missing."

"I'd like as full a description as possible. Did she usually wear jewelry with this outfit?"

"Yes. A diamond-and-gold pin. Matching earrings. A wide gold bracelet. She always wore several diamond rings."

"She had no jewelry on. So we may have a simple felony murder."

Jack took her arm as they left the room. "You okay?"

Neeve shook her head. "There's something I'm missing."

One of the detectives had heard her. He gave her his card. "Call anytime."

They headed for the door of the courthouse building. Myles was ahead, chatting with the District Attorney, his silver-white hair a full head over her dark-brown blunt-cut bob. Last year his cashmere overcoat had hung limply from his shoulders. After the operation, he'd looked pale and shrunken. Now his shoulders filled out the coat again. His step was firm and sure. And he was in his element in this situation. Police work was what made sense to him, to his life. Neeve found herself praying that nothing would interfere with that job in Washington.

As long as he works, he'll live to be one hundred, she thought. There was some crazy expression: "If you want to be happy for a year, win the lottery. If you want to be happy for life, love what you do."

Loving his work kept Myles going after Mother died.

And now Ethel Lambston was dead.

The detectives had stayed behind when they left, refolding the clothes that had been Ethel's shroud, clothing that Neeve knew would someday be seen again at a trial. Last seen wearing . . .

Myles was right. She was a silly fool to come to this place dressed like a checkerboard, those idiotic earrings faintly jangling in this dark place. Neeve was grateful she had not removed the hooded black cape that covered the striking ensemble. A woman was dead. Not an easy woman. Not a popular one. But a highly intelligent woman who fiercely called the shots as she saw them, who wanted to look well but didn't have either the time or the instinct to fend for herself in the fashion world.

Fashion. That was it. There was something about the outfit she was wearing . . .

Neeve felt a tremor go through her body. It was as though Jack Campbell felt it, too. Suddenly his arm was drawn through hers. "You cared about her a lot, didn't you?" he asked.

"Much more than I realized."

Their footsteps echoed down the long marble corridor. The marble was old and worn, cracks fissured through it like veins beneath flesh.

Ethel's jugular vein. Ethel's neck had been so thin. But unwrinkled. At nearly sixty, a lot of women started to get the telltale signs of age. "The neck goes first." Neeve remembered that that was what Renata would say when a manufacturer tried to persuade her to buy low-cut dresses in mature women's sizes.

They were at the entrance to the courthouse. The District Attorney and Myles were agreeing that Manhattan and Rockland County would cooperate closely in the investigation. Myles said, "I should keep my mouth shut. It gets awfully hard to remember that I'm not pushing the buttons at One Police Plaza anymore."

Neeve knew what she had to say and prayed that she wouldn't sound ridiculous. "I wonder . . ." The District Attorney, Myles and Jack waited. She began again. "I wonder if I could possibly speak to the woman who found Ethel's body. I don't know why, but I just feel as though I should." She swallowed over a lump in her throat.

She felt their eyes studying her. "Mrs. Conway has made a complete statement," Myra Bradley said slowly. "You can look at that if you want."

"I'd like to talk with her." Don't let them ask why, Neeve thought wildly. "I just have to."

"My daughter is the reason Ethel Lambston has been identified," Myles said. "If she'd like to speak with this witness, I think she should."

He had already opened the door, and Myra Bradley shivered in the crisp April wind. "More like March," she observed. "Look, I have absolutely no objection. We can give Mrs. Conway a call and see if she's in. We feel she's told everything she knows, but maybe something else will surface. Wait a minute."

A few moments later she returned. "Mrs. Conway is home. She'd be perfectly willing to talk with you. Here's her address and the directions." She smiled at Myles, the smile of two professional cops. "If she happens to remember that she got a good look at the guy who killed Lambston, give us a quick call. Okay?"

Kitty Conway had a fire blazing in the library, a fire that threw pyramids of blue-tipped flame from the glowing logs. "Let me know if it's too warm for you," she said apologetically. "It's just that from the moment I touched that poor woman's hand, I haven't stopped feeling cold." She paused, embarrassed, but the three sets of eyes that were observing her all seemed to signal understanding.

She liked their looks. Neeve Kearny. Better than beautiful. Interesting, magnetic face with those high cheekbones, that milk-white skin accentuating those intense brown eyes. But her face showed strain; the pupils of her eyes were enormous. It was obvious that the young man, Jack Campbell, was concerned about her. When he took her cape he'd said, "Neeve, you're still trembling."

Kitty had a sudden wave of nostalgia. Her son was the same type as Jack Campbell, a little over six feet tall, broad-shouldered, trim body, strong, intelligent expression. She deplored the fact that Mike Junior lived half a world away.

Myles Kearny. When the District Attorney phoned, she'd known immediately who *he* was. For years his name had appeared regularly in the media. Sometimes she'd seen him when she and Mike used to eat in Neary's Pub on East Fifty-seventh Street. She'd read about his heart attack and retirement, but he looked fine now. A good-looking Irishman.

Kitty was fleetingly grateful that she'd changed from her jeans and ancient oversized sweater to a silk blouse and slacks. When they wouldn't accept drinks, she insisted on making tea. "You need something to warm you up," she told Neeve. Refusing assistance, she disappeared down the corridor to the kitchen.

Myles was sitting in a high-backed wing chair with a striped red-and-burnt-orange upholstery. Neeve and Jack were side by side on a velvet sectional that was placed like a crescent around the fireplace. Myles looked around the room approvingly. Comfortable. There were few people who had the brains to buy couches and chairs in which a tall man could lean his head back. He got up and began to examine the framed family photos. The usual history of a life. The young couple. Kitty Conway hadn't lost her looks along the way, that was for sure. She and her husband with their young son. A collage of the boy's growing years. The last picture was of Kitty, her son, his Japanese wife and their little girl. Myra Bradley had told him that the woman who discovered Ethel's body was a widow.

He heard Kitty's steps in the hallway. Quickly, Myles turned to the bookshelves. One section caught his eye, a collection of well-worn books on anthropology. He began to glance through them.

Kitty placed the silver tray on the round table near the sectional, poured the tea, urged cookies on them. "I baked up a storm this morning; nerves after yesterday, I guess," she said, and walked over to Myles.

"Who's the anthropologist?" he asked.

She smiled. "Strictly amateur. I got hooked in college when the professor said that to know the future we should study the past."

"Something I used to keep reminding my detective squads," Myles said.

"He's turning on the charm," Neeve murmured to Jack. "A most unfamiliar sight."

As they sipped the tea, Kitty told them about the horse bolting down the incline, about the plastic flying into her face, about her blurred impression of a hand in a blue sleeve. She explained about the sleeve of her sweatsuit lapping over the lid of the hamper and how at that moment she'd known she had to go back to the park and investigate.

Throughout, Neeve listened attentively, her head poised to one side as though she were straining to catch every word. She still had the overwhelming feeling that she was missing something, something that was right before her, simply waiting to be pounced on. And then she realized what it was.

"Mrs. Conway, will you describe exactly what you saw when you found the body?"

"Neeve?" Myles shook his head. He was building his questions carefully and did not want to be interrupted.

"Myles, I'm sorry, but this is terribly important. *Tell me about Ethel's hand. Tell me what you saw.*"

Kitty closed her eyes. "It was like looking at a mannequin's hand. It was so white and the nails seemed a garish red. The cuff of the jacket was blue. It came to the wrist, and that little piece of black plastic was sticking to it. The blouse was blue and white, but it hardly showed beneath the cuff. It was sort of crumpled. It was crazy, but I almost straightened it."

Neeve let out a long sigh. She leaned forward and rubbed her forehead with her hands. "That's what I couldn't get. That blouse."

"What about the blouse?" Myles asked.

"It . . ." Neeve bit her lip. She was going to sound like a fool to him again. The blouse Ethel had been wearing was a part of the original three-piece ensemble. But when Ethel bought the suit, Neeve had told her she didn't think the blouse was right for it. She'd sold Ethel another blouse, all white, without the distraction of the blue stripes. She'd seen Ethel wear that outfit twice, and both times she'd had the white blouse on.

Why did she wear the blue-and-white one?

"What is it, Neeve?" Myles insisted.

"It's probably nothing. Just I'm surprised she wore that blouse with that suit. It just didn't look right with it."

"Neeve, didn't you tell the police that you recognized the outfit and tell them who the designer was?"

"Yes, Gordon Steuber. It was an ensemble from his workrooms."

"I'm sorry, I don't get it." Myles tried to conceal his irritation.

"I think I do." Kitty poured steaming tea into Neeve's cup. "Drink this," she ordered. "You look faint." She looked directly at Myles. "If I'm right, Neeve is saying that Ethel Lambston would not have deliberately dressed in that outfit as it was found on her."

"I *know* she would not have chosen to wear it that way," Neeve said. She looked directly into Myles's disbelieving eyes. "Obviously her body had been moved. Is there any way they can establish whether or not someone dressed her *after* she died?"

Douglas Brown had known that the homicide squad planned to obtain a search warrant for Ethel's apartment. Even so, it was a shock when they arrived with it. A team of four detectives converged on the apartment. He watched as they spread powder over surfaces, as they vacuumed the rugs and floors and furniture, carefully sealing and marking the plastic bags in which they stored the dust and fibers and particles which they collected as they minutely examined and sniffed at the small Oriental rug near Ethel's desk.

Seeing Ethel's body on the slab had left Doug with a queasy stomach; an incongruous reminder of the one boat ride he ever took and how violently seasick he had become. She was covered by a sheet that had been wrapped around her face like a nun's wimple, so at least he didn't have to look at her throat. To avoid thinking about her throat he concentrated on the purple-and-yellow bruise on her cheek. Then he'd nodded his head and bolted for the lavatory.

All night he had lain awake in Ethel's bed, trying to decide what to do. He could tell the police about Seamus, about his desperation to stop the alimony payments. But the wife, Ruth, would be blabbering about him. Cold sweat formed on his forehead as he realized how stupid he'd been to go to the bank the other day and insist on getting the withdrawal in hundred-dollar bills. If the police found that out . . .

Before the police came, he'd agonized about whether to leave the bills hidden around the place. If they weren't there, who could say that Ethel hadn't spent them all?

Someone would know. That crazy kid who had come in to clean might have noticed the ones he'd put back.

In the end, Douglas decided to do absolutely nothing. He'd let the cops find the bills. If Seamus or his wife tried to point a finger at him, he'd call them liars. With the slight comfort of that thought, Douglas turned his mind to the future. This was his apartment now. Ethel's money was his money. He'd get rid of all those stupid clothes and accessories, A goes with A, B goes with B. Maybe he'd pack them all just that way and pitch them into the garbage. The thought brought a grim smile. But no use getting wasteful. All the bucks Ethel spent on her clothes shouldn't go down the drain. He'd find a good second-hand shop and sell them.

When he dressed on Saturday morning, he'd deliberately chosen to wear dark-blue slacks and a tan long-sleeved sport shirt. He wanted to give the impression of subdued grief. The lack of sleep had caused circles to form under his eyes. Today that was all to the good.

The detectives went through Ethel's desk. He watched as they opened the file that read "Important Papers." The will. He still hadn't decided whether to admit he knew about it. The detective finished reading it and looked over at him. "You ever seen this?" he asked, his tone offhand.

On the spur of the moment, Douglas made his decision. "No. Those are my aunt's papers."

"She never discussed her will with you?"

Douglas managed a rueful smile. "She used to kid a lot. She said that if she could only leave me her alimony payments, I'd be set for life."

"Then you didn't know that she seems to have left you a sizable amount of money?"

Douglas swept his hand around the apartment. "I didn't think Aunt Ethel had a sizable amount of money. She bought this place when it went co-op. That must have cost her plenty. She made a good living as a writer, but not big-league."

"Then she must have been very thrifty along the way." The detective had handled the will with gloved hands, holding it at the very edges of the paper. As Douglas stared in dismay, the detective called to the fingerprint expert. "Let's dust this."

Five minutes later, his hands twisting nervously in his lap, Douglas confirmed and then denied any knowledge of the hundred-dollar bills the homicide squad had found secreted in the apartment. To divert them from that subject, he explained that until yesterday he hadn't answered the phone.

"Why?" Detective O'Brien was in charge. The question cut the air like a razor.

"Ethel was funny. I picked up the phone when I was visiting her once and she took my head off. She told me it wasn't my business who called her. But then, yesterday, I happened to think maybe she might want to get in touch with me. So I started answering."

"Could she have reached you at work?"

"I never thought of that."

"And the first call you got was a threat to her. What a coincidence you got the call almost at the very hour her body was found." Abruptly, O'Brien cut off the interrogation. "Mr. Brown, do you plan to stay in this apartment?"

"Yes, I do."

"We'll be coming in tomorrow with Miss Neeve Kearny. She'll be checking Ms. Lambston's closet for missing items of clothing. We may want to talk to you again. You'll be here." It was not a request. It was a flat statement.

For some reason Douglas was not relieved that the questioning was at an end. And then his fears were justified. O'Brien said, "We may ask you to stop in at headquarters. We'll let you know."

When they left, they took the plastic bags with the vacuum contents, Ethel's will and appointment book and the small Oriental carpet. Just before the door closed behind them, Doug heard one of them say, "No matter how hard they try, they can't get all the blood off rugs."

In St. Vincent's Hospital, Tony Vitale was still in the intensive-care unit, his condition still critical. But, as the head surgeon continued to reassure his parents, "He's young. He's tough. We believe he's going to make it."

Swathed in bandages that covered the gunshot wounds in his head, shoulder, chest and legs, intravenous fluid dripping into his veins, electronic monitors observing his every bodily change, plastic tubes in his nostrils, Tony drifted from a state of deep coma to fragments of consciousness. Those last moments were coming back to him. *Nicky Sepetti's eyes boring through him. He'd known that Nicky suspected he was a plant. He should have driven to headquarters instead of stopping to call. He should have known that his cover had been blown.*

Tony slid into darkness.

When he groped his way back to consciousness, he heard the doctor say, "Every day shows a little improvement."

Every day! How long had he been here? He tried to speak, but no sound came.

Nicky had screamed and pounded his fist on the table and ordered them to get the contract canceled.

Joey had told him it was impossible.

Then Nicky had demanded to know who ordered it.

"... Someone turned the heat on," Joey had said. "Ruined his operation. Now the Feds are on his tail. . . ." Then Joey had given the name.

As he slid back into unconsciousness, Tony remembered that name:

Gordon Steuber.

In the Twentieth Precinct on West Eighty-second Street, Seamus waited, his round, pale face damp with perspiration. He tried to remember all the warnings Ruth had given him, everything she had told him to say.

It was all a blur.

The room he was sitting in was stark. A conference table, the surface scarred from cigarette burns. Wooden chairs. The one he was sitting on caught the small of his back. A grimy window that overlooked the side street. The traffic outside was hell; cabs and buses and cars blaring at one another. The building was rimmed with squad cars. How long were they going to keep him here?

It was another half hour before the two detectives came in. A court stenographer followed them and slipped into a chair behind Seamus. He turned and watched as she set up her steno machine on her lap.

The older detective's name was O'Brien. He'd introduced himself and his partner, Steve Gomez, in the bar.

Seamus had expected them to give him the Miranda warning. It was still a shock to hear it read to him, to have O'Brien hand him a printed copy and ask him to read it. He nodded at the question did he understand it? Yes. Did he want his lawyer present? No. Did he realize that he could discontinue answering questions at any point? Yes. Did he realize that anything he said could be used against him?

He whispered, "Yes."

O'Brien's manner changed. It became subtly warmer. His tone was conversational. "Mr. Lambston, it is my duty to tell you that you are considered a possible suspect in the death of your former wife, Ethel Lambston."

Ethel dead. No more alimony checks. No more stranglehold on him and Ruth and the girls. Or had the stranglehold only begun? He could see her hands clawing at him, see the way she'd looked when she fell backward, see the way she'd struggled up and reached the letter opener. He felt the wetness of her blood on his hands.

What was the detective saying in that friendly, conversational tone? "Mr. Lambston, you quarreled with your former wife. She was driving you crazy. The alimony was bankrupting you. Sometimes things get too much for us and we blow our lids. Did that happen?"

Had he gone crazy? He could feel the hatred of that moment, the way bile rose in his throat, the way he'd clenched his fist and aimed it at that mocking, vicious mouth.

Seamus laid his head down on the table and began to cry. Sobs racked his body. "I want a lawyer," he said.

Two hours later, Robert Lane, the fiftyish lawyer Ruth had frantically managed to locate, showed up. "Are you prepared to press formal charges against my client?" he asked.

Detective O'Brien looked at him, his expression sour. "No, we are not. Not at this time."

"Then Mr. Lambston is free to go?"

O'Brien sighed. "Yes, he is."

Seamus had been sure they would arrest him. Not daring to believe what he had heard, he leaned his palms on the table and dragged his body from the chair. He felt Robert Lane put his hand under his arm and guide him from the room. He heard Lane say, "I want a transcript of my client's statement."

"You'll get it." Detective Gomez waited until the door closed, then turned to his partner. "I'd love to have locked up that guy."

O'Brien smiled, a thin, mirthless smile. "Patience. We have to wait for the lab reports. We need to check Lambston's movements on Thursday and Friday. But if you want to bet on a sure thing, bet that we'll have an indictment from the grand jury before Seamus Lambston gets to enjoy the end of his alimony payments."

When Neeve, Myles and Jack got back to the apartment, there was a message on the answering machine. Would Myles please call Police Commissioner Schwartz at his office?

Herb Schwartz lived in Forest Hills, "where ninety percent of the PCs have traditionally dwelt," Myles explained to Jack Campbell as he reached for the phone. "If Herb isn't fussing around his house on Saturday evening, something big is happening."

The conversation was brief. When Myles hung up he said, "It looks as though it's all over. The minute they brought in the ex-husband and started questioning him, he cried like a baby and demanded a lawyer. It's only a matter of time till they have enough to indict him."

"What you're saying is that he didn't confess," Neeve said. "Isn't that right?" As she spoke, she began turning on table lamps until the room was bathed in a soft, warm glow. Light and warmth. Was that what the spirit yearned for after witnessing the harsh reality of death? She could not shake off the feeling of something ominous surrounding her. From the moment she had seen Ethel's clothing laid out on that table, the word *shroud* had danced in her head. She realized now that she had immediately wondered what *she* would be wearing when she died. Intuition? Irish superstition? The feeling that someone was walking on her grave?

Jack Campbell was watching her. He knows, she thought. He senses that there's more than just the clothes. Myles had pointed out that if the blouse Ethel usually wore with the suit was at the cleaners, she would automatically choose as a substitute the one that belonged with the ensemble.

All the answers Myles came up with made such sense. Myles. He was standing in front of her; his hands were on her shoulders. "Neeve, you haven't heard a word I said. You asked me a question and I answered it. What's the matter with you?"

"I don't know." Neeve tried to smile. "Look, it's been a rotten afternoon. I think we should have a drink."

Myles scrutinized her face. "I think we should have a *stiff* drink, and then Jack and I should take you out for dinner." He looked up at Jack. "Of course, you may have plans."

"No plans except, if I may, to fix us that drink."

The scotch, like the tea at Kitty Conway's, did the job of temporarily taking from Neeve the sense of being swept along by a dark current. Myles repeated what the Commissioner had told him: The homicide detectives felt that Seamus Lambston was on the verge of admitting guilt.

"Do they still want me to go through Ethel's closet tomorrow?" Neeve wasn't sure whether she wanted to be relieved of the task.

"Yes. I don't think it's going to matter one way or the other whether Ethel had planned to go away and packed for herself or if he killed her and then tried to make it look as though she was off on one of her trips, but we don't leave loose ends."

"But wouldn't he have to keep sending the alimony indefinitely if people thought she was away? I remember Ethel told me once that if he was late with the check she'd have her accountant call and threaten suit. If Ethel's body wasn't discovered, they'd have been after him to keep paying for seven years before she'd be declared legally dead."

Myles shrugged. "Neeve, the percentage of homicides that are the result of domestic violence is awesome. And don't credit people with too many brains. They act impulsively. They go off the deep end.

Then they try to cover their tracks. You've heard me say it over and over. 'Every killer leaves his calling card.' "

"If that's true, Commish, I'd be interested to know what calling card Ethel's murderer left."

"I'll tell you what I think the calling card is. That bruise on Ethel's jaw. You didn't see the autopsy report. I did. As a kid, Seamus Lambston was a darn good Golden Glover. The bruise almost broke Ethel's jaw. With or without a confession, I'd have started looking for someone with a boxing background."

"The Legend has spoken. And you're dead wrong."

Jack Campbell sat on the leather couch sipping Chivas Regal, and for the second time in one day decided to keep his own counsel as Neeve and her father argued. Listening to them was not unlike watching a game of tennis between two well-matched opponents. He almost smiled but, observing Neeve, felt another stab of worry. She was still very pale, and the coal-black hair that framed her face accentuated the milk-white luster of her skin. He had seen those wide sherry-colored eyes brighten with amusement, but tonight it occurred to him that there was a sadness in them that went beyond Ethel Lambston's death. Whatever happened to Ethel isn't finished, Jack thought, and it has to do with Neeve.

Impatiently he shook his head. His Scottish forebears with claims of their own to second sight were getting to him. He had asked to accompany Neeve and her father to the District Attorney's office in Rockland County for the simple reason that he wanted to spend the day with Neeve. When he left her this morning, he'd gone to his place, showered, changed and headed for the Mid-Manhattan Library. There on microfilm he had read the seventeen-year-old newspapers with the screaming headlines POLICE COMMISSIONER'S WIFE MURDERED IN CENTRAL PARK. He'd absorbed every detail; studied the pictures of the funeral procession from St. Patrick's Cathedral. Neeve, ten years old, in a dark coat and bonnet-shaped hat, her small hand lost in Myles's hand, her eyes shimmering with tears. Myles's face carved in granite. The rows upon rows of policemen. They seemed to stretch the length of Fifth Avenue. The editorials that linked convicted mobster Nicky Sepetti to the execution of the Police Commissioner's wife.

Nicky Sepetti had been buried this morning. That had to have yanked both Neeve and her father back to the full memory of Renata Kearny's death. The microfilms of the old newspapers had been filled with speculation about whether Nicky Sepetti from his prison cell had also ordered Neeve's death. This morning Neeve had told Jack that her father had been dreading Nicky's release because he was worried about her, that she believed that Nicky Sepetti's death had freed Myles from that obsessive fear.

Then why am I worried about you, Neeve? Jack wondered.

The answer came into his thoughts as simply as though he'd asked the question aloud. Because I love her. Because I've been looking for her since that first day when she ran away from me on the plane.

Jack realized that all their glasses were empty. He got up and reached for Neeve's glass. "Tonight I don't think you should fly on one wing."

With the second cocktail they watched the evening news. Excerpts of Nicky Sepetti's funeral came on, including his widow's impassioned statement. "What do you think?" Neeve asked Myles quietly.

Myles snapped off the set. "What I think isn't printable."

They had dinner at Neary's Pub on East Fifty-seventh Street. Jimmy Neary, a twinkly-eyed Irishman with a leprechaun's smile, rushed to greet them. "Commissioner, it's grand to see you." They were ushered to one of the prize corner tables Jimmy reserved for his special guests. Jimmy was introduced to Jack and pointed out to him the pictures that framed the walls. "There's himself." Former Governor Carey's picture was placed where it could not be missed. "Only the cream of New York up there," Jimmy told Jack. "See where the Commissioner is." Myles's picture was directly opposite Governor Carey's.

It was a good evening. Neary's was always the gathering place for politicians and the clergy. Repeatedly people stopped at the table to greet Myles. "It's great to see you again, Commissioner. You're looking fit."

"He loves this," Neeve murmured to Jack. "He hated being sick and just about dropped out of sight this last year. I think he's ready to join the real world."

Senator Moynihan came over. "Myles, I hope to God you're taking over the Drug Enforcement Agency," he said. "We *need* you. We've got to get rid of this drug scum, and you're the man we want in charge."

When the Senator left, Neeve raised her eyes. "You talked about 'feelers.' It's gone this far!"

Myles was studying the menu. Margaret, his longtime favorite waitress, came over. "How's the shrimp Creole, Margaret?"

"Brilliant."

Myles sighed. "I knew it would be. In honor of my diet, bring me broiled flounder, please."

They ordered, and as they sipped wine Myles said, "It means spending a lot of time in Washington. It means renting an apartment there. I don't think I could have left you here alone, Neeve, if Nicky Sepetti was walking the streets. But now I do feel safe about you. The gang hated Nicky for ordering your mother's death. We kept the heat on them until most of the old crowd was up there with him."

"Then you don't believe the deathbed statement?" Jack asked.

"It's hard for those of us who were raised believing that deathbed repentance might slip you into heaven to witness a man going out with a false oath on his lips. But in Nicky's case I'll stand by my first reaction. That was a farewell gesture for his family, and obviously they fell for it. And now it's been a grueling enough day. Let's talk about something interesting. Jack, have you been in New York long enough to decide if the Mayor will win another election?"

As they were finishing coffee, Jimmy Neary stopped back at the table. "Commissioner, did you know that the Lambston woman's body was found by one of my old customers, Kitty Conway? She used to come in here with her husband. She's a grand lady."

"We met her today," Myles said.

"If you see her again, give her my best and tell her not to be such a stranger."

"Maybe I'll do better than that," Myles said casually. "Maybe I'll bring her in myself."

Jack's apartment was the first stop for the cab. As he said good night, Jack asked, "Look, I know this sounds pushy, but would there be any objection if I went along with you tomorrow to Ethel's apartment?"

Myles raised his eyebrows. "Not if you promise to fade into the background and keep your mouth shut."

"Myles!"

Jack grinned. "Your dad's absolutely right, Neeve. I accept the conditions."

When the cab pulled up to Schwab House, the doorman opened the door for Neeve. She stepped out as Myles waited for change from the driver. The doorman went back to stand at the entrance to the lobby. The night had become clear. The sky was filled with stars. Neeve walked away from the cab. She raised her head and looked up to admire the galaxy.

Across the street, Denny Adler was propped against an apartment house, a wine bottle by his side, his head sunk on his chest. Through narrowed eyes he observed Neeve step from the cab. He inhaled sharply. He had a clear shot at her and could be gone before anyone saw him. Denny reached into the pocket of the raggedy sweater-jacket he was wearing tonight.

Now.

His finger touched the trigger. He was about to pull the gun from his pocket when the door to his right opened. An elderly woman emerged from the building, holding a leash from which a small poodle strained forward. The poodle lunged toward Denny.

"Don't be afraid of Honey Bee," the woman said. "She's a friendly darling."

Outrage built like erupting lava within Denny as he watched Myles Kearny step from the cab and walk behind Neeve into Schwab House. His fingers went for the poodle's throat, but in time he managed to control the gesture and let his hand drop onto the pavement.

"Honey Bee loves to be petted," the elderly woman encouraged, "even by strangers." She dropped a quarter onto Denny's lap. "I hope this will help."

~ 10

On Sunday morning, Detective O'Brien phoned and asked for Neeve.

"Why do you want her?" Myles asked sharply.

"We'd like to talk to the cleaning woman who was in the Lambston apartment last week, sir. Does your daughter have her number?"

"Oh." Myles did not know why he experienced instant relief. "That's easy. I'll get it from Neeve."

Five minutes later, Tse-Tse called. "Neeve, I'm a witness." Tse-Tse sounded thrilled. "But could I have them meet me in your apartment at one-thirty? I've never been interviewed by the police before. I'd kind of like you and your dad to be around." Her voice lowered. "Neeve, they don't think I killed her, do they?"

Neeve smiled into the receiver. "Of course not, Tse-Tse. Sure. Dad and I are going to the twelve at St. Paul's. One-thirty will be fine."

"Should I tell them about the creepy nephew taking the money and putting it back and Ethel threatening to disinherit him?"

Neeve was shocked. "Tse-Tse, you said that Ethel was mad at him. You didn't say she threatened to disinherit him. Of course you've got to tell them that."

When she hung up the receiver, Myles was waiting, his eyebrows raised. "What was that all about?"

She told him. Myles emitted a soundless whistle.

When Tse-Tse arrived, her hair was in a prim bun. Her makeup was understated except for her false eyelashes. She was wearing a granny dress and flat shoes. "This is the costume I wore when I played the housekeeper on trial for poisoning her employer," she confided.

Detectives O'Brien and Gomez were announced a few minutes later. When Myles greeted them, Neeve thought, You'd never guess he wasn't still top man at One Police Plaza. They're practically genuflecting.

But when Tse-Tse was introduced, O'Brien looked bewildered. "Douglas Brown told us that the cleaning woman was Swedish."

His eyes bulged as Tse-Tse earnestly explained how she used different personas depending upon her current off-off-Broadway roles. "I've been playing a Swedish maid," she concluded, "and I sent a personal invitation to Joseph Papp to come to the show last night. It was closing night. My astrologer said that Saturn was on the cusp of Capricorn, so my career aspects were very strong. I really had a feeling he'd show." She shook her head sadly. "He didn't come. In fact, nobody came."

Gomez coughed vigorously. O'Brien swallowed a smile. "I'm sorry about that. Now, Tse-Tse—if I may call you that?" He began to question her.

The questioning became a dialogue as Neeve explained why she had gone with Tse-Tse to Ethel's apartment, why she had gone back to check the coats in the closet, to look over Ethel's daily calendar. Tse-Tse told about Ethel's angry phone call to her nephew a month ago, about the money that had been replaced last week.

At two-thirty O'Brien snapped his notebook closed. "You've both been very helpful. Tse-Tse, would you mind accompanying Miss Kearny to the Lambston apartment? You know the place well. I'd like to have your impressions of anything that might be missing. Come over in about an hour, if you will. I'd like to have another little chat with Douglas Brown."

Myles had been sitting in his deep leather chair, his forehead furrowed. "So now a greedy nephew enters the picture," he said.

Neeve smiled wryly. "What do you think his calling card would be, Commish?"

* * *

At three-thirty, Myles, Neeve, Jack Campbell and Tse-Tse entered Ethel's apartment. Douglas Brown was sitting on the couch, his hands twisting in his lap. When he looked up, his expression was unfriendly. His sullenly handsome face was damp with perspiration. Detectives O'Brien and Gomez were sitting across from him, their notebooks open. The surfaces of the tables and the desk appeared sooty and unkempt.

Tse-Tse murmured to Neeve, "This place was spotless when I left it."

Neeve whispered an explanation that the smear was caused by the homicide squad dusting for fingerprints, then said quietly to Douglas Brown, "I'm terribly sorry about your aunt. I liked her very much."

"Then you were one of the few," Brown snapped. He stood up. "Look, anyone who knew Ethel can swear to how irritating and demanding she could be. So she bought me a bunch of dinners. There were plenty of nights I gave up being with my friends because she wanted company. So she slipped me some of those hundred-dollar bills she kept around here. Then she'd forget where she hid the rest of them and say I took them. Then she'd find them and say she was sorry. And that's the whole of it." He stared at Tse-Tse. "What the hell are you doing in that getup, paying off a bet? If you want to make yourself useful, why don't you get out the vacuum and clean up this place?"

"I worked for Miss Lambston," Tse-Tse said with dignity, "and Miss Lambston is dead." She looked at Detective O'Brien. "What do you want me to do?"

"I'd like Miss Kearny to itemize the clothing that is missing from the wardrobe, and I'd like you to generally look around and see if there's anything missing that you notice."

Myles murmured to Jack, "Why don't you go in with Neeve? Maybe you can take notes for her." He chose to sit in a straight chair near the desk. From there he could clearly see the wall that was Ethel's photo gallery. After a moment he got up to study the pictures and was grudgingly surprised to see a montage showing Ethel at the last Republican convention on the dais with the President's immediate family; Ethel giving the Mayor a hug at Gracie Mansion; Ethel receiving the annual award for the best magazine article from the American Society of Journalists and Authors. There had obviously been more to the woman than I realized, Myles thought. I dismissed her as a rattlebrain.

The book Ethel had proposed to write. There was plenty of mob money being laundered through the fashion industry. Had Ethel stumbled on that? Myles made up his mind to ask Herb Schwartz if there was any big undercover investigation going on that had to do with the rag trade.

Although the bed was neatly made and there was nothing out of order in the room, the bedroom had the same soiled appearance as the rest of the apartment. Even the closet looked different. Obviously every garment and accessory had been pulled out, examined and haphazardly put back. "Terrific," Neeve told Jack. "That's going to make it harder."

Jack was wearing a white handmade Irish cable-knit sweater and navy corduroy slacks. When he arrived at Schwab House, Myles had opened the door for him, raised his eyebrows and said, "You two are going to look like Flossie and Freddie Bobbsey." He'd stood aside to let Jack in, and Jack faced Neeve, who was also wearing an Irish white cable-knit sweater and navy corduroy slacks. They'd laughed together, and Neeve had quickly changed to a navy-and-white cardigan.

The coincidence had lightened Neeve's dread of handling Ethel's personal effects. Now that dread was lost in her dismay at the careless handling of Ethel's treasured wardrobe.

"Harder but not impossible," Jack said calmly. "Tell me the best way to go about this."

Neeve gave him the file with the carbons of Ethel's bills. "We'll start with the latest purchases first."

She pulled out the brand-new clothing Ethel had never worn, laid it on the bed, then worked backward, reeling off to Jack the dresses and suits that were still in the closet. It soon became obvious that the missing garments were only suitable for cold weather. "So that eliminates any idea that she might have been planning to go to the Caribbean or whatever and deliberately didn't bring a coat," Neeve murmured as much to herself as to Jack. "But Myles may be right. The white blouse that went with the suit she had on when they found her isn't here. Maybe it *is* at the cleaners— Wait a minute!"

Abruptly she stopped speaking and reached far back into the closet to pull out a hanger that had been jammed between two sweaters. On it was a white silk blouse with a jabot neck and lace-trimmed sleeves. "That's what I was looking for," Neeve told Jack triumphantly. "Why didn't Ethel put it on? And if she did decide to wear the blouse that came with the outfit, why didn't she pack this one as well?"

They sat together on the chaise longue while Neeve copied from Jack's notes until she had a precise listing of the clothing that was missing from Ethel's closet. As Jack waited in silence, he looked around the room. Grimy, probably because of the police search.

Good furniture. Expensive spread and decorative pillows. But it lacked identity. There were no personal touches, no framed snapshots, no special knickknacks. The few paintings scattered on the wall were totally unimaginative, as though they had been chosen only to fill space. It was a depressing room, empty rather than intimate. Jack realized he was beginning to feel an enormous sense of pity for Ethel. His mental image of her had been so different. He'd always thought of her as a self-propelled tennis ball, bobbing from one side of the court to the other in frenzied, unstopping motion. The woman this room suggested had been a rather pathetic loner.

They went back to the living room in time to watch Tse-Tse go through the stacks of mail on Ethel's desk. "It isn't here," she said.

"What isn't there?" O'Brien asked sharply.

"Ethel had an antique dagger as a letter opener, one of those Indian jobs with a fancy red-and-gold handle."

Neeve thought that Detective O'Brien suddenly had the look of a bird dog picking up a scent.

"Do you remember the last time you saw the dagger, Tse-Tse?" he demanded.

"Yes. It was here both days this week when I cleaned, Tuesday and Thursday."

O'Brien looked at Douglas Brown. "The dagger letter opener wasn't here when we dusted yesterday. Any idea where we can find it?"

Douglas swallowed. He tried to look as though he were deep in thought. The letter opener had been on the desk on Friday morning. No one had come in except Ruth Lambston.

Ruth Lambston. She'd threatened to tell the police that Ethel was going to disinherit him. But he had already told the cops that Ethel was always finding the money she claimed he'd taken. That had been a brilliant answer. But now should he tell them about Ruth or just say he didn't know?

O'Brien was repeating the question, this time persistently. Douglas decided it was time to get the cops' attention off him. "Friday afternoon Ruth Lambston came over. She took back a letter Seamus had left for Ethel. She threatened to tell you people that Ethel was sore at me if I said one word about Seamus to you." Douglas paused, then piously added, "That letter opener was here when she came. She was standing next to the desk when I went into the bedroom. I haven't seen it since Friday. You better ask *her* why she decided to steal it."

* * *

When Ruth received the frantic call from Seamus on Saturday afternoon, she'd managed to contact the personnel director of her company at home. It was she who sent the lawyer, Robert Lane, to the police station.

When Lane brought Seamus home, Ruth was sure her husband was on the verge of a heart attack, and she wanted to take him to the emergency room of the hospital. Seamus vehemently refused, but did agree to go to bed. His eyes red-rimmed, welling with tears, he shuffled into the bedroom, a crushed and broken man.

Lane waited in the living room to talk to Ruth. "I'm not a criminal lawyer," he said bluntly. "And your husband is going to need a good one."

Ruth nodded.

"From what he told me in the cab, he might stand a chance of acquittal or reduced charges on a temporary insanity defense."

Ruth went cold. "He admitted killing her?"

"No. He told me he punched her, that she reached for the letter opener, that he grabbed it from her and in the scuffle that her right cheek was cut. He also told me that he hired some character who hangs out in his bar to make threatening phone calls to her."

Ruth's lips were stiff. "I just learned that last night."

Lane shrugged. "Your husband won't stand up under intense questioning. My advice is that he come clean and try to plea-bargain. You believe he killed her, don't you?"

"Yes, I do."

Lane stood up. "As I've said, I'm not a criminal lawyer, but I'll ask around and see who I can find for you. I'm sorry."

For hours Ruth sat quietly, the quiet of total despair. At ten o'clock she watched the news and heard the report that Ethel Lambston's ex-husband was being questioned about her death. She ran to snap off the set.

The events of the past week ran over and over again through her mind like a tape in a constant replay position. Ten days ago, the tearful call from Jeannie—"Mom, I was so humiliated. The check bounced. The bursar sent for me"—had started it all. Ruth remembered the way she had screamed and ranted at Seamus. I pushed him to the point where he went crazy, she thought.

Plea-bargain. What did that mean? Manslaughter? How many years? Fifteen? Twenty? But he had buried her body. He had gone to such trouble to conceal the crime. How had he managed to stay that calm?

Calm? Seamus? That letter opener in his hand, staring down at a woman whose throat he had cut? Impossible.

A new memory came back to Ruth, one that had been a family joke in the days when they were still able to laugh. Seamus had come into the delivery room when Marcy was born. And fainted. At the sight of the blood, he'd passed out cold. "They were more worried about your father than about you and me," Ruth used to tell Marcy. "That was the first and last time I let Dad set foot in the delivery room. He was better off standing drinks at the bar than getting in the doctor's way."

Seamus watching blood spurt from Ethel's throat, putting her body into a plastic bag, sneaking it out of her apartment. Ruth thought of the news report that the labels had been ripped from Ethel's clothes. Seamus having the cold courage to do that, then burying her in that cave in the park? It simply wasn't possible, she decided.

But if he didn't kill Ethel, if he'd left her as he claimed, then by scrubbing and disposing of the letter opener she might have destroyed evidence that might have led to someone else. . . .

It was too overwhelming for her to even consider any longer. Wearily, Ruth got up and went into the bedroom. Seamus was breathing evenly, but he stirred. "Ruth, stay with me." When she got into bed, he put his arms around her and fell asleep, his head on her shoulder.

At three o'clock, Ruth was still trying to decide what to do. Then, almost as in response to an unspoken prayer, she thought of how often she'd run into former Police Commissioner Kearny in the supermarket since he retired. He always smiled so pleasantly and said, "Good morning." Once when her bag of groceries had broken, he'd stopped to help her. She'd liked him instinctively, even though to see him was to remember that at least some of the alimony money was spent in his daughter's fancy shop.

The Kearnys lived in Schwab House on Seventy-fourth Street. *Tomorrow she and Seamus were going to go and ask to see the Commissioner. He'd know what they should do. She could trust him.* Ruth finally fell asleep thinking, I've got to trust somebody.

For the first time in years, she slept Sunday morning away. Her watch read quarter of twelve when she pulled herself up on one arm and glanced at it. The bright sunshine radiated into the room around the ill-fitting outlet-store shades. She looked down at Seamus. In sleep, he lost the anxious, fearful expression that so irritated her, and his even features retained the traces of a once handsome man. The girls get their looks from him, Ruth thought, and their humor. In the early days, Seamus had been witty and confident. And then the downspin began. The rent for the pub increased astronomically, the neighborhood became gentrified, and thc old customers disappeared one by one. And every month the alimony check.

Ruth slipped out of bed and went to the bureau. The sun mercilessly revealed the scars and nicks on it. She tried to open the drawer quietly, but it stuck and screeched in protest. Seamus stirred.

"Ruth." He was not quite awake.

"Stay there," she said, her voice soothing. "I'll call you when breakfast is ready."

The phone rang just as she took the bacon from the broiler. It was the girls. They had heard about Ethel. Marcy, the oldest, said, "Mama, we're sorry for her, but it does mean that Dad is off the hook, isn't he?"

Ruth tried to sound cheery. "It looks like that, doesn't it? We still haven't gotten used to the idea." She called Seamus, and he came to the phone.

Ruth knew the effort he was making as he said, "It's a terrible thing to be glad someone is dead, but it's not terrible to be glad a financial burden has been lifted. Now tell me. How are the Dolly sisters doing? None of the boys getting frcsh, I hope."

Ruth had prepared fresh-squeezed orange juice, bacon, scrambled eggs, toast and coffee. She waited until Seamus had finished eating and she had poured a second cup of coffee for him. Then she sat opposite him, across the heavy oak dining-room table that had been an unwanted donation from his maiden aunt, and said, "We've got to talk."

She leaned her elbows on the table, clasped her hands under her chin, saw her reflection in the spotted mirror over the china cupboard and had a fleeting realization that she looked and was drab. Her housecoat was faded; her always fine light-brown hair had become thin and mousy; her round glasses made her small face seem pinched. She dismissed the thoughts as irrelevant and continued to speak. "When you told me you had punched Ethel, that she'd been nicked with the letter opener, that you'd paid someone to threaten her, I believed that you had gone one step further. I believed that you had killed her."

Seamus looked down into the coffee cup intently. You'd think it held the secrets of the universe, Ruth thought. Then he straightened up and stared into her eyes. It was as though a good night's sleep, talking to the girls, and a decent breakfast had set him straight. "I did not kill Ethel," he said. "I frightened her. Hell, I frightened myself. I never knew I was going to punch her, but maybe that came instinctively. She got cut because she went for the letter opener. I got it from her and threw it back on the desk. But she was scared. That's when she said, 'All right, all right. You can keep your damn alimony.' "

"That was Thursday afternoon," Ruth said.

"Thursday about two o'clock. You know how quiet the place gets around that time. You know the state you were in about the bounced check. I left the bar at one-thirty. Dan was there. He'll back me up."

"Did you go back to the bar?"

Seamus finished the coffee and set the cup back on the saucer. "Yes. I had to, then I came home and got drunk. And I stayed drunk over the weekend."

"Who did you see? Did you go out for the paper?"

Seamus smiled, a hollow, mirthless smile. "I wasn't in any condition to read." He waited for her reaction, then Ruth saw tentative hope coming into his face. "You believe me," he said, his tone humble and surprised.

"I didn't believe you yesterday or Friday," Ruth said. "But I believe you now. You're a lot of things and you're *not* a lot of things, but I do know you could never take a knife or a letter opener in your hands and cut a throat."

"You got yourself some prize in me," Seamus said quietly.

Ruth's tone became brisk. "I could have done worse. Now let's get practical. I don't like that lawyer, and he admitted you need someone else. I want to try something. For the last time, swear on your life that you did not kill Ethel."

"I swear on my life." Seamus hesitated. "On the lives of my three girls."

"We need help. Real help. I watched the news last night. They talked about you. That you were being questioned. They're anxious to prove you did this. We need to tell the full truth to someone who can advise us what to do or send us to the right lawyer."

It took all afternoon of arguing, debating, cajoling, reasoning to get Seamus to agree. It was four-thirty when they put on their all-weather coats, Ruth sturdy and compact in hers, Seamus with the middle button straining on his, and walked the three blocks to Schwab House. Along the way, they spoke little. Even though the day was unseasonably brisk, people were reveling in the strong sunshine. Young children holding balloons, followed by exhausted-looking parents, made Seamus smile. "Remember when we took the girls to the zoo on Sunday afternoons? It's nice it's open again."

At Schwab House the doorman told them that Commissioner

Kearny and Miss Kearny were out. Hesitantly, Ruth asked permission to wait. For half an hour they sat side by side on a lobby sofa, and Ruth began to doubt the wisdom of her decision to come here. She was just about to suggest that they leave when the doorman held open the main door and a party of four people came in. The Kearnys and two strangers.

Before she lost her courage Ruth rushed to confront them.

"Myles, I wish you had let them talk to you." They were in the kitchen of the apartment. Jack was making a salad. Neeve was defrosting the remainder of the pasta sauce from Thursday night's dinner.

Myles was preparing a very dry martini for himself and Jack. "Neeve, there's no way I can let them spill their guts to me. You're a witness in this case as it is. I let him tell me he killed Ethel in a struggle, and I've got a moral obligation to report it."

"I'm sure that's not what he wanted to tell you."

"Be that as it may, I can promise you that both Seamus Lambston and his wife Ruth are facing hard questioning at headquarters. Don't forget, if that slimy nephew is telling the truth, Ruth Lambston stole that letter opener, and you can bet she didn't want it as a souvenir. I did the best I could. I called Pete Kennedy. He's a hell of a good criminal lawyer, and he'll see them in the morning."

"And can they afford a hell of a good criminal lawyer?"

"If Seamus Lambston has clean hands, Pete will show our guys that they're barking up the wrong tree. If he's guilty, anything Pete charges will be worth it to get the count reduced from murder two to aggravated manslaughter."

At dinner, it seemed to Neeve that Jack deliberately steered the conversation away from Ethel. He asked Myles about some of his famous cases, a subject Myles never tired of discussing. It was only when they were clearing the table that Neeve realized Jack knew a lot about cases that certainly never would have been publicized in the Midwest. "You looked up Myles in back newspapers," she accused.

He did not seem abashed. "Yes, I did. Hey, leave those pots in the sink. I'll do them. You'll ruin your nails."

It is impossible, Neeve thought, that so much has happened in a week. It felt as though Jack had always been around. What was going on?

She knew what was going on. Then an aching cold came over her. Moses glimpsing the Promised Land and knowing he will never enter it. Why did she feel like that? Why did she feel as though somehow she was winding down? Why, when she looked at the mournful snapshot of Ethel, did she see something else in it today, something secretive, as though Ethel were saying, "Wait till you see what it's like."

What is 'it'? Neeve wondered.

Death.

The ten-o'clock news was filled with more stories about Ethel. Someone had pieced together footage on her vivid background. The media had been short on exciting, headline-making news, and Ethel was helping to fill the void.

The program was just going off when the phone rang. It was Kitty Conway. Her clear, almost musical voice sounded a bit hurried. "Neeve, I'm sorry to bother you, but I just got home. When I hung up my coat I realized that your father left his hat in the closet. I'm coming into the city tomorrow in the late afternoon, so maybe I could drop it somewhere for him."

Neeve was astonished. "Wait a minute, I'll get him." As she turned the phone over to Myles, she murmured, "You never forget anything. What's up?"

"Oh, it's pretty Kitty Conway." Myles sounded delighted. "I was wondering if she'd ever find the damned hat." When he hung up the phone, he looked sheepishly at Neeve. "She's going to stop by around six o'clock tomorrow. Then I'll take her out for dinner. Want to come?"

"Certainly not. Unless you think you need a chaperone. Anyhow, I have to get to Seventh Avenue."

At the door, Jack asked, "Tell me if I'm making a pest of myself. If I'm not, how about dinner tomorrow night?"

"You know darn well you're not making a pest of yourself. Dinner's fine if you don't mind waiting until I phone you. I don't know what time that would be. I usually make my last stop at Uncle Sal's, so I'll call you from there."

"I don't mind. Neeve, just one thing. Be careful. You're an important witness in Ethel Lambston's death, and seeing those people, Seamus Lambston and his wife, made me pretty uneasy. Neeve, they're desperate. Guilty or innocent, they want this investigation stopped. Their desire to spill to your father may be spontaneous or it may be pretty calculated. The point is, murderers don't hesitate to kill again if someone gets in the way."

~ 11

Since Monday was Denny's day off from the delicatessen, his absence there would not be suspect, but he also wanted to establish the alibi that he'd spent the day in bed. "I guess I got flu," he mumbled to the disinterested clerk in the lobby of his rooming house. Big Charley had called him on the phone in this lobby yesterday. "Get rid of her now or we'll find someone who can."

Denny knew what that meant. He wouldn't be left around in case he ever tried to use his knowledge of the hit as a plea bargain. Besides, he wanted the rest of the money.

Carefully he laid his plans. He went to the corner drugstore and, coughing his way through the questions, asked the pharmacist to suggest over-the-counter medication. Back in the rooming house, he made it a point to talk to the stupid old broad who lived two doors down from him and was always trying to get friendly. Five minutes later, he left her room with a cup of evil-smelling tea in a battered mug.

"It'll cure anything," she told him. "I'll look in on you later."

"Maybe you'd make more tea for me around noon," Denny whined.

He went to the bathroom that serviced the tenants on the second and third floors and complained of cramps to the old wino who was waiting patiently for the door to open. The wino refused to give up his place on line.

In his own room, Denny carefully packed all the shabby clothes he had used when following Neeve. You never knew who among doormen might have sharp eyes and be able to describe someone who'd been hanging around Schwab House. Even that old busybody with the dog. She'd gotten a good look at him. Denny did not doubt that when the ex–Police Commissioner's daughter was wasted, the cops would be swarming for leads.

He would drop the clothes into a nearby dumpster. That was easy. The tough part was following Neeve Kearny from her shop to Seventh Avenue. But he had figured out a way. He had a new gray sweatsuit. No one around here had ever seen him wear it. He had a punk-rock wig and wide space-cadet glasses. In that outfit, he'd look like the messengers running all over town on their bikes knocking people down. He'd get a big manila envelope, watch for Neeve Kearny to come out. She'd probably cab to the fashion district. He'd follow her in another cab. He'd give the cabbie a cock-and-bull story about his bike being stolen and that lady needing the papers he was delivering.

With his own ears, he'd heard Neeve Kearny discuss a one-thirty appointment with one of those rich broads who could afford to spend big bucks for clothes.

Always leave margin for error. He'd be across the street from her place before one-thirty.

It wouldn't matter if the cabbie put two and two together after Kearny was wasted. They'd be looking for a guy with a punk-rock cut.

His plans made, Denny shoved the bundle of old clothes under the sagging bed. What a dump, he thought as he stared around the tiny room. Alive with cockroaches. Smelly. A bureau that wasn't much more than an orange crate. But when he finished the job and got the other ten thousand, he'd only have to hang around till his parole was up and then he'd take off. Boy, would he take off.

For the rest of the morning, Denny made frequent trips to the toilet, complaining about his pains to anyone who would listen. At noon, the hag down the hall knocked on his door and handed him another cup of tea and a stale roll. He made more trips to the toilet, standing inside the locked door, trying not to inhale the noxious odors and keeping others waiting until there were grumbled protests.

At quarter of one, he shuffled out and said to the old wino, "I think I feel better. I'm gonna get some sleep." His room was on the second floor and faced an alley. There was an overhang from the steep roof that jutted over the lower floors. Minutes after he had changed into the gray sweats, pulled on the punk wig and adjusted the glasses, he'd tossed the bag of beggar clothes into the alley and vaulted down.

He dropped the bundle deep into a rat-infested dumpster behind an apartment building on One Hundred and Eighth Street, caught the subway to Lexington and Eighty-sixth, picked up a large manila envelope and crayons in the five-and-ten, marked the envelope "Rush" and took up a vigil opposite Neeve's Place.

At ten o'clock on Monday morning, a Korean cargo plane, Flight 771, was cleared for landing at Kennedy Airport. Trucks from Gordon Steuber Textiles were waiting to pick up the crates of dresses and sportswear to be transported to Long Island City warehouses; warehouses that did not appear anywhere in the company records.

Others were waiting for that shipment: law-enforcement officers aware that they were about to make one of the biggest drug busts of the past ten years.

"A hell of an idea," one observed to the other as he waited in a mechanic's uniform on the tarmac. "I've seen the stuff stashed in furniture, in Kewpie dolls, in dog collars, in babies' diapers, but never in designer clothes."

The plane circled, landed, braked to a stop in front of the hangar. In an instant the field was swarming with Federal officers.

Ten minutes later, the first crate had been pried open. The seams of an exquisitely tailored linen jacket were slashed. Pure, uncut heroin poured into a plastic bag held open by the chief of the task force. "Christ," he said in awe, "there must be two million bucks' worth in this box alone. Tell them to pick up Steuber."

At 9:40 A.M., Federal officers burst into Gordon Steuber's office. His secretary tried to bar the way, but was firmly put aside. Steuber listened impassively as the Miranda warning was read to him. Without a trace of visible emotion, he watched as handcuffs were clasped around his wrists. Inwardly he was raging, a deadly, furious rage, and the target was Neeve.

As he was being led out he paused to speak to his weeping secretary. "May," he told her, "you'd better cancel all my appointments. Don't forget."

The expression in her eyes told him that she understood. She would not mention that twelve days ago, on Wednesday evening, Ethel Lambston had barged into his office and told him she was wise to his activities.

Douglas Brown did not sleep easily on Sunday night. As he tossed restlessly on Ethel's fine percale sheets, he dreamt of her, fitful dreams in which Ethel was brandishing a glass of Dom Pérignon at San Domenico: "Here's to Seamus the wimp." Dreams that portrayed Ethel saying coldly to him, "How much did you help yourself to this time?" Dreams in which the police came to take him away.

At ten o'clock on Monday morning, the Medical Examiner's Office of Rockland County phoned. As next of kin, Doug was queried about his plans for the disposal of the mortal remains of Ethel Lambston. Doug tried to sound solicitous. "It was my aunt's wish that she be cremated. Can you suggest what I should do?"

Actually Ethel had said something about being buried with her parents in Ohio, but it would be a lot cheaper to mail an urn than a casket.

He was given the name of a mortuary. The woman who answered

was cordial and solicitous and inquired about financial responsibility. Doug promised to get back to her and phoned Ethel's accountant. The accountant had been away for a long weekend and had just heard the dreadful news.

"I witnessed Miss Lambston's will," the accountant said. "I have a copy of the original. She was very fond of you."

"And I loved her dearly." Doug hung up. It still took getting used to, knowing that he was a rich man. Rich by his standards, anyhow.

If only it doesn't all get screwed up, he thought.

He had instinctively been expecting the cops, but, even so, the brisk rap on the door, the invitation to step down to headquarters for questioning, unnerved him.

At the precinct, he was startled when he received the Miranda warning. "You gotta be kidding."

"We tend to be overcautious," Detective Gomez said soothingly. "Remember, Doug, you don't need to answer questions. You can call a lawyer. Or, you can stop answering questions whenever you say the word."

Doug thought of Ethel's money; Ethel's co-op; the chick at work who had big eyes for him; throwing up his job; telling off that scum who was his immediate boss. He assumed a solicitous stance. "I'm perfectly agreeable to answering any questions."

That first one from Detective O'Brien threw him for a loop. "Last Thursday, you went to the bank and withdrew four hundred dollars which you took in hundred-dollar bills. No point in denying that, Doug. We checked it. That was the money we found in the apartment, wasn't it, Doug? Now, why would you put it there when you told us your aunt always found the money she accused you of taking?"

Myles slept from midnight till five-thirty. When he woke, he knew there was no chance of dozing off again. There was nothing he detested more than lying in bed on the off chance that he could slip back into the arms of Morpheus. He got up, reached for a bathrobe and went into the kitchen.

Over a cup of freshly perked decaffeinated coffee, he step-by-step examined the events of the week. His initial sense of release that had stemmed from Nicky Sepetti's death was fading. Why?

He glanced around the orderly kitchen. Last night he'd silently approved of the way Jack Campbell had assisted Neeve in clearing. Jack knew his way around a kitchen. Myles half smiled, thinking of his own father. A great guy. "Himself," his mother said when referring to him. But God knows, Pop had never carried a dish to the sink or minded a child or pushed a vacuum around. Today's young husbands were different. And it was a good difference.

What kind of husband had he been to Renata? Good by most people's standards. "I loved her," Myles said now, his voice barely above a whisper, "I was proud of her. We had fun together. But I wonder how well I knew her. How much of my father's son was I during our marriage? Did I ever take her seriously outside of her role as wife and mother?"

Last night, or was it the night before, he'd told Jack Campbell that Renata had taught him about wine. I was busy clearing off my rough spots in those days, Myles thought, remembering how before he met Renata he had quietly set on a program of self-improvement. Tickets to Carnegie Hall. Tickets to the Met. Dutiful visits to the Museum of Art.

It was Renata who had changed those dutiful visits to exciting expeditions of discovery. Renata, who when she came home from an opera would hum the music in her strong clear soprano. "Milo, *caro,* are you the only Irishman in the world who is tone deaf?" she would tease.

In the eleven wonderful years we had, we were only beginning to plumb all that we would have become to each other.

Myles got up and poured a second cup of coffee. Why was this awareness so strong? What was eluding him? Something. Something. Oh, Renata, he begged. I don't know why, but I'm worried about Neeve. I've done my best for her these seventeen years. But she's your kid, too. Is she in trouble?

The second cup of coffee revived his spirits and he began to feel slightly foolish. When Neeve came yawning into the kitchen, he was sufficiently recovered to say, "Your publisher is a good pot-walloper."

Neeve grinned, bent down to kiss the top of Myles's head and replied, "So it's 'pretty Kitty Conway.' I approve, Commish. It's about time you started looking over the ladies. After all, you're not getting any younger." She ducked to avoid his swat.

Neeve chose a pale-pink-and-gray Chanel suit with gold buttons, gray leather pumps and a matching shoulder bag to wear to work. She pulled her hair into a smooth chignon.

Myles nodded his approval. "I like that kind of outfit. Better than Saturday's checkerboard. I must say, you have your mother's taste in clothes."

"Approbation from Sir Hubert is praise indeed." At the door, Neeve hesitated. "Commish, are you going to indulge me and ask the Medical Examiner if there's any chance Ethel's clothes were changed after she died?"

"I hadn't thought about it."

"Please think about it. And even if you don't approve, do it for my sake. Something else: Do you think Seamus Lambston and his wife were trying to sucker us?"

"Entirely possible."

"Fair enough. But, Myles, hear me out without hushing me up, just this once. The last person who admits to seeing Ethel alive was her ex-husband Seamus. We know that was Thursday afternoon. Can someone ask him what she was wearing? My bet is that it was a multicolored light wool caftan that she just about lived in when she was home. That caftan wasn't in her closet. Ethel never traveled with it. Myles, don't look at me like that. I know what I'm talking about. The point is, suppose Seamus—or someone else—killed Ethel while she was wearing that caftan and then changed her clothes."

Neeve opened the door. Myles realized that she was expecting a derisive remark from him. He kept his tone impersonal. "Meaning . . . ?"

"Meaning that *if* Ethel's clothes were changed after she died, there is no way that ex-husband is responsible for her death. You saw the way he and his wife were dressed. They have no more idea of fashion than I have of the inner workings of the space shuttle. On the other hand, there is a slimy bastard named Gordon Steuber who would instinctively have chosen something that came from his own company and dressed Ethel the way the outfit was sold."

Just before she closed the door behind her, Neeve added, "You're always talking about a killer leaving his calling card, Commish."

Peter Kennedy, attorney at law, was frequently asked whether he was related to *the* Kennedys. He did in fact bear a strong resemblance to the late President. He was a man in his early fifties with hair more rust than gray, a square, strong face and a rangy body. Early in his career he had been an assistant attorney general and formed a lasting friendship with Myles Kearny. At Myles's urgent phone call, Pete had canceled his eleven-o'clock appointment and agreed to meet Seamus and Ruth Lambston in his midtown office.

Now he listened to them incredulously as he observed their strained, weary faces. From time to time he interjected questions. "You are saying, Mr. Lambston, that you punched your former wife so violently that she fell backwards onto the floor, that she sprang up and grabbed the dagger she used as a letter opener, that in the struggle to wrench it from her hand her cheek was nicked."

Seamus nodded. "Ethel could see I'd been almost ready to kill her."

"Almost?"

"Almost," Seamus said, his voice low and ashamed. "I mean, for one second if that punch had killed her, I'd have been glad. She made my life hell for more than twenty years. Then when she got up, I realized what could have happened. But she was scared. She told me to forget the alimony payments."

"And then . . ."

"I got out. I went to the bar. Then I went home, got drunk and stayed drunk. I knew Ethel. It woulda been just like her to file an assault charge against me. She tried to have me locked up three different times when I was late with the alimony." He laughed mirthlessly. "One of those times was the day Jeannie was born."

Pete continued his questioning and skillfully extracted the fact that Seamus had been afraid of Ethel's signing a complaint; sure that when she had time to think about it she'd demand the alimony; foolish enough to tell Ruth that Ethel had said it was all right to quit the payments; terrified when Ruth demanded he put it in writing to Ethel.

"And then you inadvertently left both the check and the letter in the mailbox and went back hoping to retrieve them?"

Seamus twisted his hands in his lap. To his own ears he sounded like a bumbling fool. Which was exactly what he was. And there was more. The threats. But somehow he couldn't bring himself to tell about them yet.

"You never saw or spoke to your former wife, Ethel Lambston, after Thursday, March thirtieth."

"No. I did not."

He hasn't told me everything, Pete thought, but it's enough for a start. He watched as Seamus Lambston leaned back on the maroon leather couch. He was beginning to relax. Soon he'd unwind enough to put everything on the table. Too much probing would be a mistake. Pete turned to Ruth Lambston. She was sitting primly next to her husband, her eyes wary. Pete realized that Ruth was becoming frightened at her husband's revelations.

"Is it possible for someone to charge Seamus with assault or whatever it is for punching Ethel?" she asked.

"Ethel Lambston's not alive to press a charge," Pete replied. Technically the police could file. "Mrs. Lambston, I think I'm a pretty good judge of character. You were the one who persuaded your husband to speak to Commissioner"—he corrected himself—"*former* Commissioner Kearny. I think you were right to know you needed help at this time. But the only way I can help you is if you tell me the truth. There is something that you are weighing and measuring, and I think I need to know what it is."

As her husband and this impressive-looking lawyer stared at her, Ruth said. "I believe I threw away the murder weapon."

By the time they left an hour later, Seamus having agreed to offer to take a lie-detector test, Pete Kennedy was no longer sure of his instincts. At the very end of the session, Seamus admitted that he had hired some wet-brained goon who hung around his pub to threaten Ethel. Either he's only stupid and scared or he's playing a pretty shrewd hand, Pete decided, and made a mental note to let Myles Kearny know that not all the clients Myles sent him were his cup of tea.

The news of Gordon Steuber's arrest crashed like a tidal wave through the fashion center. Phone lines buzzed: "No, it isn't the illegal factories. Everybody does that. It's drugs." Then the big question: "Why? He makes millions. So he got a slap on the wrist for the sweatshops. So they're investigating him for income-tax evasion. A good team of lawyers could stall that for years. But drugs!" After an hour the black humor started. "Don't get Neeve Kearny mad at you. You'll trade your wristwatch for steel bracelets."

Anthony della Salva, surrounded by fluttering assistants, was working on the final details of the fashion show for his fall line, which was to be held the following week. It was an eminently satisfying collection. The new kid he'd hired fresh out of the Fashion Institute of Technology was a genius. "You're another Anthony della Salva," he told Roget, beaming. It was Sal's highest praise.

Roget, thin-faced, lank-haired, small-bodied, muttered under his breath, "Or a future Mainbocher." But he returned Sal's beatific smile. Within two years he was sure he'd have the backing to open his own place. He'd fought tooth and nail with Sal about his use of miniatures of the Pacific Reef design as accessories in the new collection, scarves and pocket handkerchiefs and belts in the brilliant tropical shades and intricate patterns that caught the magic and mystery of the aquatic world.

"I don't want it," Sal had said flatly.

"It's still the best thing you've ever done. It's your trademark." When the collection was complete, Sal admitted that Roget was right.

It was three-thirty when Sal heard the news about Gordon Steuber. And the jokes. He immediately phoned Myles. "Did you know this was coming?"

"No," Myles said, his voice testy. "I'm not on the ear for everything that's happening at One Police Plaza." Sal's worried tone flamed the abiding sense of oncoming disaster that had haunted him all day.

"Then maybe you should be," Sal retorted. "Listen, Myles, we've all known that Steuber has mob connections. It's one thing for Neeve to blow the whistle on him because of workers without green cards. It's a hell of another proposition when she's the indirect cause of a hundred-million-dollar drug bust."

"Hundred million. I hadn't heard that figure."

"Then turn on the radio. My secretary just heard it. The point is, maybe you should think about hiring a bodyguard for Neeve. *Take care of her!* I know she's your kid, but I claim a vested interest."

"You have a vested interest. I'll talk to the guys downtown and think about it. I just tried to call Neeve. She'd already left for Seventh Avenue. This is a buying day. Is she stopping in to see you?"

"She usually winds up here. And she knows I want her to preview the new line. She'll love it."

"Tell her to call me as soon as you see her. Tell her I'll wait for the call."

"Will do."

Myles started to say goodbye, then had a sudden thought. "How's the hand, Sal?"

"Not bad. Teaches me not to be so clumsy. Much more important, I feel crummy about ruining the book."

"Quit worrying. It's drying out. Neeve has a new beau, a publisher. He's going to take it to a restorer."

"No way. That's my problem. I'll send someone up for it."

Myles laughed. "Sal, you may be a good designer, but I think Jack Campbell is the right one for this job."

"Myles, I insist."

"See you, Sal."

* * *

At two o'clock, Seamus and Ruth Lambston returned to Peter Kennedy's law office for polygraph tests. Pete had explained to them, "If we're willing to stipulate that the police polygraph can be used in the event you come to trial, I think I can talk them into not pressing assault or tampering-with-evidence charges."

Ruth and Seamus had spent the intervening two hours having lunch in a small midtown coffee shop. Neither ate more than a few bites of the sandwiches the waitress placed before them. They both ordered more tea. Seamus broke the silence. "What do you think of that lawyer?"

Ruth did not look at him. "I don't think he believes us." She turned her head and stared straight into his eyes. "But if you're telling the truth, we did the right thing."

The test reminded Ruth of her last electrocardiogram. The difference was, these wires measured different impulses. The polygraph expert was impersonally cordial. He asked Ruth about her age, where she worked, her family. When she talked about the girls, she began to relax and a note of pride crept into her voice. "Marcy . . . Linda . . . Jeannie . . ."

Then the questions came about her visit to Ethel's apartment, about her tearing up the check, about taking the letter opener, bringing it home, washing it, dropping it into the basket in the Indian shop on Sixth Avenue.

When it was over, Peter Kennedy asked her to wait in the reception room and send Seamus in. For the next forty-five minutes she sat, dulled with apprehension. We've lost control of our lives, she thought. Other people will decide if we go to trial, go to jail.

The waiting room was impressive. The handsome leather couch, studded with gold nailheads. Must have cost at least six or seven thousand dollars. The matching loveseat; round mahogany drum table holding the latest magazines; excellent modernistic prints on the paneled walls. Ruth was aware that the receptionist was stealing curious glances at her. What did the smartly dressed young woman see? Ruth wondered. A plain woman in a plain green wool dress, sensible shoes, hair that was beginning to slip from the bun. She's probably thinking we can't afford the prices here, and she's right.

The door from the corridor that led to Peter Kennedy's private office opened. Kennedy was standing there, his face warm and smiling. "Won't you come in, Mrs. Lambston? Everything's fine."

When the polygraph expert left, Kennedy laid the cards on the table. "Normally I wouldn't want to move this swiftly. But you're concerned that the longer the media refers to Seamus as a suspect, the worse it will be for your daughters. I propose that I contact the homicide squad investigating the death. I demand an immediate polygraph test to clear the atmosphere of innuendo which you find intolerable. I warn you: In order to have them agree to an immediate test, we'll have to stipulate that if you ever came to trial the results of the test would be admissible. I think they'll go along with that. I think I can also persuade them to drop any other possible charges."

Seamus swallowed. His face was shiny, as though a perpetual glow of perspiration had been glossed onto it. "Go for it," he said.

Kennedy stood up. "It's three o'clock. We might still be able to get with them today. Would you mind waiting outside until I see what I can do?"

A half hour later, he came out. "We've got a deal. Let's go."

Monday was usually a slow day in retailing, but, as Neeve remarked to Eugenia, "You can't prove it by us." From the moment she unlocked the door at nine-thirty, the place was busy. Myles had passed on Sal's concern about bad publicity stemming from Ethel's death, but after working without a break until nearly twelve, Neeve said dryly, "Apparently a lot of people wouldn't mind being caught dead in a Neeve's Place outfit." Then she added, "Phone for coffee and a sandwich, okay?"

When the order was delivered to Neeve's office, she glanced up and raised her eyebrows. "Oh, I expected Denny. He didn't quit, did he?"

The delivery boy, a gangly nineteen-year-old, plunked the bag on her desk. "Monday's his day off."

When the door closed behind him, Neeve said wryly, "No room service with that one." Gingerly she removed the lid from the steaming container.

Jack phoned a few minutes later. "Are you okay?"

Neeve smiled into the speaker. "Sure I'm okay. In fact, I'm not only okay, I'm prosperous. It's been a great morning."

"Maybe you should plan on supporting me. I'm on my way to have lunch with an agent who isn't going to be happy with my offer." Jack dropped the bantering tone. "Neeve, take down this number. It's the Four Seasons. If you need me, I'll be there for the next couple of hours."

"I'm just about to attack a tuna-fish sandwich. Bring me a doggie bag."

"Neeve, I'm serious."

Neeve's voice became quiet. "Jack, I'm fine. Just save some appetite for dinner. It'll probably be about six-thirty or seven when I call you."

Eugenia watched critically as Neeve hung up the phone. "The publisher, I gather."

Neeve opened the wrapping on the sandwich. "Uh-huh." She had just taken the first bite when the phone rang again.

It was Detective Gomez. "Miss Kearny, I've been studying the postmortem pictures of the deceased, Ethel Lambston. You have a pretty strong hunch that she may have been dressed after she died."

"Yes." Neeve felt her throat close and pushed away the sandwich. She was aware that Eugenia was staring at her; she could feel the color drain from her cheeks.

"Keeping that in mind, I had the pictures blown up pretty big. The tests aren't complete and we know the body had been moved, so it's pretty hard to be sure whether or not you're right, but tell me this: Would Ethel Lambston have left her home with a wide run in her stocking?"

Neeve remembered noticing that run when she identified Ethel's clothing. "Never."

"That's what I thought," Gomez agreed. "The autopsy report shows nylon fibers caught in a toenail. The run started when the stocking was being put on. That means if Ethel Lambston dressed herself, she went out in a designer outfit with a very unsightly-looking stocking. I'd like to talk about this in the next couple of days. You'll be around?"

As Neeve replaced the phone, she thought of what she had told Myles this morning. As far as she was concerned, Seamus Lambston, with his utter lack of fashion sense, had not dressed the bleeding corpse of his former wife. She remembered the rest of what she had told Myles. Gordon Steuber would instinctively have chosen the original blouse for the ensemble.

There was a perfunctory rap on the door, and the receptionist rushed in. "Neeve," she whispered, "Mrs. Poth is here. And, Neeve, did you know Gordon Steuber has been arrested?"

Somehow Neeve managed to keep a calm, attentive smile on her face as she helped her wealthy client select three Adolfo evening gowns that ranged in price from four to six thousand dollars apiece; two Donna Karan suits, one at fifteen hundred dollars, the other twenty-two hundred; slippers, shoes and handbags. Mrs. Poth, a strikingly chic woman in her midsixties, professed to be uninterested in the costume jewelry. "It's lovely, but I prefer my own real pieces."

In the end she said, "These are more interesting," and accepted all Neeve's suggestions.

Neeve saw Mrs. Poth to her limousine, which was parked squarely in front of the shop. Madison Avenue was busy with shoppers and strollers. It seemed as though everyone was relishing the continuing sunshine and taking in stride the unusually chilly temperature. As Neeve turned back to the store, she noticed a man in a gray sweatsuit leaning against the building across the street. She had a fleeting sense of familiarity, which she disregarded as she hurried back into the shop and to her office. There she added fresh lip gloss and reached for her pocketbook. "Mind the store," she told Eugenia. "I won't be back, so lock up, please."

Smiling easily, pausing for a quick word with some of the old customers, she made her way to the front door. The receptionist had a cab waiting. Neeve got into it quickly and did not notice that the man with the crazy punk hairstyle and the gray sweats had hailed a cab across the street.

Over and over again, from different angles, Doug answered the same questions. The time he had arrived at Ethel's. His decision to move into her apartment. The phone call threatening Ethel if she did not let Seamus off the hook. The fact that he had begun staying in the apartment from Friday the thirty-first but didn't begin to answer the phone for a week and then the first call he got was a threat. How come?

Repeatedly, Doug was told he was free to go. He could call for a lawyer; he could discontinue answering questions. His answer was, "I don't need a lawyer. I have nothing to hide."

He told them he hadn't answered the phone because he was afraid Ethel would call and order him to get out. "For all I knew, she was going to be gone for a month. I needed a place to stay."

Why had he made a bank withdrawal in hundred-dollar bills and then hidden them around his aunt's apartment?

"Okay. So I borrowed some of the bucks Ethel stashed around the apartment, and I put them back."

He had said he didn't know anything about Ethel's will, but his fingerprints were all over it.

Doug began to panic. "I just started to think that maybe something was wrong. I looked in Ethel's date book and saw that she'd canceled all her appointments after that Friday she was supposed to meet me at the apartment. That made me feel better. But the neighbor told me that dopey ex-husband of hers had had a fight with her and that he'd shown up while I was at work. Then his wife practically breaks in and tears up Ethel's alimony check. I started to think maybe something was wrong."

"And then," Detective O'Brien said, his voice laden with sarcasm, "you decided to answer the phone, and the first call you got was a threat to your aunt's life? And the second was the Rockland County District Attorney's office, notifying you that the body had been found?"

Doug felt perspiration soak his armpits. He moved restlessly, trying to find a comfortable spot in the straight-backed wooden chair. Across the table, the two detectives were observing him, O'Brien with his beefy thick-featured face, Gomez with his shiny dark hair and chipmunk chin. The mick and the spic. "I'm getting fed up with this," Doug said.

O'Brien's face hardened. "Then take a walk, Dougie. But if you're so inclined, give one more answer. The rug in front of your aunt's desk had been spattered with blood. Someone did a very thorough job of cleaning it up. Doug, before you got your present position, didn't you work in the carpet-and-furniture-cleaning department of Sears?"

Panic caused a reflex action in Doug. He jumped up, pushed the chair back so violently that it toppled over. "Screw you!" He spat out the words as he rushed to the door of the interrogation room.

Denny had taken a calculated risk in waiting to hail a cab just as Neeve Kearny got into hers. But he knew that cabbies were nosy. It made more sense to grab one, sound breathless and say, "Some creep stole my bike. Follow that cab, will ya? It's my head if this envelope don't get delivered to that broad."

The driver was a Vietnamese. He nodded indifferently and expertly cut off an approaching bus as he swung across, then up Madison Avenue and left on Eighty-fifth Street. Denny slouched in the corner, his head down. He didn't want the cabbie to have too much chance to observe him in the rearview mirror. The cabbie's only observation was, "Crackheads. If there was a market for farts, they'd steal them," The Nam's English was amazingly good, Denny thought sourly.

At Seventh Avenue and Thirty-sixth Street, the other cab made the light and they missed it. "Sorry," the driver apologized.

Denny knew that Neeve was probably getting off in the next block or so. Her cab would probably creep in this traffic. "So let them fire me. I tried." He paid off the driver and sauntered uptown. From sidelong glances, he was able to see when the cab started again, continuing down Seventh Avenue. Quickly, Denny reversed direction and sped from Seventh Avenue to Thirty-sixth Street.

As usual, the streets in the high Thirties, off Seventh Avenue, were milling with the hyperactivity of the Garment District. Outsize trucks in the process of being unloaded were double-parked along the road, snarling traffic into near-gridlock. Messengers on roller skates whizzed around the crowds of pedestrians; delivery men, indifferent to both pedestrians and vehicles, shoved cumbersome racks laden with clothing. Horns blared. Men and women in high-fashion outerwear strode rapidly, talking excitedly, totally indifferent to the people and traffic around them.

A perfect place for a hit, Denny thought with satisfaction. Halfway up the block, he saw a cab pull nearer to the curb and watched as Neeve Kearny emerged from it. Before Denny could get close to her, she rushed into a building. Denny took up an observation post across the street, shielded by one of the huge trucks. "While you're picking those fancy clothes, you better order yourself a shroud, Kearny," he mumbled to himself.

Jim Greene, at age thirty, had been recently promoted to detective. His ability to size up a situation and instinctively choose the correct course of action had recommended him to his superiors in the Police Department.

Now he had been assigned the boring but vital task of guarding the hospital bed of undercover detective Tony Vitale. It was not a desirable job. If Tony had been in a private room, Jim could have kept his vigil at the door. But in the intensive-care unit, it was necessary for him to sit in the nurses' station. There, for his eight-hour shift, he was constantly reminded of the fragility of life as monitors suddenly sounded alarms and the hospital staff rushed to stave off death.

Jim was wiry and of barely average height, a fact which made it possible for him to be as unobtrusive as possible in the small, confined area. After four days the nurses had begun to treat him as a not unwelcome fixture. And they all seemed to have a particular concern for the tough young cop who was fighting for his life.

Jim knew the guts it took to be an undercover cop, to be at the table with cold-blooded killers, to know that at any moment your cover might be blown. He knew the concern that Nicky Sepetti might order a hit on Neeve Kearny; the relief when Tony managed to tell them, "Nicky . . . no contract, Neeve Kearny . . ."

Jim had been on duty when the PC came to the hospital with Myles Kearny and had had a chance to shake Kearny's hand. The Legend. Kearny had lived up to the title. After the way his wife died, his guts must have been shredded wondering if Sepetti would go for his daughter.

The PC had told them that Tony's mother thought he was trying to tell them something. The nurses had instructions to call Jim anytime Tony was able to speak.

It happened at four o'clock Monday afternoon. Vitale's parents had just left, the exhaustion in their faces brightened by hope. Barring the unexpected, Tony was out of danger. The nurse went in to check on him. Through the glass, Jim watched, then moved rapidly as she waved him in.

Glucose was dripping into Tony's arm and oxygen was being administered by tubes taped to his nostrils. Tony's lips were moving. He whispered a word.

"He's saying his own name," the nurse told Jim.

Jim shook his head. Bending, he put his ear to Tony's lips. He heard "Kearny." Then a faint "Nee . . ."

He touched Vitale's hand. "Tony, I'm a cop. You just said 'Neeve Kearny,' didn't you? Squeeze my hand if I'm right."

He was rewarded by the faintest pressure on his palm. "Tony," he said, "when you came in here, you tried to talk about a contract. Is that what you want to tell me?"

"You're disturbing the patient," the nurse protested.

Jim looked up at her briefly. "He's a cop, a good cop. He'll be better off if he communicates what he's trying to say." He repeated the question in Vitale's ear.

Again, a featherlike pressure on his palm.

"All right. You want to tell us something about Neeve Kearny and about a contract." Jim's mind raced over the words he knew Vitale had said upon admittance to the hospital. "Tony, you said 'Nicky, no contract.' Maybe that was only part of what you wanted to say." Jim had a sudden, chilling thought. "Tony, were you trying to tell us that Sepetti didn't put out a contract on Neeve Kearny but someone else did?"

An instant passed and then his hand was gripped convulsively.

"Tony," Jim begged. "Try. I'm watching your lips. If you know who ordered it, tell me."

It was as though the other cop's questions were echoing through a tunnel. Tony Vitale felt vast, overwhelming relief at having been able to give this much warning. Now the picture was so clear in his mind Joey telling Nicky that Steuber ordered the hit. His voice simpl wouldn't come, but he was able to move his lips slowly, pucker them to form the "Stu" syllable, release them for the "ber" sound.

Jim watched intently. "I think he's trying to say something like 'Tru . . .' "

The nurse interrupted. "To me it was "Stu-ber."

With a final effort before he fell back into a deep, healing sleep, undercover detective Anthony Vitale squeezed Jim's hand and managed to nod his head.

After Doug Brown stalked from the interrogation room, Detectives O'Brien and Gomez discussed the facts of the case as far as they were known. They jointly agreed that Doug Brown was a punk; that his story was thin; that he probably had been stealing from his aunt; that his cock-and-bull alibi for not answering the phone was an outright lie; that he must have panicked when he started the story of receiving threats to Ethel just as her corpse was found.

O'Brien leaned back in the chair and attempted to put his feet on the table, his "thinking" position at his desk. The table was too high for comfort, and, annoyed, he swung his feet to the floor, muttering about the crummy furniture and then adding, "That Ethel Lambston was some judge of character. Her ex-husband is a wimp; her nephew is a thief. But of the two scumbags, I say the ex-husband wasted her."

Gomez watched his partner cautiously. He had some thoughts of his own that he wanted to introduce gradually. When he began to speak, it was as though the idea had just floated through his mind. "Let's assume she was murdered at home."

O'Brien grunted in agreement.

Gomez continued, "If you and Miss Kearny are right, somebody changed Ethel's clothes, somebody ripped out the labels, somebody probably dumped her suitcases and handbag."

Through half-closed but thoughtful eyes, O'Brien signaled agreement.

"Here's the point." Gomez knew it was time to unveil his theory. "Why would Seamus hide her body? It was only a fluke that it was discovered so soon. He'd have had to keep sending alimony to her accountant. Or, why would the nephew hide the body and rip off identification? If Ethel had rotted undisturbed, he'd have to wait seven years to get at her dough, and even then it would have involved a lot of expensive legal time. If one of them did it, they'd have *wanted* the body discovered, right?"

O'Brien raised his hand. "Don't credit these punks with brains. We just keep raking them over, making them nervous, and sooner or later one of them will say, 'I didn't mean to do it.' I still bet on the husband. For five bucks, you want the nephew?"

Gomez was saved from making the choice when the telephone in the interrogation room rang. The Police Commissioner wanted to see both detectives in his office immediately.

On the way downtown in a squad car, both O'Brien and Gomez tried to assess their activities on the case. The PC was on top of this one. Had they goofed? It was four-fifteen when they entered his office.

Police Commissioner Herbert Schwartz listened as the discussion progressed. Detective O'Brien was flat out against giving even limited immunity to Seamus Lambston. "Sir," he told Herb, his voice deferential, "I've been positive right along that the ex-husband did it. Hold off. Give me three days to solve this."

Herb was about to decide in O'Brien's favor when his secretary came in. Hurriedly, he excused himself and went to the outer office. Five minutes later he returned. "I have just been told," he said quietly, "that Gordon Steuber may have ordered a contract put on Neeve Kearny. We'll interrogate him immediately. Neeve blew the whistle on his illegal sweatshops, and that started the investigation that led to the drug bust, so it makes sense. But Ethel Lambston may also have gotten wind of his activities. So now there's a damn good chance that Steuber may have been involved with Ethel Lambston's death. I want to either pin down or eliminate the ex-husband in that murder. Go ahead with the deal his lawyer requested. And get the polygraph today."

"But . . ." O'Brien saw the expression on the PC's face and did not finish the sentence.

An hour later, in two separate interrogation rooms, Gordon Steuber, who had not yet raised ten million dollars in bail, and Seamus Lambston were being questioned. Steuber's lawyer hovered beside him as the questions crackled from Detective O'Brien.

"Do you have any knowledge of a contract put out on Neeve Kearny?"

Gordon Steuber, immaculate despite his hours in the detention pen, still assessing the seriousness of his situation, burst out laughing. "You gotta be kidding. But what a great idea."

In the next room, Seamus, under limited immunity, having told his story, was hooked up to a polygraph machine for the second time that day. Seamus kept reminding himself that this was the same as the other and he'd passed the first one. But it *wasn't* the same. The hard, unfriendly faces of the detectives, the claustrophobic smallness of the room, the realization that they were sure he'd killed Ethel, terrified him. The encouraging comments of his lawyer, Kennedy, didn't help. He knew he had made a mistake agreeing to the test.

Seamus was barely able to answer the early, simple questions. When he got to that last meeting with Ethel, it was as though he were there with her again, watching her mocking face, knowing she was enjoying his misery, knowing that she'd never let go. The rage built in him as it had that night. The questions became incidental.

"You punched Ethel Lambston."

His fist hitting her jaw. Her head snapping back. "Yeah. Yes."

"She picked up the letter opener and tried to attack you."

The hatred in her face. No. It had been *scorn.* She knew she had him. She'd shouted, "I'll have you arrested, you ape." She'd reached for the letter opener and thrust it at him. He'd twisted it from her hand and cut her face when they grappled for it. Then she'd seen what was in his eyes. She'd said, "All right, all right, no more alimony."

Then . . .

"Did you kill your former wife, Ethel Lambston?"

Seamus closed his eyes. "No. No . . ."

Peter Kennedy did not need confirmation from Detective O'Brien to tell him what he had already sensed. He had lost the gamble.

Seamus had failed the lie-detector test.

Herb Schwartz listened, his face impassive, his eyes wary, as for the second time that afternoon he conferred with Detectives O'Brien and Gomez.

In the past hour, Herb had agonized about whether or not to tell Myles that they suspected Gordon Steuber had ordered a contract on Neeve. He knew it might be enough to trigger another heart attack.

If Steuber had ordered a contract on Neeve, was it too late to stop it? Herb felt his guts wrench as he realized the probable answer. No. If Steuber had set it in motion, it would have filtered through five or six hoods before the arrangements were made. The hit man would never know who had ordered it. Likely as not, some out-of-town goon would be brought in and would be rushed away as soon as the execution had taken place.

Neeve Kearny. God, Herb thought, I can't let it happen. He'd been a thirty-four-year-old deputy commissioner when Renata was murdered. Till the day he died, he'd never forget the look on Myles Kearny's face as he knelt beside the body of his wife.

And now his daughter?

The line of inquiry that might have linked Steuber to Ethel Lambston's death no longer seemed valid. The ex-husband had failed the lie-detector test, and O'Brien made no secret that he thought Seamus Lambston had cut his former wife's throat. Herb asked O'Brien to present his reasons again.

It had been a long day. Irritated, O'Brien shrugged, then, at a steely glance from the PC, assumed a respectful demeanor. As precisely as though he were on the witness stand, he made a forceful argument damning Seamus Lambston. "He's broke. He's desperate. He had a huge fight with his wife over a bounced tuition check. He goes up to see Ethel, and the neighbor four stories up can hear them quarreling. He doesn't go to his bar all weekend. Nobody sees him. He knows Morrison State Park like his own backyard. He and his kids used to spend Sundays there. A couple of days later, he drops off a letter to Ethel saying thanks for letting me off the hook, and with that he encloses the check he's not supposed to send. He goes back to retrieve it. He admits punching and cutting Ethel. He probably confessed everything to his wife, because she stole the murder weapon and got rid of it."

"Have you found it?" Schwartz cut in.

"Our guys are looking for it now. And, sir, the bottom line is—he failed the polygraph."

"And passed the one he took in his lawyer's office," Gomez interjected. Without looking at his partner, Gomez decided he had to tell what he thought. "Sir, I spoke with Miss Kearny. She is sure that there's something wrong about the outfit Ethel Lambston was wearing. The autopsy shows the victim tore her stocking when she put it on. When that pantyhose was pulled over her right foot, her toe caught and caused a huge run clear up the front. Miss Kearny believes Ethel Lambston would not have walked out looking like that. I respect Miss Kearny's opinion. A fashion-conscious woman would not leave her home dressed like that when in ten seconds she can grab other stockings."

"Have you got the autopsy report and the morgue shots?" Herb asked.

"Yes, sir."

When the envelope was produced, Herb studied the pictures with clinical detachment. The first picture, the hand protruding from the ground; the body after it had been removed from the cavelike opening, frozen by rigor mortis into a doubled-over ball of rotting flesh. The close-ups of Ethel's jaw, purple and black and blue. The bloody nick on her cheek.

Herb turned to another print. This depicted only the area between Ethel's chin and the bottom of her throat. The ugly jagged opening made Herb wince. No matter how many years he'd been in police work, the terrible proof of man's cruelty to his fellow beings still saddened him.

It was more than that.

Herb grasped the print convulsively. The way the throat had been cut. That long slash down, then the precise line from the base of the throat up to the left ear. He'd seen that exact thrust one time before. He reached for the phone.

Waves of shock did not affect the timbre of Police Commissioner Schwartz's voice as he calmly ordered a particular file from the archives.

Neeve quickly realized that her mind was not on ordering sportswear. Her first stop was Gardner Separates. The shorts and T shirts with contrasting loose jackets were amusing and well cut. She could visualize doing the front window of the shop with these outfits in a beach-scene motif in early June. But after that decision had been made, she found herself unable to focus on the rest of the line. Pleading the pressure of time, she made an appointment for the following Monday and hastened from the overly eager clerk who pleaded to "show the new swimwear. You'll flip, it's so great."

When she reached the street, Neeve hesitated. For two cents, I'd go home, she thought. I need some quiet time. She realized she had the beginnings of a headache, a faint sense of pressure like a band around her forehead. I never get headaches, she told herself as she stood indecisively in front of the building.

She could not go home. Just before she stepped into her car, Mrs. Poth had asked her to look for a simple white gown that would do for a small family wedding. "Nothing too elaborate," she'd explained. "My daughter has already broken two engagements. The minister marks her wedding dates in pencil. But this time it just may happen."

There were several houses where Neeve planned to search for the gown. She started to turn right, then paused. The other place was probably the better choice. As she reversed direction, she glanced directly across the street. A man in a gray sweatsuit, a large envelope under his arm, a man with heavy dark glasses and a freakish punk-rock hairstyle, was rushing toward her through the stalled traffic. For an instant they had eye contact and Neeve felt as though an alarm had sounded. The sense of pressure along her forehead was accentuated. A truck pulled out, blocking the messenger from view, and, suddenly annoyed with herself, Neeve began to walk rapidly down the block.

It was four-thirty. The sunlight was hiding behind long, slanting shadows. Neeve found herself almost praying that she'd find a gown at the first stop. Then she thought, I'll quit and go see Sal.

She had given up trying to convince Myles that the blouse Ethel was wearing in death was important. But Sal would understand.

Jack Campbell went directly from his luncheon to an editorial meeting. It lasted until four-thirty. Back in his office, he tried to concentrate on the mountain of mail that Ginny had separated for him, but it was impossible. The sense of something being terribly wrong was overpowering him. Something he had missed. What was it?

Ginny stood at the door that separated Jack's office from the cubicled area where she worked, and studied him thoughtfully. In the month since Jack had taken over the presidency of Givvons and Marks, she had come to admire and like him tremendously. After twenty years of working for his predecessor, she had been afraid that she might not be able to adjust to the change, or that Jack might not want a holdover.

Both concerns were invalid. Now as she studied him, unconsciously approving of the casual good taste of his dark-gray suit and amused by the boyish way he had loosened his tie and the top button of his shirt, she realized that he was seriously worried. His hands were locked under his chin. He was staring at the wall. His forehead was furrowed. Had the editorial meeting gone well? she wondered. She knew there were still some noses out of joint that Jack had been tapped for the top job.

She knocked on the open door. Jack looked up and she watched as his eyes refocused. "Are you in deep meditation?" she asked easily. "If so, the mail can wait."

Jack attempted a smile. "No. It's just this Ethel Lambston business. There's something I've been missing about it, and I've racked my brains trying to figure it out."

Ginny sat at the edge of the chair opposite Jack's. "Maybe I can help. Think about the day Ethel came in here. You only spent abou two minutes with her and the door was open, so I heard her. She was yapping about a fashion scandal but gave absolutely no specifics. She wanted to talk big money and you threw a figure at her. I don't think you missed anything."

Jack sighed. "I guess not. But tell you what. Let me look over that file Toni sent. Maybe there's something in Ethel's notes."

At five-thirty when Ginny looked in to say good night, Jack nodded absently. He was still poring over Ethel's voluminous research. For every designer mentioned in her article, she had apparently put together a separate file containing biographical information and Xerox copies of dozens of fashion columns from newspapers and magazines like the *Times, W, Women's Wear Daily, Vogue* and *Harper's Bazaar.*

She had obviously been a meticulous researcher. Interviews with the designers contained frequent notations: "Not what she said in *Vogue.*" "Check these figures." "Never won that prize." "Try to interview governess about her claim she sewed clothes for her dolls." . . .

There were a dozen different drafts of Ethel's final article, with slashes and inserts in each version.

Jack began to skim the material until he saw the name "Gordon Steuber." Steuber. Ethel had been wearing a suit he designed when she was found. Neeve had been so insistent about the fact that the blouse taken from Ethel's body had been sold with that suit but that Ethel wouldn't have deliberately worn it.

With minute care he analyzed the material on Gordon Steuber and was alarmed to see how frequently his name was mentioned in newspaper clippings of the past three months showing he was under investigation. In the article, Ethel had credited Neeve for pointing the finger at Steuber. The next-to-final draft of her article not only dealt with the exposure of his sweatshops, his income-tax problems, but contained a sentence: "Steuber got his start in his father's business, making linings for fur coats. The word is that nobody else in the history of fashion has made more money with linings and seams in the last few years than the dapper Mr. Steuber."

Ethel had bracketed that sentence and marked it "Save." Ginny had told Jack about Steuber's arrest after the drug bust. Had Ethel discovered several weeks ago that Steuber was smuggling heroin in the linings and seams of his imports?

It ties in, Jack thought. It ties in with Neeve's theory about the clothes Ethel was wearing. It ties in with Ethel's "big scandal."

Jack debated about calling Myles, then decided to show the file to Neeve first.

Neeve. Was it really possible that he'd known her for only six days? No. Six years. He'd been looking for her since that day on the plane. He glanced at the phone. His need to be with her was overpowering. He hadn't even once held her in his arms, and now they ached for her. She'd said she'd phone him from her Uncle Sal's place when she was ready to leave.

Sal. Anthony della Salva, the famous designer. The next pile of clippings and fashion sketches and articles were about him. Glancing at the phone, willing Neeve to call *now,* Jack began to go through the file on Anthony della Salva. It was thick with illustrations of the Pacific Reef collection. I can see why people went for it, Jack thought, and I don't know beans about fashion. The dresses and gowns seemed to float from the pages. He skimmed the write-ups of the fashion reporters. "Slender tunics with drifting panels that fall like wings from the shoulders . . ."; ". . . soft, pleated sleeves on gossamer-like chiffon . . ."; ". . . simple wool daytime dresses that drape the body in understated elegance . . ." The reporters were lyrical in their praise of the colors.

> Anthony della Salva visited the Chicago Aquarium early in 1972 and found his inspiration there in the aquatic beauty of the magnificent Pacific Reef exhibit.
>
> For hours he walked through the rooms and sketched the underwater kingdom where the brilliantly beautiful creatures of the sea vie with the wondrous plant life, the clusters of coral trees and the hundreds of exquisitely colored shells. He sketched those colors in the patterns and combinations that nature had decreed. He studied the movement of the ocean dwellers so that he might capture with his scissors and fabric the floating grace that is their birthright.
>
> Ladies, put those man-tailored suits and those evening gowns with their ruffled sleeves and voluminous skirts in the back of your closet. This is your year to be beautiful. Thank you, Anthony della Salva.

I guess he *is* good, Jack thought, and started to stack the della Salva file together, then wondered what was bothering him. There was something he had missed. What was it? He had read Ethel's final draft of her article. Now he looked at the next-to-the-last version.

It was deeply annotated. "Chicago Aquarium—check date he visited it!" Ethel had clipped one of the fashion sketches of the Pacific Reef collection to the top of her working draft. Next to it she had drawn a sketch.

Jack's mouth went dry. He had seen that sketch in the last few days. He had seen it in the stained pages of Renata Kearny's cookbook.

And the Aquarium. "Check date." Of *course!* With dawning horror, he began to understand. He had to be sure. It was nearly six o'clock. That meant that in Chicago it was nearly five. Rapidly he dialed Chicago area code information.

At one minute to five, Chicago time, the number he dialed was answered. "Please call the director in the morning," an impatient voice told him.

"Give him my name. He knows me. I must speak to him immediately, and let me tell you, lady, if I find out he's there and you don't put me through, I'll get your job."

"I'll connect you, sir."

A moment later, a surprised voice asked, "Jack, what's going on?"

The question tumbled from Jack's lips. He realized his hands were clammy. Neeve, he thought, Neeve, be careful. He stared down at Ethel's article and noticed where she had written, "We salute Anthony della Salva for creating the Pacific Reef look." Ethel had crossed out della Salva's name and over it written: "the designer of the Pacific Reef look."

The answer from the curator of the Aquarium was even more frightening than he had anticipated. "You're absolutely right. And you know what's crazy? You're the second person to call about that in the last two weeks."

"Do you know who the other one was?" Jack asked, knowing what he would hear.

"Sure I do. Some writer. Edith . . . Or no, Ethel. Ethel Lambston."

Myles had an unexpectedly busy day. At ten o'clock, the phone rang. Would he be available at noon to discuss the position he was being offered in Washington? He agreed to luncheon in the Oak Room of the Plaza. In the late morning, he went to the Athletic Club for a swim and massage and secretly was delighted at the confirmation the masseur gave him: "Commissioner Kearny, your body's in great shape again."

Myles knew that his skin had lost that ghastly pallor. But it wasn't just appearance. He *felt* happy. I may be sixty-eight, he thought as he knotted his tie in the locker room, but I look all right.

I look all right to myself, he decided ruefully as he waited for the elevator. A woman may see it differently. Or, more specifically, he acknowledged as he stepped from the lobby onto Central Park South and turned right toward Fifth Avenue and the Plaza, Kitty Conway may see me in a less flattering light.

The luncheon with a Presidential aide had one purpose. Myles must give his answer. Would he accept the chairmanship of the Drug Enforcement Agency? Myles promised to make his decision in the next forty-eight hours. "We're hoping it's affirmative," the aide told him. "Senator Moynihan seems to think it will be."

Myles smiled. "I never cross Pat Moynihan."

It was when he returned to the apartment that the sense of well-being vanished. He had left a window in the den open. As he entered the room, a pigeon flew in, circled, hovered, perched on the window-sill and then flew out over the Hudson. "A pigeon in the house is a sign of death." His mother's words pounded in his ears.

Crazy, superstitious rot, Myles thought angrily, but the persistent sense of foreboding could not be shaken. He realized he wanted to talk to Neeve. Quickly he dialed the shop.

Eugenia got on. "Commissioner, she just left for Seventh Avenue. I can try to track her down."

"No. Not important," Myles said. "But if she happens to phone, tell her to give me a call."

He had just put the receiver down when the phone rang. It was Sal confirming that he too was worried about Neeve.

For the next half hour, Myles debated about calling Herb Schwartz. But for what? It wasn't that Neeve would be a witness against Steuber. It was just that she'd pointed the finger at him and set the investigation in motion. Myles acknowledged that a hundred-million-dollar drug bust was enough reason for Steuber and his co-horts to exact revenge.

Maybe I can persuade Neeve to move down to Washington with me, Myles thought, and rejected the idea as ridiculous. Neeve had her life in New York, her business. Now, if he was any judge of human events, she had Jack Campbell. Then forget Washington, Myles decided as he paced the den. I've got to stay here and keep an eye on her. Whether she liked it or not, he would hire a bodyguard for her.

He expected Kitty Conway at about six o'clock. At five-fifteen he went into his bedroom, stripped, showered in the adjoining bath-room and carefully selected the suit, shirt and tie he would wear to dinner. At twenty of six, he was fully dressed.

Long ago, he'd discovered that working with his hands had a calm-ing effect on him when he was facing an intolerable problem. He decided that for the next twenty minutes or so he'd see whether he could fix the handle that had broken off the coffeepot the other night.

Once again, he realized he was looking with anxious appraisal into the mirror. Hair pure white now but still plenty thick. No monk's tonsures in his family. What difference did that make? Why would a very pretty woman ten years his junior have any interest in an ex-police commissioner with a bum heart?

Avoiding that train of thought, Myles glanced around the bedroom. The four-poster bed, the armoire, the dresser, the mirror, were antiques, wedding gifts from Renata's family. Myles stared at the bed, remembering Renata, propped up on pillows, an infant Neeve at her breast. *"Cara, cara, mia cara,"* she would murmur, her lips brushing Neeve's forehead.

Myles grasped the footboard as he again heard Sal's worried warning, "Take care of Neeve." God in heaven! Nicky Sepetti had said, "Take care of your wife and kid."

Enough, Myles told himself as he left the bedroom and headed for the kitchen. You're turning into a nervous old biddy who'd jump at the sight of a mouse.

In the kitchen, he fished among the pots and pans until he'd pulled out the espresso pot that had scalded Sal on Thursday night. He brought it into the den, laid it on his desk, got his tool kit out of the storage closet and settled down to the role Neeve dubbed "Mr. Fixit."

A moment later, he realized that the reason the handle was off was not a matter of loose or broken screws. Then he said aloud, "This is absolutely crazy!"

He tried to remember just exactly what had happened the night Sal had burned himself. . . .

On Monday morning, Kitty Conway awoke with a sense of anticipation she had not felt for a long time. Gamely refusing the temptation to grab another forty winks, she dressed in a jogging outfit and ran through Ridgewood from seven until eight o'clock.

The trees along the lovely wide avenues had that special reddish haze that signaled spring was coming. Only last week when she had run here, she'd noticed the budding, thought of Mike and remembered a fragment of a poem: "What can spring do; except renew; my need for you?"

Last week she had looked with nostalgia at the sight of the young husband down the block waving goodbye to his wife and toddlers as he backed his car out of the driveway. It seemed only yesterday that she was holding Michael and waving goodbye to Mike.

Yesterday and thirty years ago.

Today she smiled absently at her neighbors as she approached her house. She was due at the museum at noon. She'd get home at four, just in time to dress and start for New York. She debated about getting her hair done and decided she did a better job on it herself.

Myles Kearny.

Kitty fished in her pocket for the house key, let herself in, then exhaled a long sigh. It felt good to jog, but, oh Lord, it sure made her feel her fifty-eight years.

Impulsively she opened the hall closet and looked up at the hat Myles Kearny had "forgotten." The moment she'd discovered it last night, she'd known that it was his excuse to see her again. She thought of the chapter in *Pavilion of Women* where the husband leaves his pipe as a sign he plans to return to his wife's quarters that night. Kitty grinned, saluted the hat and went upstairs to shower.

The day went quickly. At four-thirty, she debated between two outfits, a simply cut square-necked black wool that accentuated her slenderness and a two-piece blue-green print that played up her red hair. Go for it, she decided, and reached for the print.

At five past six, the concierge announced her arrival and gave her Myles's apartment number. At seven past six she was getting off the elevator and he was waiting in the hallway.

She knew immediately there was something wrong. His greeting was almost perfunctory. And yet she instinctively knew that the coolness was not directed at her.

Myles put his hand under her arm as they walked down the hall to his apartment. Inside, he took her coat and absentmindedly laid it on a chair in the foyer. "Kitty," he said, "bear with me. There's something I'm trying to dope out and it's important."

They went into the den. Kitty glanced around the lovely room, admiring its comfort and warmth and intrinsic good taste. "Don't worry about me," she said. "Get on with what you're doing."

Myles went back to his desk. "The point," he said, thinking aloud, "is that this handle didn't just come loose. It was *forced* off the pot. It was the first time Neeve used that coffeepot, so maybe it came that way, the way things are made these days. . . . But, for God's sake, wouldn't she have noticed the damn handle was hanging by a thread?"

Kitty knew Myles was not expecting an answer. She walked around the room quietly, admiring the fine paintings, the framed family pictures. She smiled unconsciously at the sight of the three scuba divers.

Through the masks it was almost impossible to detect the faces, but it was undoubtedly Myles, his wife and a seven- or eight-year-old Neeve. She and Mike and Michael used to scuba-dive in Hawaii, too.

Kitty looked at Myles. He was holding the handle against the pot, his expression intent. She walked over to stand beside him. Her glance fell on the open cookbook. The pages were stained with coffee, but the sketches were accentuated rather than diminished by the discoloration. Kitty bent over and examined them closely, then reached for the magnifying glass next to them. Again she studied the sketches, concentrating on one of them. "How charming," she said. "That's Neeve, of course. She must have been the first child to wear the Pacific Reef look. How chic can you get?"

She felt a hand snap around her wrist. "What did you say?" Myles asked. *"What did you say?"*

When Neeve arrived at Estrazy's, her first stop in her search for the white gown, she found the showroom crowded. Buyers from Saks and Bonwit's and Bergdorf as well as others like her with small private shops were there. She quickly realized that everyone was discussing Gordon Steuber.

"You know, Neeve," the buyer from Saks confided, "I'm stuck with a load of his sportswear. People are funny. You'd be amazed at how many got turned off Gucci and Nippon when they were convicted of sales-tax evasion. One of my best customers told me she won't patronize greedy felons."

A sales clerk whispered to Neeve that her best friend, who was Gordon Steuber's secretary, was frantic. "Steuber's been good to her," she confided, "but now he's in big trouble and my friend is afraid she could be, too. What should she do?"

"Tell the truth," Neeve said, "and please warn her not to have misplaced loyalty to Gordon Steuber. He doesn't deserve it."

The sales clerk managed to find three white gowns. One of them, Neeve was sure, would be perfect for Mrs. Poth's daughter. She ordered the one, took the other two on consignment.

It was five minutes past six when she arrived at Sal's building. The streets were becoming quiet. Between five and five-thirty the uproar of the Garment District ended abruptly. She went into the lobby and was surprised to see that the guard was not at his desk in the corner. Probably went to the john, she thought as she walked to the bank of elevators. As usual after six o'clock, only one elevator was in service. The door was closing when she heard footsteps scurrying down the marble floor. Just before the door snapped shut and the elevator began to rise, she caught a glimpse of a gray sweatsuit and a punk-rock haircut. Eyes met.

The messenger. In a moment of total recall, Neeve remembered noticing him when she'd escorted Mrs. Poth to her car; noticing him when she'd left Islip Separates.

Her mouth suddenly dry, she pushed the twelfth-floor button, then all the buttons of the remaining nine upper floors. At the twelfth floor she got out and rushed down the corridor the few steps to Sal's place.

The door to Sal's showroom was open. She ran in and closed it behind her. The room was empty. "Sal!" she called, almost panicked. "Uncle Sal!"

He hurried from his private office. "Neeve, what's the matter?"

"Sal, I think someone is following me." Neeve grasped his arm. "Lock the door, please."

Sal stared at her. "Neeve, are you sure?"

"Yes. I've seen him three or four times."

Those dark deep-set eyes, the sallow skin. Neeve felt the color drain from her face. "Sal," she whispered, "I know who it is. He works in the coffee shop."

"Why would he be following you?"

"I don't know." Neeve stared at Sal. "Unless Myles was right all along. Is it possible Nicky Sepetti wanted me dead?"

Sal opened the outside door. They could hear the whirring of the elevator as it made its way down. "Neeve," he said, "are you game to try something?"

Not knowing what to expect, Neeve nodded.

"I'm going to leave this door open. You and I can be talking. If someone is after you, it's better if he doesn't get scared off."

"You want me to stand where someone can see me?"

"The hell I do. Get behind that mannequin. I'll be in back of the door. If someone comes in, I can get a drop on him. The point is to detain him, to find out who sent him."

They stared at the indicator. The elevator was on the lobby floor. It began to rise.

Sal rushed into his office, opened his desk drawer, pulled out a gun and hurried back to her. "I've had a permit since I was robbed years ago," he whispered. *"Neeve, get behind that mannequin."*

As though in a dream, Neeve obeyed. The lights had been dimmed in the showroom, but, even so, she realized that the mannequins were dressed in Sal's new line. Dark fall colors, cranberry and deep blue, charcoal brown and midnight black. Pockets and scarves and belts blazoned with the brilliant colors of the Pacific Reef collection. Corals and reds and golds and aquas and emeralds and silvers and blues combined in microscopic versions of the delicate patterns as Sal had sketched them in the Aquarium so long ago. Accessories and accents, signatures of his great classic design.

She stared at the scarf that was brushing her face. *That pattern.* Sketches. *Mama, are you drawing my picture? Mama, that's not what I'm wearing. . . . Oh, bambola mia, it's just an idea of what could be so pretty . . .*

Sketches—Renata's sketches drawn three months before she died, a year before Anthony della Salva stunned the fashion world with the Pacific Reef look. Only last week Sal had tried to destroy the book because of one of those sketches.

"Neeve, say something to me." Sal's whisper pierced the room, an urgent command.

The door was ajar. From the corridor outside, Neeve heard the elevator stop. "I was thinking," she said, trying to make her voice sound normal, "I love the way you've incorporated the Pacific Reef look in the fall line."

The elevator door slid open. The faint sound of footsteps in the hall.

Sal's voice sounded genial. "I let everybody go early. They've all been breaking their necks getting ready for the show. I think this is my best collection in years." With a reassuring smile in her direction, he stepped behind the partially open door. The dimmed lights sent his shadow looming against the far wall of the showroom, the wall that was decorated with a Pacific Reef mural.

Neeve stared at the wall, touched the scarf on the mannequin. She tried to answer, but words would not come.

The door opened slowly. She saw the silhouette of a hand, the muzzle of a gun. Cautiously Denny walked into the room, his eyes darting in search of them. As Neeve watched, Sal stepped noiselessly from behind the door. He raised the gun. "Denny," he said softly.

As Denny spun around, Sal fired. The bullet went through Denny's forehead. Denny dropped the pistol and fell to the floor, without making a sound.

Stupefied, Neeve watched as Sal pulled a handkerchief from his pocket and, holding it, reached down and picked up Denny's gun.

"You shot him," Neeve whispered. "You shot him in cold blood. You didn't have to do that! You never gave him a chance."

"He would have killed you." Sal dropped his own gun on the receptionist's desk. "I was only protecting you." He began to walk toward her, Denny's pistol in his hand.

"You *knew* he was coming," Neeve said. "You *knew* his name. You planned this."

The warm, jovial mask that had been Sal's permanent expression was gone. His cheeks were puffy, and shiny with perspiration. The eyes that always seemed to twinkle were narrowed into slits that disappeared into the fleshiness of his face. His hand, still blistered and red, raised the gun and pointed it at her. Spatters of Denny's blood glistened on the shiny fabric of his suit jacket. On the carpet a widening pool of blood encircled his feet. "Of course I did," he said. "The word is out that Steuber ordered you hit. What nobody knows is that *I'm* the one who started that word and *I'm* the one who gave the contract. I'll tell Myles that I managed to get your killer, but too late to save you. Don't worry, Neeve. I'll comfort Myles. I'm good at that."

Neeve stood, rooted, unable to move, beyond fear. "My mother designed the Pacific Reef look," she told him. "You stole it from her, didn't you? And somehow Ethel found out. You're the one who killed *her! You* dressed her, not Steuber! *You* knew which blouse belonged with the ensemble!"

Sal began to laugh, a mirthless chuckle that shook his body. "Neeve," he said, "you're a lot smarter than your father. That's why I have to get rid of you. You knew there was something wrong when Ethel didn't show up. You caught on that all her winter coats were still in her closet. I figured you would. When I saw a Pacific Reef sketch in the cookbook I knew I had to get rid of it any way I could, even if it meant burning my hand. You'd have made the connection, sooner or later. Myles wouldn't have recognized it blown up to billboard size. Ethel found out that my story about getting inspiration for the Pacific Reef look in the Chicago Aquarium was a lie. I told her I could explain it and went to her place. She was smart all right. She told me she knew I'd lied, and *why* I lied—that I'd stolen that design. And she was going to prove it."

"Ethel saw the cookbook," Neeve said numbly. "She copied one of the sketches into her appointment book."

Sal smiled. "Was that how she made the connection? She didn't live long enough to tell me. If we had time, I'd show you the portfolio your mother gave me. The whole collection is there."

This wasn't Uncle Sal. This wasn't her father's boyhood friend. This was a stranger who hated her, hated Myles. "Your father and Dev, treating me like I was a big joke from the time we were kids. Laughing at me. Your mother. High-class. Beautiful. Understanding fashion the way you only can when it's born in you. Wasting all that knowledge on a clod like your father who can't tell a housedress from a coronation robe. Renata always looked down her nose at me. She knew I didn't have it, the gift. But when she wanted advice about where to take her designs, guess who she came to!

"Neeve, you still haven't figured the best part of it. You're the only one who'll ever know, and you won't be around to tell. Neeve, you damn fool, I didn't just *steal* the Pacific Reef look from your mother. *I cut her throat for it!*"

"It's Sal!" Myles whispered. "He ripped the handle off the coffeepot. He tried to ruin those sketches. And Neeve may be with him now."

"Where?" Kitty grasped Myles's arm.

"His office. Thirty-sixth Street."

"My car is outside. It has a phone."

Nodding, Myles ran for the door and down the corridor. An agonizing minute passed before the elevator came. It stopped twice to pick up passengers before the ground floor. Holding Kitty's hand, he ran across the lobby. Heedless of traffic, they dashed across the street.

"I'll drive," Myles told her. With a screeching U-turn he raced down West End Avenue, willing a squad car to see him, to follow him.

As always in a crisis, he felt himself go icy cold. His mind became a separate entity, weighing what he must do. He gave Kitty a number to dial. Silently she obeyed, and handed the phone to him.

"Police Commissioner's office."

"Myles Kearny. Put the Commissioner on."

Frantically Myles steered around the heavy evening traffic. Ignoring red lights, he left in his wake a snarl of angry motorists. They were at Columbus Circle.

Herb's voice. "Myles, I just tried to reach you. Steuber put a contract out on Neeve. We've got to protect her. And, Myles, I think there's a connection between Ethel Lambston's murder and Renata's death. The V-shaped slash in Lambston's throat—it's exactly the same as the wound that killed Renata."

Renata, her throat slashed. Renata, lying so quietly in the park. No sign of struggle. Renata who had not been mugged but who had met a man she trusted, her husband's boyhood friend. Oh Jesus, Myles thought. Oh Jesus.

"Herb, Neeve is at Anthony della Salva's place. Two-fifty West Thirty-sixth. Twelfth floor. Herb, send our guys there fast. Sal is a murderer."

Between Fifty-sixth and Forty-fourth streets, the right lanes of

Seventh Avenue were being repaved. But the workers had left. Recklessly Myles drove behind the stanchions, over the still-damp tarmac. They were passing Thirty-eighth Street, Thirty-seventh . . .

Neeve. Neeve. Neeve. Let me be on time, Myles prayed. Grant me my child.

Jack laid down the phone, still absorbing what he had just heard. His friend the director of the Chicago Aquarium had confirmed what he suspected. The new museum had opened eighteen years ago, but the magnificent display on the top floor that reproduced the dazzling sense of walking the bottom of the ocean at the Pacific Reef had not been completed until *sixteen* years ago. Not too many people were aware that there had been a problem with the tanks and the Pacific Reef floor had not been open to the public for nearly two years after the rest of the Aquarium was completed. It was not something that the director cared to include in the public-relations releases. Jack knew because he'd gone to Northwestern and used to visit the museum regularly.

Anthony della Salva had claimed that his inspiration for the Pacific Reef look had been occasioned by a visit to the Chicago Aquarium *seventeen* years ago. Impossible. Then why had he lied?

Jack stared down at Ethel's voluminous notes; the clip sheets of the interviews and write-ups about Sal; the bold question marks over Sal's rhapsodic descriptions of his first experience seeing the Pacific Reef exhibition at the Aquarium; the copy of the sketch from the cookbook. Ethel had picked up the discrepancy and pursued it. Now she was dead.

Jack thought of Neeve's absolute insistence that there was something odd about the way Ethel was dressed. He thought about Myles saying, "Every killer leaves a calling card."

Gordon Steuber wasn't the only designer who might have mistakenly clothed his victim in a seemingly appropriate outfit.

Anthony della Salva might have made exactly the same mistake.

Jack's office was silent, the silence that comes when a room that is used to the activity of visitors and secretaries and ringing phones is suddenly hushed.

Jack grabbed the phone book. Anthony della Salva had six different office addresses. Frantically, Jack tried the first one. There was no answer. The second and third had an answering machine: "Business hours are eight-thirty till five P.M. Please leave a message."

He tried the apartment at Schwab House. After six rings he gave up. As a last resort he phoned the shop. Somebody answer, he prayed.

"Neeve's Place."

"I've got to reach Neeve Kearny. This is Jack Campbell, a friend."

Eugenia's voice was warm."You're the publisher—"

Jack interrupted. "She's meeting della Salva. Where?"

"His main office. Two-fifty West Thirty-sixth Street. Is anything wrong?"

Without answering, Jack slammed down the phone.

His office was at Park and Forty-first Street. He ran through the deserted corridors, managed to catch an elevator that was just descending and hailed a cruising cab. He threw twenty dollars at the driver and shouted out the address. It was eighteen minutes past six.

Is this the way it was for Mother? Neeve thought. Did she look up at him that day and see the change come over his face? Did she have any warning?

Neeve knew she was going to die. She had felt all week that her time was running out. Now that she was beyond hope, it seemed suddenly vital to have those questions answered.

Sal had moved closer to her. He was less than four feet away. Behind him, near the door, the crumpled body of Denny, the delivery man who would fuss to open the coffee container for her, was sprawled on the floor. From the corner of her eye, Neeve could see the blood that was oozing from the wound in his head; the outsized manila envelope that he had been carrying was spattered with blood, the punk-rock haircut that had been a wig was mercifully half covering his face.

It seemed an age ago since Denny had burst into this room. How long had it been? A minute? Less than a minute. The building had felt deserted, but it was possible someone had heard the shot. Someone might investigate. . . . The guard was *supposed* to be downstairs. . . . Sal didn't have time to waste, and they both knew it.

From far off Neeve heard a faint whir. An elevator was moving. Someone might be coming. Could she delay the instant when Sal pulled the trigger?

"Uncle Sal," she said quietly, "will you tell me just one thing? Why was it necessary for you to kill my mother? Couldn't you have worked with her? There isn't a designer going who doesn't pick the brains of apprentices."

"When I see genius, I don't share, Neeve," Sal told her flatly.

The sliding of an elevator door in the hallway. Someone was there.

To keep Sal from hearing the sound of footsteps, Neeve shouted. "You killed my mother because of your greed. You comforted us and cried with us. At her casket you told Myles, 'Try to think your pretty one is sleeping.' "

"Shut up!" Sal stretched out his hand.

The muzzle of the pistol loomed before Neeve's face. She turned her head and saw Myles standing in the doorway.

"Myles, run, he'll kill you!" she screamed.

Sal spun around.

Myles did not move. The absolute authority in his voice rang through the room as he said, "Give me the gun, Sal. It's all over."

Sal held the pistol on both of them. His eyes wild with fear and hatred, he stepped back as Myles began to approach him. "Don't come any further," he cried. "I'll shoot."

"No you won't, Sal," Myles said, his voice deadly quiet now, not a trace of fear or doubt in it. "You killed my wife. You killed Ethel Lambston. In another second you would have killed my daughter. But Herb and the cops will be here any minute. They know about you. You can't lie your way out of this one. So *give me that gun.*"

His words became measured and were spoken with awesome force and contempt. He paused for a moment before speaking again. "Or else do yourself and all of us a favor and put the muzzle of that pistol in your lying mouth and blow your brains out."

Mylcs had told Kitty not to leave the car. Agonized, she waited. Please—please help them. From down the block she heard the insistent scream of sirens. Directly in front of her a cab stopped and Jack Campbell rushed out.

"Jack." Kitty pushed open the car door and ran after him into the lobby. The guard was on the phone.

"Della Salva," Jack snapped.

The guard held up his hand. "Wait a minute."

"The twelfth floor," Kitty said.

The one elevator in service was not there. The indicator showed that it was on the twelfth floor. Jack grabbed the guard by the neck. "Turn on another elevator."

"Hey, what do you think . . ."

Outside the building, squad cars screeched to a halt. The guard's eyes widened. He threw Jack a key. "This'll unlock them."

Jack and Kitty were on the way up before the police burst into the lobby. Jack said, "I think della Salva—"

"I know," Kitty said.

The elevator lumbered to the twelfth floor, stopped. "Wait here," Jack told her.

He was in time to hear Myles say in a quiet, disciplined voice: "If you're not going to use it on yourself, Sal, *hand me that gun.*"

Jack stood in the doorway. The room was heavily shadowed and the scene like a surrealistic painting. The body on the carpet. Neeve and her father with the pistol pointed at them. Jack saw the glint of metal on the desk near the door. A gun. Could he reach it in time?

Then, as he watched, Anthony della Salva dropped his hand to his side. "Take it, Myles." He pleaded, "Myles, I didn't *mean* it. I never meant it." Sal fell to his knees and put his arms around Myles's legs. "Myles, you're my best friend. Tell them I didn't mean it."

For the last time that day, Police Commissioner Herbert Schwartz conferred in his office with Detectives O'Brien and Gomez. Herb had just returned from Anthony della Salva's office. He had arrived there just behind the first squad car. He'd spoken to Myles after they'd taken that scum della Salva out. "Myles, you've tortured yourself for seventeen years thinking you didn't take Nicky Sepetti's threat seriously. Isn't it time you let go of the guilt? Do you think if Renata had come to you with the Pacific Reef design, you'd have been able to say it was genius? You may be a smart cop, but you're also somewhat color-blind. I remember Renata saying she laid out your ties for you."

Myles would be all right. What a shame, Herb thought, that "An eye for an eye and a tooth for a tooth" wasn't acceptable anymore. The taxpayers would support della Salva for the rest of his life. . . .

O'Brien and Gomez waited. The PC looked exhausted. But it had been a good day. Della Salva had admitted to murdering Ethel Lambston. The White House and the Mayor would be off their backs.

O'Brien had a few things to tell the PC. "Steuber's secretary came in on her own about an hour ago. Lambston went to see Steuber ten days ago. In effect, told him she was going to get him busted. She was probably onto his drug operation, but it doesn't matter. He didn't hit Lambston."

Schwartz nodded.

Gomez spoke up. "Sir, we know now that Seamus Lambston is innocent of his ex-wife's murder. Do you want to press the assault charge against him and the tampering-with-evidence charge against his wife?"

"Did you find the murder weapon?"

"Yes. In that Indian shop just as she told us."

"Let's give the poor bastards a break." Herb got up. "It's been a long day. Good night, gentlemen."

Devin Stanton was having a pre-dinner cocktail with the Cardinal at the Madison Avenue residence and watching the evening news. Old friends, they were discussing Devin's forthcoming red hat.

"I'll miss you, Dev," the Cardinal told him. "Sure you want the job? Baltimore can be a bathhouse in the summer."

The bulletin broke just before the program went off. Famed designer Anthony della Salva was being arraigned for the murders of Ethel Lambston, Renata Kearny and Denny Adler, and for the attempted murder of former Police Commissioner Kearny's daughter, Neeve.

The Cardinal turned to Devin. "Those are your friends!"

Devin jumped up. "If you'll excuse me, Eminence . . ."

Ruth and Seamus Lambston listened to the NBC six-o'clock news sure they would hear that Ethel Lambston's ex-husband had failed the lie-detector test. They had been astonished when Seamus was allowed to leave police headquarters, both convinced that his arrest was only a matter of time.

Peter Kennedy had tried to offer some encouragement. "Polygraph tcsts arc not infallible. If it comes tu trial, we'll have the evidence that you passed the first one."

Ruth had been taken to the Indian shop. The basket where she'd dropped the dagger had been moved. That was why the cops hadn't found it. She dug it out for them, watched the impersonal way they slipped it into a plastic bag.

"I scoured it," she told them.

"Bloodstains don't always disappear."

How could it have happened? she wondered as she sat in the heavy overstuffed velour chair that she had hated for so long but that now felt familiar and comfortable. How did we lose control over our lives?

The bulletin about the arrest of Anthony della Salva came just as she was about to turn off the set. She and Seamus stared at each other, for the moment unable to comprehend, then clumsily reached for each other.

* * *

Douglas Brown listened incredulously to the report on *The CBS Evening News,* then sat down on Ethel's bed—no, *his* bed—and held his head in his hands. It was over. Those cops couldn't prove he'd taken Ethel's money. He was her heir. He was rich.

He wanted to celebrate. He pulled out his wallet and reached for the phone number of the friendly receptionist from work. Then he hesitated. That kid who cleaned, the actress. There was something about her. That idiotic name. "Tse-Tse." She was listed in Ethel's personal telephone directory.

The phone rang three times, then was picked up. "Allo."

She must have a French roommate, Doug concluded. "May I speak to Tse-Tse, please? This is Doug Brown."

Tse-Tse, who was auditioning for the part of a French prostitute, forgot her accent. "Drop dead, twerp," she told him, and slammed down the receiver.

Devin Stanton, Archbishop designate of the Baltimore diocese, stood at the door of the living room and watched the silhouette of Neeve and Jack against the windows. Beyond them a crescent moon had finally broken through the clouds. With rising anger, Devin thought of the cruelty, greed and hypocrisy of Sal Esposito. Before his clerical training recaptured Christian charity, he muttered to himself, "That murdering bastard." Then, as he watched Neeve in Jack's arms, he thought, Renata, I hope and pray you're aware.

Behind him in the den, Myles reached for the bottle of wine. Kitty was sitting in a corner of the couch, her red hair soft and shimmering under the glow of the Victorian table lamp. Myles heard himself say, "Your hair is a lovely shade of red. I think my mother would have called it strawberry blond. Would that be right?"

Kitty smiled. "At one time. Now nature is being helped along."

"In your case nature doesn't need any help." Myles felt suddenly tongue-tied. How do you thank a woman for saving your daughter's life? If Kitty had not connected the sketch to the Pacific Reef look, he would not have reached Neeve on time. Myles thought of how Neeve and Kitty and Jack had wrapped their arms around him after the cops took Sal away. He had sobbed, "I didn't listen to Renata. I never listened. And because of that, she went to him and died."

"She went to him for an expert's opinion," Kitty had said firmly. "Be honest enough to admit you couldn't have offered her that."

How do you tell a woman that because of her presence the terrible rage and guilt you've carried all these years is in the past, that instead of feeling empty and devastated, you feel strong and eager to really live the rest of your life? There was no way.

Myles realized he was still holding the wine bottle. He looked around for her glass.

"I'm not sure where it is," Kitty told him. "I guess I laid it down somewhere."

There *was* a way to tell her. Deliberately Myles filled his own glass to the brim and handed it to Kitty. "Have mine."

Neeve and Jack stood at the window and looked out over the Hudson River, the parkway, the outline of the apartment houses and restaurants that loomed on the waterfront of New Jersey.

"Why did you go to Sal's office?" Neeve asked quietly.

"Ethel's notes on Sal were annotated with references to the Pacific Reef look. She had a whole bunch of magazine ads showing that look, and next to them she'd done a sketch. The sketch reminded me of something and I realized I'd seen the same one in your mother's cookbook."

"And you knew?"

"I remembered you telling me how Sal created that look after your mother died. Ethel's notes showed that Sal claimed he'd gotten the inspiration for the Pacific Reef look at the Aquarium in Chicago. That simply wasn't possible. Everything fell into place when I realized that. Then, knowing you were with him, I almost went crazy."

All those years ago, Renata as a ten-year-old child, hurrying home in the midst of two armies shooting at each other, had, because of a "feeling," gone into church and saved a wounded American soldier. Neeve felt Jack's arm go around her waist. The movement was not tentative, but sure and steady.

"Neeve?"

All these years she'd been telling Myles that when it happened, she would know it.

As Jack drew her closer to him, she knew that that time had finally come.

LOVES MUSIC, LOVES TO DANCE

ENDLESS THANKS to all who gave so much input and encouragement in the writing of this book—my editor, Michael V. Korda; his associate, senior editor Chuck Adams; my agent, Eugene H. Winick; Robert Ressler, Associate Director of Forensic Behavioral Services. Kudos to my daughter, Carol Higgins Clark, for her research, comments and suggestions and for burning the midnight oil with me as we raced to deadline. And of course, special thanks to the rest of my family and friends, who endured my usual self-doubting about whether or not I could tell this story; their saintly patience will have the cathedrals fighting for their bones.

For my brother Johnny's boys,
Luke and Chris Higgins,
and for his granddaughter, Laura.

With love.

What is a friend?
A single soul dwelling in two bodies.

—Aristotle

~ 1

MONDAY
February 18

The room was dark. He sat in the chair, his arms hugging his legs. It was happening again. Charley wouldn't stay locked in the secret place. Charley insisted on thinking about Erin. *Only two more,* Charley whispered. *Then I'll stop.*

He knew there was no use protesting. But it was becoming more and more dangerous. Charley was becoming reckless. Charley wanted to show off. *Go away, Charley, leave me alone,* he begged. Charley's mocking laugh roared through the room.

If only Nan had liked him, he thought. If only she'd invited him to her birthday party fifteen years ago . . . He'd loved her so much! He'd followed her to Darien with the present he'd bought her at a discount house, a pair of dancing slippers. The cardboard shoebox had been plain and cheap, and he'd taken such trouble to decorate it, drawing a sketch of the slippers on the lid.

Her birthday was on March twelfth, during spring break. He'd driven down to Darien to surprise her with the present. He'd arrived to find her house ablaze with lights. Cars were being parked by valets. He'd driven slowly past, shocked and stunned to recognize students from Brown there.

It still embarrassed him to remember that he'd cried like a baby as he turned around to drive back. Then the thought of the birthday gift made him change his mind. Nan had told him that every morning at seven o'clock, rain or shine, she jogged in the wooded area near her home. The next morning he was there, waiting for her.

He remembered, still vividly today, her *surprise* at seeing him. *Surprise,* not pleasure. She'd stopped, her breath coming in gasps, a stocking cap hiding her silky blond hair, a school sweater over her running suit, her feet in Nikes.

He'd wished her a happy birthday, watched her open the box, listened to her insincere thanks. He'd put his arms around her. "Nan,

I love you so much. Let me see how pretty your feet look in the slippers. I'll fasten them for you. We can dance together right here."

"Get lost!" She pushed him away, threw the box at him, started to jog past him.

It was Charley who had run after her, grabbed her, thrown her to the ground. Charley's hands squeezed her throat until her arms stopped flailing. Charley fastened the slippers on her feet and danced with Nan, her head lolling on his shoulder. Charley lay her on the ground, one of the dancing slippers on her right foot, replacing the Nike on her left.

A long time had passed. Charley had become a blurred memory, a shadowy figure lurking somewhere in the recesses of his mind, until two years ago. Then Charley had started reminding him about Nan, about her slender, high-arched feet, her narrow ankles, her beauty and grace when she danced with him. . . .

Eeney-meeney-miney-mo. Catch a dancer by the toe. Ten piggy toes. The game his mother used to play when he was small. *This little piggy went to market. This little piggy stayed home.*

"Play it ten times," he used to beg when she stopped. "One for each piggy toe."

His mother had loved him so much! Then she changed. He could still hear her voice. *"What are these magazines doing in your room? Why did you take those pumps from my closet? After all we've done for you! You're such a disappointment to us."*

When he reappeared two years ago, Charley ordered him to place ads in the personal columns. So many ads. Charley dictated what he had to say in the special one.

Now seven girls were buried on the property, each with a dancing slipper on the right foot, her shoe or sneaker or boot on the left. . . .

He'd begged Charley to let him stop for a while. He didn't want to do it anymore. He'd told Charley that the ground was still frozen—he couldn't bury them, and it was dangerous to keep their bodies in the freezer. . . .

But Charley shouted, "I want these last two to be found. I want them found just the way I let Nan be found."

Charley had chosen these last two the same way he had chosen the others after Nan. They were named Erin Kelley and Darcy Scott. They had each answered two different personal ads he'd placed. More important, they had each answered his *special* ad.

In all the replies he'd received, it was *their* letters and pictures that had jumped out at Charley. The letters were amusing, the cadence of the language attractive, almost like hearing Nan's voice, that self-deprecating wit, that dry, intelligent humor. And there were the pictures. Both were inviting in different ways. . . .

Erin Kelley had sent a snapshot of herself perched on the corner of a desk. She'd been leaning forward a bit as though speaking, her eyes shining, her long, slim body poised as though she were waiting to be asked to dance.

Darcy Scott's picture showed her standing by a cushioned window-seat, her hand on the drapery. She was half-turned toward the camera. Clearly, she'd been surprised when her picture was taken. There were swatches of material over her arm, an absorbed, but amused, expression on her face. She had high cheekbones, a slender frame, and long legs accentuated by narrow ankles, her slim feet encased in Gucci loafers.

How much more attractive they would be in dancing slippers! he told himself.

He got up and stretched. The dark shadows falling across the room no longer disturbed him. Charley's presence was complete and welcome. No more nagging voice begged him to resist.

As Charley willingly receded into the dark cave from which he had emerged, he reread Erin's letter and ran his fingertips over her picture.

He laughed aloud as he thought of the beguiling ad that had summoned Erin to him.

It began: *"Loves Music, Loves to Dance."*

2

TUESDAY

February 19

Cold. Slushy. Raw. Terrible traffic. It didn't matter. It was good to be back in New York.

Darcy happily tossed off her coat, ran her fingers through her hair, and surveyed the neatly separated mail on her desk. Bev Rothhouse, skinny, intense, bright, a night student at Parsons School of Design and her treasured secretary, identified the stacks by order of importance.

"Bills," she said, pointing to the extreme right. "Deposit slips next. Quite a few of them."

"Substantial, I hope," Darcy suggested.

"Pretty good," Bev confirmed. "Messages over there. You've got requests to furnish two more rental apartments. I swear, you certainly knew what you were doing when you opened a secondhand business."

Darcy laughed. "Sanford and Son. That's me."

Darcy's Corner, Budget Interior Design was what the placard on the office door read. The office was in the Flatiron Building on Twenty-third Street.

"How was California?" Bev asked.

Amused, Darcy heard the note of awe in the other young woman's voice. What Bev really meant was, "How are your mother and father? What's it like to be with them? Are they really as gorgeous as they look in films?"

The answer, Darcy thought, is, Yes, they're gorgeous. Yes, they're wonderful. Yes, I love them and I'm proud of them. It's just that I've never felt comfortable in their world.

"When are they leaving for Australia?" Bev was trying to sound offhanded.

"They left. I caught the red-eye back to New York after seeing them off."

Darcy had combined a visit home with a business trip to Lake Tahoe, where she'd been hired to decorate a model ski house for budget-priced buyers. Her mother and father were embarking on an international tour with their play. She wouldn't see them for at least six months.

Now she opened the container of coffee she'd picked up at a nearby lunch counter and settled down at her desk.

"You look great," Bev observed. "I love that outfit."

The square-neck red wool dress and matching coat were part of the Rodeo Drive shopping tour her mother had insisted upon. "For such a pretty girl, you never pay enough attention to your clothes, darling," her mother had fussed. "You should emphasize that wonderful ethereal quality." As her father frequently observed, Darcy could have posed for the portrait of the maternal ancestor for whom she had been named. The original Darcy had left Ireland after the Revolutionary War to join her French fiancé, an officer with Lafayette's forces. They had the same wide-set eyes, more green than hazel, the same soft brown hair streaked with gold, the same straight nose.

"We've grown a bit since then," Darcy enjoyed pointing out. "I'm five eight. Darcy the First was a shrimp. That helps when you're trying to look ethereal." She had never forgotten when she was six and overheard a director comment, "How ever did two such stunning people manage to produce that mousy-looking child?"

She still remembered standing perfectly still, absorbing the shock. A few minutes later when her mother tried to introduce her to someone on the set, "And this is my little girl, Darcy," she had shouted "No!" and run away. Later she apologized for being rude.

This morning when she got off the plane at Kennedy, she'd dropped her bags at the apartment, then come directly to the office, not taking time to change into her usual working garb, jeans and a sweater. Bev waited for her to start sipping the coffee, then picked up the messages. "Do you want me to start getting these people for you?"

"Let me give Erin a quick call first."

Erin picked up on the first ring. Her somewhat preoccupied greeting told Darcy that she was already at her worktable. They'd been college roommates together at Mount Holyoke. Then Erin had studied jewelry design. Recently she'd won the prestigious N. W. Ayer award for young designers.

Darcy had also found her professional niche. After four years of working her way up in an advertising agency, she had switched careers from account executive to budget interior decorating. Both women were now twenty-eight, and they were as close as they'd been when living together in school.

Darcy could picture Erin at her worktable, dressed in jeans and a baggy sweater, her red hair held back by a clip or in a ponytail, absorbed by her work, unaware of outside distraction.

The preoccupied "hello" gave way to a whoop of joy when Erin heard Darcy's voice.

"You're busy," Darcy said. "I won't keep you. Just wanted to report that I've arrived, and, of course, I wanted to see how Billy is."

Billy was Erin's father. An invalid, he'd been in a nursing home in Massachusetts for the past three years.

"Pretty much the same," Erin told her.

"How's the necklace going? When I phoned Friday you sounded worried." Just after Darcy had left last month, Erin had landed a commission from Bertolini Jewelers to design a necklace using the client's family gems. Bertolini was on a par with Cartier's and Tiffany's.

"That's because I was still terrified the design might be off base. It really was pretty intricate. But all is well. I deliver it tomorrow morning and if I say so myself, it's sensational. How was Bel-Air?"

"Glamorous." They laughed together, then Darcy said, "Update me on Project Personal."

Nona Roberts, a producer at Hudson Cable Network, had become friendly with Darcy and Erin at their health club. Nona was preparing a documentary on personal columns—about the kind of people who placed and answered the ads; their experiences, good or bad. Nona had asked Darcy and Erin to assist in the research by answering some of the ads. "You don't have to see anybody more than once," she'd urged. "Half the singles at the network are doing it and having a lot of laughs. And who knows, you might meet someone terrific. Anyhow, think about it."

Erin, typically the more daring, had been unusually reluctant. Darcy had persuaded her it could be fun. "We won't place our own ads," she argued. "We'll just answer some that look interesting. We won't give our addresses, just a phone number. We'll meet them in public places. What's to lose?"

They had started six weeks ago. Darcy had had time for only one date before she left on the trip to Lake Tahoe and Bel-Air. That man had written he was six one. As she told Erin afterward, he must have been standing on a ladder when he measured himself. Also he'd claimed he was an advertising executive. But when Darcy threw out a few names of agencies and clients, he was totally at sea. A liar and a jerk, she reported to Erin and Nona. Now, smiling in anticipation, Darcy asked Erin to fill her in on her most recent encounters.

"I'll save it all for tomorrow night when we get together with Nona," Erin said. "I'm writing every detail down in that notebook you gave me for Christmas. Suffice it to say, I've been out twice more since we talked. That brings the total to eight dates in the last three weeks. Most of them were nerds with absolutely no redeeming social value. One it turned out I'd met before. One of the new ones was really attractive and needless to say hasn't called back. I'm meeting somebody tonight. He sounds okay, but let's wait and see."

Darcy grinned. "Obviously, I haven't missed much. How many ads have you answered for me?"

"About a dozen. I thought it would be fun to send both our letters to some of the same ads. We can really compare notes if those dudes call."

"I love it. Where are you meeting tonight's prize?"

"In a pub off Washington Square."

"What does he do?"

"Corporate law. He's from Philadelphia. Just relocating here. You can make tomorrow night, can't you?"

"Sure." They were meeting Nona for dinner.

Erin's tone changed. "I'm glad you're back in town, Darce. I've missed you."

"Me too," Darcy said heartily. "Okay, see you then." She started to say good-bye, then impulsively asked, "What's the name of tonight's pig-in-a-poke?"

"Charles North."

"Sounds upscale, waspy. Have fun, Erin-go-bragh." Darcy hung up.

Bev was waiting patiently with the messages. Now her tone was frankly envious. "I swear, when you two talk, you sound like a couple of school kids. You're closer than sisters. Thinking about *my* sister, I'd say you're a lot closer than sisters."

"You're absolutely right," Darcy said quietly.

The Sheridan Gallery on Seventy-eighth Street, just east of Madison Avenue, was in the midst of an auction. The contents of the vast country home of Mason Gates, the late oil baron, had drawn an overflow crowd of dealers and collectors. Chris Sheridan observed the scene from the back of the room, reflecting with pleasure that it had been a coup to triumph over Sotheby's and Christie's for the privilege of auctioning this collection. Absolutely magnificent furniture from the Queen Anne period; paintings distinguished less by their technique than by their rarity; Revere silver that he knew would set off feverish bidding.

At thirty-three, Chris Sheridan still looked more like the linebacker he had been in college than a leading authority on antique furniture. His six-four height was accentuated by his straight carriage. His broad shoulders tapered down to a trim waist. His sandy hair framed a strong-featured face. His blue eyes were disarming and friendly. As his competitors had learned, however, those eyes could quickly take on a keen, no-nonsense glint.

Chris folded his arms as he watched the final bids on a 1683 Domenico Cucci cabinet with panels of pietra dura and central reliefs of inlaid stones. Smaller and less elaborate than the pair Cucci made for Louis XIV, it was nevertheless a magnificent, flawless piece that he knew the Met wanted desperately.

The room quieted as the bidding between the two high-stakes players, the Met and the representative of a Japanese bank, continued. A tug on his arm made Chris turn with a distracted frown. It was Sarah Johnson, his executive assistant, an art expert whom he had coaxed away from a private museum in Boston. Her expression reflected concern. "Chris, I'm afraid there's a problem," she said.

"Your mother's on the phone. She says she has to talk to you immediately. She sounds pretty upset."

"The problem is that damn program!" Chris strode toward the door, shoved it open, and, ignoring the elevator, raced up the stairs.

A month ago the popular television series *True Crimes* had run a segment about the unsolved murder of Chris's twin sister, Nan. At nineteen, Nan had been strangled while jogging near their home in Darien, Connecticut. Despite his vehement protests, Chris had not been able to prevent the camera crews from filming long shots of the house and grounds, nor from reenacting Nan's death in the nearby wooded area where her body had been found.

He had pleaded with his mother not to watch the program, but she had insisted on viewing it with him. The producers had managed to find a young actress who bore a startling resemblance to Nan. The docudrama showed her jogging; the figure watching her from the protection of the trees; the confrontation; the attempt to escape, the killer tackling her, choking her, pulling the Nike from her right foot and replacing it with a high-heeled slipper.

The commentary was delivered by an announcer whose sonorous voice sounded gratuitously horrified. "Was it a stranger who accosted beautiful, gifted Nan Sheridan? She and her twin celebrated their nineteenth birthday the night before at the family mansion. Did someone Nan knew, someone who perhaps toasted her on her birthday, become her killer? In fifteen years no one has come forward with a shred of information that might solve this hideous crime. Was Nan Sheridan the random victim of a deranged monster, or was her death an act of personal vengeance?"

A montage of closing shots followed. The house and grounds from a different angle. The phone number to call "if you have any information." The last closeup was the police photo of Nan's body as it had been found, neatly placed on the ground, her hands folded together on her waist, her left foot still wearing the Nike, her right foot in the sequined slipper.

The final line: "Where are the mates to this sneaker, to this graceful evening shoe? Does the killer still have them?"

Greta Sheridan had watched the program dry-eyed. When it was finished, she'd said, "Chris, I've gone over it in my mind so often. That's why I wanted to see this. I couldn't function after Nan died, couldn't think. But Nan used to talk to me so much about everyone at school. I . . . I just thought that seeing that program might make me recall something that could be important. Remember the day of the funeral? That huge crowd. All those young people from college. Remember Chief Harriman said that he was convinced her killer was sitting there among the mourners? Remember how they had cameras set up to take pictures of everyone in the funeral home and at church?"

Then, as though a giant hand had smashed her face, Greta Sheridan had broken into heart-rending sobs. "That girl looked so much like Nan, didn't she? Oh Chris, I've missed her so much all these years. Dad would still be alive if she were here. That heart attack was his way of grieving."

I wish I'd taken an ax to every television in the house before I let Mother watch that damn program, Chris thought as he ran down the corridor to his office. The fingers of his left hand drummed on the desk as he grabbed the phone. "Mother, what's wrong?"

Greta Sheridan's voice was tense and unsteady. "Chris, I'm sorry to bother you during the auction, but the strangest letter just came."

Another fallout from that stinking program, Chris fumed. All those crank letters. They ranged from psychics offering to conduct seances to people begging for money in exchange for their prayers. "I wish you wouldn't read that garbage," he said. "Those letters tear you apart."

"Chris, this one is different. It says that in memory of Nan, a dancing girl from Manhattan is going to die on the evening of February nineteenth in exactly the way Nan died." Greta Sheridan's voice rose. "Chris, suppose this isn't a crank letter? Is there anything we can do? Is there anyone we can warn?"

Doug Fox pulled on his tie, carefully twisted it into a precise knot, and studied himself in the mirror. He'd had a facial yesterday and his skin glowed. The body wave had made his thinning hair seem abundant and the sandy rinse completely covered the touch of gray that was emerging at his temples.

A good-looking guy, he assured himself, admiring the way his crisp white shirt followed the lines of his muscular chest and slim waist. He reached for his suit jacket, quietly appreciating the fine feel of the Scottish wool. Dark blue with faint pinstripes, accented by the small red print on his Hermès tie. He looked every inch the part of the investment banker, upstanding citizen of Scarsdale, devoted husband of Susan Frawley Fox, father of four lively, handsome youngsters.

No one, Doug thought with amused satisfaction, would suspect him of his other life: that of the single freelance illustrator with an apartment in the blessed anonymity of London Terrace on West

Twenty-third Street, plus a hideaway in Pawling and a new Volvo station wagon.

Doug took a final look in the long mirror, adjusted his pocket handkerchief, and with a glance to make sure he hadn't forgotten anything, walked to the door. The bedroom always irritated him. Antique French provincial furniture, damn place done by an upscale interior designer, and Susan still managed to make it look like the inside of Fibber McGee's closet. Clothes piled on the chaise, silver toilet articles haphazardly strewn over the top of the dresser. Kindergarten drawings taped on the wall. Let me out, Doug thought.

The kitchen was the scene of the usual mayhem. Thirteen-year-old Donny and twelve-year-old Beth jamming food in their mouths. Susan warning that the school bus was down the block. The baby waddling around with a wet diaper and grubby hands.

Trish saying she didn't want to go to kindergarten this afternoon, she wanted to stay home and watch "All My Children" with Mommy.

Susan was wearing an old flannel robe over her nightgown. She had been a very pretty girl when they were married. A pretty girl who'd let herself go. She smiled at Doug and poured him coffee. "Won't you have pancakes or something?"

"No." Would she ever stop asking him to stuff his face every morning? Doug jumped back as the baby tried to embrace his leg. "Damn it, Susan, if you can't keep him clean, at least don't let him near me. I can't go to the office looking grubby."

"Bus!" Beth yelled. "Bye, Mom. Bye, Dad."

Donny grabbed his books. "Can you come to my basketball game tonight, Dad?"

"Won't be home till late, son. An important meeting. Next time for sure, I promise."

"Sure." Donny slammed the door as he left.

Three minutes later, Doug was in the Mercedes heading for the train station, Susan's reproachful "Try not to be too late" ringing in his ears. Doug felt himself begin to unwind. Thirty-six years old and stuck with a fat wife, four noisy kids, a house in the suburbs. The American Dream. At twenty-two he'd thought he was making a smart move when he married Susan.

Unfortunately, marrying the daughter of a wealthy man wasn't the same as marrying wealth. Susan's father was a tightwad. Lend, never give. That motto had to be tattooed on his brain.

It wasn't that he didn't love the kids or that he wasn't fond enough of Susan. It was just that he should have waited to get into this paterfamilias routine. He'd thrown his youth away. As Douglas Fox, investment banker, upstanding citizen of Scarsdale, his life was an exercise in boredom.

He parked and ran for the train, consoling himself with the thought that as Doug Fields, bachelor artist, prince of the personals, his life was swift and secretive, and when the dark needs came there was a way to satisfy them.

~ 3

WEDNESDAY
February 20

On Wednesday evening, Darcy arrived at Nona Roberts's office promptly at six-thirty. She'd had a meeting with a client on Riverside Drive and phoned Nona to suggest they cab over to the restaurant together.

Nona's office was a cluttered box in a row of cluttered boxes on the tenth floor of the Hudson Cable Network. It held a somewhat battered oak desk piled with papers, several filing cabinets, the drawers of which did not fully close, shelves of reference books and tapes, a distinctly uninviting-looking love seat, and an executive swivel chair which Darcy knew no longer swiveled. A plant which Nona consistently forgot to water drooped wearily on the narrow windowsill.

Nona loved that office. Darcy privately wondered why it didn't destroy itself by spontaneous combustion. When she arrived, Nona was on the phone, so she went out seeking water for the plant. "It's begging for mercy," she said when she returned.

Nona had just completed the call. She jumped up to embrace Darcy. "A green thumb I have not." She was wearing a khaki wool jumpsuit that faithfully followed the lines of her small frame. A narrow leather belt with a white-gold clasp sculpted in the form of linked hands cinched her waist. Her medium-blond hair, streaked with touches of gray, was blunt-cut and barely reached her chin. Her animated face was interesting rather than pretty.

Darcy was glad to see that the pain in Nona's dark brown eyes had been almost completely replaced by an expression of wry humor. Nona's recent divorce had hit her hard. As she put it, "It's traumatic enough turning forty without your husband bumping you for a twenty-one-year-old nymphet."

"I'm running late," Nona apologized. "We're meeting Erin at seven?"

"Between seven and seven-fifteen," Darcy said, her fingers itching to skim the dead leaves from the plant.

"Fifteen minutes to get over there, provided I throw myself in front of an empty cab. Terrific. There's one thing I'd like to do before we go. Why don't you come with me and witness the compassionate side of television."

"I wasn't aware it had one." Darcy reached for her shoulder bag.

All the offices rimmed a large central area which was crowded with secretaries and writers at their desks. Computers hummed and fax machines clattered. At the end of the room, an announcer was on camera giving a news update. Nona waved a general greeting as she passed. "There isn't a single unattached person in that maze who isn't answering the personal ads for me. As a matter of fact, I suspect there are some supposedly attached guys who are also quietly getting together with an intriguing box number."

She led Darcy into a screening room and introduced her to Joan Nye, a pretty blonde who didn't look more than twenty-two. "Joan does the obits," she explained. "She just finished updating an important one and asked me to take a look at it." She turned to Nye. "I know it will be fine," she added reassuringly.

Joan sighed. "I hope so," she said, and pushed the button to start the film rolling.

The face of film great Ann Bouchard filled the screen. The mellifluous voice of Gary Finch, the Hudson Cable anchorman, was properly subdued as he began to speak.

> "Ann Bouchard won her first Oscar at the age of nineteen, when she replaced ailing Lillian Marker in the 1928 classic *Perilous Path*. . . ."

Film clips of Ann Bouchard in her most memorable roles were followed by highlights of her personal life: her seven husbands, her homes, her well-publicized battles with studio executives, excerpts of interviews throughout her long career, her emotional response to receiving a lifetime achievement award: "I have been blessed. I have been loved. And I love you all."

It was over. "I didn't know Ann Bouchard died," Darcy exclaimed. "My God, she was on the phone with my mother last week. When did that happen?"

"It didn't," Nona said. "We prepare the celebrity obits in advance just the way the newspapers do. And we regularly update them. The farewell to George Burns was revised twenty-two times. When the inevitable occurs, we just have to drop in the lead. The rather irreverent name for the project is the Toodle-oo Club."

"Toodle-oo Club?"

"Uh-huh. We do the final portion and say toodle-oo to the deceased." She turned to Nye. "That was terrific. I'm positively blinking back tears. Incidentally, have you answered any new personals?"

Nye grinned. "It may cost you, Nona. The other night I made a date to meet some jerk. Naturally got caught in traffic. Double-parked my car to rush in and let him know I'd be right back. Rushed out to find a cop ticketing me. Finally found a garage six blocks away and when I came back—"

"He was gone," Nona suggested.

Nye's eyes widened. "How did you know?"

"Because I've heard this from some other people. Don't take it personally. Now we'd better run." At the door Nona called over her shoulder, "Give me the ticket. I'll take care of it."

In the cab on the way to meet Erin, Darcy found herself wondering what it was that made someone pull a trick like that. Nye was genuinely attractive. Was she too young for the man she had met? When she answered the ad she must have given her age. Did he have some image in mind that Nye didn't fit?

It was a disquieting thought. As the cab bumped and lurched through Seventy-second Street traffic, she commented, "Nona, when we started answering these ads, I thought of it as a joke. Now I'm not so sure. It's like having a blind date without the security of being introduced to the guy because he's the best friend of somebody's brother. Can you imagine any man you know doing that? Even if for some reason Nye's date hated the way she dressed or wore her hair or whatever, all he had to do was have a quick drink and say he was rushing for a plane. He still gets away fast and doesn't leave her feeling like a fool."

"Darcy, let's face it," Nona said. "From all the reports I'm hearing, most of the people who place or answer these ads are pretty insecure. What's a lot more scary is that just today I got a letter from an FBI agent who'd heard about the program and said he wants to talk to me. He'd like us to include a warning that these ads are a natural for sexual psychopaths."

"What a lovely thought!"

* * *

As usual, Bella Vita offered encompassing warmth. The wonderful, familiar garlicky aroma was in the air. There was a faint hum of talk and laughter. Adam, the owner, greeted them. "Ah, the beautiful ladies. I have your table." He indicated one by the window.

"Erin should be along any minute," Darcy told him as they were seated. "I'm surprised she isn't waiting. She's always so prompt, it actually gives me a complex."

"She's probably stuck in traffic," Nona said. "Let's order wine. We know she'll have chablis."

Half an hour later, Darcy pushed her chair back. "I'm going to phone Erin. The only thing I can imagine is that when she delivered the necklace she designed for Bertolini's, there might have been some adjustment needed. She loses track of time when she's working."

The answering machine was on in Erin's studio apartment. Darcy returned to the table and realized Nona's anxious expression mirrored her own feelings. "I left a message that we're waiting for her and to call here if she can't make it."

They ordered dinner. Darcy loved this restaurant, but tonight she was hardly aware of what she was eating. Every few minutes she glanced at the door hoping that Erin would come flying in with a perfectly reasonable explanation of why she had been delayed.

She did not come.

Darcy lived on the top floor of a brownstone on East Forty-ninth Street, Nona in a co-op on Central Park West. When they left the restaurant they took separate cabs, promising that whoever heard from Erin first would contact the other.

The minute she got home, Darcy tried Erin's number again. She tried an hour later, just before she went to bed. This time she left an emphatic message. "Erin, I'm worried about you. It's Wednesday, 11:15. I don't care how late you get in, call me."

Eventually, Darcy fell into an uneasy sleep.

When she awakened at 6 a.m., her immediate thought was that Erin had not called.

Jay Stratton stared out the corner window of his thirtieth-floor apartment in Waterside Plaza on Twenty-fifth Street and the East River Drive. The view was spectacular: the East River arced by the Brooklyn and Williamsburg Bridges, the twin towers to the right, the Hudson behind them, the streams of traffic, agonizingly slow in the evening rush hour, flowing well enough now. It was seven-thirty.

Jay frowned, a gesture that caused his narrow eyes to become almost invisible. A head of dark brown hair, expensively cut and attractively threaded with gray, helped to foster his cultivated look of casual elegance. He was aware of the tendency of his waistline to thicken, and exercised vigorously. He knew he looked a bit older than his age, which was thirty-seven, but that had proved to be an advantage. He'd always been considered unusually handsome by most people.

Certainly the newspaper magnate's widow whom he'd escorted to the Taj Mahal casino in Atlantic City last week had found him attractive, though when he had mentioned that he'd like to have some jewelry created for her, her face turned to stone. "No sales pitch, please," she snapped. "Let's understand that."

He hadn't bothered with her again. Jay did not believe in wasting time. Today he'd lunched at the Jockey Club and while he waited for a table he'd started chatting with an older couple. The Ashtons were in New York on holiday celebrating their fortieth anniversary. Obviously well-heeled, they were somewhat at loose ends outside their familiar North Carolina surroundings and responded eagerly to his conversational overtures.

The husband had looked pleased at Jay's query as to whether he'd chosen a suitable piece of jewelry for his wife to commemorate their forty years together. "I keep telling Frances that she ought to let me buy her some real nice jewelry but she says to save the money for Frances Junior."

Jay had suggested that at some time in the distant future, Frances Junior might enjoy wearing a lovely necklace or bracelet and telling her own daughter or granddaughter that this was a very special gift from Grampa to Nana. "It's what royal families have been doing for centuries," he explained as he handed them his card.

The phone rang. Jay hurried to answer it. Maybe it was the Ashtons, he thought.

It was Aldo Marco, the manager at Bertolini's. "Aldo," Jay said heartily. "I was planning to call you. All's well, I trust?"

"All is certainly not well." Marco's tone was icy. "When you introduced me to Erin Kelley I was most impressed with her and her portfolio. The design she submitted was superb and as you know, we gave her our client's family gems to reset. The necklace was supposed to have been delivered this morning. Miss Kelley failed to keep the appointment and has not answered our repeated messages.

Mr. Stratton, I want either that necklace or my client's gems back immediately."

Jay ran his tongue over his lips. He realized the hand holding the phone was damp. He had forgotten about the necklace. He chose his answer carefully. "I saw Miss Kelley a week ago. She showed me the necklace. It was exquisite. There must be some misunderstanding."

"The misunderstanding is that she has failed to deliver the necklace, which is needed for an engagement party Friday night. I repeat, I want it or my client's gems back tomorrow. I hold you responsible to execute one or the other alternative. Is that clear?"

The sharp click of the phone sounded in Stratton's ears.

Michael Nash saw his last patient, Gerald Renquist, at five o'clock on Wednesday afternoon. Renquist was the retired CEO of an international pharmaceutical company. Retirement had thrown a man whose personal identity was linked to the intrigue and politics of the boardroom to the status of unwilling sideliner.

"I know I should consider myself lucky," Renquist was saying, "but I feel so damn useless. Even my wife pulled that old saw on me—'I married you for better or worse, but not for lunch.' "

"You must have had a game plan for retirement," Nash suggested mildly.

Renquist laughed. "I did. Avoid it at all cost."

Depression, Nash thought. The common cold of mental illness. He realized he was tired and not giving Renquist his full attention. Not fair, he told himself. He's paying for me to listen. Still, it was a distinct relief when at ten of six he was able to wrap up the session.

After Renquist left, Nash began to lock up. His office was on Seventy-first and Park, his apartment on the twentieth floor of the same building. He went out through the door that led to the lobby. The new tenant in 20B, a blonde in her early thirties, was waiting for the elevator. He fought down irritation at the prospect of riding up with her. The undisguised interest in her eyes was a nuisance, as were her almost inevitable invitations to drop in for a drink.

Michael Nash had the same problem with a number of his women patients. He could read their minds. Nice-looking guy, divorced, no children, mid-to-late thirties, available. A diffident reserve had become second nature to him.

At least tonight the new neighbor did not repeat the invitation.

Maybe she was learning. When they stepped from the elevator, he murmured, "Good night."

His apartment reflected the precise care he took with everything in his life. Ivory flax upholstery on the twin sofas in the living room was repeated on the dining room chairs surrounding the round oak table. That table had been a find at an antique auction in Bucks County. The area carpets had muted geometric patterns on an ivory background. A wall of bookcases, plants on the windowsills, a Colonial dry sink which served as a bar, bric-a-brac he'd gathered on trips abroad, good paintings. A comfortable, handsome room.

The kitchen and study were to the left of the living room, the bedroom suite and bath to the right. A pleasant apartment and an attractive complement to the big place in Bridgewater that had been his parents' pride and joy. Nash was often tempted to sell it, but knew he'd miss riding on weekends.

He took off his jacket and debated between watching the tail end of the six o'clock news or listening to his new compact disc, a Mozart symphony. Mozart won. As the familiar opening bars softly filled the room, the doorbell rang.

Nash knew exactly who it would be. Resigned, he answered it. The new neighbor stood holding an ice bucket—the oldest trick in the book. Thank God he hadn't started to mix his drink. He gave her the ice, explained that no, he couldn't join her, he was on his way out, and steered her to the door. When she was gone, still twittering about "Maybe next time," he made straight for the bar, mixed a dry martini, and ruefully shook his head.

Settling on the sofa near the window, he sipped the cocktail, appreciating its smooth, soothing taste, and wondered about the young woman he was meeting for dinner at eight o'clock. Her response to his ad had been downright amusing.

His publisher was ecstatic about the first half of the book he was writing, the book analyzing the people who placed or answered personal ads, their psychological needs, their flights into fantasy in the way they described themselves.

His working title was *The Personal Ads: Quest for Companionship or Departure from Reality?*

4

THURSDAY
February 21

Darcy sat at the dinette table, sipping coffee and staring unseeingly out the window at the gardens below. Barren now, scattered with unmelted snow, in the summer they were exquisitely planted and manicured to perfection. The prestigious owners of the private brownstones they backed included the Aga Khan and Katharine Hepburn.

Erin loved to come over when the gardens were in bloom. "From the street you'd never guess they exist," she'd sigh. "I swear, Darce, you sure lucked out when you found this place."

Erin. Where was she? The minute she woke up and realized that Erin had not phoned, Darcy had called the nursing home in Massachusetts. Mr. Kelley's condition was unchanged. The semi-comatose state could go on indefinitely, although he was certainly getting weaker. No, there had been no emergency call to his daughter. The day nurse really couldn't say if Erin had made her usual phone call last evening.

"What should I do?" Darcy wondered aloud. Report her missing? Call the police and inquire about accidents?

A sudden thought made her shiver. Suppose Erin had had an accident in the apartment. She had a habit of tilting back in her chair when she was concentrating. Suppose she'd been lying there unconscious all this time!

It took her three minutes to throw on a sweater and slacks, grab a coat and gloves. She waited agonizing minutes on Second Avenue before getting a cab.

"One-oh-one Christopher Street, and please hurry."

"Everybody says 'hurry.' I say take it easy, you'll live longer." The cabbie winked into the rearview mirror.

Darcy turned her head. She was in no mood to banter with the driver. Why hadn't she thought of the possibility of an accident? Last month, just before she went to California, Erin had dropped by for dinner. They'd watched the news. One of the commercials showed a frail old woman falling and getting help by touching the emergency signal on a chain around her neck. "That'll be us in fifty years," Erin had said. She'd imitated the commercial, moaning, "Hel-l-l-p, hel-l-l-p! I've fallen, and I can't get up!"

Gus Boxer, the superintendent of 101 Christopher Street, had an eye for pretty women. That was why when he hurried to the lobby to answer the persistent ring of the doorbell, his annoyed scowl was quickly replaced by an ingratiating twist of his mouth.

He liked what he saw. The visitor's light brown hair was tossed by the wind. It fell forward on her face, reminding him of the Veronica Lake movies he stayed up to watch. Her hip-length leather jacket was old but had that classy look that Gus had come to recognize since taking this job in Greenwich Village.

His appraising eyes lingered on her long, slim legs. Then he realized why she looked familiar. He'd seen her a couple of times with 3B, Erin Kelley. He opened the vestibule door and stepped aside.

"At your service," he said in what he considered to be a winning manner.

Darcy walked past him, trying not to show her distaste. From time to time, Erin complained about the sixty-year-old Casanova in dirty flannel. "Boxer gives me the creeps," she'd said. "I hate the idea he has a master key to my place. Once I walked in and found him there and he gave me some cock-and-bull story about a leak in the wall."

"Was anything ever missing?" Darcy had asked.

"No. I keep any jewelry I'm working on in the safe. There's nothing else worth pocketing. It's more that he has a nasty, flirtatious way about him that makes my skin crawl. Oh well. I've got a safety bolt when I'm inside and the place is cheap. He's probably harmless."

Darcy came straight to the point. "I'm concerned about Erin Kelley," she told the superintendent. "She was supposed to meet me last night and didn't show up. She doesn't answer her phone. I want to check her apartment. Something may have happened to her."

Boxer squinted. "She was okay yesterday."

"Yesterday?"

Thick lids drooped over faded eyes. Parted lips were moistened with his tongue. His forehead collapsed into erratic lines. "No, I'm wrong. I seen her Tuesday. Late afternoon. She come in with some groceries." His tone became virtuous. "I offered to carry 'em up for her."

"That was Tuesday afternoon. Did you see her go out or return Tuesday evening?"

"Nope. Can't say I did. But listen, I'm not a doorman. Tenants have their own keys. Delivery guys gotta use the intercom to get let in."

Darcy nodded. Knowing it was useless, she had rung Erin's apartment before she buzzed for the superintendent. "Please. I'm afraid there may be something wrong. I've got to get into her place. Do you have your passkey?"

The twisted smile returned. "You gotta understand, I don't normally let people into an apartment just because they wanna go in. But I seen you with Kelley. I know you're friends. You're like her. Classy. Good-lookin'."

Ignoring the compliment, Darcy started up the stairs.

The stairs and landings were clean but dreary. The patched walls were battleship gray, the tiles on the steps uneven. Walking into Erin's apartment had the effect of going from a cave into daylight. When Erin moved here three years ago, Darcy had helped her paint and paper. They'd hired a U-Haul and made forays into Connecticut and New Jersey for garage-sale furnishings.

They'd painted the walls a stark white. Colorful Indian rugs were scattered over the scratched but polished parquet floor. Framed museum posters were arranged over a studio couch that was covered in bright red velour and piled with vividly assorted throw pillows.

The windows faced the street. Even though the sky was overcast, the light was excellent. Under the windows a long worktable held Erin's supplies neatly placed side by side: torch, hand drill, files and pliers, ring clamps and spring tweezers, soldering block, gauges, drills. Darcy had always been fascinated to watch Erin at work, her slender fingers skillfully handling delicate gems.

Next to the table was Erin's one extravagance, a tall chest with several dozen narrow drawers. A nineteenth-century pharmaceutical cabinet, the bottom drawers were a facade concealing a safe. One easy chair, a television, and a good stereo system completed the pleasant room.

Darcy's immediate impression was a surge of relief. There was nothing out of order here. Gus Boxer at her heels, she walked swiftly into the tiny kitchen, a small windowless cubicle that they'd painted a bright yellow and decorated with framed tea towels.

The narrow hallway led to the bedroom. The pewter and brass bed and a two-on-three dresser were the only furniture in the closet-sized room. The bed was made. There was nothing out of place.

Clean, dry towels were on the rack in the bathroom. Darcy opened the medicine chest. With a practiced eye, she noted that Erin's toothbrush, cosmetics and creams were all there.

Boxer was becoming impatient. "Looks okay to me. You satisfied?"

"No." Darcy went back into the living room and walked over to the worktable. The message machine showed twelve calls had come in. She pressed playback.

"Hey, I don't know—"

She cut off Boxer's protest. "Erin is missing. Have you got that straight? She's *missing.* I'm going to listen to these messages and see if they might somehow give me an idea of where she might be. Then I'm going to call the police and inquire about accidents. For all I know, she's unconscious in a hospital somewhere. You can stay here with me or if you're busy, you can go. Which is it?"

Boxer shrugged. "I guess it's okay to leave you here."

Darcy turned her back on him, reached into her purse, and took out her notebook and pen. She did not hear Boxer leave as the messages began. The first one had come on Tuesday evening at six forty-five. Someone named Tom Swartz. Thanks for answering his ad. Just discovered a great little inexpensive restaurant. Could they meet for dinner? He'd phone again.

Erin was supposed to meet Charles North on Tuesday evening at seven o'clock at a pub near Washington Square. By quarter of seven she had undoubtedly already left, Darcy thought.

The next call came in at seven twenty-five. Michael Nash. "Erin, I certainly enjoyed meeting you and hope you might be free for dinner sometime this week. If you have a chance, call me back this evening." Nash left both his home and office numbers.

Wednesday morning the calls began at nine o'clock. The first few were run-of-the-mill business-related. The one that made Darcy's throat close was from an Aldo Marco of Bertolini's. "Miss Kelley, I am disappointed you did not keep our ten o'clock appointment. It is essential that I see the necklace and be sure there is no last-minute adjustment necessary. Please get back to me immediately."

That call had come in at eleven. There were three more follow-ups from the same man, increasing in irritation and urgency. Besides Darcy's own messages, there was another one concerning the Bertolini assignment.

"Erin, this is Jay Stratton. What's going on? Marco's bugging me for the necklace and holding me responsible for bringing you to him."

Darcy knew that Stratton was the jeweler who had given Erin's portfolio to Bertolini's. His message came in around seven Wednesday evening. Darcy started to push the rewind button, then paused. Maybe it would be better not to erase these. She looked in the phone book for the number of the nearest precinct. "I want to report someone missing," she said when the call was answered. She was told that she would have to come in personally, that this kind of information about a competent adult could not be accepted over the phone.

I'll stop there on my way home, Darcy thought. She went into the kitchen and made coffee, noting that the only milk container was unopened. Erin started her day with coffee and always drank it light. Boxer had seen her with groceries Tuesday afternoon. Darcy looked into the garbage pail under the sink. There were a few odds and ends, but no empty milk container. She wasn't here yesterday morning, Darcy thought. She never got back Tuesday night.

She brought the coffee back to the worktable. A daily reminder was in the top drawer. She flipped through it, starting with today. There were no appointments listed. Yesterday, Wednesday, there were two: Bertolini's, 10 A.M.; Bella Vita, 7 P.M. (Darcy and Nona).

In the preceding weeks, there were notations of dates with names of men unfamiliar to Darcy. They were usually scheduled between five and seven o'clock. Most of them had the meeting place listed: O'Neal's, Mickey Mantle's, P. J. Clarke's, the Plaza, the Sheraton . . . all hotel cocktail lounges and popular pubs.

The phone rang. Let it be Erin, Darcy prayed as she grabbed it. "Hello."

"Erin?" A man's voice.

"No. This is Darcy Scott. Erin's friend."

"Do you know where I can reach Erin?"

Disappointment, intense and overwhelming, swept over Darcy. "Who is this?"

"Jay Stratton."

Jay Stratton had left the message about the Bertolini jewelry. What was he saying?

". . . if you have any idea where Erin is, please tell her that if they don't get that necklace, they'll file a criminal complaint."

Darcy's eyes flickered to the pharmaceutical cabinet. She knew that Erin kept the combination in her address book under the name of the safe company. Stratton was still talking.

"I know Erin kept that necklace in a safe in her studio. Is there any possibility you can check to see if it's there?" he urged.

"Hold on a minute." Darcy put her hand over the speaker, then thought, What a dumb thing to do. There's no one here I can ask. But in a way she was asking Erin. If the necklace wasn't in the safe, it might mean that Erin had been the victim of a robbery when she attempted to deliver it. If it was there, it was almost certain proof that something had happened to her. Nothing would have kept Erin from delivering the necklace on time.

She opened Erin's address book and turned to D. Next to Dalton Safe was the series of numbers. "I have the combination," she told Stratton. "I'll wait for you to come here. I don't want to open Erin's safe without a witness. And in case the necklace is here, I'll want a receipt for it from you."

He said he'd be right over. After she replaced the receiver, Darcy decided that she'd ask the superintendent to be present as well. She didn't know anything about Jay Stratton except that Erin told her he was a jeweler and the one who got her the Bertolini commission.

While she waited, Darcy went through Erin's files. Under "Project Personal," she found sheets of personal columns torn from magazines and newspapers. On each page a number of the ads were circled. Were these the ones Erin had answered, or had thought about answering? Dismayed, Darcy realized that there were at least two dozen of them. Which, if any of them, had been placed by Charles North, the man Erin was to meet on Tuesday evening?

When she and Erin agreed to answer the personal ads, they'd gone about it systematically. They'd had inexpensive letterheads made with only their names at the top. They'd each chosen a favorite snapshot to send when requested. They'd spent a hilarious evening composing letters they had no intentions of sending. "I love to clean clean clean," Erin had suggested, "my favorite hobby is doing the wash by hand. I inherited my grandmother's scrub board. My cousin wanted it too. It caused a big family fight. I get a little nasty during my period, but I'm a very good person. Please call soon."

They had finally come up with what they decided were reasonably alluring responses. When Darcy was leaving for California, Erin had said, "Darce, I'll send yours out about two weeks before you're due back. I'll just change a sentence here or there to fit the ad."

Erin didn't own a computer. Darcy knew she typed out the responses on her electric typewriter but did not Xerox them. She kept all the input in the notebook she carried in her purse: the box numbers of the ads she answered, the names of the people she called, her impressions of the ones she dated.

Jay Stratton leaned back in the cab, his eyes half-closed. The speaker behind his right ear was blaring rock music. "Will you turn that down?" he snapped.

"Man, you trying to deprive me of my music?" The cabbie was in his early twenties. Wispy, snarled hair hung around his neck. He glanced over his shoulder, caught the look on Stratton's face, and, muttering under his breath, lowered the volume.

Stratton felt sweat forming in his armpits. He had to pull this off. He tapped his pocket. The receipts Erin had given him for the Bertolini gems and for the diamonds he'd given her last week were in his wallet. Darcy Scott sounded smart. He mustn't arouse the slightest suspicion.

The nosy superintendent must have been watching for him. He was in the foyer when Stratton arrived. Obviously, he recognized him. "I'll bring you up," he said. "I'm supposed to stay while she opens the safe."

Stratton swore to himself as he followed the squat figure up the stairs. He didn't need two witnesses.

When Darcy opened the door for them, Stratton's face was set in a pleasant, somewhat-concerned expression. He had planned to sound reassuring, but the worry in Scott's eyes warned him against banalities. Instead, he agreed with her that something must be dreadfully wrong.

Smart girl, he thought. Darcy had obviously memorized the combination of the safe. She was not about to let anyone know where Erin kept it. She had a pad and pen ready. "I want to itemize everything we find in there."

Stratton deliberately turned his back while she twisted the dial, then crouched beside her as she pulled the door open. The safe was fairly deep. Boxes and pouches lined the shelves.

"Let me hand everything out to you," he suggested. "I'll describe what we find. You write it down."

Darcy hesitated, then realized it was a sensible suggestion. He was the jeweler. His arm was brushing against hers. Instinctively, she moved aside.

Stratton looked over his shoulder. An irritated-looking Boxer was lighting a cigarette and glancing around the room, probably searching for an ashtray. It was Stratton's only chance. "I think that velvet case is the one Erin kept the necklace in." Reaching for it, he deliberately knocked a small box onto the floor.

Darcy jumped as she saw the glitter of stones scattering around her and scrambled to collect them. An instant later Stratton was beside her, cursing his carelessness. They searched the area thoroughly. "I'm sure we got them all," he said. "These are semiprecious, suitable for good costume jewelry. But more important . . ." He opened the velvet case. "Here's the Bertolini."

Darcy stared down at the exquisite necklace. Emeralds, diamonds, sapphires, moonstones, opals, and rubies were set in an elaborate design that reminded her of the medieval jewelry she'd seen in portraits at the Metropolitan Museum of Art.

"Lovely, isn't it?" Stratton asked. "You can understand why the manager at Bertolini's was so upset at the prospect of something happening to it. Erin is remarkably gifted. She not only managed to create a setting that made those stones look ten times their own considerable value, but she did it in the Byzantine style. The family who commissioned the necklace was originally from Russia. These gems were the only valuable possessions they were able to take when they fled in 1917."

Darcy could visualize Erin sitting at this worktable, her ankles around the rungs of the chair, the way she used to sit when she was studying in college. The sense of impending disaster was overwhelming. Where would Erin willingly go without delivering this necklace on time?

Nowhere *willingly,* she decided.

Biting her lip to keep it from quivering, she picked up the pen. "Will you describe this for me and I think we should identify every precious stone in it so there's no question that any are missing."

As Stratton removed other pouches, velvet cases, and boxes from the safe, she noticed that he was becoming increasingly more agitated. Finally he said, "I'm going to open the rest all at once, then we'll list them." He looked directly at her. "The Bertolini necklace is here, but a pouch I gave Erin with a quarter of a million dollars worth of diamonds is gone."

Darcy left the apartment with Stratton. "I'm going to the police station to file a missing-person report," she told him.

"You're absolutely right," he said. "I'll take care of getting the necklace to Bertolini's immediately and if we haven't heard from Erin in a week, I'll contact the insurance company about the diamonds."

It was exactly noon when Darcy entered the Sixth Precinct on Charles Street. At her insistence that something was terribly wrong, a detective came out to see her. A tall black man in his mid-forties with military bearing, he introduced himself as Dean Thompson and listened sympathetically as he tried to allay her fears.

"We really can't file a missing-person report for an adult woman simply because no one has heard from her for a day or two," he explained. "It violates freedom of movement. What I will do if you give me her description is check it against accident reports."

Anxiously, Darcy gave the information. Five feet seven, one hundred and twenty pounds, auburn hair, blue eyes, twenty-eight years old. "Wait, I have her picture in my wallet."

Thompson studied it, then handed it back. "A very attractive woman." He gave her his card and asked for hers. "We'll keep in touch."

Susan Frawley Fox hugged five-year-old Trish and guided her reluctant feet to the waiting school bus that would take her to the afternoon session of kindergarten. Trish's woebegone face was on the verge of crumbling into tears. The baby, firmly held under Susan's other arm, reached down and pulled Trish's hair. It gave the needed excuse. Trish began to wail.

Susan bit her lip, torn between annoyance and sympathy. "He didn't hurt you and you're not staying home."

The bus driver, a matronly woman with a warm smile, said coaxingly, "Come on, Trish. You sit right up here near me."

Susan waved vigorously and sighed with relief as the bus pulled away. Shifting the baby's weight, she hurried from the corner back to their rambling brick and stucco home. Patches of snow still covered isolated sections of the lawn. The trees seemed stark and bloodless against the gray sky. In a few months the property would be lush with flowering hedges and the willows would be heavily laden with cascades of leaves. Even as a small child Susan had studied the willows for the first hint of spring.

She shoved the side door open, heated a bottle for the baby, brought him to his room, changed him, and put him down for a nap. Her quiet time had begun: the hour and a half before he woke up. She knew she should get busy. The beds weren't made. The kitchen was a mess. This morning Trish had wanted to make cupcakes, and spilled batter was still lumped on the table.

Susan glanced at the baking pan on the countertop and half-smiled. The cupcakes looked delicious. If only Trish wouldn't carry on so about kindergarten. It's almost March, Susan worried. What's it going to be like when she's in the first grade and has to be gone all day?

Doug blamed Susan for Trish's reluctance to go to school. "If you'd go out more yourself, have lunch at the club, volunteer for some committees, Trish would be used to being minded by other people."

Susan put the kettle on, sponged the table, and fixed a grilled cheese and bacon sandwich. There is a God, she thought gratefully as she reveled in the blessed silence.

Over a second cup of tea, she permitted herself to face the anger that was burning inside her. Doug hadn't come home again last night. When he stayed in for late meetings he used the company suite at the Gateway Hotel near his office in the World Trade Center. He got furious when she called him there. "Damn it, Susan, unless there's an earth-shattering emergency, give me a break. I can't be called out of meetings and by the time they're over it's usually well past midnight."

Taking the tea with her, Susan got up and walked down the long hall to the master bedroom. The antique full-length standing mirror was in the right-hand corner opposite the wall of closets. Deliberately, she stood in front of it and appraised herself.

Thanks to the baby's exploring fingers, her short, curly brown hair was disheveled. She seldom bothered with makeup during the day but really didn't need it. Her skin was clear and unlined, her complexion fresh. At five feet four she could certainly afford to lose fifteen pounds. She'd been one hundred and five when she and Doug were married fourteen years ago. Sweats and sneakers had become her daily wardrobe, especially since Trish and Conner were born.

I am thirty-five years old, Susan told herself. I could lose some weight, but contrary to what my husband thinks, I am not fat. I'm not a great housekeeper, but I know I'm a good mother. A good cook, too. I don't want to spend my time outside the house when I have young children who need me. Especially since their father won't give them the time of day.

She swallowed the rest of the tea, her anger building. Tuesday night when Donny came home from the basketball game, he had been in the never-never land between ecstasy and misery. He had sunk the winning shot. "Everybody stood up and cheered for me, Mom!" Then he added, "Dad was practically the only father who wasn't there."

Susan's heart had wrenched at the pain in her son's eyes. The babysitter had canceled at the last minute, which was why she hadn't been able to be at the game either. "This is an earth-shattering event," she'd said firmly. "Let's see if we can reach Dad and tell him all about it."

Douglas Fox was not registered at the hotel. There was no conference room in use. The suite kept for personnel of Keldon Equities was not being occupied.

"Probably some dumb new operator," Susan had told Donny, trying to keep her tone even.

"Sure, that's it, Mom." But Donny wasn't fooled. At dawn, Susan had awakened to the sound of muffled sobs. She'd stood outside Donny's door, knowing that he wouldn't want her to see him crying.

My husband doesn't love me or his children, Susan told her reflected image. He lies to us. He stays in New York a couple of nights a week. He's bullied me into almost never calling him. He's made me feel like a fat, frowsy, dull, useless clod. And I'm sick of it.

She turned from the mirror and analyzed the cluttered bedroom. I could be a lot more organized, she acknowledged. I used to be. When did I give up? When did I become so damn discouraged that it wasn't worth trying to please him?

Not hard to answer. Nearly two years ago, when she was pregnant with the baby. They'd had a Swedish au pair, and Susan was sure that Doug had had an affair with her.

Why didn't I face it then? she wondered as she began to make the bed. Because I was still in love with him? Because I hated to admit my father was right about him?

She and Doug had been married a week after she was graduated from Bryn Mawr. Her father offered her a trip around the world if she'd change her mind. "Under that schoolboy charm, there's a foul-tempered sneak," he had warned her.

I went into it with my eyes open, Susan acknowledged, as she returned to the kitchen. If Dad had known the half of it, he'd have had a stroke, she thought.

There was a pile of magazines on the wall desk in the kitchen. She riffled through them until she found the one she was looking for. An issue of *People* with an article about a female private investigator in Manhattan. Professional women hired her to check out the men they were considering marrying. She also handled divorce cases.

Susan got the phone number from information and dialed it. When she reached the investigator, she was able to make an appointment for the following Monday, February 25th. "I believe my husband is seeing other women," she explained quietly. "I am thinking of divorce, and I want to know all about his activities."

When she hung up she resisted the temptation to simply sit and continue to think things through. Instead, she attacked the kitchen vigorously. Time to shape up this place. By summer, with any luck, it would be on the market.

It wouldn't be easy raising four children alone. Susan knew that Doug would pay little if any attention to the kids after the divorce. He was a splashy spender but cheap in hundreds of little ways. He'd balk at adequate child support. But it would be a lot easier to live on a tight budget than to go on with this farce.

The telephone rang. It was Doug, complaining again about the damn late meetings these last two nights. He was exhausted today and they still hadn't settled everything. He'd be home tonight, but late. Real late.

"Don't worry, dear," Susan said soothingly. "I understand perfectly."

The country road was narrow, winding, and dark. Charley didn't pass a single other car. His driveway was almost hidden by brush at the point where it intersected the road. A secret and quiet place, removed from curious eyes. He'd bought it six years ago. An estate sale. Estate giveaway was more like it. The place had been owned by an eccentric bachelor who as a hobby renovated it himself.

Built in 1902, the exterior was unpretentious. Inside, the renovation had consisted of turning the entire first floor into one open room, complete with a kitchen area and fireplace. Wide plank oak flooring shone with a satiny finish. The furniture was Pennsylvania Dutch, austere, handsome.

Charley had added a long upholstered couch covered in maroon tapestry, a matching chair, an area rug between the couch and fireplace.

The second floor was exactly as he'd found it. Two small rooms made into one decent-sized bedroom. Shaker furniture, a carved headboard bed and tall chest. Both made of pine. The original tub, free-standing on claw feet, had been left in the modernized bath.

Only the basement was different. The eight-foot freezer that no longer held an ounce of food, the freezer where, when necessary, he left the bodies of the girls. Here, ice maidens, they'd waited for their graves to be dug under the warming rays of the spring sun. There was a worktable in the basement as well, the worktable with a stack of ten cardboard shoe boxes. There was only one left to decorate.

A charming house nestled in the woods. He'd never brought anyone here until two years ago when he'd begun to dream about Nan. Before that, owning the house had been enough. When he wanted to escape, this was his retreat. The aloneness. The ability to pretend that he was dancing with beautiful girls. He'd play old movies on the VCR, movies in which he became Fred Astaire and danced with Ginger Rogers and Rita Hayworth and Leslie Caron. He'd follow Astaire's graceful movements until he could step with his every step, mimic the way Astaire would turn his body. Always he sensed Ginger and Rita and Leslie and Fred's other partners in his arms, their eyes worshipful, loving the music, loving the dance.

Then one day, two years ago, it was over. In the middle of the dance, Ginger drifted away and Nan was in Charley's arms again. Just like the moments after he killed her, waltzing on the jogging path, her light, svelte body so easy to hold, her head lolling on his shoulder.

When that memory came back, he'd run to the basement and taken the mates of the sequined dancing slipper and the Nike that he'd left on her feet from the shoe box and cradled them in his arms while he swayed to the music on the stereo. It was like being with Nan again, and he'd known what he had to do.

First he'd set up a hidden video camera so he could relive every single moment of what was to happen. Then he'd begun to bring the girls here one by one. Erin was the eighth to die here. But Erin would not join the others in the wooded fields that surrounded the house. Tonight he would move Erin's body. He had decided exactly where he would leave her.

The station wagon moved silently down the driveway, around to the back of the house. He stopped at the metal doors that led to the basement.

Charley's breath began to come in short, excited gasps. He reached for the handle to open the back door of the wagon, then stood irresolutely. Every instinct warned him not to delay. He must lift Erin's body from the freezer, carry it to the car, drive back to the city, leave it on the abandoned Fifty-sixth Street dock bordering the West Side Highway. But the thought of watching the video of Erin, of dancing with her just one more time, was irresistible.

Charley hurried around the house to the front door, let himself in, snapped on the light, and without bothering to remove his overcoat ran across the room to the VCR. Erin's tape was on top of the others on the cabinet. He popped it in and sat back on the couch, smiling in anticipation.

The tape began to play.

Erin, so pretty, smiling, coming in the door, exclaiming with delight over the house. "I envy you this haven." He fixing a drink for them. She sitting curled on the couch. He sitting across from her in the easy chair, getting up and setting a match to the kindling in the fireplace.

"Don't bother to light a fire," she'd told him. "I really must get back."

"Even for half an hour it's worth it," he'd assured her. Then he'd turned on the stereo, muted, soft, and pleasant, the songs of the forties "Our next date is going to be at the Rainbow Room," he said. "You enjoy dancing as much as I do."

Erin had laughed. The lamp beside her accentuated the glints of red in her auburn hair. "As I wrote when I answered your ad, I love to dance."

He'd stood up, held out his arms. "How about now?" Then, as though struck by a thought, said, "Wait a minute. Let's do this right. What shoe size are you? Seven? Seven and a half? Eight?"

"Seven and a half narrow."

"Perfect. Believe it or not, I have a pair of evening slippers that should fit you. My sister asked me to pick up a pair she had ordered in that size. Like the good big brother I did as I was told. Then she phoned and told me to take them back. She'd found a pair she liked better."

Erin had laughed with him. "Just like a kid sister."

"I'm not going to be bothered running around returning them." The camera stayed on her, catching her smiling, content expression as she looked around the room.

He'd gone up to the bedroom, opened the closet where boxes of new evening shoes were lined up on the shelf. He'd bought the ones he'd chosen for her in a variety of sizes. Pink and silver. Open toes and backs. Heels as narrow as stilettos. A gossamer ankle strap. He reached for the pair that were seven and a half narrow and carried them down, still wrapped in tissue.

"Try these on, Erin."

Even then, she wasn't suspicious. "They're lovely."

He'd knelt and slipped off her ankle-top leather boots, his hands impersonal. She'd said, "Oh, really, I don't think . . ." Ignoring her protest, he'd fastened the slippers on her feet.

"Will you promise to wear these next Saturday when we go to the Rainbow Room?"

She had lifted her right foot a few inches off the carpet and smiled at the sheer beauty of the shoes. "I can't accept these as a gift . . ."

"Please." He had smiled up at her.

"Well, let me buy them from you. The funny thing is, they'd go perfectly with a new dress I've only worn once."

It had been on the tip of his tongue to say, "I saw you in that dress." Instead, he'd murmured, "We'll talk about payment later." Then he'd put his hand on her ankle, letting it linger just enough to begin to alert her. He'd stood up, gone over to the stereo. The cassette he had specially prepared was already in place. "Till There Was You" was the first song. The Tommy Dorsey orchestra began to play and the unforgettable voice of the young Frank Sinatra filled the room.

He walked back to the couch and reached for Erin's hands. "Let's practice."

The look he'd been waiting for came into Erin's eyes. That tiny first flicker of awareness that something wasn't quite right. She recognized the subtle change in his tone and manner.

Erin was like the others. They all reacted the same way. Speaking too quickly, nervously. "I think I really had better start back. I have an early appointment tomorrow morning."

"Just one dance."

"All right." Her tone had been reluctant.

When they began to dance, she seemed to relax. All the girls had been good dancers, but Erin was perfection. He'd felt disloyal thinking she might even be better than Nan. She was weightless in his arms. She was grace. But when the last notes of "Till There Was You" faded away, she stepped back. "Time to go."

Then when he said, "You're not going anywhere," Erin began to run. Like the others, she slipped and slid on the floor he had polished so lovingly. The dancing slippers became her enemy as she scurried to escape him, raced toward the door to find it bolted, pushed the panic button on the alarm system to learn it was a farce. It emitted a hollow maniacal laugh when touched, a little extra bit of irony that set most of them sobbing as he reached for their throats.

Erin had been particularly satisfying. At the end she seemed to know it was useless to plead and in an animal burst of strength she fought him, clawing at the hands that gripped her slender neck. It was only when he twisted that heavy gold necklace around her throat and she began to lose consciousness that she had whispered, "Oh God, please help me, oh Daddy. . . ."

When she was dead, he danced with her again. No resistance now in that lovely body. She was his Ginger, his Rita, his Leslie, his Nan, and all the others. When the music stopped, he took off her left slipper and replaced it with her boot.

The video ended as he carried her body down to the basement, where he laid her in the freezer and placed the other slipper and boot in the waiting shoe box.

Charley got up from the sofa and sighed. He rewound the videotape, removed it, and turned off the VCR. The cassette tape he had prepared for Erin was still in the stereo. He pressed "Play."

As the music filled the room, Charley hurried downstairs and opened the freezer. Lovely, lovely, he sighed as he saw the still face, the bluish veins that showed in the ice-blue skin. Tenderly, he reached for her.

It was the first time he'd danced with one of the girls whose body he had frozen. It was a different but thrilling experience. Erin's limbs weren't pliant now. Her back would not bend in a dip. Her cheek pressed against his neck, his chin rested on the auburn hair. That hair once so soft, now beaded with frost. Minutes passed. Finally, as the third song was ending, he twirled her around one last time, then, satisfied, glided to a halt and bowed.

It had all begun with Nan fifteen years ago on March thirteenth, he thought. He kissed Erin's lips just the way he had kissed Nan's. March thirteenth was three weeks away. By then he would have brought Darcy here and it would be over.

He realized that Erin's blouse was beginning to feel damp. He must get her to the city. Holding her in one arm, he half-dragged her to the stereo.

As he turned off the dials, Charley did not notice that an onyx ring with a gold *E* slipped from Erin's frozen finger. Neither did he hear the faint ping as it landed on the floor and lay almost hidden in the fringe on the rug.

~ 5

FRIDAY
February 22

Darcy stared unseeingly at the blueprint of the apartment she was decorating. The owner was spending a year in Europe and was specific about her needs. "I want to rent the place furnished, but I'm putting my own things in storage. I don't want some klutz burning a hole in my carpets or upholstery. Fix the place up tastefully but cheaply. I hear you're a genius at that."

Yesterday after she'd left the police station, Darcy had forced herself to follow up a "Moving/Everything Must Go" sale in Old Tappan, New Jersey. She'd hit a bonanza of good furniture that was practically a giveaway. Some of it would exactly suit this apartment; the rest she'd store for future jobs.

She picked up her pen and sketching pad. The sectional should be on the long wall, arcing to face the windows. The . . . She laid down the pen and put her face in her hands. I have got to get this job finished. I've got to concentrate, she thought desperately.

A memory came unbidden. The week of finals of their sophomore year. She and Erin holing up in their room, cracking the books. The music of Bruce Springsteen coming from the stereo in the next room, echoing through the walls, tempting them to join the celebrants whose exams were over. Erin lamenting, "Darce, when Bruce is playing, I can't concentrate."

"You've got to. Maybe I can buy us earplugs."

Erin, a mischievous look on her face: "I've got a better idea." After dinner they'd gone to the library. When it was closing, they hid in stalls in the bathroom until the security guards left. They'd settled themselves on the seventh floor at the desks by the elevator, where fluorescent lights burned all night, and studied in perfect peace, letting themselves out through a window at dawn.

Darcy bit her lip, realizing she was on the verge of tears again. Impatiently, she dabbed at her eyes, reached for the phone, and called Nona. "I tried you last night, but you were out." She told her about going to Erin's apartment, about Jay Stratton, about finding the Bertolini necklace, about the missing diamonds.

"Stratton's going to wait a few days to see if Erin shows up before he makes a report to the insurance company. The police can't accept a missing-person report because it interferes with Erin's right to freedom of movement."

"That's nonsense," Nona said flatly.

"Of course it's nonsense. Nona, Erin was meeting someone Tuesday night. She'd answered his ad. That's what worries me. Do you think you should call that FBI agent who wrote to you and talk to him?"

A few minutes later, Bev poked her head in Darcy's office. "I wouldn't bother you, but it's Nona." There was sympathetic understanding in her face. Darcy had told her about Erin's disappearance.

Nona was brief. "I left a message for the FBI guy to call. I'll get back to you when he does."

"If he wants to meet you, I'd like to be there." When Darcy hung up, she looked across the room at the coffee brewer on a side table near the window. She made a new pot, deliberately heaping a generous amount of ground coffee into the filter. Erin had brought along a thermos of strong, black coffee that night they had hidden in the library. "This makes the gray cells stand at attention," she had announced after the second cup.

Now, after the second cup, Darcy was finally able to fully concentrate on the apartment plan. You're always right, Erin-go-bragh, she thought as she reached for her sketchpad.

* * *

Vince D'Ambrosio returned to his twenty-eighth-floor office from the conference room in the FBI headquarters on Federal Plaza. He was tall and trim, and no one observing him would doubt that after twenty-five years he still held the record for the mile run at his high school alma mater, St. Joe's, in Montvale, New Jersey.

His reddish-brown hair was cut short. His warm brown eyes were wide-set. His thin face broke easily into a smile. People instinctively liked and trusted Vince D'Ambrosio.

Vince had served as a criminal investigative officer in Vietnam, completed his master's degree in psychology on his return, then entered the Bureau. Ten years ago, at the FBI training academy on the Quantico Marine Base near Washington, D.C., he'd helped set up the Violent Criminal Apprehension Program. VICAP, as it was called, was a computerized national master file with a particular emphasis on serial killers.

Vince had just conducted an update session on VICAP for detectives from the New York area who had taken the VICAP course at Quantico. The purpose of today's meeting had been to alert them that the computer which tracked seemingly unrelated crimes had sent out a warning signal. There was a possible serial killer loose in Manhattan.

It was the third time in as many weeks Vince had delivered the same sobering news: "As you all are aware, VICAP is able to establish patterns in what heretofore have been considered isolated cases. The VICAP analysts and investigators have recently alerted us to a possible connection between six young women who have vanished in the past two years.

"All of them had apartments in New York. No one is sure whether they were actually *in* New York when they disappeared. They're all still officially listed as missing persons. We now believe that is a mistake. Foul play is a probability.

"The similarities between these women are striking. They are all slender and very attractive. They range in age from twenty-two to thirty-four. All are upscale in background and education. Outgoing. Extroverted. Finally, every one of them had begun to regularly answer personal ads. I am convinced we have another personal-ad serial killer out there, and a damn clever one.

"If we are right, the profile of the subject is the following: well-educated; sophisticated; late twenties to early forties; physically attractive. These women wouldn't have been interested in a diamond-in-the-rough. He may never have been arrested for a violent crime but could have a juvenile history of being a Peeping Tom, maybe stealing women's personal items at school. His hobby could be photography."

The detectives had left, all promising to be on the lookout for any reports of missing young women who fit that category. Dean Thompson, the detective from the Sixth Precinct, lingered behind the others. Vince and he had met in Vietnam and had remained friends over the years.

"Vince, a young woman came in yesterday, wanting to file a missing-person report on a friend of hers, Erin Kelley, who hasn't been seen since Tuesday night. She's a young woman who fits the profile you've described. *And* she was answering a personal ad. I'll stay on top of it."

"Keep me posted."

Now, as Vince flipped through the messages on his desk, he nodded with satisfaction when he saw that Nona Roberts had called him. He dialed her, gave his name to her secretary, and was immediately put through.

He frowned as Nona Roberts's troubled voice explained, "Erin Kelley, a young woman I talked into answering personal ads for my documentary, has been missing since Tuesday night. There is no way Erin would have dropped out of sight unless she'd been in an accident, or worse. I'd stake my life on that."

Vince looked at his list of appointments. He had meetings in the building the rest of the morning. He was due at the Mayor's office at one-thirty. Nothing he could skip. "Would three o'clock work out for you?" he asked Roberts. After he replaced the receiver, he said aloud, "Another one."

A moment after she telephoned Darcy about the three o'clock appointment with Vincent D'Ambrosio, Nona received an unexpected visit from Austin Hamilton, CEO and sole owner of Hudson Cable Network.

Hamilton had an icy, sarcastic manner which his staff regarded with intense apprehension. Nona had managed to talk Hamilton into the personal-ads documentary despite the fact that his initial reaction had been: "Who cares about a bunch of losers meeting other losers?"

She had secured his reluctant go-ahead by showing him the pages upon pages of personal ads in magazines and newspapers. "It's the social phenomenon of our society," she'd argued. "These ads aren't cheap to place. It's the old story. Boy wants to meet girl. Aging executive wants to meet wealthy divorcée. The point is, does Prince Charming find Sleeping Beauty? Or are these ads a colossal and even humiliating waste of time?"

Hamilton had grudgingly agreed that there might be a story there. "In my day," he'd pointed out, "you met people socially at prep school and college and at coming-out parties. You acquired a select group of friends and through them met other social equals."

Hamilton was a sixty-year-old professional preppie, and the consummate snob. He had, however, singlehandedly built Hudson Cable and his innovative programming was a serious challenge to the three big networks.

When he stopped in Nona's office his mood was frosty. Even though he was as always impeccably dressed, Nona decided that he still managed to remain remarkably unattractive. His Savile Row suit did not quite conceal his narrow shoulders and thickening waist. His sparse hair was tinted a silvery blond shade that did not succeed in looking natural. His narrow lips, which were capable of selectively breaking into a warm smile, were set in an almost invisible line. His pale blue eyes were chilly.

He got right to the point. "Nona, I'm damn sick of this project of yours. I don't think there's an unattached person in this building who isn't placing or answering personal ads and wasting time comparing results ad nauseam. Either wrap this project up fast or forget it."

There was a time to placate Hamilton; a time to intrigue him. Nona chose the second option. "I had no idea how explosive this personal-ads business might be." She fished on her desk for the letter from Vincent D'Ambrosio and handed it to Hamilton. His eyebrows went up as he read it.

"He's coming here at three o'clock." Nona swallowed. "As you can see, he points out that there's a dark side to these ads. A good friend of mine, Erin Kelley, answered one on Tuesday night. She's missing."

Hamilton's instinct for news overcame his petulance. "Do you think there's a connection?"

Nona turned her head, abstractly noted that the plant Darcy had watered two days ago was beginning to droop again. "I hope not. I don't know."

"Talk to me after you meet with this guy."

Disgusted, Nona realized Hamilton was salivating over the potential media value of Erin's disappearance. With a visible effort to sound sympathetic, he said, "Your friend's probably fine. Don't worry."

When he was gone, Nona's secretary, Connie Frender, poked her head in the door. "Are you still alive?"

"Barely." Nona tried to smile. Had she ever been twenty-one? she wondered. Connie was the black counterpart of Joan Nye, the Toodle-oo Club president. Young, pretty, bright, smart. Matt's new wife was now twenty-two. And I'll be forty-one, Nona thought. With neither chick nor child. Lovely thought.

"This single black female wishes to meet anyone who breathes," Connie laughed. "I've got a whole new batch of responses from some of the box numbers you wrote to. Ready to look at them?"

"Sure."

"Want some more coffee? After Awesome Austin, you probably need it."

This time Nona knew her smile was almost maternal. Connie did not seem to know that offering the boss a cup of coffee was frowned upon by some feminists. "I'd love one."

She returned with it five minutes later. "Nona, Matt's on the phone. I told him you were in conference and he said it was vital that he talk to you."

"I'm sure it is." Nona waited for the door to close and took a swig of coffee before she reached for the phone. Matthew, she thought. Meaning of the name? Gift of God. For sure. "Hi, Matt. How are you and the prom queen?"

"Nona, is it possible for you to stop being nasty?" Had he always sounded this querulous?

"No, it really isn't." Damn, Nona thought. After nearly two years, it still hurts to talk with him.

"Nona, I was wondering. Why don't you buy me out of the house? Jeanie doesn't like the Hamptons. The market's still lousy so I'll give you a real break on the price. You know you can always borrow from your folks."

Matty the moocher, Nona thought. Marriage to the child-bride had reduced Matt to this. "I don't want the house," she said quietly. "I'm going to buy my own place when we unload this one."

"Nona, you love that place. You're just doing this to punish me."

"See you." Nona broke the connection. You're wrong, Matt, she thought. I loved the house because we bought it together and cooked lobsters to celebrate our first night in it and every year we did something else to make it even greater. Now I want to start absolutely fresh. No memories.

She began to go through the new batch of letters. She'd sent out over a hundred to people who had placed recent ads requesting them to share their experiences. She'd also persuaded the cable anchorman, Gary Finch, to invite people to write in about the results of personal ads they'd either placed or answered and the reason they no longer would do it.

The result of the on-air announcement was proving to be a bonanza. A relatively small number wrote ecstatically about meeting "the most wonderful person in the world and now we're engaged" . . . "living together" . . . "married."

Many others expressed disappointment. "He said he was an entrepreneur. Meaning he's broke. Tried to borrow money the first time I met him." From Bashful Single White Male: "She criticized me all through dinner. Said I had a nerve putting in the ad that I was attractive. Boy, did she make me feel lousy." "I started getting obscene phone calls in the middle of the night." "When I got back home from work I found him sitting on my doorstep sniffing coke."

Several letters were unsigned. "I don't want you to know who I am, but I'm sure one of the men I met through a personal column is the man who burglarized my house." "I brought a very attractive fortyish executive home and found him trying to kiss my seventeen-year-old daughter."

Nona felt heartsick at the final letter in the pile. It was from a woman in Lancaster, Pennsylvania. "My twenty-two-year-old daughter, an actress, disappeared almost two years ago. When she did not return our calls, we went to her New York apartment. It was obvious that she had not been there in days. She was answering personal ads. We are frantic. There has been absolutely no trace of her."

Oh God, Nona thought, oh God. Please let Erin be all right. Her hands trembling, she began to sort through the letters, adding the most interesting to one of three files: *Happy About Ads. Disappointed. Serious Problem.* The last letter she held out to show Agent D'Ambrosio.

At one o'clock Connie brought her in a ham and cheese sandwich. "Nothing like a little cholesterol," Nona commented.

"There's no point in ordering tuna for you when you never eat it," Connie commented.

By two, Nona had dictated letters to potential guests. She made a note to herself to invite a psychiatrist or psychologist to be on the program. I ought to have someone who can do a wrap-up analysis of the whole personal-ads scene, she decided.

Vincent D'Ambrosio arrived at quarter of three. "He knows he's early," Connie told Nona, "and doesn't mind waiting."

"No, that's fine. Ask him to come in."

In less than one minute, Vince D'Ambrosio forgot the remarkable discomfort of the green love seat in Nona Roberts's office. He considered himself a good judge of people and liked Nona immediately. Her manner was straightforward, pleasant. He liked her looks. Not pretty but attractive, especially those large reflective brown eyes. She wore little if any makeup. He also liked the touches of gray in her dark blond hair. Alice, his ex-wife, was also blond but her sunny tresses were the result of regular appointments at Vidal Sassoon. Well, at least now she was married to a guy who could afford them.

It was obvious that Roberts was desperately worried. "Your letter coincides with the most recent responses I've been receiving," she told him. "People writing about meeting thieves, moochers, addicts, lechers, perverts. And now . . ." She bit her lip. "And now, someone who never would have dreamed of answering a personal ad and did it as a favor to me, is missing."

"Tell me about her."

Nona was fleetingly grateful that Vince D'Ambrosio did not waste time with empty reassurances. "Erin is twenty-seven or -eight. We met six months ago in our health club. She, Darcy Scott, and I were in the same dance classes and became friendly. Darcy will be here in a few minutes." She picked up the letter from the woman in Lancaster and handed it to Vince. "This just arrived."

Vince read it quickly and whistled silently. "Somebody didn't file a report with us. This girl isn't on our list. She brings the count up to seven missing."

In the cab on the way to Nona's office, Darcy thought of the time she and Erin had gone skiing at Stowe their senior year of college. The slopes had been icy, and most people had headed for the lodge early. At her urging, she and Erin went for one last run. Erin hit a patch of ice and fell, her leg snapping under her.

When the patrol came with the meat wagon for Erin, Darcy skied beside her, then accompanied her in the ambulance. She remembered Erin's ashen face, Erin trying to joke. "Hope this doesn't affect my dancing. I plan to be queen of the stardust ballroom."

"You will be."

At the hospital, when the X-rays were developed, the surgeon raised his eyebrows. "You really did a job on yourself, but we'll fix you up." He'd smiled at Darcy. "Don't look so worried. She'll be fine."

"I'm not just worried. I feel so damn guilty," she'd told the doctor. "Erin didn't want to make the last run."

Now as she entered Nona's office and was introduced to Agent D'Ambrosio, Darcy realized she was experiencing exactly the same reaction. The same relief that somebody was in charge, the same guilt that she had urged Erin to answer the ads with her.

"Nona only asked if we wanted to *try* them. I was the one who pushed Erin to do it," she told D'Ambrosio. He took notes as she talked about the phone call on Tuesday, about Erin's saying she was meeting someone named Charles North in a pub near Washington Square. She noticed the change in D'Ambrosio's manner when she spoke about opening the safe, about giving the Bertolini necklace to Jay Stratton, about Stratton's claim that there were diamonds missing.

He asked her about Erin's family.

Darcy stared at her hands.

Remember arriving at Mount Holyoke first day of freshman year? Erin already there, her suitcases piled neatly in the corner. They'd sized each other up, both liked what they saw. Erin's eyes widening as she recognized Mother and Dad but not losing her composure.

"When Darcy wrote to me this summer introducing herself, I didn't realize that her parents were Barbara Thorne and Robert Scott," she'd said. "I don't think I ever missed one of your films." Then she added, "Darcy, I didn't want to settle in until you were here. I thought you might have a preference about which closet or bed you wanted."

Remember the look Mother and Dad exchanged. They were thinking, what a nice girl Erin is. They asked her to join us for dinner.

Erin had come to college alone. Her father was an invalid, she explained. We wondered why she never even mentioned her mother. Later she told me that when she was six, her father developed multiple sclerosis and needed a wheelchair. Her mother took off when she was seven. "I didn't bargain for this," she'd said. "Erin, you can come with me if you want."

"I can't leave Daddy all alone. He needs me."

Over the years, Erin completely lost touch with her mother. "The last I heard she was living with some guy who owned a charter sailboat in the Caribbean." She was at Mount Holyoke on a scholarship. "As Daddy says, being immobilized gives you plenty of time to help your kid with her homework. If you can't pay for college, at least you can help her get a free ride." Oh Erin, where are you? What's happened to you?

Darcy realized that D'Ambrosio was waiting for her to answer his question. "Her father's been in a nursing home in Massachusetts for the last few years," she said. "He's not aware of much anymore. I guess I'm the closest thing Erin has to a relative besides him."

Vince saw the pain in Darcy's eyes. "In my business I've observed that having one good friend can beat having a passel of relatives."

Darcy managed a smile. "Erin's favorite quote is from Aristotle. 'What is a friend? A single soul dwelling in two bodies.' "

Nona got up, stood beside Darcy's chair, and put her hands reassuringly on her shoulders. She looked squarely at D'Ambrosio. "What can we do to help find Erin?"

A long time ago, Petey Potters had been a construction worker. *"Big jobs,"* as he liked to boast to anyone whose ear he could get. "World Trade Center. I usta be out on one of them girders. Tell ye, the wind wuz whippin' so ye wondered if ye were gonna stay up there." He'd laugh, a wheezy chortle. "Some view, lemme tell ye, some view."

But at night the thought of going back up on the girder began to get to Petey. A coupla shots of rye, a coupla beer chasers, and the warmth would flow into the pit of his stomach and spread through his body.

"You're just like your father," his wife began to scream at him. "A no-good drunk."

Petey never got insulted. He understood. He'd start to laugh when his wife ranted about Pop. Pop had been some card. He'd disappear for weeks at a time, dry out in a flophouse on the Bowery, and then come back home. "When I'm hungry, it's no problem," he'd confided to eight-year-old Petey. I go to the Salvation Army shelter, take a dive, get a meal, a bath, a bed. Never fails."

"What's 'take a dive' mean?" Petey had asked.

"When you go to the shelter, they tell you about God and forgiveness and we're all brothers and we want to be saved. Then they ask anyone who believes in the good book to come forward and acknowledge his Maker. So you get religion. You run up, fall on your knees, and shout something about being saved. That's taking a dive."

Nearly forty years later the memory still tickled the homeless derelict Petey Potters. He'd created his own shelter, a combination of wood and tin and old rags that he'd piled together into a tentlike structure against the sagging, shuttered terminal on the abandoned West Fifty-sixth Street pier.

Petey's needs were simple. Wine. Butts. A little food. Litter baskets were a constant supply of cans and bottles that could be redeemed for the deposits. When he was ambitious, Petey took a squeegee and a bottle of water and stood at the Fifty-sixth Street exit of the West Side Highway. No drivers wanted their car windows smeared by his efforts, but most people were afraid to wave him away. Only last week he'd heard an old bat explode to the driver of a Mercedes, "Jane, why do you allow yourself to be held up like this?"

Petey had loved the answer. "Because, Mother, I don't want to have the side of this car scratched if I refuse."

Petey didn't scratch anything when he was rejected. He just went on to the next car, armed with his squirt bottle, a coaxing smile on his face.

Yesterday had been one of the good days. Just enough snow so that the highway became messy and windshields got sprayed with dirty slush from the tires of cars ahead of them. Few people had refused Petey's ministrations at the exit ramp. He'd made eighteen bucks, enough for a hero sandwich, butts, and three bottles of dago red.

Last night he'd settled inside his tent, wrapped in the old army blanket the Armenian church on Second Avenue had given him, a ski cap keeping his head warm, a tattered greatcoat, its moth-eaten fur collar cozy around his neck. He'd finished the hero with the first bottle of wine, then settled down to puffing and sipping, content and warm in an inebriated haze. Pop taking a dive. Mom coming back to the apartment on Tremont Avenue, worn out from scrubbing other people's houses. Birdie, his wife. *Harpie,* not Birdie. That's what they shoulda called her.

Petey shook with mirth at the play on words. Wonder where she was now. How about the kid? Nice kid.

Petey wasn't sure when he heard the car pull up. He tried to force himself to wakefulness, instinctively wanting to protect his territory. It better not be cops trying to knock over his place. Nah. Cops didn't bother with this kind of shack in the middle of the night.

Maybe it was a druggie. Petey gripped the neck of an empty wine bottle. Better not try to come in here. But nobody came. After a few minutes he heard the car start up again; he peered out cautiously. Taillights were disappearing onto the deserted West Side Highway. Maybe somebody had to take a leak, Petey decided as he reached for the last bottle.

* * *

It was late afternoon when Petey opened his eyes again. His head had that empty, throbbing feeling. His gut burned. His mouth felt like the bottom of a birdcage. He pulled himself up. The three empty bottles offered no consolation. He found twenty cents in the pockets of the greatcoat. I'm hungry, he whined silently. Poking his head from behind the piece of tin sheeting that served as door for his shelter, he decided that it must be late afternoon. There were long shadows on the dock. His eyes moved to focus on something that was clearly not a shadow. Petey squinted, muttered a profanity under his breath, and dragged himself to his feet.

His legs were stiff and his gait clumsy as he made his unsteady way to whatever was lying on the pier.

It was a slim woman. Young. Red hair curling around her face. Petey was sure she was dead. A necklace was twisted into her throat. She was wearing a blouse and slacks. Her shoes didn't match.

The necklace sparkled in the fading light. Gold. Real gold. Petey licked his lips nervously. Bracing himself for the shock of touching the dead girl he reached around the back of her neck for the clasp of the elaborate necklace. His fingers fumbled. Thick and unsteady, they could not get the clasp to release. Christ, she felt cold.

He didn't want to break anything. Was the necklace long enough to pull over her head? Trying to ignore the bruised, blue-veined throat, he tugged at the heavy chain.

Grimy fingerprints streaked Erin's face as Petey freed the necklace and slipped it in his pocket. The earrings. They were good, too. From a distance, Petey heard the whine of a police siren. Like a startled rabbit he jumped up, forgetting the earrings. This was no place for him. He'd have to take his stuff, get himself a new shelter. When the body was found, just his being around here would be enough for the cops.

An awareness of his potential danger sobered Petey. On stumbling feet he rushed back to the shelter. Everything he owned could be tied in the army blanket. His pillow. A couple pairs of socks, some underwear. A flannel shirt. A dish and spoon and cup. Matches. Butts. Old newspapers for cold nights.

Fifteen minutes later, Petey had vanished into the world of the homeless. Panhandling on Seventh Avenue netted four dollars and thirty-two cents. He used it to buy wine and a pretzel. There was a young fellow on Fifty-seventh Street who sold hot jewelry. He gave Petey twenty-five dollars for the necklace. "This is good, man. Try to get more like this."

At ten o'clock Petey was asleep on a subway grating that radiated warm, dank air. At eleven, he was being shaken awake. A not-unkind voice said, "Come on, pal. It's going to be real cold tonight. We're going to take you to a place where you can have a decent bed and a good meal."

At quarter of six on Friday evening, Wanda Libbey, snugly secure in her new BMW, was inching her way along the West Side Highway. Complacent in the excellent shopping she'd done on Fifth Avenue, Wanda was still annoyed at herself that she'd gotten such a late start back to Tarrytown. The Friday night rush hour was the worst of the week, a time when many quit New York for their country homes. She'd never want to live in New York again. Too dirty. Too dangerous.

Wanda glanced at the Valentino purse on the passenger seat. When she'd parked in the Kinney lot this morning, she'd tucked it firmly under her arm and kept it there all day. She wasn't fool enough to have it dangling from her arm where someone might grab it.

Another damn traffic light. Oh well, in a few blocks she'd be on the ramp and past this miserable section of so-called highway.

A tap on the window made Wanda look swiftly to the right. A bearded face grinned in at her. A rag began to make swishing movements on the windshield.

Wanda's lips snapped into a rigid line. Damn. She shook her head vigorously. No. No.

The man ignored her.

I am not going to be held up by these people, Wanda fumed, jamming her finger on the button that opened the passenger window. "I don't want—" She began to shriek. The rag was thrown against the windshield. The bottle of fluid pinged off the hood. A hand reached into the car. She watched her purse disappear.

A squad car was heading west on Fifty-fifth Street. The driver suddenly straightened up. "What's that?" On the approach to the highway he could see traffic stopped, people getting out of cars. "Let's go." Siren blaring, lights flashing, the squad car lurched forward, skillfully weaving through the maze of moving traffic and double-parked vehicles.

Still screaming with rage and frustration, Wanda pointed to the pier a block away. "My purse. He ran there."

"Let's go." The squad car turned left, then made a sharp right as they roared onto the pier. The cop in the passenger seat turned on the spotlight, revealing the shack Petey had abandoned. "I'll check inside." Then he snapped, "Hey, over there. Past the terminal. What's that?"

The body of Erin Kelley, glistening with sleet, the silvery slipper flashing under the powerful beam from the spotlight, had been discovered again.

Darcy left Nona's office with Vince D'Ambrosio. They took a cab to her apartment and she gave him Erin's daily reminder and her personal-columns file. Vince studied them carefully. "Not much here," he commented. "We'll find out who placed the ads she circled. With any luck, Charles North is one of them."

"Erin isn't the greatest record keeper," Darcy said. "I could go back to her apartment and look through her desk again. It's possible I missed something."

"That could help. But don't worry. If North's a corporate lawyer from Philadelphia, it'll be easy to trace him." Vince stood up. "I'll get on this right away."

"And I'm going back to her apartment now. I'll leave with you." Darcy hesitated. The light on the answering machine was blinking. "Can you wait just a minute till I check the messages?" Attempting a smile she said, "There's always the chance Erin left one."

There were two messages. Both were about personal ads. One was genial. "Hi, Darcy. Trying you again. Enjoyed your note. Hope we can get together sometime. I'm Box 4358. David Weld, 555-4890."

The other was sharply different. "Hey, Darcy, why do you waste *your* time answering ads and *my* time trying to reach you. This is the fourth time I've called. I don't like to leave messages, but here's this one. Drop dead."

Vince shook his head. "That guy has a short leash."

"I didn't leave the answering machine on while I was away," Darcy said. "I suppose if anyone tried to reach me in response to the few letters I sent myself, they probably gave up. Erin started answering ads in my name about two weeks ago. Those are the first calls I've gotten."

* * *

Gus Boxer was surprised and not especially pleased to respond to the buzzer and find the same young woman who had wasted so much of his time yesterday. He was prepared to absolutely refuse to allow her to enter Erin Kelley's apartment again but did not get the chance. "We've reported Erin's disappearance to the FBI," Darcy told him. "The agent in charge has asked me to go through her desk."

The FBI. Gus felt a nervous tremor go through his body. But that was so long ago. He had nothing to worry about. A couple of people had left their names recently just in case a vacancy came up. One good-looking gal said it would be worth a thousand bucks under the table if he put her at the top of the list. So if Kelley's friend was able to find out something happened to her, it would mean a nice piece of change in his pocket.

"I'm just as worried about that girl as you are," he whined, the unfamiliar sympathetic tone catching in his vocal cords. "Come on up."

In the apartment, Darcy immediately turned on all the lights against the impending dusk. Yesterday, the place had seemed cheerful enough. Today, Erin's continued absence was leaving its mark. A faint edging of soot was visible on the windowsill. The long worktable needed dusting. The framed posters that always gave brightness and color to the room seemed to mock her.

The Picasso from Geneva. Erin had bought it on her one school trip abroad. "I love this even though it isn't my favorite theme," she'd commented. It depicted a mother and child.

There were no further messages on Erin's machine. A search of the desk revealed nothing significant. There was a new cassette for the answering machine in the drawer. Possibly Agent D'Ambrosio would want the old tape, the one that contained messages. Darcy switched the two.

The nursing home. This was around the time Erin usually called it. Darcy looked up the number and dialed. The head nurse on Billy Kelley's floor came to the phone. "I spoke to Erin as usual on Tuesday night around five. I told her I think her father is quite near the end. She said she would spend the weekend in Wellesley." Then she added, "I understand she's missing. We're all praying that she's all right."

There's nothing more I can do here, Darcy thought, and suddenly felt an overwhelming desire to go home.

It was quarter of six when she got back to her own place. A hot shower was called for, she decided, and a hot toddy.

At ten past six, wrapped in her favorite flannel robe, steam rising from the toddy, she settled on the couch and pushed the remote control for the television.

A story was breaking. John Miller, the investigative crime reporter for Channel 4, was standing at the entrance to a West Side pier. Behind him in a roped-off area a dozen policemen were silhouetted against the cold waters of the Hudson. Darcy turned up the volume.

". . . body of an unidentified young woman was just discovered on this abandoned Fifty-sixth Street pier. She appears to have been the victim of strangulation. The woman is slim, in her mid-twenties with auburn hair. She is wearing slacks and a multicolored blouse. A bizarre twist is that she is wearing mismatched shoes, a brown leather ankle boot on her left foot, an evening slipper on her right."

Darcy stared at the television. Auburn hair. Mid-twenties. Multicolored blouse. She'd given Erin a multicolored blouse for Christmas. Erin had been delighted. "It has all the colors of Joseph's coat," she'd said. "I love it."

Auburn. Slim. Joseph's coat.

The biblical Joseph's coat had been stained in blood when his treacherous brothers showed it to their father as proof of his death.

Somehow, Darcy managed to find in her purse the card Agent D'Ambrosio had given her.

Vince was just about to leave his office. He was meeting his fifteen-year-old son Hank at Madison Square Garden. They were going to have a quick dinner, then take in a Rangers game. As he listened to Darcy he realized that he had been expecting this call; he just hadn't thought it would come quite this soon.

"It doesn't sound good," he told her. "I'll phone the precinct where the body was found. Sit tight. I'll get back to you."

When he hung up, he called Hudson Cable. Nona was still in her office. "I'll get right over to be with Darcy," she said.

"She'll be asked if she can identify the body," Vince warned.

He called the Midtown North precinct and was put through to the head of the homicide squad. The body had not yet been removed from the crime scene. When it reached the morgue, they'd send a squad car for Miss Scott. Vince explained his interest in the case. "We'd be grateful for your assistance," he was told. "Unless this turns out to be an open-and-shut case, we'd like to have it run through VICAP."

Vince called Darcy back, told her about the squad car and that

Nona was on the way. She thanked him, her tone flat and unemotional.

Chris Sheridan left the gallery at ten past five and with long strides walked the fourteen blocks from Seventy-eighth and Madison to Sixty-fifth and Fifth. It had been a busy and highly successful week and he savored the luxurious freedom of knowing that he had the whole weekend to himself. Not a single plan.

His tenth-floor apartment faced Central Park. "Directly across from the zoo," as he told his friends. Eclectic in taste, he'd mixed antique tables, lamps, and carpets with long, comfortable upholstered couches that he'd covered in a heraldic pattern, copied from a medieval tapestry. The paintings were English landscapes. Nineteenth-century hunting prints and a silk-on-silk Tree of Life wall hanging complemented the Chippendale table and side chairs in the dining area.

It was a comfortable, inviting room, a room which in the past eight years many young women had eyed with hope.

Chris went into the bedroom, changed into a long-sleeved sport shirt and chinos. A very dry martini, he decided. Maybe later he'd go out for a plate of pasta. Drink in hand, he switched on the six o'clock news and saw the same broadcast Darcy was watching.

His compassion for the dead girl and identification with the grief her family would experience was instantly replaced by horror. Strangled! A dancing shoe on one foot! "Oh, God," Chris said aloud. Could whoever murdered that girl have been the one who sent the letter to his mother? The letter that said a dancing girl who lived in Manhattan would die on Tuesday night exactly the way Nan died.

Tuesday afternoon, after his mother called, he'd contacted Glenn Moore, the police chief of Darien. Moore had gone to see Greta, had taken the letter, reassuring her it was probably from a crank. He'd then called Chris back. "Chris, even if it's on the level, how do you begin to protect all the young women in New York?"

Now Chris dialed the Darien police station again and was put through to the chief. Moore had not yet heard about the death in New York. "I'll call the FBI," he said. "If that letter is from the killer, it's physical evidence. I have to warn you, the FBI will probably want to talk to you and your mother about Nan's death. I'm sorry, Chris. I know what that does to her."

* * *

At the entrance to Beefsteak Charlie's restaurant in Madison Square Garden, Vince threw an arm around his son's shoulders. "I swear you've grown since last week." He and Hank were now eye to eye. "One of these days, you'll be eating your blue plate off my head."

"What the heck is a blue plate?" Hank's lean face with a sprinkling of freckles across the nose was the one Vince remembered seeing in the mirror nearly thirty years ago. Only the color of his gray-blue eyes had come from his mother's genes.

The waiter beckoned to them. When they were seated, Vince explained, "A blue plate used to be the special of the evening at a cheap restaurant. Seventy-nine cents bought you a hunk of meat, a couple of vegetables, a potato. The plate was sectioned to keep the juices from running together. Your grandfather loved that kind of bargain."

They decided on hamburgers with everything piled on, french fries, salads. Vince had a beer, Hank a cola. Vince forced himself not to think about Darcy Scott and Nona Roberts going to the morgue to view the body of the murder victim. Rough as hell for both of them.

Hank filled him in about his track team. "We're running at Randall's Island next Saturday. Think you can make it?"

"Absolutely, unless . . ."

"Oh, sure." Unlike his mother, Hank understood the demands of Vince's job. "You working on anything new?"

Vince told him about the concern that a serial killer was on the loose, about the meeting in Nona Roberts's office, about the belief that Erin Kelley might be the dead woman found on the pier.

Hank listened intently. "You think you ought to be in on this, Dad?"

"Not necessarily. This may be a local homicide solely for the NYPD, but they have requested assistance from the Behavioral Science Unit at Quantico and I'll help them as much as I can." He signaled for the check. "We'd better get started."

"Dad, I'm coming in again Sunday. Why don't I go to the game alone? You know your gut is telling you to follow up on this case."

"I don't want to pull that on you."

"Look, the game is sold out. I'll make a deal with you. No scalping, but if I sell your ticket for exactly what you paid for it, I get to keep the money. I've got a date tomorrow night. I'm broke, and I can't stand to ask Mom for a loan. She sends me to that hunk of blubber she married. So anxious for us to be buddies."

Vince smiled. "I swear you've got the makings of a con man. See you Sunday, pal."

On the way to the morgue, Darcy and Nona clasped hands in the squad car. When they arrived, they were taken to a room off the lobby. "They'll come for you when they're ready," the cop who had driven them explained. "They're probably taking photographs."

Photographs. *Erin, don't worry. Send your picture if they request it. In for a penny, in for a pound.* Darcy stared straight ahead, barely conscious of the room, of Nona's arm around her.

Charles North. Erin had met him at seven o'clock on Tuesday night. A little more than a few short days ago. Tuesday morning she and Erin had joked about that date.

Darcy said aloud, "And now I'm sitting in the New York City morgue waiting to look at a dead woman who I'm sure is going to be Erin." Vaguely she felt Nona's arm tighten around her.

The cop returned. "An FBI agent's on the way. Wants you to wait for him before you go downstairs."

Vince walked between Darcy and Nona, his hands firmly under their elbows. They stopped at the glass window that separated them from the still form on the stretcher. At Vince's nod, the attendant pulled the sheet back from the victim's face.

But Darcy already knew. A strand of that auburn hair had escaped concealment. Then she was seeing the familiar profile, the wide blue eyes now closed, the lashes dark shadows, the always smiling lips so still, so quiet.

Erin. Erin. Erin-go-bragh, she thought, and felt herself begin to sink into merciful darkness.

Vince and Nona grabbed her. "No. No. I'm all right." She fought back the waves of dizziness and made herself straighten up. She pushed away the supporting arms and stared at Erin, deliberately studying the chalky whiteness of her skin, the bruises on her throat. "Erin," she said fiercely, "I swear to you I will find Charles North. I give you my word he is going to pay for what he did to you."

The sound of racking sobs echoed in the stark corridor. Darcy realized they were coming from her.

* * *

Friday had been an extremely successful day for Jay Stratton. In the morning, he'd stopped at the Bertolini office. Yesterday, when he brought in the necklace, Aldo Marco, the manager, had still been furious at the delay. Today, Marco was singing a different tune. His client was ecstatic. Miss Kelley had certainly executed the concept they had in mind when they'd decided to have the gems reset. They looked forward to continuing to work with her. At Jay's request, the twenty-thousand-dollar check was made out to Jay as Erin Kelley's manager.

From there, Stratton went to the police station to file a complaint about the missing diamonds. The copy of the official report in his hand, he'd headed for the midtown office of his insurance company. The distressed agent told him that Lloyd's of London had reinsured this packet of gems. "They'll undoubtedly post a reward," she said nervously. "Lloyd's is getting terribly upset about the theft of jewelry in New York."

At four o'clock, Jay had been in the Stanhope having drinks with Enid Armstrong, a widow who'd answered one of his personal ads. He'd listened attentively as she told him about her overwhelming loneliness. "It's been a year," she'd said, her eyes glistening. "You know, people are sympathetic and they take you out occasionally, but it's a fact of life that the world goes two-by-two and an extra woman is a nuisance. I went on a Caribbean cruise alone last month. It was absolutely miserable."

Jay made the appropriate clucking sounds of understanding and reached for her hand. Armstrong was mildly pretty, in her late fifties, good clothes but no style. He'd run into the type often enough. Married young. Stayed home. Raised the kids and joined the country club. Husband who became successful but mowed his own lawn. The kind of guy who made sure his wife was well provided for after he keeled over.

Jay studied Armstrong's wedding and engagement rings. All the diamonds were top quality. The solitaire was a beauty. "Your husband was very generous," he commented.

"I got these for our twenty-fifth anniversary. You should have seen the pinpoint he gave me when we got engaged. We were such kids." More glistening eyes.

Jay signaled for another glass of champagne. By the time he left Enid Armstrong, she was excited about his suggestion that they get together next week. She'd even agreed to consider having him redesign her rings. "I'd like to see you with one important ring that incorporates all these stones. The solitaire and baguettes in the center, banded on either side by alternating diamonds and emeralds. We'll use the diamonds in your wedding ring and I can get some fine quality emeralds for you at a very reasonable price."

Over a quiet dinner at the Water Club, he pondered the pleasure of substituting a cubic zirconia for the solitaire in Armstrong's ring. Some of them were so good even a jeweler's naked eye could be fooled. But of course he'd have the new ring appraised for her with the solitaire still in place. Amazing how single women fell for that. "How thoughtful of you to take care of the appraisal for me. I'll take it right to my insurance company."

He lingered at the bar of the Water Club after dinner. Good to relax. The business of being attentive and charming with these old girls was exhausting even though the results were lucrative.

It was nine-thirty when he walked the few blocks from the restaurant back to his apartment. At ten he was wearing pajamas and a robe newly purchased at Armani's. He settled on the couch with a bourbon on the rocks and turned on the news.

The glass shook in Stratton's trembling hands and liquor spilled unheeded on his robe as he stared at the screen and learned of the discovery of the body of Erin Kelley.

Michael Nash wondered ruefully if he should offer free analysis to Anne Thayer, the blonde who so unfortunately had bought the apartment next to his. When he left the office at ten of six on Friday afternoon, she was at the desk in the lobby, speaking to the concierge. As soon as she saw him, she dashed to stand beside him and wait for the elevator. On the way up, she chatted nonstop, as though she was on a countdown to ensnare him before they reached the twentieth floor.

"I went over to Zabar's today and got the most marvelous salmon. Fixed a platter of hors d'oeuvres. My girlfriend was supposed to come over but can't make it. Can't bear to see them go to waste. I was wondering . . ."

Nash cut her off. "Zabar's salmon is great. Put it away. It'll keep for a few days." He was aware of the commiserating glance of the elevator operator. "Ramon, I'll see you in a few minutes. I'm on my way out."

He said a firm good night to the crestfallen Miss Thayer and disappeared into his own apartment. He *was* going out, but not for an hour or so. And if he bumped into her then, maybe she'd start to get the message to leave him alone. "Dependent personality, probably neurotic, could get vicious when crossed," he said aloud, then laughed. Hey, I'm off work. Forget it.

He was spending the weekend in Bridgewater. There was a dinner party at the Balderstons' tomorrow night. They always had interesting guests. More important, he intended to use the better part of the next two days working on his book. Nash acknowledged to himself that he'd become so interested in the project that he was becoming impatient with distractions.

Just before he left, he tried Erin Kelley's number. He half-smiled as he heard the message in her lilting voice: "This is Erin. Sorry to miss your call. Please leave a message."

"This is Michael Nash. I'm sorry to miss you, too, Erin. Tried you the other day. Guess you're away. Hope there isn't a problem with your father." He left his office and home number again.

The drive to Bridgewater on Friday night was as usual a traffic-clogged nuisance. It was only when he passed Paterson on Route 80 that it began to let up. Then with each mile the terrain became more countrylike. Nash felt himself begin to relax. By the time he had driven through the gate of Scotshays, he had a total sense of well-being.

His father had bought the estate when Michael was eleven. Four hundred acres of gardens, woods, and fields. Swimming pool, tennis courts, stable. The house copied from a manor in Brittany. Stone walls, red-tiled roof, green shutters, white portico. Twenty-two rooms in all. Half of them Michael hadn't bothered with in years. Irma and John Hughes, the housekeeping couple, ran the place for him.

Irma had dinner waiting. She served it in the study. Michael settled in his favorite old leather armchair to study the notes he would use tomorrow when he wrote the next chapter of his book. That chapter would concentrate on the psychological problems of people who, when they answered personal ads, sent in pictures of themselves that had been taken twenty-five years ago. He would concentrate on what factors made them try that ploy and how they explained themselves when the date showed up.

That sort of thing had happened to a number of the girls he had interviewed. A couple of them had been indignant. Some had been downright funny describing the encounter.

At quarter of ten, Michael turned the television on in anticipation of the news, then went back to his notes. The name Erin Kelley made him look up, startled. He grabbed the remote control and pressed the volume frantically, causing the announcer's voice to shout through the room.

When the segment was finished, Michael flipped off the set and stared at the dark screen.

"Erin," he said aloud, "who could do that to you?"

Doug Fox stopped for a drink at Harry's Bar on Friday evening before heading home to Scarsdale. It was a watering hole for the Wall Street crowd. As usual the bar was four deep and the news on the television set was ignored. Doug did not see the bulletin about the body that had been found on the pier.

If she was sure he was coming home, Susan usually fed the kids first, then waited to eat with him, but tonight, when he arrived at eight, Susan was in the den reading. She barely raised her eyes when he came into the room and turned away from the kiss he tried to press on her forehead.

Donny and Beth had gone to the movies with the Goodwyns, she explained. Trish and the baby were asleep. She did not offer to prepare anything for him. Her eyes went back to her book.

For a moment Doug stood uncertainly over her, then turned and went into the kitchen. She had to pull this attitude act the one night I'm hungry, he thought bitterly. She's just sore because I didn't get home for a couple of nights and was so late last night. He opened the door of the refrigerator. The one thing Susan could do was cook. With mounting anger he decided that when he was able to make it home, the least she could do was to have something ready for him.

He yanked out packets of ham and cheese and went to the bread box. The weekly community newspaper was on the kitchen table. Doug made a sandwich, poured a beer, and began to skim the paper as he ate. The sports page caught his eye. Scarsdale had unexpectedly defeated Dobbs Ferry in the midschool tournament. The sudden-death winning basket had been sunk by second-stringer Donald Fox.

Donny! Why didn't anyone tell him?

Doug felt his palms begin to sweat. Had Susan tried to phone him Tuesday night? Donny had been disappointed and sullen when Doug told him he couldn't make the game. It would be just like Susan to suggest they call with the news.

Tuesday night. Wednesday night.

The new telephone operator at the hotel. She wasn't like the young kids who willingly accepted the hundred bucks he slipped them from time to time. "Remember, any calls come in for me when I'm not here, I'm in a meeting. If it's real late, I left a do-not-disturb."

The new operator looked like she posed for a moral majority ad. He'd been still trying to figure out how to snow her into lying for him. He hadn't worried too much, however. He'd trained Susan not to phone him when he stayed in "for meetings."

But she *had* tried him Tuesday night. He was sure of it. Otherwise, she'd have had Donny phone him at the office Wednesday afternoon. And that dumb operator had probably told her there was no meeting and no one was staying in the company suite.

Doug looked around the kitchen. It was surprisingly neat. They'd had the whole house renovated when they bought it eight years ago. The kitchen was a chef's dream. Center island with sink and chopping board. Plenty of counter space. Latest appliances. Skylight.

Susan's old man had lent them the money for the renovation. He'd also lent them most of the down payment. *Lent.* Not given.

If Susan got really sore . . .

Doug tossed the rest of the sandwich in the compactor and brought his beer into the den.

Susan watched him enter the room. My handsome husband, she thought. She'd deliberately left the newspaper on the table, knowing Doug would probably read it. Now he's sweating bullets. He figured I probably called the hotel to let Donny give him the news. Funny, when you finally faced reality, it was amazing how clearly you could see things.

Doug sat on the couch opposite her. He's afraid to give me an opening, she decided. Tucking her book under her arm, she got up. "The kids will be back about half past ten," she told him. "I'm going to read in bed."

"I'll wait for them, honey."

Honey! He must be worried.

Susan settled in bed with the book. Then, knowing she was not able to focus on the print, she laid it down and turned on the television.

Doug came into the bedroom just as the ten o'clock news began. "It's too lonesome out there." He sat on the bed and reached for her hand. "How's my girl?"

"Good question," Susan said. "How is she?"

He attempted to pass it off as a joke. Tilting her chin, he said, "She looks pretty good to me."

They both turned to watch the screen as the anchorman gave the headline news. "Erin Kelley, a prize-winning young jewelry designer, was found strangled on the West Fifty-sixth Street pier. More after this."

A commercial.

Susan glanced at Doug. He was staring at the screen, his pallor a ghastly white. "Doug, what is it?"

He did not seem to have heard her.

". . . Police are searching for Petey Potters, a drifter who was known to have been living in this shack and may have observed the body when it was abandoned on this cold, debris-strewn pier."

When the segment was completed, Doug turned to Susan. As though he had just heard her question, he snapped, "Nothing's the matter. Nothing." Beads of perspiration were forming on his forehead.

At three in the morning, Susan was awakened from her own uneasy sleep by Doug thrashing beside her. He was mumbling something. A name? ". . . no, can't . . ." The name again. Susan propped herself up on one arm and listened intently.

Erin. That was it. The name of the young woman who'd been found murdered.

She was about to shake Doug awake when he suddenly quieted. With growing horror, Susan realized why the newscast had so upset him. Undoubtedly, he'd linked it to that terrible time in college when he was one of the students questioned about the girl who had been strangled.

6
SATURDAY
February 23

On Saturday morning, Charley read the *New York Post* with intense fascination. COPYCAT MURDER was the banner-sized headline.

The similarity of Erin Kelley's death to the *True Crimes* program about Nan Sheridan was the focus of the story on the inside pages.

Someone had tipped an investigative reporter from the *Post* about the letter to Nan Sheridan's mother warning that a young woman from New York would be murdered on Tuesday night. The reporter, quoting an unidentified source, wrote that the FBI was on the trail of a possible serial killer. In the past two years, seven young women from Manhattan had disappeared after answering personal ads. Erin Kelley had been answering personal ads.

The circumstances of Nan Sheridan's death were rehashed in full. Erin Kelley's background; interviews with colleagues in the jewelry business. Their responses identical. Erin was a warm, lovely person, immensely talented. The picture the *Post* used was the one Erin had sent Charley. That delighted him.

The network was going to repeat the *True Crimes* episode about Nan's death Wednesday night. That would be so interesting to watch. Of course he'd taped it last month, but even so, to see it again, knowing that hundreds of thousands of people would be playing amateur detective. *Who did it? Who was smart enough to get away with it?*

Charley frowned. *Copycat.*

Copycat meant they thought someone else was imitating him. Anger rushed through him, stark, raging anger. They had no right not to credit him. Just as Nan had had no right not to invite him to her party fifteen years ago.

He'd go back to the secret place in the next few days. He needed to be there. He'd turn on the video and dance in step with Astaire. It wouldn't be Ginger, or Leslie, or Ann Miller in his arms.

His heart began beating faster. This time it wouldn't even be Nan. It would be Darcy.

He picked up Darcy's picture. The soft brown hair, the slender body, the wide, inquiring eyes. How much lovelier would that body be when he held it, rigid and cold in his arms?

Copycat.

Again he frowned. The anger was pounding at his temples, causing one of the terrible headaches to begin. It is I, Charley, alone who has the power of life and death over these women. I, Charley, broke through the prison of the other soul and now dominate him at will.

He would take Darcy and crush the life from her as he had crushed it from the others. And he would confound the authorities with his genius, confuse and bewilder their tiresome minds.

Copycat.

The people who wrote that should see the shoe boxes in the basement. Then they'd know. Those boxes that contained one shoe and one dancing slipper from the foot of each of the dead girls beginning with Nan.

Of course.

There was a way to prove he wasn't a copycat. His body shook with silent, mirthless laughter.

Oh yes, indeed. There was a way.

~ 7

SATURDAY February 23 THROUGH TUESDAY February 26

The next week for Darcy passed as though she was a robot who had been wound up and programmed to perform specific tasks.

Accompanied by Vince D'Ambrosio and a detective from the local precinct, she went to Erin's apartment on Saturday. There were three more calls that had been received after she'd been in the apartment on Friday morning. Darcy rewound the answering machine. One was from the manager at Bertolini's. "Miss Kelley, we gave your check to your manager, Mr. Stratton. We cannot tell you how pleased we are with the necklace."

Darcy raised her eyebrows. "I never heard Erin refer to Stratton as her manager."

The second call was from someone who identified himself as Box 2695. "Erin, it's Milton. We went out last month. I've been away. I'd like to see you again. My phone number is 555–3681. And listen, I'm sorry if I came on a little too strong last time."

The third call was from Michael Nash. "He left a message the other night," Darcy said.

Vince copied the names and numbers. "We'll leave the tape on for the next few days."

Vince had told Darcy that forensics experts from the NYPD would arrive shortly to go over Erin's apartment for possible evidence. She had asked Vince if she could come with him and get Erin's private papers. "My name is on her bank account and insurance policies as trustee for her father. She told me the papers were in her file under his name."

Erin's instructions were simple and explicit. If anything happened to Erin, as agreed, Darcy would use her insurance to pay nursing home expenses. She had contracted with a funeral director in Wellesley that when the time came he would handle her father's arrangements. Everything in her apartment, all her personal jewelry and clothing, were left to Darcy Scott.

There was a brief note for Darcy: "Darce, this is surely a just-in-case. But I know you'll keep your promise to look after Dad if I'm not around. And if that ever should happen, thanks for all the great times we had together, and have fun for both of us."

Dry-eyed, Darcy looked at the familiar signature.

"I hope you'll follow her advice," Vince said quietly.

"I will someday," Darcy told him. "But not yet. Would you make a copy for me of that personal ads file I gave you?"

"Sure," Vince said, "but why? We're going to look up the people who placed the ads she circled."

"But you're not going to date them. She answered some ads for both of us. Maybe I'll get calls from people who took her out."

Darcy left as the forensics crew arrived. She went directly home and began to make phone calls. The funeral director in Wellesley. Sympathy, then practicality. He would send a hearse to the morgue when Erin's body was released. What about clothing? Open casket?

Darcy thought about the bruises on Erin's throat. Undoubtedly, there'd be media at the funeral parlor. "Closed casket. I'll bring up clothing for her." Visitation on Monday. Funeral mass on Tuesday at St. Paul's.

St. Paul's. When she'd stayed with Erin and Billy, she had gone to St. Paul's with them.

She went back to Erin's apartment. Vince D'Ambrosio was still there. He accompanied her into the bedroom and watched as she opened the closet door.

"Erin had so much style," Darcy said unsteadily as she searched for the dress she had in mind. "She used to tell me that she felt so out of it when I walked in the room with my folks that first day at college. I was wearing a designer suit and Italian boots my mother had forced on me. I thought she looked smashing in chinos and a sweater and marvelous jewelry. Even then she was designing her own pieces."

Vince was a good listener. Abstractly, Darcy was aware that she was glad he was letting her talk. "No one's going to see her," she said, "except maybe I will, just for a minute. But I want to feel that she'd be pleased with what I chose for her. . . . Erin urged me to be more daring about clothes. I taught her to trust her own instincts. She had impeccable taste."

She pulled out a two-piece cocktail dress: pale pink fitted jacket, delicate silver buttons, flowing pink and silver chiffon skirt. "Erin just bought this to wear to a benefit, a dinner dance. She was a wonderful ballroom dancer. That was something else we shared. Nona too. We met Nona in a ballroom dancing class at our health club."

Vince remembered Nona had told him that. "From what you tell me, this dress sounds like something Erin would want to wear now."

He didn't like the fact that Darcy's pupils were so enlarged. He wished he could call Nona Roberts. She had told him she absolutely had to be on a shoot in Nanuet today. Darcy Scott ought not to be alone too much.

Darcy realized she could read D'Ambrosio's thoughts. She also realized there was no use reassuring him. The best service she could perform was to get out of here and let the fingerprint experts and God knows who else do their thing. She tried to make her voice and manner matter-of-fact as she asked, "What are you doing to find the man Erin was meeting Tuesday night?"

"We've found Charles North. What Erin told you checks out. It was a lucky break you happened to ask her about him. He moved last month from a law firm in Philadelphia to one on Park Avenue. He left yesterday for a trip to Germany. We'll be waiting for him when he gets back Monday. Detectives from this precinct are going around pubs and bars in the Washington Square area with Erin's picture. We want to see if some bartender or waiter can remember seeing her on Tuesday evening and possibly can identify North when we get him."

Darcy nodded. "I'm going to Wellesley. I'll stay there till after the funeral."

"Nona Roberts is going to join you there?"

"On Tuesday morning. She can't get up before then." Darcy tried to smile. "Please don't worry. Erin had loads of friends. I've heard from so many of the Mount Holyoke grads. They'll be there. So will a lot of our buddies from New York. And she lived in Wellesley all her life. I'm staying with the people who used to be her next-door neighbors."

She went home to pack. A call came from Australia. Her mother and father. "Darling, if only we could be with you. You know we thought of Erin as our second daughter."

"I know." *If only we could be with you.* How many times had she heard that over the years? Birthdays. Graduations. But there had been lots of times when they *were* with her. Any other kid would have been so happy to have the golden couple as parents. Why had she been a throwback to the cottage-with-a-picket-fence mentality? "It's so good to talk with you. How's the play going?"

Now they were on safe ground.

The funeral was a media event. Photographers and cameras. Neighbors and friends. Curiosity seekers. Vince had told her that hidden cameras would be recording everyone who came to the funeral parlor, the church, and the interment, in case Erin's killer was there.

The white-haired Monsignor who had known Erin all her life. "Who can forget the sight of that little girl pushing her father's wheelchair into this church?"

The soloist. ". . . All I ask of you is forever to remember me as loving you . . ."

The interment. "When every tear shall be wiped away. . . ."

The hours she spent with Billy. I'm glad you don't know, she thought. Holding his hand. If he understands anything, I hope he thinks it's Erin with him.

Tuesday afternoon on the shuttle back to New York, Nona sat beside her. "Can you take a couple of days off, Darce?" Nona asked. "This has been a pretty awful time for you."

"As soon as I know they have Charles North in custody, I will go away for a week. A couple of my friends have a condo in St. Thomas. They want me to visit."

Nona hesitated. "That's not the way it's going to work, Darcy. Vince called me last night. They picked up Charles North. Last Tuesday evening he was in a board meeting at his law firm with twenty partners. Whoever met Erin was using his name."

After he saw the broadcast and spoke to Chief Moore, Chris decided to go to Darien for the weekend. He wanted to be around when the FBI talked to his mother.

He knew Greta was planning to attend a black-tie dinner at the club. He stopped to eat at Nicola's, arrived at the house around ten and decided to watch a film. A classic movie buff, he put on *Bridge of San Luis Rey* and then wondered at his choice. The idea of lives drawn together to one particular moment in time always intrigued him. How much was fate? How much was happenstance? Was there some kind of inevitable, inexorable plan to it all?

He heard the whirring of the garage door shortly before midnight and walked to the head of the basement stairs to wait for Greta, wishing once again that she had live-in help. He did not like the idea of her coming into this big house alone late at night.

Greta adamantly refused that suggestion. Dorothy, the daily housekeeper of three decades, suited her fine. That and the weekly cleaning service. If she had a dinner party, her caterer was excellent. And that was that.

As she approached the stairs, he called down, "Hi, Mother."

Her gasp was audible. "What! Oh dear God, Chris. You startled me. I'm a bundle of nerves." She looked up, trying to smile. "I was so glad to see your car." In the dim light her fine-boned face reminded him of Nan's delicate features. Her hair, shimmering silver, was pulled back in a French knot. A sable jacket fell loosely from her shoulders. She was wearing a long black velvet sheath. Greta would be sixty on her next birthday. An elegant, beautiful woman whose smile never fully removed the sadness from her eyes.

It suddenly struck Chris that his mother always appeared to be poised waiting or listening for something, some sort of signal. When he was a kid, his grandfather had told him a World War I story about a soldier who had lost the message warning of an imminent enemy attack. Afterward the soldier always blamed himself for the terrible casualties and went through life looking in gutters and under stones for the lost message.

Over a nightcap, he told Greta about Erin Kelley and understood why the simile had occurred to him. Greta always felt that there was something Nan had told her before she died that had set off an instinctive alarm. Last week, once again, she had received a warning and been powerless to prevent a tragedy.

"The girl they found had a high-heeled evening shoe on?" Greta asked. "Like Nan? The sort of shoe you would dance in? That note said a dancing girl would die."

Chris chose his words carefully. "Erin Kelley was a jewelry designer. From what I understand, the feeling is that this is a copycat murder. Somebody got the idea from watching that *True Crimes* program. An FBI agent wants to talk to us about it."

Chief Moore phoned on Saturday. An FBI agent, Vincent D'Ambrosio, would like to drop in on the Sheridans on Sunday.

Chris was glad that D'Ambrosio emphasized that no one could have acted on the letter Greta had received. "Mrs. Sheridan," he told her, "we get tips much more specific than that one and still can't prevent a tragedy from happening."

Vince asked Chris to walk outside with him. "The Darien police have the files on your sister's death," he explained. "They're going to copy them for me. Would you mind taking me to the exact place where she was found?"

They walked down the road that led from the Sheridan property to the wooded area with the jogging path. The trees had grown higher, their branches thicker in the fifteen years, but otherwise, Chris commented, the place was pretty much the same.

A bucolic scene in a wealthy town, contrasted with an abandoned West Side pier. Nan Sheridan had been a nineteen-year-old kid. A student. A jogger. Erin Kelley was a twenty-eight-year-old career woman. Nan had come from a well-to-do social family. Erin was on her own. The only two similarities were in the manner of death and the footwear. They both had been strangled. They both had been wearing one fancy shoe. Vince asked Chris if while Nan was at school, she did any blind dating through personal ads.

Chris smiled. "Believe me, Nan had enough guys flocking around that she didn't need to answer ads to get a date. Anyhow, there was none of that personal-ads stuff when we were in college."

"You went to Brown?"

"Nan did. I was at Williams."

"I assume any special boyfriends were checked out?"

They were walking along the path that threaded through the woods. Chris stopped. "This is where I found her." He shoved his hands in the pockets of his windbreaker. "Nan thought anyone who got tied up with one guy was crazy. She was something of a flirt. She liked to have a good time. She never willingly missed a party, and she danced every dance."

Vince turned to face him. "This is important. You're sure the fancy slipper your sister was wearing when she was found was not one of her own."

"Absolutely. Nan hated spike heels. She simply wouldn't have bought that shoe. And of course, there was no trace of the mate in her closet."

As he drove back to New York, Vince continued to weigh the comparisons and differences between Nan Sheridan and Erin Kelley. It's got to be a copycat murder, he told himself. *Dancing girl.* That's what was bugging him. The note Greta Sheridan had received. Nan Sheridan had danced every dance. Had that come out on the *True Crimes* program? Erin Kelley had met Nona Roberts in a dancing class. Was it a coincidence?

On Tuesday afternoon, Charles North was interrogated for the second time by Vincent D'Ambrosio. He had been met at Kennedy Airport on Monday evening and his astonishment at being greeted by two FBI agents had been quickly replaced by anger. "I never heard of Erin Kelley. I never answered a personal ad. I think they're ridiculous. I cannot imagine who would use my name."

It was a simple matter to ascertain that North had been in a board meeting at seven o'clock on the previous Tuesday evening, the hour Erin Kelley supposedly planned to meet him.

This time the questioning was in FBI headquarters on Federal Plaza. North was of medium height with a stocky build. A slightly florid face suggested a three-martini drinker. Nevertheless, Vince decided, he had a distinct air of authority and sophistication that probably appealed to women. Forty years old, he had been married twelve years prior to his recent divorce. He made it very clear that he deeply resented the request that he drop in at Vince's office for a second interview.

"I think you must understand that I have just become a partner in a prestigious law firm. It certainly will be a great embarrassment if I am in any way linked to that young woman's death. An embarrassment for me personally and most certainly for my firm."

"I'm very sorry to embarrass you, Mr. North," Vince said coldly. "I can assure you that at this moment you are not a suspect in Erin Kelley's death. But Erin Kelley is dead, the victim of a brutal homicide. It is possible that she is one of a number of young women who have answered personal ads and disappeared. Someone used your name to place that ad. A very clever someone who knew you would have left your Philadelphia firm by the time he arranged to meet Erin Kelley."

"Will you please tell me why that would matter to anyone?" North snapped.

"Because some women who answer personal ads are smart enough to check out the man they agree to date. Suppose Erin Kelley's killer thought she might be that careful. What better name to use than someone who had just left his law firm in Philadelphia to relocate in New York. Suppose Erin had looked you up in the Pennsylvania Bar Register and called your old office. She would have been told that you just left the firm to relocate in New York. She might even have been able to ascertain that you're divorced. Now she has no qualms about meeting Charles North."

Vince leaned forward across his desk. "Like it or not, Mr. North, you are a link to Erin Kelley's death. Someone who knows your activities used your name. We're going to be following up a lot of leads. We're going to contact the people whose ads Erin Kelley may have answered. We're going to pump her friends' memories to see if she mentioned any names we don't have. In each and every case, we're going to talk to you to see if that person is someone who somehow is connected to you."

North stood up. "I see that I'm being told, not asked. Just one thing. Has my name been released to the media?"

"No, it has not."

"Then see that it isn't. And when you call at the office, don't identify yourself as FBI. Say," he smiled mirthlessly, "say it's personal business. Not personal *ad* business, of course."

When he left, Vince leaned back in his chair. I don't like wise guys, he thought. He picked up the intercom. "Betsy, I want a complete background check on Charles North. I mean everything. And here's another one. Gus Boxer, the superintendent at 101 Christopher

Street. That's the apartment building where Erin Kelley lived. His face has been bugging me since Saturday. We've got a file on him, I'm sure of it."

Vince snapped his fingers. "Wait a minute. That's not his name. I remember. It's *Hoffman.* He was the super ten years ago in the building where a twenty-year-old woman was murdered."

Dr. Michael Nash was not surprised when on his return to Manhattan Sunday night there was a call on his answering machine asking him to contact FBI agent Vincent D'Ambrosio. Obviously, they were following up on the people who had left messages for Erin Kelley.

He returned the call on Monday morning and arranged for Vince to stop by before his first appointment on Tuesday.

Vince arrived at Nash's office promptly at 8:15 Tuesday morning. The receptionist was waiting for him and ushered him in to where Nash was already at his desk.

It was a clubby kind of room, Vince decided. Several comfortable chairs, walls a sunny yellow, curtains that let the daylight in but shielded the occupants from the view of passersby on the sidewalk. The traditional couch, a leather version of the chaise longue Alice had bought years ago, was at a right angle to the desk.

A restful room, and the expression in the eyes of the man at the desk was both kind and thoughtful. Vince thought of Saturday afternoons. Confession. "Bless me, Father, for I have sinned." The transgressions evolved from disobeying his parents to recitation of more lusty offenses in teenage years.

It always bothered him to hear someone say that analysis had replaced confession. "In confession you blame yourself," he'd point out. "In analysis you blame everyone else." His own master's degree in psychology had only strengthened that viewpoint.

He had the feeling Nash sensed his gut-level hostility to most shrinks. Sensed it and understood it.

They eyed each other. Well-dressed in an unobtrusive way, Vince thought. Vince was aware that he was no good at picking out the right tie for his suit. Alice used to do that for him. Not that he cared. He'd rather wear a brown tie with a blue suit than hear her harping at him all the time. "Why don't you leave the Bureau and get a job where you can earn some real money?" Today he'd grabbed the nearest tie and pulled it on in the elevator. It was brown and green. His suit was a blue pinstripe.

Alice was now Mrs. Malcolm Drucker. Malcolm wore Hermés ties and custom-made suits. Recently, Hank told Vince that Malcolm had blown up to size fifty-two. Fifty-two short.

Nash was wearing a gray tweed jacket, a red and gray tie. Nice-looking guy, Vince conceded. Strong chin, deep-set eyes. Skin a touch windburned. Vince liked a man to look as though he didn't hide indoors in lousy weather.

He got right to the point. "Dr. Nash, you left two messages for Erin Kelley. They suggest that you knew her, had dated her. Is that the case?"

"Yes. I am in the process of writing a book analyzing the social phenomenon of the personal ad situation. Kearns and Brown is my publisher; Justin Crowell, my editor."

Just in case I thought he was really trying to get a date, Vince thought, then warned himself to knock it off. "How did you come to go out with Erin Kelley? Did you answer her ad or did she answer yours?"

"She answered mine." Nash reached in his drawer. "I was anticipating your question. Here is the ad she answered. Here is her letter. I met her for a drink on January thirtieth at the Pierre. She was a lovely young woman. I expressed surprise that anyone so attractive would need to seek companionship. She quite frankly told me that she was answering ads at the behest of a friend who is doing a documentary. I don't usually acknowledge that I'm doing research on these meetings, but I was up-front with her."

"And that was the only time you saw her?"

"Yes. I've been terribly busy. I'm almost at the end of my book and wanted to get it finished. I'd planned to call Erin again when I turned it in. Last week I realized that it's going to take another month to complete and rushing it simply didn't work."

"And so you called her."

"Yes, early in the week. Then again last Thursday. No, it was Friday, just before I left for the weekend."

Vince studied the letter Erin had written to Nash. His ad was clipped to it: DWM, Physician, 37, 6′1″, attractive, successful, good sense of humor. Enjoys skiing, riding, museums, and concerts. Seeking creative, attractive s/d/wf. Box 3295.

Erin's typewritten note had said,

> Hi, Box 3295. Perhaps I'm all of the above. No, not quite. I do have a good sense of humor. I'm twenty-eight, 5′7″, 120 pounds, and my best friend tells me I'm very attractive! I'm a jewelry designer on my way to being successful. I'm a good skier; can

ride if the horse is slow and fat. Definitely a museum-goer. In fact, I get a lot of ideas for my jewelry by haunting them. And music is a must. See you? Erin Kelley, 212–555–1432.

"You can understand why I called," Nash said.

"And you never saw her again."

"I never got the chance." Michael Nash stood up. "I'm sorry. I have to cut this short. My first patient is arriving earlier than usual. But I'm here if you want me. If there's any way I can help, please allow me."

"How do you think you can help, Doctor?" Vince got to his feet as he asked the question.

Nash shrugged. "I don't know. I suppose it's the instinctive desire to want a killer brought to justice. Erin Kelley obviously loved life and had much to offer. She was only twenty-eight years old." He held out his hand. "You don't think much of us shrinks, do you, Mr. D'Ambrosio? Your version is that neurotic, self-centered people pay good money to come in here and complain. Let me explain how I view my job. My professional life is devoted to trying to help people who for whatever reason are in danger of sinking. Some cases are easy. I'm like a lifeguard who swims out because he notices that someone is over his head and simply escorts him back in. Other cases are much tougher. It's as though I'm trying to rescue a shipwreck victim during a hurricane. It takes a long time to get close to him and tidal waves are forcing me back. It's pretty satisfying when I'm able to complete the rescue."

Vince put Erin's letter in his briefcase. "You may be able to help us, Doctor. We're going to be tracking down the people Erin met through personal ads. Would you be willing to interview some of them and give your professional opinion of what makes them tick?"

"Absolutely."

"By any chance, are you a member of AAPL?" Psychiatrists who belonged to the American Association of Psychiatry and the Law, Vince knew, were particularly skilled in dealing with psychopaths.

"No, I'm not. But, Mr. D'Ambrosio, my research has shown that the vast majority of people who place or answer these ads do so because of loneliness or boredom. Others may have more sinister motives."

Vince turned and walked to the door. As he twisted the knob, he looked back. "I'd say that was true in Erin Kelley's case."

* * *

On Tuesday night, Charley drove to the retreat and went directly to the basement. He took down the stack of shoe boxes and laid them on top of the freezer. Clipped onto each of them was the name of the girl who belonged with them. Not that he needed reminding, of course. He remembered every single one in perfect detail. Besides that, except for Nan, he had a videotape of each of them. And he had videotaped the *True Crimes* program about Nan's death. They'd done a good job of finding a girl who looked like her.

He opened Nan's box. The scuffed Nike and the black sequined satin slipper. The slipper was garish. His taste had improved since then.

Should he send Nan's and Erin's things back at the same time? Carefully, he considered the idea. It was such an interesting decision.

No. If he did that the police and the media would realize immediately that their theory about a copycat murder was wrong. They'd know that one set of hands had snuffed out both lives.

Maybe it would be more fun to toy with them for a while.

Maybe start by returning Nan's shoe and the one from the first of the other girls. That had been Claire, two years ago. An ash-blond musical-comedy actress from Lancaster. She could dance so beautifully. Gifted. Really gifted. Her wallet was in the box with her white sandal and the gold slipper. Surely by now her family had given up her apartment. He'd send the package to the address in Lancaster.

Then every few days he'd send another package. Janine. Marie. Sheila. Leslie. Annette. Tina. Erin.

He'd time it so they'd all be delivered by March thirteenth. Fifteen days from now.

On that night, no matter how he accomplished it, Darcy would be here dancing with him.

Charley stared at the freezer. Darcy was going to be the last one. Maybe he'd keep her with him always. . . .

When Darcy got back to her apartment from the airport Tuesday evening, there were a dozen messages on the answering machine. Condolences from old friends. Seven calls had come in from personal ads Erin must have answered for her. The pleasant-voiced

David Weld again. This time he left a number. So did Len Parker, Cal Griffin, and Albert Booth.

A call from Gus Boxer saying he had a tenant for Erin Kelley's apartment. Could Miss Scott get the place cleared out by the weekend? If she did, she wouldn't have to pay the March rent.

Darcy rewound the tape, wrote down the names and phone numbers of the personal ad callers, and changed cassettes. Vince D'Ambrosio might want to have a record of those voices.

She heated a can of soup, ate it on a tray in bed. When she was finished she reached for the phone and the list of men who had called for a date. She dialed the first number. As it began to ring she slammed the phone back in the cradle. Tears gushed down her cheeks as she sobbed, "Erin, I want to call *you.*"

8

WEDNESDAY
February 27

At nine o'clock, Darcy went to the office. Bev was already there. She had coffee brewing and fresh juice and warm bagels. A new plant was on the windowsill. Bev hugged her briefly, her extravagantly mascaraed eyes filled with sympathy. "You can guess everything I want to say."

"Yes, I can." Darcy realized the coffee aroma was enticing. She reached for a bagel. "I didn't know I was hungry."

Bev assumed a businesslike attitude. "We had two calls in yesterday. People who saw the magic you did on the Ralston Arms apartment. Want you to redo for them. Also, would you take on that residential hotel on Thirtieth and Ninth? New owners. Claim they have more taste than money."

"Before I do anything else, I have to clear out Erin's apartment." Darcy took a gulp of coffee and pushed back her hair. "I dread it."

It was Bev who suggested she simply move all the furniture to the warehouse. "You told me it was a terrific setup. Could you use Erin's things piece by piece on jobs? One of the women who called wants to redo her daughter's bedroom in a really special way. The kid's sixteen and is coming home from the hospital after a long siege. She'll be laid up for quite a while."

It was good to think of Erin's pewter and brass bed being enjoyed by a girl like that. It made it easier. "I'd better check that it's all right for me to move everything out." She called Vince D'Ambrosio.

"I know the NYPD is finished going over the place," he told her.

Bev arranged for the van to go to Christopher Street the next day. "I'll meet it. Just show me what you want." At noon she went with Darcy to Erin's apartment. Boxer let them in.

"Sure appreciate you releasing the place," he whined. "Nice person taking it."

I wonder how much you got under the table, Darcy thought. I never want to come here again.

There were a few blouses and scarves that she decided to keep as mementos. The rest of Erin's clothes she gave to Bev. "You're Erin's size. Just please don't wear them to the office."

The jewelry Erin had made. Swiftly she gathered it, not wanting to think now about Erin's talent. What else was bothering her? Finally she laid all the jewelry on the worktable. Earrings, necklaces, pins, bracelets. Gold. Silver. Semiprecious stones. All imaginative, whether formal or fun pieces. *What was bothering her?*

The new necklace Erin had completed with the chunky gold copies of Roman coins. Erin had joked about it. "It'll retail for about three thousand dollars. I designed it for a fashion show in April. Can't afford to keep it for myself, but until then I'm going to wear it a few times."

Where was that necklace?

Had Erin been wearing it when she went out that last time? That and her initial ring and her watch. Were they with the clothes she'd been wearing when her body was found?

Darcy scooped Erin's personal jewelry into a suitcase along with the contents of the safe. She'd have the loose gems appraised and sold for Billy's nursing home expenses. She did not look back when she closed the door of apartment 3B for the last time.

On Wednesday afternoon at four o'clock, a detective from the Sixth Precinct, armed with Erin Kelley's picture, was making the rounds of the pubs in the Washington Square area. So far his search had been fruitless. Several bartenders freely acknowledged knowing Erin. "She'd drop in once in a while. Sometimes with a date. Sometimes meeting someone. Last Tuesday. No. Didn't see her at all last week."

Charles North's picture produced no effect at all. "Never saw that one."

Finally, at Eddie's Aurora on West Fourth Street, a bartender positively stated: "Yeah, that girl was here last Tuesday. I went to Florida Wednesday morning. Just got back. That's why I'm sure about the date. I started talking to her. Told her I was finally getting away for some sun. She said she was a typical redhead, her skin always burned. She was expecting to meet someone and waited around for about forty minutes. He never showed up. Nice girl. Finally, she paid her bill and left."

The bartender was sure it was Tuesday; sure Erin Kelley had come in at seven o'clock; sure she had been stood up. He accurately described the clothes she had been wearing, including an unusual necklace that resembled old Roman coins. "Necklace was real different. Looked expensive. I told her not to wander around outside without pulling her coat collar over it."

The detective reported to Vince D'Ambrosio from the pay phone in the bar. Vince immediately phoned Darcy, who verified that Erin had had a gold coin necklace. "I thought it might have been found on her." She told Vince that Erin's initial ring and watch were also missing.

"She was wearing a watch and earrings when she was found," Vince said quietly, and asked if he could come over.

"Sure," Darcy said. "I'll be working late."

When Vince arrived at the office, he was carrying a copy of Erin's personal ad file. "We did an exhaustive examination of all Erin's papers. In them we found a receipt for one of those private safe deposit boxes that are accessible twenty-four hours a day. Erin signed up for that only last week. She told the manager that she was a jewelry designer and was uncomfortable about the value of some of the stones she was keeping in her apartment."

Darcy listened attentively as Vince D'Ambrosio told her that Erin had been stood up on Tuesday night. "She left that bar alone at about quarter of eight. We're leaning to the theory that it was a felony murder. She was wearing the necklace Tuesday night, but not when she was found. We don't know about the ring."

"She always wore that ring," Darcy said.

Vince nodded. "She may have had the pouch of diamonds in her possession." He wondered if he was getting through to Darcy Scott. She was sitting at her desk, a pale yellow sweater accentuating the blond highlights in her brown hair, her expression totally controlled, her eyes more green than hazel today. He hated to be giving her copies of Kelley's personal ads file. He was sure that she was going to start writing to the ones that were circled.

Unconsciously, his voice deepened as he stressed, "Darcy, I know the sense of rage you're feeling at losing a friend like Erin. The point is, I beg you not to answer these personal ads with some crazy idea that you'll find the man who called himself Charles North. We're going to do everything we can to find Erin's killer. But the fact remains that even though Erin may not have been one of his victims, there is a serial murderer using these ads to meet young women, and I don't want you to be his next date."

Doug Fox had not strayed from Scarsdale over the weekend. He'd devoted himself to Susan and the children and been pleasantly compensated for his efforts by having Susan tell him that she'd arranged for a babysitter Monday afternoon. She wanted to do some shopping and proposed that they meet for dinner in New York that night and ride home together.

She had not told him that before shopping, she had the appointment with an investigative agency.

Doug had taken her to San Domenico for dinner and made it his business to be especially charming, even telling her that sometimes he forgot how really pretty she was.

Susan had laughed.

Tuesday night Doug had arrived home at midnight. "Damn late meetings," he'd sighed.

Wednesday morning he felt secure enough to tell Susan he'd be taking clients out to dinner and might as well stay at the Gateway. He was relieved at how understanding she was. "A client is a client, Doug. Just don't wear yourself out."

Wednesday afternoon when he left the office, he went straight to the apartment in London Terrace. He was meeting a divorced thirty-two-year-old real estate broker in SoHo for drinks at seven-thirty. But first he wanted to change into casual clothes and make a phone call.

He hoped that tonight he'd reach Darcy Scott.

* * *

On Wednesday afternoon, Jay Stratton received a call from Merrill Ashton of Winston-Salem, North Carolina. Ashton had been thinking long and hard about Stratton's suggestion that he buy Frances an important piece of jewelry for their fortieth wedding anniversary. "If I discuss it with her, she'll talk me out of it," Ashton said, a smile in his voice. "Point is, I have to be in New York next week on business. You got anything to show me? I was thinking maybe a diamond bracelet."

Jay assured him that he most certainly did have something to show him. "I just bought some particularly fine diamonds which are being set in a bracelet right now. It would be perfect on your wife."

"I'd want an appraisal."

"Of course you would. If you like the bracelet, you can take it to a jeweler in Winston-Salem whom you trust and if he doesn't agree that the value is there, we don't have a deal. Are you prepared to spend forty thousand dollars? One for each year of your marriage?"

He heard the hesitation in Ashton's reply. "Well, that's a bit steep."

"A truly exquisite bracelet," Jay assured him. "Something that Frances Junior will proudly leave to her own daughter."

They arranged to meet for a drink next Monday, March fourth.

Was it all going too well, Stratton wondered as he laid the portable phone on the coffee table. The twenty-thousand-dollar check for the Bertolini necklace. Would anyone think to come looking for it? The insurance on the pouch of diamonds. With Erin's body found, the chance that she had been robbed could not be disputed. He'd give Ashton the gemstones at a reasonable but not questionable price. A jeweler in Winston-Salem wasn't going to be looking for stones listed as missing or stolen.

A wave of pure pleasure swept over him. Stratton laughed, remembering what his uncle had said to him twenty years ago. "Jay, I've sent you to an Ivy League school. You've got the brains to get good marks on your own, and you still cheat. Your father will never be dead while you're around."

When he told his uncle that he'd conned the dean at Brown into letting him reapply if he joined the Peace Corps for two years, his uncle had sarcastically snapped, "Be careful. There's nothing to steal in the Peace Corps and you might actually have to do some work."

Not that much work. At twenty he'd started over at Brown as a freshman. Never get caught, his father had warned him. And if you do, no matter how you fix it, make sure you don't have a record.

He'd of course been older than the other students. They'd all looked like babyfaced kids, even the ones who were obviously rich.

Except for one.

The phone rang. It was Enid Armstrong. Enid Armstrong? Of course, the teary-eyed widow.

She sounded excited. "I talked to my sister about your suggestion of what I should do to my ring and she said, 'Enid, if that will give you a lift, do it. You deserve to pamper yourself.' "

On the channel 4 six o'clock news, reporter John Miller had an ongoing report about Erin Kelley. It had been learned that a quarter of a million dollars in diamonds was missing from her safe. Lloyd's of London had posted a fifty-thousand-dollar reward for their return. The police still believed that she had been the victim of a copycat murderer who might not have known that she was carrying valuables. The report ended with a reminder that the *True Crimes* dramatization of Nan Sheridan's death was being repeated at eight o'clock.

Darcy snapped the off button on the remote control. "It had nothing to do with a robbery," she said aloud. "It had nothing to do with a copycat murder. No matter what they say, it had everything to do with a personal ad."

Vince D'Ambrosio would undoubtedly learn the identity of some of the people Erin had dated. But Erin had been meeting for the first time the man who called himself Charles North, and he hadn't shown up. Suppose he'd been just coming into the bar and met her at the door? Suppose he'd been one of the ones to whom she'd sent a picture? Suppose he'd said, "Erin Kelley, I'm Charles North. I got stuck in traffic. This place looks crowded. Let's go somewhere else."

It makes sense, Darcy thought. If there is a serial killer out there and if he's been responsible for other deaths, he won't stop now. If only she knew which ads Erin had actually answered, which ads she'd answered for both of them.

It was seven o'clock, a good time to try returning the calls that had been left on her machine. In the next forty minutes she reached three people, left messages for the other four. Now she had a date for drinks with Len Parker at McMullen's on Thursday, drinks with David Weld at Smith and Wollensky's Grill on Friday, and brunch with Albert Booth at the Victory Café on Saturday.

What about the guys who had left messages on Erin's machine? A couple of them had given phone numbers that she'd taken down. Maybe she'd call them back, tell them about Erin in case they didn't already know, and try to get a date with them. If they were meeting a lot of girls, they might have heard someone talk about a date who turned out to be weird.

The first two didn't answer. The next one picked up immediately. "Michael Nash."

"Michael, I'm Darcy Scott, a good friend of Erin Kelley's. I imagine you know what happened to her."

"Darcy Scott." The pleasant voice deepened with concern. "Erin told me about you. I'm so terribly sorry. I spoke with an FBI agent yesterday and assured him I'd like to help in any way I can. Erin was a lovely girl."

Darcy realized her eyes were filling with tears. "Yes, she was."

Obviously, he caught the catch in her voice. "This is terribly rough for you. Can I take you out for dinner some night soon? Talking about it may help."

"I'd like that."

"Tomorrow?"

Darcy thought swiftly. She was meeting Len at six. "If eight o'clock is all right with you."

"It's fine. I'll make a reservation at Le Cirque. Incidentally, how will I know you?"

"Medium brown hair, five eight. I'll wear a blue wool dress with a white collar."

"I'll be the most average-looking guy in the place. I'll be waiting at the bar."

Darcy hung up feeling somehow comforted. At least I'll get some use out of the Rodeo Drive clothes, she thought, and realized that instinctively she was making a mental note to call Erin and tell her that.

She got up and massaged the back of her neck. A dull headache made her realize she hadn't eaten since noon. It was now quarter of eight. A quick, hot shower, she decided. Then I'll heat some soup and watch that program.

The soup, appetizing enough when piping hot, slumped into a thick concoction of bits of vegetables swimming in tomato stock as Darcy stared at the screen. The photograph of the dead nineteen-year-old, her one foot in a scuffed Nike, the other in a sequined black satin pump, was horrifying. Was that the way Erin had looked when she'd been found? Hands folded on her waist, the tips of the mismatched shoes pointing in the air? What kind of sick brain could see that picture and want to duplicate it? The program closed with a reference to the fact that a copycat murderer might be responsible for the death of Erin Kelley.

When it was over, she snapped off the set and buried her face in her hands. Maybe the FBI was right about the copycat murder. It could not have been sheer coincidence that a few weeks after that program was shown, Erin had died in the same way.

But why Erin? And did the slipper she was wearing fit? If it did, how did her killer know her size? Maybe I'm crazy, she thought. Maybe I should back off and leave this to people who know what they're doing.

The phone rang. She was tempted not to answer it. Suddenly she felt too tired to talk to anyone. But it might be news about Billy. The nursing home had her number to call for emergencies. She picked up the receiver. "Darcy Scott."

"In person. Well, *at last.* I've been trying you every few days. I'm Box 2721. Doug Fields."

9

THURSDAY
February 28

On Thursday morning, Nona, working with her assistant producer, Liz Kroll, completed the planning of the documentary. Liz, a thin-faced, sharp-featured young woman, had interviewed the potential guests, culling the duds as she put it.

"We've got a nice mix," she assured Nona. "Two couples who ended up married. The Caírones fell in love at first sight and are mushy enough to satisfy the romantic slobs. The Quinlans answered each other's ads and are pretty funny telling how their letters crossed in the mail. We've got someone who looks like young Abe Lincoln confiding how shy he is and that he's still hunting for the perfect girl. We've got a gal whose ad mistakenly read that she was a wealthy divorcée. She got seven hundred answers and has dated fifty-two of them so far. We've got a woman who had dinner with her date and at the end he picked a fight with her, stalked off, and stuck her with the check. The next guy practically attacked her when he drove her home. Now he hangs around her house. She woke up one morning and saw him looking in her bedroom window. If your friend Erin

Kelley had actually met her date that night, we'd have a heck of a terrific wrap-up."

"Wouldn't we ever," Nona said quietly, and realized that she had never liked Liz.

Kroll did not seem to notice. "That FBI agent, Vince D'Ambrosio, is cute. I talked to him yesterday. He's going to show pictures of those missing girls on the program and warn people that they all answered personal ads. Then he'll ask if anybody has any information, that kind of thing. That worries me a little. We don't want to sound like *True Crimes,* but what can you do?" She got up to go. "One more thing. You know that Barnes woman from Lancaster whose daughter Claire has been missing for two years? I had a brainstorm yesterday. What about having her on the show? Just a brief segment. I bumped into Hamilton and he thought it was a great idea but said to check with you."

"Nobody bumps into Austin Hamilton." Nona felt anger cut through the dull lethargy that had been encompassing her with each passing day. Not for a single minute could she get Erin out of her mind. That face, always ready to break into a smile, that slender, graceful body. Like the others in the waltz class where they'd met, Nona was a pretty good dancer, but both Erin and Darcy were outstanding. Particularly Erin. Everyone else stopped to watch when she waltzed with the instructor. And I got friendly with them and told them about this great idea I had for a personal ad documentary. If only Vince D'Ambrosio were right. He believed Erin had been the random victim of a copycat murderer. Please God, let it be that, Nona prayed. Let it be that.

But if Erin had died because she'd answered personal ads, let this program help to save someone else. "I'll call Mrs. Barnes in Lancaster," she told Kroll, her tone a clear dismissal.

Darcy sat on the windowsill of the bedroom she was redecorating for the teenager who would soon be coming home from the hospital. Erin's pewter and brass bed would be perfect. The charming turn-of-the-century lady's vanity that she'd picked up in Old Tappan last week had deep drawers. It really was like a small dresser and wouldn't crowd the room. The present double dresser, a battered mahogany veneer object, was a horror. More overhead shelves in the closet would take care of bulky items like sweaters.

She was aware that the girl's mother, a weary look on her pleasant face, was studying her anxiously. "Lisa's been in a dreary room in the hospital for such a long time that I thought having her room done over might give her a lift. She's in for so much therapy, but she's spunky. She told the doctors she'll be back in dancing class in another couple of years. Ever since she could toddle, the minute she heard music she'd start to dance."

Lisa had been run over by a messenger on a bike who'd been cycling at top speed against the traffic on a one-way street. He'd smashed into her, breaking her legs, ankles, and foot bones. "She loves to dance," her mother added wistfully.

"Loves music, loves to dance." Darcy smiled, thinking of the framed poster with that title that had been in Erin's bedroom. Erin always said that it was the first thing she saw in the morning and it brightened her day. She firmly squelched the instinctive desire to keep it as a memoir. "I have just the thing for that wall," she said, and felt the constant pain ease a little. It was almost as though Erin was nodding in approval.

The Harkness on East Forty-fifth Street was the discreet investigative firm Susan Fox retained to probe into the nocturnal wanderings of her husband, Douglas. The retainer of fifteen hundred dollars had seemed symbolic to her. That was just what she had squirreled away in a personal account, saving for Doug's August birthday. She'd smiled sadly as she wrote the check.

On Wednesday she had called Carol Harkness. "My husband has one of his famous nonmeetings tonight."

"We'll have Joe Pabst, one of our best people, following him," she was assured.

On Thursday, Pabst, jovial-featured, heavy-set, reported to his boss. "This guy's a piece of work. He leaves his office, cabs up to London Terrace. He's got an apartment there; been subletting from the owner, an engineer named Carter Fields, for two years. He's registered as Douglas Fields. Pretty neat. That way, nobody questions an illegal sublet and he don't run into anyone tracking him down at work or at home. Same initials, too. That's lucky. Don't have to worry about his monogrammed cufflinks."

Pabst shook his head in reluctant admiration. "The neighbors think he's an illustrator. Super tells me he's got a lot of signed pen-and-ink stuff framed in the apartment. I gave the super the garbage about him being up for a government assignment. Slipped the usual twenty bucks to keep the mouth shut."

At thirty-eight, Carol Harkness looked like one of the women executives in the AT&T commercials. Her well-cut black suit was brightened only by a gold lapel pin. Her ash-blond hair was shoulder length. Her hazel eyes had a cool, impersonal expression. The daughter of a New York City detective, the love of police work was in her blood.

"Did he stay there or go out?" she asked.

"Went out. About seven o'clock. You should have seen the difference in him. Hair combed so it looked real curly. Turtleneck sweater. Jeans. Leather jacket. Don't get me wrong, not cheap-looking. Kind of the way the arty types with money dress. He met some gal in a bar in SoHo. Attractive. Thirty or so. Classy. I got the table behind them. They had a coupla drinks, then she said she had to leave."

"Anxious to dump him?" Harkness asked quickly.

"No way. She had big eyes for him. He's a good-looking guy and can turn on the charm. They have a date Friday night. They're going dancing at some nightclub downtown."

His forehead creased in concentration, Vince D'Ambrosio studied the autopsy report on Erin Kelley. It stated that she had eaten approximately an hour before she died. Her body showed no sign of decomposition. Her clothing had been soaked through. These facts were initially attributed to the sleet and cold the day she was found. The autopsy revealed that her organs were partially thawed. The medical examiner concluded that her body had been frozen immediately after her death.

Frozen! Why? Because it was too dangerous for the killer to dispose of the body immediately? Where had she been kept? Had she died on Tuesday night? Or was it possible that she had been held captive somewhere and died as late as Thursday?

Had she been planning to put the pouch of diamonds in the security vault? From all accounts, Erin Kelley was a level-headed young woman. Certainly, she didn't seem like the kind who would confide to a stranger that she was carrying a fortune in jewels in her purse.

Or would she?

They'd been running down the identity of the people who'd placed some of the ads they believed Erin answered. So far they'd all been like that lawyer, North. Absolute proof of where they'd been Tuesday night. Some of them picked up their own mail at the magazines or newspapers where they'd run the ads. Three of the forwarding addresses for the others turned out to be mail drops. Probably married guys who didn't want to take any chance of their wives opening the mail.

It was nearly five when Vince received a call from Darcy Scott. "I've been wanting to talk to you all day, but I've been out of the office on jobs," she explained.

Best thing for her, Vince thought. He liked Darcy Scott. After Kelley's body was found, he'd asked Nona Roberts about Scott's family and had been astonished to learn that she was the offspring of two superstars. Nothing Hollywood about that girl. Genuine. It was amazing some guy hadn't snapped her up yet. He asked her how it was going.

"It's going okay," Darcy said.

Vince tried to analyze what he was hearing in her voice. The first time he met her in Nona's office her low, strained tone suggested acute worry. At the morgue, until she'd broken down, she'd spoken in the emotionless monotone of a person in shock. Now there was a certain briskness. Determination. Vince knew instantly that Darcy Scott was still convinced that Erin's death was the result of answering personal ads.

He was about to talk to her about that when she asked, "Vince, something has been bothering me. Did that high-heeled shoe Erin was wearing fit? I mean, was it her size?"

"It was the same size as her boot, seven and a half narrow."

"Then how did whoever put it on her happen to have a shoe exactly her size?"

Smart girl, Vince thought. Carefully, he weighed his words. "Miss Scott, that's something we're working on now. We're trying to trace that shoe through the manufacturer to learn where it was purchased. It's not cheap, in fact the pair probably cost several hundred dollars. That narrows considerably the number of outlets in the New York area that might carry it. I promise I'll keep you posted on developments." He hesitated, then added, "I hope you've given up the idea of following up any personal ads Erin Kelley answered for you."

"As a matter of fact," Darcy told him, "I have my first date with one of them in an hour."

* * *

Len Parker at six. They were meeting at McMullen's on Seventy-sixth and Third. A trendy place, Darcy thought, and certainly safe. A favorite with the New York "in" crowd. She'd been there on dates a few times and liked the owner, Jim McMullen. She was only going to have a glass of wine with Parker. He'd told her he was meeting some friends at the Athletic Club to play basketball.

She had told Michael Nash that she would be wearing a blue wool dress with a white collar. Now that she had it on, she felt over-dressed. Erin always teased her about the clothes her mother showered on her. "When you get around to wearing them, you make the rest of us look as though we shop in John's Bargain Store."

Not true, Darcy thought as she applied another smidgen of mid-night-gray eye shadow. Erin always looked great, even in college when she had so little money to buy clothes.

She decided to wear the silver and azurite pin Erin had given her for her birthday. "Funky but fun," Erin had pronounced it. The pin was shaped like a bar of music. The notes were lined in azurite, exactly the sea-blue shade of the dress. Silver bracelets and earrings and narrow suede boots completed the outfit.

Carefully, Darcy appraised herself in the mirror. On the trip to California, her mother had bullied her into going to her personal hairdresser. He'd changed her part, cut off a few inches, then accentuated the natural blond highlights in her hair. She had to admit that she liked the results. She shrugged. Okay, I look good enough that Len Parker probably won't walk out on me when I show up.

Parker was tall, bone-thin, but not unattractive. A college teacher, he told her he had recently moved to New York from Wichita, Kansas, and didn't know many people. Over a glass of wine he confided that a friend had suggested he place a personal ad. "They're really expensive. You'd be surprised. It makes a lot more sense to answer other people's ads, but I'm sure glad you answered mine." His eyes were light brown but large and expressive. He stared at Darcy. "I really have to say this. You're very pretty."

"Thank you." Why was it that something about him made her uncomfortable? Was he really a teacher, or was he like the one date she'd had before she went to California? That guy had claimed to be an advertising executive and didn't know the first thing about the agencies she brought up with him.

Parker fidgeted on the bar stool, rocking it slightly. His voice was low and with the hubbub of conversation from the people nearby, Darcy had to lean over to hear him.

"Very pretty," he emphasized. "You know, not all the girls I've met are pretty. When you read the letters they send, you'd think they were Miss Universe. And who shows up? Olive Oyl."

He signaled for another glass of wine. "You?"

"I'm fine." Carefully, she chose her words. "Surely all of them weren't that bad. I bet you've met some really pretty girls."

He shook his head emphatically. "Not like you. No way."

It was a long hour. Darcy heard about Parker's trouble finding an apartment. The prices, wow. Some girls think you should take them out for fancy dinners. Come on. Who can keep that up?

Finally, Darcy was able to get Erin's name in. "I know. My friend and I both met some strange people through these ads. Her name was Erin Kelley. Did you meet her by any chance?"

"Erin Kelley?" Parker swallowed convulsively. "Wasn't that the girl who got murdered last week? No, I never met her. And she was your friend? Gee, I'm sorry. That's lousy. Did they find the killer yet?"

She did not want to discuss Erin's death. There was no way, even if Erin met this man once, that she'd have gone out with him a second time. She looked at her watch. "I have to run. And you'll be late for your basketball game."

"Oh, that's all right. I'll skip it. Stay for dinner. They have good hamburgers here. Expensive, but good."

"I really can't. I'm meeting someone."

Parker frowned. "Tomorrow night? I mean, I know I'm not much to look at and teachers are famous for not making much money, but I'd really like to see you again."

Darcy slipped her arms into her coat. "I really can't. Thank you."

Parker stood up and punched the bar. "Well, you can pay for the drinks. You think you're too good for me. I'm too good for you."

She was relieved to see him stalk out of the restaurant. When the bartender came with the check, he said, "Miss, don't bother with that nut. Did he pull his college-professor stuff? He's on the maintenance staff at NYU. He gets more free drinks and meals through those ads he places. You got off cheap."

Darcy laughed. "I think I did, too." A thought struck her. She reached in her purse for Erin's picture. "By any chance, did he ever show up with this girl?"

The bartender, who looked as though he might be an actor, studied the picture carefully, then nodded. "He sure did. Around two weeks ago. She was a knockout. She walked out on him."

* * *

At six o'clock, Nona was surprised and pleased to receive a call from Vince D'Ambrosio. "You're obviously another one who doesn't keep regular hours," he said. "I'd like to talk to you about your program. Are you free for dinner in about an hour?"

She was.

"Okay, make a reservation at a good steak place in your neighborhood."

Smiling, she hung up. D'Ambrosio was clearly a meat-and-potatoes man, but she'd bet her bottom dollar that his cholesterol level was fine. She realized that she was unreasonably glad that she'd worn her new Donna Karan jumpsuit today. The cranberry shade suited her and the gold belt with the clasped hands accentuated her small waist. Nona knew that her waistline was her one vanity. Then she had a flash of overwhelming sadness. Erin had made that belt for her for Christmas.

Shaking her head as though to negate the reality of Erin's death, she got up and walked around her desk, rotating her shoulders. She'd spent the entire day working on the documentary and felt as though her body was a mass of knots. At three o'clock, Gary Finch, the Hudson Cable anchorman, had reviewed it with her. At the end of the session, Finch, a notorious perfectionist, smiled and said, "It's going to be great."

"Approbation from Sir Hubert is praise indeed." Nona stretched and tried to decide whether or not to call Emma Barnes in Lancaster again. She'd already tried three or four times. Admittedly, Liz was smart to suggest having Barnes appear on the program to talk about her missing daughter who had answered personal ads. Liz was bright and imaginative. But she was trying to skunk me when she discussed Barnes with Hamilton, Nona decided. She wants my job. Let her try.

She gave one last, long stretch, sat at her desk, and dialed the Lancaster number. Once more the Barnes household did not answer.

Vince arrived promptly at seven. He was wearing a well-cut gray pinstriped suit accompanied by a brown and beige tie. It's for sure no woman picks out his ties, Nona thought, remembering how fussy Matt had been about what tie went with which shirt and what suit.

* * *

The restaurant was on Broadway, a few blocks from Nona's apartment. "Let's save the serious stuff for dessert," Vince suggested. Over salads they briefly sketched their personal lives. "If you were placing a personal ad, what would you say about yourself?" he asked.

Nona reflected. "Divorced White Female, age 41, cable television producer."

He sipped his scotch. "Go on."

"Manhattan born and bred. Think anyone who lives anywhere else is mentally ill."

He laughed. She noticed that caused friendly creases in the corners of his eyes.

Nona sipped her wine. "This is terrific burgundy," she commented. "I hope you're planning to have some when the steak comes."

"I am. Finish your ad, please."

"Barnard graduate. I didn't even leave Manhattan for college, you see. I did have a year abroad, and I do like to travel as long as I'm not gone more than three weeks."

"Your ad's getting expensive."

"I'll wind it up. Clean but not particularly tidy. You've noticed my office. Do not have green thumb. Good cook but hate fussy food. Love jazz. And oh, yes, I'm a good dancer."

"That's how you got friendly with Erin Kelley and Darcy Scott, in a dance class," D'Ambrosio commented, and then watched as pain darkened Nona's eyes. Hurriedly he added, "My ad's a little shorter. I work for the government. Divorced White Male, 43 years old, FBI agent, brought up in Waldwick, New Jersey, graduated from NYU. Can't dance without tripping over my own feet. Like to travel as long as it isn't Vietnam. Three years there was enough. And last, but certainly not least, I have a fifteen-year-old son, Hank, who's a swell kid."

As she had promised, the steaks were superb. Over coffee they talked about the program. "We're taping it in two weeks," Nona said. "I'd like to save you for last so people are left with a sobering warning about the potential danger of answering these ads. You're going to show the pictures of the missing girls, aren't you?"

"Yes. There's always the chance a viewer may have information about one of them."

It was biting cold when they left the restaurant. A frosty winter wind made Nona gasp. Vince took her arm as they crossed the street. He did not remove it the rest of the way to her apartment.

He accepted her invitation to come up for a nightcap. Nona remembered happily that her cleaning lady, Lola, had been in. The place would look presentable.

The seven-room apartment was in a prewar building. She could see D'Ambrosio's eyebrows raise as he took in the large foyer, the high ceilings, the long windows on Central Park West, the paintings in the living room, the massive Jacobean furniture. "Very nice," he commented.

"My folks gave it to me as is when they moved to Florida. I'm an only child, and this way when they come up to New York, my father feels comfortable. He hates hotels." She went to the bar. "What'll it be?"

She poured Sambuca for both of them, then paused. "It's only quarter past nine. Do you mind if I take a minute to phone some one?" She reached in her purse. As she looked up the Barnes's number, she explained why she was calling them.

This time the phone was picked up immediately. Nona froze as she realized the sound she was hearing was a woman screaming. A man's voice gave a distracted greeting. In shocked bewilderment he said, "Whoever this is, please get off the phone. I must call the police immediately. We've been away all day and just opened the mail. There was a package addressed to my wife."

The screams were now a shrieking crescendo. Nona motioned to Vince to pick up the portable telephone on the table beside him.

"Our daughter," the bewildered voice went on. "She's been missing for two years. That package has one of Claire's own shoes and a high-heeled satin slipper in it." He began to shout, "Who sent this? Why did they send it? Does this mean Claire is dead?"

Darcy was handed out of the cab by the doorman, entered Le Cirque, and felt herself begin to unwind. She had not realized how much energy she had put into the meeting with Len Parker. Her head was still buzzing with the realization that he had met Erin. Why had he denied it? Erin had walked out on him. Certainly, she'd never dated him again. Was it simply that he didn't want to be questioned and have to admit the lies about his background?

Every time her mother and father were in New York they dined at Le Cirque. It was a wonderful restaurant. Darcy found herself wondering why she didn't come here more often. *How ever did two such stunning people manage to produce that mousy-looking child?* And how could one sentence remain so imbedded in memory?

The bar was to the left. Small and charming, it was not a hangout but a place to wait for a guest or a table. A young couple was standing near it, chatting animatedly. A single man was at the end. *The most ordinary-looking person you'll see.*

Michael Nash had not been kind to himself. Dark blond hair, a face that was saved from being conventionally handsome by a rather sharp chin, a long, trim body, dark blue suit with faint pinstripes, silver and blue tie. As he looked at her with obvious recognition and pleasure, Darcy was aware that Michael Nash's eyes were an unusual shade, somewhere between sapphire and midnight blue.

"Darcy Scott." It was a statement, not a question. He signaled to the maître d' and put his hand under her elbow.

They were seated at a prime table in full view of the entrance. Michael Nash must be a frequent and valued customer of Le Cirque.

"A drink? Wine?"

"White wine, please. And a glass of water."

He ordered a bottle of Pellegrino with the Chardonnay, then smiled. "Now that for the moment we've taken care of the necessaries, as an old friend puts it, Darcy, it's good to meet you."

For the next half hour, she realized that he was deliberately steering the conversation away from Erin. It was only after she had begun to sip the wine and pick at a roll that he said, "Mission accomplished. I think you are finally starting to feel safe."

Darcy stared at him. "Whatever do you mean?"

"I mean that I was watching for you. I saw the way you hurried in. Everything about you suggested a high level of tension. What happened?"

"Nothing. I'd really like to talk about Erin."

"I would too. But Darcy . . ." He stopped. "Look, I can't get out of the business of doing what I do all day. I'm a psychiatrist." His smile was apologetic.

She felt herself at last begin to relax. "I'm the one who should apologize. You're absolutely right. I did feel pretty tense coming here." She told him about Len Parker.

He listened attentively, his head slightly tilted. "You'll of course report this man to the police."

"The FBI, actually."

"Vincent D'Ambrosio? As I told you when you called, he came to my office on Tuesday. Unfortunately, I could tell him very little. I met Erin for a drink several weeks ago. I had the immediate feeling that a girl like her had no need to answer personal ads. I challenged her with that and she told me about the program her friend is putting together. She mentioned you. Said her best friend was answering ads with her."

Darcy nodded, hoping that her eyes were not going to fill with tears.

"I don't usually explain that the reason I'm going this route is because of a book I'm working on, but I did tell Erin. We exchanged some stories about our various dates. I've tried to remember everything she said, but she didn't give any names and they were funny stories. Certainly, I had no hint that anyone worried her."

" 'Close encounters of the worst kind,' she used to call them."

Nash laughed. "She told me that. I asked if we could plan dinner soon, and she agreed. I was trying to wrap up my book and she was completing a necklace she had designed. I said I'd get back to her. When I tried, there was no answer. From what Vincent D'Ambrosio said, it was already too late."

"That was the night she thought she was meeting someone named Charles North. I still think that even though he didn't show up, her death has to do with a personal ad she answered."

"Thinking that, why are you answering personal ads now?"

"Because I'm going to find that man."

He looked troubled but did not comment. They studied the menu, both selecting the Dover sole. As they ate, Nash seemed to be deliberately trying to keep her mind off Erin's death. He told her about himself. "My father made his money in plastics. Literally lived out that famous line from *The Graduate.* Then bought a rather garishly ornate mansion in Bridgewater. He was a decent, fine man, and every time I wonder why three of us needed twenty-two rooms, I remember how happy he was showing them off."

He touched on his divorce. "I married the week after I graduated from college. Terrible mistake for both of us. It wasn't a financial problem, but medical school, especially when it involves the continuing study of psychoanalysis, is a long, hard road. We didn't have time for each other. By the end of four years, she'd had enough. Sheryl lives in Chicago now and has three children."

It was Darcy's turn. Carefully, she steered around giving the names of her famous parents, jumping quickly to leaving the advertising agency and setting up her budget decorating business.

"Somebody once told me I'm a new version of Sanford and Son, and I guess it's true, but I love it." She thought of the room she was decorating for the recuperating sixteen-year-old.

If he noticed gaps in the background, he did not comment. The salads arrived just as a producer friend of her parents stopped at the table. "Darcy!" A warm kiss, a hug. He introduced himself to Michael Nash. "Harry Curtis." He turned back to Darcy. "You get prettier every day. I hear your parents are touring in Australia. How's it going?"

"They just got there."

"Well, give them my love." Another hug and Curtis left for his own table.

Nash's eyes did not signal curiosity. That's the way it works with shrinks, Darcy thought. They wait for you to tell them. She did not offer an explanation of what Curtis had said.

It was a pleasant dinner. Nash confessed to two passions, riding and tennis. "They're what keep me in Bridgewater." Over espresso, he returned to the subject of Erin's death. "Darcy, I don't usually offer advice to people, even free advice, but I wish you'd drop the idea of answering these ads. That FBI fellow seemed perfectly competent to me and if I'm any judge, he's not going to rest until whoever murdered Erin is paying the price."

"He told me that in so many words. I guess we all do what we have to do." She managed a smile. "The last time I spoke to Erin, she said she'd met one nice guy and wouldn't you know it, he hadn't called back. I'd bet my bottom dollar it was you."

He took her home in a cab, told the driver to wait, and walked her to the door. The wind was sharp and he turned so that he was protecting her from its full blast as she turned the key. "May I call you again?"

"I'd like that." For a moment she thought he was going to kiss her cheek, but he simply pressed her hand and went back to the waiting cab.

The wind pulled at the door, causing it to close slowly. As the lock clicked, the sound of footsteps made her turn. Through the glass she could see the figure of a man rushing up the steps. An instant sooner and he would have been in the vestibule with her. As she stared at him, her mouth too dry to scream, Len Parker pounded at the door, kicked it, then turned and ran down the block.

10
FRIDAY
March 1

Greta Sheridan debated between getting up or trying to sleep for another hour. A gusty March wind was rattling the windowpanes and she remembered that Chris had been after her to have these windows replaced.

The early-morning light filtered through the drawn draperies. She loved a cold room for sleeping. The quilt and blankets were warm and the blue and white moire canopy gave the bed a comforting enclosed feeling.

She had been dreaming of Nan. The anniversary of her death, March thirteenth, was two weeks away. Nan had turned nineteen the day before. This year she would have been celebrating her thirty-fourth birthday.

Would have been. Impatiently, Greta tossed back the covers, reached for her velour robe, and got up. Pulling on her slippers, she went into the hallway and down the winding staircase to the main floor. She understood why Chris was concerned. It was a large house and it was generally known that she lived alone. "You don't know how easy it is for a professional to disarm a security system," he had warned several times.

"I love this house." Every room held so many happy memories. Somehow, Greta felt that to leave this place would be to leave them as well. And, she thought with an unconscious smile, if Chris would finally settle down one of these days and give me some grandchildren, it will be a wonderful place for them to visit.

The *Times* was at the side door. As the coffee perked, Greta began to read. There was a brief item on an inside page about that girl who'd been found dead in New York last week. Copycat murder. What a horrible thought. How could there be two such evil people, the one who had snuffed out Nan's life and the one who had killed Erin Kelley? Would Erin Kelley still be alive if that program had not been aired?

And what was it that she had been trying to remember when she insisted on watching it? Nan. Nan, she thought. You told me something that I should have realized was important.

Nan, chatting about school, her classes, her friends, her dates. Nan looking forward to the summer program in France. Nan who loved to dance. "I Could Have Danced All Night." The song could have been written for her.

Erin Kelley had also been found wearing one high-heeled shoe. High heel? What was it about those two words? Impatiently, Greta opened the *Times* to the crossword puzzle.

The phone rang. It was Gregory Layton. She'd met him at the club dinner the other night. In his early sixties, he was a federal judge and lived in Kent about forty miles away. "An attractive widower," Priscilla Clayburn had whispered to her. He *was* attractive, and he was asking her to have dinner with him tonight. Greta accepted and replaced the receiver, realizing that she was looking forward to the evening.

Dorothy came in at the stroke of nine. "Hope you don't have to go out this morning, Mrs. Sheridan. That wind is mean." She was carrying the mail, including a bulky package under her arm. She laid everything on the table and frowned. "That's a funny looking thing. I mean, no return address. I hope it's not a bomb or something."

"Probably more of that awful crank mail. Damn that program." Greta started to pull at the string on the package and had a sudden sense of panic. "It does look funny. Let me call Glenn Moore."

Police Chief Moore had just arrived in his office at headquarters. "Don't touch that package, Mrs. Sheridan," he told her crisply. "We'll be right over." He called the state police. They promised to rush a portable security surveillance unit to the Sheridan household.

At ten o'clock, handling the package with infinite caution, an officer in the bomb squad positioned it to be X-rayed.

From the living room to which she and Dorothy had been banished, Greta heard the man's relieved laughter. Dorothy at her heels, she hurried back to the kitchen.

"These won't blow up, ma'am," she was assured. "Nothing in there except a pair of mismatched shoes."

Greta saw Moore's startled expression, felt the blood drain from her face as the package was ripped open, revealing a shoe box with the sketch of an evening slipper on the cover. The lid came off. Inside, nestled together in tissue, were a high-heeled sequined slipper and a scuffed running shoe.

"Oh, Nan! Nan!" Greta did not feel Moore grab her as she fainted.

* * *

At three o'clock on Friday morning, Darcy was yanked from restless sleep by the insistent ringing of the phone. Reaching for it, she saw the time on the clock radio. Her "hello" was quick and breathless.

"Darcy." Her name was whispered. The voice sounded familiar, but she couldn't place it.

"Who is this?"

The whisper became a shout. "Don't you ever close the door in my face again! Hear me? Hear me?"

Len Parker. She slammed down the phone, pulled the covers around her. A moment later the phone began to ring again. She did not pick it up. The ringing continued. Fifteen, sixteen, seventeen rings. She knew she should take the receiver off the hook but could not bear to touch it, knowing that Parker was on the other end.

Finally it stopped. She yanked the jack from the wall, rushed into the living room, and put the answering machine on automatic pickup, then hurried back to bed, slamming the bedroom door behind her.

Had he done this to Erin? Followed her when she walked out on him? Maybe followed her to the bar where she was supposed to meet someone named Charles North? Maybe forced her into a car?

She'd call Vince D'Ambrosio in the morning.

For the next two hours she lay awake, finally falling into a sleep that once again was troubled with vague, restless dreams.

At seven-thirty, she awakened with an instant sense of fear, then remembered the reason for it. A long, hot shower relieved some of the tension. She pulled on jeans, a turtleneck sweater, her favorite boots.

The answering machine showed only hangups.

Juice and coffee at the table by the window. Staring down into the lifeless garden. At eight o'clock the phone rang. Not Len Parker, please. Her "hello" was guarded.

"Darcy, I hope it's not too early to call. I just wanted to tell you how much I enjoyed being with you last night."

She exhaled, a relieved sigh. "Oh, Michael, I can't tell you how much I enjoyed being with you too."

"Something happened. What was it?"

The concern in his voice was comforting. She told him about Len Parker, the episode on the steps, the phone call.

"I blame myself that I didn't see you upstairs."

"Please don't."

"Darcy, call that FBI agent and report this Parker character, and can I implore you to stop answering those ads?"

"I'm afraid not. But I will call Vince D'Ambrosio right away."

When she said good-bye, she hung up feeling oddly consoled.

She called Vince from the office. A wide-eyed Bev stood by her desk as she spoke to another agent. Vince had flown to Lancaster. The other agent took the information. "We're working with the police department. We'll get right onto that character. Thanks, miss."

Nona phoned and told her why Vince had gone to Lancaster. "Darce, this is so scary. It's one thing if someone saw that *True Crimes* episode and was perverted enough to repeat it, but this means someone may have been doing this for a long time. Claire Barnes has been missing for two years. She and Erin were so alike. She was just about to get her first big break in a Broadway musical. Erin had just gotten her first big break with Bertolini's."

Her first big break with Bertolini's. The words rippled through Darcy's mind as she made and received phone calls, went through Connecticut and New Jersey papers for notices of estate and moving sales, made a quick trip to the rental apartment she was furnishing, and finally stopped for a sandwich and coffee at a lunch counter. That was where she realized what had been bothering her. *Her first big break with Bertolini's.* Erin had told her she was to receive twenty thousand dollars for designing and executing the necklace. In the rush of events, she forgot about the strange message on Erin's answering machine. She'd call them as soon as she got back to the office to confirm.

Aldo Marco came to the phone. Was this a family member making inquiries?

"I'm executor of Erin Kelley's estate." The words sounded appalling to her ears.

Payment had already been made to Miss Kelley's manager, Jay Stratton. Was there a problem?

"I'm sure there isn't." So Stratton presumed to act as Erin's manager.

He was not home. The message she left was brusque. Please call her immediately about Erin's check.

Jay Stratton phoned just before five o'clock. "I'm sorry. Of course I should have gotten to you sooner. I've been away. How shall I make out the check?" He told Darcy that while he was out of town he'd thought of nothing but Erin. "That beautiful, talented girl. I firmly believe that someone knew about that jewelry, killed her for it, and then tried to make it look like a copycat murder."

You of all people knew about the jewelry. It was an effort to listen to Stratton, to respond pleasantly to his sympathetic comments. He would be out of town again for a few days. She agreed to meet him Monday evening.

For minutes after she said good-bye to him, Darcy stared straight ahead, lost in thought, then said aloud, "After all, as you say, Mr. Stratton, two of Erin's closest friends really ought to know each other better." She sighed. She'd better get some work done before it was time to dress for her date with Box 1527.

Vince flew to Lancaster on the earliest flight Friday morning. He had urged Claire Barnes's father not to tell anyone outside the family about the package of shoes. But when he arrived at the airport the local paper had the story in headlines. He phoned the Barnes's home and learned from the maid that Mrs. Barnes had been rushed to the hospital last night.

Lawrence Barnes was a heavy-set executive type who, Vince decided, in other circumstances would have a commanding presence. Seated at the bedside, a young woman next to him, he was anxiously looking down at his heavily sedated wife. Vince showed him his card and was followed out into the corridor.

Barnes introduced the young woman as his other daughter, Karen. "A reporter happened to be in the emergency room when we got here," Barnes said tonelessly. "He heard Emma screaming about the package and that Claire was dead."

"Where are the shoes now?"

"At home."

Karen Barnes drove him to get them. A corporate lawyer in Pittsburgh, she had never shared her parents' hope that one day Claire would suddenly show up. "There was no way, if she were alive, she would have given up the chance to be in Tommy Tune's show."

The Barnes's home was a large Colonial in an impressive neighborhood. Zoning at least an acre, Vince thought. There was a television mobile unit on the street. Karen drove quickly past it, into the driveway, and around to the back of the house. A policeman prevented the reporter from stopping her.

The living room was filled with framed family pictures, many of them showing Karen and Claire in their growing-up years. Karen picked one of them off the piano. "I took this one of Claire the last time I saw her. We were in Central Park just a few weeks before she disappeared."

Slender. Pretty. Blond. Mid-twenties. Joyous smile. You can pick 'em, Buster, Vince thought bitterly. "May I take this? I'll make copies and get the original right back to you."

The package was on the foyer table. Ordinary brown wrapper, address label you could buy anywhere, block printing. Postmarked New York City. The box had no markings except for a delicately drawn sketch of a high-heeled slipper on the lid. The mismatched shoes. One a white Bruno Magli sandal, the other a gold slingback with an open toe and narrow high heel. They were the same size, six narrow.

"You're sure this sandal is hers?"

"Yes. I have an identical pair. We bought them together that last day in New York."

"How long had your sister been responding to personal ads?"

"About six months. The police checked out anyone whose ad she had answered, at least anyone they could find."

"Did she ever place any?"

"Not that I know of."

"Where did she live in New York?"

"On West 63rd Street. An apartment in a brownstone. My father paid the rent for nearly a year after she disappeared, then gave it up."

"Where did you put her belongings?"

"The furniture wasn't worth shipping. Her clothes and books and whatever are upstairs in her old room."

"I'd like to see them."

* * *

There was a cardboard file box on a shelf in the closet. "I packed that," Karen told him. "Her address book, date book, stationery, some mail, that sort of thing. When we reported her missing, the New York police went through all her personal papers."

Vince lifted down the box and opened it. A date book now two years old was on top. He skimmed through it. From January till August the pages were filled with appointments. Claire Barnes had not been seen after August fourth.

"What makes it hard is that Claire had her own kind of shorthand." Karen Barnes's voice quavered. "You see where it says 'Jim.' That meant Jim Haworth's studio, where she took dancing lessons. See, August fifth, 'Tommy.' That meant rehearsal for the Tommy Tune show, *Grand Hotel.* She'd just been hired."

Vince turned the pages back. On July fifteenth at five o'clock he saw "Charley."

Charley!

In a noncommittal tone he pointed to the entry. "Do you know who this one is?"

"No. Although she did mention a Charley who took her dancing once. I don't believe the police were able to locate him." Karen Barnes's face paled. "That slipper. It's the sort of thing you'd wear to a dance."

"Exactly. Miss Barnes, keep that name between the two of us, please. By the way, how long had your sister lived in her apartment?"

"Just about a year. Before that she had a place in the Village."

"Where?"

"Christopher Street. At 101 Christopher Street."

At quarter of five, Darcy handed Bev the last of the bills to be paid, and on impulse phoned the mother of the recuperating teenager. The girl was coming home at the end of next week. The painter Darcy hired, a cheerful moonlighting security guard, was already on the job. "We'll have the room all set by Wednesday," Darcy assured the woman.

Thank heaven I had the brains to bring some clothes with me this morning, she thought as she changed from her sweater and jeans to an oval-necked, long-sleeved black silk blouse, a calf-length Italian silk skirt in tones of green and gold, a matching stole. Gold chain, a narrow gold bracelet, gold earrings—the jewelry all designed by Erin.

In a crazy way she felt as though she was donning Erin's coat of arms as she rode into battle.

She released her hair from the clip and brushed it loose around her face.

Bev came back just as she finished applying eyeshadow. "You look fabulous, Darcy." Bev hesitated. "I mean, it always seemed to me that you kind of tried to play down your looks and now, I mean, oh God, I'm not saying it right. I'm sorry."

"Erin pretty much said the same thing," Darcy reassured her. "She was always bullying me to use more makeup or wear some of the fancy duds my mother sends me."

Bev was wearing a skirt and sweater Darcy had seen on her frequently. "By the way, how do Erin's clothes fit?"

"Perfect. I'm so glad to get them. The tuition just jumped again and I swear, with today's prices, I was getting ready to do a Scarlett O'Hara and make a dress out of curtains."

Darcy laughed. "That's still my favorite scene in *Gone With the Wind.* Look, I know I asked you to avoid wearing Erin's things to the office, but she'd be the first to say enjoy them. So feel free."

"Are you sure?"

Darcy reached past the faithful leather jacket for her cashmere cape. "Of course I'm sure."

She was meeting Box Number 1527, David Weld, at the grill at Smith and Wollensky's at five-thirty. He'd said he'd be at the last seat at the bar, "or standing near it." Brown hair. Brown eyes. About six feet tall. Wearing a dark suit.

It was easy to pick him out.

A pleasant guy, Darcy decided fifteen minutes later as they sat across from each other at one of the small tables. Born and raised in Boston. Worked for Holden's, the department store chain. Had been coming back and forth for the last few years as they expanded into the Tri-State Area.

She judged him to be in his mid-thirties, then wondered if there was something about that age that sent unattached singles scurrying to the personal ads.

It was easy to direct the conversation. He'd gone to Northeastern. His father and grandfather had been executives with Holden's. He'd worked there from the time he was a kid. After school. Saturdays. Summer vacations. "Never occurred to me to do anything else," he confided. "Retailing runs in the family."

He had never met Erin. He'd read about her death. "That's what makes you feel funny placing these ads. I mean, all I want is to meet some nice people." Pause. *"You're nice."*

"Thank you."

"I'd be very pleased to have dinner with you if you can stay." He looked hopeful but the request was made with dignity.

No ego problem here, Darcy thought. "I honestly can't, but I bet you've met some nice people answering these ads, haven't you?"

He smiled. "A couple of very nice ones. One of them, if you can believe it, just started to work for Holden's in the Paramus, New Jersey, store. She's a buyer. Same kind of job I had before I went into the management end."

"Oh? What was that?"

"I was shoe buyer for our New England stores."

Vince got back to his office at Federal Plaza at three o'clock Friday afternoon. There was an urgent message for him to call Police Chief Moore in Darien. From him, Vince learned about the package that had arrived at the Sheridan home.

"You're sure they're the mates of the ones Nan Sheridan was wearing?"

"We've compared them. We have both sets now."

"Has the press gotten hold of this?"

"Not so far. We're trying to keep it quiet, but no guarantees. You've met Chris Sheridan. That was his first concern."

"It's mine, too," Vince said quickly. "What we now know is that this killer started fifteen years ago, if not sooner. He has to have a reason for sending those shoes back at this time. I want to talk to one of our psychiatrists to get his opinion. But if anyone questioned about Nan Sheridan's death also can be linked to Claire Barnes, we've got something positive to go on."

"How about Erin Kelley? Don't you include her?"

"I'm still keeping an open mind. Her death may have been connected to the missing jewelry and made to look like a copycat murder." Vince arranged to pick up the shoes the next day and hung up.

His assistant, Ernie Cizek, a new young agent from Colorado, briefed him on Darcy's call about Len Parker.

"This guy's a weirdo," Cizek said. "Works in maintenance at NYU. An electrical whiz. Can fix anything. Loner. Paranoid about money. But get this! The family is loaded. Parker's got a hefty income. A trustee banks an allowance for him. He only made one large withdrawal, some years ago. The trustee thinks he bought property. Seems to live on his maintenance salary in a cheap walkup on Ninth Avenue. Has an old station wagon. No garage. He parks it on the street."

"Police record?"

"Same sort of thing that the Scott girl complained about. Following girls home. Shouting at them. Banging on doors. He's a great one for placing personal ads. Everybody brushes him off. So far no physical attacks. Restraining orders but no convictions."

"Bring him in now."

"I've talked to his shrink. He says he's harmless."

"Sure he's harmless. Just like Peeping Toms supposedly never act out their fantasies. We both know better, don't we?"

Susan's announcement that she was planning to take the children to visit her father in Guilford, Connecticut, for the weekend was received with eager agreement by her husband. Doug had made the date to go dancing with the divorced real estate broker and was wondering if he should break it. He had been late two nights this week and even though Susan had seemed to enjoy their New York dinner on Monday night, there was something about her attitude that he could not put his finger on.

Susan's visiting her father with the kids till Sunday gave him two nights off. He did not offer to go with her. It would have been an empty gesture. Susan's father had never liked him, always made cracks about how important Doug must be that he worked so many nights. "Funny, with all that hard work, you needed to borrow so much from me to buy the house, Doug. I'd be glad to go over your budget with you and see where the problem is."

Sure you would.

"Have a good time, honey," Doug told Susan when he was leaving on Friday morning. "And give my best to your Dad."

That afternoon, while the baby slept, Susan phoned the investigative agency for a report. Calmly she took down the information they gave her. The meeting with the woman in the SoHo bar. The date they'd made to go dancing. The apartment in London Terrace under the name Douglas Fields. "Carter Fields is his old buddy," she told the investigator. "They're two of a kind. Don't bother to follow him again. I don't want to hear any more."

* * *

Her father lived year-round in the pre-Revolutionary house that had been their summer home. Several heart attacks had left him with a permanent pallor that tore at Susan's heart. But there was nothing fragile about his demeanor or voice. After dinner, Beth and Donny went next door to visit friends. Susan put Trish and the baby to bed, then fixed demitasse and brought it into the library.

She knew her father was studying her as she prepared his cup with sweetener and a lemon peel.

"Exactly when do I hear the reason for this unexpected, although most welcome, visit?"

Susan smiled. "Now, I guess. I'm going to divorce Doug."

Her father waited.

Promise not to say "I told you so," Susan prayed silently, then went on, "I've had an investigative agency following him. He has a sublet in New York under the name Douglas Fields. Calls himself a freelance illustrator. Doug does sketch very well as you know. Has plenty of dates. In the meantime, he rants on to me about how hard he works, 'all those night meetings.' Donny can see through his lies and is angry and contemptuous. He'll be better off to expect nothing from his father than to keep on hoping that it will change."

"Would you like to move in here, Susan? There's plenty of room."

She flashed him a grateful smile. "You'd go crazy in a week. No. The Scarsdale house is too large. Doug insisted we buy it to impress the people at the club. We couldn't afford it then, and I'm beginning to understand why we can't afford it now. I'll sell it, get a smaller place, put the baby in a day care center next year— there's a terrific one in town. Then I'll get a job."

"It won't be easy."

"It'll be a lot better than it is now."

"Susan, I'm trying not to say, 'I told you so,' but there it is. That fellow is a born womanizer and he's got a vicious streak. Remember your eighteenth birthday? That night he was so drunk when he brought you home that I threw him out? The next morning every window in my car was broken."

"You still can't be sure it was Doug."

"Come on, Susan. If you're going to start facing facts, face them all. And tell me this. Weren't you covering for him when he was questioned in that girl's death?"

"Nan Sheridan?"

"Of course, Nan Sheridan."

"Doug simply isn't capable—"

"Susan, what time did he pick you up the morning she died?"

"Seven o'clock. We wanted to get back to Brown for a hockey game."

"Susan, before she died I got the truth out of Grandma. You were in tears because you thought Doug had stood you up again. He got to our place after nine. At least grant me the satisfaction of telling the truth now."

The front door banged shut. Donny and Beth came in. Donny's face looked relaxed and happy. It was becoming a carbon copy of Doug's face at that age. She'd had a crush on Doug from their sophomore year in high school.

Susan felt a stab of pain. I'll never get over him completely, she acknowledged. *Doug pleading with her, "Susan, my car broke down. They're trying to accuse me. They want to blame somebody. Please say I was here at seven."*

Donny came over to kiss her. She reached back and smoothed his hair, then turned to her father. "Dad, come on. You know how confused Grandma was. Even back then she didn't know one day from another."

11

SATURDAY

March 2

It was 2:30 a.m. Saturday morning when he got to the place. By then his need to be there was overwhelming. When he was in the place, Charley could be his own person. No more skulking behind the other one. Able to dance in synch with Astaire, smiling down at the phantom in his arms, crooning in her ear. The wonderful solitude of the place, the draperies drawn against the unseemly gaze of a casual interloper, the bolts securing him from the outside world, the limitless sense of self, unrestrained by listeners or observers, free to roam in the delicious memories.

Nan. Claire. Janine. Marie. Sheila. Leslie. Annette. Tina. Erin. All of them smiling at him, so glad to be with him, never getting the chance to turn on him, sneer at him, look at him with contempt. In the end, when they understood, it had been so wonderfully satisfying. He regretted that he hadn't given Nan a chance to realize what was happening, to beg. Leslie and Annette had pleaded for their lives. Marie and Tina had cried.

Sometimes the girls came back to him one by one. Other times they appeared together. *Change partners and dance with me.*

By now the first two packages would have arrived. Oh, if only one could be the proverbial fly on the wall, watching the moment when they were opened, when the puzzled expression changed to comprehension.

Copycat.

They wouldn't call him that anymore. Now had Janine been next, or Marie? Janine. September twentieth, two years ago. He'd send her package now.

He went to the basement. The boxes with the shoes were such an amusing sight. Pulling on the plastic gloves he always used when he handled anything that belonged to the girls, he reached for the one behind the place card marked "Janine." He'd send it to her family in White Plains.

His eye lingered on the last place card. "Erin." He began to giggle. Why not send hers now? That would really put their copycat notion in the gutter. She'd told him her father was in a nursing home. He'd send them to her New York address.

But suppose no one in her apartment building was smart enough to give the package to the police? What a waste to have it gathering dust in some storeroom.

What about sending the shoes care of the morgue? After all, that was her last address in New York. How funny that would be.

First, make sure to wipe the shoes and boxes thoroughly just to make sure there were absolutely no prints on them. Get out the identification. He'd plucked their wallets from their purses, then buried the purses.

Wrap fresh tissue around the mismatched sets. Close the lids. He admired his sketches. He was getting better. The one on Erin's box was as good as any professional could do.

Brown wrapping paper, sealing tape. Address label. Any one of them could have been bought anywhere in the United States.

He addressed Janine's package first.

Now it was Erin's turn. The New York telephone book would give the address of the morgue.

Charley frowned. Suppose some dumb klutz in the mailroom didn't open it, just gave it back to the postman. "Nobody with that name works here." Without a return address the package would go into the dead-letter office.

There was one other possibility. Would it be a mistake? No. Not really. He giggled again. This will certainly keep them guessing!

He began to print the name of the person he had chosen to receive Erin's boot and special slipper.

DARCY SCOTT . . .

On Saturday, Darcy met Box 1143, Albert Booth, for brunch at the Victory Café. She judged him to be about forty. In their telephone conversation she'd managed to learn that his ad claimed he was a computer expert, enjoyed reading, skiing, golfing, waltzing, leisurely strolls through museums, and listening to records. He also said he had a good sense of humor.

That, Darcy decided, after Booth asked her "if meeting a box number made her feel boxed in," stretched truth to the breaking point. By the time she had finished her first cup of coffee, she also doubted just about everything else he'd claimed except computer expert. He had a soft couch-potato look that did not hint of a skier, golfer, waltzer, or walker.

His conversation consisted solely of the past, present, and future of computers. "Forty years ago a computer took two big rooms of heavy equipment to do what the one on your desk is doing now."

"I finally bought one just last year."

He looked shocked.

Over eggs Benedict, he shared his disgust with the way clever students were manipulating school records by breaking into computer systems. "They should go to jail for five years. And pay a big fine too."

Darcy was sure that desecration of the sanctuary or ark of the temple would not have been any more serious to him.

Over the last cup of coffee, he finally finished expounding his theory that future wars would be won or lost by experts able to crack enemy computers. "Change all the figures, see what I mean. You think you have two thousand nuclear warheads in Colorado. Somebody changes it to two hundred. You have armies deployed. The statistics change. Where's the Fifth Division? The Seventh? You don't know anymore. Right?"

"Right."

Booth smiled suddenly. "You're a good listener, Darcy. Not many girls are good listeners."

It was the opening she needed. "I've just started to answer personal ads. You certainly meet a variety of people. What are most of them like?"

"Most of them are pretty boring." Albert leaned across the table. "Listen, you want to know who I took out just two weeks ago?"

"Who?"

"That girl who was murdered. Erin Kelley."

Darcy hoped she would not overreact. "What was *she* like?"

"Pretty girl. Nice. She was worried about something."

Darcy gripped her coffee cup. "Did she tell you what was worrying her?"

"She sure did. She told me she was finishing some necklace and it was her first really big job and as soon as she was paid she was going to look for a new apartment."

"Any reason?"

"She said the superintendent was always brushing against her when she passed him and making excuses to be in her apartment. Looking for a water leak, a heat blockage, that kind of thing. She said she supposed he was harmless, but it was kind of creepy to walk into her bedroom and find him there. I guess it had just happened again the day before I met her."

"Don't you think you ought to let the police know about this?"

"No way. I work for IBM. They don't want any of their employees ever to be mentioned in the papers unless they're getting married or buried. I tell the police and they start checking on me. Right? But I wonder. Do you think I ought to drop them an anonymous note?"

The vast resources of the FBI swung into high gear for the search for the retail outlet where the high-heeled evening slipper that had been returned to the home of Claire Barnes and the one found on Erin Kelley's body had been purchased. In the case of Nan Sheridan, fifteen years ago the police had traced the slipper to a shoe outlet on Route 1 in Connecticut. No one then had had any memory of who had bought it.

The Claire Barnes slipper was expensive, a Charles Jourdan, sold in fine department stores all over the country. Two thousand pairs, to be exact. Impossible to trace. Erin Kelley's was a Salvatore Ferragamo, a current model.

Agents and NYPD detectives began to fan through department stores, shoe salons, discount outlets.

* * *

Len Parker was brought in for questioning. He began immediately to rant about how rude Darcy had been to him. "I just wanted to apologize. I knew I'd been mean. Maybe she did have a dinner date. I followed her and she wasn't lying. I waited outside in the cold while she ate in that fancy restaurant."

"You just stood there?"

"Yes."

"And then?"

"She got right in a cab with some guy. I took one too. Got out down the block. The guy walked her to the door and left. I ran up. After all I went through to apologize, she slammed the door in my face."

"How about Erin Kelley? Did you follow her?"

"Why should I? She walked out on me. Maybe that was my fault. I was in a bad mood when I saw her. I told her all women were rotten gold diggers."

"Then why didn't you admit that to Darcy Scott? When she asked you, you denied meeting Erin."

"Because I knew I'd end up here."

"You live on Ninth Avenue and Forty-eighth Street?"

"Yes."

"Your trustee at the bank thinks you have another residence. You withdrew a large sum of money five or six years ago."

"It was my money to spend as I please."

"Did you buy another residence?"

"Prove it."

On Saturday afternoon when he was finished with Len Parker, Vince D'Ambrosio drove to 101 Christopher Street and rang the bell. Gus Boxer, his face set in surly lines, came to the door. He was wearing a long-sleeved undershirt. Tattered suspenders held up shapeless trousers. He acted unimpressed by the FBI badge. "I'm off duty. What do ye want?"

"I want to talk to you, Gus. Your place or headquarters? And drop the righteous indignation. I have your file on my desk, Mr. Hoffman."

Boxer's eyes darted nervously. "Come on in. And keep your voice down."

"I wasn't aware I'd raised it."

Boxer led the way to his ground-floor apartment. As Vince had expected from the way the man dressed, the apartment was a further extension of his personality. Shabby, stained upholstery. Remnants of a once-beige rug. A rickety table piled with porn magazines.

Vince riffled through them. "Quite a collection you have here."

"Any law against it?"

Vince slapped down the magazines. "Listen, Hoffman, we've never gotten anything on you, but your name has an unhealthy way of coming up on the computer. Ten years ago you were the super of an apartment where a twenty-year-old girl was found dead in the basement."

"I had nothing to do with that."

"She'd filed a complaint with the management that she found you in her apartment going through her closet."

"I was looking for a water leak. There was a waterpipe in the wall behind that closet."

"That's the same story you gave Erin Kelley two weeks ago, isn't it?"

"Who said that?"

"She told someone that she was going to move as soon as possible because she'd found you in her bedroom."

"I was—"

"Looking for a water leak. I know. Now let's talk about Claire Barnes. How many times did you drop in on her unexpectedly when she lived here?"

"Never."

When he left Boxer, Vince went directly to his office, arriving there just in time to get a call from Hank. Was it okay if he didn't get in until eight or so? There was a basketball game at school and some of the gang were going out for pizza afterward.

A great kid, Vince told himself again as he assured Hank that was fine. Worth all the years of trying to make a go of his marriage to Alice. Well at least she was happy now. The pampered wife of a guy whose wallet was as fat as his waistline. And he? I'd like to meet someone, Vince admitted to himself, then realized that Nona Roberts's face was suddenly filling his mind.

His assistant Ernie told him there'd been a break. A detective from the Midtown North Precinct had picked up Petey Potters, the derelict who lived on the pier where Erin Kelley's body was found. They were bringing Petey into the precinct for questioning. Vince turned and ran for the elevators.

* * *

Petey was having trouble with his vision. Seeing double. That happened sometimes after he'd had a coupla bottles of dago red. That meant that instead of three cops he was seeing three sets of twin cops. Nobody's eyes were friendly.

Petey thought about the dead girl. How cold she'd felt when he'd lifted the necklace.

What was the cop saying? "Petey, there are fingerprints on Erin Kelley's throat. We're going to compare them with yours."

Through a haze, Petey thought of one of his friends who'd happened to stab a guy. He was in prison for five years now and the guy he stabbed had hardly been scratched. Petey had never been in trouble with the cops. Never. He wouldn't hurt a fly.

He told them that. He could tell they didn't believe him.

"Look," he volunteered in a burst of confidence. "I found that girl. I didn't have enough money to buy even a cuppa coffee." Tears formed in his eyes at the memory of how thirsty he'd been. "I could tell the necklace was real gold. It had a long chain with lots of fancy coins attached. Figured if I didn't take it, the first guy who found her would. Including some cops I've heard about." He was sorry he'd added that.

"What'd you do with the necklace, Petey?"

"Sold it for twenty-five bucks to that big dude who works Seventh Avenue around Central Park South."

"Buy-and-Sell Bert," one of the cops remarked. "We'll pick him up."

"When did you find the body, Petey?" Vince asked.

"When I woke up late morning." Petey squinted. His eyes took on a crafty expression. Everything was coming into focus. "But real early, I mean when it was still pitch dark, I heard a car drive onto the pier, pass my place, and stop. I figured it might be a drug deal so I stayed inside. Honest."

"Even when you knew it was driving away?" one of the detectives asked. "You didn't even peek?"

"Well, when I was sure it was going . . ."

"Did you get a look at it, Petey?"

They believed him. He knew it. If he could only tell them something else to make them feel like he was trying to cooperate. Petey forced the alcoholic haze to retreat for a split second from his brain. All the days of standing with a bottle of sudsy water and a squeegee at the Fifty-sixth Street exit of the West Side Highway rushed through his mind. He'd had plenty of chance to know what the backs of cars looked like.

Again he could see the taillights of the car disappearing off the pier. Something about the rear window. "It was a station wagon," he said with a triumphant wheeze. "On Birdie's grave, it was a station wagon."

As the haze rushed back, Petey had to force himself not to cackle. Birdie was probably still alive.

Darcy and Nona had planned to have dinner together on Saturday night. Other friends were calling, inviting her to join them, but Darcy was in no mood yet to see anyone.

They arranged to meet at Jimmy Neary's Restaurant on East Fifty-seventh Street. Darcy arrived first. Jimmy had saved the left back corner table for them. "A damn shame," he said as he greeted Darcy. "Erin was one of the prettiest lasses ever to walk through this door, God rest her." He patted Darcy's hand. "You were a grand friend to her. And don't think I don't know it. Sometimes when she'd come in for a quick bite, I'd sit with her for the moment. I told her to watch her step answering those crazy ads."

Darcy smiled. "I'm surprised she told you about them, Jimmy. She'd have known you wouldn't approve."

"Be sure I didn't. She reached in her jacket pocket for a handkerchief last month and pulled out one that she'd torn from a magazine. It fell to the floor and when I picked it up, it caught my eye. I said to her, 'Erin Kelley, I hope you're not into that foolishness.' "

"That's what I'm afraid of," Darcy told him. "Erin was a fabulous jewelry designer but not much of a record keeper. The FBI is trying to trace anyone Erin wrote to or met, but I'm sure the list isn't complete." Darcy decided against saying that she was also answering personal ads. "Do you remember what that ad said?"

Neary's brow furrowed in thought. "No, but I got a fair glance at it, and I will. Something about singing or—ah, it'll come. Look, here's Nona and she has someone with her."

Vince followed Nona to the table. "I'm only going to stop by for a minute," he told Darcy. "I don't want to interfere with your dinner, but I was trying to reach you, phoned Nona, and found out you were here."

"It's fine, and I wish you'd stay." Darcy noticed that Nona's eyes had a brightness she had never seen in them before. "You got the message about Erin's telling one of her dates that she'd found the superintendent in her apartment again?"

"I saw Boxer today." Vince raised an eyebrow. *"Again?"*

"Erin told me he pulled that last year, but she always dismissed him as being harmless. Apparently as of two weeks ago she changed her mind."

"We're following up on him as well as other people. I'd like to hear about the guy from last night."

"He was a nice guy . . ."

Liz came to take their orders. She gave Darcy a quick, sympathetic smile. She always took such good care of us, Darcy thought. She had told Erin that growing up in Ireland she'd been a redhead too.

Dubonnet for Darcy and Nona. A beer for Vince.

Darcy and Nona decided on the red snapper. Nona said crisply to Vince, "You've got to eat sometime."

He ordered the corned beef and cabbage.

Vince got back to Darcy's other date. "I want to know about everybody you met. You've already seen two who admitted knowing Erin. Please let me decide on who is or isn't important."

She told him about David Weld. "He's an executive from Boston with the Holden chain. I gather he's been back and forth to New York for the last few years as they opened new stores." She felt as though she could read Vince D'Ambrosio's mind. *Back and forth to New York for the last two years.* Darcy said, "The one thing that did strike me is that he's been a shoe buyer."

"Shoe buyer! What's this guy's name?" Vince made a note in his book. "David Weld, Box 1527. Believe me, we'll check him out. Darcy, Nona told you about the shoes that were returned to the parents of the girl from Lancaster?"

"Yes."

He hesitated, glanced around, and saw that the people at the next table were absorbed in their own conversation. "We're trying to keep this one quiet. Another pair of mismatched shoes were delivered yesterday. They were the mates of the ones Nan Sheridan was found wearing fifteen years ago."

Darcy gripped the table. "Then Erin's death may not be a copycat crime."

"We just don't know. We're digging to see if anyone who knew Claire Barnes also knew Nan Sheridan."

"And Erin?" Nona asked.

"That would of course clinch the fact we have another Ted Bundy who's been getting away with serial murders for years." Vince put down his fork. "I've got to tell it to you straight. A lot of people who answer these ads turn out to be a far different cry from the way they describe themselves. All the young women our computer targeted as being possible serial-killer victims are in your age bracket, in your intelligence bracket, in your looks bracket. In other words, our killer may date fifty girls and then one turns him on. I know I can't dissuade you from answering these ads. Frankly, you've turned up some mighty interesting people for us to investigate. Nevertheless, you're not trained to be a decoy. You're a thoroughly nice, vulnerable young woman who doesn't have the ability to protect herself if she suddenly finds that she's painted into a corner."

"I don't intend to let myself get painted into a corner."

Vince had a quick coffee and left. He explained that his son, Hank, was coming in on a train from Long Island and he wanted to be in the apartment when he arrived.

Nona's eyes followed him as he stopped to pay the check. "Did you notice his tie?" she asked. "Today it was a blue and black check with a brown tweed jacket."

"So? Surely that doesn't bother you."

"No, I like it. Vince D'Ambrosio is so determined to find whoever killed these girls that I swear he blocks out anything unimportant. I happened to call the Barnes home in Lancaster just after they opened the package with the shoes and I tell you, hearing them broke my heart. Today I called Nan Sheridan's brother to ask him to be on the program. I could hear that same pain in his voice. Oh, Darcy, please God, be careful."

12

SUNDAY

March 3

On Sunday morning at nine o'clock, Michael Nash phoned. "I've been thinking about you, even worrying about you. How's it going?"

She had slept reasonably well. "Okay, I guess."

"Up to a drive to Bridgewater, New Jersey, and an early dinner?" He did not wait for her to answer. "In case you haven't looked out the window, it's a beautiful day. Really feels like spring. My housekeeper is a great cook and has to be treated for frustration if I don't bring company home at least once over the weekend."

Somehow, she had dreaded this day. If they didn't have other plans, she and Erin had often met for brunch on Sundays and spent the afternoon at Lincoln Center or in a museum. "That sounds fine." They arranged that he'd pick her up at eleven-thirty.

"And don't get all gussied up. In fact, if you like to ride, wear a pair of jeans. I've got a couple of darn good horses."

"I love to ride."

His car was a two-seater Mercedes. "Very fancy," Darcy said.

Nash was wearing a turtleneck sport shirt, jeans, a herringbone jacket. The other night at dinner, she'd had the impression of how kind his eyes were. Today they were still kind, but there was something else. Maybe, she told herself, just the look a guy got when he was interested in a woman. Darcy realized that the thought pleased her.

The drive was pleasant. As they progressed south on Route 287, the suburbs disappeared. Houses that could be glimpsed from the road were now farther and farther apart. Nash talked with affectionate warmth about his parents. "To paraphrase that old commercial, 'My father made his money the old-fashioned way, he earned it.' He was just starting to hit it big when I was born. For ten years we moved every year, one house larger than the other, until he bought the present place when I was eleven. As I told you, my tastes are somewhat simpler, but God he was so proud the day we moved in. Carried my mother over the threshold."

Somehow it was easy to talk with Michael Nash about her famous parents and the Bel-Air mansion. "I always felt like a changeling there, as though the princess daughter of the royal couple must be living in a cottage and I was an impostor in her place." *How ever did two such stunning people manage to produce that mousy-looking child?*

Erin was the only one who knew about that. Now Darcy found herself telling Michael Nash. Then she added, "Hey, this is Sunday. You're off duty, doctor. Be careful, you've got a way of being too good a listener."

He glanced at her. "And when you grew up, you never looked in the mirror and realized what an outrageous statement that was?"

"Should I have?"

"I would say so." He was steering the car off the highway, through the quaint town, along a country road. "The fence starts the property."

It was a full minute before they turned into the gate. "My God, how many acres do you have?"

"Four hundred."

At the Le Cirque dinner he had said the house was too ornate. Darcy silently agreed but nevertheless decided that it was an imposing and substantial mansion. The trees and plants were still bare of leaves and flowers, but the evergreens that edged the long driveway were full and luxuriant. "If you decide you've enjoyed yourself and come back next month, the grounds will be worth the trip," Nash commented.

Mrs. Hughes, the housekeeper, had prepared a light lunch. Sandwiches quartered with the crusts cut off—chicken, ham and cheese—then cookies, coffee. She looked approvingly at Darcy, severely at Michael. "I hope this is enough, miss. Doctor said that since you'll be having an early dinner I mustn't overdo now."

"It's perfect," Darcy told her sincerely. They ate in the breakfast room off the kitchen. Michael then gave her a quick tour of the house.

"Interior-decorator picture perfect," he said. "Don't you agree? Antiques that cost a fortune. I suspect half of them are fakes. Someday I'll change everything, but for now it just isn't worth the effort. Unless I'm having guests I live in the study. Here we are."

"Now this is a comfortable room," Darcy said with real pleasure. "Warm. Lived-in. Wonderful view. Good lighting. It's the kind of look I try to give a place when I refurbish."

"You really haven't told me much about your job. I want to hear, but how about that ride now? John has the horses ready."

Darcy had begun riding when she was three. It was one of the few activities she had not shared with Erin. "She was afraid of horses," Darcy told Michael as she swung onto the coal-black mare.

"Then riding won't be memory lane for you today. That's good."

The air, fresh and clean, seemed to at last cleanse the scent of funeral flowers from her nostrils. They cantered across Michael's property, slowed the horses to a walk as they went across town, joined other riders whom he introduced as his neighbors.

At six o'clock, they had dinner in the small dining room. The temperature had dropped. A fire was blazing, the white wine chilling, a decanter of red wine on the sideboard. John Hughes, now in uniform, served the beautifully prepared meal. Crabmeat cocktail. Veal medallions. Tiny asparagus. Roast potatoes. Green salad with pepper cheese. Sherbet. Espresso.

Darcy sighed as she sipped the coffee. "I can't thank you enough. If I'd been home by myself all day, it would have been pretty rough."

"If I'd been here alone all day, it would have been pretty boring."

She could not help overhearing Mrs. Hughes comment to her husband as they were leaving, "Now there is one lovely girl. I hope Doctor brings her back."

13

MONDAY

March 4

On Monday evening, Jay Stratton met Merrill Ashton in the Oak Bar of the Plaza. The bracelet, a band of diamonds in a charming Victorian setting, won Ashton's instant approval. "Frances is just going to love that," he enthused. "I'm sure glad you convinced me to order it for her."

"I knew you'd be pleased. Your wife is a very pretty woman. That bracelet will look lovely on her arm. As I told you, I want you to have it appraised when you get home. If the jeweler tells you it's worth one cent less than forty thousand dollars, the deal is off. In fact, he'll undoubtedly tell you that you drove a hard bargain. But the fact is that I'm hoping that next Christmas you'll think of another piece for Frances. A diamond necklace? Diamond earrings? We'll see."

"So this is your loss leader for me?" Ashton chuckled as he reached for his checkbook. "That's good business."

Jay felt the peculiar thrill that came with taking risks. Any decent jeweler would tell Ashton that at fifty thousand the bracelet would still be a bargain. Tomorrow he had a lunch date with Enid Armstrong. He couldn't wait to get his hands on her ring.

Thank you, Erin, he thought as he accepted the check.

Ashton invited Jay to have a quick bite before he left for the airport. He was taking a 9:30 plane home to Winston-Salem. Stratton explained that he was meeting a client at seven. He did not add that Darcy Scott was hardly the kind of client he wanted. He had a check in his pocket for seventeen thousand five hundred dollars; the twenty thousand from Bertolini less his commission.

Effusive good-byes. "Give my very best to Frances. I know how happy you'll make her."

Stratton did not notice another man quietly leave a nearby table and follow Merrill Ashton into the lobby.

"If I may have a word with you, sir."

Ashton accepted the card that was offered to him. *Nigel Bruce, Lloyd's of London.*

"I don't understand," Ashton sputtered.

"Sir, if Mr. Stratton comes out, I don't want to be observed. Would you mind if we step into the jewelry shop right over there? One of our experts will meet us. We'd like to have a look at the jewelry you just purchased." The investigator took pity on Ashton's bewildered expression. "It's routine."

"Routine! Are you suggesting that the bracelet I just bought was stolen?"

"I'm not suggesting anything, sir."

"The hell you're not. Well, if there's anything funny about this bracelet, I want to know right now. That check isn't certified. I can have payment stopped in the morning."

The investigative reporter for the *New York Post* had done his job well. Somehow he managed to learn that a package had been delivered to Nan Sheridan's home and that it contained the mates of the mismatched shoes she'd been wearing when her body was found. Nan Sheridan's picture; Erin's picture; Claire Barnes's picture. Splashed side by side on the front page. SERIAL KILLER ON THE LOOSE.

Darcy read the paper in a cab on the way to the Plaza.

"Here we are, miss."

"What? Oh, all right. Thank you."

She was glad that she had had wall-to-wall appointments that day. Once again, she had brought clothes to the office. This time she changed into the red wool Rodeo Drive ensemble. As she got out of the cab, she remembered that she'd worn this outfit the last time she spoke to Erin. If only I'd seen her just once more, she thought.

It was ten of seven, a bit early for her meeting with Jay Stratton. Darcy decided to pop into the Oak Room. Fred, the maître d' of the restaurant, was an old friend. Ever since she could remember, when she and her parents had come to New York they had stayed at the Plaza.

Something Michael Nash had said yesterday was gnawing at her. Hadn't he been suggesting that she was still harboring a child's resentment at a careless, even cruel remark that had no present validity? She found herself looking forward to the next time she saw Nash. I suppose it's like getting a free consultation, but I'd like to ask him about it, she acknowledged as a beaming Fred rushed to greet her.

Promptly at seven she went next door to the bar. Jay Stratton was at a corner table. The only other time she had met him had been at Erin's apartment. Her first impression had been distinctly unfavorable. He'd been angry about the missing Bertolini necklace, then after it was found switched to a display of anxiety over the missing pouch of diamonds. He'd been infinitely more concerned about the necklace than about the fact that Erin was missing. Tonight it was like being with a different person. He was really trying to turn on the charm. Somehow, she was sure she'd seen the real Jay Stratton the first time.

She asked him where he had met Erin.

"Don't laugh. She happened to answer a personal ad I placed. I knew her casually and called her. One of those serendipity things. Bertolini had asked me about resetting those jewels and when I read Erin's letter I remembered that wonderful piece she did that won the N.W. Ayer award. And so we got together. It was strictly business although she did ask me to escort her to a benefit. A client had given her the tickets. We danced the nightaway."

Why had he felt it necessary to add "strictly business"? Darcy wondered. And would it have been strictly business for Erin? Only six months ago Erin had said almost wistfully, "You know, Darcc, I'm at the point where I'd really like to meet some nice guy and fall madly in love."

The Jay Stratton who was sitting across the table, attentive, handsome, able to understand Erin's talent, might well have fit the bill.

"What ad of yours did she answer?"

Stratton shrugged. "Frankly, I place so many of them I forget." He smiled. "You look shocked, Darcy. I'll explain to you what I explained to Erin. I will marry a very rich woman someday. I haven't met her yet, but be assured I will. I meet many women through these ads. It is not very difficult to persuade older women, ever so gently, to relieve their loneliness by treating themselves to a particularly beautiful piece of jewelry or by resetting their own rings, necklaces, or bracelets. They're happy. I'm happy."

"Why are you telling me this?" Darcy asked. "I hope it's not your way of letting me down easily. I didn't think of tonight as a date. For me, it's 'strictly business.' "

Stratton shook his head. "God forbid I should be so presumptuous. I'm telling you exactly what I told Erin after she explained to me her purpose in answering the ads. Your producer friend's documentary, isn't it?"

"Yes."

"What I'm trying to say and probably not doing it very well is that there was no romantic spark between Erin and me. The next point I'd like to make is to profoundly apologize for my behavior the first time we met. Bertolini is a valued client of mine. I'd never worked with Erin before. I didn't know her well enough to be totally sure that she wouldn't go away on a whim and forget the deadline for delivery. Believe me, I've had very uncomfortable moments of communing with myself and realizing the impression I must have made on you when you were heartsick with worry about your missing friend and I was talking client deadlines."

A wonderful speech, Darcy thought. I should warn him I've lived most of my life with two of the best actors in this country. She wondered if it would be appropriate to burst into applause. Instead she said, "You do have the check for the necklace?" "Yes. I didn't know how to make it out. Do you think 'Estate of Erin Kelley' will be appropriate?"

Estate of Erin Kelley. All the years Erin had cheerfully done without the things that most of their friends considered essential. So proud that she could keep her father in a private nursing home. Just on the threshold of major success. Swallowing over a lump in her throat, Darcy said, "That will do."

She looked down at the check. Seventeen thousand five hundred dollars made out to the Estate of Erin Kelley, drawn on Chase Manhattan Bank, and signed by Jay Charles Stratton.

14
TUESDAY
March 5

On Tuesday morning when Agent D'Ambrosio entered Sheridan Galleries, he took a quick look around before he was ushered upstairs to Chris Sheridan's office. The furniture reminded him of the contents of Nona Roberts's living room. Funny. One of the things that had always been on his list was to take courses in art and antique furniture. The Bureau's Art Theft program had only whetted his appetite in that area.

In the meantime, Vince thought as he followed a secretary down the corridor, I live with Alice's mistakes. At the time of the divorce he'd gotten tired of expecting a fair shake from her. "Take what you want if it's so important to you," he'd offered.

She'd certainly taken him at his word.

Sheridan was on the phone. He smiled and waved Vince to a seat. Without appearing to be paying attention, Vince took in the conversation. Something about a collection being wildly overvalued.

Sheridan was saying, "Tell Lord Kilman that they may promise him that amount but they can't deliver. We'll be happy to set reasonable opening bids. The market isn't as strong as it was a few years ago, but is he prepared to wait it out another three to five years? Otherwise, I think if he looks carefully at our estimates he'll realize that many of the pieces he acquired fairly recently will still turn him a handsome profit."

Confident. Knowledgeable. Innate warmth. That was the way Vince had sized up Chris Sheridan last week when he'd gone to Darien. At that time, Sheridan had been wearing a sports shirt and windbreaker. Today he was dressed in a charcoal gray suit, white shirt, red and gray tie, very much the executive.

Chris hung up and reached across the desk to shake hands. Vince apologized for giving him such short notice and got right to the point. "When I saw you last week, I was pretty sure that Erin Kelley's death was a copycat murder because of the *True Crimes* program about your sister. I'm not sure about that anymore." He told him about Claire Barnes and the package that had been returned to her home.

Chris listened attentively. "Another one."

It seemed to Vince that all the residual pain of his sister's murder was in those two words.

"Is there anything I can do to help?" Chris asked.

"I don't know," Vince said frankly. "Whoever killed your sister must have known her. The matching shoe size can't be a coincidence. We have three possibilities. The same murderer has continued to kill young women all through these years. The same murderer stopped killing and started again several years ago. The third possibility is that Nan's murderer confided his modus operandi to someone else who decided to take over. The last one is the least likely."

"Then you're going to try to connect someone whom Nan knew to someone these other women knew?"

"Exactly. Although in Erin Kelley's case, because of the missing diamonds, there is still a possibility that we have a different culprit. That's why we're planning to explore both avenues. The reason I'm here is that I'm going to try to link one person with Nan, Erin Kelley, and Claire Barnes."

"Someone who knew my sister fifteen years ago and recently met those girls through personal ads?"

"You've got it. Darcy Scott was Erin Kelley's closest friend. They'd been answering the ads only because a television producer friend is doing a documentary and asked them to take part in the research. Darcy was out of town for a month. She gave Erin a sample of the letter she was sending, and some photographs. We know Erin answered some of those ads for both of them. Darcy Scott is hoping that whoever killed Erin will contact her."

Chris frowned. "You mean, you're allowing another young woman to be set up as a possible victim?"

Vince raised his hand as though to wave away the suggestion. "You don't know Darcy Scott. I'm not allowing anything. It's what she's determined to do. The one thing I have to grant her is she's already met some pretty interesting characters and come up with information that might be helpful."

"I still think it's a lousy idea," Chris said flatly.

"So do I and now that we've established that, here's how I hope you can help. The faster we get this guy, the less chance Darcy Scott or some other young woman might get hurt. We're going to Brown to get a roster of everyone who was in the student body or on the faculty when your sister was there. We'll check those names against anyone we know Erin met or Darcy meets on these dates. I also think it would be a good idea if, besides the school yearbooks that we can get ourselves, you dig out any snapshots, albums, whatever, of your sister's friends or acquaintances. You've got to understand that not everybody who answers a personal ad uses his own name. I want Darcy Scott to look over Nan's pictures to see if she can spot anyone she meets along the way."

"Of course we've got endless snapshots of Nan," Chris said slowly. "Ten years ago, after my father died, I managed to persuade my mother to pack up most of them and put them in the attic. Mother admitted that Nan's room was getting to be a shrine."

"Good for you," Vince said. "You must have been pretty persuasive."

Chris smiled quickly. "I pointed out that it was one of the brightest rooms in the house and would be great for a visiting grandchild someday. The problem is, as my mother frequently reminds me, I haven't delivered." The smile disappeared. "I can't get up to Connecticut until the weekend. I'll bring everything down on Sunday."

Vince stood up. "I appreciate this. I know how tough this has been on your mother, but if it turns out that we find the guy who was responsible for your sister's death, believe me, in the long run it will give her a lot of peace."

As he turned to go, his beeper sounded. "Do you mind if I call my office?"

Sheridan handed him the phone, watched as D'Ambrosio's forehead furrowed. "How is Darcy?"

Chris Sheridan felt a cold wave of apprehension. He didn't know this girl but experienced a sudden unreasoning fear for her. He had never told anyone that when Nan went for a jog the morning after their birthday party, he had heard her go out. Still half asleep, he'd started to get up. Some instinct was urging him to follow her. He'd shrugged it off and gone back to sleep.

Vince hung up the phone and turned back to Chris. "Is there any way you could possibly get those pictures immediately? The White Plains police phoned. The father of Janine Wetzl, another one of the missing girls, just received the sort of package your mother and the Barnes family got. Her own shoe and a high-heeled white satin slipper." He slapped his hand on the table. "And while one agent was taking that call, Darcy Scott phoned. She had just opened a package that came in the morning mail. The mates of the shoes found on Erin Kelley's body were sent to her."

Chris knew that the frustrated anger he saw on Agent D'Ambrosio's face mirrored his own expression. "Why the hell is he doing this?" Chris blurted. "To prove the girls are dead? To taunt? What makes him tick?"

"When I know that, I'll know who he is," Vince said quietly. "And now, do you mind if I use your phone again? I have to call Darcy Scott."

From the moment Darcy saw the package, she'd known. The mailman arrived just as she was leaving for work. He'd handed her the package and the letters and magazines and junk mail. Afterward, Darcy remembered that he'd looked puzzled when she did not respond to his greeting.

Like an automaton she'd walked stiffly upstairs to her apartment and laid the package on the table by the window. Deliberately keeping her gloves on, she opened it, unknotting the twine and slitting the sealing tape at the flaps.

The sketch of the slipper on the lid. Remove the lid. Separate the tissue. Look down at Erin's boot and a pink and silver slipper nestled together.

The slipper is so pretty, she thought. It would have gone beautifully with the dress Erin was buried in.

She did not have to look up Vince D'Ambrosio's number, her brain produced it effortlessly. He was not there but they promised to locate him. "Can you wait for him?"

"Yes."

He called a few minutes later, was at the apartment within half an hour. "This is rough for you."

"I touched the heel of the slipper with my glove," she confessed. "I simply had to know if it was Erin's size. It was."

Vince looked at her compassionately. "Maybe you should take it easy today."

Darcy shook her head. "That would be the worst thing in the world for me to do." She attempted a smile. "I've got a big project scheduled, and then, guess what? I have a date tonight."

* * *

When Vince left with the package, Darcy went directly to the newly purchased hotel on West Twenty-third Street. Small, a total of thirty guest rooms, rundown, badly in need of paint, it still had tremendous possibilities. The owners, a couple in their late thirties, explained that the cost of basic repairs would leave very little for refurbishing. They were delighted with her suggestion that they decorate in the style of an English country inn. "I can get plenty of sofas and upholstered chairs and lamps and tables in very good condition at private sales," she'd told them. "We can give this place a lot of charm. Look at the Algonquin. The most intimate bar in Manhattan and you'd be hard put to find a chair that isn't threadbare."

She walked through the rooms with them, making notes on their various sizes and shapes, and marking what furniture was usable. The day passed quickly. She had intended to go home and change for her date, but then decided against it. When Doug Fields called to reconfirm, he'd told her that he dressed casually. "Slacks and a sweater are pretty much a uniform for me."

They were meeting at six at the Twenty-third Street Bar and Grill. Darcy got there exactly on time. Doug Fields was fifteen minutes late. He burst into the bar, clearly irritated and filled with apologies. "I swear I've never seen this block so messed up. So many cars, you'd swear it was an assembly line in Detroit. I'm so sorry, Darcy. I never keep people waiting. It's a thing with me."

"It really doesn't matter." He's good-looking, Darcy thought. Attractive. Why had he found it necessary to immediately insist that he never kept people waiting?

Over a glass of wine, she listened to him on two levels. He was amusing, self-confident, well-spoken. Extremely likable. He'd been raised in Virginia, went to the University there, dropped out of law school. "I'd have made a lousy lawyer. Don't have enough of the 'go for the jugular.' "

Go for the jugular. Darcy thought of the bruises on Erin's throat.

"Switched to art school. Pointed out to my father that instead of cracking the books, I was doing caricatures of the profs. It was a good decision. I love illustrating and do well at it."

"There's an old saying, 'If you want to be happy for a year, win the lottery. If you want to be happy for life, love what you do.' " Darcy hoped she sounded relaxed. This was the kind of guy Erin would have enjoyed meeting, the kind who after a date or two she would have trusted. An artist? The sketch? Was everybody suspect?

The inevitable question came. "Why would a pretty girl like you need to answer personal ads?"

This time the question was easy to parry. "Why would a good-looking, successful guy like you need to place personal ads?"

"That's easy," he said promptly. "I was married for eight years and now I'm not. I'm not interested in getting serious. You get introduced to somebody at a friend's house, take her out a few times, and bingo, everybody's looking at the two of you waiting for the big announcement. This way, I meet a lot of nice women. Lay the cards on the table just like this and see if it clicks. Tell me, how many dates from ads have you had this week?"

"You're the first one."

"Last week, then. Starting with Monday."

Monday I was standing over Erin's casket, Darcy thought. Tuesday I was watching that casket being lowered. Wednesday I was home watching the reenactment of Nan Sheridan's murder. Thursday she had met Len Parker. Friday, David Weld, the mild-mannered, rather shy man who described himself as a department store executive and claimed not to have known Erin. Saturday, Albert Booth, a computer analyst who was enthralled with the wonders of desktop publishing and who knew Erin was frightened of her superintendent.

"Oh, come on, admit you had dates last week," Doug urged. "I called you Wednesday and you weren't free until tonight."

Startled, Darcy realized that a number of times recently, someone had to repeat a question. "I'm sorry. Yes, I did go out a couple of times last week."

"And had fun?"

She thought of Len Parker pounding on the door. "You could call it that."

He laughed. "That speaks volumes. I've met some winners too. Now you've gotten my life history, how about telling me about yourself?"

She gave a carefully edited version.

Doug raised one eyebrow. "I sense a lot of omissions but maybe when you get to know me a bit better, you'll fill me in."

She refused a second glass of wine. "I really have to be going."

He did not argue. "Actually, I do too. When am I going to see you again, Darcy? Tomorrow night? Let's make it dinner."

"I really am busy."

"Thursday?"

"I'm working on a job that's going to tie me up. Will you call in a few days?"

"Yes. And if you keep turning me down, I promise I won't persist. But I hope you don't."

He really is nice, Darcy thought, or else he's a heck of a good actor.

Doug put her in a cab, then quickly waved one down for himself. In the apartment, he tore off the sweater and slacks and rushed into the suit he'd worn to the office. At quarter of eight he was on the train to Scarsdale. At quarter of nine he was reading a bedtime story to Trish while Susan broiled a steak for him. She certainly understood how maddening these late meetings were. "You work too hard, Doug, dear," she had said soothingly when he stamped into the house, ranting about missing the earlier train by a hairbreadth.

Through hours of intense questioning, Jay Stratton remained calm. His only explanation for the diamonds in the bracelet that he had sold to Merrill Ashton was that it must have been a ghastly error. Erin Kelley had been commissioned to create settings for a number of fine diamonds. Stratton claimed that somehow he had made a mistake and inadvertently substituted other fine stones for some of the ones that were meant to be in the diamond pouch he had given Kelley. That was not to say that those others were not of equal value. Take a look at his various insurance policies.

A search warrant revealed no other missing diamonds in his apartment or in his safety deposit box. He was booked on suspicion of receiving stolen goods and bail was set. Disdainfully, he strode from the precinct with his lawyer.

Vince had shared the interrogation with detectives from the Sixth Precinct. They all knew he was guilty, but as Vince said, "There goes one of the most convincing con men I've ever come across and believe me, I've run into a lot of them."

The crazy thing, Vince thought as he left for his office, is that Darcy Scott ends up being a witness *for* Stratton. She'd opened the safe for him and would swear that the pouch wasn't there. And of course the big question was, would Stratton have had the nerve to claim those diamonds were missing unless he knew that Erin Kelley would never show up to say what happened to them?

In the office, Vince snapped out orders. "I want to know everything, and I mean *everything,* about Jay Stratton. Jay Charles Stratton."

15

WEDNESDAY

March 6

Chris Sheridan studied Darcy Scott, liking what he saw. She was wearing a leather jacket belted at the waist, tan slacks that disappeared into scuffed but fine leather boots, a knotted silk scarf that accentuated the hollow in the nape of her neck. Her brown hair, darted with blond highlights, was soft and loose around her face. Hazel eyes, soft brown flecked with green, were framed by dark lashes. Charcoal brows accentuated her porcelain complexion. He judged her to be in her late twenties.

She reminds me of Nan. The realization shocked him. But they don't look alike, he thought. Nan had been the typical Nordic beauty with her pink and white skin, vivid blue eyes, hair the color of daffodils. Then where was the resemblance? It was in the absolute grace with which Darcy moved. Nan had walked like that, as though if music began to play, she would glide into a dance step.

Darcy was aware of Chris Sheridan's scrutiny. She had been making some observations of her own. She liked his strong features, the slight bump on the bridge of his nose, probably the result of a break. The width of his shoulders and an overall impression of disciplined fitness suggested athletic prowess.

A few years ago, her mother and father had both had plastic surgery. "A nip here, a tuck there," her mother had said, laughing. "Don't look so disapproving, darling Darcy. Remember, our looks are an important part of our stock in trade."

How totally irrelevant to remember that now, Darcy thought. Was she simply trying to escape the delayed shock of opening the package with Erin's boot and the dancing slipper? She'd been composed all day yesterday, then woke up this morning at four o'clock to find her face and pillow wet with tears. She bit her lip at the memory, but could not prevent new tears from welling in her eyes. "I'm sorry," she said quickly, and tried to sound brisk. "It was good of you to go to Connecticut for the pictures last night. Vince D'Ambrosio told me you had to change your plans."

"They weren't important." Chris sensed that Darcy Scott wanted him to ignore her distress. "There's an awful lot of stuff," he said matter-of-factly. "I have it laid out on a table in the conference room. My suggestion is that you take a look at it. If you want to bring everything home or to your office, I can have it delivered. If you want part of it, we can arrange that too. I know most of the people in the pictures. Some, of course, I don't. Anyhow, let's take a look."

They went downstairs. Darcy realized that in the fifteen minutes she'd been in Chris Sheridan's office, the crowd inspecting the items for the next auction had increased substantially. She loved auctions. Growing up she had regularly gone to them with the dealer representing her parents. They never could go themselves. If either one of them was known to be interested in acquiring a painting or antique, the price shot up instantly. It was hearing her mother and father recite the history of their acquisitions that made her uncomfortable.

She was walking next to Sheridan toward the rear of the building when she spotted a cylinder writing desk and darted over to it. "Is this really a Roentgen?"

Chris ran his hand over the mahogany surface. "Yes, it is. You know your antiques. Are you in the business?"

Darcy thought of the Roentgen in the library of the Bel-Air house. Her mother loved to tell the story of how Marie Antoinette had sent it to Vienna as a gift to her mother, the Empress, which was why it had escaped being sold during the French Revolution. This one had obviously been shipped out of France as well.

"Are you in the business?" Chris repeated.

"Oh, I'm sorry." Darcy smiled, thinking of the hotel she was refurbishing with garage sale trappings. "In a way you could say that."

Chris raised his eyebrows but did not ask for an explanation. "Down this way." A wide foyer led to a double-doored room. Inside, a protective cloth covered a Georgian banquet table. Albums, yearbooks, framed pictures, snapshots, and carousels of slides were neatly placed rowlike on the table.

"Don't forget, these were all taken somewhere between fifteen and eighteen years ago," Sheridan warned.

"I know." Darcy considered the mass of material. "How much do you use this room?"

"Not that often."

"Then would it be possible to leave everything here and let me come in and out? The thing is, when I'm in the office I'm always busy. My apartment isn't large, and anyhow I'm not there very much."

Chris knew it was none of his business but could not stop himself. "Agent D'Ambrosio told me you were answering personal ads." He watched the withdrawal in Darcy Scott's expression.

"Erin didn't want to answer those ads," Darcy said. "I persuaded her. The only way I can possibly atone for that is to try to help find her killer. Is it all right if I come back and forth? I promise I won't bother you or your staff."

Chris realized what Vince D'Ambrosio had meant when he said that Darcy Scott was going to do what she wanted about the personal ads. "You won't be any bother. One of the secretaries is always here by eight. The cleaning staff is around until ten at night. I'll leave word for them to let you in. Better yet, let me give you a key."

Darcy smiled. "I promise not to make off with a Sèvres. Is it okay if I stay for a while now? I have a few hours free."

"Of course. And remember, I know many of those people. Try me if you want a name."

At three-thirty Sheridan returned, followed by a maid carrying a tea tray. "I thought you might need a break. I'll join you if I may."

"That would be fine." Darcy realized she had a vague headache and remembered she had skipped lunch. She accepted a cup of tea, poured a few drops of milk from the delicate Limoges pitcher, and tried not to look too anxious as she reached for a sugar cookie. She waited until the maid left, then commented, "I know how hard it must have been for you to put all this together. Memory Lane is pretty shattering."

"My mother did most of it. She surprises me. She fainted when that package of shoes arrived, but now, whatever she can do to track down Nan's killer and to stop him from harming anyone else is all she cares about."

"And you?"

"Nan was six minutes older than I. She never let me forget it. Called me 'little brother.' She was outgoing. I was shy. We kind of balanced each other. Long ago I gave up the hope of seeing her killer in court. Now that hope is within reach again." He looked at the stack of pictures she had separated. "Anyone you know?"

Darcy shook her head. "Not so far."

At quarter of five, she poked her head in his office. "I'm running along now."

Chris jumped up. "Here's the key. I meant to give it to you when I came down."

Darcy pocketed it. "I'll probably come back early in the morning."

Chris could not resist. "Have you got one of those dates now? I'm sorry. I have no right to ask. I'm only concerned because I think it's so dangerous."

This time he was glad to see Darcy Scott did not stiffen. She simply said, "I'll be fine," and with a half-wave left him.

He stared after her, remembering the one time he had gone hunting. The doe had been drinking water from a stream. Sensing danger, it had lifted its head, listening, poised for flight. An instant later it sank to the ground. He had not joined in the exultant cheers the others in the party accorded the marksman. His instinct had been to shout a warning to the deer. That same instinct was crying out to him now.

"How's the program going?" Vince asked Nona as he tried to find a comfortable spot on the green love seat in her office.

"It is and it isn't." Nona sighed. Wearily, she ran a hand through her hair. "The hardest thing is to find a balance. When you wrote and asked me to include a segment about the possible dangers of answering those ads, I had no idea what the next week would bring. I still think my original concept is right. I want to give an overall picture and then end with a warning." She smiled at him. "I'm glad you called and suggested pasta."

It had been a long day. At four-thirty, Vince had had a brainstorm. He'd had a list made of the dates the eight young women had disappeared and ordered researchers to start collecting personal ads from New York area newspapers and magazines that had appeared three months previous to those dates.

A sense of accomplishment at the new possible lead had made him realize that he was gut-level tired. The thought of going back to the apartment and finding some food in the neglected refrigerator had been depressing. Instead, almost inadvertently, he'd reached for the phone and dialed Nona.

Now it was seven o'clock. He'd just arrived at her office and Nona was ready to pack it in.

The phone rang. Nona raised her eyes to heaven, reached for it, and identified herself. Vince watched as her expression changed.

"You're right, Matt. Always a safe bet that you'll find me here. What can I do for you?" She listened. "Matt, get it straight. I'm not in the market to buy you out. Not today. Not tomorrow. If you'll remember, last year when we had a buyer you didn't think it was enough. The usual. Now I can wait. You can wait. What the heck is the rush? Does Jeanie need braces or something?"

Nona laughed as she hung up. "That was the man I promised to love, honor, and cherish all the days of my life. Trouble is, he forgot to remember."

"It's been known to happen."

They went to Pasta Lovers on West Fifty-eighth Street. "I duck in here a lot when I'm by myself," Nona told him. "Wait till you taste the pasta. It would drive anyone's blues away."

A glass of red wine. The salad. Warm bread. "It's the connection," Vince heard himself saying. "There's got to be a connection between one man and all those girls."

"I thought you were convinced that except for Nan Sheridan the connection is the personal ads."

"It is. But don't you see? He can't just *happen* to have the right-sized slipper for each one of them. Granted, he could have bought the slippers after he killed the girls, but he certainly had the one he left on Nan Sheridan's foot with him when he attacked her. This type of killer usually follows a pattern."

"So you're talking about someone who met these girls, somehow managed to learn their shoe size without any of them getting bad vibes, and then was able to get them in a situation where they disappeared without a trace."

"You've got it." Over linguine with clam sauce, he told her about his plan to analyze personal ads that had been placed in the New York area in the three months before each of the women disappeared, to see if the same one showed up. "And of course that could be another dead end," he acknowledged. "For all we know, the same guy is placing a dozen different ads."

They both ordered decaf cappuccino. Nona began talking about the documentary. "I still haven't settled on a psychiatrist," she said. "I certainly don't want to get one of those professional show-biz experts who pop up whenever you turn the dial."

Vince told her about Michael Nash. "Very articulate guy. Writing a book about personal ads. He'd met Erin."

"Darcy told me about him. A very good idea, Agent D'Ambrosio."

Vince took Nona home in a cab, and had it wait while he saw her inside her building. "I have a hunch we're both pretty beat," he said in answer to her suggestion of a nightcap. "But please give me a raincheck."

"You've got it." Nona grinned. "I am tired, and anyhow, my cleaning woman hasn't been around since last Friday. I don't think you're ready for the real me."

It was all Vince could do to remember that he was technically on the job. That did not stop him from wondering how it would feel to hold Nona Roberts in his arms.

Back at his apartment, there was a message on his answering machine. Ernie, his assistant. "No emergency, but I thought you'd be interested in hearing this, Vince. We have the roster of students from Brown for the time Nan Sheridan was there. Guess who was a returning student and in some of her classes? None other than our friend the jeweler, Jay Stratton."

Darcy's five-thirty date was to meet Box 4307, Cal Griffin, in the bar at Tavern on the Green. He's not in his early thirties, was her first impression. Griffin was closer to fifty. A beefy man who combed his hair across the top of his head to conceal his bald spot, he was expensively and conservatively dressed. He was from Milwaukee, but, as he explained, got into New York regularly.

A suggestive wink followed. Don't get him wrong, he was a happily married man, but when he came in on business it would sure be good to have a friend. Another wink. Believe you me, he knew how to treat a woman. What show haven't you seen? He knew how to get house seats. What's your favorite restaurant? Lutèce? Expensive, but worth every penny.

Darcy managed to ask him the last time he'd been in New York.

Too long. Last month he'd taken the wife and kids—great teenagers but you know teenagers—skiing in Vail. They had a house there. They were building a bigger place. Money's no object. Anyhow, the kids brought their friends and it was bedlam. That rock and roll stuff. Drive you crazy, wouldn't it? They had a great stereo system in the house.

Darcy had ordered a Perrier. Halfway through it, she made a business of glancing at her watch. "My boss was real mad at me for leaving," she said. "I'm going to have to cut this short."

"Forget him," Griffin ordered. "You and I are going to have a nice night."

They were sitting at a banquette. A beefy arm went around her. A moist kiss was planted on her ear.

Darcy did not want to make a scene. "Oh, my God," she said, pointing to a nearby table where a man was sitting alone, his back to them. "That's my husband. I've got to get out of here."

The arm disappeared from around her waist. Griffin looked shaken. "I don't want trouble."

"I'll just slip away," Darcy whispered.

On the way home in the cab, she tried not to laugh out loud. Well, one thing's for sure—it's not that one.

The phone was ringing as she turned her key in the lock. It was Doug Fields. "Hi, Darcy. Why are you so unforgettable? I know you said you were busy tonight, but my plans changed and I decided to take a chance. How about a hamburger at P. J. Clarke's or something?"

Darcy realized that she had forgotten to tell Vince D'Ambrosio about Doug Fields. A nice guy. Attractive. An illustrator. The kind Erin might easily have been interested in. "That sounds great," she answered. "What time?"

How stupid does Doug think I am? Susan wondered as she sat at the kitchen table with Donny and went over his geometry homework. The guidance counseler had phoned her this afternoon. Was there a problem at home? Donny, always a good student, was slipping in all his subjects. He seemed distracted and depressed.

"Well, that's it," she said cheerfully. "As *my* geometry teacher used to say, 'It shows what you can do, Miss Frawley, when you put your mind to it.' "

Donny smiled and gathered up his books. "Mom . . ." He hesitated.

"Donny, you've always been able to talk to me. What is it?"

He looked around.

"The little kids are in bed. Beth is taking one of her thirty-minute showers. We can talk," Susan assured him.

"And Dad is in one of his meetings," Donny said bitterly.

He suspects, Susan thought. There was no use trying to protect him. This was as good a time as any to be straight with him. "Donny, Dad isn't in a meeting."

"You know?" Relief flooded the troubled face.

"Yes, I do. But how did you find out?"

He looked down. "Patrick Driscoll, one of the guys on the team, was in New York Friday night when we were visiting Grandpa. Dad was in a restaurant with some woman. They were holding hands and kissing. Patrick said it was gross. His mother wants to tell you. His dad won't let her."

"Donny, I'm planning to divorce your father. It's not something I want, but living like this isn't great for any of us. This way we won't always be waiting for him to come home, always putting up with his lies. I hope he makes it his business to see you kids, but I can't guarantee it. I'm sorry. I'm terribly, terribly sorry." She realized she was crying.

Donny patted her shoulder. "Mom, he doesn't deserve you. I promise I'll help with the other kids. I swear I'll do a better job than he did with us."

Donny may look like Doug, but thank God, Susan thought, he's got enough of my genes in him that he'll never act like his father. She kissed Donny's cheek. "Let's keep this between us for now. Okay."

Susan went to bed at eleven o'clock. Doug was still not home. She turned on the late news and watched horrified as the anchorman updated the story of the missing young women and the packages of mismatched shoes that were being returned to their families.

The announcer was saying, "Although the FBI refuses to comment, inside sources tell us that the latest shoes to be returned are the mates of the ones Erin Kelley was wearing when her body was found. If true, she is probably linked to the disappearance of two young women originally from Lancaster and White Plains, who had been living in Manhattan, and the long-unsolved murder of Nan Sheridan."

Nan Sheridan. Erin Kelley.

"Oh my God," Susan moaned. Her hands clenched in fists, she stared at the screen.

Pictures of Claire Barnes, Erin Kelley, Janine Wetzl and Nan Sheridan were flashed on the screen.

The announcer was saying, "The trail of death seems to have begun on that cold March morning, fifteen years ago next week, when Nan Sheridan was strangled on the jogging path near her home."

Susan felt her own throat close. Fifteen years ago she had lied for Doug when he was questioned about Nan's death. If she hadn't, would these other young women not have disappeared? That night almost two weeks ago when the announcement came about Erin Kelley's death, Doug had had a nightmare. Called out *Erin* in his sleep.

". . . The FBI is cooperating with the New York Police Department in an attempt to trace the evening shoes back to the purchaser. The file on Nan Sheridan's death has been reopened . . ."

Suppose they questioned Doug again? Suppose they question *me,* Susan thought. Did she have a duty to tell the police she had lied fifteen years ago?

Donny. Beth. Trish. Conner. What would their lives be like if they grew up as the children of a serial killer?

The police commissioner of New York was being interviewed. "We believe we're dealing with a vicious serial killer."

Vicious.

"What shall I do?" Susan whispered to herself. Her father's words rang in her ears. "Vicious *streak* . . ."

Two years ago when she challenged him about his relationship with the *au pair,* his face had contorted with rage. The fear she had experienced at that moment swept through her again. As the news ended, Susan finally faced the fact she had never allowed herself to consider. "I thought he was going to hurt me that night."

Shall we dance? *Shall we dance? Shall we dance? On a bright cloud of music shall we fly? . . . Shall we still be together with our arms around each other, shall we dance? Shall we dance? Shall we dance?*

Charley laughed aloud at the sheer exultation of the music. Whirling and stepping in synch with Yul Brynner, he stamped his foot, twisted, twirled an imaginary Darcy in his arms. They'd dance to this next week! Then Astaire! What joy! What joy! It was only seven days away: Nan's fifteenth anniversary!

On the clear understanding that this kind of thing can happen, shall we dance? Shall we dance? Shall we dance?

The music stopped. He reached for the remote control and

snapped off the video. If only he could spend the night. But that would be foolish. Do what he had come to do.

The basement stairs creaked and he frowned. Must take care of that. Annette had fled down these stairs. Listening to the frantic tapping of the heels on the bare wood had enthralled him. If Darcy tried to escape him that same way, he didn't want a creaking noise to interfere with the sound of her slippers on their futile flight.

Darcy. How hard it had been to sit across the table from her. He had wanted to say "Come with me" and bring her here. Like the Phantom of the Opera inviting his beloved to the netherworld.

The shoe boxes. Five of them now. Marie and Sheila and Leslie and Annette and Tina. Suddenly he realized he wanted to send them all back at once. Be finished with it. And then there would be only one.

Only Darcy's package would be here next week. Maybe he'd never return it.

He opened the latch of the freezer, lifted the heavy door, and stared down into the empty space. Awaiting a new ice maiden, Charley thought. This one he wouldn't give back.

16

THURSDAY
March 7

"How well did you know Nan Sheridan?" Vince snapped. He and a detective from the Midtown North precinct were taking turns questioning Jay Stratton.

Stratton remained unruffled. "She was a student at Brown when I was there."

"You dropped out of Brown and came back the year she was a sophomore?"

"That's right. I wasn't much of a student my freshman year. My uncle, who was my guardian, thought it would do me a lot of good to mature a bit. I went into the Peace Corps for two years."

"I repeat: How well did you know Nan Sheridan?"

How well indeed, Stratton thought. Lovely Nan. *To dance with her was to feel a will-o'-the-wisp in your arms.*

D'Ambrosio's eyes narrowed. He had seen something in Stratton's face. "You haven't answered me."

Stratton shrugged. "There's no answer to give. Certainly I remember her. I was there when the whole student body was talking endlessly about the tragedy."

"Were you invited to her birthday party?"

"No, I was not. Nan Sheridan and I happened to be in several classes together. Period."

"Let's talk about Erin Kelley. You were in an awfully big hurry to report those missing diamonds to the insurance company."

"As Miss Scott can certainly verify, my first response when I spoke with her was irritation. I really didn't know Erin well. It was her work I knew. When she didn't keep the appointment to turn over the necklace to Bertolini, I convinced myself that she simply lost track of time. The moment I met Darcy Scott I realized how foolish that was. Her terrible concern made me see the situation clearly."

"Do you often mix up valuable gemstones?"

"Certainly not."

Vince tried another tack. "You didn't know Nan Sheridan well, but did you know anyone who had a crush on her? Besides you, of course," he added deliberately.

~ 17

FRIDAY
March 8

On Friday afternoon, Darcy went to the West Side apartment where she'd redecorated the room for Lisa, the recuperating teenager. She brought with her plants for the windowsill, some throw pillows, a porcelain vanity set that she'd picked up at a house sale. And Erin's much-loved poster.

The large pieces were already in; the pewter and brass bed, the dresser, the night table, the rocker. The Indian rug that had been in Erin's living room was perfect in this space. Candy-striped wall paper gave the room a feeling of movement. Almost like a carousel, Darcy thought. The tieback curtains and spread were the same candy stripe as the paper. A starched white cotton dust ruffle picked up the glistening white of the ceiling and trim.

Carefully, Darcy positioned the poster. It depicted an Egret painting, one of his early, lesser known works: a young dancer soaring through the air, her arms extended, her toes pointed. He'd called it, "Loves Music, Loves to Dance."

She drove picture hooks into the wall, thinking of all the dance classes she and Erin had taken. "Why jog in the freezing rain when you can get just as much exercise dancing?" Erin would ask. "There's an old slogan, 'To put a little fun in your life, try dancing.' "

Darcy stepped back to be sure the poster was hanging straight. It was. Then what was gnawing at her? *The personal ads.* But why now? Shrugging, she closed her toolbox.

She went directly to Sheridan Galleries. So far, all the poring over the pictures had proven useless. She had come across Jay Stratton's picture, but Vince D'Ambrosio had already picked his name from the student roster. Yesterday, Chris Sheridan had pointed out that she probably had a better chance of winning the lottery than of having a familiar face jump out at her.

She'd been afraid that he might have regretted his decision to let her use his conference room, but that wasn't the case. "You look wiped out," he'd said to her late yesterday afternoon. "I understand you've been here since eight o'clock this morning."

"I was able to rearrange some appointments. This seems more important."

Last night had been Box 3823, Owen Larkin, an internist from New York Hospital. He'd been pretty full of himself. "Trouble with being an unattached doctor is that all the nurses keep offering to have you over for a home-cooked meal." He was from Tulsa and hated New York. "The minute I finish my residency I'm on my way back to God's country. You can keep these crowded cities."

Casually, she'd brought up Erin's name. His tone confidential, he'd told her, "I didn't meet her, but one of my friends at the hospital who answers these ads did. Just once. He's keeping his fingers crossed that she didn't keep records. The last thing he needs is to be questioned in a murder investigation."

"When did he see her?"

"Early February."

"I wonder if I've ever met him."

"Not unless you met him around that time. He'd broken up with his girlfriend and they got back together."

"What's his name?"

"Brad Whalen. Say, is this some kind of inquisition? Let's talk about you and me."

Brad Whalen. Another name for Vince D'Ambrosio to check out.

Chris was standing at his office window when he saw the cab pull up and Darcy get out of it. He shoved his hands in his pockets. It was windy and he watched as Darcy closed the door of the cab and turned to the building. She pulled her jacket around her neck and bent forward slightly as she crossed the sidewalk.

Yesterday had been busy. He had some important Japanese clients examining the silver from the von Wallens estate to be auctioned next week. He'd spent the better part of the afternoon with them.

Mrs. Vail, the housekeeper for the gallery, had made sure that morning coffee, a light lunch, and tea were brought to Darcy Scott. "That poor girl is going to ruin her eyes, Mr. Sheridan," Vail had fussed.

At four-thirty, Chris had gone to the conference room. He'd realized what a blunder he'd made when he suggested the task was hopeless. He hadn't meant it to come out like that. It was just that when you analyzed it, the chances of Darcy Scott's meeting someone who had known Nan, and recognizing him in a picture fifteen years old, were, to say the least, very slim.

Yesterday she'd asked him if Nan had ever dated anyone named Charles North.

Not to his knowledge. When he came to Darien, Vince D'Ambrosio had asked him and his mother the same question.

Chris realized that he wanted to go downstairs now and talk to Darcy. He wondered if she would get the feeling again that he was anxious to be rid of her.

The phone rang. He let his secretary pick it up. A moment later she buzzed through. "It's your mother, Chris."

Greta came directly to the point. "Chris, you know that business about someone named Charles. As long as we had to get all those pictures down, I decided to go through the rest of Nan's things. No use leaving the job to you someday. I reread her letters. There's one from the September before . . . before we lost her. She'd just started the fall semester. She wrote about dancing with a fellow named Charley who teased her about wearing Capezios.

"Here's exactly the way she put it: 'Can you believe that a guy in my generation thinks girls should wear spike heels?' "

* * *

"I was finished with my patients at three o'clock and thought it would be a lot easier to come over and talk with you than discuss this on the phone." Michael Nash shifted slightly, trying to find a comfortable position on the green love seat in Nona's office. He could not help analyzing why an obviously bright and outgoing person like Nona Roberts would submit her visitors to this torturous object.

"Doctor, I'm sorry." Nona yanked files from the one comfortable chair next to her desk. "Please."

Nash moved willingly.

"I really should get rid of that thing," Nona apologized. "It's just I never get around to it. There's always something more interesting to do than fool around with arranging furniture." Her smile was guilty. "But for heaven's sake, don't tell Darcy that."

He returned the smile. "In my profession, I'm sworn to secrecy. Now, how can I help you?"

A really attractive man, Nona thought. Late thirties. A maturity that probably comes with the territory of being a psychiatrist. Darcy had told her about the visit to his place in New Jersey. Don't marry for money, as Nona's old aunts used to say, but it's just as easy to love a rich man as a poor one. Not, God knows, that Darcy needed to marry money. Her folks had been making millions since before she was born. But Nona had always sensed a loneliness in Darcy, a little girl lost. Without Erin, that was bound to get worse. It would be wonderful if she met the right guy now.

She realized that Dr. Michael Nash was looking at her with an amused expression. "Will I pass?" he asked.

"Absolutely." She fished for the documentary file. "Darcy probably told you why she and Erin got into answering personal ads."

Nash nodded.

"We've got the program pretty much together, but I want to have a psychiatrist do an overall viewpoint about the kind of people who place or answer ads and what motivates them. Maybe it would be possible to give some hints as to what kind of behavior should raise warning signals. Am I saying it right?"

"You're saying it very explicitly. I gather that the FBI agent will concentrate on the serial killer aspect."

Nona felt herself tense. "Yes."

"Ms. Roberts, Nona, if I may, I wish you could see the expression on your face right now. You and Darcy are alike. You must stop torturing yourselves. You are no more responsible for Erin Kelley's death than the mother who takes her child for a walk and sees it crushed by an out-of-control car. Some things must be considered acts of fate. Grieve for your friend. Do anything you can to alert others that there is a madman out there. But don't try to play God."

Nona tried to keep her voice steady. "I wish I could hear that about five times a day. If it's bad for me, it's ten times worse for Darcy. I hope you've told her that."

Michael Nash's smile reached his eyes. "My housekeeper has called three times this week with suggested menus if I'll only bring Darcy back. She's going to drive to Wellesley to see Erin's father on Sunday, but she will have dinner with me on Saturday."

"Good! And now how about the program. We tape next Wednesday. It will be aired Thursday night."

"I usually shy away from this sort of thing. Too many of my colleagues rush to be on television panels or in the witness box at criminal trials. But maybe I can contribute something here. Count me in."

"Terrific." They stood up together. Nona waved her hand at the desks in the open area outside her office. "I understand you're writing a book about personal ads. If you need any more research, most of the uncommitted people out there have been playing the game."

"Thanks, but my own file is pretty thick. I'll be turning my book in by the end of the month."

Nona watched Nash's long, easy stride as he made his way to the elevator. She closed the door of her office and dialed Darcy's apartment.

When the answering machine came on, she said, "I know you're not home yet, but I had to tell you. I just met Michael Nash and he's a doll."

Doug's warning antenna was signaling him. When he phoned Susan this morning, saying he didn't want to wake her up by calling when he knew he couldn't get home last night, she'd been warm and pleasant.

"That was sweet of you, Doug. I did get to bed early."

The warning signal had come after he'd hung up and realized that she didn't ask him if he'd be on time tonight. Up till a couple of weeks ago, she'd always pulled that martyred, anxious routine. "Doug, those people have to realize you have a family. It's not fair to expect you to stay for meetings night after night."

She'd seemed pretty happy when she'd met him for dinner in New York. Maybe he should call back and suggest she meet him again tonight.

Or maybe he'd better get home early, make a fuss over the kids. They had been away last weekend.

If Susan ever got mad, really mad, especially with the way the personal ad murders were getting played up and all the interest in Nan . . . !

Doug's office was on the forty-fourth floor of the World Trade Center. Unseeingly, he stared down at Lady Liberty.

It was time to play the role of devoted husband and father.

Something else. He'd better stop using the apartment for a while. His clothes. His sketches. The ads. When he got a chance next week, he'd bring them up to the cottage.

Maybe he'd better think about leaving the station wagon there too.

Was it possible? Darcy blinked and reached for the magnifying glass. This five-by-seven snapshot of Nan Sheridan and her friends on the beach. The maintenance man in the background. Did he look familiar or was she crazy?

She did not hear Chris Sheridan come in. His quiet greeting, "I don't want to interrupt you, Darcy," made her jump.

Chris rushed to apologize. "I knocked. You didn't hear me. I'm terribly sorry."

Darcy rubbed her eyes. "You shouldn't have to knock. It's your place. I guess I'm getting jumpy."

He looked at the magnifying glass in her hand. "Do you think you've come across something?"

"I can't be sure. It's just this guy . . ." She pointed to the figure behind the cluster of girls, "looks a little like someone I know. Do you remember where this picture was taken?"

Chris studied it. "On Belle Island. That's a few miles from Darien. One of Nan's best friends has a summer home there."

"May I take this?"

"Of course." Concerned, Chris watched as Darcy slipped the snapshot into her carrying case and began to stack the pictures she had perused into orderly piles. Her movements were slow, almost mechanical, as though she were terribly tired.

"Darcy, do you have one of your dates tonight?"

She nodded.

"Drinks, dinner?"

"I try to keep them to a glass of wine. By then, I think I can get a handle on whether or not they either met Erin or sound funny if they deny knowing her."

"You don't drive off with them or go to their homes?"

"Lord, no."

"That's good. You look as though you wouldn't have much strength to fight back if someone made a pass at you." Chris hesitated. "Believe it or not, I'm not here to ask questions about something that isn't my business. I just wanted you to know that my mother came across a letter from Nan, written six months before she died. In it she refers to a Charley who thought girls ought to wear spike heels."

Darcy looked up at him. "Have you told Vince D'Ambrosio?"

"Not yet. I will, of course. But I'm wondering if it would be a good idea for you to talk to my mother. It was digging out all these pictures that made her go through Nan's letters. No one had asked her to do that. I just think that if there is anything my mother knows, it might come to the surface faster if she talks to another woman who understands the kind of pain she's been living with all these years."

Nan was six minutes older than I. She never let me forget it. She was outgoing. I was shy.

Chris Sheridan and his mother had probably come to terms with Nan Sheridan's death, Darcy thought. The *True Crimes* program, Erin's murder, the returned shoes, and now me. They've been forced to rip open whatever scars had healed. For them as well as me, there'll be no peace until this is over.

The distress in Chris Sheridan's face for the moment robbed it of the aura of sophistication and executive confidence that had been so noticeable a few days ago.

"I'd like to meet your mother," Darcy said. "She lives in Darien, doesn't she?"

"Yes. I'll drive you."

"I'm going up to Wellesley early Sunday morning to visit Erin Kelley's father. If it's all right, I'll stop late Sunday afternoon on my way home."

"Sounds like a long day for you. Tomorrow wouldn't be better?"

Darcy thought it was ridiculous at her age to blush. "I have plans for tomorrow."

She got up to go. Robert Kruse was meeting her at Mickey Mantle's at five-thirty. As of now, no one else had called. She had run out of personal ad dates.

Next week she'd start writing to the ads Erin had circled.

* * *

Len Parker had been angry at work. A maintenance man at NYU, there was nothing he couldn't fix. Not that he'd studied much. It was just the feel of wires in his hands, the feel of a lock and key, doorjambs, switches. He was supposed to do only routine maintenance, but often when he saw something wrong, he'd fix it without talking about it. It was the one thing that gave him peace.

But today, his thoughts had been confused. He'd yelled at his trustee for hinting that he might have a house somewhere. Whose business? Whose?

His family? What about them? His brothers and sisters. Never even invited him to visit. Glad to wash their hands of him.

That girl, Darcy. Maybe he'd been mean to her, but she didn't realize how cold it had been standing waiting outside that fancy restaurant to apologize to her.

He'd told Mr. Doran, the trustee, about that. Mr. Doran said, "Lenny, if you'd only understand that you have enough money to eat in Le Cirque or anywhere else every night of your life."

Mr. Doran just didn't understand.

Lenny could remember his mother yelling at his father all the time. "You'll put your children in the streets with your crazy investments." Lenny used to cower in bed. He hated to think of being out in the cold.

Was that when he started going outside in his pajamas so he'd be used to it when it really happened? No one knew he did that. By the time his father made all that money, he was used to being in the cold.

It was hard to remember. He got so confused. Sometimes he imagined things that didn't happen.

Like Erin Kelley. He'd looked up her address. She'd told him she lived in Greenwich Village and there she was: Erin Kelley, 101 Christopher Street.

One night he'd followed her, hadn't he?

Was he wrong?

Was it just a dream that she went to that bar and he stood outside? She sat and had something. He didn't know what it was. Wine? Club soda? What difference? He'd tried to decide whether or not to go in and join her.

Then she'd come out. He'd been about to go up and talk to her when the station wagon pulled up.

He couldn't remember if he'd gotten a look at the driver. Some times he dreamed about a face.

Erin got in.

That was the night they say she disappeared.

The thing was that Lenny wasn't sure if he'd just dreamed that. And if he told that to the cops, would they try to say he was crazy and make him go back to the place where they locked him up?

18

SATURDAY

March 9

At noon on Saturday, FBI agents Vince D'Ambrosio and Ernie Cizek sat in a dark-gray Chrysler across the street from the entrance to 101 Christopher Street.

"There he goes," Vince said. "All dressed up for his day off."

Gus Boxer was exiting from the building. He was wearing a red and black check lumber jacket over loose-fitting dark brown polyester pants, heavy laced boots, a black cap with a rim that half-covered his face.

"You call that dressed up?" Ernie exclaimed. "In that getup I thought he was paying off a bet."

"You just never saw him in his underwear and suspenders. Let's go." Vince opened the driver's door.

They had checked with the building managers. Boxer was off from noon every other Saturday till Monday morning. In his absence, a substitute super, José Rodriguez, handled complaints and did minor repairs.

Rodriguez answered their ring. A sturdy man in his mid-thirties with a direct manner, Vince wondered why the management didn't keep him full-time. He and Ernie showed their Bureau credentials. "We're going from apartment to apartment questioning the tenants about Erin Kelley. A number of them were not in the last time we went through."

Vince did not add that today he was going to get very specific about what the tenants thought of Gus Boxer.

On the fourth floor, he hit gold. An eighty-year-old woman answered the door, taking care not to remove the security chain. Vince showed his badge. Rodriguez explained, "It's all right, Miss Durkin. They just want to ask a few questions. I'll stay right here where you can see me."

"Can't hear," the old woman yelled.

"I just want to . . ."

Rodriguez touched D'Ambrosio's arm. "She can hear better than you or me," he whispered. "Come on, Miss Durkin, you liked Erin Kelley. Remember how she always asked you if you needed anything from the store and how she'd take you to church sometimes? You want the cops to get the guy who did that to her, don't you?"

The door opened the length of the chain. "Ask your questions." Miss Durkin looked severely at Vince. "And don't shout. It gives me a headache."

For the next fifteen minutes, the two agents got an earful of what a native New York octogenarian thought of how the city was being run. "I've lived here all my life," Miss Durkin informed them crisply, her wavy gray hair bobbing as she spoke. "We never used to lock our doors. Why would you? Who'd bother you? But now, all this crime and no one doing a thing about it. Disgusting. I tell you, they should ship all those drug dealers to the ends of the earth and let them sail off."

"I agree with you, Miss Durkin," Vince said wearily. "Now about Erin Kelley."

The old woman's face saddened. "A sweeter girl you'd never find. I'd like to get my hands on whoever did that to her. Now a few years ago, I happened to be sitting at the window looking at that apartment building across the street. A woman was murdered. They came around asking questions but May and I—she lives next door—decided to keep our mouths shut. We saw it. We know who did it. But that woman was no better than she ought to be, and there was good reason."

"You witnessed a murder and didn't tell the police?" Ernie asked incredulously.

She snapped her lips closed. "If I said that, I didn't say it the way I meant. What I meant was, I have my suspicions and so does May. But that's as far as it goes."

Suspicions! She saw that murder, Vince thought. He also knew that no one would ever get her or her friend May to testify. With an inward sigh, he said, "Miss Durkin, you sit by the window. I have a feeling you're a good observer. Did you see Erin Kelley leave with anyone that evening?"

"No. She left alone."

"Was she carrying anything?"

"Only her shoulder bag."

"Was it large?"

"Erin always carried a large shoulder bag. She often carried jewelry and didn't want anything that could be yanked from her hand."

"Then it was generally known she carried jewelry?"

"I guess so. Everyone knew she was a designer. From the street, you could see her sitting at her worktable."

"Did she date much?"

"She dated. But I wouldn't say much. Of course, she might have been meeting people outside. That's the way young people do it now. In my day, a young man picked you up at your home or you didn't set foot out the door. It was better then."

"I'm inclined to agree." They were still standing in the hall. "Miss Durkin, I wonder if we might just step inside for a moment. I don't want to be overheard."

"Your feet aren't muddy, are they?"

"No, ma'am."

"I'll wait right here, Miss Durkin," Rodriguez promised.

The apartment had the same layout as the one where Erin Kelley had lived. It was meticulously neat. Overstuffed horsehair furniture protected with antimacassars, standing lamps with elaborate silk shades, polished end tables, framed family pictures of bewhiskered men and severe women. Vince was carried back to the memory of his grandmother's parlor in Jackson Heights.

They were not invited to sit down.

"Miss Durkin, tell me, what do you think of Gus Boxer?"

A ladylike snort. "That one! Believe me, this is one of the few apartments he doesn't barge into looking for one of his famous water leaks. And this is the one that has it. I don't like that man. I don't know why the management keeps him on. Goes around in those disgusting clothes. Surly. The only thing I can figure is that they get him cheap. Just a week before she disappeared, I heard Erin Kelley tell him that if she found him in her apartment again, she'd call the police."

"Erin told him that?"

"You bet she did. And she was right."

"Was Gus Boxer aware of the amount of jewelry Erin Kelley handled?"

"Gus Boxer is aware of everything that goes on in this place."

"Miss Durkin, you've been very helpful. Is there anything else you can think of to tell us?"

She hesitated. "For a few weeks before Erin disappeared, from time to time a young fellow used to hang out across the street. Always when it was getting dark so you couldn't see him clearly. Now I don't know what he was up to. But that Tuesday night that Erin left here for the last time, I could make out that she was alone and carrying that big shoulder bag. My glasses had fogged up and I'm not sure if it was that same fellow across the street, but I think it was, and when Erin started walking down the block, he went in the same direction."

"You didn't see him clearly that night, but you saw him other times. What did he look like, Miss Durkin?"

"Beanpole. Collar up. Hands in his pockets, kind of hugging his arms against his body. Thin face. Dark, messy hair."

Len Parker, Vince thought. He glanced at Ernie, who obviously had the same idea.

"I've been looking forward to this." Darcy leaned back in the passenger seat of the Mercedes and smiled at Michael. "It's been quite a week."

"So I gathered," he said drily. "It was all I could do to catch you in at home or at your office."

"I know. I'm sorry."

"Don't be sorry about anything. It's a great day for a ride, isn't it?"

They were on Route 202 nearing Bridgewater. "I never knew very much about New Jersey," Darcy commented.

"Except comedians' jokes. Everyone judges it by that turnpike strip with all the refineries. Believe it or not, it has a longer coastline than most other states on the eastern seaboard and has among the highest number of horses per capita in the nation."

"So there!" Darcy laughed.

"So there. Who knows? With my missionary zeal, maybe I'll make you a convert."

Mrs. Hughes was bathed in smiles. "Oh, Miss Scott, I've been planning the nicest dinner since Doctor said you were coming."

"How nice of you."

"The guest room at the head of the stairs is all ready. You can just freshen up there after your ride."

"Great."

If anything, the day was even more perfect than last Sunday. Cool. Sunny. A hint of spring in the air. Darcy managed to give herself completely to the enjoyment of the canter.

When they stopped to let the horses rest, Michael said, "I don't have to ask if you're having a good time. It shows."

The late afternoon turned sharply cooler. A fire had been laid in Michael's study. The draft from the chimney was brisk, causing the flames to leap up.

Michael poured wine for her, made an old-fashioned for himself, sat beside her on the comfortable leather couch, stretched his feet on the coffee table. His arm went around the back of the sofa. "Do you know," he said, "I've spent more time this week thinking about what you told me. It's terrible that a chance remark can hurt a child so much. But Darcy, can you honestly say that sometimes you don't look in the mirror and see the fairest of all?"

"I certainly do not." Darcy hesitated. "God forbid I should angle for a free consultation, but I've been meaning to talk to you about that. No, never mind."

His hand ruffled her hair. "What? Shoot. Spit it out."

She looked directly at him, concentrating on the kindness in his eyes. "Michael, I get the feeling that you understand how devastating that remark was for me, but that you think I've been—how can I put this—subconsciously blaming my mother and father all these years."

Michael whistled. "Hey, you'd put me out of business. Most people take a year of therapy before they come to that kind of conclusion."

"You haven't answered me."

He kissed her cheek. "And I don't intend to. Come on, I think Mrs. Hughes has the fatted calf on the table."

They got back to her apartment at ten o'clock. He parked the car and walked her to the door. "This time I don't leave until I make sure you're safely inside. I wish you'd let me drive you to Wellesley tomorrow. That's a heck of a long round-trip for one day."

"I don't mind it. And I have to make a stop on the way back."

"More garage sales?"

She did not want to talk about the Nan Sheridan pictures. "Something like that. Another fishing expedition."

He put his hands on her shoulders, tilted up her face, brought his lips down to hers. His kiss was warm but brief. "Darcy, call me when you get home tomorrow night. I just want to be sure you're safe."

"I will. Thank you."

She stood inside the door until the car disappeared down the block. Then, humming, she ran up the stairs.

Hank was coming in early Saturday evening. We have so little time together, Vince fretted as he opened the door to his apartment. When they were married, he and Alice had been living in Great Neck. There hadn't been much point in his commuting after they split up, so when they sold the house he'd taken this apartment at Second Avenue and Nineteenth Street. The Gramercy Park area. Not Gramercy Park, of course. Not on his salary.

But he liked his apartment. On the ninth floor, his windows offered a typical midtown view. To the right a peek of the Park with its elegant brownstones, straight down the murderous traffic on Second Avenue, across the street a blend of residential and office buildings with storefront restaurants, delis, Korean produce markets, a video store.

He had two bedrooms, two baths, a fair-sized living room, a dinette, a minuscule kitchen. The second bedroom was for Hank, but he'd put bookshelves and a desk in it and it also served as a study.

The living room and dinette were furnished in Alice-in-Mistakeville decor. The year before they broke up, she'd gone pastel modern in the living room. Pale peach and white sectional, pale peach carpet, peach and teal no-arms easy chair. Glass tables. Lamps that looked like bones in a desert. She'd wished that stuff on him, taking all the traditional furniture that he liked. One of these days, when he got around to it, Vince was going to get rid of everything and buy good old-fashioned, comfortable furniture. He was sick of feeling as though he'd stumbled into Barbie's Dream House.

Hank hadn't arrived yet. Vince stripped, stood under a hot shower, pulled on underwear, a sweater, chinos, and loafers. He opened a beer, stretched out on the sectional, and reviewed the case.

This was one baffling investigation. Look under any rock and you'll find a new clue.

Boxer. Erin had threatened to go to the police about him. Yesterday, Darcy Scott had called saying she thought she had a picture of Nan Sheridan at Belle Island with a maintenance man in the background who might have been Boxer. They'd picked up the picture and were checking it out.

Miss Durkin had seen someone who sure as blazes sounded like that looney, Len Parker, hanging around Christopher Street, and she thought he had followed Erin Kelley the night she disappeared.

There was a direct connection between that con man Jay Stratton and Nan Sheridan. A direct connection between Jay Stratton and Erin Kelley.

Vince heard the turn of a key in the latch. Hank bounded in. "Hi Dad." Dropped his overnight bag. Quick hug.

Vince felt the tousled hair brush his cheek. He always had to check himself from showing the fierce love he felt for his son. The kid would be embarrassed. "Hi, pal. How's it going?"

"Great. I think. I aced the chemistry."

"You studied hard enough."

Hank took off his school jacket, flung it into space. "Boy, it's great to have midterms over." He took long steps into the kitchen and opened the refrigerator door. "Dad, it looks as though you could use Meals-on-Wheels."

"I know. It's been quite a week." Inspiration seized Vince. "I found a terrific new pasta restaurant the other night. It's on West Fifty-eighth Street. We can take in a movie after."

"Great." Hank stretched. "Oh boy, it's good to be here. Mom and Blubber are sore at each other."

It's none of my business, Vince thought, but couldn't help himself. "Why?"

"She wants a Rolex for her birthday. A sixteen, five Rolex."

"Sixteen thousand five hundred dollars? And I thought she was expensive when I was married to her."

Hank laughed. "I love Mom, but you know her. She thinks big. What's going on with the serial murder case?"

The phone rang. Vince frowned. Not again on Hank's night, he thought, observing that Hank's reaction was to look interested. "Maybe there's been a break," Hank said as Vince picked up the phone.

It was Nona Roberts. "Vince, I hate to call you at home, but you did give your number. I was out on location all day and stopped by the office just now. There's a message from Dr. Nash. His editor doesn't want him talking about personal ads now when his own book is scheduled for fall publication. Have you any other ideas about a shrink who might be particularly tuned in to this subject?"

"I deal with a few who are members of AAPL. That's an organization of shrinks who are specialists in psychiatry and law. I'll try and get one of them for you by Monday."

"Thanks a lot. Again, forgive me for bothering you. I'm off to Pasta Lovers for another bowl of that spaghetti."

"If you get there first, ask for a table for three. Hank and I are just leaving." Vince realized he sounded presumptuous. "Unless, of course, you're with your own friends." Or *friend,* he thought.

"I'm by myself. That sounds great. See you there." The phone clicked in his ear.

Vince looked at Hank. "Is that okay with you, Chief?" he asked. "Or would you have preferred just the two of us?"

Hank reached for the jacket that had landed on the armless easy chair. "Not at all. It's my duty to check out your dates."

19

SUNDAY
March 10

Darcy left for Massachusetts at seven o'clock Sunday morning. How many times had she and Erin driven up together to see Billy, she wondered as she steered the car onto the East River Drive. Sharing the driving, stopping midway for carry-out coffee at McDonald's, always deciding they really ought to get around to buying a thermos like the one they had had in college.

The last time they'd agreed on that, Erin had laughed. "Poor Billy will be dead and buried before we ever get that thermos."

Now it was Erin who was dead and buried.

Darcy drove straight through and got to Wellesley at eleven-thirty. She stopped at St. Paul's and rang the doorbell of the rectory. The monsignor who had celebrated Erin's funeral mass was there. She had coffee with him. "I left word at the nursing home," she told him, "but I wanted you to know as well. If Billy needs anything, if he starts sinking, or if he becomes conscious and aware, please send for me."

"He's not going to become aware anymore," the monsignor said quietly. "I think that's a special mercy for him."

She attended the noon mass and thought of the eulogy less than two weeks ago. "Who can forget the sight of that little girl pushing her father's wheelchair into this church?"

She went to the cemetery. The ground had not yet settled over Erin's grave. The dark brown soil was still uneven; a glaze of frost over it shimmered in the slanting rays of the weak March sun. Darcy knelt, removed her glove, and placed her hand on the grave. "Erin. Erin."

From there she went to the nursing home and sat by Billy's bed for an hour. He did not open his eyes, but she held his hand and kept up a steady stream of small talk. "Bertolini's is crazy about the necklace Erin designed. They want her to do a lot more work for them."

She talked about her own business. "Honestly, Billy, if you saw Erin and me rummaging through attics looking for goodies, you'd think we were crazy. She has a great eye and has picked out some furniture that I would have missed."

As she left, she leaned over and kissed his forehead. "God bless, Billy."

There was a faint pressure on her hand. He does know I'm here, she thought. "I'll be back soon," she promised.

Her car was a Buick station wagon with a cellular built-in phone. The traffic was slow heading south, and at five o'clock she called the Sheridan home in Darien. Chris answered. "I'm running later than I expected," she explained. "I don't want to interfere with your mother's plans—or your plans, for that matter."

"No plans," he assured her. "Just come along."

She pulled into the Sheridan property at quarter of six. It was almost dark, but outside lights illuminated the handsome Tudor mansion. The long driveway had a roundabout at the main entrance. Darcy parked just past the bend.

It was obvious that Chris Sheridan had been watching for her. The front door opened and he came out to greet her. "You made good time at that," he said. "It's nice to see you, Darcy."

He was wearing an oxford cloth shirt, corduroy pants, and loafers. As he extended his hand to assist her from the car, she was again aware of the breadth of his shoulders. She was also glad to see that he was not in a jacket and tie. On the way down it had occurred to her that she was arriving at dinnertime and her own corduroy pants and wool sweater might not be suitable garb.

The interior of the house had the charming combination of lived-in comfort and exquisite taste. Persian carpets were scattered in the high-ceilinged foyer. A Waterford chandelier and matching sconces enhanced the magnificent carving on the curving staircase. Paintings Darcy longed to study covered the stairway wall.

"Like most people, my mother uses the den more than any other room," Chris told her. "Through here."

Darcy glanced at the living room as they passed. Chris noticed and said, "The whole house is done in American antiques. Anywhere from early Colonial to Greek Revival. My grandmother was hooked on antiques and I guess we learned by osmosis."

Greta Sheridan was sitting in a comfortable armchair by the fireplace. *The New York Times* was scattered around her. The Sunday magazine section was open to the puzzle page and she was studying a crossword dictionary. She got up gracefully. "You must be Darcy Scott." She took Darcy's hand. "I'm so sorry about your friend."

Darcy nodded. What a beautiful woman, she thought. Many of the film stars who were her mother's intimates would enjoy Greta Sheridan's high cheekbones, patrician features, slender frame. She was wearing pale blue wool slacks, a matching cowl neck sweater, diamond earrings, and a diamond pin in the shape of a horseshoe.

To the manor born, Darcy thought.

Chris poured sherry. A platter of cheese and crackers was on the coffee table. He poked at the fire. "By the end of the day, you know it's still March."

Greta Sheridan asked about the trip. "You have more courage than I to go up in the morning to Massachusetts and back a few hours later."

"I'm in the car a lot."

"Darcy, we've known each other for five days," Chris commented. "Will you please tell me exactly what you do?" He turned to Greta. "The first time I took Darcy through the main floor of the gallery, she spotted the Roentgen writing desk out of the corner of her eye. Then she told me she was 'sort of in the business.' "

Darcy laughed. "You won't believe, but here goes."

Greta Sheridan was fascinated. "What a sensational idea. If you're interested, I'll be a scout for you. You'd be amazed at the wonderful furnishings people discard or sell for next to nothing in this area."

At six-thirty, Chris said, "I'm the chef. I hope you're not a vegetarian, Darcy. We're having steaks, baked potato, salad. Gourmet delight time."

"I'm not a vegetarian. It sounds wonderful."

When he had left, Greta Sheridan began to talk about her daughter and the reenactment of her murder on the *True Crimes* television series. "When I received that letter telling me a dancing girl was going to die in New York in Nan's honor, I thought I would go mad. There's nothing worse than not being able to prevent a tragedy you know is going to happen."

"Except to feel you had a hand in causing it," Darcy said. "I know that the only way I can make up to Erin for urging her to answer those cursed ads is to stop her killer from hurting anyone else. You obviously feel the same way. I understand how it must be tearing you apart to go through Nan's letters and pictures, and I'm grateful."

"I've found some others. They're here." Greta pointed to a stack of small albums on the raised hearth. "These were on a high shelf of the library and missed getting put away." She reached for the top one. Darcy pulled up a chair beside her and together they bent over it. "Nan got interested in photography that last year," Greta said. "We gave her a Canon for Christmas, so these were all taken between late December and early March."

The salad days, Darcy thought. She had albums like this of the Mount Holyoke crowd. The only difference was Mount Holyoke was a women's college. In these pictures there were as many guys as coeds. They began to go through them.

Chris appeared in the doorway. "Five-minute warning."

"You're a good cook," Darcy said approvingly as she ate the last bite of steak.

They began talking about Nan's reference to someone named Charley who had liked girls to wear spike heels. "That's what I was trying to remember," Greta said. "On the program and in the newspapers they were talking about high-heeled slippers. It was the letter from Nan about spike heels that was gnawing at me. Unfortunately, it really hasn't helped much, has it?"

"Not yet," Chris said.

* * *

Chris carried a tray with coffee into the study.

"You make a marvelous butler," his mother said affectionately.

"Since you refuse to have live-in help, I've had to learn."

Darcy thought of the Bel-Air mansion with its permanent staff of three live-ins.

When she finished the coffee, she got up to go. "I hate to break this up, but it will be over an hour before I get home and if I relax too much, I'll end up falling asleep at the wheel." She hesitated. "Can I just look at that first book again?"

In that first album, on the next to the last page, there was a group scene. "The tall fellow in the school sweater," Darcy said. "The one with his face turned from the camera. There's something about him." She shrugged. "I just have a feeling I may have met him somewhere."

Greta and Chris Sheridan studied the picture. "I can pick out some of the kids," Greta said, "but not that one. How about you, Chris?"

"No. But look, Janet is in it. She was one of Nan's big buddies," he explained to Darcy. "She lives in Westport." He turned to his mother. "She loves to visit you. Why not ask her to drop in soon?"

"She's so busy with the children. I could drive down there."

As Darcy said good-bye, Greta Sheridan smiled and said, "Darcy, I've been studying you all night. Except for the color of your hair, has anyone ever told you that you have a striking resemblance to Barbara Thorne?"

"Never," Darcy said honestly. It was not the moment to say that Barbara Thorne was her mother. She smiled back. "But I have to tell you, Mrs. Sheridan, that's a very nice thing to say."

Chris walked her to the car. "You're not too tired to drive?"

"Oh no. You should see the long treks I take when I'm out on one of my hunts for furniture."

"We really are in the same business."

"Yes, but you take the high road . . ."

"Will you be coming to the gallery tomorrow?"

"I'll be there. Good night, Chris."

Greta Sheridan was waiting at the door. "She's a lovely girl, Chris. Lovely."

Chris shrugged. "I think so too." He remembered how Darcy had blushed when he'd asked her about coming up yesterday.

"But don't start matchmaking, Mother. I've got a hunch she's taken."

Over the weekend Doug had been everything any woman could ask of a devoted husband and father. Even knowing his behavior was all a sham, Susan managed to assuage her fear that Doug might be a serial killer.

He went to Donny's basketball practice, then got together a scrimmage in the outdoor court with the kids who could stay. He took everyone out to Burger King for lunch. "Nothing like health food," he'd joked.

The place was full of young families. This is the sort of togetherness we've been lacking, Susan thought. But now it's too late. She looked across the table at Donny, who had hardly said a word.

Back home, Doug played with the baby, helping him build a castle of interlocking blocks. "Let's put the little prince inside." Conner squealed with delight.

He took Trish for a ride on her scooter. "We can beat anyone on the block, can't we, toots?"

He had a friendly father-daughter conversation with Beth. "My little girl is getting prettier every day. I'm going to have to build a fence around this house to keep away all the boys who'll be coming after you."

While she was getting dinner, he nuzzled Susan's neck. "We should go dancing some night, honey. Remember how we used to dance in college?"

Like a cold wind, that ended the fantasy that maybe she had been ridiculous in suspecting him of anything stronger than womanizing. *Dancing shoes found on dead bodies.*

Later, in bed, Doug reached for her. "Susan, have I ever told you how much I love you?"

"Many times, but one stands out in my mind." *When I lied for you after Nan Sheridan died.*

Doug pulled up on one elbow, stared down at her in the dark. "Now when was that?" he asked teasingly.

Don't let him know what you're thinking. "The day we were married, of course." She laughed nervously. "Oh, Doug, no. Please, I'm really tired." She could not bear his touch. She realized she was afraid of him.

"Susan, what the hell is the matter with you? You're trembling."

Sunday was more of the same. Family togetherness. But Susan could spot the wary expression in Doug's eyes, the lines of worry around his mouth. *Do I have an obligation to report my suspicions to the police? And if I admit that I lied for him fifteen years ago, could I go to prison too? And if that happened, what would become of the children? And if he suspected I was going to tell the police that I lied for him about the morning Nan died, how would he try to stop me?*

20
MONDAY
March 11

On Monday morning, Vince called Nona. "I've got a shrink for your program. Dr. Martin Weiss. A nice guy. Sensible. A member of AAPL and very knowledgeable. He says it straight and he's willing to do the show. Want to take down his number?"

"Absolutely." Nona repeated it, then added, "I like Hank, Vince. He's terrific."

"He wants to know if you'd like to see him pitch when baseball starts."

"I'll bring the Cracker Jacks."

Nona phoned Dr. Weiss. He agreed to come to the studio at four o'clock on Wednesday. "We tape at five. It will be aired Thursday night at eight."

Darcy spent a good part of Monday in the warehouse tagging furniture for the hotel. At four o'clock she arrived at Sheridan Galleries.

An auction was taking place. She saw Chris standing on the side of the first row, his back to her. She slipped down the corridor to the conference room. Many of the snapshots were dated. She wanted to find others in that same time frame. Maybe she'd come across another picture of the student who had seemed vaguely familiar.

At six-thirty she was still at it. Chris came in. She looked up, smiling. "The bidding out there sounded hot and heavy. Was it a good day?"

"Very. No one told me you were here. I noticed the light was on."

"I'm glad you did. Chris, does this fellow look like the one I pointed out yesterday?"

He studied it. "Yes, it does. My mother left a message a few minutes ago. She saw Janet today. That guy was one of the many questioned in Nan's death. He had a crush on her, I gather. His name was Doug Fox." At Darcy's shocked expression he asked, "You know him then?"

"As Doug Fields. Through a personal ad."

"Honey, they called an emergency meeting. I can't talk, but a company we've recommended to our biggest client is going under."

Somehow Susan got through the evening. She gave the baby and Trish a bath and helped Donny and Beth with their homework.

At last she was able to turn out the lights and go to bed. For hours she lay sleepless. He'd managed to stay home for a weekend. Now he was on the loose again. And if he was responsible for the deaths of those girls, she was equally guilty.

It would be so easy if she could only run away. Bundle the kids in the car and drive as far as they could go.

But it didn't work like that.

The next afternoon when she'd seen Trish off on the school bus and put Conner down for his nap, Susan picked up the phone and asked information for the number of the FBI headquarters in Manhattan.

She dialed and waited. A voice said, "Federal Bureau of Investigation."

It was not too late to disconnect. Susan shut her eyes, forced her voice above a whisper. "I want to talk to someone about the dancing-shoe murders. I may have some information."

* * *

On Monday evening, Darcy met Nona for dinner at Neary's and filled her in about Doug Fox. "Vince was out when I tried to reach him," she said. "I left word with his assistant." She broke off a piece of roll and lightly buttered it. "Nona, Doug Fox, or Doug Fields as he introduced himself to me, is exactly the kind of guy Erin would have enjoyed and trusted. He's good-looking, bright, artistic, and he's got one of those boyish faces that would appeal to a nurturer like Erin."

Nona looked grave. "It's pretty scary that he was questioned in Nan Sheridan's death. You'd better not see him again. Of course, Vince did say that a lot of guys don't give their right names when they answer these ads."

"But how many others were questioned in Nan Sheridan's death?"

"Just don't get your hopes up. So far, it isn't really more of a lead than the fact that Jay Stratton also went to Brown or that Erin's superintendent worked near Nan Sheridan's home fifteen years ago."

"I just want it to be over," Darcy sighed.

"Let's not talk about it anymore. You've been eating and breathing it. How's work going?"

"Oh, I've been neglecting it, of course. But I did have a nice call today about a room I did for a sixteen-year-old girl who had a terrible accident. I used some of Erin's things to furnish it. The mother wanted me to know that her daughter Lisa came home from the hospital Saturday and loves the room. And you know what the mother said really got Lisa excited?"

"What?"

"Remember the poster Erin had on the wall opposite her bed? The one of the Egret painting?"

"Sure I do. 'Loves Music, Loves to Dance.' "

They hadn't noticed that Jimmy Neary had come up to their table. *"That's it,"* he said vehemently. "By heaven, that's it. That's the way the ad began that fell out of Erin's pocket, right here on this very spot."

21
TUESDAY
March 12

Susan hired a babysitter on Tuesday and took the train down to New York. Vince had asked her to come in. "I can understand how difficult this is for you, Mrs. Fox," he'd said carefully. He did not tell her that they already had a connection to her husband. "We'll do everything to keep our investigation from the media, but the more we know, the easier that will be."

At eleven o'clock, Susan was in FBI headquarters. "You can contact the Harkness Agency," she told Vince. "They've been trailing Doug. I would like to think he's just a philanderer, but if it's more than that, I can't let it go on."

Vince saw the agony in the face of the pretty young woman opposite him. "No, you can't let it go on," he said quietly. "However, it's a long jump from knowing your husband is playing around to thinking that he might be a serial killer. How did you make that jump?"

"I was only twenty and I was so in love with him." It was as though Susan was talking to herself.

"How long ago was that?"

"Fifteen years."

Vince kept his face impassive. "What happened at that time, Mrs. Fox?"

Her eyes fixed somewhere on the wall behind him, Susan told Vince about lying for Doug when Nan Sheridan died and how Doug had called out Erin's name in his sleep the night her body was discovered.

When she was finished, Vince said, "The Harkness Agency knows where his apartment is?"

"Yes." After she revealed everything she knew or suspected, Susan felt a vast weariness. Now all she had to do was live with herself for the rest of her life.

"Mrs. Fox, this is one of the hardest things you'll ever have to do. We need to check with the Harkness Agency. The fact that they were following your husband could be of great value. Can you act normally with him for the next day or two? Don't forget, our investigation may clear him."

"It isn't hard to keep up appearances with my husband. Most of the time he doesn't notice me except to complain."

When she left, Vince called in Ernie. "We have our first big break and I don't want to blow it. This is what we'll do. . . ."

On Tuesday afternoon, Jay Charles Stratton was booked for grand theft. The NYPD detectives, in conjunction with the Lloyd's of London security staff, had found the jeweler who fenced some of his stolen diamonds. The rest of the gems that were listed as being in the missing pouch were traced to a private safe deposit box rented under the name Jay Charles.

It had been a long meeting and the tension in the office all day was brutal. How do you explain to your best clients that a company's accountants pulled the wool over your eyes? That sort of thing wasn't supposed to happen anymore.

Doug called home several times and was surprised to hear the babysitter pick up the phone. Something was definitely up. He'd make it his business to get home tonight. It wasn't that hard to straighten Susan out. His confidence oozed away. She wasn't beginning to suspect . . . Or was she?

On Tuesday evening, Darcy went straight home from work. All she wanted to do was heat a can of soup and go to bed early. The tension of the last two weeks was catching up with her. She knew it.

At eight o'clock Michael phoned. "I've heard tired voices, but yours just might win first prize."

"I'm sure it would."

"You've been driving yourself too hard, Darcy."

"Don't worry. I intend to come straight home from the office for the rest of the week."

"That's a good idea. Darcy, I'll be out of town for a few days, but keep Saturday for me, won't you? Or Sunday? Or better still, both days?"

Darcy laughed. "Let's plan on Saturday. Have fun."

"It isn't fun. It's a psychiatric convention. I've been asked to fill in for a friend who's had to cancel. You want to know what it's like to have four hundred shrinks in one room at the same time?"

"I can't imagine."

~ 22
WEDNESDAY
March 13

Dday, Nona thought as she slipped off her cape and tossed it on the love seat. It was not quite eight A.M. She was grateful to see that Connie was already there and the coffee brewing.

Connie followed her in. "It's going to be a great program, Nona." She was carrying freshly washed mugs.

"I think Cecil B. DeMille did one of his epics faster than I handled this one," Nona said wryly.

"You've been doing all your regular shows while putting this together," Connie pointed out.

"I suppose. Let's be sure to reconfirm all the guests by phone. You did send them a follow-up letter?"

"Of course." Connie looked astonished that she'd ask.

Nona grinned. "I'm sorry. It's just that Hamilton has been such a pain about this program, and Liz is determined to take the credit for what's good in it and leave me holding the bag if there are any snafus . . ."

"I know."

"Sometimes I wonder who runs this office, Connie, you or me. There's only one area where I wish we weren't alike."

Connie waited.

"I wish you talked to plants. You're like me. You never even see them." She pointed to the plant on the windowsill. "That poor thing is gasping. Pour something liquid on it, will you?"

* * *

Len Parker was tired Wednesday morning. Yesterday he hadn't been able to stop thinking about Darcy Scott. When he left work he'd hung around her apartment building and seen her step out of a cab around six-thirty or seven. He'd waited until ten, but she hadn't come out. He really wanted to talk to her. Other times he was mad at her for being so mean to him. There was something he had thought about the other day that had been important, but now it was gone. He wondered if he'd remember again.

He put on his maintenance uniform. Nice thing about wearing a uniform, it didn't cost you anything for work clothes.

Vince's secretary had taken a message from Darcy Scott before he got to the office on Wednesday morning. She'd be out all day on different jobs but wanted him to know that Erin had probably answered an ad that began *"Loves Music, Loves to Dance."* That certainly sounded like the kind of ad those missing girls would have answered too, Vince thought.

Following up on the personal ads was a grueling job. Anyone who didn't want his real identity known could fake a few ID's, open a checking account, and rent a private box where magazines and newspapers could forward the responses to the nameless ads. No home address to trace. The people who ran those private box services were in the business of offering secrecy to their clients.

It was going to be a long haul. But this ad had a ring to it. He got on the phone to the researchers. They were closing in on Doug Fox, also known as Doug Fields. The Harkness Agency's file on him was an FBI investigator's dream.

Fields had been subletting the apartment for two years, starting just about the time Claire Barnes disappeared.

Joe Pabst, the Harkness man, had sat near Fox in the SoHo restaurant. It was clear he had met the woman through a personal ad.

He'd made a date to take her dancing.

He had a station wagon.

Pabst was sure that Fox had some sort of hideout. He'd overheard him telling the real estate broker in SoHo that he had a retreat he'd love to have her visit.

He was passing himself off as an illustrator. The super of the London Terrace building had been in and out of Fields's apartment and said that there were sketches lying around that were really good.

And he had been questioned in Nan Sheridan's death.

But it was all circumstantial, Vince reminded himself. Did Fox place ads, or answer them, or both? Would it be better to tap his London Terrace phone for a while, see what that turned up?

Should they bring him in for questioning? It was a tough one to call.

Well, at least Darcy Scott was already alerted to the possibility that Fox was the one. She wouldn't let herself get painted into a corner by him.

And wouldn't it be a bonus if it turned out that Fox had placed the ad they knew Erin Kelley had been carrying around? *"Loves Music, Loves to Dance."*

At noon, Vince got a VICAP alert from headquarters in Quantico. Calls had come in from police departments all over the country. Vermont. Washington, D.C. Ohio. Georgia. California. Five more packages of mismatched shoes had been returned. All of them contained a shoe or boot and a high-heeled slipper. All of them were sent to families of the young women who had turned up in the VICAP file, the young women who had lived in New York and been reported missing in the last two years.

At three-thirty, Vince was ready to leave his office for Hudson Cable Network. His secretary stopped him as he passed her desk and handed him the phone. "Mr. Charles North. He says it's important."

Vince felt his eyebrows go up. Don't tell me that stuffy ambulance chaser is starting to cooperate, he thought. "D'Ambrosio," he said crisply.

"Mr. D'Ambrosio, I have been doing a great deal of thinking."

Vince waited.

"There is only one possible explanation I can come up with to account for how my plans may have fallen on the wrong ears."

Vince felt a stir of interest.

"When I came to New York in early February to make final living arrangements, I attended a benefit at the Plaza as the guest of my senior partner. The 21st Century Playwrights' Festival Benefit. It was quite a glittery crowd. Helen Hayes, Tony Randall, Martin Charnin, Lee Grant, Lucille Lortel. I was introduced to a great many people during the cocktail hour. The senior partner at my firm was anxious that I become known. I spoke to a group of four or five people right before dinner was announced. One of them asked me for my card, but I can't think of his name."

"What did he look like?"

"You're speaking to someone with a very poor memory for both faces and names, which I am sure must be puzzling to someone in your profession. I'm vague about him. About six feet. Late thirties or early forties. Late thirties, I would think. Well-spoken."

"Do you think that if we got a roster of the people who attended that benefit it might stir your memory?"

"I don't know. It might."

"Okay, Mr. North. I'm grateful for this. We'll get the list and perhaps you can ask your senior partner if he recognizes the names of any of the people you spent time with."

North sounded alarmed. "And how would I explain the need for that information?"

The faint stirring of gratitude that Vince had felt for the man's attempt to be helpful disappeared. "Mr. North," he snapped, "you're a lawyer. You should be used to getting information without giving it." He hung up and yelled for Ernie. "I need the guest list for the 21st Century Playwrights' Benefit at the Plaza in early February," he said. "Shouldn't be hard to get. You know where I'll be."

It was March thirteenth, Nan's anniversary. Yesterday had been their thirty-fourth birthday.

Long ago Chris had started to celebrate his on the twenty-fourth, Greta's birthday. It was easier for both of them. His mother had phoned yesterday before he left for work. "Chris, I thank my stars every day that I have you. Happy birthday, dear."

This morning he'd phoned her. "The tough day, Mother."

"I guess it always will be. Are you sure you want to be on that program?"

"Want to? No. But I think if it does anything to help solve this case, it's worth it. Maybe someone watching it will remember something about Nan."

"I hope so." Greta sighed. Her tone changed. "How's Darcy? Chris, she is so dear."

"I think this whole business is wearing her down."

"Will she be on the program as well?"

"No. And she doesn't want to watch it being taped."

It was a quiet day at the gallery. Chris had a chance to catch up on paperwork. He'd left instructions that if Darcy came in he was to be notified. But there was no sign of her. Maybe she wasn't well. At two he phoned her office. Her secretary said she was working on some outside job all day and then planned to go directly home.

At three-thirty, Chris was hailing a cab to go to Hudson Cable.

Let's get this over with, he thought grimly.

The guests for the program gathered in the greenroom. Nona introduced them. The Corras, a couple in their mid-forties. They'd separated. Each had placed a personal ad. They'd answered each other's ad. That had been the catalyst that brought them back together.

The Daleys, a serious-looking couple in their fifties. Neither had ever married. They'd both been embarrassed about placing and answering ads. They'd met three years ago. "It was good from the very beginning," Mrs. Daley said. "I've always been much too reticent. I was able to put on paper what I couldn't say to any one." She was a research scientist. He was a college professor.

Adrian Greenfield, the vivacious divorcèe in her late forties. "I'm having more fun," she told the others. "Actually, they made a printing error. They were supposed to say that I was well-liked. Instead, they put down that I was wealthy. I swear, you need a U-Haul for the mail I've gotten."

Wayne Harsh, the shy president of a toy manufacturing company. In his late twenties. Every mother's dream of the kind of guy her daughter will bring home, Vince decided. Harsh was enjoying his dates. In his ad he'd written that it frustrated him to see the toys he manufactured being enjoyed by kids all over the world while he is childless. Anxious to meet sweet, bright woman in her twenties who wants a nice guy who'll be home on time and won't drop his laundry on the floor.

The lovebirds, the Cairones. They fell in love on their first personal ad date. At the end of the evening he had gone over to the piano at the bar where they met and played "Get Me to the Church on Time." They were married a month later.

"Until they came along, I was worried that we didn't have any young couples," Nona had confided to Vince when he arrived. "Those two make you believe in romance."

Vince saw the psychiatrist, Dr. Martin Weiss, come in and got up to greet him.

Weiss was a man in his late sixties with a strong face, a good head of silver hair, penetrating blue eyes. They went over to the coffeepot.

"Thank you for doing this on short notice, Doctor," Vince said.

"Hello, Vince."

Vince turned as Chris came up to them. He remembered that this was the anniversary of Nan Sheridan's death. "Not the best day for you," he said.

At quarter of five, Darcy leaned back in the cab, her eyes closed. At least today she'd made up for lost time. The painters would start next Monday at the hotel. This morning she'd brought down a brochure from the Pelham Hotel in London. "This is an absolutely elegant and intimate hotel. It's like your place in the sense that the rooms aren't large, the reception area is small, the parlor off it is perfect for receiving visitors. Notice the little bar in the corner. You can have the same thing. And study the rooms. We're not going to be nearly that grand, of course, but we can give it the effect."

It was obvious they were delighted.

Now, Darcy thought, I've got to get in touch with the window designer at Wilston's. She'd been shocked to realize that when a window display was taken down, the fabrics were often sold for peanuts. Yards and yards of top-quality goods.

She shook her head, trying to dislodge a nagging headache. I don't know whether I'm getting a bug or if I just ache, but it's another early night for me. The cab was pulling up to her building.

In the apartment her answering machine was blinking. Bev had left a message. "Darcy, you got the craziest call about twenty minutes ago. Call me right away."

Quickly, Darcy dialed her office. "Bev, what's the message?"

"It was some woman. Spoke real low. I could hardly hear her. She wanted to know where she could get in touch with you. I didn't want to give your home number so I said I'd give you a message. She said she was in the bar the night Erin disappeared, afraid to admit it because her date wasn't her husband. She saw Erin meet someone who was coming in just as Erin was leaving. They walked away together. She got a good look at him."

"How can I get back to her?"

"You can't. She wouldn't leave her name. She wants you to meet her at that bar. It's Eddie's Aurora on West Fourth Street off Washington Square. She said to come alone and sit at the bar. She'll be there by six unless she can't get away. Don't wait any longer than that. She'll call tomorrow if you don't get together tonight."

"Thanks, Bev."

"Listen, Darcy, I'm going to stay late. I have an exam to study for and there's no peace and quiet in my apartment with my roommate's friends always hanging around. Call me back, won't you? I'd just like to know that you're okay."

"I'll be fine. But yes, I'll call you back."

Darcy forgot that she was tired. It was five of five. She had just time to freshen her face, brush her hair, and change from her dusty jeans to a skirt and sweater. Oh, Erin, she thought. Maybe it's ending.

Nona watched the credits roll as the guests chatted quietly, still on-camera but off-mike. "Amen," she said as the screen went dark. She jumped up and ran down the steps to the set. "You were wonderful," she said. "Every one of you. I can't thank you enough."

A relaxed smile from some of the participants. Chris, Vince, and Dr. Weiss got up together.

"I'm glad it's over," Chris said.

"Understandable," Martin Weiss said. "From what I've heard today, both you and your mother have shown remarkable strength through all this."

"You do what you have to do, Doctor."

Nona came up to them. "The others are leaving, but I wish you people would come back to my office for a cocktail. You've certainly earned it."

"Oh, I don't think . . ." Weiss shook his head, then hesitated. "I must check in with my office. If I can do it from there?"

"Of course."

Chris debated. He realized how low he was feeling. Darcy's secretary had said she was going straight home. He wondered if he could talk her into a quick dinner. "Can I get on line for the phone too?"

"Dial away."

The beeper went off on Vince's belt. "I hope you have a lot of phones around here, Nona."

Vince dialed from the secretary's desk and received a message to call Ernie at the 21st Century Playwrights' Festival office. When he reached him, Ernie was brimming with news.

"I've got the guest list. Guess who was there that night?"

"Who?"

"Erin Kelley and Jay Stratton."

"Holy smoke." He thought of the description North had given him of the man who had taken his card. Tall. Late thirties or early forties. Well-spoken. But Erin Kelley! That afternoon in Kelley's apartment Darcy had selected a pink and silver dress for Erin to be buried in. Darcy had told him Erin bought it to wear *to a benefit.* Then when he'd picked up the package of shoes that had been mailed to Darcy's apartment, she'd said that the evening slipper in the package went better with Erin's pink and silver dress than the ones Erin had bought herself. He suddenly knew why the shoes went so well with it. Her killer had been at the benefit and seen her wearing that dress.

"Meet me in Nona Roberts's office," he told Ernie. "We might as well go downtown together."

In the office Dr. Weiss seemed more relaxed. "No problems. I was concerned that one patient might need to see me tonight. Ms. Roberts, I'm going to take advantage of your kindness. My youngest son is a communications major and will be graduating from college in June. How does he get a foothold in this business?"

Chris Sheridan had moved the phone from Nona's desk to the windowsill. Absently, he fingered the dusty plant. Darcy wasn't home. When he'd called her office, her secretary had been evasive. Something about expecting to hear from her later. "A very important meeting had come up."

His intuition was pounding at him. Something was wrong.

He knew it.

Darcy wasn't supposed to wait any longer than six o'clock. She stayed until six-thirty, then decided to give up for tonight. Obviously the woman who called hadn't been able to meet her. She paid for the Perrier and left.

She stepped out onto the street. The wind had stirred up again and seemed to cut through her body. I hope I can get a cab, she said to herself.

"Darcy. I'm so glad I caught you. Your secretary said you'd be here. Hop in."

"Oh, you're a lifesaver. What luck."

Len Parker huddled in a doorway across the street and watched the vanishing taillights. It was just like last time when Erin Kelley came out and someone called her from that station wagon.

Suppose this was the same person who had killed Erin Kelley? Should he call that FBI agent? His name was D'Ambrosio. Len had his card.

Would they think he was crazy?

Erin Kelley had walked out on him and Darcy Scott had refused to have dinner with him.

But he'd been mean to them.

Maybe he should call.

He'd spent a lot of money on cabs following Darcy Scott these last couple of days.

And the phone call would only cost a quarter.

Chris turned from the window. He had to ask. Vince D'Ambrosio had just come back into the room. "Do you know if Darcy is answering another one of those damn ads tonight?" he demanded.

Vince saw the concern on Sheridan's face and ignored the belligerent tone. He knew it was not directed at him. "I understood from Nona that Darcy was planning an early night."

"She was." The smile vanished from Nona's face. "When I called her office, her secretary said she was going straight home from that hotel she's redoing."

"Well, something changed her mind," Chris retorted. "Her secretary sounds very mysterious."

"What's her office number?" Vince grabbed the phone. When Bev answered, he identified himself. "I'm concerned about Miss Scott's plans. If you know what they are, I want to hear them."

"I'd really rather let her get back to you—" Bev began, but was interrupted.

"Listen, miss, I have no intention of interfering with her private life, but if this has to do with a personal ad, I want to know. We're getting very close to solving this case but no one is in custody."

"Well, promise not to interfere—"

"Where is Darcy Scott?"

Bev told him. Vince gave her Nona's number. "Ask Miss Scott to call me immediately when you hear from her." He hung up. "She's meeting a woman who claims she saw Erin Kelley leave Eddie's Aurora in the Village the night she disappeared, and can describe the man she met outside. This woman hasn't come forward because she was with a guy who wasn't her husband."

"Do you believe it?" Nona asked.

"I don't like the sound of it. But if Darcy meets her in that bar, it should be okay. What time is it?"

"Six-thirty," Dr. Weiss said.

"Then Darcy should be phoning her office any minute. She was only supposed to wait until six for that caller to show up."

"Didn't the same thing happen to Erin Kelley?" Chris demanded. "As I understand it, she went to Eddie's Aurora, was stood up, left, and disappeared."

Vince felt the skin on the back of his neck start to crawl. "I'll phone there." When he reached the bar, he fired rapid questions, listened, then slammed down the receiver. "The bartender says a young woman answering Darcy's description walked out a few minutes ago. Nobody showed up to meet her."

Chris swore under his breath. The moment when he'd found Nan's body fifteen years ago today filled his mind with sickening clarity.

An escort from reception tapped on the half-open door. "Mr. Cizek from the FBI says you're expecting him," she told Nona.

Nona nodded. "Show him in."

Cizek was pulling the thick guest list for the Playwrights' gala from a bulging manila envelope as he came through the door. It was stuck. When he tried to yank it out, the clip fell off and the pages scattered. Nona and Dr. Weiss helped to retrieve them.

Chris was clenching and unclenching his fists, Vince noticed. "We have two strong suspects," he told Chris, "and we have a tail on both of them."

Dr. Weiss was examining one of the pages he picked up. As though he was thinking aloud he commented, "I'd have thought he was too busy with his personal ads to go to parties."

Vince looked up quickly. "Who are you talking about?"

Weiss seemed embarrassed. "Dr. Michael Nash. Forgive me. That was an unprofessional comment."

"Nothing is unprofessional at this point," Vince said sharply. "It could be very important that Dr. Nash was at the benefit. You sound as if you don't like him. Why?"

All eyes were on Martin Weiss. He seemed to be debating with himself, then said slowly, "This must go no farther than this room. One of Nash's former patients, who now consults with me, noticed him in a restaurant with a young woman she knew. The next time she saw that young woman she teased her about it."

Vince felt his nerves tingling the way they always did when he sensed a break in the case. "Go on, Doctor."

Weiss looked uncomfortable. "My patient's young friend said that she had met the man when she answered his personal ad and wasn't surprised to learn that he had lied about his name and background. She felt distinctly uneasy with him."

Vince sensed that Dr. Weiss was deliberately choosing his words. "Doctor," he said, "you know what we're up against. You've got to level with me. What is your candid opinion of Dr. Michael Nash?"

"I consider it unethical for him to do research for a professional book under false pretenses," Weiss said cautiously.

"You're hedging," Vince told him. "If you were on the witness stand, how would you describe him?"

Weiss looked away. "Loner," he said flatly. "Repressed. Pleasant on the surface but basically antisocial. Probably has deep-rooted problems that began to manifest themselves in childhood. However, he's a natural dissembler and could fool most professionals."

Chris felt blood pounding in his temples. "Has Darcy been seeing this guy?"

"Yes," Nona whispered.

"Doctor," Vince continued rapidly, "I want to get in touch with that young woman immediately and find out what ad he placed."

"My patient brought it in to show me," Weiss said. "I have it in my office."

"Would you remember if it began *'Loves Music, Loves to Dance'?*" Vince asked.

As Weiss said, "Why yes, that's right," Vince's beeper went off. He grabbed the phone, dialed, and barked his name. Nona, Chris, Dr. Weiss, and Ernie waited in absolute silence as they saw the lines on Vince D'Ambrosio's forehead deepen. Still holding the receiver he told them, "That Len Parker looney just phoned in. He was following Darcy. She came out of that bar and got into the same station wagon Erin Kelley drove off in the night she disappeared." He paused, then said tersely, "It's a black Mercedes registered to Dr. Michael Nash of Bridgewater, New Jersey."

* * *

"You have a different car."

"I mostly use this one in the country."

"You got back early from the convention."

"The speaker I was to replace felt well enough to come after all."

"I see. Michael, you're sweet, but I think I'd just as soon go home tonight."

"What'd you have for dinner last night?"

Darcy smiled. "A can of soup."

"You lean your head back and rest. Sleep if you can. Mrs. Hughes is going to have a fire blazing, a terrific dinner, and then you can sleep all the way home." He reached over and gently stroked her hair. "Doctor's orders, Darcy. You know I like taking care of you."

"It's nice to be taken care of. Oh!" She reached for the car phone. "Is it all right if I call my secretary? I promised to check in with her."

He placed his hand over hers and squeezed it. "I'm afraid it will have to wait until we get to the house. The phone is broken. Now you just relax."

Darcy knew Bev would be there at least a few more hours. She closed her eyes and began to drift off. She was asleep by the time they went through the Lincoln Tunnel.

"We'll have Nash's apartment checked," Vince said. "But he'd never take her there or to his office. The doorman would see them."

"Darcy told me his place in Bridgewater is a four-hundred-acre estate. She's been there a couple of times." Nona was gripping the sides of the desk to steady herself.

"Then if he suggested going there with him tonight, she wouldn't be suspicious." Vince felt growing anger at himself.

Ernie returned from the next office. "I've checked surveillance. Doug Fox is home in Scarsdale. Jay Stratton is at the Park Lane with some old broad."

"That lets them out." It makes sense, Vince thought furiously. Nash left word on Erin's answering machine to call him at his apartment the night he drove off with her. I never thought to check that out. He leaves a phony message with Darcy's secretary and probably acts as though the secretary told him where to find Darcy. We know

Darcy trusts him. Sure, she gets into his car. And if that weirdo Parker hadn't been trailing her, she'd have vanished into thin air too.

"How are we going to find Darcy?" Chris asked desperately. Agonizing fear that made it hard to breathe was crushing his chest. He knew that sometime in this past week, he had fallen hard for Darcy Scott.

Vince was on the line snapping orders to headquarters. "Alert the Bridgewater police," he was saying. "Have them meet us there."

"Be careful, Vince," Ernie warned. "We have absolutely no proof of anything, and the only witness is certifiably nuts."

Chris spun on him. "*You* be careful." He felt Weiss grip his arm.

"Get directions to Nash's place," Vince was saying. "And have a chopper at the Thirtieth Street pad in ten minutes."

Five minutes later, they were in a patrol car, lights flashing, sirens screaming, racing down Ninth Avenue. Vince was in the front seat with the driver, Nona, Chris, and Ernie Cizek in the back. Chris had flatly declared that he was going with Vince. Nona had looked at Vince, her eyes begging.

Vince did not share the chilling information received from the Bridgewater police. Nash's estate had a number of outer buildings scattered over the four hundred acres, including some in wooded areas. A search could take a long time.

And every minute we lose, the clock is running out for Darcy, he thought.

"We're here, sweetheart."

Darcy stirred. "I did fall asleep, didn't I?" She yawned. "Forgive me for being such boring company."

"I was glad you were sleeping. Rest heals the spirit as well as the body."

Darcy looked out. "Where are we?"

"Only ten miles from the house. I have a little retreat where I get my writing done and I forgot my manuscript the other day. You don't mind if we stop for it? As a matter of fact, we can have a glass of sherry here."

"As long as we don't stay too long. I do want to get home early, Michael."

"You will. I promise. Come on in. Sorry it's so dark."

His hand was under her arm. "How did you ever find this place?" Darcy asked as he opened the door.

"Pure luck. I know it doesn't look like much outside, but the interior is quite nice."

He pushed the door open and reached for the light switch. Beneath it, Darcy noticed a button marked "Panic."

She looked around the large room. "Oh, this is handsome," she said, taking in the seating area by the fireplace, the open kitchen, the polished floors. Then she noticed the big-screen television and elaborate stereo speakers. "That's magnificent equipment. Isn't it wasted in a writing retreat?"

"No, it isn't." He was removing her coat. Darcy shivered even though the room was comfortably warm. There was a bottle of wine in a silver holder on the coffee table by the sofa.

"Does Mrs. Hughes take care of this place?"

"No. She doesn't know it exists." He walked the length of the room and switched on the stereo.

The opening bars of "Till There Was You" sounded from the wall speakers.

"Come here, Darcy." He poured sherry into a glass and handed it to her. "On a cold night this tastes wonderful, doesn't it?"

He was smiling at her affectionately. Then what was wrong? Why did she suddenly sense something different? His voice seemed slightly blurred, almost as though he'd been drinking. His eyes. That was it. There was something about his eyes.

Her instinct was to run for the door, but that was ridiculous. She searched frantically for something to say. Her eyes rested on the staircase. "How many rooms do you have upstairs?" To her own ears the question sounded abrupt.

He didn't seem to notice. "Just a smallish bedroom and bath. This is one of those really old-fashioned cottages."

The smile was still there, but his eyes were changing, the pupils widening. *Where were his computer and printer and books and all the usual trappings of a writer?*

Darcy felt perspiration form on her forehead. What was the matter with her? Was she going crazy suspecting . . . what? It was just nerves. This was Michael.

Holding his sherry, he settled in the large chair opposite the sofa and stretched out his legs. His eyes never left her face.

"Let me look around." She walked aimlessly through the room, pausing as though to examine one of the few pieces of bric-a-brac, running her hand over the countertop that separated the kitchen area from the rest of the room. "What beautiful cabinets."

"I had them made, but I installed them myself."

"You did!"

His voice was genial but a hard edge came into it. "I told you my father was a self-made man. He wanted me to be able to turn my hand to anything."

"He did a good job teaching you." There was no way she could stand here any longer. She turned, walked toward the sofa, and stepped on something solid that was almost covered by the fringe of the rug in the seating area.

Ignoring it, Darcy sat down quickly. Her knees were shaking so much she felt as though they would buckle under her. *What was the matter? Why was she so afraid?*

This was Michael, kind, considerate Michael. She did not want to think about Erin now, but Erin's face was looming in her mind. She took a quick sip of sherry to relieve the dryness in her mouth.

The music stopped. Michael looked annoyed, got up and went to the stereo. From the shelf above it, he took a pile of cassettes and began to examine them. "I didn't realize that tape was so close to the end."

It was as though he was talking to himself. Darcy gripped the stem of the glass. Now her hands were trembling. A few drops of sherry spilled on the floor. She grabbed the cocktail napkin and bent to pat it dry.

As she began to straighten up, she noticed that something was actually caught in the fringe of the rug, something that glinted in the light from the lamp beside the sofa. That's what she must have stepped on. It was probably a button. She reached for it. The tips of her thumb and index finger slipped into hollow space and met. It wasn't a button, it was a ring. Darcy picked it up and stared unbelieving.

A gold *E* on an onyx background in an oval setting. *Erin's ring.*

Erin had been in this house. Erin had answered Michael Nash's personal ad.

Sheer horror washed over Darcy. Michael had lied when he claimed he'd only met Erin once for a drink at the Pierre.

The stereo suddenly started to blare. "Sorry," Michael said. His back was still to her.

"Change Partners and Dance." He was humming the opening bars with the orchestra as he lowered the volume and turned to her.

Help me, Darcy prayed. Help me. He must not see the ring. He was staring at her. She clasped her hands together, managed to slip the ring on her finger as Michael came to her, his arms outstretched.

"We've never danced together, Darcy. I'm good, and I know you are."

Erin's body had been found with a dancing slipper on her foot. Had she danced with him here in this room? Had she died in this room?

Darcy leaned back on the sofa. "I didn't think you cared about dancing, Michael. When I talked about the classes Nona and Erin and I took together, I didn't think you were very interested."

He dropped his arms, reached for his glass of sherry. He perched on the chair this time, so much on the edge that it seemed as though his legs, planted on the floor, were preventing him from falling.

Almost as though any moment he might spring at her.

"I love dancing," he said. "I didn't think it would be healthy for you to be thinking about the fun you had taking those classes with Erin."

Darcy tilted her head as though considering his answer. "You don't stop riding in cars because someone you cared about was in an automobile accident, do you?" She did not wait for a response, but tried to change the subject. She examined the stem of the glass. "Lovely glassware," she commented.

"I bought a set of these in Vienna," he said. "I swear they make the sherry taste even better."

She smiled with him. Now he sounded like the Michael she knew. The strange look in his eye vanished for an instant. *Keep him like that, her intuition warned. Talk to him. Make him talk to you.*

"Michael." She made her voice hesitant, confidential. "Can I ask you something?"

"Of course." He looked interested.

"The other day, I think you were suggesting that I've been making my parents pay for that remark that hurt me so much when I was a kid. Can I possibly be that selfish?"

During the twenty-minute helicopter ride, no one spoke. His mind racing, Vince had gone over every detail of the investigation. Michael Nash. I sat in his office, thinking he sounded like one of the few shrinks who makes sense. Was this a wild-goose chase? What was to say that someone with Nash's money hadn't some sort of retreat in Connecticut or upstate New York?

Maybe he did, but with all his property, the odds were that he would bring his victims here. Over the whir of the propeller Vince could hear in his head the names of serial killers who buried their victims in the attics or basements of their own homes.

The chopper circled over the country road. "There!" Vince pointed to the right where twin high beams were gleaming upward, making paths through the darkness. "The Bridgewater police said they'd park right outside Nash's place. Put it down."

The mansion was outwardly tranquil. There were lights shining from several windows on the main floor. Vince insisted that Nona stay outside with the pilot. Ernie and Chris at his heels, he ran from the side lawn up the long driveway and rang the bell. "Leave the talking to me."

A woman answered, using the intercom. "Who is it?"

Vince clenched his teeth. If Nash was in there, they were giving him plenty of warning. "FBI agent Vincent D'Ambrosio, ma'am. I must speak to Dr. Nash."

A moment later the door opened slightly. The security chain was still in place. "May I see your identification, sir?" The courteous tone of a trained servant, this time a man.

Vince passed it through.

"Hurry them," Chris urged.

The security chain was released, the door opened. Housekeeping couple, Vince thought. They had that look. He asked them to identify themselves.

"We're John and Irma Hughes. We work for Dr. Nash."

"Is he here?"

"Yes, he is," Mrs. Hughes answered. "He's been in all evening. He's completing his book and doesn't wish to be disturbed."

"Darcy, you really have great introspection," Michael said. "I told you that last week. You're feeling a little guilty about your attitude toward your parents, aren't you?"

"I think I am." Darcy could see that his pupils were closer to normal size. The blue-gray color was visible in his eyes.

The next song on the tape began to play. "Red Roses for a Blue Lady." Michael's right foot began to move in synch with the music.

"*Should* I feel guilty?" she asked quickly.

* * *

"Where is Dr. Nash's room?" Vince demanded. "I'll take responsibility for disturbing him."

"He always locks the door when he wants privacy, and won't answer. He's very firm about not being interrupted when he's in his room. We haven't even seen him since we got home from shopping late this afternoon, but his car is in the driveway."

Chris had had enough. "He's not upstairs. He's driving around in a station wagon doing God knows what." Chris started for the staircase. "Where the hell is his room?"

Mrs. Hughes looked pleadingly at her husband, then led them up the stairs. Her repeated knocking brought no response.

"Have you a key?" Vince demanded.

"Doctor has forbidden me to use it when he leaves his door locked."

"Get it."

As Vince had expected, the massive bedroom was empty. "Mrs. Hughes, we have a witness who saw Darcy Scott get into the doctor's station wagon tonight. We believe she is in imminent danger. Does Dr. Nash have a studio or a cottage on this property or some other place he might have taken her?"

"You must be mistaken," the woman protested. "He's brought Miss Scott here twice. They're great friends."

"Mrs. Hughes, you haven't answered my question."

"On this estate there are barns and a stable and some storage facilities. There's no other building where he'd bring a young lady. He also has an apartment and office in New York."

Her husband was nodding in agreement. Vince could see they were telling the truth.

"Sir," Mrs. Hughes said timidly, "we've worked for Dr. Nash for fourteen years. If Miss Scott is with him, I can assure you you have nothing to worry about. Dr. Nash wouldn't hurt a fly."

How long had they been talking? Darcy didn't know. The music was soft in the background. "Begin the Beguine" was playing. How often had she seen her mother and father dance to this music?

"Mother and Daddy were the ones who really taught me to dance," she told Nash. "Sometimes they'd just put on records and fox-trot or waltz. They're really good."

His eyes were still kind. They were the eyes she'd seen the other times she'd been with him. As long as he didn't suspect that she knew about him, maybe he would leave with her, take her to the house for dinner. I've got to make him want to keep talking to me.

Mother had always said, "Darcy, you have a real talent for acting. Why do you keep resisting it?"

If I have it, let me prove it now, she prayed.

All her life she'd heard her mother and father discussing how a scene should be played. She must have learned something.

I can't let him see how scared I am, Darcy thought. Channel my nervousness into the performance. How would her mother play this scene, a woman trapped in the home of a serial killer? Mother would stop thinking about Erin's ring on her finger and do exactly what Darcy was trying to pull off. She'd play it as though Michael Nash was a psychiatrist and she was a patient confiding in him.

What was Michael saying?

"Have you noticed, Darcy, that when you let yourself talk about your parents you become animated? I think you enjoyed your childhood much more than you realized."

People always clustered around them. Remember the time the crowd was so great that she lost her mother's hand?

"Tell me, Darcy, what are you thinking? Say it. Let it out."

"I was so frightened. I couldn't see them. I knew that moment that I hated . . ."

"What did you hate?"

"The crowds. Being torn from them . . ."

"It wasn't their fault."

"If they weren't so famous . . ."

"You've resented that fame . . ."

"No." It was working. His voice was his own. I don't want to talk about this, she thought, but I must. I've got to be honest with him. It's my only chance. Mother. Daddy. Help me. Be here for me. "They're so far away." She didn't know she'd said it aloud.

"Who are?"

"My mother and father."

"You mean now?"

"Yes. They're touring in Australia with their play."

"You sound so forlorn, frightened even. Are you frightened, Darcy?"

Don't let him think that. "No, I'm just sorry that I won't see them for six months."

"Do you think the time you were separated from them that day was the first time you felt abandoned?"

She wanted to shout, "I feel abandoned now." Instead, she turned her mind to the past. "Yes."

"You hesitated. Why?"

"There was another time, when I was six. I was in the hospital and they didn't think I was going to live . . ." She tried not to look at him. She was so afraid the eyes would become empty and dark again.

She was reminded of the character in "One Thousand and One Nights" who had told stories to stay alive.

Chris was engulfed with a sense of helplessness. Darcy had been in this house a few days ago with the man who had killed Nan and Erin Kelley and all those other girls, and she was going to be his next victim.

They were in the kitchen, where Vince had an open line on one phone to the Bureau, a second one to the state police. More copters were on the way.

Nona was standing near Vince, looking as though she was about to pass out. The Hugheses, their expressions bewildered and frightened, were sitting, shoulders touching, at the long refectory table. A local cop was talking to them, questioning them about Nash's activities. Ernie Cizek was in the chopper, which was flying low over the grounds. Chris could hear the sound of the engine through the closed window. They were looking for Michael Nash's black Mercedes station wagon. Local squad cars were fanning out across the property checking the outer buildings.

Grimly, Chris remembered how lucky he'd been when he bought a Mercedes station wagon last year. The salesman had talked him into having the Lojack system installed. "It's built right into the wiring," he'd explained. "If your car is ever stolen, it can be located within minutes. You phone in your Lojack code number to the police, it's fed into a computer, and a transmitter activates the system in your vehicle. Many police cars are equipped to follow the signal."

Chris had owned the station wagon only one week before it was stolen outside the gallery with a one hundred thousand dollar painting in the back. He'd dashed back inside his office for his briefcase, and when he came out the car was gone. He'd phoned to report the theft, and within fifteen minutes the station wagon had been traced and recovered.

If only Nash had picked up Darcy in a stolen car that could be traced.

"Oh my God!" Chris ran across the room and grabbed Mrs. Hughes's arm. "Does Nash keep his personal files here or in New York?"

She looked startled. "Here. In a room off the library."

"I want to see them."

Vince said, "Hold it," into the phone. "What have you got, Chris?"

Chris didn't answer. "How long has the doctor owned the station wagon?"

"About six months," John Hughes replied. "He trades in regularly."

"Then I'll bet he has it."

The files were contained in a row of handsome mahogany cabinets. Mrs. Hughes knew where the key was hidden.

The Mercedes file was easy to find. Chris grabbed it. His exultant cry brought the others running. From the folder he pulled the Lojack pamphlet. The code number for Nash's black Mercedes was listed.

The Bridgewater cop realized what Chris had found. "Give me that," he said. "I'll phone it in. Our squad cars have the system."

"You were in the hospital, Darcy." Michael's voice was calm.

Her mouth was so dry. She wanted a glass of water, but she didn't dare distract him. "Yes, I had spinal meningitis. I remember feeling so sick. I thought I was going to die. My parents were at the bedside. I heard the doctor say he didn't think I'd make it."

"How did your mother and father react?"

"They were hugging each other. My father said, 'Barbara, we have each other.' "

"And that hurt you, didn't it?"

"I knew they didn't need me," she whispered.

"Oh, Darcy, don't you know that when you think you're going to lose someone you love, the instinctive reaction is to look for someone or something to hang on to? They were trying to cope, or more accurately, preparing to cope. Believe it or not, that's healthy. And ever since then, you've been trying to shut them out, haven't you?"

Had she? Always resisting the clothes her mother bought for her, the gifts they showered on her, scorning their lifestyle, something they'd worked all their lives to achieve. Even her job. Was that one-upmanship to prove something? "No, it isn't."

"What isn't?"

"My job. I really do love what I do."

"Love what I do." Michael repeated the words slowly, in cadence. A new song had begun on the tape. "Save the Last Dance for Me." He stood up. "And I love to dance. *Now,* Darcy. But first I have a present for you."

Horrified, she watched as he got up and reached behind the chair. He turned to her, a shoe box in his hand. "I bought you pretty slippers to dance in, Darcy."

He knelt in front of the sofa and pulled off her boots. Every instinct warned Darcy not to protest. She dug her nails into her palms to keep from screaming. Erin's ring had turned and she could feel the impression of the raised *E* against her skin.

Michael was opening the shoe box and parting the tissue. He took one shoe out and held it up for her to admire. It was an open-toed, high-heeled satin slipper. Gossamer ankle straps were almost transparent bands of gold and silver. Michael took Darcy's right foot in his hand and eased it into the shoe, double-knotting the long straps. He reached into the box, removed the other slipper, and caressed her ankle as he guided her foot along the insole.

When she had both shoes on, he looked up and smiled. "Do you feel like Cinderella?" he asked.

She could not answer.

The radar indicates the wagon is parked about ten miles away in a northwest direction," the Bridgewater cop said tersely as the squad car raced down the country road. Vince, Chris, and Nona were with him. "The signal's getting stronger," he said a few minutes later. "We're getting closer."

"Until we're there, we're not close enough," Chris exploded. "Can't you go faster?"

They rounded a curve. The driver slammed on the brakes. The squad car skidded, then straightened. "Oh hell!"

"What's the matter?" Vince snapped.

"They're digging up the road down here. We can't get through. And the damn detour will waste time."

Music filled the room but could not drown out his maniacal laugh. Darcy's footsteps were flying in synch with his. "I don't often do a Viennese waltz," he shouted, "but tonight it was what I planned for you." Twirling, bobbing, turning. Darcy's hair flew around her face. She was gasping but he seemed not to notice.

The waltz ended. He did not remove his arms from around her. His eyes were glittering, dark, empty holes again.

"Can't Get Started with You." Easily, he slipped into a graceful fox trot. Effortlessly, she followed him. He was holding her tightly, crushing her. She couldn't breathe. Is this what he did to the others? Got them to trust him. Brought them to this desolate house. Where were their bodies? Buried around here somewhere?

What chance did she have to get away from him? He'd catch her before she could get to the door. When they came in, she'd noticed the panic button. Was it hooked up to a security system? Knowing that someone was on the way, he might not kill her.

Now there was a growing urgency about Michael. His arm was like steel as he glided and stepped in perfect time to the music. "Do you want to know my secret?' he whispered. "This isn't my house. It's Charley's house."

"Charley?"

Backstep. Glide. Turn.

"Yes, that's my real name. Edward and Janice Nash were my aunt and uncle. They adopted me when I was a year old and changed my name from Charley to Michael."

He was staring down at her. Darcy could not bear to look into those eyes.

Backstep. Sidestep. Glide.

"What happened to your real parents?"

"My father killed my mother. They electrocuted him. Whenever my uncle was mad at me, he said I was getting just like him. My aunt was nice to me when I was little, but then she stopped loving me. She said they'd been crazy to adopt me. She said bad blood shows."

A new song. Frank Sinatra crooning, "Hey there, Cutes, put on your dancing boots and come dance with me."

Step. Step. Glide.

"I'm glad you're telling me this, Michael. It helps to talk, doesn't it?"

"I want you to call me Charley."

"All right." She tried not to sound tentative. He mustn't see her fear.

"Don't you want to know what happened to my mother and father? I mean, the people who raised me?"

"Yes, I do." Darcy thought of how tired her legs were. She was not used to the spike heels. She felt as though the tight ankle straps were cutting off her circulation.

Sidestep. Turn.

Sinatra urged, "Romance with me on a crowded floor . . ."

"When I was twenty-one, they were in a boating accident. The boat blew up."

"I'm sorry."

"I'm not. I rigged the boat. I *am* just like my real father. You're getting tired, Darcy."

"No. No. I'm fine. I enjoy dancing with you." Stay calm . . . stay calm.

"You can rest soon. Were you surprised when you got Erin's shoes back?"

"Yes, very surprised."

"She was so pretty. She liked me. On our date I told her about my book and she talked about the program and about how you and she were answering personal ads. That was really funny. I'd already decided you'd be next after her."

Next after her.

"Why did you choose us?"

"And while the rhythm pings, what coo-coo things I'll be saying," Sinatra sang.

"You both answered the special ad. All the girls I brought here did. But Erin wrote to one of my other ads too, the one I showed the FBI agent."

"You're very clever, Charley."

"Do you like the spike heels I bought for Erin? They match her dress."

"I know they do."

"I was at the Playwrights' Benefit too. I recognized Erin from the picture she sent me and I looked up her name on the seating list to make sure I was right. She was sitting four tables away. It was fate that I already had a date to meet her the very next night."

Step. Step. Glide. Turn.

"How did you know Erin's shoe size? My size?"

'It was so easy. I bought Erin's shoes in different sizes. I wanted just that pair for her. Remember last week when you had a pebble in your boot and I helped you take it out? I saw your size then."

"And the others?"

"Girls like to be flattered. I'd say, 'You have such pretty feet. What size are you?' Sometimes I bought shoes specially. Other times I'd take them from the ones I already had."

"The real Charles North didn't place any personal ads, did he?"

"No. I met him at that benefit too. He kept talking about himself and I asked him for his business card. I never use my own name when I call people who answer the special ad. You made it easy. You called me."

Yes, she had called him.

"You say Erin liked you when you met her the first time. Weren't you afraid she'd recognize your voice when you called and said you were Charles North?"

"I phoned her from Penn Station, where there's a lot of noise. I told her I was running to catch a train to Philadelphia. I lowered my voice and spoke faster than usual. Just like this afternoon when I talked to your secretary." The timbre of his voice changed, became high-pitched. "Don't I sound like a woman now?"

"Suppose I hadn't been able to go to that bar tonight? What would you have done?"

"You told me you didn't have any plans for this evening. I knew you'd do anything to find the man Erin met the night she disappeared. And I was right."

"Yes, Charley, you were right."

He nuzzled her neck.

Step. Step. Glide.

"I'm so glad you both answered my special ad. You know what it is, don't you. It begins, *'Loves Music, Loves to Dance.'* "

"Because what is dancing but making love set to music playing?" Sinatra continued.

"That's one of my favorite songs," Michael whispered. He twirled her, never relaxing his grip on her hand. When he drew her back in, his tone became confidential, even regretful. "It was Nan's fault that I started killing girls."

"Nan Sheridan?" Chris Sheridan's face filled Darcy's mind. The sadness in his eyes when he talked about his sister. The authority and presence he had in the gallery. The way his staff obviously loved him. His mother. The easy relationship between them. She could hear him saying, "I hope you're not a vegetarian, Darcy. Gourmet delight time."

His concern that she was answering these ads. How right he'd been. I wish I'd had a chance to get to know you, Chris. I wish I'd had a chance to tell my mother and father I loved them.

"Yes, Nan Sheridan. After I graduated from Stanford, I spent a year in Boston before I started med school. I used to drive down to Brown a lot. That's where I met Nan. She was a wonderful dancer. You're good, but she was wonderful."

The familiar opening bars of "Good Night, Sweetheart."

No, Darcy thought. No.

Backstep. Sidestep. Glide.

"Michael, something else I meant to ask you about my mother," she began.

He pushed her head down on his shoulder. "I told you to call me Charley. Don't talk anymore," he said firmly. "We'll just dance."

"Time will heal your sorrow," floated through the room. Darcy didn't recognize the singer's voice.

"Good night, sweetheart, good night." The last notes faded into the air.

Michael dropped his arms and smiled at Darcy. "It's time," he said in a friendly voice, although his expression was blankly terrifying. "I'll give you to the count of ten to try to get away. Isn't that fair?"

They were back on the road. "The signal is coming from the left. Wait a minute, we're going too far," the Bridgewater cop said. "There must be a side road here somewhere." The wheels screeched as they made a U-turn.

The sense of impending disaster had grown in Chris to the explosive point. He opened the car window. "There, for God's sake, *there's* a driveway."

The squad car ground to a halt, backed up, turned sharply right, raced along the rutted ground.

Darcy slipped and slid on the polished floor. The high-heeled slippers were her enemies as she ran for the door. She took a precious instant to stop and try to yank the shoes off, but she couldn't. The double knots on the straps were too tight.

"One," Charley called from behind her.

She reached the door and tugged at the bolt. It did not release. She twisted the knob. It did not turn.

"Two. Three. Four. Five. Six. I'm counting, Darcy."

The panic button. She jammed her finger against it.

Hahahahahahaha. . . . A hollow, mocking laugh echoed through the room. Hahahaha. . . . The sound was coming from the panic button.

With a shriek, Darcy jumped back. Now Charley was laughing too.

"Seven. Eight. Nine . . ."

She turned, saw the stairway, began to run to it.

"Ten!"

Charley was rushing toward her, his hands outstretched, his fingers bent, his thumbs rigid.

"No! No!" Darcy tried to reach the staircase, skidded. Her ankle turned. Sharp, stabbing pain. Moaning, she hobbled onto the first step and felt herself pulled back.

She didn't know she was screaming.

"There's the Mercedes," Vince cried. The squad car slammed to a stop behind it.

He sprang out of the car, Chris and the cop with him. "Stay back," Vince shouted to Nona.

"Listen." Chris held up his hand. "Someone's screaming. It's Darcy." He and Vince threw themselves against the thick oak door. It didn't budge.

The cop pulled out his gun and pumped six bullets into the lock.

This time when Chris and Vince attacked the door, it opened.

Darcy tried to kick Charley with the sharp stiletto heels. He spun her around, seeming not to feel the heels stabbing at his legs. His hands were around her neck. She tried to claw them away. Erin, Erin, is this the way it was for you? She couldn't scream anymore. She opened her mouth, frantic to gulp in air, and could find none. Were those moans coming from her? She tried to keep fighting but couldn't raise her arms again.

Vaguely, she heard loud staccato sounds. Was someone trying to help her? It's . . . too . . . late . . . she thought as she felt herself fall into darkness.

Chris got through the doorway first. Darcy was dangling like a rag doll, her arms drooping at her sides, her legs buckled under her. Long, powerful fingers were squeezing her throat. Her screams had stopped.

With a cry of rage, Chris flew across the room and tackled Nash, who sagged and fell, pulling Darcy with him. His hands convulsed, then tightened their grip around her neck.

Vince threw himself next to Nash, snapped his arm around Nash's neck, forcing his head back. The Bridgewater cop grabbed Nash's thrashing feet.

Charley's hands seemed to have a life of their own. Chris could not pry his fingers loose from Darcy's throat. Nash seemed to be possessed of superhuman strength and impervious to pain. Desperately Chris sank his teeth into the right hand of the man who was snuffing out Darcy's life.

With a howl of pain Charley yanked back his right hand and relaxed the left one.

Vince and the cop twisted his arms behind him and snapped handcuffs on his wrists as Chris grabbed Darcy.

Nona had been watching from the doorway. Now she rushed into the house and dropped to her knees at Darcy's feet. Darcy's eyes were not focusing. There were ugly red bruises on her slender throat.

Chris covered Darcy's mouth with his own, pinched her nostrils closed, forced breath down into her lungs.

Vince looked at Darcy's staring eyes and began to pound her chest.

The Bridgewater cop was guarding Michael Nash, who was handcuffed to the banister. Nash began to recite in a singsong voice, "Eeney, meeney, miney, mo, Catch a dancer by the toe . . ."

She's not responding, Nona thought frantically. She grasped Darcy's ankles and for the first time realized Darcy was wearing dancing slippers. I can't stand it, Nona thought, I can't stand it. Almost unaware of what she was doing, Nona began to struggle with the knots on the ankle straps.

"One little piggy went to market. One little piggy stayed home. Sing it again, Mama. I have ten piggy toes."

We may be too late, Vince thought furiously as he searched for some response from Darcy, but if we are, you lousy bastard, you'd better not think that spouting nursery rhymes now will help you prove insanity.

Chris raised his head as he gulped in air and for a split second stared at Darcy's face. The same look as Nan when he found her that morning. The bruised throat. The blue-white tone to her skin. *No! I won't let it happen. Darcy, breathe.*

Nona, weeping now, had finally untied one of the ankle straps. She pushed it back and began to pull the high-heeled slipper from Darcy's foot.

She felt something. Was she wrong? No.

"Her foot is moving!" she cried. "She's trying to get it out of the shoe."

At the same instant, Vince saw a pulse begin to beat in Darcy's throat and Chris heard a long, drawn-out sigh come from her lips.

23
THURSDAY
March 14

The next morning, Vince phoned Susan. "Mrs. Fox, your husband may be a philanderer but he's not a criminal. We have the serial killer in custody and we have absolute proof that he is solely responsible for the dancing-shoe deaths starting with Nan Sheridan."

"Thank you. I guess you can understand what this means to me."

"Who was that?" Doug had stayed home from work. He felt lousy. Not sick, just lousy.

Susan told him.

He stared at her. "You mean you told the FBI you thought I was a murderer! You actually thought I killed Nan Sheridan and all those other women!" His face darkened in incredulous rage.

Susan stared back at him. "I thought that was a possibility, and that by lying for you fifteen years ago I might also be responsible for those other deaths."

"I swore to you that I never went near Nan the morning she died."

"Obviously you didn't. Then where were you, Doug? At least level with me now."

The anger faded from his face. He looked away, then turned back with a cajoling smile. "Susan, I told you then. I repeat it. The car broke down that morning."

"I want the truth. You owe it to me."

Doug hesitated, then said slowly, "I was with Penny Knowles. Susan, I'm sorry. I didn't want you to know because I was afraid of losing you."

"You mean Penny Knowles was about to get engaged to Bob Carver and didn't want to take a chance on losing out on the Carver money. She'd have let you be accused of murder before she'd speak up for you."

"Susan, I know I played around a lot then . . ."

"Then?" Susan's laugh was harsh. "You played around *then?* Listen to me, Doug. All these years my father has never gotten over the fact that I perjured myself for you. Go pack your clothes. Move into your bachelor apartment. I'm filing for divorce."

All day he begged for another chance. "Susan, I promise."

"Get out."

He would not leave before Donny and Beth came home from school. "I'll see a lot of you kids, I promise." When he walked down the driveway, Trish ran after him and grabbed his knees. He carried her back and handed her to Susan. "Susan, please."

"Good-bye, Doug."

They watched him drive away. Donny was crying. "Mom, last weekend. I mean, if he was like that all the time . . ."

Susan tried to blink back her own tears. "Never say never, Donny. Your father has a lot of growing up to do. Let's see if he can handle it."

"Are you going to watch your program?" Vince asked Nona when he phoned Thursday afternoon.

"Absolutely not. We prepared a special wrap. I wrote it. I lived it."

"What do you feel like eating tonight?"

"A steak."

"Me too. What are you doing over the weekend?"

"It's supposed to be mild. I thought I'd drive out to the Hamptons. After the last few weeks, I must go down to the sea again."

"You have a house there."

"Yes. I think I'm changing my mind about buying Matt out. I love my place and he really is very forgettable. Want to come along for the ride?"

"I'd love to."

Chris brought an antique cane for Darcy to use while her sprained ankle mended.

"It's very grand," she told him.

He wrapped his arms around her. "Are you all set? Where are your things?"

"Just that bag." Greta had phoned insisting that Chris bring Darcy to Darien for a long weekend.

The phone rang. "I'll skip it," Darcy said. "No, wait. I tried to reach my folks in Australia. Maybe the operator finally caught up with them."

It was both her mother and father on the line. "I'm absolutely fine. I just wanted to say . . ." She hesitated, ". . . that I really miss you guys. I . . . I love you. . . ." Darcy laughed. "What do you mean, I must have met somebody?"

She winked at Chris. "As a matter of fact, I have met a nice young man. His name is Chris Sheridan. You'll approve. He's in my business, only upscale. He has an antiques gallery. He's good-looking, nice, and has a way of showing up when you need him. . . . How did I meet him?"

Only Erin, she thought, could really appreciate the irony of her answer. "Believe it or not, I met him through the personal ads."

She looked up at Chris and their eyes met. He smiled. I'm wrong, she thought. Chris understands too.

ALL AROUND THE TOWN

My sincere thanks and profound gratitude to Walter C. Young, M.D., Medical Director of the National Center for the treatment of Dissociative Disorders in Aurora, Colorado; Trish Keller Knode, A.T.R., L.P.C., art therapist; and Kay Adams, M.A., journal therapist, for the Center. Their guidance, assistance and encouragement have been infinitely invaluable in allowing me to tell this story.

Kudos and heartfelt thanks to my editor Michael V. Korda; his associate, senior editor Chuck Adams; my agent, Eugene H. Winick; Ina Winick, M.S.; and my publicist, Lisl Cade. And of course my terrific family and friends.

Bless you, my dears, one and all.

For my newest grandson,
Justin Louis Clark,
with love and joy.

Part One

~ 1

June 1974
Ridgewood, New Jersey

Ten minutes before it happened, four-year-old Laurie Kenyon was sitting cross-legged on the floor of the den rearranging the furniture in her dollhouse. She was tired of playing alone and wanted to go in the pool. From the dining room she could hear the voices of Mommy and the ladies who used to go to school with her in New York. They were talking and laughing while they ate lunch.

Mommy had told her that because Sarah, her big sister, was at a birthday party for other twelve-year-olds, Beth, who sometimes minded her at night, would come over to swim with Laurie. But the minute Beth arrived she started making phone calls.

Laurie pushed back the long blond hair that felt warm on her face. She had gone upstairs a long time ago and changed into her new pink bathing suit. Maybe if she reminded Beth again . . .

Beth was curled up on the couch, the phone stuck between her shoulder and ear. Laurie tugged on her arm. "I'm all ready."

Beth looked mad. "In a minute, honey," she said. "I'm having a very important discussion." Laurie heard her sigh into the phone. "I *hate* baby-sitting."

Laurie went to the window. A long car was slowly passing the house. Behind it was an open car filled with flowers, then a lot more cars with their lights on. Whenever she saw cars like that Laurie always used to say that a parade was coming, but Mommy said no, that they were funerals on the way to the cemetery. Even so, they made Laurie *think* of a parade, and she loved to run down the driveway and wave to the people in the cars. Sometimes they waved back.

Beth clicked down the receiver. Laurie was just about to ask her if they could go out and watch the rest of the cars go by when Beth picked up the phone again.

Beth was *mean,* Laurie told herself. She tiptoed out to the foyer and peeked into the dining room. Mommy and her friends were still talking and laughing. Mommy was saying, "Can you *believe* we graduated from the Villa thirty-two years ago?"

The lady next to her said, "Well, Marie, at least *you* can lie about it. You've got a four-year-old daughter. I've got a four-year-old *granddaughter!*"

"We still look pretty darn good," somebody else said, and they all laughed again.

They didn't even bother to look at Laurie. They were mean too. The pretty music box Mommy's friend had brought her was on the table. Laurie picked it up. It was only a few steps to the screen door. She opened it noiselessly, hurried across the porch and ran down the driveway to the road. There were still cars passing the house. She waved.

She watched until they were out of sight, then sighed, hoping that the company would go home soon. She wound up the music box and heard the tinkling sound of a piano and voices singing, " 'Eastside, westside . . .' "

"Little girl."

Laurie hadn't noticed the car pull over and stop. A woman was driving. The man sitting next to her got out, picked Laurie up, and before she knew what was happening she was squeezed between them in the front seat. Laurie was too surprised to say anything. The man was smiling at her, but it wasn't a nice smile. The woman's hair was hanging around her face, and she didn't wear lipstick. The man had a beard, and his arms had a lot of curly hair. Laurie was pressed against him so hard she could feel it.

The car began to move. Laurie clutched the music box. Now the voices were singing: " 'All around the town . . . Boys and girls together . . .' "

"Where are we going?" she asked. She remembered that she wasn't supposed to go out to the road alone. Mommy would be mad at her. She could feel tears in her eyes.

The woman looked so angry. The man said, "All around the town, little girl. All around the town."

2

Sarah hurried along the side of the road, carefully carrying a piece of birthday cake on a paper plate. Laurie loved chocolate filling, and Sarah wanted to make it up to her for not playing with her while Mommy had company.

She was a bony long-legged twelve-year-old, with wide gray eyes, carrot red hair that frizzed in dampness, milk-white skin and a splash of freckles across her nose. She looked like neither of her parents—her mother was petite, blond and blue eyed; her father's gray hair had originally been dark brown.

It worried Sarah that John and Marie Kenyon were so much older than the other kids' parents. She was always afraid they might die before she grew up. Her mother had once explained to her, "We'd been married fifteen years and I'd given up hope of ever having a baby, but when I was thirty-seven I knew you were on the way. Like a gift. Then eight years later when Laurie was born—oh, Sarah, it was a miracle!

When she was in the second grade, Sarah remembered asking Sister Catherine which was better, a gift or a miracle?

"A miracle is the greatest gift a human being can receive," Sister Catherine had said. That afternoon, when Sarah suddenly began to cry in class, she fibbed and said it was because her stomach was sick.

Even though she knew Laurie was the favorite, Sarah still loved her parents fiercely. When she was ten she had made a bargain with God. If He wouldn't let Daddy or Mommy die before she was grown, she would clean up the kitchen every night, help to take care of Laurie and never chew gum again. She was keeping her side of the bargain, and so far God was listening to her.

An unconscious smile touching her lips, she turned the corner of Twin Oaks Road and stared. Two police cars were in her driveway, their lights flashing. A lot of neighbors were clustered outside, even the brand-new people from two houses down, whom they hadn't even really met. They all looked scared and sad, holding their kids tightly by the hand.

Sarah began to run. Maybe Mommy or Daddy was sick. Richie Johnson was standing on the lawn. He was in her class at Mount Carmel. Sarah asked Richie why everyone was there.

He looked sorry for her. Laurie was missing, he told her. Old Mrs. Whelan had seen a man take her into a car, but hadn't realized Laurie was being kidnapped . . .

3

1974–1976
Bethlehem, Pennsylvania

They wouldn't take her home.

They drove a long time and took her to a dirty house, way out in the woods somewhere. They slapped her if she cried. The man kept picking her up and hugging her. Then he would carry her upstairs. She tried to make him stop, but he laughed at her. They called her Lee. Their names were Bic and Opal. After a while she found ways to slip away from them, in her mind. Sometimes she just floated on the ceiling and watched what was happening to the little girl with the long blond hair. Sometimes she felt sorry for the little girl. Other times she made fun of her. Sometimes when they let her sleep alone she dreamt of other people, Mommy and Daddy and Sarah. But then she'd start to cry again and they'd hit her, so she made herself forget Mommy and Daddy and Sarah. *That's good,* a voice in her head told her. *Forget all about them.*

4

At first the police were at the house every day, and Laurie's picture was on the front page of the New Jersey and New York papers. Beyond tears, Sarah watched her mother and father on "Good Morning, America," pleading with whoever took Laurie to bring her back.

Dozens of people phoned saying they'd seen Laurie, but none of the leads was useful. The police had hoped there'd be a demand for ransom, but there was none.

The summer dragged on. Sarah watched as her mother's face became haunted and bleak, as her father reached constantly for the nitroglycerin pills in his pocket. Every morning they went to the 7 A.M. mass and prayed for Laurie to be sent home. Frequently at night Sarah awoke to hear her mother's sobbing, her father's exhausted attempts to comfort her. "It was a miracle that Laurie was born. We'll count on another miracle to bring her back to us," she heard him say.

School started again. Sarah had always been a good student. Now she pored over the books, finding that she could blot out her own relentless sorrow by escaping into study. A natural athlete, she began taking golf and tennis lessons. Still she missed her little sister, with aching pain. She wondered if God was punishing her for the times she'd resented all the attention paid to Laurie. She hated herself for going to the birthday party that day and pushed aside the thought that Laurie was strictly forbidden to go out front alone. She promised that if God would send Laurie back to them she would always, *always* take care of her.

~ 5

The summer passed. The wind began to blow through the cracks in the walls. Laurie was always cold. One day Opal came back with long-sleeved shirts and overalls and a winter jacket. It wasn't pretty like the one Laurie used to wear. When it got warm again they gave her some other clothes, shorts and shirts and sandals. Another winter went by. Laurie watched the leaves on the big old tree in front of the house begin to bud and open, and then all the branches were filled with them.

Bic had an old typewriter in the bedroom. It made a loud clatter that Laurie could hear when she was cleaning up the kitchen or watching television. The clatter was a good sound. It meant that Bic wouldn't bother with her.

After a while, he'd come out of the bedroom holding a bunch of papers in his hand and start reading them aloud to Laurie and Opal. He always shouted and he always ended with the same words, "Hallelujah. Amen!" After he was finished, he and Opal would sing together. Practicing, they called it. Songs about God and going home.

Home. It was a word that her voices told Laurie not to think about anymore.

Laurie never saw anyone else. Only Bic and Opal. And when they went out, they locked her in the basement. It happened a lot. It was scary down there. The window was almost at the ceiling and had boards over it. The basement was filled with shadows, and sometimes they seemed to move around. Each time, Laurie tried to go to sleep right away on the mattress they left on the floor.

Bic and Opal almost never had company. If someone did come to the house, Laurie was put down in the basement with her leg chained to the pipe, so she couldn't go up the stairs and knock on the door. "And don't you dare call us," Bic warned her. "You'd get in big trouble, and, anyhow, we couldn't hear you."

After they'd been out they usually brought money home. Sometimes not much. Sometimes a lot. Quarters and dollar bills, mostly.

They let her go out in the backyard with them. They showed her how to weed the vegetable garden and gather the eggs from the chicken coop. There was a newborn baby chick they told her she could keep as her pet. She played with it whenever she went outside. Sometimes when they locked her in the basement and went away they let her keep it with her.

Until the bad day when Bic killed it.

Early one morning they began to pack—just their clothes and the television set and Bic's typewriter. Bic and Opal were laughing and singing, "Ha-lay-loo-ya."

"A fifteen-thousand-watt station in Ohio!" Bic shouted, "Bible Belt, here we come!"

They drove for two hours. Then from the backseat where she was scrunched against the battered old suitcases, Laurie heard Opal say, "Let's go into a diner and get a decent meal. Nobody will pay any attention to her. Why should they?"

Bic said, "You're right." Then he looked quickly over his shoulder at Laurie. "Opal will order a sandwich and milk for you. Don't you talk to anybody, you hear?"

They went to a place with a long counter and tables and chairs. Laurie was so hungry that she could almost taste the bacon she could smell frying. But there was something else. She could remember being in a place like this with the other people. A sob that she couldn't force back rose in her throat. Bic gave her a push to follow Opal, and she began to cry. Cry so hard she couldn't get her breath. She could see the lady at the cash register staring at her. Bic grabbed her and hustled her out to the parking lot, Opal beside him.

Bic threw her in the backseat of the car, and he and Opal rushed to get in front. As Opal slammed her foot on the gas pedal, he reached for her. She tried to duck when the hairy hand swung forward and back across her face. But after the first blow she didn't feel any pain. She just felt sorry for the little girl who was crying so hard.

~ 6

June 1976
Ridgewood, New Jersey

Sarah sat with her mother and father watching the program about missing children. The last segment was about Laurie. Pictures of her taken just before she disappeared. A computerized image that showed how she would probably look today, two years after she'd been kidnapped.

When the program ended, Marie Kenyon ran from the room screaming, "I want my baby. I want my baby."

Tears running down her face, Sarah listened to her father's agonized attempt to comfort her mother. "Maybe this program will be the instrument of a miracle," he said. He did not sound as if he believed it.

It was Sarah who answered the phone an hour later. Bill Conners, the police chief of Ridgewood, had always treated Sarah as an adult. "Your folks pretty upset after the program, honey?" he asked.

"Yes."

"I don't know whether to get their hopes up, but a call has come in that may be promising. A cashier in a diner in Harrisburg, Pennsylvania, is positive she saw Laurie this afternoon."

"This afternoon!" Sarah felt her breath stop.

"She'd been worried because the little girl suddenly became hysterical. But it was no tantrum. She was practically choking herself trying to stop crying. The Harrisburg police have Laurie's updated picture."

"Who was with her?"

"A man and woman. Hippie types. Unfortunately the description is pretty vague. The cashier's attention was on the kid, so she hardly got a glimpse of the couple."

He left it to Sarah to decide whether it was wise to tell her parents, to raise her parents' hopes. She made another bargain with God. "Let this be their miracle. Let the Harrisburg police find Laurie. I'll take care of her forever."

She hurried upstairs to offer her mother and father the new reason to hope.

7

The car started to have trouble a little while after they left the diner. Every time they slowed down in traffic the engine sputtered and died. The third time it happened and cars had to pull out from behind them, Opal said, "Bic, when we break down for good and a cop comes along, you'd better be careful. He might start asking questions about her." She jerked her head toward Laurie.

Bic told her to look for a gas station and pull off the road. When they found one, he made Laurie lie down on the floor and piled garbage bags filled with old clothes over her before they drove in.

The car needed a lot of work; it wouldn't be ready till the next day. There was a motel next to the gas station. The attendant said it was cheap and pretty comfortable.

They drove over to the motel. Bic went inside the office and came back with the key. They drove around to the room and rushed Laurie inside. Then, after Bic drove the car back to the gas station, they watched television for the rest of the afternoon. Bic brought in hamburgers for dinner. Laurie fell asleep just when the program came on about missing children. She woke up to hear Bic cursing. *Keep your eyes shut,* a voice warned her. *He's going to take it out on you.*

"The cashier got a good look at her," Opal was saying. "Suppose she's watching this. We'll have to get rid of her."

The next afternoon, Bic went to get the car by himself. When he came back he sat Laurie on the bed and held her arms against her. "What's my name?" he asked her.

"Bic."

He jerked his head at Opal. "What's her name?"

"Opal."

"I want you to forget that. I want you to forget us. Don't you ever talk about us. Do you understand, Lee?"

Laurie did not understand. *Say* yes, a voice whispered impatiently. *Nod your head and say yes.*

"Yes," she said softly and felt her head nodding.

"Remember the time I cut the head off the chicken?" Bic asked.

She shut her eyes. The chicken had flopped around the yard, blood spilling out from its neck. Then it had fallen on her feet. She had tried to scream as the blood sprayed over her, but no sound came out. She never went near the chickens after that. Sometimes she dreamed that the headless chicken was running after her.

"Remember?" Bic asked, tightening his grip on her arms.

"Yes."

"We have to go away. We're going to leave you where people will find you. If you ever tell anyone my name or Opal's name or the name we called you or where we lived or anything that we did together, I'm going to come with the chicken knife and cut your head off. Do you understand that?"

The knife. Long and sharp and streaked with blood from the chicken.

"Promise you won't tell anybody," Bic demanded.

"Promise, promise," she mumbled desperately.

They got in the car. Once more they made her lie on the floor. It was so hot. The garbage bags stuck to her skin.

When it was dark they stopped in front of a big building. Bic took her out of the car. "This is a school," he told her. "Tomorrow morning a lot of people will come, and other kids you can play with. Stay here and wait for them."

She shrank from his moist kiss, his fierce hug. "I'm crazy about you," he said, "but remember, if you say one word about us . . ." He lifted his arm, closed his fist as though he was holding a knife and made a slashing motion on her neck.

"I promise," she sobbed, "I promise."

Opal handed her a bag with cookies and a Coke. She watched them drive off. She knew that if she didn't stay right here they'd come back to hurt her. It was so dark. She could hear animals scurrying in the woods nearby.

Laurie shrank against the door of the building and wrapped her arms around her body. She'd been hot all day and now she was cold and she was so scared. Maybe the headless chicken was running around out there. She began to tremble.

Look at the 'fraidy cat. She slipped away to be part of the jeering voice that was laughing at the small figure huddled at the entrance to the school.

8

Police Chief Connors phoned again in the morning. The lead looked promising, he said. A child who answered Laurie's description had been found when the caretaker arrived to open a school in a rural area near Pittsburgh. They were rushing Laurie's fingerprints there.

An hour later he phoned back. The prints were a perfect match. Laurie was coming home.

9

John and Marie Kenyon flew to Pittsburgh. Laurie had been taken to a hospital to be checked out. The next day on the noon edition of the TV news, Sarah watched as her mother and father left the hospital, Laurie between them. Sarah crouched in front of the set and gripped it with her hands. Laurie was taller. The waterfall of blond hair was shaggy. She was very thin. But it was more than that. Laurie had always been so friendly. Now even though she kept her head down, her eyes darted around as if she were looking for something she was afraid to find.

The reporters were bombarding them with questions. John Kenyon's voice was strained and tired as he said, "The doctors tell us Laurie is in good health, even though she is a touch underweight. Of course she's confused and frightened."

"Has she talked about the kidnappers?"

"She hasn't talked about anything. Please, we're so grateful for your interest and concern, but it would be a great kindness to allow our family to reunite quietly." Her father's voice was almost pleading.

"Is there any sign that she was molested?"

Sarah saw the shock on her mother's face. "Absolutely not!" she said. Her tone was appalled. "We believe that people who wanted a child took Laurie. We only hope they don't put another family through this nightmare."

Sarah needed to release the frantic energy that was churning inside her. She made Laurie's bed with the Cinderella sheets that Lauric loved. She arranged Laurie's favorite toys around her room, the twin dolls in their strollers, the dollhouse, the bear, her Peter Rabbit books. She folded Laurie's security blanket on the pillow.

Sarah bicycled to the store to buy cheese and pasta and chopped meat. Laurie loved lasagna. While Sarah was making it, she was constantly interrupted by phone calls. She managed to convince everyone to put off visiting for at least a few days.

They were due home at six o'clock. By five-thirty the lasagna was in the oven, the salad in the refrigerator, the table set for four again. Sarah went upstairs to change. She studied herself in the mirror. Would Laurie remember her? In the past two years she'd grown from five-four to five-seven. Her hair was short. It used to be shoulder-length. She used to be straight up and down. Now that she was fourteen her breasts had begun to fill out. She wore contact lenses instead of glasses.

That last night, before Laurie had been kidnapped, Sarah remembered that she had worn jeans and a long T-shirt to dinner. She still had the T-shirt in her closet. She put it on with jeans.

Crews with television cameras were in the driveway when the car pulled up. Groups of neighbors and friends waited in the background. Everyone began to cheer when the car door opened and John and Marie Kenyon led Laurie out.

Sarah ran to her little sister and dropped on her knees. "Laurie," she said softly. She stretched out her hands and watched as Laurie's hands fled to cover her face. She's afraid I'll hit her, Sarah thought.

It was she who picked Laurie up and took her inside the house as her parents once again spoke to the media.

Laurie did not show any sign that she remembered the house. She did not speak to them. At dinner she ate silently, her eyes looking down at the plate. When she had finished she got up, brought her plate to the sink and began to clear the table.

Marie stood up. "Darling, you don't have to—"

"Leave her alone, Mom," Sarah whispered. She helped Laurie clear, talking to her about what a big girl she was and how Laurie always used to help her with the dishes. Remember?

Afterwards they went into the den and Sarah turned on the television. Laurie pulled away trembling when Marie and John asked her to sit between them. "She's frightened," Sarah warned. "Pretend she isn't here."

Her mother's eyes filled with tears, but she managed to look absorbed in the program. Laurie sat cross-legged on the floor, choosing a spot where she could see but not be seen.

At nine o'clock when Marie suggested a nice warm bath and going to bed, Laurie panicked. She pressed her knees against her chest and buried her face in her hands. Sarah and her father exchanged glances.

"Poor little tyke," he said. "You don't have to go to bed now." Sarah saw in his eyes the same denial she had seen in her mother's. "It's just everything is so strange for you, isn't it?"

Marie was trying to hide the fact that she was weeping. "She's afraid of us," she murmured.

No, Sarah thought. She's afraid to go to bed. Why?

They left the television on. At quarter of ten, Laurie stretched out on the floor and fell asleep. It was Sarah who carried her up, changed her, tucked her into bed, slipped the security blanket between her arms and under her chin.

John and Marie tiptoed in and sat on either side of the small white bed, absorbing the miracle that had been granted them. They did not notice when Sarah slipped from the room.

Laurie slept long and late. In the morning Sarah looked in on her, drinking in the blessed sight of the long hair spilling on the pillow, the small figure nestling the security blanket against her face. She repeated the promise she had made to God. "I will always take care of her."

Her mother and father were already up. Both looked exhausted but radiant with joy. "We kept going in to see if she was really there," Marie said. "Sarah, we were just saying we couldn't have made it through these two years without you."

Sarah helped her mother prepare Laurie's favorite breakfast, pancakes and bacon. Laurie pattered into the room a few minutes later, the nightgown that used to be ankle length now stopping at her calves, her security blanket trailing behind her.

She climbed on Marie's lap. "Mommy," she said, her tone injured. "Yesterday I wanted to go in the pool and Beth kept talking on the phone."

Part Two

~ 10

September 12 1991
Ridgewood, New Jersey

During the mass, Sarah kept glancing sideways at Laurie. The sight of the two caskets at the steps of the sanctuary had clearly mesmerized her. She was staring at them, tearless now, seemingly unaware of the music, the prayers, the eulogy. Sarah had to put a hand under Laurie's elbow to remind her to stand or kneel.

At the end of the mass, as Monsignor Fisher blessed the coffins, Laurie whispered, "Mommy, Daddy, I'm sorry. I won't go out front alone again."

"Laurie," Sarah whispered.

Laurie looked at her with unseeing eyes, then turned and with a puzzled expression studied the crowded church. "So many people." Her voice sounded timid and young.

The closing hymn was "Amazing Grace."

With the rest of the congregation, a couple near the back of the church began to sing, softly at first, but he was used to leading the music. As always he got carried away, his pure baritone becoming louder, soaring above the others, swelling over the thinner voice of the soloist. People turned distracted, admiring.

" 'I once was lost but now am found . . .' " Through the pain and grief, Laurie felt icy terror. The voice. Ringing through her head, through her being.

I am lost, she wailed silently. *I am lost.*

They were moving the caskets.

The wheels of the bier holding her mother's casket squealed.

She heard the measured steps of the pallbearers.

Then the clattering of the typewriter.

" '. . . was blind but now I see.' "

"No! No!" Laurie shrieked as she crumpled into merciful darkness.

* * *

Several dozen of Laurie's classmates from Clinton College had attended the mass, along with a sprinkling of faculty. Allan Grant, Professor of English, was there and with shocked eyes watched Laurie collapse.

Grant was one of the most popular teachers at Clinton. Just turned forty, he had thick, somewhat unruly brown hair, liberally streaked with gray. Large dark brown eyes that expressed humor and intelligence were the best feature in his somewhat long face. His lanky body and casual dress completed an appearance that many young women undergraduates found irresistible.

Grant was genuinely interested in his students. Laurie had been in one of his classes every year since she entered Clinton. He knew her personal history and had been curious to see if there might be any observable aftereffects of her abduction. The only time he'd picked up anything had been in his creative writing class. Laurie was incapable of writing a personal memoir. On the other hand, her critiques of books, authors and plays were insightful and thought-provoking.

Three days ago she had been in his class when the word came for her to go to the office immediately. The class was ending and, sensing trouble, he had accompanied her. As they hurried across the campus, she'd told him that her mother and father were driving down to switch cars with her. She'd forgotten to have her convertible inspected and had returned to college in her mother's sedan. "They're probably just running late," she'd said, obviously trying to reassure herself. "My mother says I'm too much of a worrier about them. But she hasn't been that well and Dad is almost seventy-two."

Somberly the dean told them that there had been a multivehicle accident on Route 78.

Allan Grant drove Laurie to the hospital. Her sister, Sarah, was already there, her cloud of dark red hair framing a face dominated by large gray eyes that were filled with grief. Grant had met Sarah at a number of college functions and been impressed with the young assistant prosecutor's protective attitude toward Laurie.

One look at her sister's face was enough to make Laurie realize that her parents were dead. Over and over she kept moaning "my fault, my fault," seeming not to hear Sarah's tearful insistence that she must not blame herself.

Distressed, Grant watched as an usher carried Laurie from the nave of the church, Sarah beside him. The organist began to play the recessional hymn. The pallbearers, led by the monsignor, started to walk slowly down the aisle. In the row in front of him, Grant saw a man making his way to the end of the pew. "Please excuse me. I'm a doctor," he was saying, his voice low but authoritative.

Some instinct made Allan Grant slip into the aisle and follow him to the small room off the vestibule where Laurie had been taken. She was lying on two chairs that had been pushed together. Sarah, her face chalk white, was bending over her.

"Let me . . ." The doctor touched Sarah's arm.

Laurie stirred and moaned.

The doctor raised her eyelids, felt her pulse. "She's coming around but she must be taken home. She's in no condition to go to the cemetery."

"I know."

Allan saw how desperately Sarah was trying to keep her own composure. "Sarah," he said. She turned, seemingly aware of him for the first time. "Sarah, let me go back to the house with Laurie. She'll be okay with me."

"Oh, would you?" For an instant gratitude replaced the strain and grief in her expression. "Some of the neighbors are there preparing food, but Laurie trusts you so much. I'd be so relieved."

" 'I once was lost but now am found . . .' "

A hand was coming at her holding the knife, the knife dripping with blood, slashing through the air. Her shirt and overalls were soaked with blood. She could feel the sticky warmth on her face. Something was flopping at her feet. The knife was coming . . .

Laurie opened her eyes. She was in bed in her own room. It was dark. What happened?

She remembered. The church. The caskets. The singing.

"Sarah!" she shrieked, "Sarah! Where are you?"

11

They were staying at the Wyndham Hotel on West Fifty-eighth Street in Manhattan. "Classy," he'd told her. "A lot of show business people go there. Right kind of place to start making connections."

He was silent on the drive from the funeral mass into New York. They were having lunch with the Reverend Rutland Garrison, pastor of the Church of the Airways, and the television program's executive producer. Garrison was ready to retire and in the process of choosing a successor. Every week a guest preacher was invited to co-host the program.

She watched as he discarded three different outfits before settling on a midnight blue suit, white shirt and bluish gray tie. "They want a preacher. They're gonna get a preacher. How do I look?"

"Perfect," she assured him. He did too. His hair was now silver even though he was only forty-five. He watched his weight carefully and had taught himself to stand very straight so that he always seemed to stand above people, even taller men. He'd practiced widening his eyes when he thundered a sermon until that had become his usual expression.

He vetoed her first choice of a red-and-white checked dress. "Not classy enough for this meeting. It's a little too Betty Crocker."

That was their private joke when they wanted to impress the congregations who came to hear him preach. But there was nothing joking about him now. She held up a black linen sheath with a matching jacket. "How's this?"

He nodded silently. "That will do." He frowned. "And remember . . ."

"I never call you Bic in front of anyone," she protested coaxingly. "Haven't for years." He had a feverish glitter in his eyes. Opal knew and feared that look. It had been three years since the last time he was brought in by local police for questioning because some little girl with blond hair had complained to her mother about him. He'd always managed to scorn the complainant into stammering apologies, but even so it had happened too often in too many different towns. When he got that look it meant he was losing control again.

Lee was the only child he'd ever kept. From the minute he spotted her with her mother in the shopping center, he'd been obsessed by her. He followed their car that first day and after that cruised past their house hoping to get a glimpse of the child. He and Opal had been doing a two-week stint, playing the guitar and singing at some crummy nightclub on Route 17 in New Jersey and staying in a motel twenty minutes from the Kenyon home. It was going to be their last time singing in a nightclub. Bic had started gospel singing at revivals and then preaching in upstate New York. The owner of a radio station in Bethlehem, Pennsylvania, heard him and asked him to start a religious program on his small station.

It had been bad luck that he'd insisted on driving past the house one last time on their way back to Pennsylvania. Lee was outside alone. He'd scooped her up, brought her with them, and for two years Opal lived in a state of perpetual fear and jealousy that she didn't dare let him see.

It had been fifteen years since they dumped her in the school yard, but Bic had never gotten over her. He kept her picture hidden in his wallet, and sometimes Opal would find him staring at it, running his fingers over it. In these last years, as he became more and more successful, he worried that someday FBI agents would come up to him and tell him he was under arrest for kidnapping and child molestation. "Look at that girl in California who got her daddy put in prison because she started going to a psychiatrist and remembering things best forgotten," he would sometimes say.

They had just arrived in New York when Bic read the item in the *Times* about the Kenyons' fatal accident. Over Opal's beseeching protests, they'd gone to the funeral mass. "Opal," he had told her, "we look as different as day and night from those two guitar-playing hippies Lee remembers."

It was true that they looked totally different. They'd begun to change their appearance the morning after they got rid of Lee. Bic shaved his beard off and got a short haircut. She'd dyed her hair ash blond and fastened it in a neat bun. They'd both bought sensible clothes at JC Penney, the kind of stuff that made them blend in with everyone else, gave them the middle-American look. "Just in case anyone in that diner got a good look at us," he'd said. That was when he'd warned her never to refer to him as Bic in front of anyone and said that from now on, in public he'd call her by her real name, Carla. "Lee heard our names over and over again in those two years," he'd said. "From now on I'm the Reverend Bobby Hawkins to everyone we meet."

Even so she'd felt the fear in him when they hurried up the steps of the church. At the end of the mass as the organist began to play the first notes of "Amazing Grace," he'd whispered, "That's our song, Lee's and mine." His voice soared over all the others. They were in the seats at the end of the pew. When the usher carried Lee's limp body past them, Opal had to grab his hand to keep him from reaching out and touching her.

"I'll ask you again. Are you ready?" His voice was sarcastic. He was standing at the door of the suite.

"Yes." Opal reached for her purse, then walked over to him. She had to calm him down. The tension in him was something that shot through the room. She put her hands on the sides of his face. "Bic, honey. You gotta relax," she said soothingly. "You want to make a good impression, don't you?"

It was as though he hadn't heard a word she'd said. He murmured,

"I still have the power to scare that little girl half to death, don't I?" Then he began sobbing, hard, dry, racking sobs. "God, how I love her."

12

Dr. Peter Carpenter was the Ridgewood psychiatrist Sarah called ten days after the funeral. Sarah had met him occasionally, liked him, and her inquiries justified her own impressions. Her boss, Ed Ryan, the Bergen County prosecutor, was Carpenter's most emphatic supporter. "He's a straight shooter. I'd trust any one of my family with him, and you know that for me that's saying a lot. Too many of those birds are yo-yos."

She asked for an immediate appointment. "My sister blames herself for our parents' accident," she told Carpenter. Sarah realized as she spoke that she was avoiding the word "death." It was still so unreal to her. Gripping the phone, she said, "There was a recurrent nightmare she's had over the years. It hasn't happened in ages, but now she's having it regularly again."

Dr. Carpenter vividly remembered Laurie's kidnapping. When she was abandoned by her abductors and returned home, he had discussed with colleagues the ramifications of her total memory loss. He was keenly interested in seeing the girl now, but he told Sarah, "I think it would be wise if I talk to you before I see Laurie. I have a free hour this afternoon."

As his wife often teased, Carpenter could have been the model for the kindly family doctor. Steel gray hair, pink complexion, rimless glasses, benign expression, trim body, looking his age, which was fifty-two.

His office was deliberately cozy: pale green walls, tieback draperies in tones of green and white, a mahogany desk with a cluster of small flowering plants, a roomy wine-colored leather armchair opposite his swivel chair, a matching couch facing away from the windows.

When Sarah was ushered in by his secretary, Carpenter studied the attractive young woman in the simple blue suit. Her lean, athletic body moved with ease. She wore no makeup, and a smattering of freckles was visible across her nose. Charcoal brown brows and lashes accentuated the sadness in her luminous gray eyes. Her hair was pulled severely back from her face and held by a narrow blue band. Behind the band a cloud of dark red waves floated, ending just below her ears.

Sarah found it easy to answer Dr. Carpenter's questions. "Yes. Laurie was different when she came back. Even then I was certain she must have been sexually abused. But my mother insisted on telling everyone that she was sure loving people who wanted a child had taken her. Mother needed to believe that. Fifteen years ago people didn't talk about that kind of abuse. But Laurie was so frightened to go to bed. She loved my father but would never sit on his lap again. She didn't want him to touch her. She was afraid of men in general."

"Surely she was examined when she was found?"

"Yes, at the hospital in Pennsylvania."

"Those records may still exist. I wish you'd arrange to send for them. What about that recurring dream?"

"She had it again last night. She was absolutely terrified. She calls it the knife dream. Ever since she came back to us, she's been afraid of sharp knives."

"How much personality change did you observe?"

"At first a great deal. Laurie was an outgoing sociable child before she was kidnapped. A little spoiled, I suppose, but very sweet. She had a play group and loved to visit back and forth with her friends. After she came back she would never stay overnight in anyone's house again. She always seemed a little distant with her peers.

"She chose to go to Clinton College because it's only an hour-and-a-half drive away and she came home many weekends."

Carpenter asked, "What about boyfriends?"

"As you'll see, she's a very beautiful young woman. She certainly got asked out plenty and in high school did go to the usual dances and games. She never seemed interested in anyone until Gregg Bennett, and that ended abruptly."

"Why?"

"We don't know. Gregg doesn't know. They went together all last year. He attends Clinton College as well and would often come home weekends with her. We liked him tremendously, and Laurie seemed so happy with him. They're both good athletes, especially fine golfers. Then one day last spring it was over. No explanations. Just over. She won't talk about it, won't talk to Gregg. He came to see us. He has no idea what caused the break. He's in England this semester, and I don't know that he's even heard about my parents."

"I'd like to see Laurie tomorrow at eleven."

The next morning Sarah drove Laurie to the appointment and promised to return in exactly fifty minutes. "I'll bring in some stuff for dinner," she told her. "We've got to perk up that appetite of yours."

Laurie nodded and followed Carpenter into his private office. With something like panic in her face, she refused to recline on the couch, choosing to sit across the desk from him. She waited silently, her expression sad and withdrawn.

Obvious profound depression, Carpenter thought. "I'd like to help you, Laurie."

"Can you bring back my mother and father?"

"I wish I could. Laurie, your parents are dead because a bus malfunctioned."

"They're dead because I didn't have my car inspected."

"You forgot."

"I didn't forget. I decided to break the appointment at the gas station. I said I'd go to the free inspection center at the Motor Vehicle Agency. That one I forgot, but I deliberately broke the first appointment. It's my fault."

"Why did you break the first appointment?" He watched closely as Laurie Kenyon considered the question.

"There was a reason but I don't know what it was."

"How much does it cost to have the car inspected at the gas station?"

"Twenty dollars."

"And it's free at the Motor Vehicle Agency. Isn't that a good enough reason?"

She seemed to be immersed in her own thoughts. Carpenter wondered if she had heard him. Then she whispered, "No," and shook her head.

"Then why do you think you broke the first appointment?"

Now he was sure she had not heard him. She was in a different place. He tried another tack. "Laurie, Sarah tells me that you've been having bad dreams again, or rather the same bad dream you *used* to have has come back."

Inside her mind, Laurie heard a loud wail. She pulled her legs against her chest and buried her head. The wailing wasn't just inside her. It was coming from her chest and throat and mouth.

13

The meeting with Preacher Rutland Garrison and the television producers was sobering.

They had eaten lunch in the private dining room of Worldwide Cable, the company that syndicated Garrison's program to an international audience. Over coffee, he made himself very clear. "I began the 'Church of the Airways' when ten-inch black-and-white TVs were luxuries," he said. "Over the years this ministry has given comfort, hope and faith to millions of people. It has raised a great deal of money for worthwhile charities. I intend to see that the right person continues my work after me."

Bic and Opal had nodded, their faces set in expressions of deference, respect and piety. The following Sunday they were introduced on the "Church of the Airways." Bic spoke for forty minutes.

He told of his wasted youth, his vain desire to be a rock star, of the voice the good Lord had given him and how he had abused it with vile secular songs. He spoke of the miracle of his conversion. Yea, verily, he understood the road to Damascus. He had traveled it in the footsteps of Paul. The Lord didn't say, "Saul, Saul, why persecuteth thou Me?" No, the question hurt even more. At least Saul thought he was acting in the name of the Lord when he tried to blot out Christianity. As he, Bobby, stood in that crowded dirty nightclub, singing those filthy lyrics, a voice filled his heart and soul, a voice that was so powerful and yet so sad, so angry and yet so forgiving. The voice asked, "Bobby, Bobby, why do you blaspheme me?"

Here he began to cry.

At the end of the sermon, Preacher Rutland Garrison put a fatherly arm around him. Bobby beckoned to Carla to join him. She came onto the set, her eyes moist, her lips quivering. He introduced her to the Worldwide audience.

They led the closing hymn together. " 'Bringing in the sheaves . . .' "

After the program the switchboard came alive with calls praising the Reverend Bobby Hawkins. He was invited to return in two weeks.

On the drive back to Georgia, Bic was silent for hours. Then he said, "Lee's at the college in Clinton, New Jersey. Maybe she'll go back. Maybe she won't. The Lord is warning me it's time to remind her of what will happen if she talks about us."

Bic was going to be chosen as Rutland Garrison's successor. Opal could sense it. Garrison had been taken in the same as all the others. But if Lee started remembering . . . "What are you going to do about her, Bic?"

"I got ideas, Opal. Ideas that came to me full blown while I was praying."

14

On her second visit to Dr. Carpenter, Laurie told him that she was returning to college the next Monday. "It's better for me, better for Sarah," she said calmly. "She's so worried about me that she hasn't gone back to work, and work will be the best thing for her. And I'll have to study like crazy to make up for losing nearly three weeks."

Carpenter was not sure what he was seeing. There was something different about Laurie Kenyon, a brisk matter-of-fact attitude that was at total variance with the crushed, heartbroken girl he had seen a week earlier.

That day she had worn a gold cashmere jacket, beautifully cut black slacks, a gold, black and white silk blouse. Her hair had been loose around her shoulders. Today she had on jeans and a baggy sweater. Her hair was pulled back and held by a clip. She seemed totally composed.

"Have you had any more nightmares, Laurie?"

She shrugged. "I'm positively embarrassed remembering the way I carried on last week. Look, a lot of people have bad dreams and they don't go mewing around about them. Right?"

"Wrong," he said quietly. "Laurie, since you feel so much stronger, why don't you stretch out on the couch and relax and let's talk?" Carefully he watched her reaction.

It was the same as last week. Absolute panic in her eyes. This time the panic was followed by a defiant expression that was almost a sneer. "There's no need to stretch out. I'm perfectly capable of talking sitting up. Not that there's much to talk about. Two things went wrong in my life. In both cases I'm to blame. I admit it."

"You blame yourself for being kidnapped when you were four?"

"Of course. I was forbidden to go out front alone. I mean really forbidden. My mother was so afraid that I'd forget and run into the road. There was a teenager who lived down the block, and he had a lead foot on the accelerator. The only time that I remember my mother really scolding me was when she caught me on the front lawn, alone, throwing a ball in the air. And you know I'm responsible for my parents' death."

It was not the time to explore that. "Laurie, I want to help you. Sarah told me that your parents believed that you were better off not to have psychological counseling after your abduction. That probably is part of the reason you're resisting talking to me now. Why don't you just close your eyes and rest and try to learn to feel comfortable with me? In other sessions we may be able to work together."

"You're so sure there will be other sessions?"

"I hope so. Will there be?"

"Only to please Sarah. I'll be coming home weekends, so they'll have to be on Saturdays."

"That can be arranged. You're coming home every weekend?"

"Yes."

"Is that because you want to be with Sarah?"

The question seemed to excite her. The matter-of-fact attitude disappeared. Laurie crossed her legs, lifted her chin, reached her hand back and opened the clip that held her hair in a ponytail.

Carpenter watched as the shining blond mass fell around her face. A secretive smile played on her lips. "His wife comes home weekends," she said. "There's no use hanging around the college then."

15

Laurie opened the door of her car. "Starting to feel like fall," she said.

The first leaves were falling from the trees. Last night the heat had gone on automatically. "Yes, it does," Sarah said. "Now look, if it's too much for you . . ."

"It won't bc. You put all the creeps in prison, and I'll make up all the classes I missed and keep my cum laude. I still may even have a shot at magna. You left me in the dust with your summa. See you Friday night." She started to give Sarah a quick hug, then clung to her. "Sarah, don't you ever let me switch cars with you."

Sarah smoothed Laurie's hair. "Hey, I thought we'd agreed that Mom and Dad would get real upset about that kind of thinking. After you see Dr. Carpenter on Saturday, let's go for a round of golf."

Laurie attempted a smile. "Winner buys dinner."

"That's because you know you'll beat me."

Sarah waved vigorously until the car was no longer in sight, then turned back to the house. It was so quiet, so empty. The prevailing wisdom was to make no dramatic changes after a family death, but her instinct told her that she should start hunting immediately for another place, perhaps a condo, and put the house on the market. Maybe she'd phone Dr. Carpenter and ask him about that.

She was already dressed for work. She picked up her briefcase and shoulder bag, which were on the table in the foyer. The delicate eighteenth-century table, inlaid with marble, and the mirror above it were antiques that had belonged to her grand-mother. Where would they and all the other lovely pieces, all the first-edition volumes of classics that lined John Kenyon's library fit in a two-bedroom condo? Sarah pushed the thought away.

Instinctively she glanced in the mirror and was shocked at what she saw. Her complexion was dead white. There were deep circles under her eyes. Her face had always been thin, but now her cheeks were hollowed out. Her lips were ashen. She remembered her mother saying that last morning, "Sarah, why not wear a little makeup? Shadow would bring out your eyes . . ."

She dropped her shoulder bag and briefcase back on the table and went upstairs. From the vanity in her bathroom she took her seldom-used cosmetic case. The image of her mother in her shell-pink dressing gown, so naturally pretty, so endearingly maternal, telling her to put on eyeshadow brought at last the scalding tears she had forced back for Laurie's sake.

It was so good to get to her airless office with its chipped-paint walls, stacks of files, ringing telephone. Her coworkers in the prosecutor's office had come to the funeral home en masse. Her closest friends had been at the funeral, had phoned and stopped at the house these past few weeks.

Today they all seemed to understand that she wanted to get back to a semblance of normality. "Good to have you back." A quick hug. Then the welcome "Sarah, let me know when you have a minute . . ."

Lunch was a cheese on rye and black coffee from the courthouse cafeteria. By three o'clock Sarah had the satisfying feeling that she'd made a dent in responding to the urgent messages from plaintiffs, witnesses and attorneys.

At four o'clock, unable to wait any longer, she called Laurie's room at college. The phone was picked up immediately. "Hello."

"Laurie, it's me. How's it going?"

"So-so. I went to three classes, then cut the last one. I just felt so tired."

"No wonder. You haven't had a decent night's sleep. What are you doing tonight?"

"Going to bed. Got to clear out my brain."

"Okay. I'm going to work late. Be home around eight. Why don't I give you a call?"

"I'd like that."

Sarah stayed at the office until seven-fifteen, stopped at a diner and bought a hamburger to go. At eight-thirty she phoned Laurie.

The ringing at the other end continued. Maybe she's showering, maybe she's had some kind of reaction. Sarah held the receiver as the staccato sound buzzed and buzzed in her ear. Finally an impatient voice answered. "Laurie Kenyon's line."

"Is Laurie there?"

"No, and please, if the phone isn't answered in five or six rings, give me a break. I'm right across the hall and I've got a test to prepare for."

"I'm sorry. It's just that Laurie was planning to go to bed early."

"Well, she changed her plans. She went out a few minutes ago."

"Did she seem to be all right? I'm her sister and I'm a bit concerned."

"Oh, I didn't realize. I'm so sorry about what happened to your mother and father. I think Laurie was okay. She was all dressed up, like for a date."

Sarah called again at ten, at eleven, at twelve, at one. The last time, a sleepy Laurie answered. "I'm fine, Sarah. I went to bed right after dinner and have been asleep since then."

"Laurie, I rang so long the girl across the hall came over and picked up your phone. She told me you went out."

"Sarah, she's wrong. I swear to God I was right here." Laurie sounded frightened. "Why would I lie?"

I don't know, Sarah thought.

"Well, as long as you're okay. Get back to sleep," she said and replaced the receiver slowly.

16

Dr. Carpenter could sense the difference in Laurie's posture as she leaned back in the roomy leather chair. He did not suggest that she lie on the couch. The last thing he wanted was to have her lose this tentative trust in him that he sensed she was developing. He asked her how the week at college had been.

"Okay, I guess. People were awfully nice to me. I have so much catching up to do that I'm burning the midnight oil." She hesitated then stopped.

Carpenter waited then said mildly, "What is it, Laurie?"

"Last night when I got home, Sarah asked me if I'd heard from Gregg Bennett."

"Gregg Bennett?"

"I used to go out with him. My mother and father and Sarah liked him a lot."

"Do you like him?"

"I did, until . . ."

Again he waited.

Her eyes widened. "He wouldn't let go of me."

"You mean he was forcing himself on you?"

"No. He kissed me. And that was all right. I liked it. But then he pressed my arms with his hands."

"And that frightened you."

"I knew what was going to happen."

"What was going to happen?"

She was looking off into the distance. "We don't want to talk about that."

For ten minutes she was silent, then said sadly, "I could tell that Sarah didn't believe I hadn't been out the other night. She was worried."

Sarah had called him about that. "Maybe you were out," Dr. Carpenter suggested. "It would be good for you to be with friends."

"No. I don't care about dating now. I'm too busy."

"Any dreams?"

"The knife dream."

Two weeks ago she had become hysterical when she was asked about it. Today her voice was almost indifferent. "I have to get used to it. I'm going to keep having it until the knife catches up with me. It will, you know."

"Laurie, in therapy we call acting out an emotionally disturbing memory *abreaction.* I'd like you to abreact for me now. Show me what you see in the dream. I think you dread going to sleep because you're afraid you'll have the dream. Nobody can do without sleep. You don't have to talk. Just show me what is happening in the dream."

Laurie got up slowly, then raised her hand. Her mouth twisted into a cunning thin-lipped smile. She started walking around the desk toward him, her steps deliberate. Her hand jerked up and down as she swung an imaginary blade. Just before she reached him she stopped. Her posture changed. She stood, riveted to the spot, staring. Her hand tried to wipe away something from her face and hair. She looked down and jumped back terrified.

She collapsed on the floor, her hands over her face, then crouched against the wall, shivering and making hurting sounds like a wounded animal.

Ten minutes passed. Laurie quieted, dropped her hands and got up slowly.

"That's the knife dream," she said.

"Are you in the dream, Laurie?"

"Yes."

"Who are you, the one who has the knife or the one who is afraid?"

"Everybody. And in the end we all die together."

"Laurie, I'd like to talk to a psychiatrist I know who's had a great deal of experience with people who have suffered childhood trauma. Will you sign a release to let me discuss your case with him?"

"If you like. What difference can it make to me?"

17

At seven-thirty Monday morning, Dr. Justin Donnelly walked rapidly up Fifth Avenue from his Central Park South apartment to Lehman Hospital on Ninety-sixth Street. He constantly competed with himself to cover the two mile distance a minute or two faster each day. But short of actually jogging, he could not better his twenty-minute record.

He was a big man who always looked as if he'd be at home in cowboy boots and a ten-gallon hat, not an inaccurate image. Donnelly had been raised on a sheep station in Australia. His curly black hair had a permanently tousled look. His black mustache was luxuriant, and when he smiled, it accentuated his strong white teeth. His intense blue eyes were framed by dark lashes and brows that women envied. Early in his psychiatric training he had decided to specialize in multiple personality disorders. A persuasive ground-breaker, Donnelly fought to establish a clinic for MPD in New South Wales. It quickly became a model facility. His papers, published in prominent medical journals, soon brought him international recognition. At thirty-five he was invited to set up a multiple personality disorder center at Lehman.

After two years in Manhattan, Justin considered himself a dyed-in-the-wool New Yorker. On his walks to and from the office he affectionately drank in the newly familiar sights: the horses and carriages arriving at the park, the glimpse of the zoo at Sixty-fifth Street, the doormen at the swank Fifth Avenue apartment buildings. Most of them greeted him by name. Now as he strode past, several remarked about the fine October weather.

It was going to be a busy day. Justin usually tried to keep the ten-to-eleven time slot free for staff consultations. This morning he'd made an exception. An urgent phone call Saturday from a New Jersey psychiatrist had piqued his interest. Dr. Peter Carpenter wanted to consult with him immediately about a patient who he suspected was an MPD and potentially suicidal. Justin had agreed to a ten o'clock meeting today.

He reached Ninety-sixth and Fifth in twenty-five minutes and consoled himself that the heavy pedestrian traffic had slowed his progress. The main entrance to the hospital was on Fifth Avenue. The MPD clinic was entered by a discreet private door on Ninety-sixth. Justin was almost invariably the first one there. His office was a small suite at the end of the corridor. The outer room, painted a soft ivory and simply furnished with his desk and swivel chair, two armchairs for visitors, bookcases and a row of files, was enlivened by colorful prints of sailboats in Sydney Harbor. The inner room was where he treated patients. It was equipped with a sophisticated video camera and tape recorder.

His first patient was a forty-year-old woman from Ohio who had been in treatment for six years and was diagnosed as schizophrenic. It was only when an alert psychologist began to believe that the voices the woman kept hearing were those of alter personalities that she had come to him. She was making good progress.

Dr. Carpenter arrived promptly at ten. Courteously grateful to Justin for seeing him on such short notice, he immediately began to talk about Laurie.

Donnelly listened, took notes, interjected questions. Carpenter concluded, "I'm not an expert on MPD, but if ever there were signs of it, I've been seeing them. There's been a marked change in her voice and manner during her last two visits. She definitely is unaware of at least one specific incident when she left her room and was out for hours. I'm sure she's not lying when she claims to have been asleep at that time. She has a recurring nightmare of a knife slashing at her. Yet during abreaction at one point she was acting out holding the knife and doing the slashing. Then she switched to trying to avoid it. I've made a copy of her file."

Donnelly read down the pages swiftly, stopping to circle or check when something jumped out at him. The case fascinated him. A beloved child kidnapped at the age of four and abandoned by the kidnappers at age six, with total memory loss of the intervening two years! A recurring nightmare! A sister's perception that since her reunion with the family, Laurie had responded to stress with child-like anxiety. Tragic parental death for which Laurie blamed herself.

When he laid the file down, he said, "The records from the hospital in Pittsburgh where she was examined indicated probable sexual abuse over a long period of time and counseling was strongly recommended. I gather there was none."

"There was total denial on the part of the parents," Dr. Carpenter answered, "and therefore no therapy whatsoever."

"Typical of the pretend-it-didn't-happen thinking of fifteen years ago, plus the Kenyons were significantly older parents," Donnelly observed. "It would be a good idea if we could persuade Laurie to come here for evaluation, and I'd say the sooner the better."

"I have a feeling that will be very difficult. Sarah had to beg her to come to me."

"If she resists, I'd like to see the sister. She should watch for signs of aberrant behavior and of course she must not take any talk of suicide lightly."

The two psychiatrists walked to the door together. In the reception room a dark-haired teenaged girl was staring moodily out the window. Her arms were covered with bandages.

In a low voice, Donnelly said, "You have to take it seriously. The patients who have experienced trauma in their childhood are at high risk for self-harm."

~ 18

That evening when Sarah got home from work the mail was neatly stacked on the foyer table. After the funeral, Sophie, their long-time daily housekeeper, had proposed cutting down to two days a week. "You don't need me more than that anymore, Sarah, and I'm not getting any younger."

Monday was one of the days she came in. That was why the mail was sorted, the house smelled faintly of furniture polish, the draperies were drawn and the soft light of lamps and sconces gave a welcoming glow to the downstairs rooms.

This was the hardest part of the day for Sarah, coming into an empty house. Before the accident, if she was expected home, her mother and father would be waiting to have their predinner cocktail with her.

Sarah bit her lip and pushed aside the memory. The letter on top of the pile was from England. She ripped open the envelope, certain it was from Gregg Bennett. She read the letter quickly then again, slowly. Gregg had just learned about the accident. His expression of sympathy was profoundly moving. He wrote about his affection for John and Marie Kenyon, about the wonderful visits to their home, how rough it must be for her and Laurie now.

The final paragraph was disturbing: "Sarah, I tried to phone Laurie, and she sounded so despondent when she answered. Then she screamed something like, 'I won't, I won't,' and hung up on me. I'm terribly worried about her. She's so fragile. I know you're taking good care of her, but be very careful. I'll be back at Clinton in January and would like to see you. My love to you, and kiss that girl for me, please. Gregg."

Her hands trembling, Sarah carried the mail into the library. Tomorrow she'd call Dr. Carpenter and read this to him. She knew he had given Laurie antidepressants, but was she taking them? The answering machine was blinking. Dr. Carpenter had called and left his home number.

When she reached him, she told him about Gregg's letter then listened, shocked and frightened, to his careful explanation of why he had seen Dr. Justin Donnelly in New York and why it was imperative that Sarah see him as soon as possible. He gave her the number of Donnelly's service. Her voice low and strained, she had to repeat her phone number twice to the operator.

Sophie had roasted a chicken, prepared a salad. Sarah's throat closed as she picked at the food. She had just made coffee when Dr. Donnelly returned her call. His day was full, but he could see her at six tomorrow evening. She hung up, reread Gregg's letter and, with a frantic sense of urgency, dialed Laurie. There was no answer. She tried every half hour until finally at eleven o'clock she heard the receiver being picked up. Laurie's "Hello" was cheerful enough. They chatted for a few minutes, then Laurie said, "How's this for a pain? After dinner I propped myself up on the bed to research this damn paper and fell asleep. Now I've got to burn the midnight oil."

~ *19*

At eleven o'clock on Monday evening, Professor Allan Grant stretched out on his bed and switched on the night table lamp. The long bedroom window was partially open, but the room was not cool enough for his taste. Karen, his wife, used to teasingly tell him that in a previous incarnation he must have been a polar bear. Karen hated a cold bedroom. Not that she was around much to joke about it anymore, he thought as he threw back the blanket and swung his feet onto the carpet.

For the last three years, Karen had been working at a travel agency in the Madison Arms Hotel in Manhattan. At first she'd stayed overnight in New York only occasionally. Then more and more often she'd phone in late afternoon. "Sweetie, we're so busy, and I've got stacks of paperwork. Can you fend for yourself?"

He'd fended for himself for thirty-four years before he'd met her six years ago on a tour of Italy. Getting back in the habit wasn't that hard. Karen now had an apartment in the hotel and usually stayed there most of the week. She did come home weekends.

Grant padded across the room and cranked the window wide open. The curtains billowed in, followed by an eminently satisfying blast of chilly air. He hurried toward the bed but hesitated and turned in the direction of the hallway. It was no use. He was not sleepy. Another bizarre letter had come in his office mail today. Who the hell was Leona? He had no students by that name, had never had.

The house was a comfortable-size ranch model. Allan had bought it before he and Karen were married. For a time she'd seemed interested in decorating it and replacing shabby or dull furniture, but now it was beginning to look as it had in his bachelor days.

Scratching his head and yanking up pajama bottoms, which always seemed to settle around his hips, Grant walked down the hallway past the guest bedrooms, across the center hall, past the kitchen, living and dining rooms, and into the den. He turned on the overhead lights. After rummaging successfully for the key to the top drawer of his desk, he opened it, got out the letters and began to reread them.

The first one had come two weeks ago: "Darling Allan, I'm reliving now the glorious hours we spent together last night. It's hard to believe that we haven't always been madly in love, but maybe it's because no other time counts for us, does it? Do you know how hard it is for me not to shout from the rooftops that I'm crazy about you? I know you feel the same way. We have to hide what we are to each other. I understand that. Just keep on loving me and wanting me the way you do now. Leona."

All the letters were in the same vein. One arrived every other day, each talking about wild love scenes with him in his office or this house.

He'd had enough informal workshops here that any number of students knew the layout. Some of the letters referred to the shabby brown leather chair in the den. But never once had he had a student alone in the house. He wasn't that much of a fool.

Grant studied the letters carefully. They were obviously typed on an old machine. The *o* and the *w* were broken. He'd gone through his student files, but no one used a machine like that. He also did not recognize the scrawled signature.

Once again he agonized about whether to show them to Karen and to the administration. It would be hard to predict how Karen would react. He didn't want to upset her. Neither did he want her to decide to give up her job and stay home. Maybe he would have wanted that a few years ago, but not now. He had a big decision to make.

The administration. He'd bring the Dean of Student Affairs in on this the minute he found out who was sending them. The trouble was he simply didn't have a clue, and if anyone believed they contained an iota of truth, he could kiss his future at this college goodbye.

He read the letters once more, searching for a writing style, phrases or expressions that might bring one of his students to mind. Nothing. Finally he replaced them in the drawer, locked it, stretched and realized that he was dead tired. And chilly. It was one thing to sleep in a cold room under warm blankets, another to be in the path of a direct draft when you're sitting there in cotton pajamas. Where the heck was the draft coming from?

Karen always closed the draperies when she was home but he never bothered. He realized that the sliding glass door from the den to the patio was open a few inches. The door was heavy and slow to move on the track. He probably hadn't closed it completely the last time he went out. The lock was a pain in the neck too. Half the time it didn't catch. He walked over, shoved the door closed, snapped the lock and without bothering to see if it had caught, turned out the light and went back to bed.

He hunched under the covers in the now satisfyingly cold bedroom, closed his eyes and promptly fell asleep. In his wildest dreams he could not have imagined that half an hour ago a slender figure with long blond hair had been curled up in his brown leather chair and had only slipped away at the sound of his approaching footsteps.

20

Fifty-eight-year old private investigator Daniel O'Toole was known in New Jersey as Danny the Spouse Hunter. Under his hard-drinking, hail-fellow-well-met exterior, he was a remarkably thorough worker and quietly discreet in compiling information.

Danny was used to people using false names when they hired him to check on possibly erring husbands or wives. It didn't bother him. As long as he received his retainer and follow-up bills were paid promptly, his clients could call themselves anything they pleased.

Even so it was a bit surprising when a woman identifying herself as Jane Graves phoned his Hackensack office Tuesday morning, hinting at a possible insurance claim and engaging him to investigate the activities of the Kenyon sisters. Was the older sister working at her job? Was the younger sister back in college, completing her studies? Did she come home often? How were they reacting to the death of their parents? Were there any signs of breakdown? Very important, was either young woman seeing a psychiatrist?

Danny sensed something fishy. He had met Sarah Kenyon a few times in court. The accident that killed the parents had been caused by a speeding chartered bus with failed brakes. It was entirely possible that there was a suit pending against the bus company, but insurance companies usually had their own investigators. Still a job was a job, and because of the recession the divorce business was lousy. Breaking up was really hard to do when money was tight.

Taking a gamble, Danny doubled his usual retainer and was told the check would be in the mail immediately. He was instructed to send his reports and further bills to a private post office box in New York.

Smiling broadly, Danny replaced the receiver.

21

Sarah drove into New York after work on Tuesday evening. She was on time for the six o'clock appointment with Dr. Justin Donnelly, but when she entered his reception area he was hurrying out of his office.

With a quick apology he explained that he had an emergency and asked her to wait. She had an impression of height and breadth, dark hair and keen blue eyes—then he was gone.

The receptionist had obviously gone home. The phones were quiet. After ten minutes of scanning a news magazine and registering nothing, Sarah put it down and sat quietly absorbed in her own thoughts.

It was after seven o'clock when Dr. Donnelly returned. "I'm very sorry," he said simply as he brought her into his office.

Sarah smiled faintly, trying to ignore her hunger pangs and the unmistakable beginning of a headache. It had been a long time since noon when she'd gulped a ham on rye and coffee.

The doctor indicated the chair across from his desk. She sat there, aware that he was studying her, and got to the point immediately.

"Dr. Donnelly, I had my secretary go to the library and copy material on multiple personality disorder. I'd only known about it vaguely, but what I read today frightens me."

He waited.

"If what I understand is accurate, a primary cause is childhood trauma, particularly sexual abuse over a prolonged period. Isn't that right?"

"Yes."

"Laurie certainly had the trauma of being kidnapped and held captive away from home for two years when she was a small child. The doctors who examined her when she was found believe she was abused."

"Is it okay if I call you Sarah?" he asked.

"Of course."

"All right then, Sarah. If Laurie has become a multiple personality, it probably started back at the time of her abduction. Assuming she was abused, she must have been so frightened, so terrified, that one small human being couldn't absorb everything that was happening. At that point, there was a shattering. Psychologically Laurie, the child as you knew her, withdrew from the pain and fear and alter personalities came to help her. The memory of those years is locked away in them. It would seem that the other personalities have not been apparent until now. From what I understand, after Laurie came home at age six she gradually returned to pretty much her old self except for a recurring nightmare. Now, in the death of your parents, she's experienced another terrible trauma, and Dr. Carpenter has seen distinct personality changes in her during her recent sessions with him. The reason he came to me so quickly is that he's afraid she might be suicidal."

"He didn't tell me that." Sarah felt her mouth go dry. "Laurie's been depressed, of course, but . . . Oh God, surely you don't think that's possible?" She bit her lip to keep it from quivering.

"Sarah, can you persuade Laurie to see me?"

She shook her head. "It's a job to make her see Dr. Carpenter. My parents were wonderful human beings but they had no use for psychiatry. Mother used to quote one of her college teachers. According to him there are three types of people: the ones who go for therapy when they're under stress; the ones who talk out their troubles with a friend or a cabdriver or bartender; the ones who hug their problems to themselves. The teacher claimed that the rate of recovery is exactly the same in all three types. Laurie grew up listening to that."

Justin Donnelly smiled. "I'm not sure that opinion isn't shared by quite a lot of people."

"I know Laurie needs professional help," Sarah said. "The problem is she doesn't want to open up to Dr. Carpenter. It's as though she's afraid of what he might find out about her."

"Then at least for now it's important to work around her. I've reread her file and made some notes."

At eight o'clock, observing Sarah's drawn, tired face, Dr. Donnelly said, "I think we'd better stop here. Sarah, listen for any reference to suicide, no matter how offhand it might seem, and report it to Dr. Carpenter and me. I'm going to be perfectly honest. I'd like to stay involved in Laurie's case. My work is research into multiple personality disorder and it's not often we catch a patient at the beginning of the emergence of alter personalities. I'll be discussing Laurie with

Dr. Carpenter after her next several sessions with him. Unless there's a radical change, I have a hunch that we'll get more information from you than from Laurie. Be very observant."

Sarah hesitated then asked, "Doctor, isn't it a fact that until Laurie unlocks those lost years, she'll never really be well?"

"Think of it this way, Sarah. My mother broke her nail down to the quick once and an infection developed. A few days later the whole finger was swollen and throbbing. She kept doctoring it herself because she was afraid to have it lanced. When she finally went to the emergency room she had a red streak up her arm and was on the verge of blood poisoning. You see, she had ignored the warning signs because she didn't want the immediate pain of treatment."

"And Laurie is exhibiting warning signs of psychological infection?"

"Yes."

They walked together through the long corridor to the front door. The security guard let them out. There was no wind but the October evening had an unmistakable bite in the air. Sarah started to say good night.

"Is your car nearby?" Donnelly asked.

"Miracle of miracles, I found a parking spot right down the block."

He walked her to it. "Keep in touch."

What a nice guy, Sarah thought as she drove away. She tried to analyze her own feelings. If anything she was more worried now about Laurie than she had been before she saw Dr. Donnelly, but at least now she had a sense of solid help available to her.

She drove across Ninety-sixth Street past Madison and Park avenues, heading for the FDR Drive. At Lexington Avenue she impulsively turned right and headed downtown. She was famished, and Nicola's was only a dozen blocks away.

Ten minutes later she was being ushered to a small table. "Gee, it's great to see you again, Sarah," Lou, Nicola's longtime waiter, told her.

The restaurant was always cheery, and the delectable sight of steaming pasta being carried from the kitchen lifted Sarah's spirits. "I know what I want, Lou."

"Asparagus vinaigrette, linguine with white clam sauce, Pellegrino, a glass of wine," he rattled off.

"You've got it."

She reached into the bread basket for a warm crusty roll. Ten minutes later, just after the asparagus was served, the small table to her left was taken. She heard a familiar voice say, "Perfect, Lou. Thanks. I'm starving."

Sarah glanced up quickly and found herself looking into the surprised then obviously pleased face of Dr. Justin Donnelly.

22

Seventy-eight-year-old Rutland Garrison had known from the time he was a boy that he was called to the ministry. In 1947 he had been inspired to recognize the potential reach of television and persuaded the Dumont station in New York to allocate time on Sunday mornings for a "Church of the Airways" religious hour. He had been preaching the Lord's word ever since.

Now his heart was quite simply wearing out and his doctor had warned him to retire immediately. "You've done enough in your lifetime for a dozen men, Reverend Garrison," he'd said. "You've built a Bible college, a hospital, nursing homes, retirement communities. Now be good to yourself."

Garrison knew more than anyone how vast sums could be diverted from worthy causes to greedy pockets. He did not intend that his ministry fall into the hands of anyone of that ilk.

He also knew that by its very nature a television ministry needed a man in the pulpit who could not only inspire and lead his flock but also preach a rousing good sermon.

"We must choose a man with showmanship but not a showman," Garrison cautioned the members of the Church of the Airways Council. Nevertheless in late October, after Reverend Bobby Hawkins's third appearance as guest preacher, the council voted to invite him to accept the pulpit.

Garrison had the power of veto over council decisions. "I am not sure of that man," he told the members angrily. "There's something about him that troubles me. There's no need to rush into a commitment."

"He has a messianic quality," one of them protested.

"The Messiah Himself was the one who warned us to beware of false prophets." Rutland Garrison saw from the tolerant but somewhat irritated expressions on the faces of the men around him that they all believed his objections were based solely on his unwillingness to retire. He got up. "Do what you want," he said wearily. "I'm going home."

That night Reverend Rutland Garrison died in his sleep.

23

Bic had been edgy since the last time he'd preached in New York. "That old man has it in for me, Opal," he told her. "Jealous because of all the calls and letters they're getting about me. I called one of those council members to see why I haven't heard from them again and that's the reason."

"Maybe it's better if we stay here in Georgia, Bic," Opal suggested. She turned away from his scornful glance. She was at the dining room table, surrounded by stacks of envelopes.

"How were the donations this week?"

"Very good." Every Thursday on his local program and when he spoke at meetings, Bic made appeals for different overseas charities. Opal and he were the only ones allowed to touch the donations.

"They're not good compared to what the 'Church of the Airways' takes in whenever I speak."

On October 28 a call came from New York. When Bic hung up the phone he stared at Opal, his face and eyes luminescent. "Garrison died last night. I'm invited to become the pastor of the Church of the Airways. They want us to move permanently to New York as soon as possible. They want us to stay at the Wyndham until we select a residence."

Opal started to run to him, then stopped. The look on his face warned her to leave him alone. He went into his study and closed the door. A few minutes later she heard the faint sounds of music and knew that once again he had taken out Lee's music box. She tiptoed over to the door and listened as high-pitched voices sang, "All around the town . . . Boys and girls together . . ."

24

It was so hard to keep Sarah from realizing how afraid she was. Laurie stopped telling Sarah and Dr. Carpenter when she had the knife dream. There was no use talking about it. Nobody, not even Sarah, could understand that the knife was getting closer and closer.

Dr. Carpenter wanted to help her, but she had to be so careful. Sometimes the hour with him went by so swiftly, and Laurie knew she had told him things she didn't remember talking about.

She was always so tired. Even though almost every night she stayed in her room and studied, she was always struggling to keep up with assignments. Sometimes she'd find them finished on her desk and not remember having done them.

She was getting so many loud thoughts that pounded in her head like people shouting in an echo chamber. One of the voices told her she was a wimp and stupid and caused trouble for everyone and to shut her mouth around Dr. Carpenter. Other times a little kid kept crying inside Laurie's mind. Sometimes the child cried very softly, sometimes she sobbed and wailed. Another voice, lower and sultry, talked like a porno queen.

Weekends were so hard. The house was so big, so quiet. She never wanted to be alone in it. She was glad Sarah had listed it with a real estate agency.

The only time Laurie felt like herself was when she and Sarah played golf at the club and had brunch or dinner with friends. Those days made her think of playing golf with Gregg. She missed him in an aching, hurting way but was so afraid of him now, the fear blotted out all the love. She dreaded the thought that he'd be coming back to Clinton in January.

25

Justin Donnelly had already gathered from his meeting with Dr. Carpenter that Sarah Kenyon was a remarkably strong young woman, but he had not been prepared for the impact she had on him when he met her. That first evening in his office she'd sat across the desk from him, lovely and poised, only the pain in her eyes hinting at the grief and anxiety she was experiencing. Her quietly expensive dark blue tweed suit had made him remember that wearing subdued colors was once considered an appropriate gesture for someone in mourning.

He'd been impressed that her immediate response to the possibility of her sister suffering from multiple personality disorder had been to gather information about it even before she saw him. He'd admired her intelligent understanding of Laurie's psychological vulnerability.

When he'd left Sarah at her car, it had been on the tip of Justin's tongue to suggest dinner. Then he'd walked into Nicola's and found her there. She'd looked pleased to see him, and it felt easy and natural to suggest that he join her and free up the last small table for the couple who came in just behind him.

It was Sarah who had set the tone of the conversation. Smiling, she passed him the basket of rolls. "I imagine you had the same kind of lunch on the run I did," she'd told him. "I'm starting to work on a murder case and I've been talking to witnesses all day."

She'd talked about her job as an assistant prosecutor, then skillfully turned the conversation to him. She knew he was Australian. Over osso bucco Justin told her about his family and growing up on a sheep station. "My paternal great-grandfather came over from Britain in chains. Of course for generations that wasn't mentioned. Now it's a matter of pride to have an ancestor who was a guest of the Crown in the penal colony. My maternal grandmother was born in England, and the family moved to Australia when she was three months old. All her life Granny kept sighing how she missed England. She was there twice in eighty years. That's the other kind of Aussie mind-set."

It was only as they sipped cappuccino that the talk turned to his decision to specialize in the treatment of multiple personality disorder patients.

After that evening, Justin spoke to Dr. Carpenter and Sarah at least once a week. Dr. Carpenter reported that Laurie was increasingly uncooperative. "She's dissembling," he told Justin. "On the surface she agrees that she should not feel responsible for her parents' death, but I don't believe her. She talks about them as though it's a safe subject. Tender memories only. When she becomes emotional she talks and cries like a small child. She continues to refuse to take the MMPI or Rorschach tests."

Sarah reported that she saw no indication of suicidal depression. "Laurie hates going to Dr. Carpenter on Saturdays," she told him. "Says it's a waste of money and it's perfectly normal to be very sad when your parents die. She does brighten up when we go to the club. A couple of her midterm marks were pretty bad, so she told me to call her by eight o'clock if I want to talk to her in the evening. After that she wants to be able to study without interruption. I think she doesn't want me checking up on her."

Dr. Justin Donnelly did not tell Sarah that both he and Dr. Carpenter sensed that in Laurie's behavior they were witnessing a calm before the storm. Instead he continued to urge her to keep a careful watch on Laurie. Whenever he hung up he realized he was starting to look forward to Sarah's calls in a highly unprofessional way.

26

In the office, the murder case Sarah was prosecuting was a particularly vicious one in which a twenty-seven-year-old woman, Maureen Mays, had been strangled by a nineteen-year-old youth who forced his way into her car in the parking lot of the railroad station.

It was a welcome change to plunge into final preparation as the trial date drew near. With intense concentration, she pored over the statements of the witnesses who had seen the defendant lurking in the station. If only they had done something about it, Sarah thought. They all had the feeling that he was up to no good. She knew that the physical evidence of the victim's desperate attempt to save herself from her attacker would make a strong impression on the jury.

The trial began December second, no longer open and shut, as a hearty, likable sixty-year-old defense attorney, Conner Marcus, attempted to tear apart Sarah's case. Under his skillful questioning, witnesses admitted that it had been dark in the parking area, that they did not know if the defendant had opened the door to the car or if Mays had opened it to allow him in.

But when it was Sarah's turn on redirect examination, all of the witnesses firmly declared that when James Parker came on to Maureen Mays in the train station, she had clearly rebuffed him.

The combination of the viciousness of the crime and the showmanship of Marcus caused the media to descend in droves. Spectators' benches filled. Courtroom junkies placed bets on the outcome.

Sarah was in the rhythm that in the past five years had become second nature to her. She ate, drank and slept the matter of State v. James Parker. Laurie began going back to college on Saturdays after she saw Dr. Carpenter. "You're busy and it's good for me to get involved too," she told Sarah.

"How's it going with Dr. Carpenter?"

"I'm starting to blame the bus driver for the accident."

"That's good news." On her next weekly call to Dr. Donnelly, Sarah said, "I only wish I could believe her."

Thanksgiving was spent with cousins in Connecticut. It wasn't as bad as Sarah had feared. At Christmas she and Laurie flew to Florida and went on a five-day Caribbean cruise. Swimming in the outside pool on the Lido deck made Christmas with all its attendant memories seem far away. Still Sarah found herself longing for the holiday court recess to be over so that she could get back to the trial.

Laurie spent much of the cruise in the cabin, reading. She had signed on for Allan Grant's class in Victorian women writers and wanted to do some advance study. She had brought along their mother's old portable typewriter, supposedly to make notes. But Sarah knew she was also writing letters on it, letters she would rip from the machine and cover if Sarah entered the cabin. Had Laurie become interested in someone? Sarah wondered. Why be so secretive about it?

She's twenty-one, Sarah told herself sternly. Mind your own business.

27

On Christmas Eve, Professor Allan Grant had an unpleasant scene with his wife, Karen. He'd forgotten to hide the key to his desk drawer and she'd found the letters. Karen demanded to know why he'd kept them from her; why he had not turned them over to the administration if, as he claimed, they were all ridiculous fabrications.

Patiently and then not so patiently, he explained. "Karen, I saw no reason to upset you. As far as the administration is concerned, I can't even be sure that a student is sending them, although I certainly suspect it. What is the dean going to do except just what you're doing right now, wonder how much truth there is in them?"

The week between Christmas and New Year's Day the letters stopped coming. "More proof that they're probably from a student," he told Karen. "Now I *wish* I'd get one. A postmark would be a big help."

Karen wanted him to spend New Year's Eve in New York. They'd been invited to a party at the Rainbow Room.

"You know I hate big parties," he told her. "The Larkins invited us to their place." Walter Larkin was the Dean of Student Affairs.

On New Year's Eve it snowed heavily. Karen called from her office. "Darling, turn the radio on. The trains and buses are all delayed. What do you think I should do?"

Allan knew what he was supposed to answer. "Don't get stuck in Penn Station or on the highway in a bus. Why don't you stay in town?"

"Are you sure you don't mind?"

He didn't mind.

Allan Grant had entered marriage with the definite idea that it was a lifetime commitment. His father had walked out on his mother when Allan was a baby and he'd vowed he'd never do that to any woman.

Karen was obviously very happy with their arrangement. She liked living in New York during the week and spending weekends with him. At first it had worked pretty well. Allan Grant was used to living alone and enjoyed his own company. But now he was experiencing growing dissatisfaction. Karen was one of the prettiest women he'd ever seen. She wore clothes like a fashion model. Unlike him, she had a good business sense, which was why she handled all their finances. But her physical attraction for him had long since died. Her amusing hardheaded common sense had become predictable.

What did they really have in common? Allan asked himself yet again as he dressed to go to the dean's home. Then he put the nagging question aside. Tonight he'd just enjoy the evening with good friends. He knew everyone who would be there and they were all attractive, interesting people.

Especially Vera West, the newest member of the faculty.

28

In early January, the campus of Clinton College had been a crystal palace. A heavy storm inspired students to create imaginative snow sculptures. The below-freezing temperature preserved them in pristine beauty, until the arrival of an unseasonably warm rain.

Now the remaining snow clung to soggy brown grass. The remnants of the sculptures seemed grotesque in their half-melted state.

The frivolous postexam euphoria was over and business as usual began in the classrooms.

Laurie walked quickly across the campus to Professor Allan Grant's office. Her hands were clenched in the pockets of the ski jacket she was wearing over jeans and a sweater. Her tawny blond hair was pulled back and clipped in a ponytail. In preparation for the conference she had started to dab on eyeshadow and lipliner, then scrubbed them off.

Don't try to kid yourself. You're ugly.

The loud thoughts were coming more and more often. Laurie quickened her steps as though somehow she might be able to outrun them. *Laurie, everything is your fault. What happened when you were little is your fault.*

Laurie hoped she hadn't done badly in the first test on Victorian authors. She'd always gotten good marks till this year, but now it was like being on a roller coaster. Sometimes she'd get an A or B+ on a paper. Other times the material was so unfamiliar that she knew she must not have been paying attention in class. Later she'd find notes she didn't remember taking.

Then she saw him. Gregg. He was walking across the driveway between two dormitories. When he'd gotten back from England last week he'd called her. She'd shouted at him to leave her alone and slammed down the phone.

He hadn't spotted her yet. She ran the remaining distance to the building.

Mercifully the corridor was empty. She leaned her head against the wall for an instant, grateful for the coolness.

'Fraidy cat.

I'm not a 'fraidy cat, she thought defiantly. Straightening her shoulders, she managed a casual smile for the student emerging from Allan Grant's office.

She knocked on the partly open door. A pleasant warmth and a sense of brightness permeated her at his welcoming, "Come on in, Laurie." He was always so kind to her.

Grant's tiny office was painted a sunny yellow. Crammed bookshelves lined the wall to the right of the window. A long table held reference books and student papers. The top of his desk was tidy, holding only a phone, a plant and a fishbowl in which a solitary goldfish swam aimlessly.

Grant motioned toward the chair opposite his desk. "Sit down, Laurie." He was wearing a dark blue sweater over a white turtleneck shirt. Laurie had the fleeting thought that the effect was almost clerical.

He was holding her last paper in his hand, the one she'd written on Emily Dickinson. "You didn't like it?" she asked apprehensively.

"I thought it was terrific. It's just I don't see why you changed your mind about old Em."

He liked it. Laurie smiled in relief. But what did he mean about changing her mind?

"Last term when you wrote about Emily Dickinson, you made a strong case for her life as a recluse, saying that her genius could only be fully expressed by removing herself from contact with the many. Now your thesis is that she was a neurotic filled with fear, that her poetry would have reached greater heights if she hadn't suppressed her emotions. You conclude, 'A lusty affair with her mentor and idol, Charles Wadsworth, would have done her a lot of good.' "

Grant smiled. "I've sometimes wondered the same thing, but what made you change your mind?"

What indeed? Laurie found an answer. "Maybe my mind works like yours. Maybe I started to wonder what would have happened if she had found a physical outlet for her emotions instead of being afraid of them."

Grant nodded. "Okay. These couple of sentences in the margin . . . You wrote them?"

It didn't even look like her writing, but the blue cover had her name on it. She nodded.

There was something about Professor Grant that was different. The expression on his face was thoughtful, even troubled. Was he just trying to be nice to her? Maybe the paper was lousy after all.

The goldfish was swimming slowly, indifferently. "What happened to the others?" she asked.

"Some joker overfed them. They all died. Laurie, there is something I want to talk to you about . . ."

"I'd rather die from overeating than being smashed in a car, wouldn't you? At least you don't bleed. Oh, I'm sorry. What did you want to talk about?"

Allan Grant shook his head. "Nothing that won't keep. It isn't getting much better, is it?"

She knew what he meant.

"Sometimes I can honestly agree with the doctor that if there was any fault, it was with the bus with faulty brakes that was going much too fast. Other times, no."

The loud voice in her head shouted: *You robbed your mother and father of the rest of their lives just as you robbed them of two years when you waved at that funeral procession.*

She didn't want to cry in front of Professor Grant. He'd been so nice, but people got sick of always having to bolster you up. She stood up. "I . . . I have to go. Is there anything else?"

With troubled eyes, Allan Grant watched Laurie leave. It was too soon to be sure, but the term paper he was holding had given him the first solid clue as to the identity of the mysterious letter writer who signed herself "Leona."

There was a sensual theme in the paper that was totally unlike Laurie's usual style but similiar to the tone of the letters. It seemed to him that he recognized some unusually extravagant phrases as well. That wasn't proof, but at least it gave him a place to start looking.

Laurie Kenyon was the last person he'd have dreamt could be the writer of those letters. Her attitude toward him had been consistently that of a respectful student toward a teacher whom she admired and liked.

As Grant reached for his jacket, he decided he would say nothing to either Karen or the administration about his suspicions. Some of those letters were downright salacious. It would be embarrassing for any innocent person to be questioned about them, particularly a kid living through the kind of tragedy Laurie was. He turned out the light and started home.

From behind a row of evergreens, Leona watched him go, her nails digging into her palms.

Last night she had hidden outside his house again. As usual he'd left the draperies open, and she'd watched him for three hours. He'd heated a pizza around nine and brought it and a beer to his den. He'd stretched out in that old leather chair, kicked off his shoes and rested his feet on the ottoman.

He was reading a biography of George Bernard Shaw. It was so endearing the way Allan would run his hand through his hair unconsciously. He did it in class occasionally as well. When he finished the beer he looked at the empty glass, shrugged, then went into the kitchen and came back with a fresh one.

At eleven he watched the news then turned out the light and left the den. She knew he was going to bed. He always left the window open, but the bedroom draperies were drawn. Most nights she simply went away after he turned out the light, but one night she'd pulled at the handle of the sliding glass door and discovered that the lock didn't catch. Now some nights she went inside and curled up in his chair and pretended that in a minute he'd call her. "Hey, darling, come to bed. I'm lonesome."

Once or twice she'd waited till she was sure he was asleep and tiptoed in to look at him. Last night she was cold and very tired and went home after he turned out the den light.

Cold and very tired.

Cold.

Laurie rubbed her hands together. It had gotten so dark all of a sudden. She hadn't noticed how dark it was when she left Professor Grant's office a minute ago.

29

"Ridgewood is one of the finest towns in New Jersey," Betsy Lyons explained to the quietly dressed woman who was going over pictures of real estate properties with her. "Of course it is in the upscale price bracket, but even so, with market conditions as they are, there are some excellent buys around."

Opal nodded thoughtfully. It was the third time she had visited Lyons Realty. Her story was that her husband was being transferred to New York and she was doing preliminary househunting in New Jersey, Connecticut and Westchester.

"Let her get to trust you," Bic had instructed. "All these real estate agents are taught to keep an eye on prospective buyers so they don't get light-fingered when they're being shown around houses. Right off, tell whoever sees you that you're looking in different locations, then, after a visit or two, that you like New Jersey best. First time you go in, say you didn't want to go as high as Ridgewood prices. Then drop hints that you think it's a nice town and you really could afford it. Finally get her to show you Lee's house on one of the Fridays we come out. Distract her and then . . ."

It was early Friday afternoon. The plan was in motion. Opal had won Betsy Lyons's confidence. It was time to see the Kenyon place. The housekeeper was in on Monday and Friday mornings. She would be gone by now. The older sister was busy in court, involved in a highly publicized trial. Opal would be alone inside Lee's home with someone who would be off guard.

Betsy Lyons was an attractive woman in her early sixties. She loved her job and was good at it. She frequently bragged that she could spot a phony a mile away. "Listen, I don't waste my time," she would tell new agents. "Time is money. Don't think because people obviously can't afford the houses they want to see that you should automatically steer them away. Daddy might be sitting in the background with a bundle of cash he made in his 7-Eleven. On the other hand, don't assume because people look as though they can pay steep prices that they're really serious. Some of the wives just want to get inside pricey houses to see the decorating. *And never take your eyes off any of them.*"

The thing that Betsy Lyons liked about Carla Hawkins was that she was so on the level. Straight off, she'd put her cards on the table. She was looking in other locations. She didn't gush at every house she saw. Neither did she point out what was wrong with it. Some people did that whether or not they had any plans to buy. "The baths are too small." Sure, honey. You're used to a Jacuzzi in the bedroom.

Mrs. Hawkins asked intelligent questions about the houses that sparked mild interest in her. There was obviously money there. A good real estate agent learned to spot expensive clothes. The bottom line was that Betsy Lyons had a feeling that this could turn into a big sale.

"This is a particularly charming place," she said, pointing to the picture of an all-brick ranch house. "Nine rooms, only four years old, in mint condition, a fortune in landscaping and on a cul-de-sac."

Opal pretended interest, poring over the specifics listed under the picture. "That would be interesting," she said slowly, "but let's keep looking. Oh, what's this?" She had finally come to the page with the picture of the Kenyon home.

"Now if you want a really beautiful, roomy, comfortable house, this is a buy," Lyons said enthusiastically. "Over an acre of property, a swimming pool, four large bedrooms, each with its own bath; a living room, dining room, breakfast room, den and library on the main floor. Eight thousand square feet, crown molding, wainscoting, parquet floors, butler's pantry."

"Let's see both of these this morning," Opal suggested. "That's about as much as I'm up to with this ankle."

Bic had fastened an Ace bandage on her left ankle. "You tell that agent you sprained it," he told her. "Then when you say you must have dropped a glove up in one of the bedrooms she won't mind leaving you in the kitchen."

"I'll check about the ranch," Lyons said. "They have young children and want us to call ahead. I can go in the Kenyon place any weekday without notice."

They stopped at the ranch house first. Opal remembered to ask all the right questions. Finally they were on their way to the Kenyon home. Mentally she reviewed Bic's instructions.

"Rotten weather, isn't it," Lyons said as she drove through the quiet streets of Ridgewood. "But it's nice to think that spring is on the way. The Kenyon property is alive with flowering trees in the spring. Dogwood. Cherry blossoms. Mrs. Kenyon loved gardening and there are three blooms a year. Whoever gets this place will be lucky."

"Why is it being sold?" It seemed to Opal that it would be unnatural not to ask the question. She hated driving down this road. It reminded her of those two years. She remembered how her heart pounded when they turned at the pink corner house. That house was painted white now.

Lyons knew there was no use trying to hide the truth. Problem was, some people steered clear of a hard-luck house. Better to say it right out than let them nose around and find out for themselves was her motto. "There are just two sisters living here now," she said. "The parents were killed in an automobile accident last September. A bus slammed into them on Route 78." Skillfully she attempted to make Opal concentrate on the fact that the accident had taken place on Route 78 and not in the house.

They were turning into the driveway. Bic had told Opal to be sure to notice everything. He was real curious about the kind of place where Lee lived. They got out of the car, and Lyons fished for the key to the lock.

"This is the central foyer," she said as she opened the door. "See what I mean about a well-kept place? Isn't this beautiful?"

Be quiet, Opal wanted to tell her as they walked around the first floor. The living room was to the left. Archway. Big windows. Upholstery predominantly blue. Dark polished floor with a large Oriental and a contrasting small rug in front of the fireplace. Opal felt a nervous impulse to laugh. They had taken Lee from this place to that dumpy farm. Wonder she didn't crack up on the spot.

In the library, portraits lined the walls. "Those are the Kenyons," Betsy Lyons pointed out. "Handsome couple, weren't they? And those are watercolors of the girls when they were little. From the time Laurie was born, Sarah was always such a little mother to her. I don't know if, being in Georgia, you would have known about it but . . ."

As she heard the story of the disappearance seventeen years earlier, Opal felt her heart begin to race. On an end table there was a picture of Lee with an older girl. Lee was wearing the pink bathing suit she'd had on when they picked her up. With the cluster of framed photos in this room, it was crazy that her eye fell on that one. Bic was right. There was a reason why God had sent them here to be on guard against Lee now.

She chose to fake a sneeze, pull her handkerchief from her coat pocket and drop a glove in Lee's bedroom. Even if Betsy Lyons hadn't told her, it was easy to figure which one was Lee's. The sister's room was loaded with law books over the desk.

Opal followed Lyons down the stairs, then asked to see the kitchen again. "I love this kitchen," she sighed. "This house is a dream." At least that was honest, she thought with some amusement. "Now I'd really better be going. My ankle is telling me to stop walking." She sat on one of the tall stools in front of the island counter.

"Of course." Betsy Lyons could smell a potential sale warming up.

Opal reached in her coat pocket for her gloves, then frowned. "I know I had both of them when we came in." She fished in the other pocket, brought out her handkerchief. "Oh, I know. I bet when I sneezed, I pulled out my glove with the hankie. That was in the bedroom with the blue carpet." She began to slide from the stool.

"You wait right there," Betsy Lyons ordered. "I'll run up and look for it."

"Oh, would you?"

Opal waited until a faint padding on the staircase assured her that Lyons was on her way to the second floor. Then she jumped from the stool and raced to the row of blue-handled knives attached to the wall next to the stove. She grabbed the largest one, a long carving knife, and dropped it in her oversize shoulder bag.

She was back on the stool, slightly bent over, her hand rubbing her ankle, when Betsy Lyons returned to the kitchen, a triumphant smile on her face, the missing glove clutched in her fingers.

~ 30

The first part of the week had passed in a blur. Sarah worked through Thursday night, poring over her closing statement.

She read intently, clipping, inserting, preparing three-by-five cards with the highlights of the points she wanted to hammer at the jury. The morning light began to filter into the bedroom. At seven-fifteen, Sarah read her closing paragraph. "Ladies and gentlemen, Mr. Marcus is a skilled and experienced defense attorney. He hammered away at each of the witnesses who had been in the station that night. Admittedly it was not broad daylight but neither was it so dark they could not see James Parker's face. Every one of them had seen him approach and be rebuffed by Maureen Mays in the railroad station. Every one of them told you, without hesitation, that James Parker is the person who got into Maureen's car that night. . . .

"I would say, ladies and gentlemen, the evidence has shown to you beyond any reasonable doubt that James Parker murdered this fine young woman and forever robbed her husband, mother, father and siblings of her love and supeport.

"There is nothing any of us can do to bring her back, but what you, the jury, can do is to bring her murderer to justice."

She had covered all the points. The solid mass of evidence was undeniable. Still Conner Marcus was the best criminal attorney she'd ever been up against. And juries were unpredictable.

Sarah got up and stretched. The adrenaline that always pulsed through her body during a trial would reach fever pitch when she began her final arguments. She was counting on that.

She went into the bathroom and turned on the shower. It was a temptation to linger under the cascade of hot water. Her shoulders especially seemed to be tied up in knots. Instead she turned off the hot water and twisted the cold-water tap completely to the right. Grimacing, she endured the icy blast.

She toweled dry quickly, pulled on a long, thick terry-cloth robe, stuck her feet in slippers and ran downstairs to make coffee. While she waited for it to seep through the coffee maker, she did stretching exercises and looked around the kitchen. Betsy Lyons, the real estate agent, seemed to think that she had a hot prospect for the house. Sarah realized she was still ambivalent about selling it. She had told Lyons she absolutely would not lower the price.

The coffee was ready. She dug out her favorite mug, the one her squad of detectives gave her when she was the assistant prosecutor in charge of the sex-crimes unit. It was inscribed "For Sarah, who made sex so interesting." Her mother had not been amused.

She carried the coffee upstairs and sipped while she dabbed on a touch of lipstick, blusher and eyeshadow. That had become a morning ritual, a loving tribute to her mother. Mom, if you don't mind I'll look tailored today, she thought. But she knew Marie would have approved of the blue-and-gray tweed suit.

Her hair. A cloud of curls . . . no, a mass of frizz. Impatiently she brushed it. "The sun will come out tomorrow . . ." she sang softly. All I need is a red dress with a white collar and a dopey-looking dog.

She checked her briefcase. All her notes for the closing argument were there. This is it, she thought. She was almost at the bottom of the stairs when she heard the kitchen door open. "It's me, Sarah," Sophie called. Footsteps padded across the kitchen. "I have to go to the dentist, so I thought I'd come a bit early. Oh, you look nice."

"Thanks. You didn't have to come so early. After ten years, don't you think you should just take some time off when you need it?" They smiled at each other.

The prospect of the house being sold distressed Sophie, and she'd said as much.

"Unless, of course, you girls get an apartment near here so I can look after you," she'd told Sarah.

This morning she looked troubled. "Sarah, you know the good set of knives next to the stove?"

Sarah was buttoning her coat. "Yes."

"Did you take one of them out for anything?"

"No."

"I just noticed the biggest carving knife is missing. It's the queerest thing."

"Oh, it's got to be around somewhere."

"Well, I can't tell you where."

Sarah felt suddenly uneasy. "When was the last time you saw it?"

"I'm not sure. I missed it on Monday and began looking around. It isn't in the kitchen, I'll tell you that. How long it's been gone, I have no idea." Sophie hesitated. "I don't suppose Laurie would have had any use for it at school?"

Sophie knew about the knife dream. "I hardly think so." Sarah swallowed over the sudden constriction in her throat. "Got to run." As she opened the door, she said, "If, by any chance, you come across that knife, leave a message for me at the office, will you? Just a simple 'I found it.' Okay?"

She saw the compassion in Sophie's face. She thinks Laurie took it, Sarah thought. My God!

Frantically she ran to the phone and dialed Laurie's number. A sleepy voice. Laurie had picked up on the first ring.

"Sarah? Sure. I'm fine. In fact I got a couple of my marks back. They're good. Let's celebrate somehow."

Relieved, Sarah hung up and rushed outside to the garage. A four-car garage with only her car in it. Laurie always left hers in the driveway. The other empty spaces were a constant reminder of the accident.

As she pulled out, she decided that for the moment Laurie sounded okay. Tonight she'd call Dr. Carpenter and Dr. Donnelly and tell them about the knife. But now she had to put it out of her mind. It wasn't fair to Maureen Mays or her family to do less than her best in court today. But why in the name of God would Laurie take the carving knife?

31

"Sarah's jury is still out," Laurie told Dr. Carpenter as she sat across from him in his office. "I envy her. She's so committed to what she does, to being a prosecutor, that she can block out everything she doesn't want to think about."

Carpenter waited. The temperature had changed. Laurie was different. It was the first time he had seen her express hostility toward Sarah. There was pent-up anger flashing in her eyes. Something had happened between her and Sarah. "I've been reading about that case," he said mildly.

"I'll bet you have. Sarah the prosecutor. But she's not as subtle as she thinks she is."

Again he waited. "I no sooner got home last night than she came in. All apologies. Sorry she hadn't been home to welcome me. Big sister. I said, 'Look, Sarah, at some point even I have to take care of myself. I'm twenty-one, not four.' "

"Four?"

"That's the age I was when she should have stayed home from her damn party. I wouldn't have been kidnapped if she'd stayed home."

"You've always blamed yourself for being kidnapped, Laurie."

"Oh, me too. But big sister had a hand in it. I bet she hates me."

Dr. Carpenter had intended as one of his goals to wean Laurie away from dependence on her sister, but this was something new. It was like being with a totally different patient. "Why would she hate you?"

"She has no time for a life of her own. You should have *her* as a patient. Boy, that would be something to hear! All her life being big sister. I read her old diary this morning. She's been keeping one since she was a little kid. She wrote a lot about me being kidnapped and then coming back and that she thought I was different. I guess I really chilled her out." There was satisfaction in Laurie's tone.

"Do you make it a habit to go through Sarah's diaries?"

The look Laurie gave him was pure pity. "You're the one who wants to know what everyone is thinking. What makes you better?"

It was the way she was sitting, the belligerent posture, knees pressed together, hands grasping the arms of the chair, head thrust forward, features rigid. Where was the soft, troubled young face, the hesitant Jackie Onassis voice?

"That's a good question, but I don't have any one-sentence answer to it. Why are you annoyed at Sarah?"

"The knife. Sarah thinks I sneaked a carving knife out of the kitchen."

"Why would she think that?"

"Only because it's missing. I sure as hell didn't take it. Sophie, our housekeeper, started the whole thing. I mean I don't mind admitting that a lot of things fall in my camp, but not this one, Doc."

"Did Sarah accuse you or just ask you about the knife? There's a big difference, you know."

"Buddy, I know an accusation when I hear one."

"I had the feeling that you were afraid of knives. Was I wrong, Laurie?"

"I wish you'd call me Kate."

"Kate? Any reason?"

"Kate sounds better than Laurie—more mature. Anyhow, my middle name is Katherine."

"That could be very positive. Putting away of childish things. Is that the way you feel now, that you're putting away childish things?"

"No. I just don't want to be afraid of knives."

"I was under the strong impression that you were desperately afraid of them."

"Oh no. Not me. Laurie is afraid of everything. A knife is her 'worst-case scenario.' You know, Doctor, there are some people who bring grief and pain to the rest of the universe. Our gal Laurie, for example."

Dr. Peter Carpenter realized that he now knew that Kate was the name of one of Laurie Kenyon's alter personalities.

~ 32

On Saturday morning they parked near Dr. Carpenter's office. Bic had deliberately rented the same color late-model Buick that Laurie drove. Only the interior was a different shade of leather. "If anyone happens to question my opening this door, I'll point to the other car," he explained, then answered her unspoken question. "We have observed that Lee never locks her car. Her tote bag filled with textbooks is always on the floor of the front seat. I'll just slip in that knife right at the bottom. Doesn't matter when she finds it. The point is that she's sure to come across it soon. Just a little reminder for her of what happens if she starts thinking on us with her head doctor. And now do what you must do, Opal."

Lee always left Dr. Carpenter's office at exactly five of twelve. At six of twelve Opal casually opened the door of the private entrance to his upstairs office. A narrow foyer with a flight of stairs led to his suite. She glanced around as though she'd made a mistake and meant to use the main door of the professional building at the corner of Ridgewood Avenue. There was no one on the stairs. Quickly she unwrapped the small package she was holding, dropped its contents in the center of the foyer and left. Bic was already in the rented car.

"A blind person couldn't miss it," Opal told him.

"Nobody was paying any attention to you," he assured her. "Now we'll just wait here a minute and see what happens."

Laurie stamped down the stairs. She was going directly back to college. Who the hell needed to be sitting having her head taken apart? Who needed to be fussed over by long-suffering Sarah? That was something else. It was time she concentrated on those trust funds and knew exactly how much money she was worth. Plenty. And when the house sold, she didn't want any talk of other people investing it for her. She was sick of having to deal with the wimp who said "Yes, Sarah; no, Sarah; whatever you say, Sarah."

She was at the bottom of the stairs. Her boot touched something soft, something squishy. She looked down.

The lifeless eye of a chicken stared up at her. Straggly feathers clung to its skull. The severed neck was crusted with dried blood.

Outside, Bic and Opal heard the first screams. Bic smiled. "Sound familiar?" He turned the key in the ignition, then whispered, "But now I should be comforting her."

33

The jury was filing in when Sarah's secretary hurried into the courtroom. Word had spread that a verdict had been reached, and there was a scramble for seats. Sarah's heart pounded as the judge asked, "Mr. Foreman, has the jury agreed upon a verdict?"

"Yes we have, your Honor."

This is it, Sarah thought as she stood at the prosecution table, facing the bench. She felt a tug on her arm and turned to see her secretary, Janet. "Not now," she said firmly, surprised that Janet would interrupt when a verdict was being rendered.

"Sarah, I'm sorry. A Dr. Carpenter has taken your sister to the emergency room of Hackensack Medical Center. She's in shock."

Sarah gripped the pen she was holding until her knuckles turned white. The judge was looking at her, clearly annoyed. She whispered, "Tell him I'll be there in a few minutes."

"On the charge of murder what is your verdict, guilty or not guilty?"

"Guilty, your Honor."

A cry of "not fair!" went up from the family and friends of James Parker. The Judge rapped his gavel, warned against further outbursts, ascertained that the verdict was unanimous and began to poll the jury.

Bail was revoked for James Parker. A sentencing date was set and he was led away in handcuffs. Court was adjourned. Sarah had no time to relish her victory. Janet was in the corridor holding her coat and shoulder bag. "Now you can go right to your car."

Dr. Carpenter was waiting for her in the emergency room. Briefly he explained what had happened. "Laurie had just left my office. As she approached the outside door on the ground floor, she began to scream. By the time we reached her, she had fainted. She was in deep shock but she's coming around now."

"What caused it?" The concerned kindness of the doctor brought hot tears to the back of Sarah's eyes. There was something about Carpenter that reminded her of her father. She longed for him to be with her now.

"Apparently she stepped on the head of a dead chicken, became hysterical then went into shock."

"The head of a chicken! In the lobby of your office!"

"Yes. I have a deeply disturbed patient who is involved in a cult and this is the sort of thing he would do. Does Laurie have an inordinate fear of chickens or mice or any animals?"

"No. Except she never eats chicken. She loathes the taste of it."

A nurse came out of the curtained-off area. "You can go in."

Laurie was lying quietly. Her eyes were closed. Sarah touched her hand. "Laurie."

Slowly she opened her eyes. It seemed to be an effort, and Sarah realized that she must be heavily sedated. Her voice was weak but crystal clear as she said, "Sarah, I'll kill myself before I see that doctor again."

34

Allan was in the kitchen eating a sandwich.

"Sweetie, I'm sorry I didn't get down last night, but it was really important to prepare my pitch for the Wharton account." Karen threw her arms around his neck.

He pecked at her cheek and stepped back from her embrace. "That's okay. Want some lunch?"

"You should have waited. I'd have taken care of that."

"You could have been another hour."

"You never care about food." Karen Grant poured Chianti from the decanter and handed a glass to Allan. She clinked her glass against his. "Cheers, darling."

"Cheers," he said unsmilingly.

"Hey, Professor, something's wrong."

"What's wrong is that as of about an hour ago, I became certain that Laurie Kenyon is the mysterious Leona, the one writing those letters."

Karen gasped. "You're absolutely sure?"

"Yes, I was grading papers. The one she turned in had a note attached that her computer went on the blink and she had to finish it on the old portable typewriter she keeps as a backup. There's no question it's the same one the letters were written on—including the one that came yesterday." He reached in his pocket and handed it to Karen.

It read: "Allan, my dearest, I'll never forget tonight. I love to watch you sleep. I love to see the way you turn and scrunch up when you're getting more comfortable, the way you pull up the covers. Why do you let the room get so cold? I shut the window a little. Did you notice, darling? I'll bet not. In some ways you could be the prototype for the absentminded professor. But only in some ways. Don't ever permit me to be absent from your mind. Always remember. If your wife doesn't want you enough to be with you all the time, I do. My love to you. Leona."

Karen reread the letter slowly. "Good Lord, Allan, do you think that girl actually came in here?"

"I don't think so. She certainly fantasizes all those trysts in my office. She's fantasizing this too."

"I'm not sure about that. Come on."

He followed her into the bedroom. Karen stood in front of the long window. She reached for the crank and turned it. The window opened outward noiselessly. She easily stepped over the low sill onto the ground then turned to him. Her hair blew in her face as a draft of cold air sent the curtain whirling. "Easy to get in, easy to get out," she said as she stepped back into the room. "Allan, maybe she is fantasizing, but she could have been here. You sleep like a dead man. From now on you can't leave that window open so wide."

"This has gone far enough. I'm damned if I'll change my sleeping habits. I've got to talk to Sarah Kenyon. I'm terribly sorry for Laurie, but Sarah has got to get her whatever help she needs."

He reached Sarah's answering machine and left a brief message: "It really is very important that I talk to you."

At two-thirty Sarah returned the call. Karen listened as Allan's voice changed from cool to solicitous. "Sarah, what's the matter? Laurie? Has anything happened to her?" He waited. "Oh God, that's lousy. Sarah, don't cry. I know how tough this has been for you. She'll be okay. Give it some time. No, I just wanted to see how you thought she was doing. Sure. Talk to you soon. 'Bye."

He replaced the receiver and turned to Karen. "Laurie's in the hospital. She had some sort of shock reaction on her way out of the shrink's office. I guess she's okay now, but they wanted her to stay overnight. Her sister is about at the end of her rope."

"Will Laurie come back to school?"

"She's determined to be here on Monday for classes." He shrugged helplessly. "Karen, I couldn't lay these letters on Sarah Kenyon now."

"You will turn them over to the office?"

"Of course. I'm sure Dean Larkin will have one of the psychologists speak to Laurie. I know she goes to a psychiatrist in Ridgewood, but maybe she needs counseling here as well. The poor kid."

35

Laurie was propped up in bed reading the Bergen *Record* when Sarah arrived at the hospital late Sunday morning. Her greeting to Sarah was cheerful. "Hi. You brought the clothes. Terrific. I'll get dressed and let's go to the club for brunch."

It was what she had said she wanted to do when she'd phoned an hour earlier. "Are you sure it won't be too much for you?" Sarah asked anxiously. "You were pretty sick yesterday."

"It may be too much for *you.* Oh, Sarah, why don't you move and not leave a forwarding address? Honest to God, I'm such a damn nuisance to you." Her smile was both apologetic and rueful as Sarah bent down and hugged her.

Sarah had come in not knowing what to expect. But this was the real Laurie, sorry if she put anyone out, ready to have fun. "You look better than you have in ages," she said sincerely.

"They gave me something, and I slept like a rock."

"It's a mild sleeping pill. Dr. Carpenter has ordered that and an antidepressant for you."

Laurie stiffened. "Sarah, I wouldn't let him give me any pills, and he's been trying. You know I hate those things. But I will do *this:* I'll start the pills. But no more therapy, ever."

"You *will* have to check with Dr. Carpenter about any reaction to the medication."

"Over the phone. That I don't mind."

"And Laurie, you know Dr. Carpenter consulted with a psychiatrist, Dr. Donnelly, in New York about you. If you won't see him, will you allow me to talk to him?"

"Oh, Sarah, I wish you wouldn't, but okay, if it makes you happy." Laurie jumped out of bed. "Let's get out of this place."

In the club friends invited them to join their table. Laurie ate well and was in good spirits. Looking at her, Sarah found it hard to believe that only yesterday she herself had been near despair. She winced thinking of how she had been crying on the phone with that nice Professor Grant.

When they left the club, Sarah did not drive directly home. Instead she went in the opposite direction.

Laurie raised an eyebrow. "Where?"

"About ten minutes from the house. Glen Rock. They're about to open up some condominiums that are supposed to be great. I thought we'd take a look."

"Sarah, maybe we should just rent for a while. I mean, suppose you decide to go with a law firm in New York? You've had offers. Anyplace we live should be tied to you, not me. If I do give a shot at pro golf I'll be following the sun."

"I'm not going with a private firm. Laurie, when I sit with the families of these victims and I see their grief and anger, I know that I can't work on the other side looking for one damn loophole in the law to set them free. I can sleep a lot better prosecuting murderers than defending them."

There was a model with three levels that they both liked. "Nice layout," Sarah commented. "Dearly as I love the house, those up-to-date bathrooms are something else." She told the agent who was showing them around, "We seem to have serious interest in our home. When we know we have a sale we'll be back."

She linked her arm companionably with Laurie's as they walked to the car. It was a clear, cold day and the light wind had a bite. Even so there was a sense that spring was only six weeks away. "Nice grounds," Sarah commented. "And just think. We wouldn't have to worry about having them tended. Happy thought, isn't it?"

"Dad loved puttering outside and Mom was happiest on her knees in the garden. Wonder how we both missed it?" Laurie's tone was affectionate and amused.

Was she beginning to be able to talk about their parents without instantly being reduced to raw pain and self-recrimination? Please God, Sarah thought prayerfully. They reached the parking lot. It was busy with prospective buyers coming and going. Word of mouth about the new section of the Fox Hedge condos had been excellent. Laurie spoke hurriedly. "Sarah, let me say just one thing. When we get home, I don't want to talk about yesterday. The house has gotten to be a place where you study me with such a worried expression, where you ask questions that are not as casual as they seem. From now on, don't grill me about how I sleep, what I eat, do I date, that kind of thing. Let *me* tell you what I want to talk about. You do the same with me. Okay?"

"Okay," Sarah said matter-of-factly. You *have* been treating her like a little kid who has to tell Mommy everything, she told herself. Maybe it's a good sign that she's starting to resent it. But what happened yesterday?

It was as though Laurie could read her mind. "Sarah, I don't know what made me faint yesterday. I do know that it's a terrible ordeal to have Dr. Carpenter keep after me with leading questions that are nothing but traps. It's like trying to lock all the doors and windows when an intruder is breaking in."

"He's not an intruder. He's a healer. But you're not ready for him. Agreed on everything."

"Good."

Sarah drove past the security guards at the gate, noticing how all arriving cars were stopped and checked. Laurie had obviously taken that in as well. She said, "Sarah, let's put a deposit on that corner unit. I'd love to live here. With that gate and those guards, we'd be safe. I want to feel safe. And that's what scares me so much. I never do."

They were on the road. The car began to pick up momentum. Sarah had to ask the question that was torturing her. "Is that why you took the knife? Was it necessary for you to have it in order to feel safe? Laurie, I can understand that. Just as long as you don't let yourself get so depressed that you'd . . . hurt yourself. I'm so sorry to ask, but that's what scares me."

Laurie sighed. "Sarah, I have no intention of committing suicide. I know that's what you're getting at. I do wish you could believe me. On my oath, I did *not* take that knife!"

That night, back at college, in order to repack her tote bag Laurie dumped its contents on her bed. Textbooks, spiral pads, and loose-leaf binders tumbled out. The very last object was the one that had been concealed at the bottom of the deep carryall. It was the missing carving knife from the set on the kitchen wall.

Laurie backed away from the bed. "No! No! No!" She sank to her knees and buried her face in her hands. "I didn't take it Sare-wuh," she sobbed. "Daddy said I mustn't play with knives."

A jeering voice crashed through her mind. *Oh, shut up, kid. You know why you have it. Why not take the hint and stick it in your throat. God, I need a cigarette.*

36

Gregg Bennett told himself that he didn't give a damn. Being honest, what he really meant was that he *shouldn't* give a damn. There were plenty of attractive women on this campus. He'd be meeting plenty more in California. He'd have his degree in June and be on his way to Stanford to study for his MBA.

At twenty-five Gregg was and felt considerably older than his fellow students. He still looked back in bewilderment at the nineteen-year-old dope who had quit college after his freshman year to become an entrepreneur. Not that the experience had hurt. Even getting his ears pinned back had been a long-range blessing. If nothing else he found out exactly how much he didn't know. He'd also learned that international finance was the career for him.

He'd been back from England a month and the January blahs had by now caught up with him. At least he'd been able to get in some skiing at Camelback over the weekend. The powder snow had made the runs great.

Gregg lived in a studio apartment over the garage of a private home two miles from the campus. It was a nice setup that suited him well. He had no desire to share a place with three or four other guys and end up with constant partying. This place was clean and airy; the pullout couch was comfortable for both sitting and sleeping; he could prepare simple meals in the kitchenette.

When he first arrived at Clinton, he'd noticed Laurie around the campus. Who wouldn't? But they'd never been in a class together. Then, a year and a half ago they'd sat next to each other in the auditorium at a showing of *Cinema Paradiso.* The picture had been terrific. As the lights went on, she turned to him and asked, "Wasn't that wonderful?"

That was the beginning. If a girl that attractive gave him the signal that she wanted him to come on to her, Gregg was more than willing to make the next move. But there was something about Laurie that held him back. He'd known instinctively that he'd get nowhere if he tried anything too quickly; as a result, their relationship had developed more as a friendship. She was so darn sweet. Not sugar sweet—she could be bitingly funny and she could be strong-willed. On their third date he told her that it was obvious she'd been a spoiled kid. They'd gone golfing and the starter had overbooked. They had to wait an extra hour for tee-off time. She'd been sore.

"I bet you never had to wait. I bet Mommy and Daddy called you their little princess," he had told her. She'd laughed and said, actually they had. Over dinner that night she told him about having been abducted. "The last thing I remember was standing in front of my house in a pink bathing suit and someone picking me up. The next thing, I woke up in my own bed. The only problem is that was two years later."

"I'm sorry I said you were spoiled," he'd told her. "You deserved to be."

She'd laughed. "I was spoiled before and after. You hit the nail on the head."

Gregg knew that to Laurie he was a trusted friend. It wasn't that simple for him. You don't spend a lot of time with a girl who looks like Laurie, he thought, with that marvelous ripple of blond hair, those midnight blue eyes and perfect features, without wanting to spend all the time you'll ever have with her. But then when she started inviting him home some weekends, he'd been sure she had begun to fall in love too.

Then suddenly it came to an end one Sunday morning last May. He remembered it clearly. He had slept late, and Laurie took it into her head to stop by after church with bagels and cream cheese and smoked salmon. She rapped on the door, then when he didn't hear, yelled, "I know you're in there."

He grabbed a robe, opened the door and just looked at her. She was wearing a linen dress and sandals and looking cool and fresh as the morning itself. She came in, put on the coffee, set out the bagels and told him not to bother making up the bed. She was driving home and could only stay a few minutes. After she left, he could sack out all day if he wanted.

When she was leaving, she put her arms around his neck and kissed him lightly, telling him he needed a shave. "But I still like your looks," she'd teased. "Nice nose, strong chin, cute cowlick." She'd kissed him again, then turned to go. That was when it had happened. Impulsively Gregg followed her to the door, put his hands on her arms, swooped her up and hugged her. She went crazy. Sobbing. Kicking her legs to push him away. He dropped her, angrily asked her what the hell was the matter. Did she think he was Jack the Ripper? She ran out of the apartment and never even spoke to him again except to tell him to leave her alone.

He would have liked to do just that. The only problem was that over last summer, working an internship in New York, and during the fall term, studying at the Banking Institute in London, he'd never gotten her out of his mind. Now that he was back, she was still adamant about refusing to see him.

On Monday evening Gregg wandered over to the cafeteria at the student center. He knew Laurie sometimes dropped by there. He deliberately joined a group that included some of the people from her residence. "It makes sense," one of them was saying at the other end of the table. "Laurie goes out about nine o'clock a lot of weeknights. His wife stays in New York during the week. I tried kidding Laurie about it, but she just ignored me. Obviously she was meeting someone but she sure wasn't talking about it."

Gregg's ears pricked up. Casually he moved his chair to hear better.

"Anyhow, Margy works afternoons in the administration office. She picks up a lot of dirt and knew something was up when Sexy Allan came in looking worried."

"I don't think Grant is sexy. I think he's just a very nice guy." The objection came from a dark-haired student with an air of common sense about her.

The gossiper waved aside the objection. "*You* may not think he's sexy, but a lot of people do. Anyhow, Laurie certainly does. I hear she's been sending him a bunch of love letters and signing them 'Leona.' He turned the letters over to the administration and claims that everything in them is fantasy. Maybe he's afraid if she's writing to him about their little romance she might be blabbing to other people too. I guess he's making a preemptive strike before anything gets back to his wife."

"What did she write?"

"What *didn't* she write? According to the letters, they were making out in his office, his house, you name it."

"No kidding!"

"Well, his wife's away a lot. These things happen. Remember how at her parents' funeral, he went racing down the aisle after her when she fainted?"

Gregg Bennett did not bother to pick up the chair that he knocked over as he strode from the cafeteria.

37

When Laurie checked her mail on Tuesday, she found a note asking her to phone the Dean of Student Affairs for an appointment at her earliest convenience. What's that about? she wondered. When she made the call, the dean's secretary asked if she was free to come in at three o'clock that day.

At the end of the ski season last year, she'd bought a blue-and-white ski jacket on sale. It had hung in her closet unused this winter. Why not, she thought as she reached for it. Perfect for this weather, it's pretty and I might as well get some use out of it. She matched it with blue jeans and a white turtleneck sweater.

At the last minute she twisted her hair into a chignon. Might as well look like the sophisticated senior about to leave the halls of learning for the great world outside. Maybe when she was out of the college atmosphere and among working adults she'd lose this crazy feeling of being a scared kid.

It was another cold, clear day, the kind that made her take deep breaths and throw back her shoulders. It was such a relief to know that Saturday morning she wouldn't be sitting in that damn office with Dr. Carpenter trying to look kindly but always probing, always digging.

She waved to a group of students from her residence then wondered if they were looking at her in a funny kind of way. Don't be silly, she told herself.

The knife. How had it gotten to the bottom of her tote bag? She certainly hadn't put it there. But would Sarah believe her? "Look, Sarah, the stupid thing was stuck between my books. Here it is. Problem solved."

And Sarah would reasonably ask, "How did it get in your bag?" Then she'd probably suggest talking to Dr. Carpenter again.

The knife was in the back of the closet now, hidden in the sleeve of an old jacket. The elastic cuff would keep it from falling. Should she simply throw it away, let the mystery go unsolved? But Dad valued that set of knives and always said they could cut anything clean as a whistle. Laurie hated the thought of something being cut clean as a whistle.

As she walked across the campus to the administration building she mulled over the best way to place the knife back in the house.

Hide it in a kitchen cupboard? But Sarah had said that Sophie had looked everywhere in the kitchen for it.

An idea came to her that seemed simple and foolproof: Sophie was always looking for things to polish. Sometimes she'd take the knives down and do them when she was going over the silver flatware. That was it, Laurie thought! I'll sneak the knife into the silver chest in the dining room, way to the back so it won't be seen easily. Even if Sophie had looked there, she might think she'd missed it. The point was Sarah would know that was at least a good possibility.

The solution brought relief until inside her head a derisive voice shouted, *Very clever, Laurie, but how do you explain the knife to yourself? Do you think it jumped into your bag?* The mocking laugh made her curl her fingers into fists.

"Shut up!" she whispered fiercely. "Go away and leave me alone."

Dean Larkin was not alone. Dr. Iovino, the Director of the Counseling Center, was with him. Laurie stiffened when she saw him. A voice in her mind shouted, *Be careful. Another shrink. What are they trying to pull now?*

Dean Larkin invited her to sit down, asked her how she was feeling, how her classes were going, reminded her that everyone was aware of the terrible tragedy in her family and that he wanted her always to understand that the entire faculty had the deepest concern for her well-being.

Then he said he'd excuse himself. Dr. Iovino wanted to have a little talk with her.

The dean closed the door behind him. Dr. Iovino smiled and said, "Don't look scared, Laurie. I just wanted to talk to you about Professor Grant. What do you think of him?"

That was easy. "I think he's wonderful," Laurie said. "He's a great teacher and he's been a good friend."

"A good friend."

"Of course."

"Laurie, it's not uncommon for students to develop a certain attachment to a faculty member. In a case like yours, where you especially needed compassion and kindness, it would be unusual if in loneliness and grief you didn't misinterpret that kind of relationship. Fantasize about it. What you daydreamed it *might* be, became in your mind what it *is.* That's very understandable."

"What are you *talking* about?" Laurie realized that she sounded like her mother the time she became annoyed at a waiter who had suggested he'd like to phone Laurie for a date.

The psychologist handed her a stack of letters. "Laurie, did you write these letters?"

She skimmed them, her eyes widening. "These are signed by someone named Leona. What in the world gave you the idea I wrote them?"

"Laurie, you have a typewriter, don't you?"

"I write my assignments on a computer."

"But you do *have* a typewriter?"

"Yes, I do. My mother's old portable."

"Do you keep it here?

"Yes. As a backup. Every once in a while, the computer has gone down when I had an assignment due."

"You turned in this term paper last week?"

She glanced at it. "Yes, I did."

"Notice that the *o* and *w* are broken wherever they appear on these pages. Now check that against the broken *o* and *w* that regularly appear in the letters to Professor Grant. They were typed on the same machine."

Laurie stared at Dr. Iovino. His face became superimposed with the face of Dr. Carpenter. *Inquisitors! Bastards!*

Dr. Iovino, heavyset, his manner one of all-is-well-don't-worry, said, "Laurie, comparing the signature 'Leona' with the written addenda to your term paper shows a great similarity in the handwriting."

The voice shouted: *He's not only a shrink. He's a handwriting expert now.*

Laurie stood up. "Dr. Iovino, as a matter of fact, I've let a number of people use that typewriter. I feel this conversation is nothing short of insulting. I am shocked that Professor Grant leapt to the conclusion that I wrote this trash. I'm shocked that you would send for me to discuss it. My sister is a prosecutor. I've seen her in court. She would make mincemeat of the kind of 'evidence' that you purport connects me with these disgusting outpourings."

She picked up the letters and threw them across the desk. "I expect a written apology, and if this has leaked out just as everything that happens in this office seems to leak out, I demand a public apology and retraction of this stupid accusation. As for Professor Grant, I considered him a good friend, an understanding friend at this very difficult time in my life. Clearly I was wrong. Clearly the students who call him 'Sexy Allan' and gossip about his flirtatious attitude are right. I intend to tell him that myself, immediately." She turned and walked rapidly from the room.

She was due in Allan Grant's class at 3:45. It was now 3:30. With any luck she'd catch him in the hallway. It was too late to go to his office.

She was waiting when he strode down the corridor. His cheery greetings to other students as he made his way to the classroom ended when he spotted her. "Hi, Laurie." He sounded nervous.

"Professor Grant, where did you get the preposterous idea that I wrote those letters to you?"

"Laurie, I know what a tough time you've been having and . . ."

"And you thought you'd make it easier by telling Dean Larkin that I was fantasizing sleeping with you? Are you crazy?"

"Laurie, don't be upset. Look, we're getting an audience. Why don't you see me in my office after class?"

"So we can strip for each other and I can see your gorgeous body and satisfy my lust for it?" Laurie did not care that people were stopping and listening to their exchange. "You are disgusting. You are going to regret this." She spat out the words. "As God is my witness, you are going to regret this."

She broke through the crowd of stunned students and ran back to the dorm. She locked the door, fell on the bed and listened to the voices that were now shouting at her.

One said, *Well at least you stood up for yourself for a change.*

The other screamed, *How could Allan have betrayed me? He was warned not to show those letters to anyone. You bet he's going to regret it. It's a good thing you have the knife. Kiss-and-Tell will never have to worry about hearing from us again.*

38

Bic and Opal flew to Georgia directly after the Sunday program. That night there was a farewell banquet for them.

On Tuesday morning they started driving to New York. In the trunk were Bic's typewriter, their luggage and a can of gasoline carefully wrapped in towels. No other personal possessions would be forwarded. "When we pick a house, we'll get ourselves a state-of-the-art entertainment center," Bic decreed. Till then they would live in the suite at the Wyndham.

As they drove, Bic explained his reasoning to Opal. "That case I told you, where a grown-up woman remembered something her daddy did and Daddy's in prison now. She had vivid memories of what happened in her house and in the van. Now suppose the Lord tests us by allowing Lee to start remembering little bits of our life with her. Suppose she talks about the farmhouse, the way the rooms are laid out, the short steps to the upstairs? Suppose somehow they find it and start going back to see who rented it those years? That house is visible proof that she was under our protection. Other than that, well, Lee's a troubled woman. No one ever saw her with us 'cept that cashier who couldn't describe us. So we got to get rid of the house. The Lord has dictated that."

It was dark when they drove through Bethlehem and arrived in Elmville. Even so they were able to see that little had changed in the fifteen years since they'd left. The shabby diner off the highway, the one gas station, the row of frame houses whose porch lights revealed peeling paint and sagging steps.

Bic avoided Main Street and drove a circuitous route the five miles to the farm. As they neared it, he turned off the headlights. "Don't want anyone to happen to get a look at this car," he said. "Not likely of course. There's never anyone on this road."

"Suppose a cop comes along?" Opal was worried. "Suppose he asks why you don't have lights on?"

Bic sighed. "Opal, you have no faith. The Lord is caring for us. Besides, the only places this road leads to are swamps and the farm." But when they reached the farmhouse, he did drive the car behind a clump of trees.

There was no sign of life. "Curious?" Bic asked. "Want to take a peek?"

"I just want to get out of here."

"Come with me, Opal." It was a command.

Opal felt herself sliding on the ice-crusted ground and reached for Bic's arm.

There was no sign that anyone was living in the house. It was totally dark. Windowpanes were broken. Bic turned the door handle. The door was locked, but when he pressed his shoulder against it, it squeaked open.

Bic set down the gasoline can and took a pencil-thin flashlight from his pocket. He directed the beam of light around the room. "Looks pretty much the same," he observed. "They sure didn't refurnish. That's the very rocking chair where I used to sit with Lee on my lap. Sweet, sweet child."

"Bic, I want to get out of here. It's cold and this place always gave me the creeps. That whole two years I was always so worried someone would come along and see her."

"No one did. And now if this place exists in her memory that's the only place it will exist. Opal, I'm going to sprinkle this gasoline around. Then we'll go outside and you can light the match."

They were in the car and moving rapidly away when the first flames shot above the tree line. Ten minutes later they were back on the highway. They had not encountered another car in their half-hour visit to Elmville.

39

On Monday Sarah had been interviewed by *The New York Times* and the Bergen *Record* about the Parker conviction. "I realize that he has a right to argue that the victim was the enticer, but in this case, it makes my blood boil."

"Are you sorry you didn't ask for the death penalty?"

"If I'd thought I could have made it stick, I would have asked for it. Parker stalked Mays. He cornered her. He killed her. Tell me that isn't cold-blooded, premeditated murder."

In the office, her boss, the Bergen County prosecutor, led the congratulations. "Conner Marcus is one of the two or three best criminal defense attorneys in this country, Sarah. You did a hell of a job. You could make yourself a bundle if you wanted to switch to the other side of the courtroom."

"Defend them? No way!"

Tuesday morning the phone rang as Sarah settled at her desk. Betsy Lyons, the real estate agent, was bubbling with news. There was another potential buyer seriously interested in the house. Problem was the woman was pregnant and anxious to get settled before the new baby arrived. How soon would the house be available if they decided to buy?

"As fast as they want it," Sarah said. Making that commitment felt as if she were taking a weight off her shoulders. Furniture or anything else she and Laurie decided to keep could be stored.

Tom Byers, a thirty-year-old attorney who was making a name for himself in the patent infringement field, poked his head in. "Sarah, congratulations. Can I buy you a drink tonight?"

"Sure." She liked Tom a lot. It would be fun to have a drink with him. But he'd never be special, she thought, as Justin Donnelly's face popped into her mind.

* * *

It was seven-thirty when she unlocked the front door of the house. Tom had suggested going on to dinner, but she'd taken a rain check. The unwinding process that always followed an intense trial had been taking place all afternoon, and as she told Tom, "My bones are starting to ache."

She changed immediately to pajamas and a matching robe, stuck her feet in slippers and looked in the refrigerator. Bless Sophie, she thought. There was a small pot roast already cooked. Vegetables, potatoes and gravy were in individual plastic-wrapped dishes waiting to be heated.

She was just about to carry the dinner tray into the den when Allan Grant phoned. Sarah's cheerful greeting died on her lips as she heard him say, "Sarah, I started to tell you this the other day. I know now that it wasn't fair not to warn both you and Laurie before I went to the administration."

"Warn about what?"

As she listened, Sarah felt her knees go weak. Holding the receiver with one hand, she pulled out a kitchen chair and sat down. The typewriter. The letters Laurie had been writing on the cruise and the way she'd been so secretive about them. When Allan told her about his confrontation with Laurie, Sarah closed her eyes and wished she could close her ears instead. Allan concluded, "Sarah, she needs help, a lot of help. I know she's seeing a psychiatrist, but . . ."

Sarah did not tell Allan Grant that Laurie had refused to continue seeing Dr. Carpenter. "I . . . I can't tell you how sorry I am, Professor Grant," she said. "You've been so kind to Laurie, and this is very difficult for you. I'll call her. I'll somehow find whatever help she needs." Her voice broke. "Goodbye. Thank you."

There was no way she could put off talking to Laurie, but what was the best approach to take? She dialed Justin Donnelly's home number. There was no answer.

She reached Dr. Carpenter. His questions were brief. "Laurie adamantly denies writing the letters? I see. No, she's not lying. She's blocking. Sarah, call her, reassure her of your support, suggest she come home. I don't think it's wise for her to be around Professor Grant. We've got to get her in to see Dr. Donnelly. I knew that at the Saturday session."

The dinner was forgotten. Sarah dialed Laurie's room. There was no answer. She tried every half hour until midnight. Finally she phoned Susan Grimes, the student who roomed across the hall from Laurie.

Susan's sleepy voice became instantly alert when Sarah identified herself. Yes, she knew what had happened. Of course she'd look in on Laurie.

While she waited, Sarah realized she was praying. Don't let her have done anything to herself. Please God, not that. She heard the sound of the receiver being picked up.

"I looked in. Laurie's fast asleep. I can tell; she's breathing evenly. Do you want me to wake her up?"

Relief flooded through Sarah. "I'll bet she took a sleeping pill. No, don't disturb her and please forgive me for bothering you."

Exhausted, Sarah went up to bed and fell asleep instantly, secure in the knowledge that at least she didn't have to worry about Laurie anymore tonight. She'd call her first thing in the morning.

40

That really puts the icing on a perfect day, Allan Grant thought as he replaced the receiver after his call to Sarah. She'd sounded heartsick. Why wouldn't she? Her mother and father dead five months, her kid sister well into a nervous breakdown.

Allan went into the kitchen. One corner of the largest cabinet held the liquor supply. Except for a beer or two at night, he was not a solitary drinker, but now he poured a generous amount of vodka in a tumbler and reached for the ice cubes. He hadn't bothered much with lunch, and the vodka burned his throat and stomach. He'd better get something to eat.

There were only leftovers in the refrigerator. Grimacing, he dismissed them as potential dinner material, opened the freezer and reached for a frozen pizza.

While it heated, Allan sipped the drink and continued to debate with himself how badly he had botched the business with Laurie Kenyon. Both Dean Larkin and Dr. Iovino had been impressed by Laurie's adamant denials. As the dean pointed out, "Allan, Miss Kenyon is quite right when she says that it's a typewriter anyone in her residence might have used, and that a similarity in handwriting style is hardly proof that she is the author of those letters."

So now they feel that I've started something that may embarrass the college, Allan thought. Great. How do I deal with her in class until the end of the term? Is there any chance at all that I'm wrong?

As he took the pizza from the oven, he said aloud, "There's no chance that I'm wrong. Laurie wrote those letters."

Karen phoned at eight. "Darling, I've been thinking about you. How did it go?"

"Not well, I'm afraid." They talked for twenty minutes. When they finally hung up, Allan felt a lot better.

At ten-thirty the phone rang again. "I'm really okay," he said. "But, God—it's so good to finally have it out on the table. I'm going to take a sleeping pill now and go to bed. See you tomorrow." He added, "I love you."

He put the radio on the SLEEP button, tuned the dial to CBS and promptly fell asleep.

Allan Grant never heard the soft footsteps, never sensed the figure bending over him, never woke up as the knife slid through the flesh over his heart. A moment later, the sound of the flapping curtains muffled the choking gasps that escaped him as he died.

~ 41

It was the knife dream again, but this time it was different. The knife wasn't coming at her. She was holding it and moving it up and down, up and down. Laurie sat bolt upright in bed, clamping her hand over her mouth to keep from shrieking. Her hand felt sticky. Why? She looked down. Why was she still wearing jeans and her jacket? Why were they so stained?

Her left hand was touching something hard. She closed her fingers around it and a quick stab of pain raced through her hand. Warm, wet blood trickled from her palm.

She threw back the bedclothes. The carving knife was half-hidden under the pillow. Smears of dried blood covered the sheets. What had happened? When did she cut herself? Had she been bleeding that much? Not from that cut. Why had she taken the knife from the closet? Was she still dreaming? Was this part of the dream?

Don't waste a minute, a voice shouted. *Wash your hands. Wash the knife. Hide it in the closet. Do as I tell you. Hurry up. Take off your watch. The band is filthy. The bracelet in your pocket. Wash that too.*

Wash the knife. Blindly she ran into the bathroom, turned on the taps in the tub, held the knife under the gushing water.

Put it in the closet. She raced back into the bedroom. *Throw your watch in the drawer. Get those clothes off. Strip the bed. Throw everything in the tub.*

Laurie stumbled into the bathroom, flipped the handle to the shower setting and dropped the bedding into the tub. As she stripped, she flung her clothes into the water. She stared as it turned red.

She stepped into the tub. The sheets billowed around her feet. Frantically she scrubbed the stickiness from her hands and face. The cut on her palm continued to bleed even when she wrapped a washcloth around it. For long minutes she stood, eyes closed, the water cascading over her hair and face and body, shivering even as the bathroom filled with steam.

Finally she stepped out, wrapped her hair in a towel, pulled on her long terry-cloth robe and plugged the drain. She washed her clothes and the bedding until the water ran clear.

She bundled everything into a laundry bag, dressed and went down to the dryer in the basement. She waited while the dryer spun and whirled. When it clicked off, she folded the sheets and her clothing neatly and brought them back to her room.

Now remake the bed and get out of here. Be at your first class and stay calm. You're really in a mess this time. The phone's ringing. Don't answer it. It's probably Sarah.

On the walk across the campus, she met several other students, one of whom rushed to assure her that she had a real sexual harassment case, a kind of reverse one, but she ought to press it against Professor Grant. What a nerve he had to accuse her that way.

She nodded in an absent way, wondering who the little kid was who kept crying so hard, a muffled kind of crying like her head was buried in a pillow. The image came to her of a small child with long blond hair lying on a bed in a cold room. Yes, she was the one who was crying.

Laurie did not notice when the other students left her to go to their own classes. She was unaware of the stares as they glanced back at her. She did not hear one of them say, "She is really weird."

Automatically she entered the building, took the elevator to the third floor. She started down the corridor. As she passed the classroom where Allan Grant was scheduled to teach, she poked her head in the doorway. A dozen students were gathered in a circle waiting for him. "You're wasting your time," she told them. "Sexy Allan is dead as a doornail."

Part Three

42

When Sarah could not reach Laurie in her room Wednesday morning, she called Susan Grimes again. "Please leave a note on Laurie's door to call me at the office. It's very important."

At eleven o'clock Laurie phoned from the police station.

Total numbness took over Sarah's emotions. She took precious minutes to phone Dr. Carpenter, told him what had happened, and asked him to contact Dr. Donnelly. Then she grabbed her coat and purse and rushed to the car. The hour-and-a-half-long drive to Clinton was hell.

Laurie's halting, stunned voice saying, "Sarah, Professor Grant has been found murdered. They think I did it. They arrested me and brought me to the police station. They said I could make one call."

Her only question to Laurie, "How did he die?" She'd known the answer before Laurie told her. Allan Grant had been stabbed. Oh God, merciful God, why?

Sarah arrived at the police station and was told that Laurie was being interrogated. Sarah demanded to see her.

The desk lieutenant knew Sarah was an assistant prosecutor. He looked at her sympathetically. "Miss Kenyon, you know that the only one allowed in while she's being questioned is her lawyer."

"I'm her lawyer," Sarah said.

"You can't—"

"As of this minute, I've quit my job. You can listen while I call in my resignation."

The interrogation room was small. A video camera was filming Laurie, who was seated on a rickety wooden chair, staring into the lens. Two detectives were with her. When she saw Sarah, Laurie rushed into her arms. "Sarah, this is crazy. I'm so sorry about Professor Grant. He was so good to me. I was so angry yesterday because of those letters that he thought I'd written. Sarah, tell them to find whoever wrote them. That's the crazy person who must have killed him." She began to sob.

Sarah pressed Laurie's head against her shoulder, instinctively rocking her, vaguely realizing it was the way their mother used to comfort them when they were little.

"Sit down, Laurie," the younger detective said firmly. "She's signed a Miranda warning," he told Sarah.

Sarah eased Laurie back onto the chair. "I'm staying right here with you. I don't want you to answer any more questions now."

Laurie buried her face in her hands. Her hair fell forward.

"Miss Kenyon, may I speak with you? I'm Frank Reeves." Sarah realized that the older detective looked familiar. He had testified in one of her trials. He drew her to the side. "I'm afraid it's an open-and-shut case. She threatened Professor Grant yesterday. This morning, before his body was discovered, she announced to a roomful of students that he was dead. There was a knife that is almost certainly the murder weapon hidden in her room. She tried to wash her clothing and bedding, but there are faint bloodstains on them. The lab report will clinch it."

"Sare-wuh."

Sarah spun around. It was Laurie but it wasn't Laurie in the chair. Her expression was different, childlike. The voice was that of a three-year-old. *Sare-wuh.* That's how the toddler Laurie used to pronounce her name. "Sare-wuh, I want my teddy."

Sarah held Laurie's hand as she was arraigned on the complaint. The judge set bail at one hundred fifty thousand dollars. She promised Laurie, "I'll have you out of here in a few hours." Beyond pain, she watched a handcuffed, uncomprehending Laurie led away.

Gregg Bennett came into the courthouse as she was filling out forms for the bondsman. "Sarah."

She glanced up. He looked as shocked and heartsick as she felt. She had not seen him for months; Laurie had once seemed so happy with this nice young man.

"Sarah, Laurie would never willfully hurt anyone. Something must have snapped in her."

"I know. Insanity will be her defense. Insanity at the time of the killing." As she said the words, Sarah thought of all the defense attorneys whom she had defeated in court who had tried that strategy. It seldom worked. The best it usually did was to create enough doubt to keep the accused from the death sentence.

She realized that Gregg had put his hand on her shoulder. "You look as though you could use some coffee," he told her. "Still take it black?"

"Yes."

He returned carrying two steaming Styrofoam cups as she completed the last page of the application; then he waited with her while it was processed. He's such a nice guy, Sarah thought. Why didn't Laurie fall in love with him? Why a married man? Had she chosen Allan Grant as a father substitute? As the shock wore off, she thought of Professor Grant, of how he'd rushed to be with Laurie when she fainted. Was there any chance he had led her on in subtle ways? Led her on, at a time when she was emotionally bereft? Sarah realized that possible defenses were forming in her mind.

At quarter-past six, Laurie was freed on bond. She came out of the jail accompanied by a uniformed matron. When she saw them, her knees began to buckle. Gregg rushed to catch her. Laurie moaned as he grabbed her. Then she began to shriek, "Sarah, Sarah, don't let him hurt me."

43

At eleven o'clock Wednesday morning the phone rang in the Global Travel Agency in the Madison Arms Hotel on East Seventy-sixth Street in Manhattan.

Karen Grant was on her way out the door. She hesitated, then called over her shoulder, "If it's for me say I'll be back in ten minutes. I have to get this settled before I do anything else."

Connie Santini, the office secretary, picked up the receiver. "Global Travel Agency, good morning," she said, then listened. "Karen just stepped out. She'll be back in a few minutes." Connie's tone was brisk.

Anne Webster, owner of the agency, was standing at the file cabinet. She turned. The twenty-two-year-old Santini was a good secretary but sounded too abrupt on the telephone for Anne's taste. "Always get a name immediately," Anne would preach. "If it's a business call, always ask if someone else can help."

"Yes, I'm sure she'll be back right away," Connie was saying. "Is something wrong?"

Anne hurried over to Karen's desk, picked up the extension and nodded to Connie to hang up. "This is Anne Webster. May I help you?"

Any number of times in her sixty-nine years Anne had received bad news over the phone about a relative or friend. When this caller identified himself as Dean Larkin of Clinton College, she knew with icy certainty that something was wrong with Allan Grant. "I'm Karen's employer and friend," she told the dean. "Karen is right across the lobby in the jeweler's. I can get her for you."

She listened as Larkin hesitantly said, "Perhaps it would be wise if I tell you. I'd drive in but I'm so afraid Karen might hear about it on the radio or a reporter might phone her before I can get there . . ."

A horrified Anne Webster then heard the terrible news of Allan Grant's murder. "I'll take care of it," she said. Tears were welling in her eyes as she hung up the receiver and told the secretary what had happened. "One of Allan's students has been writing love letters to him. He turned them over to the administration. Yesterday the student made a terrible scene and threatened him. This morning when Allan was late for class, this student told everyone he was dead. They found him in bed, stabbed through the heart. Oh, poor Karen."

"She's coming," Connie said. Through the glass wall that separated the travel agency from the lobby, they could see Karen approaching. Her step was springy. A smile was playing on her lips. Her dark hair was swirling around her collar. Her Nippon suit, red with pearl buttons, enhanced her model-size figure. Obviously the errand had been a success.

Webster bit her lip nervously. How should she begin to break the news? Say there'd been an accident and wait until they were in Clinton to say more? Oh God, she prayed, give me the strength I'll need.

The door was opening. "They apologized," Karen said triumphantly. "Admitted it was their fault." Then her smile faded. "Anne, what's wrong?"

"Allan is dead." Webster could not believe she had blurted out those words.

"Allan? Dead?" Karen Grant's tone was questioning, uncomprehending. Then she repeated, "Allan. Dead."

Webster and Santini saw her complexion fade to an ashen pallor and rushed to her. Each taking an arm, they eased her into a chair. "How?" Karen asked, her voice a monotone. "The car? The brakes have been getting soft. I warned him. He's not good at taking care of things like that."

"Oh, Karen." Anne Webster put her arms around the trembling shoulders of the younger woman.

It was Connie Santini who gave what details they knew, who called the garage and told them to have Karen's car brought around immediately, who collected coats and gloves and purses. She offered to go with them and drive. It was Karen who vetoed the suggestion. The office needed to be covered.

Karen insisted on driving. "You don't know the roads, Anne." On the way down, she was tearless. She talked about Allan as though he were still alive. "He's the nicest guy in the whole world . . . He's so good . . . He's the smartest man I've ever known . . . I remember . . ."

Webster was grateful that the traffic was light. It was as though Karen were on automatic pilot. They were passing Newark Airport, going onto Route 78.

"I met Allan on a trip," Karen said. "I was leading a group to Italy. He joined it at the last minute. That was six years ago. It was over the holidays, and his mother had died that year. He told me that he realized he had no place to go for Christmas and he didn't want to stay around the college. By the time we got back to Newark Airport we were engaged. I called him my Mr. Chips."

It was a few minutes past noon when they arrived in Clinton. Karen began to sob as she saw the cordoned area around her home. "Up till this minute I thought it was a bad dream," she whispered.

A policeman stopped them at the driveway, then quickly stepped aside to let the car pass through. Cameras flashed as they got out of the car. Anne put a comforting arm around Karen as they hurried the few steps to the front door.

The house was filled with police. They were in the living room, the kitchen, the hallway that led to the bedrooms. Karen started down the hallway. "I want to see my husband," she said.

A gray-haired man stopped her, led her into the living room. "I'm Detective Reeves," he said. "I'm very sorry, Mrs. Grant. We've taken him away. You can see him later."

Karen began to tremble. "That girl who killed him. Where is she?"

"She's under arrest."

"Why did she do this to my husband? He was so kind to her."

"She claims she's innocent, Mrs. Grant, but we found a knife that may be the murder weapon in her room."

At last the dam broke. Anne Webster had known that it would. Karen Grant let out a strangled cry that was half laugh, half sob, and became hysterical.

~ 44

Bic turned on the noon news as they were eating lunch in his office in the television studio on West Sixty-first Street. The breaking story was headlined: FATAL ATTRACTION MURDER AT CLINTON COLLEGE.

Opal gasped and Bic turned white as the picture of the child, Laurie, flashed on the screen. "As a four-year-old, Laurie Kenyon was the victim of an abduction. Today, at twenty-one, Kenyon is accused of stabbing to death a popular professor to whom she is alleged to have written dozens of love letters. Allan Grant was found in bed . . ."

A picture of a house flashed on the screen. The area around it was roped off. There was a shot of an open window. "It is believed that Laurie Kenyon entered and left Allan Grant's bedroom by this window." Squad cars lined the streets.

A student, her eyes popping with excitement, was interviewed. "Laurie was yelling at Professor Grant about having sex with him. I think he was trying to break off with her and she went crazy."

When the segment was over, Bic said, "Turn that off, Opal."

She obeyed.

"She gave herself to another man," Bic said. "She was creeping into his bed at night."

Opal didn't know what to do or say. Bic was trembling. His face was sweaty. He took off his jacket and rolled up his sleeves, then held out his arms. The lush curly hair on them was now steel gray. "Remember how scared she'd be when I held my arms out to her?" he asked. "But Lee knew I loved her. She's haunted me all these years. You've witnessed that, Opal. And while I suffered these last months, seeing her, being near enough to touch her, worrying that she'd talk about me to that doctor, threaten all I've worked for, she was writing filth to someone else."

His eyes were enormously wide, brilliantly bright, firing darts of lightning. Opal gave him the answer that was expected of her. "Lee should be punished, Bic."

"She will be. If the eye offends, pluck it out. If the hand offends, cut it off. Lee is clearly under Satan's influence. It is my duty to send her to the healing forgiveness of the Lord by compelling her to turn the blade upon herself."

45

Sarah drove up the Garden State Parkway, Laurie beside her, sleeping. The matron had promised to call Dr. Carpenter and tell him they were on the way home. Gregg had thrust Laurie into Sarah's arms, protesting, "Laurie, Laurie, I'd never hurt you. I love you." Then, shaking his head, he'd said to Sarah, "I don't understand."

"I'll call you," Sarah told him hurriedly. She knew his phone number was in Laurie's address book. Last year Laurie had called Gregg regularly.

When she reached Ridgewood and turned into their street, she was dismayed to see three vans parked in front of the house. A crowd of reporters with cameras and microphones were clustered there, blocking the driveway. Sarah leaned on the horn. They let her pass but ran beside the car until it stopped at the porch steps. Laurie stirred, opened her eyes, looked around. "Sarah, why are these people here?"

To Sarah's relief, the front door opened. Dr. Carpenter and Sophie rushed down the steps. Carpenter pushed his way through the reporters, opened the passenger door and put his arm around Laurie. Cameras flashed and questions were shouted at Laurie as he and Sophie half carried her up the steps into the house.

Sarah knew she had to make a statement. She got out of the car and waited as the microphones were thrust at her. Forcing herself to appear calm and confident, she listened to the questions: "Is this a fatal attraction murder? . . . Will you plea bargain? . . . Is it true you quit your job to defend Laurie? . . . Do you believe she's guilty?"

Sarah chose to answer the last query. "My sister is legally and morally innocent of any crime and we will prove that in court." She turned and pushed her way through the inquisitors.

Sophie was holding open the door. Laurie was lying on the couch in the den, Dr. Carpenter beside her. "I've given her a strong sedative," he whispered to Sarah. "Get her upstairs and into bed immediately. I've left a message for Dr. Donnelly. He's expected back from Australia today."

It was like dressing a doll, Sarah thought as she and Sophie pulled the sweater over Laurie's head and slipped the nightgown in its place. Laurie did not open her eyes nor seem to be aware of them.

"I'll get another blanket," Sophie said quietly. "Her hands and feet are ice cold."

The first mewing sound came as Sarah was turning on the night-light. It was a heartbroken weeping that Laurie was trying to muffle in the pillow.

"She's crying in her sleep," Sophie said. "The poor child."

That was it. If she were not looking at Laurie, Sarah would have thought the sound was coming from a frightened child. "Ask Dr. Carpenter to come up."

Her instinct was to put her arms around Laurie and comfort her, but she forced herself to wait until the doctor was in the room. He stood beside her in the dim light and studied Laurie. Then, as the sobs faded and Laurie's grip on the pillow relaxed, she began to whisper. They bent over to hear. "I want my daddy. I want my mommy. I want Sare-wuh. I want to go home."

46

Thomasina Perkins lived in a small four-room row house in Harrisburg, Pennsylvania. Now seventy-two, she was a cheerful presence whose one fault was that she loved to talk about the most exciting event of her life—her involvement in the Laurie Kenyon case. She had been the cashier who had called the police when Laurie became hysterical in the diner.

Her greatest regret was that she hadn't gotten a good look at the couple and couldn't remember what name the woman had called the man when they rushed Laurie out of the diner. Sometimes Thomasina would dream about them, especially the man, but he never had a face, just longish hair, a beard and powerful arms with a heavy growth of curly hair.

Thomasina heard about Laurie Kenyon's arrest on the six o'clock television news. That poor family, she thought sadly. All that trouble. The Kenyons had been so grateful to her. She had appeared with them on "Good Morning, America" after Laurie returned home. That day John Kenyon had quietly given her a check for five thousand dollars.

Thomasina had hoped that the Kenyons would keep in touch with her. For a while she wrote regularly to them, long newsy letters describing how everyone who came into the diner wanted to hear about the case and how they'd get tears in their eyes when

Thomasina described how frightened Laurie looked and how pitifully she had been crying.

Then one day she received a letter from John Kenyon. He thanked her again for her kindness but said maybe it would be better if she didn't write to them anymore. The letters upset his wife so much. They were all trying to put the memory of that terrible time behind them.

Thomasina had been intensely disappointed. She wanted so much to be invited to visit them and to be able to tell new stories about Laurie. But even though she continued to send Christmas cards every year, they never responded again.

Then she'd sent a sympathy note to Sarah and Laurie when she read about the accident in September and received a lovely note from Sarah saying her mother and father always felt that Thomasina was God's way of answering their prayers and thanking her for the fifteen happy years their family had enjoyed since Laurie's return. Thomasina framed the note and made sure any visitors became aware of it.

Thomasina loved to watch television, especially on Sunday morning. She was deeply religious, and the "Church of the Airways" was her favorite program. She'd been devoted to Reverend Rutland Garrison and was heartbroken when he died.

Reverend Bobby Hawkins was so different. Thomasina wasn't sure about him. He gave her a funny feeling. However, there was something mesmerizing about watching him and Carla together. She couldn't take her eyes off them. And he certainly was a powerful preacher.

Now Thomasina fervently wished that it was Sunday morning so that when Reverend Bobby told everyone to put their hands on the television and ask for a personal miracle, she could ask that Laurie's arrest would turn out to be a mistake. But it was Wednesday, not Sunday, and she'd have to wait the whole rest of the week.

At nine o'clock the phone rang. It was the producer of the local television show "Good Morning, Harrisburg." He apologized for the late call and asked if Thomasina would consider being on the program in the morning to talk about Laurie.

Thomasina was thrilled. "I was looking over the files of the Kenyon case, Miss Perkins," the producer said. "Boy, what a pity you couldn't remember the name of that guy who was with Laurie in the diner."

"I know," Thomasina acknowledged. "It's like it still rattles somewhere in my brain, but he's probably either dead or living in South America by now anyhow. What good would it do?"

"It would do a lot of good," the producer said. "Your testimony is the only eyewitness proof that Laurie may have been abused by her abductors. They'll need a lot more evidence than that to create sympathy for her in court. We'll talk about it tomorrow on the program."

When she put down the phone, Thomasina sprang up and rushed into the bedroom. She reached for her best blue silk dress with the matching jacket and examined it carefully. No stains, thank heaven. She laid out her good corset, her Sunday oxfords, the pair of Alicia Pantihose from JC Penney she'd been saving for a special occasion. Since she'd stopped working she hadn't bothered putting pin curls in her hair at night, but now she carefully set every one of the thinning strands.

Just as she was about to get into bed, Reverend Bobby's advice to pray for a miracle flashed into her mind.

Thomasina's niece had given her lavender stationery for Christmas. She got it out and searched for the new Bic pen she'd bought at the supermarket. Settling at the dinette table she wrote a long letter to Reverend Bobby Hawkins telling him all about her involvement with Laurie Kenyon. She explained that years ago she had refused to undergo hypnosis to help her remember the name the woman had called the man. She'd always believed that to go under hypnosis meant that you were putting your soul in the power of another, and that it would be displeasing to God. What did Reverend Bobby think? She'd be guided by him. Please write soon.

She wrote a second letter to Sarah, explaining what she was doing.

As an afterthought, she enclosed an offering of two dollars in Reverend Bobby Hawkins's envelope.

47

Dr. Justin Donnelly had gone home to Australia for Christmas vacation, with plans to stay a month. It was summer there and for those four weeks he visited his family, saw his friends, caught up with his old colleagues and reveled in the chance to unwind.

He also spent a great deal of time with Pamela Crabtree. Two years ago, when he'd left for the United States, they'd been close to making a commitment but agreed neither was ready. Pamela had her own career as a neurologist and was developing a considerable reputation in Sydney.

Over the holiday season they dined together, sailed together, went to the theater together. But as much as he'd always looked forward to being with Pamela, as much as he admired her and enjoyed her company, Justin sensed a vague feeling of dissatisfaction. Perhaps there were more than professional conflicts holding them back.

Justin's gnawing sense of unease gradually centered on the realization that he was thinking more and more of Sarah Kenyon. He'd only seen her that one time in October, yet he missed their weekly conversations. He wished he hadn't been so reluctant to suggest that they have dinner together again.

Shortly before he returned to New York, Pamela and he talked it through and agreed that whatever had been between them was over. With a vast sense of relief, Justin Donnelly boarded the plane to New York, arriving exhausted from the long trip at noon on Wednesday. When he got to the apartment he fell into bed and slept until ten o'clock, then checked his messages.

Five minutes later he was on the phone to Sarah. The sound of her voice, tired and strained, tore at his gut. Dismayed, he listened as she told him what had happened. "You must get Laurie in to see me," he told her. "Tomorrow I've got to sort out things in the clinic. Friday morning at ten?"

"She won't want to come."

"She has to."

"I know." There was a pause, then Sarah said, "I'm so glad you're back, Dr. Donnelly."

So am I, Justin thought as he replaced the receiver. He knew Sarah had not yet fully absorbed the ordeal she was facing. Laurie had committed murder in one of her altered states, and that might put the persona who was Laurie Kenyon already beyond his help.

48

Brendon Moody returned to Teaneck, New Jersey, late Wednesday night from a week of fishing with his buddies in Florida. His wife, Betty, was waiting up for him. She told him about Laurie Kenyon's arrest.

Laurie Kenyon! Brendon had been a detective with the Bergen County prosecutor's office seventeen years ago when four-year-old Laurie disappeared. Until his retirement, he'd been on the homicide squad there and knew Sarah very well. Shaking his head, he turned on the eleven o'clock news. The campus murder was the main story. The segment included shots of Allan Grant's home, Grant's widow being escorted into the house, Laurie and Sarah emerging from the police station, Sarah making a statement in front of the Kenyons' Ridgewood house.

With growing dismay, Brendon watched and listened. When the report was over, he snapped off the set. "That's a tough one," he said.

Thirty years ago, when Brendon was courting Betty, her father had said derisively, "That little bantam thinks he's the cock of the walk." There was an element of truth in the remark. Betty always felt that when Brendon was upset or angry, a certain electricity went through him. His chin went up; his thinning gray hair became tousled; his cheeks became flushed; his eyes behind rimless glasses seemed magnified.

At sixty Brendon had lost none of the feisty energy that had made him the top investigator in the prosecutor's office. In three days they were supposed to visit Betty's sister in Charleston. Knowing that she was giving him carte blanche to beg off from the trip, she said, "Isn't there something you can do?" Brendon was now a licensed private investigator, taking only cases that interested him.

Brendon's smile was both grim and relieved. "You bet there is. Sarah needs to have someone down on that campus gathering and sifting every possible tidbit of information she can get. This looks like an open-and-shut case. Bets, you've heard me say it a thousand times and I'll say it again. When you go in with that attitude the only thing you can hope for is a few years off the sentence. You gotta go in believing your client is as innocent as the babe in the manger. That's how you find extenuating circumstances. Sarah Kenyon is a hell of a nice woman and a hell of a good lawyer. I always predicted she'd have a gavel in her hand someday. But she needs help now. Real help. Tomorrow I go see her and sign on."

"If she'll have you," Betty suggested mildly.

"She'll have me. And Bets, you know how you hate the cold. Why don't you go down to Charleston and visit Jane on your own?"

Betty untied her robe and got into bed. "I might just as well. From now on, knowing you, you'll be eating, sleeping and dreaming this case."

49

"Carla, describe Lee's bedroom in detail to me."

Opal was holding the coffeepot, about to pour coffee for Bic. She paused then carefully tilted the spigot over his cup. "Why?"

"I have many times warned you not to question my requests." The voice was gentle, but Opal shivered.

"I'm sorry. You just surprised me." She looked across the table, trying to smile. "You look so handsome in that velvet jacket, Bobby. Now let's see. Like I told you, her room and her sister's room are on the right side of the staircase. The real estate agent said that the Kenyons turned smaller rooms into baths, so the four bedrooms each have a bath. Lee's room has a double bed with a velvet headboard, a dresser, desk, a standing bookcase, nighttables and a slipper chair. It's very feminine, blue-and-white flowered pattern on the spread and headboard and draperies. Two nice-sized closets, cross ventilation, pale blue carpet."

She could tell he was not yet satisfied and narrowed her eyes in concentration. "Oh yes, there are family pictures on her desk and a telephone on the night table."

"Is there a picture of Lee as a child in the pink bathing suit she was wearing when she joined us?"

"I think so."

"You think so?"

"I'm sure there is."

"You're forgetting something, Carla. Last time we discussed this, you told me that there was a stack of family albums on the bottom shelf of the bookcase and it looked as though Lee might have been going through them or perhaps was rearranging them. There appeared to be a great many loose pictures of Lee and her sister as young children."

"Yes. That's right." Opal sipped her coffee nervously. A few minutes ago she'd been telling herself that everything would be all right. She'd been reveling in the luxury of the pretty sitting room of their hotel suite, enjoying the feel of her new brushed-velvet Dior robe. She looked up and her gaze met Bic's stare. His eyes were flashing, messianic. With a sinking heart she knew he was going to demand something dangerous of her.

50

At quarter of twelve on Thursday Laurie awakened from her sedated sleep. She opened her eyes and looked around the familiar room. A bewildering cacophony of thoughts shouted through her mind. Somewhere a child was crying. Two women in her head were screaming at each other. One of them was yelling, *I was mad at him but I loved him and I didn't want that to happen.*

The other was saying, *I told you to stay home that night. You fool. Look what you've done to her.*

I didn't tell everybody that he was dead. You're the fool.

Laurie pressed both hands to her ears. Oh God, had she dreamt it all? Was Allan Grant really dead? Could anyone believe that she had hurt him? The police station. That cell. Those cameras taking her picture. It hadn't happened to her, had it? Where was Sarah? She got out of bed and ran to the door. "Sarah! Sarah!"

"She'll be back soon." It was Sophie's familiar voice, reassuring, soothing. Sophie was coming up the stairs. "How do you feel?"

Relief flowed through Laurie. The voices in her head stopped quarreling. "Oh, Sophie. I'm glad you're here. Where's Sarah?"

"She had to go to her office. She'll be back in a couple of hours. I have a nice lunch all fixed for you, consommé and tuna salad just the way you like it."

"Just the consommé, Sophie. I'll be down in ten minutes."

She went into the bathroom and turned on the shower. Yesterday she had washed sheets and clothes while she showered. What a strange thing to do. She adjusted the shower head until the hot water was a needle-sharp waterfall massaging the knotted muscles in her neck and shoulders. The groggy headache brought on by the sedatives began to clear and the enormity of what had happened started to sink in. Allan Grant, that lovely, warm human being had been murdered with the missing knife.

Sarah asked me if I had taken the knife, Laurie thought as she turned off the taps and stepped from the shower. She wrapped one of the giant bath towels around her body. Then I found the knife in my tote bag. Somebody must have taken it from my room, the same person who wrote those disgusting letters.

She wondered why she didn't feel more emotion for Allan Grant. He had been so kind to her. When she opened the closet door, trying to decide what to wear, she thought she understood. The shelves of sweaters. Mother had been with her when she bought most of them.

Mother, whose joy was to give and give. Daddy's mock dismay when they arrived home with the packages. "I'm subsidizing the entire retail business."

Laurie wiped tears from her eyes as she dressed in jeans and a pullover. After you've lost two people like them, you haven't much grief left for anyone else.

She stood in front of the mirror, brushing her hair. It really needed a trim. But she couldn't make an appointment today. People would be staring at her, whispering about her. But I didn't do anything, she protested to her reflection in the mirror. Again a sharp, focused memory of Mother. How many times had she said, "Oh, Laurie, you look so like me when I was your age."

But Mother had never had that anxious, frightened look in her eyes. Mother's lips always curved in a smile. Mother made people happy. She didn't cause trouble and pain for everyone.

Hey, why should you take all the blame, a voice sneered. *Karen Grant didn't want Allan. She kept making excuses to stay in New York. He was lonesome. He had pizza for dinner half the time. He needed me. It was just that he didn't know it yet. I hate Karen. I wish she was dead.*

Laurie went over to the desk.

Minutes later, Sophie knocked and called in a worried voice, "Laurie, lunch is ready. Are you all right?"

"Will you please leave me alone? The damn consommé won't evaporate will it?" Irritated, she finished folding the letter she'd just written and inserted it in an envelope.

The mailman came around twelve-thirty. She watched from the window until he started up the walk, then hurried downstairs and opened the door as he reached the porch.

"I'll take it and here's one for you."

As Laurie closed the door, Sophie rushed from the kitchen. "Laurie, Sarah doesn't want you to go out."

"I'm not going out, silly. I just picked up the mail." Laurie put her hand on Sophie's arm. "Sophie, you'll stay with me until Sarah comes back, won't you? I don't want to be alone here."

~ 51

Early Wednesday evening a pale but composed Karen Grant drove back to New York with her partner, Anne Webster. "I'm better off in the city," she said. "I couldn't bear to stay in the house."

Webster offered to stay overnight, but Karen refused. "You look more exhausted than I am. I'm going to take a sleeping pill and go right to bed."

She slept long and deeply. It was nearly eleven when she awakened on Thursday morning. The three top floors of the hotel were residential apartments. In the three years she'd had her apartment, Karen had gradually added touches of her own: Oriental scatter rugs in tones of cardinal red, ivory and blue that transformed the bland off-white hotel carpeting; antique lamps; silk pillows; Lalique figurines; original paintings by promising new artists.

The effect was charming and luxurious and personal. Yet Karen loved the amenities of hotel living, especially the room service and maid service. She also loved the closet full of designer clothes, the Charles Jourdan and Ferragamo shoes, the Hermés scarves, the Gucci handbags. It was such a satisfying feeling to know that the uniformed desk clerks were always watching to see what she'd be wearing when she stepped off the elevator.

She got up and went into the bathroom. The thick terry-cloth robe that enveloped her from neck to toe was on the hook there. She pulled the belt tightly around her waist and studied herself in the mirror. Eyes still swollen a bit. Seeing Allan on that slab in the morgue had been awful. In one rush she'd thought of all the marvelous times they'd had together, of the way she used to thrill to the sound of his footsteps coming down the hall. The tears had been genuine. There would be more weeping when she looked at his face for the last time. Which reminded her, she'd have to make the necessary arrangements. Not now, however; now she wanted breakfast.

On the telephone, she pressed *4* for room service. Lilly was taking orders. "I'm so sorry, Mrs. Grant," she said. "We're all just shocked."

"Thank you." Karen ordered her usual: fresh juice, fruit compote, coffee, hard roll. "Oh, and send all the morning papers."

"Of course."

She was sipping the first cup of coffee when there was a discreet knock on the door. She flew to open it. Edwin was there, his handsome patrician features set in an expression of solicitous concern. "Oh, my dear," he sighed.

His arms closed around her, and Karen laid her face against the soft cashmere jacket she had given him for Christmas. Then she clasped her hands around his neck, careful not to dishevel his precisely combed dark blond hair.

52

Justin Donnelly met Laurie on Friday morning. He had seen newspaper pictures of her but still was not prepared for her striking good looks. Breathtaking blue eyes, shoulder-length golden blond hair that made him think of an illustration of a princess in a fairy tale. She was dressed simply in dark blue slacks, a white high-necked silk blouse and a blue-and-white jacket. There was an innate elegance despite the palpable fear he could sense emanating from her.

Sarah was sitting near her sister, but a little in back of her. Laurie had refused to come into the office alone. "I promised Sarah I'd talk to you, but I cannot do it without her."

Perhaps it was Sarah's reassuring presence, but even so, Justin was surprised to hear Laurie's direct question. "Dr. Donnelly, do you think I killed Professor Allan Grant?"

"Do you think I have reason to believe that?"

"I would guess that everyone has good reason to suspect me. I quite simply did not and would not kill any human being. The fact that Allan Grant could possibly link me to the sort of anonymous trash he'd received was humiliating. But we don't kill because someone misreads a nasty situation."

"We, Laurie?"

Was it embarrassment or guilt that flickered in her expression for a fleeting moment? When she did not answer, Justin said, "Laurie, Sarah has talked with you about the serious charges against you. Do you understand what they are?"

"Certainly. They're absurd, but I haven't listened to my father and Sarah talk about the cases she was prosecuting or the sentences the defendants got without knowing what this can mean."

"It would be pretty reasonable to be frightened of what's ahead for you, Laurie."

Her head went down. Her hair fell forward, shielding her face.

Her shoulders rounded. She clasped her hands in her lap and drew up her feet so that they did not touch the floor but dangled above it. The soft weeping that Sarah had heard several times in the last few days began again. Instinctively, Sarah reached out to comfort Laurie, but Justin Donnelly shook his head. "You're so scared, aren't you, Laurie," he commented kindly.

She shook her head from side to side.

"You're not scared?"

Her head bobbed up and down. Then between sobs she said, "Not Laurie."

"You're not Laurie. Will you tell me your name?"

"Debbie."

"Debbie. What a pretty name. How old are you, Debbie?"

"I'm four."

Dear God, Sarah thought as she listened to Dr. Donnelly talking to Laurie as though he were speaking to a little child. He is right. Something terrible must have happened to her in those two years she was gone. Poor Mother, always determined to believe that some child-hungry couple took her and loved her. I knew there was a difference when she came home. If she had had help back then, would we be here now? Suppose Laurie has a totally separate personality that wrote those letters and then killed Allan Grant? Should I let him get to it? Suppose she confesses? What was Donnelly asking Laurie now?

"Debbie, you're very tired aren't you?"

"Yes."

"Would you like to go to your room and rest? I'll bet you have a pretty bedroom."

"No! No! No!"

"That's all right. You can stay right here. Why don't you nap sitting in that chair, and if Laurie's around will you ask her to come back and talk to me?"

Her breathing became even. A moment later she lifted her head. Her shoulders straightened. Her feet touched the floor and she brushed her hair back. "Of course I'm frightened," Laurie told Justin Donnelly, "but since I had nothing to do with Allan's death, I know I can count on Sarah to find the truth." She turned, smiled at Sarah and then looked directly at the doctor again. "If I were Sarah, I'd wish I'd stayed an only child. But here I am, and she's always been there for me. She's always understood."

"Understood what, Laurie?"

She shrugged. "I don't know."

"I think you do."

"I really don't."

Justin knew it was time to tell Laurie what Sarah already knew. Something terrible had happened during the two years that she had been missing, something so overwhelming that as a little child she could not handle it alone. Others came to help her, maybe one or two, maybe more, and she had become in effect a multiple personality. When she was returned home, the loving environment had made it unnecessary for the alter personalities to come forward except perhaps very occasionally. The death of her parents had been so painful that the alters were needed again.

Laurie listened quietly. "What kind of treatment are you talking about?"

"Hypnosis. I'd like to videotape you during the sessions."

"Suppose I confess that some part of me . . . some person, if you will—*did* kill Allan Grant? What then?"

It was Sarah's turn to answer. "Laurie, I'm very much afraid that as it stands a jury will almost inevitably convict you. Our only hope is to prove extenuating circumstances or that you were incapable of knowing the nature of the crime."

"I see. So it is possible that I killed Allan, that I wrote those letters? Not just possible. Probable. Sarah, have there been other people who claimed multiple personality as a defense against a murder charge?"

"Yes."

"How many of them got off?"

Sarah did not answer.

"How many of them, Sarah?" Laurie persisted. "One? Two? None? That's it, isn't it? Not one of them got off. Oh my God. Well, let's go ahead. We might as well know the truth even though it's very clear the truth won't set me free."

She seemed to be fighting back tears, then her voice became strident, angry. "Just one thing, Doctor. Sarah stays with me. I will *not* be alone with you in a room with a closed door and I will not lie on that couch. Got it?"

"Laurie, I'll do anything I can to make this easier for you. You're a very nice person who's had a very bad break."

She laughed, a jeering laugh. "What's nice about that stupid wimp? She's never done anything but cause trouble since the day she was born."

"Laurie," Sarah protested.

"I think Laurie's gone away again," Justin said calmly. "Am I right?"

"You're right. I've got my hands full with her."

"What is your name?"

"Kate."

"How old are you, Kate?"

"Thirty-three. Listen, I didn't mean to come out. I just wanted to warn you. Don't think you're going to hypnotize Laurie and get her to talk about those two years. You're wasting your time. See you."

There was a pause. Then Laurie sighed wearily. "Would it be all right if we stopped talking now? I have such a headache."

53

On Friday morning, Betsy Lyons received a firm offer of five hundred and seventy-five thousand dollars for the Kenyon home from the couple who wanted to move in quickly because the wife was expecting a baby. She called Sarah but could not reach her until the afternoon. To her dismay, Sarah told her the house was off the market. Sarah was sympathetic but firm. "I'm terribly sorry, Mrs. Lyons. First of all I wouldn't entertain an offer that low, but anyhow there is no way I can worry about moving at this time. I know how much work you've put into this sale, but you do understand."

Betsy Lyons did understand. On the other hand the real estate business was desperately slow and she was counting on the commission.

"I'm sorry," Sarah repeated, "but I can't see planning to leave this house before fall at the earliest. Now I do have someone here. I'll talk to you another time."

She was in the library with Brendon Moody. "I had decided it would be a good idea if Laurie and I moved to a condominium," she explained to the detective, "but under the circumstances . . ."

"Absolutely," Brendon agreed. "You're better to take the place off the market. Once this case comes to trial, you'll have reporters posing as potential buyers just to get a look inside."

"I never thought of that," Sarah confessed. Wearily she pushed back a strand of hair that had fallen on her forehead. "Brendon, I can't tell you how glad I am that you want to take on this investigation." She had just finished telling him everything, including what had happened during the session with Laurie at Justin Donnelly's office.

Moody had been taking notes. His high forehead puckered in concentration, his rimless glasses magnifying his snapping brown eyes, his precise bow tie and conservative dark brown suit gave him the air of a meticulous auditor. It was an image that Sarah knew was both accurate and dependable. When he was conducting an investigation, Brendon Moody missed nothing.

She waited while he reread his notes carefully. It was a familiar procedure. That was the way they had worked together in the prosecutor's office. She heard Sophie going up the stairs. Good. She was checking on Laurie again.

Sarah thought back for a moment to the drive home from Dr. Donnelly's office. Laurie had been deeply despondent, saying, "Sarah, I wish I had been in my car when that bus hit it. Mom and Dad would still be alive. You'd be working at the job you love. I'm a pariah, a jinx."

"No, you're not," Sarah had told her. "You were a four-year-old kid who had the hard luck to get kidnapped and be treated God only knows how badly. You're a twenty-one-year-old who's in a hell of a mess through no fault of her own, so stop blaming yourself!"

Then it was Sarah's turn to cry. Blinding tears obscured her vision. Frantically she wiped them away, trying to focus on the heavy Route 17 traffic.

Now she reflected that in a way her outburst might have been a blessing in disguise. A shocked, contrite Laurie had said, "Sarah, I'm so damn selfish. Tell me what you want me to do."

She'd answered, "Do exactly what Dr. Donnelly asks. Keep a journal. That will help him. Stop fighting him. Cooperate with the hypnosis."

"All right, I think I have everything," Moody said briskly, breaking Sarah's reverie. "I have to agree. The *physical aspects* are pretty cut and dried."

It gave Sarah a lift to hear him accentuate "physical aspects." Clearly he understood where the defense was heading.

"You're going for stress, diminished mental capacity?" he asked.

"Yes." She waited.

"What kind of fellow was this Grant guy? He was married. Why wasn't his wife home that night?"

"She works for a travel agency in New York and apparently stays in the city during the week."

"Don't they have travel agencies in New Jersey?"

"I would think so."

"Any chance that the professor was the kind who compensated for the absence of his wife by leading on his students?"

"We're on the same wavelength." Suddenly the library, with its cheery mahogany bookcases, family pictures, paintings, blue Oriental rug, butter-soft leather couches and chairs, assumed the electric atmosphere of the stuffy cubicle that had been her domain in the prosecutor's office. Her father's antique English desk became the battered, shabby relic she'd worked at for nearly five years. "There's a recent case where a defendant was convicted of raping a twelve-year-old," she told Moody.

"I would hope so," he said.

"The legal issue was that the victim is chronologically twenty-seven years old. She suffers from multiple personality disorder and convinced a jury that she'd been violated when she was in her twelve-year-old persona and not capable of giving informed consent. He was found guilty of statutory rape of a person who was found to be mentally defective. The verdict was overturned on appeal, but the point is, a jury believed the testimony of a woman with multiple personality disorder."

Moody leaned forward with the swiftness of a hound catching its first scent of the prey. "You're talking about turning it around."

"Yes. Allan Grant was particularly solicitous of Laurie. When she fainted in church at the funeral mass, he rushed to be with her. He offered to take her home and stay with her. Looking back, I wonder if that wasn't pretty unusual concern." She sighed. "At least it's a starting point. We don't have much else."

"It's a good starting point," Moody said decisively. "I've got a few things to clear up, then I'll get down to Clinton and start digging."

The phone rang again. "Sophie will get it," Sarah said. "Bless her. She's moved in with us. Says we can't be alone. Now let's settle the terms . . ."

"Oh, we'll talk about that later."

"No, we won't," she said firmly. "I know you, Brendon Moody."

Sophie tapped on the door, then opened it. "I'm sorry to interrupt, Sarah, but that real estate agent is on the phone again and she says it's very important."

Sarah picked up the receiver, greeted Betsy Lyons, then listened. Finally she said slowly, "I suppose I owe this to you, Mrs. Lyons. But I have to be clear. That woman cannot keep looking at the house. We'll be out on Monday morning and you can bring her in betweer ten o'clock and one o'clock, but that is it."

When Sarah hung up she explained to Brendon Moody. "There' a prospective buyer who's been hemming and hawing about thi place. Apparently she's pretty much decided on it at full price. She wants one more walk through and then indicates she'll be willing to wait to occupy it until it's available. She'll be here on Monday."

54

The funeral service for Professor Allan Grant was held on Saturday morning at St. Luke's Episcopal Church near the Clinton campus. Faculty members and students crowded together to pay their final respects to the popular teacher. The rector's homily spoke of Allan's intellect, warmth and generosity. "He was an outstanding educator . . . That smile would brighten the darkest day . . . He made people feel good about themselves . . . He could sense when someone was having a tough time. Somehow he found a way to help."

Brendon Moody was at the service in the capacity of observer, not mourner. He was especially interested in studying Allan Grant's widow, who was wearing a deceptively simple black suit with a string of pearls. Somewhat to his surprise, Brendon had developed over the years a reasonably accurate sense of fashion. On a faculty salary, even with her travel agent job thrown in, Karen Grant would find it pretty tough to buy designer clothes. Did either she or Grant have family money? It was raw and windy out and she had not elected to wear a coat into church. That meant she must have left one in the car. The cemetery would be a damn cold place on a day like this.

She was weeping as she followed the casket from the church. Good-looking woman, Brendon thought. He was surprised to see the president of the college and his wife accompany Karen Grant into the first limousine. No family member? No close friend? Brendon decided to continue to pay his respects. He'd go to the burial service.

His question about Karen's coat was answered there. She emerged from the limousine wearing a full-length Blackglama mink.

55

The Church of the Airways had a twelve-member council that met on the first Saturday of the month. Not all of the members approved of the rapid changes the Reverend Bobby Hawkins was instituting on the religious hour. The Well of Miracles particularly was anathema to the senior member of the council.

Viewers were invited to write in explaining their need for a miracle. The letters were placed in the well, and just before the final hymn, Reverend Hawkins extended his hands over it and emotionally prayed that the requests be granted. Sometimes he invited a member of the studio congregation who was in need of a miracle to come up for a special blessing.

"Rutland Garrison must be spinning in his grave," the senior member told Bic at the monthly council meeting.

Bic eyed him coldly. "Have the donations increased substantially?"

"Yes, but—"

"But *what?* More money for the hospital and the retirement home, more for the South American orphanages that have always been my personal charity, more of the faithful voicing their needs to the Lord."

He looked around the table from one member to the other. "When I accepted this ministry I said that I must steer it into wider waters. I've studied the records. In the past several years donations have been steadily decreasing. Isn't that true?"

There was no answer.

"Isn't that true?" he thundered.

Heads nodded.

"Very well. Then I suggest that he who is not with me is against me and ought to resign from this august body. The meeting is adjourned."

He strode from the conference room and down the corridor into his private office where Opal was going through the Well of Miracles mail. Her system was to glance at the requests and separate any unusual ones for Bic to possibly read aloud on the program. The letters were then dropped in one pile to be placed in the Well of Miracles. The donations were in another pile for Bic to tabulate.

Opal dreaded having to show him one letter she had put aside.

"They're seeing the light, Carla," he informed her. "They're coming to understand that my way is the Lord's way."

"Bic," she said timidly.

He frowned. "In this office you must never—"

"I know. I'm sorry. It's just . . . Read this." She thrust Thomasina Perkins' rambling letter into his outstretched hand.

~ *56*

After the funeral, Karen and the faculty members went to the home of the president of the college where a buffet luncheon was waiting. Dean Walter Larkin told Karen that he could not forgive himself for not realizing how sick Laurie Kenyon was. "Dr. Iovino, the Director of the Counseling Center, feels the same way."

"What has happened is a tragedy, and there's no use trying to place blame on ourselves or others," Karen said quietly. "I ought to have persuaded Allan to show those letters to the administration even before he was sure Laurie was writing them. Allan himself ought not to have left that bedroom window wide open. I should hate that girl, but all I can remember is how sorry Allan felt for her."

Walter Larkin had always thought that Karen was something of a cold fish but now he wondered if he'd been unfair. The tears in her eyes and her quivering lip certainly weren't faked.

At breakfast the next morning, he commented on that to his wife, Louise. "Oh, don't be such a romantic, Walter," she told him crisply. "Karen was bored stiff with campus life and faculty teas. She'd have been gone long ago if Allan hadn't been so generous with her. Look at the clothes she wears! You know what I think? Allan was finally waking up to the truth about the woman he was married to. I bet he wouldn't have put up with it much longer. That poor Kenyon girl gave Karen a one-way, first-class ticket to New York."

57

Opal appeared at the real estate office promptly at ten o'clock on Monday morning. Betsy Lyons was waiting for her. "Mrs. Hawkins," she said, "I'm afraid that this will be the only time I can bring you to the Kenyon house, so please, try to make a note of anything you want to see or ask about."

It was the opening Opal needed. Bic had told her to try to pump the real estate agent for any information about the case. "That family has so much tragedy." She sighed. "How is that poor girl?"

Betsy Lyons was relieved to see that Carla Hawkins did not seem to be linking the house to the shocking headlines of Laurie Kenyon's arrest on the murder charge. She rewarded her by being less closemouthed than usual. "As you can imagine, the whole town is buzzing. Everyone feels so sorry for them. My husband is a lawyer, and he says they'll have to go with a diminished capacity defense but it will be hard to prove. Laurie Kenyon never acted odd or crazy in all the years I've known her. Now we'd better be on our way."

Opal was quiet on the drive to the house. Suppose leaving this picture of Lee backfired and gave her a flash of memory? But even if it did, it would remind her of Bic's threat.

Bic had been pretty scary that day. He'd encouraged Lee to really love that silly chicken. Lee's eyes, usually downcast and sad, would brighten when she went in the backyard. She'd rush over to the chicken, put her arms around it and hug it. Bic had taken the butcher knife from the kitchen drawer and winked at Opal. "Watch this performance," he'd said.

He'd run outside, slashing the knife back and forth in front of Lee. She'd been terrified and hugged the chicken tighter. Then he'd reached down and grabbed it by the neck. It began to squawk, and Lee in an unusual show of courage tried to pull it from Bic. He'd slapped her so hard she fell backwards, then as she scrambled to her feet, he'd lifted his arm and swung it in an arc, cutting that chicken's head off in one blow.

Opal had felt her own blood go cold as he threw the body of the chicken at Lee's feet where it flapped around spattering her with blood. Then Bic had held up the head of the dead creature and pointed the knife at Lee's throat, chopping the air with it, his eyes fearsome and glittering. In a terrible voice, he'd sworn that that's what would happen to her if she ever talked about them. Bic was right. A reminder of that day would shut Lee up or drive her completely crazy.

Betsy Lyons was not displeased by her passenger's silence. It was her experience that when people were about to commit themselves to a purchase, they tended to become serious and introspective. It was a worry that Carla Hawkins had not brought her husband to see the house at least once though. As she steered the car into the Kenyon driveway, Betsy asked about that.

"My husband is leaving the decision entirely up to me," Opal said calmly. "He trusts my judgment. I know exactly what will make him happy."

"That's a compliment to you," Betsy assured her with fervent haste.

Lyons was about to insert the key in the lock when the door opened. Opal was dismayed to see the stocky figure in the dark skirt and cardigan who was introduced as the housekeeper, Sophie Perosky. If the woman trailed around the house with them, Opal might not be able to plant the picture.

But Sophie stayed in the kitchen, and planting the photo was easier than Opal expected. In every room, she stood by the windows to observe the view. "My husband asked me to be sure that we're not too near any other houses," she explained. In Lee's room, she spotted a spiral notebook on the desk. The cover was partially raised and the tip of a pen could be seen protruding from under it. "What are the exact dimensions of this room?" she asked as she leaned over the desk to look out the window.

As she had expected, Betsy Lyons fished in her briefcase for the house plan. Opal glanced down swiftly and flipped open the notebook. Just the first three or four pages had writing on them. The words "Dr. Donnelly wants me . . ." jumped out at her. Lee must be keeping a journal. With all her being, Opal wished she could read the entry.

It took only an instant to take the picture from her pocket and slip it about twenty pages back in the book. It was the photo Bic had taken of Lee that first day, just after they reached the farm. Lee had been standing in front of the big tree, shivering in her pink bathing suit, crying, hugging herself tightly.

Bic had cut Lee's head from the picture and stapled the fragment to the bottom. Now the picture showed Lee's face, eyes puffy with tears, hair tangled, staring up at her own decapitated body.

"You really do have a great deal of privacy from the other houses," Opal commented as Betsy Lyons announced that the room was twelve by eighteen feet, really a wonderful size for a bedroom.

~ 58

Justin Donnelly had arranged his schedule so that he could see Laurie every morning, Monday to Friday, at ten o'clock. He'd also set up appointments for her with the art and journal therapists. On Friday he had given her a half-dozen books on multiple personality disorder.

"Laurie," he'd said, "I want you to read these and understand that most of the patients with your problem are women who were abused as children. They blocked out what happened to them just as you're blocking it out. I think that the personalities who helped you to cope those two years you were missing were just about dormant until you lost your parents. Now they've come back in full force. When you read these books, you're going to see that alter personalities are often trying to help you, not hurt you. That's why I hope you'll do your best to consciously let me talk to them."

On Monday morning he had his video camera set up in his office. He knew that if Sarah decided to use any of the tapes at the trial, he had to be extremely careful not to look as though he was putting words in Laurie's mouth.

When Sarah and Laurie came in, he showed them the camera, explained that he was going to record the sessions and told Laurie, "After a while I'll play them back for you." Then he hypnotized her for the first time. Clinging to Sarah's hand, Laurie obediently riveted her attention on him, listened as he urged her to relax, closed her eyes, visibly settled back, let her hand slip from her sister's.

"How do you feel, Laurie?"

"Sad."

"Why are you sad, Laurie?"

"I'm always sad." Her voice was higher, hesitant, with a trace of a lisp.

Sarah watched as Laurie's hair fell forward, as her features seemed to become fluid and change until a childlike expression came over them. She listened as Justin Donnelly said, "I think I'm talking to Debbie. Am I right?"

He was rewarded by a shy nod.

"Why are you sad, Debbie?"

"Sometimes I do bad things."

"Like what, Debbie?"

"Leave that kid alone! She doesn't know what she's talking about."

Sarah bit her lip. The angry voice she'd heard on Friday. Justin Donnelly did not seem perturbed. "Kate, is that you?"

"You know it's me."

"Kate, I don't want to hurt Laurie or Debbie. They've been hurt enough. If you want to help them, why don't you trust me?"

An angry, bitter laugh preceded the statement that chilled Sarah. "We can't trust any man. Look at Allan Grant. He acted so nice to Laurie, and look at the fix he put her in. Good riddance to him, I say."

"You don't mean that you're glad he's dead?"

"I wish he'd never been born."

"Do you want to talk about that, Kate?"

"No, I don't."

"Would you write about it in your journal?"

"I was going to write this morning but that stupid kid had the book. She can't spell worth a damn."

"Do you remember what you were going to write about?"

A derisive laugh. "It's what I'm *not* going to write that would interest you."

On the way home in the car, Laurie was again visibly exhausted. Sophie had lunch waiting, and after Laurie picked at it she decided to lie down.

Sarah settled at the desk and went through her messages. The grand jury would consider the complaint against Laurie on Monday the seventeenth. That was only two weeks away. If the prosecutor was convening the jury that fast, he must be convinced he had a very strong case already. As indeed he did.

A stack of mail had piled up on her desk. She scanned the envelopes, not bothering to open any until she came to the one with the carefully printed return address in the corner. Thomasina Perkins! She was the cashier who long ago had spotted Laurie in the restaurant. Sarah could remember how her father's heartfelt gratitude to the woman had eroded when her frequent letters arrived, filled with increasingly lurid memories of the trauma Laurie exhibited in the restaurant. But there was no doubt Thomasina Perkins meant well. She had written a very kind note in September. This was probably another expression of sympathy. Sarah slit the envelope and read the single sheet of paper. In it, Perkins had given her phone number. Sarah dialed rapidly.

Thomasina picked up on the first ring. She was thrilled to realize it was Sarah calling. "Oh, wait till I tell you my news," she bubbled. "Reverend Bobby Hawkins phoned me himself. He doesn't believe in hypnosis. He invited me to be a guest on next Sunday's program. He's going to pray over me so that God will whisper in my ear the name of that terrible man who kidnapped Laurie."

59

Reverend Bobby Hawkins skillfully turned the Thomasina Perkins problem into a potential advantage. A trusted staff member was instantly sent to Harrisburg to check on her. It was a reasonable thing to do. The Reverend Hawkins and the council needed to be sure there was no investigative reporter putting her up to writing the letter. Bic also wanted details of Thomasina's health, particularly her hearing and vision.

The results of the probe were gratifying. Thomasina wore trifocals and had been operated on for cataracts. Her description of the two people she'd seen with Laurie had been vague from the beginning.

"She clearly doesn't recognize us on the TV screen and won't in person," Bic told Opal as he read the report. She'll be an inspiration to our congregation."

The following Sunday morning, a delighted Thomasina, her hands clasped together in the attitude of prayer, gazed worshipfully up into Bic's face. He laid his hands on her shoulders. "Years ago, this good woman brought about a miracle when the Lord gifted her with the ability to see that a child was in need. But the Lord did not grant Thomasina the ability to remember the name of the villainous man who was accompanying Laurie Kenyon. Now Lee is in need again. Thomasina, I command you to listen and remember the name that has been drifting in your unconscious all these years."

Thomasina could hardly contain herself. Here she was, a celebrity on international television; there was no way she could fail to obey Reverend Bobby's command. She strained her ears. The organ was playing softly. From somewhere she heard a whisper: "Jim . . . Jim . . . Jim . . ."

Thomasina straightened her shoulders, threw out her arms and cried, "The name I have been seeking is Jim!"

60

Sarah had told Justin Donnelly about Thomasina Perkins and the reason for her appearance on the "Church of the Airways" program. At ten o'clock on Sunday morning Donnelly turned on the television set and at the last minute decided to tape the program.

Thomasina did not appear until the hour was almost over. Then, incredulously, Donnelly witnessed the Reverend Bobby's histrionics and Perkins' revelation that "Jim" was the abductor's name. That guy claims he can bring on miracles and he couldn't even get Laurie's name straight, Donnelly thought in disgust as he snapped off the set. He referred to her as *Lee.* Nevertheless he carefully labeled the video cassette and put it in his briefcase.

Sarah phoned a few minutes later. "I don't like to call you at home," she apologized, "but I have to ask. What did you think? Is there any chance that Miss Perkins was right about the name?"

"No," Donnelly said flatly. He heard her sigh.

"I'm still going to ask the Harrisburg police to run 'Jim' through the computers," she told him. "There might be a file on a child abuser by that name who was active seventeen years ago."

"I'm afraid you're wasting your time. The Perkins woman was taking a wild guess. After all, she had Almighty God on the line, didn't she? How's Laurie doing?"

"Pretty well." She sounded cautious.

"Did she watch the program?"

"No, she refuses to listen to any kind of gospel music. Besides, I'm trying to keep her mind off all this. We're going to play a round of golf. It's fairly pleasant out considering it's February."

"I always meant to try golf. That should be relaxing for both of you. Has Laurie been writing in the journal?"

"She's upstairs scribbling away now."

"Good. See you tomorrow." Donnelly hung up and decided that the best way to shake his feeling of restlessness was to take a long walk. He realized that for the first time since he'd lived in New York, the prospect of a totally unstructured Sunday was not appealing to him.

61

Thomasina had hoped that after the "Church of the Airways" program the Reverend Bobby Hawkins and his lovely wife, Carla, might invite her to lunch at a nice place like the Tavern on the Green and maybe suggest that they drive her around New York to see the sights. Thomasina hadn't been to New York in thirty years.

But something happened. The minute the cameras were turned off, Carla whispered something to Reverend Bobby and they both looked upset. The upshot of it was that they sort of brushed Thomasina off with a hurried goodbye and thank you and keep praying. Then an escort brought her to the car that would take her to the airport.

On the ride, Thomasina tried to console herself with the glory of her appearance on the program, of the new stories she'd have to tell. Maybe "Good Morning, Harrisburg" would want her back to talk about the miracle.

Thomasina sighed. She was tired. She'd barely closed her eyes last night for the excitement and now her head ached and she wanted a cup of tea.

She arrived at the airport with nearly two hours to wait for her plane and went into one of the cafeterias. Orange juice, oatmeal, bacon, eggs, a Danish and a pot of tea restored her usual good nature. It had been a very exciting experience. The Reverend Bobby seemed so Godlike that she'd shivered when he prayed over her.

She pushed back her empty plate, poured a second cup of tea and, while she sipped it, thought of the miracle. God had spoken directly to her, saying, "Jim, Jim."

Not for the world would she contradict anything the Almighty told her, but as Thomasina dipped the paper napkin in her water glass and scrubbed away at a spot of bacon grease on her good blue dress she was ashamed of the guilty thought that imposed itself in her mind: That just isn't the name I remember hearing.

62

On Monday morning, ten days after her husband's funeral, Karen Grant entered the travel agency, a heavy stack of mail in her arms.

Anne Webster and Connie Santini were already there. They had been discussing once again the fact that Karen had not invited them to join her at the reception even though they clearly heard the college president tell her to be sure to include any close friends who had attended the service.

Anne Webster still puzzled over the omission. "I'm certain it was just that Karen was so upset."

Connie had other ideas. She was sure Karen didn't want any of the faculty asking them about the travel agency. It would have been just like Anne to artlessly say that business had been terrible for several years. Connie would have bet her bottom dollar that at Clinton College, Karen had given the impression that Global Travel was on a level with Perillo Tours.

The discussion ended with Karen's arrival. She greeted them briefly and said, "The dean had someone pick up the mail at the house. There's an awful pile. Most of it sympathy cards, I suppose. I hate to read them, but I guess I can't avoid it."

With an exaggerated sigh, she settled at her desk and reached for a letter opener. Minutes later she gasped, "Oh, my God."

Connie and Anne jumped up and rushed to her. "What is it? What's wrong?"

"Call the police in Clinton," Karen snapped. Her face was the color of chalk. "It's a letter from Laurie Kenyon, signing herself 'Leona' again. Now that crazy girl is threatening to kill *me!*"

63

The Monday morning session with Laurie was unproductive. She'd been quiet and depressed. She told Justin about playing golf. "I was terrible, Dr. Donnelly. I just couldn't concentrate. So many loud thoughts." But he couldn't get her to discuss the loud thoughts. None of the alters would talk to him either.

When Laurie went into art therapy, Sarah told Donnelly that she had begun to prepare her for the grand jury hearing. "I think everything is really starting to sink in," she explained. "Then last night I caught her going through some photo albums she keeps in her room." Sarah's eyes began to fill with tears that she hastily blinked away. "I told her it wasn't a great idea to look at pictures of Mom and Dad just now."

They left at noon. At two o'clock, Sarah phoned. In the background, Justin Donnelly could hear Laurie screaming.

Her voice trembling, Sarah said, "Laurie's hysterical. She must have been going through the albums again. There's a picture she's torn to bits."

Now Donnelly could make out what Laurie was shrieking. "I promise I won't tell. I promise I won't tell."

"Give me directions to your house," he snapped. "And then get two Valiums into her."

Sophie let him in.

"They're in Laurie's room, Doctor." She led the way upstairs. Sarah was sitting on the bed, holding a sedated Laurie.

"I made her take the Valiums," Sarah told him. "She quieted down, but now she's almost out of it." She released Laurie and eased her head onto the pillow.

Justin bent over Laurie and began to examine her. Her pulse was erratic, her breathing shallow, her pupils dilated, her skin cold to the touch. "She's in shock," he said quietly. "Do you know what brought it on?"

"No. She seemed to be all right after we got home. She said she was going to write in her journal. Then I heard her screaming. I think she must have started going through the album because she tore up a picture. There are pieces of it all over her desk."

"I want those pieces collected," Justin said. "Try not to miss any of them." He began to tap Laurie's face. "Laurie, it's Dr. Donnelly. I want you to talk to me. Tell me your full name."

She did not respond. Donnelly's fingers tapped her face with greater force. "Tell me your name," he said insistently. Finally Laurie opened her eyes. As they focused on him, they took on a surprised expression followed by one of relief.

"Dr. Donnelly," she murmured. "When did you come?"

Sarah felt herself go limp. The last hour had been agony. The sedative had calmed Laurie's hysteria, but then her total withdrawal was even more frightening. Sarah had been terrified that Laurie was slipping so far away she would not make it back.

Sophie was standing in the doorway. "Would a cup of tea be good for her?" she asked softly.

Justin heard. He looked over his shoulder. "Please."

Sarah went over to the desk. The picture was virtually shredded. In those few moments from the time Laurie started shrieking till Sarah and Sophie reached her, she had managed to reduce it to minuscule pieces. It would be a miracle if it could be put together.

"I don't want to stay here," Laurie said.

Sarah whirled around. Laurie was sitting up, hugging herself. "I can't stay here. Please."

"Okay," Justin said calmly. "Let's go downstairs. We could all use a cup of tea." He supported Laurie as she got to her feet. They were halfway down the stairs, Sarah behind them, when the chimes rang in the foyer signaling someone was at the front door.

Sophie bustled to answer it. Two uniformed policemen were on the porch. They were carrying a warrant for Laurie's arrest. By contacting the widow of Allan Grant with a threatening letter, she had violated the terms of her bail and it had been revoked.

That evening, Sarah sat in Justin Donnelly's office in the clinic. "If you hadn't been there, Laurie would be in a jail cell right now," she told him. "I can't tell you how grateful I am."

It was true. When Laurie was brought before the judge, Donnelly had convinced him that she was under intense psychological stress and required hospitalization in a secured facility. The judge had amended his order, to permit inpatient hospitalization. On the drive from New Jersey to New York, she had been in a trancelike sleep.

Justin chose his words carefully. "I'm glad to have her here. She needs to be watched and monitored constantly right now."

"To keep her from sending threatening letters?"

"And to keep her from harming herself."

Sarah got up. "I've taken enough of your time for one day, Doctor. I'll be back first thing in the morning."

It was nearly nine o'clock. "There's a place around the corner where the menu is good and the service is fast," Donnelly told her. "Why don't you grab a quick bite with me and then I'll send for a car to take you home?"

Sarah had already phoned Sophie to tell her that Laurie was checked into the hospital and to be sure to keep her own plans for the evening. The thought of something to eat and a cup of coffee with Justin Donnelly instead of going home to the empty house was comforting. "I'd like that," she said simply.

Laurie was standing at the window of her room. She liked the room. It wasn't large, so she could see all of it in one glance. She felt safe in it. The outside window didn't open. She had tried it. There was an interior window that looked out on the hallway and the nurses' station. It had a drape but she'd left it partially open. She didn't ever want to be in the dark again.

What had happened today? The last thing she remembered was sitting at the desk writing. She'd turned the page and then . . .

And then it all went blank until I saw Dr. Donnelly bending over me, she thought. Then we were going down the stairs and the police came.

The police said she had written a letter to Allan Grant's wife. Why would I write to her? Laurie wondered. They said I threatened her. That's silly, she thought. When would I have written the letter? When would I have mailed it?

If Karen Grant had received a threatening letter in the last few days it was proof that somebody else must have sent it. She couldn't wait to point that out to Sarah.

Laurie leaned her forehead against the window. It felt so cool. She was tired now and would go to bed. A few people were on the sidewalk, hurrying down the block, their heads down. You could tell it was chilly out.

She saw a man and a woman cross the street in front of the clinic. Was that Sarah and the doctor? She couldn't be sure.

She turned, crossed the room and got into bed, pulling the covers around her. Her eyes were so heavy. It was good to drift away. It would be so good never to have to wake up again.

64

On Tuesday morning, Brendon Moody drove to the Clinton College campus. His plan was to canvas the residents of the building where Laurie had her studio apartment. After Allan Grant's funeral, he'd given it the once-over. Five years old, it had been erected to serve the needs of upperclassmen. The rooms were good-sized and included a kitchenette and private bath. It was popular housing for students like Laurie who could afford to pay the surcharge for privacy.

Laurie's apartment had been thoroughly searched and then released by lab technicians from the prosecutor's office. Brendon made it his first stop.

It was totally disheveled. The bed was stripped. The door of the closet was ajar and the clothing looked as though it had been examined and replaced haphazardly on the hangers. The drawers of the dresser were partially open. The contents of the desk were strewn on its surface.

Moody knew that the investigators had taken the typewriter on which the letters to Allan Grant had been written and the rest of the stationery. He knew that the bed sheets and Laurie's bloodstained clothing and watchband and bracelet had been confiscated.

What then was he looking for?

If asked the question, Brendon Moody would have said "Nothing," and meant that he had no particular agenda in mind. He looked around, getting a feel for the premises.

It was obvious that in its normal condition the room was quite attractive. Tie-back, floor-length ivory curtains, an ivory dust ruffle on the bed, framed prints of Monet and Manet, paintings on the walls, a half-dozen golf trophies on a shelf over the bookcase. She had not stuck pictures of classmates and friends in the mirror frame over the dresser, the way so many students did. There was only a single family picture on the desk. Brendon studied the photograph. The Kenyons. He'd known the parents. This shot must have been taken in the pool area behind their house. The family had obviously been happy and content together.

Put yourself in Laurie's place, Moody thought. The family is destroyed. You blame yourself. You're vulnerable and latch onto a guy who's kind to you, who's both an attractive man and old enough to be a sort of father figure, and then he rejects you. And you explode.

Open and shut. Brendon prowled around, examining, evaluating. He stood over the tub in the bathroom. Traces of blood had been found in it. Laurie had been smart enough to wash the sheets and her clothing here, bring them down to the dryer, then fold and put them away. She'd tried to clean the watchband too. Brendon knew what the prosecutor could do with that evidence. Try to prove panic and confusion when the killer had systematically attempted to destroy evidence.

As Brendon was about to leave the room, he looked around one more time. He had found absolutely nothing, not one shred of evidence that could be used to help Laurie. Why did he have the nagging sense that somehow, someway, he was missing something?

65

Sarah had a sleepless night. The day kept replaying in her mind: Laurie's bloodcurdling screams; the torn picture; the policemen at the door; Laurie being taken out in handcuffs; Justin swearing he'd get her released in his custody as they followed the squad car to Clinton. It was dawn when Sarah finally slept, an uneasy, troubled sleep in which she dreamt of courtrooms and guilty verdicts.

She woke up at eight o'clock, showered, put on a tan cashmere shirt, matching slacks and dark brown ankle boots and went downstairs. Sophie was already in the kitchen. Coffee was brewing. In the breakfast area, a flowered pitcher held freshly squeezed orange juice. A compote of cut-up oranges, grapefruit, apples and cantaloupe was attractively arranged in a Tiffany bowl. An English toast rack was positioned next to the toaster.

Everything looks so normal, Sarah thought. It's just as though Mom and Dad and Laurie will come downstairs any minute. She pointed to the toast rack. "Sophie, remember how Dad used to call that thing a toast *cooler.* He was right."

Sophie nodded. Her round, unlined face showing distress, she poured juice into Sarah's glass. "I was worried last night—not being here when you got back. Was Laurie really willing to go into the hospital?"

"She did seem to understand that it was the clinic or jail." Wearily Sarah rubbed her forehead. "Something happened yesterday. I don't know what it was, but Laurie said she'll never spend another night in her bedroom. Sophie, if that woman who came back to see the house the other day wants it, I'm going to sell."

She did not hear the expected protest. Instead Sophie sighed. "I think maybe you're right. This isn't a happy home anymore. Maybe it's too much to expect it to be after what happened in September."

It was both a relief and a blow to realize that Sophie agreed with her. Sarah finished the juice, swallowing over the large lump in her throat. "I'll skip everything except the coffee." A thought struck her. "Do you think you found most of the pieces of that picture Laurie tore up yesterday?"

Sophie's lips creased in a triumphant smile. "Better than that. I put it together." She produced it. "See, I assembled it on the sheet of paper and then, when I was sure it was right, I glued it. Only trouble is the pieces were so small that the glue ran all over them. It's kind of hard to tell much about it."

"Why it's just a picture of Laurie when she was a kid," Sarah said. "That certainly can't be what caused her to get so upset." She studied it, then shrugged helplessly. "I'll put it in my briefcase right now. Doctor Donnelly wants to see it."

With troubled eyes, Sophie watched Sarah push back her chair. She'd so hoped that pasting the picture together would somehow be helpful and show what had brought on Laurie's hysterical outburst. She remembered something and fished inside the pocket of her apron. It wasn't there. Of course it wasn't. The staple that she'd removed from one of the scraps of the picture was in the pocket of the housedress she'd been wearing yesterday. It certainly couldn't be important, she decided as she poured coffee into Sarah's cup.

66

On Tuesday morning, while listening to the eight o'clock CBS news, Bic and Opal heard about Laurie Kenyon's threatening letter to Karen Grant, the revoking of her bail and her confinement in the locked facility of a clinic for multiple personality disorder.

Nervously Opal asked, "Bic, do you think they'll get her to talk in that place?"

"Intense efforts will be made to have her recall her childhood," he said. "We must know what is going on. Carla, call that real estate woman."

Betsy Lyons caught Sarah as she was about to leave for New York. "Sarah," she bubbled, "have I got good news for you! Mrs. Hawkins phoned. She's crazy about the house, wants to close on it as soon as possible and is willing to give you up to a year to live in it. She only asks to be able to come in occasionally with her decorator, at your convenience. Sarah, remember I told you that in this market you might have to come down from seven hundred fifty thousand? My dear, she didn't bicker about the price at all and is paying cash."

"I guess it's meant to be," Sarah said quietly. "I'm glad people who want the house that much are going to have it. You can tell them they can move in by August. The condominium should be ready then. I don't care if they come in with their decorator. Laurie will be staying in the hospital, and if I'm home I'll be working in the library."

Betsy called Carla Hawkins. "Congratulations. It's all set. Sarah is perfectly willing for you to bring in your decorator. She says if she's home she'll be working in the library." Betsy's tone became confidential. "You know, she's going to defend her sister at the trial. Poor darling, she'll have her hands full."

Bic had picked up the extension and listened to the conversation. After a final, "Congratulations again. I'm sure you'll be so happy in that beautiful house," Lyons said goodbye.

Smiling, Bic replaced the receiver. "I'm sure we'll be very happy together," he said and went to the desk. "My special phone book, Carla. Where is it?"

She hurried over. "Right here, Bic, in this drawer." She handed it to him. "Bic, what interior decorator do you want me to get?"

He sighed, "Oh, Carla." Thumbing through the book, he found the name he was looking for and dialed a number in Kentucky.

67

Sarah remembered that Laurie had gone into the clinic with only the clothes she was wearing. Grateful that she wasn't already on her way to New York, she went to Laurie's room and with Sophie's help packed a bag.

At the clinic the bag's contents were examined, and a nurse quietly removed a leather belt and laced sneakers. "Just a precaution," she said.

"You all think that she's suicidal," Sarah told Justin a few minutes later, then looked away from the understanding in his eyes. She knew she could bear anything except sympathy. I can't lose it, she warned herself, again swallowing over the constriction in her throat.

"Sarah, I told you yesterday that Laurie is fragile and depressed. But there is one thing I can promise you—and this is our great hope—she doesn't want you hurt anymore. She'll do anything to prevent that."

"Does she realize that the worst way she could hurt me would be to harm herself?"

"Yes, I do think she knows that. And I believe she is starting to trust me. She knows that I convinced the judge to let her come here instead of going to jail. Were you able to figure out what it was she tore up yesterday?"

"Sophie managed to put it together." Sarah removed the reconstructed photograph from her bag and showed it to him. "I don't understand why this picture would upset her," she said. "It's similar to a lot of others in the album and around the house."

Justin Donnelly studied it. "With all the cracks and glue, it's hard to tell much. I'll have the nurse bring her in."

Laurie was wearing some of the clothes Sarah had brought, jeans and a blue sweater that accentuated her cornflower blue eyes. Her hair was loose. She wore no makeup and looked to be about sixteen. Seeing Sarah, she ran to her and the sisters embraced. As Sarah smoothed down Laurie's hair, she thought, When we come to trial, this is the way she's got to look. Young. Vulnerable.

The thought helped her to get a grip on herself. She realized that when she concentrated on defending Laurie, her own emotions were safely harnessed.

Laurie sat in one of the armchairs. Clearly she had no intention of going near the couch. She made that apparent immediately.

"I'll bet you thought you'd coax her into lying down." It was the strident voice again.

"I think it's Kate who's talking, isn't it?" Justin asked pleasantly.

The look of a sixteen-year-old had vanished. Laurie's face had hardened. No, firmed, Sarah thought. She seems older.

"Yes, it's Kate. And I want to thank you for keeping the wimp out of jail yesterday. That really would have done her in. I tried to stop her from writing that crazy letter to Allan's wife the other day, but she wouldn't listen and see what happened."

"Laurie wrote the letter?" Justin asked.

"No, Leona wrote it. The wimp would have written a letter of condolence. That would have been just as bad. I swear I can't stand her, and as for those other two! One of them always mooning about Allan Grant, the other, the little kid, always crying. If she doesn't shut up soon, I'll throttle her."

Sarah could not take her eyes from Laurie. This alter personality who called herself Kate dwelt inside Laurie, directed or tried to direct Laurie's actions. If she came out on the witness stand with that arrogance and bullying attitude, no jury would ever acquit Laurie.

Justin said, "You know, I haven't turned on the video camera yet.

You came out awfully fast this morning. Is it okay if I turn it on now?"

An annoyed shrug. "Go ahead. You will anyhow."

"Kate, Laurie got awfully upset yesterday, didn't she."

"You should know. You were there."

"I was there after she got upset. I just wondered if you could tell me what caused it?"

"That discussion is forbidden."

Donnelly did not seem fazed. "All right, so we won't discuss it. Could you show me what Laurie was doing when she got upset."

"No way, pal." She turned her head. "Oh shut up that sniffling."

"Is Debbie crying?" Justin asked.

"Who else?"

"I don't know. How many of you are there?"

"Not many. Some of the others went away after Laurie was back home. Just as well. It was getting crowded. I said, *shut up.*"

"Kate, maybe if I spoke to Debbie, I could find out what's bothering her."

"Go ahead. I can't do a thing with her."

"Debbie, please don't be afraid. I promise nothing will hurt you. Talk to me again, won't you?" Justin Donnelly's voice was gentle, coaxing.

The changeover happened in an instant. The hair falling forward, the features smoothed out, the mouth puckered, lips quivering, the hands clasped in her lap, the dangling legs. Tears began to gush down her cheeks.

"Hi, Debbie," Justin said. "You've been crying a lot today, haven't you."

She nodded vigorously.

"Did something happen to you yesterday?"

She nodded assent.

"Debbie, you *know* I like you. You know I keep you safe. Do you think you can trust me?"

A tentative nod.

"Then can you tell me what scared you?"

She shook her head from side to side.

"You can't tell me. Then maybe you can show me. Were you writing in the journal?"

"No. Laurie was writing." The voice was soft, childlike and sad.

"Laurie was writing, but you could tell what she was writing, couldn't you?"

"Not everything, I just started to learn how to read."

"All right. Show me what Laurie was doing."

She picked up an imaginary pen, made the motion of opening a book and began to write in the air. She hesitated, held up the pen as though thinking, looked around and then her hand reached down to turn another page.

Her eyes widened. Her mouth opened in a silent scream. She jumped up, threw the book away from her and began a tearing motion, both hands working vigorously, her face contorted in horror.

Abruptly she stopped, dropped her hands and shouted, "Debbie, get back inside! Listen, Doctor, I may be sick of that little kid, but I take care of her. You burn that picture, do you hear me? Just don't make her look at it again."

Kate had taken charge.

At the end of the session, an attendant came for Laurie. "Can you come back later?" Laurie begged Sarah as she was leaving.

"Yes. Whatever time Dr. Donnelly says is okay."

When Laurie was gone, Justin handed the picture to Sarah. "Can you see anything about this that might frighten her?"

Sarah studied it. "You can't see much with all those cracks and that glue drying over it. You can tell she looks cold, the way she's hugging herself. She's wearing that same bathing suit in the picture with me that we have in the library. It was taken a few days before she was kidnapped. In fact that's the bathing suit she was wearing when she disappeared. Do you think that might have triggered the fear?"

"Very possibly." Dr. Donnelly put the picture in the file. "We'll keep her busy today. She'll be in art therapy this morning and a journal-writing session this afternoon. She still refuses to take any of the standardized tests. I'll be available to see her between and around other patients. I hope the time will come when she's willing to talk to me without you. I think that may happen."

Sarah stood up. "What time shall I come back?"

"Right after she has dinner. Six o'clock work out for you?"

"Of course." As she left, Sarah was calculating the time. It was now nearly noon. With luck she'd be home by one. She'd have to be on her way back by four-thirty to avoid the worst of the commuter traffic. That still gave her three-and-a-half hours at her desk.

Justin walked her to the door of the reception area, then watched her go. Her slim back was straight, her tote bag over her shoulder, her head high. Chin up, he thought, good girl. Then as he watched her walk down the corridor he saw her shove both hands in her pockets as though seeking warmth from a chill only she could feel.

Part Four

68

The grand jury convened on February 17 and did not take long to indict Laurie for the purposeful and knowing murder of Allan Grant. A trial date was set for October fifth.

The next day Sarah met Brendon Moody in Solari's, the popular restaurant around the corner from the Bergen County courthouse. As lawyers and judges came in, they all stopped to speak to Sarah. She should be eating with them, joking with them, Brendon thought, not meeting them this way.

Sarah had spent the morning in the courthouse library researching insanity and diminished mental capacity defenses. Brendon could see the worry in her eyes, the way the smile faded as soon as anyone who greeted her turned away. She looked pale, and there were hollows in her cheeks. He was glad that she had ordered a decent lunch and commented on that.

"Everything tastes like sawdust, but there's no way I can let myself get sick at this stage of the game," Sarah said wryly. "How about you, Brendon? How's the food around the campus?"

"Predictable." Brendon took an appreciative bite of his cheeseburger. "I'm not getting very far, Sarah." He pulled out his notes. "The best and maybe the most dangerous witness is Susan Grimes, who lives across the hall from Laurie. She's the one you called a couple of times. Since October she's noticed Laurie going out regularly between eight and nine o'clock at night and not coming back till eleven or later. She said Laurie looked different on those occasions, pretty sexy, lots of makeup, hair kind of wild, jeans tucked into high-heeled boots—not her usual style at all. She was sure Laurie was meeting some guy."

"Is there any indication that she was ever actually *with* Allan Grant?"

"You can pinpoint specific dates from some of the letters she wrote to him, and they don't hold up," Moody said bluntly. He pulled out his notepad. "On November sixteenth, Laurie wrote that she loved being in Allan's arms the night before. The night before was Friday, November fifteenth, and Allan and Karen Grant were at a faculty party together. Same kind of fantasizing for December second, twelfth, fourteenth, January sixth and eleventh. I could go on right up to January twenty-eighth. The point is, I hoped to prove that Allan Grant had been leading her on. We know she was hanging around his house, but we haven't a shred of evidence that he was aware of it. In fact everything points the other way."

"Then you're saying that all this was in Laurie's mind, that we can't even suggest that Grant might have been taking advantage of her despondency?"

"There's someone else I want to talk to, a teacher who's been away on sick leave. Her name's Vera West. I'm picking up some rumors about her and Grant."

The pleasant background hum of voices and laughter and dishes being placed on tables, all the familiar sounds that had been part of her workday world seemed suddenly intrusive and foreign to Sarah. She knew what Brendon Moody was saying. If Laurie had fantasized all the encounters with Allan Grant, if in his wife's absence Allan had begun a romance with another woman and Laurie had learned about it, it gave more credence to the prosecutor's contention that she had killed him in a jealous rage. "When will you question Vera West?" she asked.

"Soon, I hope."

Sarah swallowed the rest of her coffee and signaled for the check. "I'd better get back. I'm going to meet the people who are buying our house. Guess what? This Mrs. Hawkins who's been coming out is none other than the wife of the Reverend Bobby Hawkins."

"Who's that?" Brendon asked.

"The hot new preacher on the 'Church of the Airways' program. That's the one Miss Perkins was on when she came up with the name 'Jim' as the man Laurie was with in the diner years ago."

"Oh, that guy. What a faker. How come he's buying your house? That's quite a coincidence with him being involved with the Perkins woman."

"Not really. His wife had been looking at the house before all this happened. The Perkins woman wrote to him, not the other way round. Have we gotten any feedback yet from the Harrisburg police on 'Jim'?

Brendon Moody was hoping Sarah would not ask him about that. Choosing his words carefully, he said, "Sarah, as a matter of fact we just did. There's a Jim Brown from Harrisburg who's a known child molester. He has a record a mile long. He was in the area when Laurie was spotted in the diner. Miss Perkins was shown his picture at that time but couldn't identify him. They wanted to bring him in for questioning. After Laurie was found, he disappeared without a trace."

"He never showed up again?"

"He died in prison six years ago in Seattle."

"What was the offense?"

"Kidnapping and assault of a five-year-old girl. She testified at his trial about the two months she was with him. I've read the testimony. Bright little kid. Came out with some pretty harrowing stuff. It was all over the papers at the time."

"Which means that even if he was Laurie's abductor it won't do us any good. If Laurie has a breakthrough and remembers him and is able to describe what he did to her, the prosecutor would bring the Seattle newspapers into court and claim that she'd just parroted that case."

"We don't know that this guy had anything to do with Laurie at all," Moody said briskly. "But, yes, if he did, no matter what Laurie remembers about him, it will sound as if she's lying."

Neither one of them spoke the thought that was in their minds. The way it was going, they might have to ask the prosecutor to consider plea-bargaining for Laurie. If that proved necessary, it would mean that by the end of the summer Laurie would be in prison.

69

Bic and Opal drove with Betsy Lyons to the Kenyon home. For this meeting they had both dressed conservatively. Bic was wearing a gray pin-striped suit with a white shirt and bluish gray tie. His topcoat was dark gray, and he carried gray kidskin gloves.

Opal's hair had just been lightened and shaped at Elizabeth Arden's. Her gray wool dress had a velvet collar and cuffs. Over it she wore a black fitted coat with a narrow sable collar. Her shoes and bag, purchased at Gucci, were black lizard.

Bic was sitting next to Lyons in the front seat of her car. As she chatted, indicating various points of interest in the town, Lyons kept glancing sideways at Bic. She'd been startled when another agent had asked, "Betsy, do you know who that guy *is?"*

She knew he was in television. She certainly hadn't realized he had his own program. She decided that the Reverend Hawkins was a terribly attractive and charismatic man. He was talking about moving to the New York area.

"When I was called to the Church of the Airways ministry, I knew that we'd want to have a home nearby. I'm just not a city person. Carla has had the undesirable job of scouting for us. And she has kept coming back to this town and this house."

Praise the Lord, Betsy Lyons thought.

"My one hesitation," the preacher was saying in his courteous, gentle voice, "is that I was so afraid that Carla was letting herself in for a disappointment. I honestly thought that the house might be taken off the market permanently."

So did I, Betsy Lyons thought, shivering at the prospect. "The girls will be happier in a smaller place," she confided. "Look, this is the street. You drive down Lincoln Avenue and pass all these lovely homes, then the road bends here and it's Twin Oaks Road."

As they turned onto Twin Oaks Road, she rattled off the names of the neighbors. "He owns the Williams Bank. The Kimballs live in the Tudor. She's Courtney Meier, the actress."

In the backseat, Opal clutched her gloves nervously. It seemed to her that every time they came to Ridgewood it was as though they were skating on thin ice and insistently, consistently testing it, pushing nearer and nearer the breaking point.

Sarah was waiting for them. Attractive, Opal decided, as for the first time she got a close look at her. The kind who gets better looking as she gets older. Bic would have passed her by when she was a little kid. Opal wished Lee hadn't had golden hair down to her waist. She wished Lee hadn't been standing by the road that day.

Mutton dressed as lamb, Sarah thought as she extended her hand to Opal. Then she wondered why in the name of God that old Irish expression, a favorite of her grandmother's, had jumped into her mind at this moment. Mrs. Hawkins was a well-dressed, fashionably coiffed woman in her mid-forties. It was the small lips and tiny chin that gave her a weak, almost furtive expression. Or maybe it was that the Reverend Bobby Hawkins had such a magnetic presence. He seemed to fill the room, to absorb all the energy in it. He spoke immediately about Laurie.

"I don't know if you're aware that we prayed on our holy hour that memory of the name of your sister's abductor would be returned to a Miss Thomasina Perkins."

"I saw the program," Sarah told him.

"Have you looked into the name, Jim, to see if there is any possible connection? The Lord works in strange ways, sometimes directly, sometimes indirectly."

"There is nothing we're not checking in my sister's defense," Sarah said with closure in her voice.

He took the hint. "This is a beautiful room," he said, looking around the library. "My wife kept saying how happy I'd be working here with the bookcases and those big windows. I like to be always in the light. Now I don't want to take any more of your time. If we can just go through the house with Mrs. Lyons one last time, then my lawyer can contact your lawyer about passing papers . . ."

Betsy Lyons took the couple upstairs, and Sarah returned to work, filing the notes she had made in the law library. Suddenly she realized she'd better get started for New York.

The Hawkinses and Betsy Lyons looked in to say they were leaving. Reverend Hawkins explained that he would like to bring his architect in as soon as possible but certainly didn't want to have him going over the library while Sarah was working. What would be a good time?

"Tomorrow or the next day between nine and twelve, or late afternoon," Sarah told him.

"Tomorrow morning, then."

When Sarah returned from the clinic and went into the library the next afternoon, she had no way of knowing that from now on every word spoken in that room would be turning on sophisticated voice-activated equipment and that all her conversations would be transmitted to a tape recorder hidden in the wall of the guest-room closet.

~ 70

In mid-March, Karen Grant drove to Clinton for what she hoped would be the last time. In the weeks since Allan's death, she had spent Saturdays going through the house, weeding out the accumulation of six years of marriage, selecting the pieces of furniture she wanted in the New York apartment, arranging for a used-furniture dealer to pick up the rest. She had sold Allan's car and put the house in the hands of a real estate agent. Today there was going to be a memorial service for Allan in the chapel on campus.

Tomorrow she was leaving for four days in St. Thomas. It would be good to get away, she thought as she drove swiftly down the New

Jersey Turnpike. The travel business perks were wonderful. She'd been invited to Frenchman's Reef, one of her favorite places.

Edwin would be going too. Her pulse quickened and unconsciously she smiled. By fall they wouldn't have to sneak around anymore.

The memorial service was like the funeral. It was overwhelming to hear Allan eulogized. Karen heard herself sobbing. Louise Larkin, seated next to her, put an arm around her. "If only he'd listened to me," Karen whispered to Louise. "I warned him that girl was dangerous."

There was a reception afterwards at the Larkin home. Karen had always admired this house. It was over one hundred years old and had been beautifully restored. It reminded her of the houses in Cooperstown where so many of her high school friends lived. She had grown up in a trailer park and could still remember when one of the kids in school asked derisively if her folks were going to have a sketch of their mobile home on their Christmas card.

The Larkins had invited not only faculty members and administrative staff but a dozen or so students. Some of them offered fervent condolences, some paused to tell a favorite story about Allan. Karen's eyes moistened as she told people that she missed Allan more and more each day.

Across the room, forty-year-old Vera West, newest member of the faculty, nursed a glass of white wine. Her round, pleasant face was framed by short, naturally wavy brown hair. Tinted glasses concealed her hazel eyes. She did not need the glasses for vision. She was afraid that the expression in her eyes was too revealing. She sipped her wine, trying not to remember that at a faculty party a few months ago Allan, not his wife, had been across the room. Vera had hoped that the sick leave would give her the time she needed to get a grip on her emotions—emotions no one must suspect her of having. As she pushed back the single strand of hair that always managed to fall on her forehead, she thought of the verse written by a nineteenth-century poet: "Sorrow which is never spoken is the heaviest load to bear."

Louise Larkin joined her. "It's so good to have you back, Vera. We've missed you. How are you feeling?" Larkin's eyes were inquisitive.

"Much better, thank you."

"Mononucleosis is so debilitating."

"Yes, it is." After Allan's funeral, Vera had fled to her cottage in

Cape Cod. Mono was the excuse she'd used when she phoned the dean.

"Karen really looks quite marvelous for someone who's had such a devastating loss, don't you think, Vera?"

Vera raised the glass to her lips, sipped, then said calmly, "Karen's a beautiful woman."

"I mean, you've lost so much weight, and your face is so drawn. I swear, if I were a stranger and had to make a guess between the two of you, I'd pick you as the mourner." Louise Larkin squeezed Vera's hand and smiled sympathetically.

71

Laurie awakened to the faint murmur of voices in the corridor. It was a comforting sound, one she'd been hearing for three months now. February. March. April. It was the beginning of May. Outside, before coming here, whether on the street, on the campus, or even at home, she had begun to feel as though she was free-falling, unable to stop her descent. Here in the clinic, she felt suspended in time. Her plunge had been slowed. She was grateful for the reprieve even though she knew that in the end no one could save her.

She sat up slowly and hugged her legs. This was one of the best moments of the day, when she'd awaken to know the knife dream hadn't wrenched her awake during the night, that whatever stalked her was being held at bay.

It was the sort of thing that they wanted her to write in the journal. She reached over to the night table for the spiral notebook and pen. She had time to jot down a few thoughts before dressing and going to breakfast. She propped up the pillows, pulled herself up and opened the book.

There were pages of writing in it that hadn't been there last night. Over and over a childish hand had written, "I want my mommy. I want to go home."

Later that morning as she and Sarah sat across the desk from Justin Donnelly, Laurie carefully studied the doctor as he read the journal. He was such a big man, she thought, with those broad shoulders, those strong features, that mass of dark hair. She liked his eyes. They were intensely dark blue. She normally didn't like mustaches, but his seemed so right, especially above those even white teeth. She liked his hands too. Wide but with long fingers. Tanned but no hint of fuzz on them. Funny, she could think a mustache looked great on Dr. Donnelly, but she hated fuzz on a man's hands or arms. She heard herself saying that.

Donnelly looked up. "Laurie?"

She shrugged. "I don't know why I said that."

"Would you repeat it?"

"I said I hate fuzz on a man's hands or arms."

"Why do you think that just occurred to you?"

"She's not going to answer that."

Sarah had come to recognize Kate's voice immediately.

Justin wasn't fazed. "Come on, Kate," he said good-humoredly. "You can't keep getting away with bullying Laurie. She wants to talk to me. Or Debbie does. I think it was Debbie writing in the book last night. It looks like her handwriting."

"Well it certainly isn't mine." Over the past three months the tone had become less strident. A certain wary understanding had been struck between Justin and the alter personality, Kate.

"May I speak to Debbie now?"

"Oh, all right. But don't get her crying again. I'm sick of that kid's sniffling."

"Kate, you're a bluff," Justin said. "You protect Debbie and Laurie and we both know it. But you've got to let me help you. It's too big a job for you."

The hair falling forward was the usual signal. It wrenched Sarah's heart to hear the frightened child who called herself Debbie. Was this the way it was for Laurie those two years she was away, weeping, terrified, longing for the people she loved?

"Hi, Debbie," Justin said. "How's the big girl today?"

"Better, thank you."

"Debbie, I'm so glad you started writing in the journal again. Do you know why you wrote this last night?"

"I knew the book was empty. I shook it first."

"You shook the book? What did you expect to find?"

"I don't know."

"What were you afraid to find, Debbie?"

"More pictures," she whispered. "I have to go now. They're looking for me."

"Who? Who is looking for you?"

But she was gone.

A lazy laugh. Laurie had crossed her legs, slumped a little in the chair. In a deliberately provocative gesture, she ran her hand through her hair.

"There she goes, trying to hide, hoping they won't find her."

Sarah stiffened. This was Leona, the alter personality who wrote the letters to Allan Grant. This was the scorned woman who had killed him. She'd only come out twice before in these months.

"Hi, Leona." Justin leaned across the desk, his manner that of offering flattering attention to an attractive woman. "I've been hoping you'd pay us a visit."

"Well, a girl's got to live. You can't keep moping around forever. Got a cigarette?"

"Sure." He reached in the drawer, held out the pack, lit the cigarette for her. "Have you been moping around, Leona?"

She shrugged. "Oh, you know how it is. I was pretty crazy about Professor Kiss-and-Tell."

"Allan Grant?"

"Yes, but listen, it's over, right? I'm sorry for him, but these things happen."

"What things?"

"I mean him giving me away to the shrink and the dean at school."

"You were angry at him for that, weren't you."

"You bet I was. So was Laurie, but for different reasons. She really put on a class-A performance when she buttonholed him in the hall."

I'll have to plea bargain, Sarah thought. If this personality got on the stand, displaying not a shred of remorse about Allan Grant's death . . .

"You know that Allan's dead . . ."

"Oh, I'm used to that now. What a shock though."

"Do you know how he died?"

"Sure I do. Our kitchen knife." The bravado crumbled. "I sure wish to God I'd left it in my room when I dropped in on him that night. I really was crazy about him, you know."

72

In the three months between the beginning of February and the end of April, Brendon Moody had made frequent visits to Clinton College. He had become a familiar figure, chatting with students in the Rathskeller or the student center, talking to the faculty, falling in step with residents of Laurie's dormitory.

At the end of that time he had learned little that would be useful in Laurie's defense, although there were a few things he'd come up with that might possibly lighten her sentence. For the first three years of college she'd been an exemplary student, popular with both faculty and fellow students. "Well liked, but, if you know what I mean, not close," a student from the third floor of her apartment building volunteered. "It's just natural after a while for friends to talk pretty openly about their dates or their families or what's on their minds. Laurie never did that. She was with the crowd and agreeable, but if anyone teased her about Gregg Bennett, who obviously was crazy about her, she'd laugh it off. There was always something very private about her."

Brendon Moody had looked thoroughly into Gregg Bennett's background. Family money. Bright. Had quit college to become an entrepreneur, gotten his ears pinned back and returned for his degree. Carried a double major with honors in both. Graduating in May. Would be starting Stanford next September in the master's program. The kind of guy you'd want your daughter to bring home to meet the family, Brendon thought, and then reminded himself they'd said the same thing about serial killer Ted Bundy.

All the students were in agreement that the change in Laurie after her parents' death was dramatic. Moody. Withdrawn. Complained of headaches. Skipped classes. Assignments late. "Sometimes she'd pass me right by and not even say hello, or she'd look at me as though she'd never seen me before," one junior explained.

Brendon did not tell anyone about Laurie's multiple personality disorder. Sarah was saving that for the trial and did not want a plethora of publicity on the subject.

A significant number of students had noticed Laurie regularly going out alone at night and returning late. They'd commented on it among themselves, trying to guess whom she was meeting. A few had started to put two and two together because of the way Laurie frequently arrived at Allan Grant's classes early and lingered to talk with him afterwards.

The dean's wife, Louise Larkin, enjoyed talking with Moody. It was from her that he got the hint that Allan Grant had become interested in one of the new teachers in the English department. Following Mrs. Larkin's lead, he spoke to Vera West, but she stonewalled him.

"Allan Grant was a good friend to everybody," West said when Brendon talked with her. She ignored any implication in his questions.

Start sifting again, Brendon thought grimly. The problem was that the school year would be over soon, and a lot of the seniors who knew Laurie Kenyon well would be graduating. People like Gregg Bennett.

With that thought in mind, Brendon called Bennett and asked if they could get together again for a cup of coffee. Gregg was on his way out for the weekend, however, so they agreed to meet on Monday. As always, Bennett asked how Laurie was doing.

"From what her sister tells me, she's coming along pretty well," Brendon told him.

"Remind Sarah to call me if there's anything I can do."

Another unproductive week, Brendon thought as he drove home. To his disgust, he learned that his wife was having a Tupperware party at their home that evening. "I'll grab something at Solari's," he said, planting an irritated kiss on the top of her forehead. "How you let yourself get roped into that nonsense, I can't fathom."

"Have fun, dear. It will do you good to catch up with the regulars."

That night Brendon got his long-awaited break. He was sitting at the bar, talking with some of the old crowd from the prosecutor's office. The talk led to Sarah and Laurie Kenyon. The general feeling was that Sarah would be better off to plea bargain. "If they drop the charge to aggravated manslaughter, Laurie might get between fifteen and thirty, probably serve one third . . . be out by the time she's twenty-six or -seven."

"Judge Armon has been assigned, and he doesn't cut deals," one of the other assistant prosecutors said. "Anyhow, the fatal attraction killers aren't popular with any judge at sentencing time."

"I'd hate to see a good-looking kid like Laurie Kenyon locked up with some of those tough babes," another commented.

Bill Owens, a private investigator for an insurance company, was standing next to Brendon Moody. He waited till the subject was changed. Then he said, "Brendon, it can't get around that I tipped you off."

Moody's head did not turn, but his eyes darted to the side. "What's up?"

"You know Danny O'Toole?"

"Danny the Spouse Hunter? Sure. Who's he been spying on lately?"

"That's the point. He was a little drunk here the other night, and as usual, something came up about the Kenyon case. Listen to this. After the parents were killed, Danny was hired to investigate the sisters. Something about an insurance claim. When the younger one was arrested, the job ended."

"Sounds fishy," Moody said. "I'll get right on it. And thanks."

73

"The people who bought our house are getting on Sarah's nerves," Laurie volunteered to Dr. Donnelly.

Justin was surprised. "I hadn't realized that."

"Yes, Sarah said they're around too much. They'll be taking over the house in August and asked permission to do some planting."

"Have you ever watched them on television, Laurie?"

She shook her head. "I don't like that kind of program."

Justin waited. On his desk he had the report from the art therapist. Little by little a pattern was forming in Laurie's sketches. The last half dozen had been collages, and in each she had included two specific scenes: one showed a rocking chair with a thick, deep cushion, and next to it a stick figure of a woman, the other, a thick-trunked tree with wide, heavy branches in front of a windowless house.

Justin pointed to those illustrations on each of the papers. "Remember doing these?"

Laurie looked at them indifferently. "Sure. I'm not much of an artist, am I?"

"You'll do. Laurie, look at that rocking chair. Can you describe it?"

He saw her start to slip away. Her eyes widened. Her body became tense. But he did not want one of the alter personalities to block him. "Laurie, try."

"I have a headache," she whispered.

"Laurie, you trust me. You've just remembered something, haven't you? Don't be afraid. For Sarah's sake, tell me about it, let it out."

She pointed to the rocking chair, then clamped her lips together and squeezed her arms against her sides.

"Laurie, show me. If you can't talk about it, show me what happened."

"I will." The lisping, childlike voice.

"Good girl, Debbie." Justin waited.

She hooked her feet under his desk and tilted back the chair. Her arms crushed against her sides as though held in place by an outside force. She brought down the chair onto the floor with a thud and tilted it back again. Her face was contorted in fear. " 'Amazing grace, how sweet the sound,' " she sang in a frail, little-girl voice.

The chair thudded and tilted in perfect imitation of a rocker. With her body arched and arms immobile, she was miming a young child being held on a lap. Justin glanced down at the top drawing. That was it. The cushion looked like a lap. A small child held by someone and singing as she was being rocked. Back and forth. Back and forth.

" '. . . And grace will lead me home.' " The chair stopped. Her eyes closed again. Her breathing became quick, painful gasps. She stood and went up on her toes as though she was being lifted. "Time to go upstairs," she said in a deep voice.

74

"Here they come again," Sophie observed tartly as the familiar dark blue Cadillac pulled up into the driveway.

Sarah and Brendon Moody were in the kitchen waiting for the coffee to perk. "Oh God," Sarah said, her tone irritated. "It's my fault for letting it happen," she said to Brendon. "Tell you what. Sophie, bring the coffee into the library when it's ready and tell them I'm in a meeting. I'm just not in the mood to be prayed over."

Brendon scurried behind her and closed the library door as the chimes sounded through the house. "I'm glad you didn't give them a key," he said.

Sarah smiled. "I'm not that crazy. The thing is that there are so many things in this house that I can't use, and they're willing and anxious to buy them. I've been having appraisals. They're bringing in experts to have their own appraisals, and it's beginning to feel as though I have star boarders."

"Why not get it over with at once?" Brendon asked.

"Mostly my fault. I tell them what I'm willing to sell, then I take a look at all the stuff in this house and realize no way am I going to fit it into a condo, and so I tell them all this other stuff is available too. Or they come to me and ask about that painting or that table or that lamp. And so it goes." Sarah pushed back her hair. The day was warm and humid, and her hair had frizzed into a cloud resembling dark autumn leaves around her face.

"That's something else," she added as she sat down at the desk.

"Dad never went for air-conditioning, and they intend to put in a new system. They'd like to be able to move on it as soon as we close, and that means engineers and whatever now."

Keep your mouth shut, Brendon told himself as he settled in the leather chair opposite the desk. He knew that the Hawkinses had paid top dollar for the house, and if they were buying the furniture Sarah could not use, it meant she didn't have to try to find buyers or store it. Laurie's hospitalization was costing a fortune, and the student insurance policy she carried was covering only a small portion of it. To say nothing of the costs of preparing a defense, and Sarah not working, he thought.

"You've had a chance to go over your insurance policies?" he asked.

"Yes. Brendon, I don't get it. There is no outstanding or questionable claim. My father kept his records straight. His insurance went to Mother, and then, in the event of her predeceasing him, to us. Since he outlived her by a few minutes, it came directly to us. Unfortunately everything except the house is tied up in trusts, which would have made a lot of sense if all this hadn't happened. We get payouts of fifty thousand dollars each for five years for a total of a quarter of a million each, and there's no way we can invade the principal of those trusts."

"What about the bus company?" Brendon asked. "Have you filed suit against them?"

"Of course," Sarah said. "But why would they have us checked? We weren't involved in the accident."

"Oh, hell," Brendon said, "I was hoping to get somewhere with this angle. I'll get the investigator drunk and pump him, but that's probably what it's about. Just the bus company. How's Laurie?"

Sarah considered. "She's better in a lot of ways. I think she's coming to terms with losing Dad and Mom. Dr. Donnelly is wonderful."

"Any memory of Allan Grant's death?"

"Nothing. However, she is starting to let things out about what happened to her those years she was away. Just bits and pieces. Justin, I mean Dr. Donnelly, is sure that she was molested in that time. But even showing her the videotapes of her therapy sessions when her alter personalities come out isn't helping her to have a real breakthrough." Sarah's voice lost its calm tone and became desperate. "Brendon, it's May. In three months I have found nothing to use as a defense for her. She seems to have three alter personalities. Kate, who is kind of a protector, almost like a cross nanny. Calls Laurie a wimp and gets angry at her, but then tries to shield her. She keeps blocking memory. Leona is a sexpot. That personality did have a fatal attraction for Allan Grant. Just last week she told Dr. Donnelly that she's so sorry she brought the knife with her that night."

"Sweet Jesus," Brendon muttered.

"The last personality is Debbie, a four-year-old kid. She cries all the time." Sarah raised her hands, then let them fall. "Brendon, that's it."

"Will she ever remember what happened?"

"Possibly, but no one can predict how long it will take. She does trust Justin. She understands that she can end up in prison. But she can't seem to make the breakthrough." Sarah looked at him. "Brendon, don't suggest I plea bargain."

"I have no intention of suggesting that," Brendon growled. "At least not yet."

Sophie entered the library, carrying a tray of coffee. "I left them alone upstairs," she said. "That's all right, isn't it?"

"Of course," Sarah said. "After all, Sophie, he's a preacher. Surely he's not stuffing trinkets in his pockets."

"Today they're having a big debate about combining your bathroom and Laurie's and putting in a Jacuzzi. I thought clergymen lived simply." She banged the tray on the desk.

"Not necessarily," Brendon commented. He dropped three lumps of sugar in the coffee and stirred it vigorously. "Sarah, Gregg Bennett honestly doesn't know what triggered Laurie's reaction to him last year. I think he's still pretty crazy about her. The evening before Grant died, some of the students were discussing Laurie's crush on the professor and Gregg overheard them. Stormed out of the student center."

"Jealous?" Sarah asked quickly.

Brendon shrugged. "If he was, it doesn't seem to have any bearing on Allan Grant's death unless . . ."

"Unless Laurie gets her memory back."

There was a tap on the door. Sarah raised her eyes. "Prepare yourself to be blessed," she murmured, then called, "come in."

Bic and Opal, their faces set in solicitous smiles, stood in the doorway. They were dressed casually. Bic had taken off his jacket, and his shortsleeved T-shirt revealed muscular arms covered with soft graying hair. Opal wore slacks and a cotton blouse. "Not to disturb, just to see how it's going," she said.

Sarah introduced Brendon Moody to them. He grunted a greeting.

"And how is that little girl?" Bic asked. "You don't know how many people we have praying on her."

75

Justin Donnelly did not want to admit to Sarah that he now believed Laurie would not recover significant memory in time for the trial. With two members of his staff, Pat and Kathie, the art and journal therapists, he reviewed the tapes of his therapy sessions with Laurie. "Notice how the alter personalities trust me now and are willing to talk, but they all stonewall me when I try to go back to the night of January twenty-eighth or the years of Laurie's abduction. Let's discuss the three alter personalities again.

"Kate is thirty-three, which makes her fairly close to Sarah's age. I think she was created by Laurie to be a protector, which is how Laurie sees Sarah. Totally unlike Sarah, Kate is usually annoyed at Laurie, calls her a wimp, gets disgusted with her for getting in trouble. I think that shows Laurie's feeling that she deserves to have Sarah angry at her.

"Debbie, the four-year-old child, wants to talk but is too frightened or maybe just doesn't understand what happened. I suspect she is pretty much as Laurie was at that age. Sometimes she shows flashes of humor. Sarah Kenyon said that Laurie was a precociously funny child before she was kidnapped.

"Leona is a pretty sexy lady. There's no question she was crazy about Allan Grant and jealous of his wife. There's no question that she was so angry about what she perceived as his betrayal of her that she might have been capable of killing him, but now she talks about him with a kind of affection, the way you might talk about an old lover. The fight's over. The anger's faded and you remember the good parts."

They were in the staff room adjacent to Justin's office. The late spring sun was streaming in the windows. From where he sat, Justin could look over at the solarium. Several of the patients were there, enjoying the sunshine. As he watched, Laurie walked into the solarium, arm in arm with Sarah.

Pat, the art therapist, was holding several new drawings. "Have you got the snapshot that Laurie tore up at home?" she asked.

"Right here." Justin riffled through the file.

The therapist studied the photograph, compared it with some of Laurie's sketches, then laid them side by side. "Okay, see this." She pointed to a stick figure. "And this. And this. What do you make of it?"

"She's starting to put a playsuit or a bathing suit on the stick figure," Justin commented.

"Right. Now notice how in these three, the figure has long hair. In these two, look at the difference. Very short hair. She's drawn a face of sorts that gives me the impression of a boy's face. The arms are folded the way they are in the picture that's glued together. I think there's a possibility that she's recreating that image of herself but changing it to a boy. I wish to God the print wasn't so mutilated. She sure did a terrific job of shredding it."

Kathie, the journal therapist, was holding Laurie's latest composition. "This is the handwriting of her alternate Kate. But notice how different it is from the way it was in February. It's more and more like Laurie's penmanship. And listen to what it says. 'I'm getting so tired. Laurie will be strong enough to accept what has to be. She'd like to walk in Central Park. She'd like to take the golf clubs, drive to the club and tee off. It would have been fun for her to be on the golf circuit. Was it less than a year ago they called her the best young woman golfer in New Jersey? Maybe prison isn't much different than here. Maybe it's secure like this place. Maybe the knife dream will stay far away in prison. Nobody can sneak into prison with guards around. They can't come with knives in the night. They check all the incoming mail in prison. That means that pictures can't walk into books by themselves.' " The journal therapist handed the composition to Justin. "Doctor, this may be a sign that Kate is accepting guilt and punishment for Laurie."

Justin stared out the window. Sarah and Laurie were sitting side by side. Whatever Sarah was saying, Laurie was laughing. They could have been two very attractive young women on their terrace at home or at a country club.

The art therapist had followed his gaze. "I was talking to Sarah yesterday. I think she's going on sheer nerve now. The day the prison door closes behind Laurie, you may have a new patient, Dr. Donnelly."

Justin stood up. "They're due in my office in ten minutes. Pat, I think you're right. She's drawing different versions of the torn snapshot. Do you know anyone who might be able to take it apart, clean off all that glue, reassemble it and blow it up so we can get a better look?"

She nodded. "I can try."

He turned to Kathie. "Do you think that if Laurie or Kate realizes the effect her imprisonment will have on Sarah that she'll be less resigned to an automatic conviction?"

"Possibly."

"Okay. And there's something else I'm going to do. I'm going to talk to Gregg Bennett, Laurie's ex-boyfriend, and try to find out all the circumstances of the day she became so frightened of him."

76

As Brendon Moody slid onto a bar stool at Solari's next to Danny the Spouse Hunter, he noted that Danny's cherubic face was beginning to sag at the jawline. Broken capillaries on his nose and cheeks were tributes to his appreciation of dry Manhattans.

Dan greeted Moody with his usual exuberance. "Ah, there you are, Brendon. A sight for sore eyes."

Brendon grunted a greeting, resisting the urge to tell Dan what he could do with his acquired brogue. Then, reminding himself of the reason he was here and of Danny's fondness for dry Manhattans and the Mets, he ordered a round and asked Danny how he figured the team would do this season.

"Brilliant. A pennant," Danny crowed happily. "The lads have it together, by jingo."

I knew you when you could speak English, Brendon thought, but said, "Grand. Grand."

An hour later as Brendon nursed his first drink, Danny finished his third. It was time. Brendon directed the conversation to Laurie Kenyon. "I've been on the case," he said in a confidential whisper.

Danny's eyes narrowed. "So I've heard. Poor girl went bonkers, did she not?"

"Looks it," Brendon acknowledged. "Guess she went nuts after the parents were killed. Too bad she didn't get regular professional counseling then."

Danny glanced around. "Ah, but she did," he whispered. "And forget where you heard it. I hate to think they'd keep you in the dark."

Brendon looked shocked. "You mean she was seeing some shrink?"

"Right over in Ridgewood."

"How do you know, Danny?"

"Between the two of us?"

"Of course."

"Right after the parents died my services were engaged just to do a background check on the sisters and their activities."

"No kidding. Insurance company, I suppose. Something about a claim against the bus company?"

"Now, Brendon Moody, you know the client-investigator relationship is strictly confidential."

"Of course it is. But that bus was going too fast; the brakes were bad. The Kenyons never had a chance. Naturally an insurance company would be pretty nervous and want to get a line on the potential plaintiffs. Who else would be checking on them?"

Danny remained stubbornly silent. Brendon signaled the bartender, who shook his head. "I'll drive my good friend home," Brendon promised. He knew it was time to change the subject. An hour later, after he hoisted Danny into the passenger seat of his car, he started talking about the Kenyons again. As he pulled up in the driveway of Danny's modest split level he hit pay dirt.

"Brendon, me lad, you're a good friend," Danny said, his voice thick and slow. "Don't think I don't know but that you've been pumping me. Between you and me and the lamppost, I don't know who hired me. All very mysterious. A woman it was. Called herself Jane Graves. Never did meet her. Called every week to get a progress report. Had it sent to a private mail drop in New York City. You know who I think it might be? The widow of the late professor. Wasn't the poor dingbat Kenyon girl writing mash notes to him? And didn't the demand for my services end the day after the murder?"

Danny pushed open the car door and staggered out. "A grand good night to ye, and next time ask me straight. It won't cost you so many drinks."

~ 77

The "architect" Bic had brought to the Kenyon home on one of his early visits was an ex-convict from Kentucky. It was he who wired the library and telephone with sophisticated, voice-activated equipment, and concealed a recorder in the guest bedroom above the study.

As Bic and Opal roamed upstairs with measuring tapes, fabrics and paint samples, it was an easy matter for them to change the cassettes. The minute they were in the car, Bic began playing the tapes and he continued to listen to them over and over in their Wyndham Hotel suite.

Sarah had begun to have regular evening telephone conversations with Justin Donnelly, and these were gold mines of information. At first Opal had to make a concerted effort to conceal her sullen annoyance at Bic's absolute passion for any news of Lee. But as the weeks went by she was torn between fear of discovery and fascination at the talk about Laurie's flashes of recall. Sarah's discussion with the doctor about the rocking chair memory especially gratified Bic.

"The little darlin'," he sighed. "Remember how pretty she was and how nice she could sing. We taught her well." He shook his head. "My, my." Then he frowned. "But, she's starting to talk."

Bic had opened the hotel windows, allowing the warm May air to fill the room, the faint breeze rippling the curtains. He was letting his hair grow a little longer, and today it was disheveled. He was wearing only old slacks and a T-shirt, which exposed the thick curly hair on his arms that Opal called her favorite pillow. She stared at him, worshipping him with her eyes.

"What are you thinking, Opal?" he asked.

"You'll say I'm crazy."

"Try me."

"It just occurred to me that right at this minute, with your hair mussed and you in your T-shirt and your jacket off, all you need is that gold earring you used to wear and the Reverend Hawkins would disappear. You'd be Bic the nightclub singer again."

Bic stared at her for a long minute. I shouldn't have told him that, she thought aghast. He won't want to think that's possible. But then he said, "Opal, the Lord directed you to that revelation. I was thinking on the old farmhouse in Pennsylvania and that rocking chair where I used to sit with that sweet baby in my arms, and a plan was forming. Now you've completed it."

"What is it?"

The benevolent expression faded. "No questions. You know that. Never any questions. This is between me and the Blessed Lord."

"I'm sorry, Bobby." She deliberately addressed him that way, knowing it would mollify him.

"That's all right. One thing I am learning from all that listening is that I don't wear short sleeves around those people. The business of fuzzy arm hair is coming up pretty regular. And did you notice something else?"

She waited.

Bic smiled coldly. "This whole situation may be starting a little romantic brush fire. Listen to the way that doctor and Sarah talk to each other. Tone of voice, warmer and warmer. He's more and more concerned about her. It will be nice for her to have someone for comfort after Lee joins the heavenly choir."

~ 78

Karen Grant glanced up from her desk and smiled brightly. The small, balding man with the wrinkled forehead looked vaguely familiar. She invited him to sit down. He presented his card, and she understood why she had recognized him. He was the investigator working for the Kenyons, and he'd been at the funeral. Louise Larkin had told her that he had been questioning people on the campus.

"Mrs. Grant, if this isn't a good time, just say so." Moody glanced around the office.

"Absolutely fine," she assured him. "It's a quiet morning."

"I gather the travel business in general is pretty quiet these days," Moody said casually. "At least that's what my friends tell me."

"Oh, like everything else, it's gotten leaner and meaner. Can I sell you a trip?"

Sharp lady, Brendon thought, and just as attractive up close as across a grave site. Karen Grant was wearing a turquoise linen suit and matching blouse. The blue-green color brought out the green in her eyes. That oufit didn't come from K Mart, Brendon decided. Neither did the crescent of jade and diamonds on her lapel. "Not today," he said. "If I may I'd like to ask a few questions about your late husband."

The smile faded. "It's very hard to talk about Allan," she said. "Louise Larkin told me about you. You're working on Laurie Kenyon's defense. Mr. Moody, I'm terribly sorry for Laurie, but she did take my husband's life and she threatened mine."

"She doesn't remember anything about it. She's a very sick girl," Brendon said quietly. "It's my job to try to help a jury to understand that. I've been going over copies of the letters she, or someone, sent to Professor Grant. How long were you aware that he was receiving them?"

"At first, Allan didn't show them to me. I guess he was afraid I'd be upset."

"Upset?"

"Well, they were patently ludicrous. I mean some of the 'remembrances' were of nights when Allan and I were together. It was obvious they were all fantasy, but even so, they were certainly unpleasant. I happened to see the letters in his desk drawer and I asked about them."

"How well did you know Laurie?"

"Not well. She's a marvelous golfer, and I'd seen write-ups about her in the papers. I met her parents at some college affairs, that sort of thing. I felt terribly sorry for her after they died. I know Allan thought that she was heading for a breakdown."

"You were in New York the night he died?"

"I was at the airport meeting a client."

"When did you last speak to your husband?"

"I called him at about eight o'clock that night. He was terribly upset. He told me about the scene with Laurie Kenyon. He felt he hadn't handled the situation properly. He thought he should have sat down with Sarah and Laurie before having Laurie called in by the dean. He said that he honestly believed she had no recollection of writing those letters. She was so angry and shocked when she was accused."

"You do realize that if you testify to that on the witness stand it could be helpful to Laurie."

Now tears welled in Karen Grant's eyes. "My husband was the nicest, kindest human being I've ever known. He of all people would not want me to hurt that girl."

Moody's eyes narrowed. "Mrs. Grant, was there any point when you had a few doubts about whether or not your husband was falling in love with Laurie?"

She looked astonished. "That's ridiculous. She's twenty or twenty-one. Allan was forty."

"It's been known to happen. I certainly wouldn't blame you if you wanted to be sure, say maybe have it checked out."

"I don't know what you're talking about."

"I mean possibly hire a private investigator like myself . . ."

The tears dried. Karen Grant was visibly angry. "Mr. Moody, I wouldn't have insulted my husband like that. And you're insulting me." She stood up. "I don't think we have anything more to say to each other."

Moody rose slowly. "Mrs. Grant, please forgive me. Try to understand that my job is to find some reason for Laurie's actions. You said that Professor Grant thought Laurie was nearing a breakdown. If there was something going on between them, if he then betrayed her to the administration and she then snapped . . ."

"Mr. Moody. Do not try to defend the girl who murdered my

husband by ruining his reputation. Allan was a private man and intensely embarrassed by student crushes. You cannot change that fact to save his murderer."

As he nodded apologetically, Brendon Moody's glance was sweeping the office. Attractively furnished with a red leather settee and chairs. Framed posters of exotic travel scenes on walls. Fresh flowers on Karen Grant's desk and on the coffee table by the couch. Her desk, however, was clear of paperwork, and the phone had not rung since he'd been in the office. "Mrs. Grant, I'd like to leave on a happier note. My daughter is an American Airlines hostess. Loves the job. Says the travel business gets into your blood. I hope you feel that way and your job is helping you to adjust to the loss of your husband."

He thought she seemed slightly mollified. "I'd be lost without it."

There was no sign of anyone else. "How many people work here?" he asked casually.

"My secretary is on an errand. Anne Webster, the owner, is out ill today."

"Then you're in charge?"

"Anne is retiring soon. I'll be taking over completely."

"I see. Well, I've taken enough of your time."

Moody did not leave the hotel immediately. Instead he sat in the lobby and observed the travel agency. Two hours later not a single person had entered it. Through the glass wall he could see that Karen did not pick up the phone even once. Putting down the newspaper he had used to disguise his presence, he moseyed over to the bell captain's desk and began to chat with him.

79

Gregg Bennett drove up the Turnpike to the exit for the Lincoln Tunnel. It was a warm, hazy day, more like July than the last week in May. He rode with the top down on his new Mustang convertible, a graduation gift from his grandfather. The gift made him uncomfortable. "Granpa, I'm twenty-five, old enough to earn the money for my own cars," he'd protested. Then his mother pulled him aside.

"For heaven's sake, Gregg, don't be such a stiff-neck. Granpa is so proud that you've been accepted at Stanford that he's busting his buttons."

In truth, Gregg preferred the ten-year-old secondhand Ford he'd driven at Clinton. He could still see himself throwing the golf bags in the trunk, Laurie getting in beside him, teasing him about his game.

Laurie.

He turned the car onto the Route 3 approach to the tunnel. As usual traffic was backed up, and he glanced at the clock on the dashboard. Three-forty. It was okay. He'd left plenty of time to get to the clinic. He hoped he looked all right. He had debated about what to wear, then chosen a tan linen jacket, open-neck shirt, chinos and loafers. Laurie wouldn't know him if he got too gussied up. His mouth went dry at the thought that after all these months he would be seeing her again.

Sarah was waiting for him in the reception area. He kissed her cheek. It was obvious to him that she'd been going through hell. Deep circles underlined her eyes. Her dark brows and lashes made her skin seem transparent. She immediately brought him in to meet Laurie's doctor.

Donnelly was gravely honest. "Someday Laurie may be able to tell us about those years she was missing and about Allan Grant's death, but as it stands now, she can't tell us in time to prepare her defense. What we're trying to do is to in effect go around her, to recreate a scene in which she had a dissociative reaction and see if we can learn what set her off. You've told Sarah and Detective Moody about the episode in your apartment a year ago—we'd like to recreate it.

"Laurie's agreeable to the experiment. We're going to videotape you with her. We need you to describe in her presence, what you were doing, what you were saying, where you were in relation to each other. Please, for her sake don't edit or hide anything. I mean anything."

Gregg nodded.

Dr. Donnelly picked up the phone. "Will you bring Laurie in, please?"

Gregg didn't know what to expect. Certainly it wasn't the attractive Laurie dressed in a short cotton skirt and T-shirt, a narrow belt cinching her slender waist, sandals on her feet. She stiffened when she saw him. Some instinct made Gregg decide not to get up. He waved at her casually. "Hi, Laurie."

She watched him warily as she took a seat next to Sarah, then nodded but said nothing.

Justin turned on the camera. "Gregg, Laurie came to visit you about a year ago and for some unknown reason, she panicked. Tell us about it."

Gregg had gone over that morning so often in his mind that there was no hesitation. "It was Sunday. I slept late. At ten o'clock Laurie rang the bell and woke me up."

"Describe where you live," Justin cut in.

"A rented studio over a garage a couple of miles from the campus. Compact kitchen, countertop with stools, convertible sofa bed, bookcases, dresser, two closets, decent-sized john. Actually it's not bad as these things go."

Sarah watched Laurie close her eyes as though remembering.

"All right," Justin said. "Did you expect Laurie to drop in?"

"No. She was going home for the day. Actually she had invited me to go with her, but I had a term paper due. She'd been to the nine o'clock mass, then stopped at the bakery. When I opened the door, she said something like, 'Coffee for a hot bagel? Fair trade?' "

"What was her attitude?"

"Relaxed. Laughing. We'd played golf on Saturday and it had been a close round. She'd beaten me by only a stroke. Sunday morning she was wearing a white linen dress and looked terrific."

"Did you kiss her?"

Gregg glanced at Laurie. "On the cheek. I'd get signals from her. Occasionally she could be pretty responsive when I'd start to kiss her, but I was always careful. It was like you could scare her away. When I kissed her or put my arm around her, I'd do it slowly and casually and see if she'd tense up. If she did, I quit right away."

"Didn't you find that pretty frustrating?" Justin asked quickly.

"Sure. But I think I always knew there was something in Laurie that was afraid, and that I would have to wait for her to trust me." Gregg looked directly at Laurie. "I'd never hurt her. I'd kill before I let anyone else hurt her."

Laurie was staring at him, no longer avoiding his gaze. It was she who spoke next. "I sat next to Gregg at the counter. We had two cups of coffee and split the third bagel. We were talking about when we could get in another round of golf. I felt so happy that day. It was such a beautiful morning and everything felt so fresh and clean." Her voice faltered as she said "clean."

Gregg stood up. "Laurie said she had to be on her way. She kissed me and started to leave."

"There was no sign of fear or panic at that point?" Justin interjected.

"None."

"Laurie, I want you to stand near Gregg just as you did that day. Pretend you're about to leave his apartment."

Hesitantly Laurie stood up. "Like this," she whispered. She reached out for an imaginary doorknob, her back to Gregg. "And he . . ."

"And I started to pick her up . . ." Gregg said. "I mean jokingly. I wanted to kiss her again."

"Show me how," Justin commanded.

"Like this." Gregg stood behind Laurie, pressed his hands against her arms and started to raise her.

Her body stiffened. She began to whimper. Instantly Gregg released her.

"Laurie, tell me why you're afraid," Justin said swiftly.

The whimper changed into stifled, childlike weeping, but she did not answer.

"Debbie, you're the one crying," Justin said. "Tell me why."

She pointed down and to the right. A frail, small voice sobbed, "He's going to take me there."

Gregg looked shocked and puzzled. "Wait a minute," he said. "If we were in my apartment, she'd be pointing to the sofabed."

"Describe it," Justin snapped.

"I'd just gotten up, so it was still open and unmade."

"Debbie, why were you afraid when you thought Gregg was taking you to the bed? What might happen to you there? Tell us."

She had dropped her face in her hands. The soft childlike crying continued. "I can't."

"Why not, Debbie? We love you."

She looked up and ran to Sarah. "Sare-wuh, I don't know what happened," she whispered. "Whenever we got to the bed, I floated away."

~ 80

Vera West was counting the days until the term ended. She was finding it increasingly difficult to keep up the calm façade that she knew was absolutely necessary. Now as she walked across the campus in the late afternoon, her leather zipbag bulging with final term papers clasped in her arms, she found herself praying that she would reach the sanctuary of her rented cottage before she began to cry.

She loved the cottage. It was on a wooded cul-de-sac and at one time had been the home of the gardener of the large manor house nearby. She had taken the job in the English Department at Clinton because after going back to school for her doctorate at age thirty-seven and receiving it at forty, she'd felt restless, ready for a change from Boston.

Clinton was the kind of jewellike smaller college she loved. A theater buff, she also enjoyed the nearness to New York.

Along the way, a few men had been interested in her. At times she wistfully wished she could find someone who would seem special but had decided she was destined to follow in the footsteps of her unmarried aunts.

Then she'd met Allan Grant.

Until it was too late, it never occurred to Vera that she was falling in love with him. He was another faculty member, a very nice human being, a teacher whose intellect she admired, whose popularity she understood.

It had begun in October. One night Allan's car wouldn't start, and she'd offered him a ride home from a Kissinger lecture in the auditorium. He'd invited her in for a nightcap and she'd accepted. It hadn't occurred to her that his wife wasn't there.

His house was a surprise. Expensively furnished. Surprisingly so, considering what she knew to be his salary. But there was no sense of an effort having been made to pull it together. It looked as though it could stand a good cleaning. She knew that Karen, his wife, worked in Manhattan but didn't realize that she had an apartment there.

"Hi, Dr. West."

"What—oh, hello." Vera tried to smile as she passed a group of students. From the air of buoyancy about them it was obvious that the term was nearly over. None of these students would be dreading the emptiness of the summer, the emptiness of the future.

That first evening at Allan's home, she'd offered to get the ice while he prepared a scotch and soda for them. In the freezer individual packages of pizza, lasagna, chicken-pot pies and God knows what else were piled together. Good heavens, she'd wondered, is that the way this poor guy eats?

Two nights later, Allan dropped off a book at her place. She'd just roasted a chicken, and the inviting aroma filled the cottage. When he commented on it, she impulsively invited him to dinner.

Allan was in the habit of taking a long predinner walk. He began to stop by occasionally, and then more often on the nights Karen was in New York. He would phone, ask if she wanted company and if so, what could he bring? Calling himself the man who came to dinner, he'd arrive with wine or a wedge of cheese or some fruit. He always left by eight or eight-thirty. His manner toward her was always attentive, but no different than if the room had been filled with people.

Even so, Vera began to lie awake at night wondering how long it would be before people started to gossip about them. Without asking, she was sure that he did not tell his wife about their time together.

Allan showed her the "Leona" letters as soon as they began to arrive. "I'm not going to let Karen see these," he said. "They'd only upset her."

"Surely she wouldn't put any stock in them."

"No, but underneath that sophisticated veneer, Karen is pretty insecure, and she does depend on me more than she realizes." A few weeks later he told her that Karen had found the letters. "Just what I expected. She's upset and worried."

At the time, Vera had thought that Karen sent some pretty mixed signals. Worried about her husband but away so much. Foolish lady.

At first, Allan seemed to deliberately avoid any kind of personal discussion. Then gradually he began to talk about growing up. "My dad split when I was eight months old. My mother and grandmother . . . what a pair. They did anything to make a dollar." He'd laughed. "I mean just *about* anything. My grandmother had a big old house in Ithaca. She rented rooms to old people. I always said I was raised in a nursing home. Four or five of them were retired teachers, so I had a lot of help with my homework. My mother worked in the local department store. They saved every penny they could for my education and invested it wisely. I swear they were disappointed when I won a full scholarship to Yale. They were both good cooks. I can still remember how great it was to get home on a cold afternoon after I finished my paper route, open the door, feel that blast of warmth and breathe in all the good smells from the kitchen."

Allan had told her all that a week before he died. Then he'd said, "Vera, that's the way I feel when I come here. Warmth and a sense of coming home to someone I want to be with and who I hope wants me." He'd put his arm around her. "Can you be patient with me? I've got to work something out."

The night he died, Allan had been with her for the last time. He'd been depressed and upset. "I should have spoken to Laurie and her sister first. I jumped the gun by going to the dean. Now the dean has as much as said that my manner with these kids is too friendly. He flat out asked me if Karen and I were having problems, if there was any reason she was away so much." At the door that night, he'd kissed her slowly and said, "It's going to change. I love and need you very much."

Some instinct had warned her to tell him to stay with her. If only she'd listened to it and to hell with the gossips. But she let him go. A little after ten-thirty she'd phoned him. He sounded remarkably cheerful. He'd spoken to Karen and it was all out on the table. He had taken a sleeping pill. Again he had said, "I love you," the last words she would ever hear from him.

Too restless to go to bed herself, Vera had watched the eleven o'clock news and started tidying up the living room, fluffing pillows, straightening magazines. In the wing chair she'd noticed something gleaming. The ignition key to Allan's car. It must have slipped out of his pocket.

She was filled with unreasoning worry about him. The key was an excuse to call again. She dialed his number, letting the phone ring and ring. There was no answer. The sleeping pill must really have taken effect, she'd reassured herself.

Today, suddenly reminded again of her loneliness, Vera hurried, head down, along her cobblestone walk, Allan's face filling her mind. Her arms ached for him. She reached the steps. *"Allan. Allan. Allan."*

Vera didn't realize she'd spoken his name aloud until she looked up into the keen eyes of Brendon Moody, who was waiting for her on the porch.

81

Seated at a corner table in Villa Cesare in Hillsdale, a few miles from Ridgewood, Sarah wondered why in heaven's name she had let herself get talked into having dinner with the Reverend Bobby and Carla Hawkins.

The couple had shown up at her door five minutes after she returned from New York. They'd been just driving around, they explained, getting to know their new neighborhood, and she'd passed them on Lincoln Avenue.

"You looked as though you needed a little help," the Reverend Bobby said. "I just felt the Lord telling me to turn around, drop by and say hello."

When she'd reached home at seven o'clock after leaving the clinic and saying goodbye to Gregg Bennett, Sarah had realized she was tired and hungry. Sophie was out, and the minute Sarah opened the door of the empty house she knew she didn't want to stay there.

Villa Cesare was a longtime favorite restaurant, a great place to eat. Clams casino, shrimp scampi, a glass of white wine, cappuccino; that always-friendly, welcoming atmosphere, she thought. She was walking out the door when the Hawkinses arrived; somehow they ended up joining her.

As she nodded to familiar faces at other tables, Sarah told herself, these are caring people and I'll accept any prayers I can get. Lost in her thoughts, she suddenly realized that Reverend Hawkins was asking about Laurie.

"It's all a matter of time," she explained. "Justin—I mean Dr. Donnelly—doesn't have any doubt that eventually Laurie will let down her defenses and talk about the night Professor Grant died, but it seems as though that memory is entwined with her fear of whatever happened to her in the past. The doctor feels that at some point she'll achieve a spontaneous breakthrough. Pray God she does."

"Amen," Bobby and Carla said in unison.

Sarah realized her guard was down. She was talking about Laurie too much. These people were, after all, strangers whose only connection to her was that they had bought the house.

The house. Safe ground. "Mother planned the landscaping so we'd always have color," she said as she selected a crusty roll. "The tulips were marvelous. You saw them. The azaleas will be out in a week or so. They're my favorites. Ours are great, but the D'Andreas' are spectacular. They're in the corner house."

Opal smiled brightly. "Which house is that? The one with green shutters or the white one that used to be pink?"

"The one that used to be pink. God, my father hated it when the old owners painted it that color. I remember he said he was going to go to the town hall and petition to have his taxes lowered."

Opal felt Bic's eyes glaring at her. The enormity of her mistake almost made her gasp. Why had the pink corner house popped into her mind now? How many years since it had been painted?

But fortunately Sarah Kenyon did not seem to notice the slip. She began talking about the condominium and how well it was coming along. "It will be ready by August first," she said. "So we'll be on target to vacate the house for you. You've been very kind to wait so long to occupy it."

"Is there any chance that Laurie may get home?" Bic asked casually as the waiter served him veal piccata.

"Pray for that, Reverend Hawkins," Sarah told him. "Dr. Donnelly has said she is absolutely no threat to anyone. He wants a psychiatrist appointed by the prosecutor's office to examine her and agree that she should become an outpatient. He believes that in order to cooperate in her defense, Laurie must overcome the feeling that she needs to be behind locked doors in order to feel safe."

"There is nothing I want more than to see your little sister at home in Ridgewood," Bic said as he patted Sarah's hand.

That night when Sarah settled in bed, she had the nagging feeling that something she should have noticed had escaped her attention.

It must have been something Laurie said, she decided as she drifted off to sleep.

82

Justin Donnelly walked from the clinic to his Central Park South apartment, so engrossed in his own meditation today that for once he did not drink in the changing panorama of New York. At seven o'clock, the sun was still forty minutes from setting. The hazy warmth had brought out a steady stream of people, strolling along Fifth Avenue, browsing through the book stands on the sidewalk flanking the park or appraising the amateurish art.

The pungent smell of souvlaki that wafted to his nostrils as the weary vendors pushed their carts to overnight shelters, the sight of the patient horses as they stood fastened to festively decorated carriages at the corner of Fifth and Central Park South, the line of limousines in front of the Plaza Hotel—all these things escaped him. Justin's thoughts were totally on Laurie Kenyon.

She was by far the most interesting patient he'd ever encountered. It was common for women who had been molested as small children to feel that they had somehow invited or caused the abuse. Most of them at some point came to understand they had been powerless to prevent what had happened to them. Laurie Kenyon was resisting that knowledge.

But there was progress. He'd stopped in to see her before he left the clinic. Dinner was over, and she was sitting in the solarium. She'd been quiet and pensive. "Gregg was awfully nice to have come today," she'd volunteered and then added, "I know he'd never hurt me."

Justin had taken a chance. "He did more than not hurt you, Laurie. He helped you to see that by jokingly picking you up, he triggered a memory that, if you let it out, will help you to get well. The rest is up to you."

She'd said, "I know it is. I'll try. I promise. You know, Doctor, what I'd like to do more than anything in the world?" She hadn't waited for an answer. "I'd like to fly to Scotland and play golf at St. Andrews. Does that seem crazy to you?"

"It sounds terrific to me."

"But of course it will never happen."

"Not unless you help yourself."

As Justin turned in to his building, he wondered if he'd pushed her too far. He wondered if calling the psychiatrist appointed by the prosecutor's office and asking him to reevaluate Laurie for the purpose of reinstating bail was a mistake.

A few minutes later he was sitting on the terrace of his apartment, sipping his favorite Australian Chardonnay, when the phone rang. It was the clinic. The head nurse apologized for calling. "It's Miss Kenyon. She says she must speak to you at once."

"Laurie!"

"Not Laurie, Doctor. Her alter Kate. She wants to tell you something terribly important."

"Put her on!"

The strident voice said, "Dr. Donnelly, listen, you ought to know. There's a kid who wants to talk to you something fierce, but Laurie's afraid to let him."

"Who is the kid, Kate?" Justin asked quickly. I'm right, he thought. Laurie does have another alter who hasn't surfaced yet.

"I don't know his name. He won't tell me what it is. But he's nine or ten and smart and took a hell of a lot for Laurie. He's tired of shutting his mouth. Keep working on her. You're wearing her down. He came within inches of talking to you today."

The receiver clicked in Justin's ear.

83

On June 15 the Reverend Bobby Hawkins received a phone call from Liz Pierce of *People* magazine requesting an interview. She'd been assigned to do a feature on him for a September issue, she said.

Bic protested, then said that he was flattered and pleased. "It will be a joy to spread the word of my ministry," he assured Pierce.

But when he hung up the phone, the warmth disappeared from his voice. "Opal, if I refuse, that reporter might think I was hiding something. At least this way I can influence what she writes."

84

Brendon Moody looked compassionately at Sarah. The mid-June day was sticky, but she still had not turned on the window air conditioner in the library. She was wearing a dark blue linen jacket with a white collar and a white skirt. It was only eight-thirty, but she was already dressed to go to New York. Four months of this, Brendon thought, eating, drinking, breathing a defense that's going nowhere; spending the day in a psychiatric clinic and being grateful her sister is there instead of in the Hunterdon County jail. And he was about to shoot down her last hope for a viable defense.

Sophie knocked and without waiting for a response opened the door and came in carrying a tray with cups of coffee, rolls and orange juice. "Mr. Moody," she said, "I hope you can make Sarah swallow this roll. She's at the point where she eats nothing and is becoming skin and bones."

"Oh, Sophie," Sarah protested.

"Don't, 'oh, Sophie,' me—it's the truth." Sophie put the tray down on the desk, her face puckered with worry. "Is the miracle man going to show up today?" she asked. "I swear, Sarah, you should charge those people rent."

"They should charge me rent," Sarah said. "They've owned this house since March."

"And the agreement was that you'd move out in August."

"They don't bother me. In fact they've been very nice to me."

"Well, I've been watching them on TV every Sunday lately, and let me tell you, they are some pair. As far as I'm concerned that man is taking the name of the Lord in vain what with promising miracles in return for cash and talking as though God drops in to chat with him every day."

"Sophie," Sarah protested.

"All right, all right, you're busy." Shaking her head, Sophie marched from the library, her heavy footsteps signaling her disapproval.

Sarah handed Brendon a coffee cup. "As we were saying, or did we get around to saying anything?"

Brendon took the coffee, added three heaping teaspoons of sugar and stirred noisily. "I wish I had good news," he said, "but I don't. Our best hope was that Allan Grant was taking advantage of Laurie's depression and grief and then drove her over the edge by giving her letters to the administration. Well, Sarah, if he was taking advantage of her, we'll never be able to prove it. His marriage was rotten. I could sense that and I've followed up on the wife. She's a piece of goods. According to the hotel staff, she's had quite a variety of different male friends. For the past year or so, however, she's stuck to the same one and seems pretty crazy about him. Name is Edwin Rand. He's one of those polished, good-looking types who's lived off women all his life. About forty or forty-five. A travel writer who doesn't make enough money to live on but gets invited to resorts all over the world. He's made an art of the freebie."

"Did Allan Grant know about him?" Sarah asked.

"Can't be sure. When Karen was at home they seemed okay together."

"But suppose he did know and was hurt and rejected and turned to Laurie, who was crazy about him?"

Sarah seemed to come alive as she spoke. Poor kid, Brendon thought, grabbing at anything that would be the basis for a defense.

"It doesn't wash," he said flatly. "Allan had been seeing a member of the faculty, Vera West. West broke down when she told me that the last time she spoke to him was at about ten-thirty the night he died. He was in good spirits and said that he was relieved because it was all out on the table."

"Meaning?"

"She took it to mean that he'd told his wife he wanted a divorce."

Brendon looked away from the despair in Sarah's eyes. "Actually, you could make a prima facie case against the wife," he told her. "Allan Grant's mother left him a trust fund. He got in the neighborhood of $100,000 a year income from it. Couldn't touch the principal—and that's close to a million and a half and still growing—until he was sixty. The mother obviously realized he had no money sense.

"From what I hear, Karen Grant was treating that income as her personal allowance. In the event of a divorce, that trust was not community property. Whatever she makes at the travel agency wouldn't support her pricey apartment and designer clothers. The writer boyfriend would have been history. With Allan's death, however, she got it all.

"The only problem," Brendon concluded, "is that Karen Grant certainly didn't borrow the knife, kill her husband and then return the knife to Laurie afterwards."

Sarah didn't notice that her coffee was barely lukewarm. Sipping it helped to release the tightened muscles in her neck and throat.

"I've heard from the Hunterdon County prosecutor's office," she told him. "The psychiatrist they sent to examine Laurie reviewed the tapes of her therapy sessions. They accept the possibility that she suffers from multiple personality disorder."

She ran her hand over her forehead as though trying to brush away a headache. "In return for Laurie's pleading guilty to manslaughter, they won't press for the maximum penalty. She'd probably be out in five years, maybe less. But if we go to court, the charge will be purposeful and knowing murder. There's a good chance they could make it stick."

85

"It's been a month since Kate phoned to tell me that there's another alter personality, a nine- or ten-year-old boy, who wants to talk to me," Justin Donnelly told Sarah. "As you know, since then, Kate disclaims any knowledge of that personality."

Sarah nodded. "I know." It was time to tell Justin Donnelly that she and Brendon Moody had agreed that it was in Laurie's best interest that they accept the offer of a plea bargain. "I've reached a decision," she began.

Justin listened, his eyes never leaving Sarah's face. If I were an artist, he thought, I would sketch that face and caption it "Grief."

"So you see," Sarah concluded, "the psychiatrists for the state do believe that Laurie was abused as a child and there is substantial indication of multiple personality disorder. They know the jury is going to sympathize with her, and it's unlikely she'd be convicted of murder. But the penalty for aggravated manslaughter is also a possible thirty years. On the other hand, if she pleads guilty to second-degree manslaughter, intentionally killing in the heat of passion with reasonable provocation, at worst she could be sentenced to a maximum of ten years. It would be up to the judge if she got a mandatory five years without parole. He could also give her as little as a five-year flat term with no parole ineligibility stipulation, and she could be out in a year or two. I don't have the right to gamble with nearly thirty years of Laurie's life."

"How can she plead guilty to a crime she doesn't remember committing?" Justin asked.

"It's legal. Her statement will be something to the effect that while she has no memory of the crime, she and her lawyer, having reviewed the evidence, are satisfied that she committed it."

"How long can you hold off?"

Sarah's voice became unsteady. "What would be the point? I think if anything, taking the pressure off Laurie to remember might in the long run be beneficial to her. Let it go."

"No, Sarah." Justin pushed back his chair and walked over to the window, then was sorry he had. Across the garden, Laurie was standing in the solarium, her hands resting on the glass wall, looking out. Even from where he was, he could sense the feeling of a trapped bird longing to fly. He turned to Sarah. "Give me a little longer. How soon do you think the judge will allow her to go home?"

"Next week."

"All right. Are you busy tonight?"

"Well, let's see." Sarah spoke rapidly, obviously trying to rein in her emotions. "If I go home, one of two things will happen. The Hawkinses will come bursting in to deposit more of their possessions and want to take me to dinner. Or else Sophie, whom I love dearly, will be there, sorting through my parents' closets and relieving me of the job I've put off—giving away their clothes. The third alternative is that I'll try to figure out a brilliant defense for Laurie."

"Surely you have friends who ask you out."

"I have lots of friends," Sarah said. "Good friends, cousins too, terrific people who want to help. But, you see, at the end of the day I can't start explaining to everyone what's going on. I can't stand listening to the empty promises that something will turn up, that it's all going to be just fine. I can't bear to hear that none of this would have happened if Laurie hadn't been kidnapped all those years ago. I know that. That knowledge is driving me mad. Oh yes, I also don't want to hear that after all Dad was in his seventies and Mother had that operation a few years ago and the prognosis wasn't great and maybe it was a blessing they went together. You see, I do accept that. *But I don't want to hear it."*

Justin knew that one comforting word would reduce Sarah to tears. He didn't want that to happen. Laurie would be joining them momentarily. "I was going to suggest that you have dinner with me tonight," he said mildly. "Here's something I want you to see now."

From Laurie's file, he pulled out an eight-by-ten photograph. Faint lines crisscrossed back and forth over it.

"This is an enlargement of the picture Laurie tore up the day she was admitted here," he explained. "The man who reconstructed it did a good job. Tell me what you see in it."

Sarah looked down at the photograph, and her eyes widened. "The way this was before, I didn't see that Laurie was crying. That tree. That dilapidated house. And what's that, a barn behind it? There's nothing like that in Ridgewood. Where was this taken?"

Then she frowned. "Oh, wait a minute. Laurie went to a nursery school three afternoons a week. They used to take the kids on excursions to parks and lakes. There are farmhouses like this around Harriman State Park. But why would this picture have upset her the way it did?"

"I'm going to try to find out," Justin said, switching on the video camera as Laurie opened the door.

Laurie forced herself to look at the picture. "The chicken coop behind the farmhouse," she whispered. "Bad things happen there."

"What bad things, Laurie?" Justin asked.

"Don't talk, you jerk. He'll find out and you know what he'll do to you."

Sarah dug her nails into her palms. This was a voice she had never heard before, a young, strong, boyish voice. Laurie was frowning. Even though her face seemed to have lost its contours, her mouth was set in a determined line. One hand was smacking the other.

"Hi," Justin said casually. "You're new. What's your name?"

"Get back inside, you!" It was Leona's catlike tone. "Listen, Doctor, I know that bossy Kate has been trying to go around me. It won't happen."

"Leona, why are you always the troublemaker?" Justin demanded.

Sarah realized he was trying a new tactic. His voice was belligerent.

"Because people are always pulling things on me. I trusted Allan and he made a fool of me. I trusted you when you told us to keep a journal, and you stuck that picture in it."

Laurie's hair was tumbling over her face. She was brushing it back with an unconsciously seductive gesture.

"That's impossible. You didn't find this picture in your journal, Leona."

"I certainly did. Just the way I found that damn knife in my tote bag. I was so nice when I went to Allan's for the showdown and he looked so peaceful I didn't even wake him up, and now people are blaming me because he's dead."

Sarah held her breath. Don't react, she told herself. Don't distract her.

"Did you try to wake him up?" Justin might have been commenting on the weather.

"No. I was going to show him. I mean there's no way I can escape. The kitchen knife that was missing. Sarah. Sophie. Dr. Carpenter. Everybody wants to know why I took it. I did *not* take the knife. Then Allan makes a fool of me. You know what I decided to do?" She did not wait for an answer. "I was going to show that guy. Kill myself right in front of him. Let him be sorry for what he did to me. No use going on living. Nothing's ever going to be good for me."

"You went to his house and the big window was open?"

"No. I don't go in windows. The terrace door to the study. The lock doesn't catch. He was already in bed. I went into his room. For Pete's sake, have you got a cigarette?"

"Of course." Donnelly waited until Leona had settled back, the lit cigarette between her fingers, before he asked, "What was Allan doing when you went in?"

Her lips curved in a smile. "He was snoring. Can you believe it? My big scene wasted. He's curled up in bed like a little kid, arms all wrapped around the pillow, hair sort of tousled, and he's snoring." Her voice softened and became hesitant. "My daddy used to snore. Mommy used to say that was the only thing about him she'd change. He could wake up the dead when he started snoring."

Yes, Sarah thought, yes.

"And you had the knife?"

"Oh, that. I put my tote bag down on the floor by the bed. I had the knife in my hand by then. I laid the knife on top of the bag. I was so tired. And you know what I thought?"

"Tell me."

The voice changed completely, became that of four-year-old Debbie. "I thought of all the times I wouldn't let my daddy hold me or kiss me after I came back from the house with the chicken coop and I laid down on the bed next to Allan and he never knew, he just kept on snoring."

"Then what happened, Debbie?"

Oh please, God, Sarah thought.

"Then I got scared, afraid he'd wake up and be mad at me and tell the dean on me again, so I got up and tiptoed out. And he never even knew I was there."

She giggled happily like a little girl who had played a trick and gotten away with it.

* * *

Justin took Sarah to dinner at Neary's Restaurant on East Fifty-seventh Street.

"I'm a regular here," he told her, as a beaming Jimmy Neary rushed to greet them. Justin introduced Sarah. "Here's someone you've got to fatten up, Jimmy."

At the table he said, "I think you've had a tough enough day. Want to hear about Australia?"

Sarah wouldn't have believed that she could eat every bite of a sliced steak sandwich and french fries. When Justin had ordered a bottle of Chianti, she'd protested. "Hey, you can walk home. I've got to drive."

"I know. It's only nine o'clock. We're going to take a long walk back to my place and have coffee there."

New York on a summer evening, Sarah thought as they sat on his small terrace, sipping espresso. The lights on the trees surrounding the Tavern on the Green, the lush foliage, the horses and carriages, the strollers and joggers. All this was a world away from locked rooms and prison bars.

"Let's talk about it," she said. "Is there any chance that what Laurie, or rather Debbie, told us today—about lying down with Allan Grant and then leaving him sleeping—is true?"

"As far as Debbie knows it's probably true."

"You mean that Leona might have taken over when Debbie started to leave?"

"Leona or an alter personality we haven't met so far."

"I see. I thought Laurie remembered something when she saw that picture. What could it be?"

"I believe there probably was a chicken coop wherever Laurie was kept during those two years. That picture reminded her of something that happened there. As time goes on we may be able to learn what it was."

"But time is running out." Sarah did not know she was going to cry until she felt the tears gushing down her cheeks. She held her hands over her mouth, trying to stifle racking sobs.

Justin put his arms around her. "Let it out, Sarah," he said tenderly.

86

It was Brendon Moody's theory that if you waited long enough you'd get a break. His break came on June 25, from an unexpected source. Don Fraser, a junior at Clinton, was arrested for selling drugs. Realizing he'd been caught red-handed, he hinted that in exchange for leniency, he could tell them something about Laurie Kenyon's whereabouts the night she killed Allan Grant.

The prosecutor guaranteed nothing but said he'd do what he could. Dealing drugs within a thousand feet of a high school could mean a mandatory three-year sentence. Since the place where Fraser was picked up was just at the edge of the thousand-foot zone, the prosecutor agreed that he would not press for the within-school-zone offense if Fraser came up with something significant.

"And I want immunity from prosecution for what I'm telling you," Fraser insisted.

"You'd have made a good lawyer," the prosecutor told him sourly. "I'll say it again. You give us something helpful, and we'll help you. That's as far as I'll go right now. Take it or leave it."

"All right. All right. I happened to be on the corner of North Church and Maple the night of January twenty-eighth," Fraser began.

"Happened to be! What time was that?"

"Ten after eleven."

"All right. What happened then?"

"I'd been talking to a couple of friends. They'd left and I'd been waiting for someone else who never showed up. It was cold, so I figured I'd take off and go back to the dorm."

"This is ten after eleven."

"Yes." Fraser picked his words carefully. "All of a sudden this chick comes out of nowhere. I knew it was Laurie Kenyon. Everybody knows who she is. She was always getting her picture in the paper because of golf and then when her folks died."

"How was she dressed?"

"Ski jacket. Jeans."

"Was there any sign of blood on her?"

"No. Not a bit."

"Did you talk to her?"

"She came over to me. The way she was acting, I thought she was going to try to pick me up. There was something real sexy about her."

"Back up a minute. North Church and Maple is about ten blocks from the Grant home, isn't it?"

"About that. Anyhow she came up to me and said she needed a cigarette."

"What did you do?"

"Now this doesn't get used against me?"

"No. What did you do?"

"I thought she meant grass, so I pulled some out."

"And then?"

"She got mad. She said she didn't like that stuff and wanted a real cigarette. I had some with me and told her I'd sell her a pack."

"You didn't offer her one?"

"Hey, why should I?"

"Did she buy cigarettes from you?"

"No. She went to reach for her purse and then said something funny. She said, 'Damn it. I'll have to go back. That stupid kid forgot to bring it.' "

"What kid? Forgot to bring what?"

"I don't know what kid. I'm sure she was talking about her purse. She said to wait twenty minutes. She'd be back."

"Did you wait?"

"I figured why not? Maybe my other friend would show up too."

"You stood there."

"No. I didn't want to be seen. I got off the sidewalk and stood between two bushes on the lawn of the corner house."

"How long before Laurie got back?"

"Maybe fifteen minutes. But she never stopped. She was running like hell."

"This is very important. Was she carrying her bag?"

"She was hanging onto something with both hands, so I guess so."

~ *87*

Bic and Opal listened with rapt attention to the tape of Sarah's conversation with Brendon Moody about the testimony of the student drug dealer. "It's consistent with what Laurie told us," Sarah explained to Moody. "Debbie, the child alter, remembers leaving Allan Grant. None of Laurie's personalities will talk about what happened after she went back."

Bic remarked ominously, "Sneaking out of a man's house—going back and committing murder—terrible."

Opal tried to stifle her jealousy, comforting herself with the knowledge that it wasn't going to go on much longer. Sarah Kenyon would be out of the house in a matter of weeks, and Bic wouldn't have access to the condominium.

Bic was replaying the last part of the tape. "The judge is going to allow Lee to leave the clinic on July eighth. That's next Wednesday," he said. "We're going to pay a visit to Ridgewood to welcome Lee home."

"Bic, you don't mean to face her."

"I know what I mean, Opal. We'll both be conservatively dressed. We won't talk about prayer or God, much as it hurts me not to bring the Lord into our every activity. The point is, we must befriend her. Then, just in case she does get too much memory back, we'll be all mixed up in her mind. We won't stay long. We'll apologize for intruding and take our leave. Now try this on and let's see how cute you look."

He handed her a box. She opened it and took out a wig. She went to the mirror, put it on and adjusted it, then turned for him to see. "My Lord, it's just perfect," he observed.

The phone rang. Opal picked it up.

It was Rodney Harper from station WLIS in Bethlehem.

"You remember me?" he asked. "I was the station manager when you broadcast from here all those years ago. Proud to say I own the place now."

Opal motioned for Bic to pick up the extension as she said, "Rodney Harper. Of course I remember you."

"Been meaning to congratulate you on all your success. You folks have sure gone a long way. Reason I called today is that a woman from *People* magazine was in here talking to me about you."

Opal and Bic exchanged glances. "What did she ask?"

"Oh just about what kind of folks you were. I said Bobby was the best damn preacher we ever had in these parts. Then she wanted to know if I had a picture of you from those days."

Opal saw the sudden alarm on Bic's face and knew it mirrored her own. "And did you?"

"I'm sorry to say we can't find a one. We moved the station to a new facility about ten years ago and got rid of a heap of stuff. I guess your pictures got caught in the throwaway bags."

"Oh that doesn't matter," Opal said as she felt her stomach muscles begin to relax. "Wait a minute. Bobby's on the line and wants to say hello."

Bic cut in with a robust greeting. "Rodney, my friend, it's a treat to hear your voice. I'll never forget you gave us our first big break. If we hadn't been in Bethlehem on your station and getting known, I don't know we'd be on the 'Church of the Airways' today. Even so, if you do come across some old picture, I'd appreciate if you just tore it up. Looked too darn much like a hippie in those days, and it kind of doesn't go with preaching to the older folks in the 'Church of the Airways.' "

"Sure, Bobby. Just one thing I hope you won't mind. I did take that reporter from *People* to see the farmhouse where you lived those two years you were with us. Son of a gun. I missed the fact it had burned down. Kids or some bum, I suppose, broke in and got careless with matches."

Bic rounded his thumb and first finger, then winked at Opal. "These things happen, but I'm real sorry to hear that. Carla and I loved that snug little place."

"Well, they took a couple of pictures of the property. I heard the reporter say she wasn't sure if she'd even use them in the article, but at least the chicken coop was still standing and that was proof enough for anyone that you came from humble beginnings."

88

Karen Grant reached her desk at nine o'clock and sighed with relief that Anne Webster wasn't already in the office. Karen was having a hard time hiding her anger at the agency's retiring owner. Webster did not want to complete the sale of the agency to Karen until mid-August. She had been invited on an inaugural flight of New World Airlines to Australia and didn't intend to miss it. Karen had been hoping to go on that one. Edwin had been invited too, and they'd planned to enjoy it together.

Karen had told Anne that there was really no need for her to come in to the office anymore. Business was slow and Karen could handle it herself. After all, Anne was almost seventy, and the trip from Bronxville to the city was taxing. But Anne was proving unexpectedly stubborn about hanging on and was making a crusade of taking regular clients out to lunch and assuring them that Karen would take just as good care of them as she had.

Of course there was a reason for that. For three years Webster would get a percentage of the profits, and there was no question that even though the travel business had been abysmal for nearly two years, the mood was changing and people were starting to do more traveling.

As soon as Anne was totally out of the way, Edwin could use her office. But they'd wait until the late fall to move in together. It would look better for Karen to testify as the grieving widow at Laurie Kenyon's trial. Except for Anne hanging around and that damn detective dropping in so much, Karen was blissfully happy. She was so crazy about Edwin. Allan's trust fund was now in her name. One hundred thousand or better a year for the next twenty years, and in the meantime those stocks were increasing in value. In a way she wasn't sorry not to get the principal now. She might not always be crazy about Edwin, and if anything, his tastes were more expensive than hers.

She loved jewelry. It was hard to pass the L. Crown boutique in the lobby without looking in the showcase. It used to be that when she bought something that caught her eye she'd worry that one day Allan would come out of his dreamworld and ask to see the bankbook. He believed she was putting the bulk of the trust fund money in a savings account. Now she didn't have that worry, and between Allan's life insurance and the trust fund, he'd left her in great shape. When that damn house in Clinton sold, she was going to treat herself to an emerald necklace. Trouble was, a lot of people were squeamish about buying a house where someone had been murdered. She'd already reduced the selling price twice.

This morning she was debating about what to give Edwin for his birthday. Well, she still had two weeks to make up her mind.

The door opened. Karen forced a welcoming smile as Anne Webster came in. Now I'll hear how she didn't sleep well last night but got her usual nap on the train, she thought.

"Good morning, Karen. My, don't you look lovely. Is that another new dress?"

"Yes, I just got it yesterday." Karen couldn't resist telling the designer's name. "It's a Scaasi."

"It looks it." Anne sighed and brushed back a strand of gray hair that had escaped from the braid that circled the top of her head. "My, I'm feeling my age this morning. Awake half the night and then, as usual, dead asleep on the train. I was sitting next to Ed Anderson, my next-door neighbor. He always calls me the sleeping beauty and says that someday I'll wake up in the freight yard."

Karen laughed with her. My God, how many times more do I have to hear the sleeping beauty story? she thought. Only three weeks, she promised herself. The day we close the deal, Anne Webster will be history.

On the other hand . . . This time she gave Anne a genuinely warm smile. "You *are* a sleeping beauty!"

They chuckled together.

~ 89

Brendon Moody was watching when, at quarter of ten, Connie Santini, the secretary, came in and Karen Grant left the travel agency office. Something was bothering him about Anne Webster's account of the evening she had spent with Karen Grant at Newark Airport. He had talked to Webster a week ago, and today he wanted to talk to her again. He walked over to the agency. As he opened the door, he attempted to plaster on his face the smile of a casual visitor. "Good morning, Mrs. Webster. I was passing this way and thought I'd drop by. You're looking well. It's good to see you again. I was afraid that by now you'd be retired."

"How nice of you to remember, Mr. Moody. No, I decided to wait and have the closing in mid-August. Frankly right now business is really picking up and I sometimes wonder if I should have held off selling. But then when I get up in the morning and rush for a train and leave my husband reading the papers over coffee, I say, enough's enough."

"Well, you and Karen Grant certainly know how to give custom service," Moody commented as he sank into a chair. "Remember you told me that the night Professor Grant died, you and Karen were at Newark Airport? Not too many travel agents will personally go to the airport to meet even the very best client."

Anne Webster looked pleased at the compliment. "The lady we met is quite elderly," she said. "She loves to travel and usually has a contingent of friends and relatives with her, at her expense. Last year we booked her and eight others at full first-class fare on a round-the-world cruise. The night we met her, she had cut short a trip and returned alone because she wasn't feeling well. Her chauffeur happened to be away, so we volunteered to pick her up at the airport. It's little enough to do to keep her happy. Karen drove and I sat in back talking to her."

"The plane arrived at nine-thirty, as I remember," Brendon said casually.

"No. It was supposed to arrive at nine-thirty. We got to the ariport at nine. The flight had been delayed in London. They said it would get in at ten, so we went to the VIP Lounge."

Brendon consulted his notes. "Then, according to your statement, it did arrive at ten."

Anne Webster looked embarrassed. "I was wrong. I thought about it later and realized it was nearly twelve-thirty."

"Twelve-thirty!"

"Yes. When we reached the lounge they said that the computers were down and there would be that long a delay. But Karen and I were watching a film on the TV in the lounge, so the time passed very quickly."

"I'll bet it did." The secretary laughed. "Now Mrs. Webster, you know you probably slept through the whole thing."

"I certainly did not," Anne Webster said indignantly. "They had *Spartacus* on. That was my favorite movie years ago, and now they've restored the footage that had been cut out. I never closed an eye."

Moody let it go. "Karen Grant has a friend Edwin who's a travel writer, doesn't she?" He did not miss the expression on the secretary's face, the tightened lips. She was the one he wanted to question when she was alone.

"Mr. Moody, a woman in business meets many men. She may have lunch or dinner with them, and it does offend me that in this day and age anyone can read anything improper in their meetings." Anne Webster was adamant. "Karen Grant is an attractive, hardworking young woman. She was married to a brilliant professor who understood her need to carve out her own life. He had an independent income and was extremely generous to her. She always talked about Allan in the most glowing terms. Her relationships with other men were totally on the up-and-up."

Connie Santini's desk was behind and to the right of Webster's. Catching Brendon's glance, she raised her eyes to heaven in the classic expression of total disbelief.

~ 90

The July 8 staff meeting at the clinic was almost over. There was only one patient left to discuss—Laurie Kenyon. As Justin Donnelly well knew, her case was the one that had engrossed everyone.

"We're making breakthroughs," he said. "Maybe even significant breakthroughs to what happened to her in those missing two years. The problem is that we don't have enough time. Laurie will go home this afternoon and will be an outpatient from now on. In a few weeks she'll go to court and plead guilty to manslaughter. The deadline from the prosecutor on the plea offer to manslaughter expires then."

The room was quiet. In addition to Dr. Donnelly, there were four others at the conference table: two psychiatrists, the art therapist, and the journal therapist. Kathie, the journal therapist, shook her head. "Doctor, it doesn't matter which alter personality writes in the journal, not one of them admits killing Allan Grant."

"I know that," Justin said. "I've asked Laurie to let us take her to Grant's house in Clinton to act out what happened that night. She certainly gave us a vivid picture of being in that rocking chair on someone's lap during abreaction, but she's stonewalling me on doing the same thing with Grant's death."

"Which suggests that neither she nor her alters want to remember what happened there?"

"Possibly."

"Doctor, her recent drawings have been much more detailed when she does the stick figure of a woman. Look at these." Pat, the art therapist, passed some of them around. "Now they really look as though the figure of the woman is wearing a pendant of some sort. Will she talk about that?"

"No. All she says is that's it's clear she's no artist."

When Laurie came to Justin's office an hour later, she was wearing a pale pink linen jacket and pleated white skirt. Sarah was with her and acknowledged Justin's compliment on the outfit with quiet pleasure. "It caught my eye when I was shopping last night," she explained, "and this is an important day."

"Freedom," Laurie said quietly, "brief, frightening, but still welcome."

Then Laurie unexpectedly said, "Maybe it's about time I tried your couch, Doctor."

Justin tried to sound offhand. "Be my guest. Any reason why today?"

She kicked off her shoes and stretched out. "Maybe it's just that I'm so comfortable with you two, and I feel like my old self in this new outfit, plus it will be nice to see the house again before we move." She hesitated. "Sarah tells me that after I plead guilty I'll have about six weeks before sentencing. The prosecutor has agreed to consent before the judge to my remaining free on bail till the sentence. I know that the minute I'm sentenced I have to go to prison, so I'm going to have a wonderful time for those six weeks. We're going to play golf and we're going to fix up the condominium so I'll be able to think about it while I'm away."

"I hope you're not going to forget to come in for your sessions with me, Laurie."

"Oh no. We'll come in every day. It's just that there's so much I want to do. I'm dying to drive again. I used to love driving. Gregg has a new convertible. I'm going golfing with him next week." She smiled. "It's nice to look forward to going out with him and not be afraid that he'll hurt me. That's why I'm able to lie down. I know you won't hurt me either."

"No, I won't," Justin said. "Are you in love with Gregg, Laurie?"

She shook her head. "That's too strong. I'm too mixed up to love anybody, at least the way you mean. But the first step is just enjoying being with someone, isn't it?"

"Yes, it is. Laurie, could I speak to Kate?"

"If you want." She sounded indifferent.

For weeks now, Justin had not had to hypnotize Laurie to summon the alter personalities. Now Laurie sat up, thrust back her shoulders, narrowed her eyes. "What is it this time, Doctor?" It was Kate's voice they were hearing.

"Kate, I'm a bit troubled," Justin said. "I want Laurie to make her peace with herself and with everything that happened, but not until the whole truth has come out. She's burying it deeper, isn't she?"

"Doctor, I am getting thoroughly sick of you! Can't you get it straight? She's willing to take her medicine. She swore she'd never sleep in the house again, but now she's looking forward to going back to it. She knows that her parents' death was a terrible accident and not her fault. That guy in the service station where she had the appointment to have her car checked had hairy arms. It wasn't her fault he scared the bejesus out of her. She really understands that. Aren't you ever satisfied?"

"Hey, Kate, all along you've known the reason Laurie broke that appointment to have her car inspected, yet you never told me. Why are you telling me now?"

Sarah thought of Sam, the attendant at the service station in town. She'd just filled the car with gas there yesterday. Sam had started work at the end of last summer. He was a big guy with thick arms. Yesterday he'd been wearing a short-sleeved shirt, and she'd noticed that even the backs of his hands were covered by a mass of thick curly hair.

Kate shrugged. "I'm telling you because I'm tired of keeping secrets. Besides, the wimp will be safe in prison."

"Safe from what? Safe from whom?" Justin asked urgently. "Kate, don't do this to her. Tell us what you know."

"I know that while she's out they can get to her. She can't escape and she knows it too. If she doesn't go to prison soon, they'll make it happen."

"Who threatened her? Kate, please." Justin was cajoling, pleading.

She shook her head. "Doctor, I'm tired of telling you that I don't know everything and the kid who does isn't going to talk to you. He's the smart one. You wear me out."

Sarah watched as the aggressive look faded from Laurie's features, as she slipped down and stretched out again on the couch, as her eyes closed and her breathing became even again.

"Kate isn't going to be around much longer," Justin whispered to Sarah. "For some reason she'll feel her job is done. Sarah, look at these." He held out Laurie's drawings. "See this stick figure. Do you make anything of this necklace she's wearing?"

Sarah frowned. "It looks familiar. I feel as though I've seen it."

"Compare these two," Justin said. "They're the most detailed of the batch. You see how the center seems to be oval-shaped and set in a square with brilliants. Does that mean anything to you?"

"I wonder . . ." Sarah said. "My mother had some nice pieces of jewelry. They're all in the safe-deposit box. One of them is a pendant. It has small diamonds all around the center stone—what is it—an aquamarine . . . no, it's not that. I can see it . . . it's—"

"Don't say that word. That's a forbidden word." The command was spoken in a young, alarmed but sturdy boyish voice. Laurie was sitting up, staring intently at Sarah.

"What's a forbidden word?" Justin asked.

"Don't say it." The boyish voice coming from Laurie's lips was part pleading, part commanding.

"You're the little boy who came to talk to us last month," Justin said. "We still don't know your name."

"It's not allowed to say names."

"Well, maybe it's forbidden for you, but Sarah can. Sarah, do you remember the stone that was in the center of your mother's pendant?"

"It was an opal," Sarah said quietly. "What does *opal* mean to you?" Justin demanded, turning to Laurie.

On the couch, Laurie shook her head. Her expression became her own. She looked puzzled. "Did I drop off? I'm suddenly so sleepy. What did you ask me? Opal? Well, that's a gemstone, of course. Sarah, didn't Mama have a pretty opal pendant?"

~ 91

As always, Opal felt the tension building inside her as they passed the sign that read ENTERING RIDGEWOOD. We look totally different, she assured herself, smoothing down the skirt of her navy-and-white print dress, a conservatively cut outfit with a V neck, long sleeves and a narrow belt. With it she wore navy shoes and a matching purse. Her only jewelry was a single strand of pearls and her wedding ring. She'd had her hair trimmed and colored a few hours ago. Now every ash blond strand was coiffed sleekly against her head. Large, blue-tinted sunglasses covered her eyes and subtly redefined the contours of her face.

"You look real classy, Carla," Bic had said approvingly before they left the Wyndham. "Don't worry. There isn't a snowball's chance in hell that Lee will recognize you. And what do you think of me?"

He was dressed in a crisp, white, long-sleeved shirt, a tan, single-breasted summer suit, and a tan-and-white tie with flecks of brown. His hair was now completely silver. Even though he'd let it grow a little longer, he had it combed back so that there was no suggestion of the wavy curls that he'd been so proud of in the early days. He'd also shaved the hair from the backs of his hands. He was very much the image of a distinguished clergyman.

Their car turned into Twin Oaks Road. "That used to be the pink house," Bic said sarcastically as he pointed. "Try not to refer to it again, and don't call the little girl Lee. Call her Laurie when you speak to her, which shouldn't be much at all."

Opal wanted to remind Bic that he was the one who had referred to her as Lee on the program, but she didn't dare. Instead she went over the few words she would exchange with Laurie when they came face to face with her.

There were three cars in the driveway. One they recognized as belonging to the housekeeper. The second, a BMW, was Sarah's. But the third, an Oldsmobile with New York plates—whose car was that?

"There's someone visiting," Bic said. "That might be the Lord's way of providing us with a witness who can testify that Lee met us, should the need arise."

It was just five o'clock. The afternoon sun's slanting rays brightened sections of the deep green lawn and glistened through the brilliant blue hydrangeas that bordered the sides of the house.

Bic pulled into the driveway. "We'll just stay a minute even if they encourage us to linger."

It was the last thing on Sarah's mind to encourage the Hawkinses to linger. She and Laurie and Justin were sitting in the den, and a smiling Sophie, having embraced Laurie for a full minute, was making tea.

While Laurie was packing her bags, Justin had surprised Sarah by suggesting he accompany them.

"I think it might be wise for me to be with you when Laurie gets home," he explained. "I don't necessarily anticipate an adverse reaction, but she hasn't been there in five months, and a lot of memories are going to come flooding in. We can swing by my apartment building in your car, I'll pick up mine and follow you out."

"And you also want to be there to see if you can catch any breakthroughs," Sarah had added.

"That too."

"Actually, I'd be glad if you'd come. I think I'm as frightened as Laurie is of this homecoming."

Unconsciously Sarah had stretched out her hand, and Justin had taken it. "Sarah, when Laurie begins serving that sentence, I want you to promise that you'll get some counseling yourself. Don't worry. Not from me. I'm sure you don't want that. But it's going to be rough."

For an instant, feeling the warmth of his hand closing over hers, Sarah had felt less afraid of everything—of Laurie's reaction to being at home, of the day in court next week when she would stand next to Laurie and hear her plead guilty to manslaughter.

When the doorbell rang, Sarah was especially grateful to have Justin there. Laurie, who had happily showed the doctor around the house, suddenly looked alarmed. "I don't want to see anyone."

Sophie muttered, "Ten to one it's that pair."

Sarah bit her lip in exasperation. God, these people were getting to be omnipresent. She could hear Reverend Hawkins explaining to Sophie that they had been looking for a box containing important papers and realized it had been mistakenly included in the things they'd shipped to New Jersey. "If I could just run down to the basement and get it, we'd be so grateful," he said.

"It's the people who bought the house," Sarah explained to Justin and Laurie. "Don't worry. I'm not going to invite them to so much as sit down, but I suppose I should speak to them. I'm sure they've noticed my car."

"I don't think you'll have to bother going to them," Justin said as footsteps came across the foyer. A moment later, Bic was standing in the doorway, Opal behind him.

"Sarah, my dear, my apologies. Some business records my accountant needs desperately. And, is this Laurie?"

Laurie had been sitting next to Sarah on the sofa. She stood up. "Sarah has told me about you and Mrs. Hawkins."

Bic did not leave the doorway. "We are delighted to meet you, Laurie. Your sister is a wonderful girl and talks about you a great deal."

"A wonderful girl," Opal echoed, "and we're so happy to be buying this lovely house."

Bic turned to look at Justin. "Reverend and Mrs. Hawkins, Dr. Donnelly," Sarah murmured.

To her relief, after an acknowledgment of the introduction, Hawkins said, "We will not intrude on your reunion. If we may we'll just go down and get the material we need and let ourselves out the side door. Good day one and all."

In that minute or two, Sarah realized that the Hawkinses had managed to spoil the temporary happiness of Laurie's homecoming. Laurie fell silent and did not respond when Justin talked breezily about growing up in Australia on a sheep station.

Sarah was grateful when Justin accepted the invitation to dinner. "Sophie has cooked enough for an army," she said.

Laurie clearly wanted Justin to stay as well. "I feel better that you're here, Dr. Donnelly."

Dinner was unexpectedly pleasant. The chill that the Hawkinses had brought to the house vanished as they ate Sophie's delicious dinner of pheasant and wild rice. Justin and Sarah sipped wine, Laurie had Perrier. As they were finishing coffee, Laurie quietly excused herself. When she came back downstairs, she was carrying a small bag. "Doctor," she said, "I can't help it. I have to go back with you and sleep in the clinic. Sarah, I'm so sorry, but I know something terrible is going to happen to me in this house and I just don't want it to be tonight."

~ 92

When Brendon Moody phoned Sarah the next morning, he could hear the sounds of doors opening and closing, of furniture being moved. "We're getting out of here," Sarah told him. "It's not good for Laurie to be in this house. The condo isn't quite ready, but they can complete the finishing touches sometime later." She told him how Laurie had returned to the clinic the night before.

"I'm going to pick her up late this afternoon," she said, "and when I do, we'll go straight to the condo. She can help me put it together. The activity might be good for her."

"Just don't give the Hawkinses a key to your new place," Brendon said sourly.

"I don't intend to. Those two set my teeth on edge. But remember . . ."

"I know. They paid top dollar. They let you stay after the closing. How did you ever get a mover that fast?"

"It took a lot of doing."

"Let me come over and help. I can at least pack books or pictures."

The moving was well under way when Brendon arrived. Sarah, her hair held back by a bandana, and dressed in a pair of khaki shorts and a cotton blouse, was busily tagging the furniture the Hawkinses had purchased.

"I won't get everything out today," she told Brendon, "but turnabout is fair play. I'm supposed to have the use of this place till August twenty-fifth. I'll feel free to come in and out and sort the things I'm not sure of now."

Sophie was in the kitchen. "Never thought I'd see the day I'd be glad to leave this house," she told Brendon. "The nerve of those two Hawkins people. They asked if I'd help them get settled when they move in for good. The answer is no."

Brendon felt his antennae going up. "What don't you like about them, Sophie? You've heard Sarah say that they've done her a big favor."

Sophie snorted. Her round, usually pleasant face grimaced in disgust. "There's something about them. Mark my words. How many times do you have to study rooms and closets to decide if you're going to enlarge them or cut them up? Too much talk as far as I'm concerned. I swear these last months their car has been on radar to this place. And all those boxes they left in the basement. Pick up one of them. They're light as a feather. I bet they're not half-full. But that hasn't stopped them from delivering another and another. Just an excuse for dropping in, is what I call it. What do you want to bet, the Reverend uses Laurie's story on one of his programs?"

"Sophie, you're a very clever woman," Brendon said softly. "You may have hit the nail on the head."

Sarah entrusted Brendon with packing the contents of her desk, including the deep drawer that contained all of Laurie's files. "I need them in the same order," she told him. "I just keep going through them hoping and hoping that something will jump out at me."

Brendon noticed the top file was marked "Chicken." "What's this?"

"I told you that the photograph of Laurie Dr. Donnelly had restored and enlarged had a chicken coop in the background and that something about it terrified Laurie."

Moody nodded. "Yes, you did."

"That's been nagging me particularly, and I've just realized why. Last winter Laurie was seeing Dr. Carpenter, a Ridgewood psychiatrist. A few days before Allan Grant died, she was leaving Carpenter's office and went into shock. What seems to have set her off is that she stepped on the head of a chicken in the lobby of his private entrance."

Moody's head tilted up in the position of a bird dog picking up a scent. "Sarah, are you telling me that the severed head of a chicken just *happened* to be on the floor at the entrance to a psychiatrist's office?"

"Dr. Carpenter had been treating a very disturbed man who would come by unexpectedly and who the police thought was involved in cult worship. Moody, it never occurred to me or Dr. Carpenter at the time that this could be in any way connected to Laurie. Now I wonder."

"I don't know what I think," he told her. "But I do know that some woman had Danny O'Toole reporting on your activities. Danny knew that Laurie had been seeing a psychiatrist in Ridgewood. He mentioned it to me. That means whoever was paying him knew it too."

"Brendon, is it possible that someone who knew the effect it would have on Laurie actually *planted* that chicken head?"

"I don't know. But I'll tell you this much. I felt in my bones that the idea of an insurance company hiring Danny didn't ring true. Danny thought his client was Allan Grant's wife. I never quite bought that."

He could see that Sarah was trembling with fatigue and emotion. "Take it easy," he said. "Tomorrow I'll drop in on Danny O'Toole, and I can promise you, Sarah, before I get finished we'll both know who ordered that report on you and Laurie."

93

On the drive back to the clinic the night before, Laurie had been very quiet. The night nurse reported to Justin the next morning that she had slept fitfully and had talked aloud in her sleep.

"Did you hear what she said?" Justin asked.

"A word here or there, Doctor. I went in several times. She kept mumbling something about the tie that binds."

"The tie that binds?" Justin frowned. "Wait a minute. That's a phrase from a hymn. Let's see. He hummed a few notes. Here it is. 'Blest be the tie that binds . . .' "

When Laurie came in later for the therapy session, she looked calm but tired. "Doctor, Sarah just phoned. She won't be here till late this afternoon. Guess what? We're moving into the condo today. Isn't that terrific?"

"Hey, that's fast." Smart of Sarah, Justin thought. That house has too many memories now. He still wasn't sure what had changed Laurie so drastically yesterday. It had happened when the Hawkins couple stopped in. But they'd barely stayed a minute. Was it the fact that they were strangers and therefore represented some sort of threat to Laurie?

"What I like about the condo is that there's a security guard at the gate," Laurie said. "If anyone rings the bell, there's a television monitor so you'll never make a mistake and let a stranger in."

"Laurie, yesterday you said that something terrible was going to happen to you in the house. Let's talk about that."

"I don't want to talk about it, Doctor. I'm not going to stay there anymore."

"All right. Last night, in your sleep, you were apparently quite a chatterbox."

She looked amused. "Was I? Daddy used to say that if there was something I didn't get out during the day, I'd manage to have my say at night."

"The nurse couldn't understand a lot of it, but she did hear you say 'the tie that binds.' Do you remember what you were dreaming when you said that?"

The doctor watched as Laurie's lips became ashen, her eyelids drooped, her hands folded, her legs dangled. " 'Blest be the tie that binds . . .' " The childlike voice, true and clear, sang the words then faded into silence.

"Debbie, it's you, isn't it? Tell me about the song. When did you learn it?"

She resumed singing. " 'Our hearts in Christian love . . .' "

Abruptly she clamped her mouth shut. "Chill out and leave her alone, mister," a boyish voice ordered. "If you must know, she learned that one in the chicken coop."

94

This time Brendon Moody did not ply Danny the Spouse Hunter with liquor. Instead, he went to Danny's Hackensack office at 9 A.M., determined to get him at his most sober. Whatever condition that may be, Brendon thought as he sat across the shabby desk from him.

"Danny," he said. "I'm not going to mince words. You may have heard Laurie Kenyon is home."

"I heard."

"Anyone contact you to run a check on her again?"

Danny looked pained. "Brendon, you know perfectly well that the client-investigator relationship is as sacred as the confessional."

Brendon slammed his fist on the desk. "Not in this case. And not in any case where a person may be in jeopardy thanks to the good offices of the investigator."

Danny's florid complexion paled. "What's that supposed to mean?"

"It means that someone who knew Laurie's schedule may have deliberately tried to frighten her by putting the severed head of a chicken where she'd be sure to find it. It means that I'm damn sure no insurance company hired you and I don't believe Allan Grant's widow did either.

"Danny, I have three questions for you, and I want them answered. First, who paid you and how were you paid? Second, where did you send the information you gathered on the Kenyon sisters? Third, where is the copy of that information? After you've answered the questions, give a copy of your report to me."

The two men exchanged glares for a moment. Then Danny got up, took out a key, unlocked the file and riffled through the folders. He pulled out one and handed it to Brendon. "All the answers are in here," he said. "I was called by a woman who introduced herself as Jane Graves and said she represented one of the possible defendants in the Kenyon accident case. Wanted an investigation of the sisters. As I told you, that began right after the parents' funeral and continued until Laurie Kenyon was arrested for the murder of Allan Grant. I sent the reports to a private mail drop in New York City, enclosing my bill. The original retainer as well as all further bills were paid by a cashier's check from a bank in Chicago."

"A cashier's check," Brendon snorted. "A private mail drop. And you didn't think that was fishy?"

"When you're chasing spouses the way I do, you find the one who retains you often goes to great lengths to avoid being identified," Danny retorted. "You can make a copy of that file on my Xerox machine. And remember, you didn't get it from me."

The next day, Brendon Moody stopped by the condo. Sarah was there with Sophie, but Laurie had gone into New York. "She drove herself. She really wanted to. Isn't that great?"

"She's not nervous?"

"She locks the car doors at all times. She'll park next door to the clinic. She has a carphone now. That makes her feel safe."

"It's always best to be cautious," Brendon said, then decided to change the subject. "Incidentally, I like this place."

"So do I. It will be great when we get it in shape, which shouldn't take too long. I want Laurie to be able to enjoy it, really enjoy it before . . ." Sarah did not finish the sentence. Instead she said, "With all these levels, we do get our exercise. But this top floor makes a terrific study, don't you think? The bedrooms are the next floor down, then the living room, dining room, kitchen are entry level and the rec room opens out to the back."

It was clear to Brendon that Sarah welcomed the work involved in moving to take her mind off Laurie's problems. Unfortunately, there were some things Sarah had to know. He laid the file on her desk. "Take a look at this."

She began to read, her eyes widening in astonishment. "My God, it's our lives down to our every movement. *Who* would want this kind of information about us? Why would *anyone* want it?" She looked up at Moody.

"I intend to find out who it is if I have to blast open the records of that bank in Chicago," Moody said grimly.

"Brendon, if we can prove Laurie was under extraordinary duress from someone who knew how to terrify her, I'm sure the judge will be swayed."

Brendon Moody turned away from the look of naked hope on Sarah's face. He decided not to tell her that on gut instinct alone he was beginning to circle around Karen Grant. There are a number of things rotten in Denmark, he thought, and at least one of them has to do with that lady. Whatever it was, he was determined to find the answer.

95

The private postal box in New York had been rented under the name J. Graves. Rental payments had been made in cash. The clerk in charge of the boxes, a small man with slicked-back hair and an unpressed suit, had absolutely no memory of whoever made the pickups. "That box changed hands three times since February," he told Moody. "I'm paid to sort mail, not run Club Med."

Moody knew that this kind of mail drop was retained by purveyors of porno literature and get-rich-quick schemes, none of whom wanted to leave a paper trail that might lead back to them. His next call was to the Citizen's Bank in Chicago. He was keeping his fingers crossed on that one. In some banks it was possible to walk in, plunk down money and buy a cashier's check. Other institutions would only issue that kind of check for depositors. Muttering a prayer, he dialed the number.

The bank manager told Moody that it was bank policy that cashier's checks could only be sold to depositors who withdrew the funds from their savings or checking accounts. Bingo, Brendon thought. Then, predictably, the manager told him that without a subpoena no information would be forthcoming about any depositors or accounts. "I'll get the subpoena, don't worry," Moody told the manager grimly.

He dialed Sarah.

"I have a friend from law school who practices in Chicago," she said. "I'll get him to request the court for the subpoena. It will take a couple of weeks, but at least we're *doing* something."

"Don't get too excited about it yet," Moody cautioned. "I do have one theory. Karen Grant certainly had the money to hire Danny. We know that in her own personality Laurie liked and trusted Professor Grant. Suppose she told him something about things that frightened her and he discussed them with his wife."

"You mean Karen Grant may have believed there was something between Allen and Laurie and tried to scare Laurie off?"

"It's the only explanation I can come up with, and I could be all wet. But Sarah, I'll tell you this: That woman is a cold-blooded phony."

96

On July 24, with Sarah at her side, Laurie pled guilty to manslaughter in the death of Professor Allan Grant.

The press rows of the courtroom were packed with reporters from television and radio networks, newspapers and magazines. Karen Grant, in a black sheath and gold jewelry, was seated behind the prosecutor. From the visitors' section, students from Clinton and the usual contingent of courtroom junkies watched the proceedings, hanging on every word.

Justin Donnelly, Gregg Bennett and Brendon Moody sat in the first row behind Laurie and Sarah. Justin felt an overwhelming sense of helplessness as the clerk called, "All rise for the Court," and the judge strode in from his chambers. Laurie was wearing a pale blue linen suit that accentuated her delicate beauty. She looked more like eighteen than twenty-two as she answered the judge's questions in a low but steady voice. Sarah was the one who seemed the more fragile of the two, Justin thought. Her dark red hair flamed against her pearl gray jacket. The jacket hung loosely on her, and he wondered how much weight she had lost since this nightmare had begun.

There was an air of pervasive sadness throughout the courtroom as Laurie calmly answered the judge's questions. Yes, she understood what her plea meant. Yes, she had carefully reviewed the evidence. Yes, she and her lawyer were satisfied that she had killed Allan Grant in a fit of anger and passion after he turned her letters over to the school administration. She finished by saying, "I am satisfied from the evidence that I committed this crime. I don't remember anything about it but I know I must be guilty. I'm so terribly sorry. He was so good to me. I was hurt and angry when he turned those letters in to the administration, but that was because I didn't remember writing them either. I'd like to apologize to Professor Grant's friends and students and fellow members of the faculty. They lost a wonderful human being because of me. There's no way I can ever make that up to them." She turned to look at Karen Grant. "I'm so very, very sorry. If it were possible I would gladly give my life to bring your husband back."

The judge set the sentencing date for August 31. Sarah closed her eyes. Everything was moving too fast. She had lost her parents less than a year ago, and now her sister was to be taken away from her too.

A sheriff's officer led them to a side exit to escape the media. They drove away quickly, Gregg at the wheel, Moody beside him, Justin in the backseat with Laurie and Sarah. They were heading for Route 202 when Laurie said, "I want to go to Professor Grant's house."

"Laurie, you've been adamant about not going there. Why now?" Sarah asked.

Laurie pressed her head with her hands. "When I was in court before the judge, the loud thoughts were pounding like tom-toms. A little boy was shouting that I was a liar."

Gregg made an illegal U-turn. "I know where it is."

The realtor's multiple-listing sign was on the lawn. The white ranch-style house had a closed and shuttered look. The grass was in need of cutting. Weeds were sprouting around the foundation shrubbery. "I want to go in," Laurie said.

"There's a phone number for the real estate agent," Moody pointed out. "We could call and find out about getting the key."

"The lock doesn't catch on the sliding glass door to the den," Laurie said. She chuckled. "I should know. I opened it often enough."

Chilled, Sarah realized that the sultry laugh belonged to Leona.

They followed silently as she led them around the side of the house onto the flagstone patio. Sarah noticed the privacy screen of tall evergreens that shielded the patio from the side road. In her letters to Allan Grant, Leona had written about watching him through this door. No wonder she had not been noticed by passersby.

"At first it seems to be locked, but if you just jiggle it a little . . ." The door slid open, and Leona stepped inside.

The room smelled musty. There was still some furniture scattered haphazardly in it. Sarah watched as Leona pointed to an old leather chair with an ottoman in front of it. "That was his favorite chair. He'd sit there for a couple of hours. I used to love to watch him. Sometimes after he went to bed, I'd curl up in it."

"Leona," Justin said. "You came back for your pocketbook the night Allan Grant died. Debbie told us you had left him sleeping, and your tote bag and the knife were on the floor beside him. Show us what happened."

She nodded and began to walk with careful, silent footsteps to the hallway that led to the bedroom. Then she stopped. "It's so quiet. He isn't snoring anymore. Maybe he's awake." On tiptoe she led the way to the door of the bedroom, then stopped.

"The door was open?" Justin asked.

"Yes."

"Was there a light on?"

"The night-light in the bathroom. Oh no!"

She stumbled to the center of the room and gazed down. Immediately her stance changed. "Look at him. He's dead. They're going to blame Laurie again." The young boyish voice that came from Laurie's throat was shocked. "Got to get her out of here."

The boy again, Justin thought. I must get to him. He's the key to all this.

Sarah watched horrified as Laurie, who was not Laurie, her feet wide apart, her features somehow reassembled with fuller cheeks and narrowed lips, closed her eyes, bent down and with both hands made a yanking gesture.

She's taking the knife from the body, Sarah thought. Oh dear God. Justin, Brendon and Gregg were standing in a line with her like spectators at a surrealistic play. The empty room suddenly seemed to be furnished by Allan Grant's deathbed. The carpet had been cleaned, but Sarah could imagine it spattered with blood as it had been that night.

Now the boy alter personality was reaching for something on the carpet. Her tote bag, Sarah thought. He's hiding the knife in it.

"Got to get her out of here," the frightened young voice said again. The feet that were not really Laurie's feet rushed to the window, stopped. The body that was not her body turned. The eyes that were not her eyes swept the room. She bent down as though picking up something and mimed shoving it in a pocket.

That's why the bracelet was found with Laurie's jeans, Sarah thought.

The window was being cranked open. Still clutching the imaginary bag, the boy alter stepped over the low sill into the backyard.

Justin whispered, "Follow him out."

It was Leona who was waiting for them. "That night the kid didn't have to open the window," she said matter-of-factly. "It was already open when I went back. That's why the room had gotten so cold. I hope you brought cigarettes, Doctor."

97

Bic and Opal did not attend Laurie's court appearance. For Bic the temptation had been great, but he realized that he would undoubtedly be recognized by the media. "As a minister of the Lord and family friend it would be appropriate for me to be present," he said, "but Sarah is refusing all our invitations to share dinner or to visit with Lee."

They spent a lot of time in the New Jersey house now. Opal hated it. It upset her to see how often Bic would go into the bedroom that had been Lee's. The room's only piece of furniture was a decrepit rocking chair similar to the one they'd had on the farm. He'd sit in it for hours, rocking back and forth, fondling the faded pink bathing suit. Sometimes he'd sing hymns. Other days he'd listen to Lee's music box playing the same tinkling song over and over again.

" 'All around the town . . . Boys and girls together . . .' "

Liz Pierce, the *People* magazine reporter, had been in touch with Bic and Opal several times, checking on facts and dates. "You were in upstate New York and that's where you found your calling. You were preaching on the radio station in Bethlehem, Pennsylvania, then in Marietta, Ohio; Louisville, Kentucky; Atlanta, Georgia, and finally New York. That's right, isn't it?"

It always chilled Opal that Pierce had the dates in Bethlehem so accurately. But at least no one there had ever seen Lee. There wasn't a person who wouldn't swear that they'd lived alone. It would be all right, she told herself.

The same day Lee pled guilty to manslaughter, Pierce called to arrange for more photographs. They'd been chosen as the *People* magazine cover story for the August 31 issue.

98

Brendon Moody had driven to the Hunterdon County courthouse in his own car. He'd planned to go home from there, but after what he'd witnessed in Allan Grant's bedroom he wanted a chance to talk quietly to Dr. Justin Donnelly. That was why when Sarah suggested he join them for lunch at the condo, Brendon readily accepted.

He got his opening when Sarah asked Donnelly to start a fire in the barbecue. Moody followed him onto the patio. In a low voice, he asked, "Is there any chance that Laurie or the alter personalities were telling the truth, that she'd left Allan Grant alive and came back to find him dead?"

"I'm afraid it's more probable that an alter personality we haven't met is the one who took Grant's life."

"Do you think there is any possibility at all that she is totally innocent?"

Donnelly carefully arranged the charcoal briquettes in the bar becue and reached for the lighter fluid. "Possibility? I suppose anything is possible. You observed two of Laurie's alter personalities today, Leona and the boy. There may be a dozen more who haven't surfaced yet, and I'm not sure that they ever will."

"I still have a gut feeling—" Brendon clamped his lips together as Sarah came out to the patio from the kitchen.

~ 99

"Thank you for going to the courthouse with us Friday, Dr. Donnelly," Laurie told Justin. She was lying on the couch; she seemed calm, almost tranquil. Only the way she clasped her hands together hinted at inner turmoil.

"I wanted to be with you and Sarah, Laurie."

"You know, when I was making the statement I was more worried about Sarah than myself. She's suffering so much."

"I know she is."

"This morning at about six o'clock I heard her crying and went into her room. Funny, all these years she's been the one to come to me. You know what she was doing?"

"No."

"Sitting up in bed making a list of more people she'd ask to write to the judge for me. She's been hoping that I'll only have to serve two years before I'm eligible for parole, but now she's worried that Judge Armon might give me five years without parole. I hope you'll stay in touch with Sarah when I'm in prison. She's going to need you."

"I intend to stay in touch with Sarah."

"Gregg is terrific, isn't he, Doctor."

"Yes, he is."

"I don't want to go to prison," Laurie burst out. "I want to stay home. I want to be with Sarah and Gregg. *I don't want to go to prison.*"

She sat bolt upright, swung her feet down onto the floor and clenched her hands into fists. Her face hardened. "Listen, Doctor, you can't let her get those ideas. Laurie's got to be locked up."

"Why, Kate, why?" Justin asked urgently.

She did not answer.

"Kate, remember a couple of weeks ago, you told me the boy was ready to talk to me. He came out yesterday in the Grants' house. Were he and Leona telling the truth about what happened? Is there someone else I should talk to?"

In an instant Laurie's face changed again. The features became smooth, the eyes narrowed. "You shouldn't be asking so many questions about me." The boyish voice was polite but determined.

"Hi," Justin said easily. "I was glad to see you again yesterday. You took very good care of Laurie the night the professor died. You're very smart for a nine-year-old. But I'm grown up. I think I could help you take care of Laurie. Isn't it about time you trusted me?"

"You don't take care of her."

"Why do you say that?"

"You let her tell people she killed Dr. Grant, and she didn't do it. What kind of friend are you?"

"Maybe someone else who hasn't talked to me yet did it?"

"There are just four of us, Kate and Leona and Debbie and me, and none of us killed anyone. That's why I kept trying to make Laurie stop talking to the judge yesterday."

~ *100*

Brendon Moody could not let go of his gut reaction to Karen Grant. The last week of July, as he impatiently waited for the subpoena to be issued by the Chicago court, he wandered around the lobby of the Madison Arms Hotel. It was obvious that Anne Webster had finally retired from the agency. Her desk had been replaced by a handsome cherrywood table, and in general the decor of the agency had become more sophisticated. Moody decided it was time to pay another visit to Karen Grant's ex-partner, this time at her home in Bronxville.

Anne was quick to let Brendon know that she had been deeply offended by Karen's attitude. "She kept after me to move up the sale. The ink wasn't dry on the contract when she told me that it was not necessary for me to come into the office at all, that she would handle everything. Then immediately she replaced my things with new furniture for that boyfriend of hers. When I think of how I used to stick up for her when people made remarks about her, let me tell you, I feel like a fool. Some grieving widow!"

"Mrs. Webster," Moody said, "this is very important. I think there is a chance that Laurie Kenyon is not guilty of Allan Grant's murder. But she'll go to prison next month unless we can prove that someone else did kill him. Will you please go over that evening again, the one you spent at the airport with Karen Grant? Tell me every detail, no matter how unimportant it seems. Start with the drive out."

"We left for the airport at eight o'clock. Karen had been talking to her husband. She was terribly upset. When I asked her what was wrong, she said some hysterical girl had threatened him and he was taking it out on her."

"Taking it out on her? What did she mean by that?"

"I don't know. I'm not a gossip and I don't pry."

If there's anything I'm sure of, it's that, Brendon thought grimly. "Mrs. Webster, what did she mean?"

"Karen had been staying at the New York apartment more and more these last months, ever since she met Edwin Rand. I have the feeling that Allan Grant let her know he was mighty sick of the situation. On the way to the airport, she said something like, I should be straightening this out with Allan, not running a driving service.

"I reminded her that the client was one of our most valuable, and that she had a real aversion to hired cars."

"Then the plane was late."

"Yes. That really upset Karen. But we went to the VIP lounge and had a drink. Then *Spartacus* came on. It's my—"

"Your favorite movie of all time. Also a very long one. And you do tend to fall asleep. Can you be sure that Karen Grant sat and watched the entire movie?"

"Well, I do know she was checking on the plane and went to make some phone calls."

"Mrs. Webster, her home in Clinton is forty-two miles from the airport. Was there any span of time when you did not see her for somewhere between two to two-and-a-half hours? I mean was it possible that she might have left you and driven to her home?"

"I really didn't think I slept but . . ." She paused.

"Mrs. Webster, what is it?"

"It's just that when we picked up our client and left the airport, Karen's car was parked in a different spot. It was so crowded when we arrived that we had quite a walk to the terminal, but when we left it was right across from the main door."

Moody sighed. "I wish you had told me this before, Mrs. Webster."

She looked at him, bewildered. "You didn't ask me."

~ 101

It was just like it had been in those months before Lee was locked up in the clinic, Opal thought. In rented cars, she and Bic began to follow her again. Some days they'd be parked across the street and watch Lee hurry from the garage to the clinic entrance, then wait however long it took until she came out again. Bic would spend the time staring at the door, so afraid of missing even one glimpse of her. Beads of perspiration would form on his forehead, his hands would grip the wheel when she reemerged.

"Wonder what she's been talking about today?" he'd ask, fear and anger in his voice. "She's alone in the room with that doctor, Opal. Maybe he's being tempted by her."

Weekdays Lee went to the clinic in the morning. Many afternoons she and Sarah would golf together, usually going to one of the local public courses. Afraid that Sarah would notice the car following them, Bic began to phone around to the starters to inquire about a reservation in the name of Kenyon. If there was one, he and Opal would occasionally drive to that course and try to run into Sarah and Lee in the coffee shop.

He never lingered at the table, just greeted them casually and kept going, but he missed nothing about Lee. Afterwards, he'd emotionally comment about her appearance. "That golf shirt just clings to her tender body . . . It was all I could do not to reach over and release the clip that was holding back that golden hair."

Because of the "Church of the Airways" program, they had to be in New York the better part of the weekend. Opal was secretly grateful for that. If they did get a glimpse of Lee and Sarah on Saturday or Sunday, the doctor and the same young man, Gregg Bennett, were always with them. That infuriated Bic.

One mid-August day he called to Opal to join him in Lee's room. The shades were drawn, and he was sitting in the rocker. "I have been praying for guidance and have received my answer," he told her. "Lee always goes to and returns from New York alone. She has a phone in her car. I have been able to get the number of that phone."

Opal cringed as Bic's face contorted and his eyes flashed with that strange compelling light. "Opal," he thundered, "do not think I have not been aware of your jealousy. I forbid you to trouble me with it again. Lee's earthly time is almost over. In the days that are left, you must allow me to fill myself with the sight and sound and scent of that pretty child."

102

Thomasina Perkins was thrilled to receive a note from Sarah Kenyon asking her to write a letter on Laurie's behalf to the judge who was going to sentence her.

You remember so clearly how terrified and frightened Laurie was, Sarah wrote, *and you're the only person who ever actually saw her with her abductors. We need to make the judge understand the trauma Laurie suffered when she was a small child. Be sure to include the name you thought you heard the woman call the man as they rushed Laurie from the diner.* Sarah concluded by writing that a known child abuser by that name had been in the Harrisburg area then and, while of course they couldn't prove it, she intended to suggest the possibility that he was the kidnapper.

Thomasina had told the story of seeing Laurie and calling the police so often that it could practically write itself. Until she got to the sticking point.

That day the woman had *not* called the man Jim. Thomasina knew that now with absolute certainty. She couldn't give that name to the judge. It would be like lying under oath. It troubled her to know that Sarah had wasted time and money tracking down the wrong person.

Thomasina was losing faith in Reverend Hawkins. She'd written to him a couple of times thanking him for the privilege of being on his show and explaining that, while she would never suggest that God had made a mistake, maybe they should have waited and kept listening to Him. It was just that God had given her the name of the counter boy first. Could they try again?

Reverend Hawkins hadn't bothered to answer her. Oh, she was on his mailing list, that was for sure. For every two dollars she donated, she got a letter asking for more.

Her niece had taped Thomasina's appearance on the "Church of the Airways" program, and Thomasina loved to watch it. But as her resentment of Reverend Hawkins grew she noticed more and more things about the taped segment. The way his mouth was so close to her ear when she heard the name. The way he didn't even get Laurie's name straight. He had referred to her at one point as Lee.

Thomasina's conscience was clear when she mailed a passionate letter to the judge, describing Laurie's panic and hysteria in lurid terms but without mentioning the name *Jim.* She sent a copy of the letter and an explanation to Sarah, pointing out the mistake the Reverend Hawkins himself had made by referring to Laurie as Lee.

~ 103

"It's getting closer," Laurie told Dr. Donnelly matter-of-factly as she kicked off her shoes and settled back on the couch.

"What is, Laurie?"

He expected her to talk about prison, but instead she said, "The knife."

He waited.

It was Kate who spoke to him now. "Doctor, I guess we've both done our best."

"Hey, Kate," he said, "that doesn't sound like you." Was Laurie becoming suicidal? he wondered.

A wry laugh. "Kate sees the handwriting on the wall, Doctor. Got a cigarette?"

"Sure. How's it going, Leona?"

"It's pretty nearly gone. Your golf is getting better."

"Thank you."

"You really like Sarah, don't you?"

"Very much."

"Don't let her be too unhappy, will you?"

"About what?"

Laurie stretched. "I have such a headache," she murmured. "It's as though it isn't just at night anymore. Even yesterday when Sarah and I were on the golf course I could suddenly see the hand that's holding the knife."

"Laurie, the memories are coming closer and closer to the surface. Can't you let them out?"

"I can't let go of the guilt." Was it Laurie or Leona or Kate speaking? For the first time Justin couldn't be sure. "I did such bad things," she said, "disgusting things. Some secret part of me is remembering them."

Justin made a sudden decision. "Come on. We're going to take a walk in the park. Let's sit in the playground for a while and watch the kids."

* * *

The swings and slides, the jungle gym and seesaws were filled with young children. They sat on a park bench near the watchful mothers and nannies. The children were laughing, calling to each other, arguing about whose turn it was to be on the swing. Justin spotted a little girl who looked to be about four. She was happily bouncing a ball. Several times the nanny called to the child, "Don't go so far away, Christy." The child, totally absorbed in keeping the ball bouncing, did not seem to hear. Finally the nanny got up, hurried over and firmly caught the ball. "I said, stay in the playground," she scolded. "If you chased that ball in the road, one of those cars would hit you."

"I forgot." The small face looked forlorn and repentant, then, turning and seeing Laurie and Justin watching her, immediately brightened. She ran to them. "Do you like my beautiful sweater?" she asked.

The nanny came up. "Christy, you mustn't bother people." She smiled apologetically. "Christy thinks everything she puts on is beautiful."

"Well, it is," Laurie said. "It's a perfectly beautiful new sweater."

A few minutes later they started back for the clinic. "Suppose," Justin said, "that little girl, very absorbed in what she was doing, wandered too close to the road and someone grabbed her, put her in a car, disappeared with her and abused her. Do you think that years later she should blame herself?"

Laurie's eyes were welling with tears. "Point taken, Doctor."

"Then forgive yourself as readily as you would forgive that child if something she couldn't help had happened to her today."

They went back into Justin's private office. Laurie stretched out on the couch. "If that little girl had been picked up today and put in a car . . ." she hesitated.

"Maybe you can imagine what might happen to her," Justin suggested.

"She wanted to go back home. Mommy would be angry that she went down to the road. There was a new neighbor whose son was seventeen years old and a fast driver. Mommy said the little girl must not run out in front anymore. She might get hurt by the car. They loved the little girl so much. They called her their miracle."

"But the people wouldn't take her home?"

"No. They drove and drove. She was crying, and the woman slapped her and said shut up. The man with the fuzzy arms picked her up and put her on his lap." Laurie's hands clenched and unclenched.

Justin watched as she clutched her shoulders. "Why are you doing that?"

"They told the little girl to get out of the car. It's so cold. She has to go to the bathroom, but he wants to take her picture so he makes her stand by the tree."

"The picture you tore up the day you first camc to stay at the clinic made you remember that, didn't it."

"Yes. Yes."

"And the rest of the time the little girl stayed with him . . . the rest of the time *you* stayed with him . . ."

"He raped me," Laurie screamed. "I never knew when it would happen, but always after we sang the songs in the rocking chair he took me upstairs. Always then. Always then. He hurt me so much."

Justin rushed to comfort the sobbing girl. "It's okay," he said. "Just tell me this. Was it your fault?"

"He was so big. I tried to fight him. I couldn't make him stop," she shrieked. *"I couldn't make him stop."*

It was the moment to ask. "Was Opal there?"

"She's his wife."

Laurie gasped and bit her lip. Her eyes narrowed.

"Doctor, I told you that was a forbidden word." The nine-year-old boy would not allow any more memories to escape that day.

104

On August 17, while Gregg took Laurie to dinner and a play, Sarah and Brendon went to Newark Airport. They arrived at 8:55. "This is approximately the time Karen Grant and Anne Webster got here the night Allan Grant died," Moody told Sarah as they drove into the parking area. "The plane their client was on was more than three hours late, as were a lot of other planes that night. That means that the parking lot would be pretty full. Anne Webster said they had to walk quite a distance to the terminal."

Deliberately he parked his car almost at the end of the facility. "It's a pretty good hike to the United terminal," he observed. "Let's clock it at a normal pace. It should take five minutes at least."

Sarah nodded. She had told herself not to grasp at straws, not to be like so many family members of defendants she had prosecuted. Denial. Their husband or daughter or sister or brother was incapable of committing a crime, they'd argue. Even in the face of overwhelming evidence they'd be convinced there'd been some kind of horrible mistake.

But when she'd talked to Justin, he had been cautiously encouraging about Moody's theory that Karen Grant had both the opportunity and the motive to kill her husband. He said that he was beginning to accept the possibility that Laurie had no more than the four alter personalities they had met, all of whom consistently told him that Laurie was innocent.

As Sarah walked with Moody into the air-conditioned terminal, she welcomed the coolness and the relief from the muggy mid-August evening. The check-in lines reminded her of the wonderful trip to Italy she and Laurie had taken with their parents a little more than a year ago. Now it seemed as if that had been several lifetimes ago, she thought sadly.

"Remember, it was only after Karen Grant and Mrs. Webster got here that they learned the computer system had gone down and the plane was rescheduled for twelve-thirty arrival." Moody paused as he looked up at the listings of arrivals and departures. "What's your reaction if you're Karen Grant and edgy about your relationship with your husband? Maybe more than edgy if when you phoned him he'd told you he wanted a divorce?"

An image of Karen Grant came to Sarah's mind. In all these months she'd thought of Karen Grant as a grieving widow. In court at Laurie's plea bargain she'd been wearing black. It was odd, Sarah thought now as she remembered the scene. Maybe she was carrying it a bit far—not many people in their early thirties wear black as a sign of mourning anymore.

Sarah remarked on this fact to Brendon as they walked toward the VIP lounge. He nodded. "The widow Grant is always playing a part, and it shows. We know she and Anne Webster went up to the lounge and had a drink. The movie *Spartacus* started at nine o'clock that night on The Movie Channel. The receptionist who was here that night is on duty now," he told Sarah. "We'll talk to her."

The receptionist did not remember the night of January 28, but she did know and like Anne Webster. "I've been on the job ten years," she explained, "and I've never known a better travel agent. Only problem with Anne Webster is that whenever she kills time here, she takes over the television. She always puts on one of the movie stations and gets mighty stubborn if someone else wants to watch the news or something."

"Real problem," Brendon said sympathetically.

The receptionist laughed. "Oh, not really. I always tell the people who want to watch something different to just wait five minutes. Anne Webster can conk out faster than anyone I know. And once she's asleep, we change the channel."

* * *

They drove from the airport to Clinton. On the way, Moody theorized. "Let's say Karen was hanging around the airport that night, getting more and more worried that she can't talk her husband out of wanting a divorce. Webster is either engrossed in a movie or asleep and won't miss her. The plane won't be in until twelve-thirty."

"So she got in her car and went home," Sarah said.

"Exactly. Assume she let herself into the house with her key and went to the bedroom. Allan was asleep. Karen saw Laurie's tote bag and the knife and realized that if he were found stabbed to death, Laurie would be blamed for it."

On the way they discussed the fact that the subpoena to the bank in Chicago had not, so far, helped them.

The account had been opened in the name of Jane Graves, using an address in the Bahamas that turned out to be another mail drop. The deposit had been a draft from a numbered bank account in Switzerland.

"Almost impossible to get any information about Swiss depositors," Brendon said. "I'm inclined to think now that it was Karen Grant who hired Danny. She may have been stashing some of Allen Grant's trust fund away, and as a travel agent, she knows her way around."

When they reached Clinton, the realtor's sign was still on the lawn of Allan Grant's home.

They sat in the car for several minutes, looking at the house. "It could happen. It makes sense," Sarah said. "But how do we prove it?"

"I talked to the secretary, Connie Santini, again today," Moody said. "She confirms everything we know. Karen Grant was living her own life exactly as she wanted to live it, using Allan Grant's income as a personal allowance. Putting on a show as the grieving widow, but it *is* a show. Her spirits have never been better, according to the secretary. I want you with me on August twenty-sixth when Anne Webster gets back from Australia. We're going to talk to that lady together."

"August twenty-sixth," Sarah said. "Five days before Laurie goes to prison."

105

"It's the last week,"Laurie told Justin Donnelly on August 24.

He watched as she leaned back on the couch, her hands clasped behind her head.

"Yesterday was fun wasn't it, Justin? I'm sorry. I'd rather call you Doctor in here."

"It was fun. You really are a terrific golfer, Laurie. You beat us all hands down."

"Even Gregg. Well, I'll be out of practice soon enough. Last night I was awake for a long time. I was thinking about that day when I was kidnapped. I could see myself in my pink bathing suit, going down the driveway to watch the people in the funeral procession. I thought it was a parade.

"When the man picked me up, I was still holding my music box. That song keeps going through my head . . . 'Eastside, westside, all around the town . . . Boys and girls together . . .' " She stopped.

Justin waited quietly.

"When the man with the hairy arms put me in the car, I asked him where we were going. The music box was still playing."

"Did anything special bring on those thoughts?"

"Maybe. Last night after you and Gregg left, Sarah and I sat up for a long time talking about that day. I told her that when we drove past the corner house, the one that was that ugly pink color, old Mrs. Whelan was on the porch. Isn't it funny to remember something like that?"

"Not really. All the memories are there. Once they're all out, the fear that they cause will go away."

" 'Boys and girls together . . .' " Laurie sang softly. "That's why the others came to be with me. We were boys and girls together."

"Boys? Laurie, is there another boy?"

Laurie swung her feet off the couch. One hand began smacking the other. "No, Doctor. There's only me." The young voice dropped to a whisper. "She didn't need anyone else. I always sent her away when Bic hurt her."

Justin had not caught the whispered name.

"Who hurt her?"

"Oh, gee," the boy alter said. "I didn't mean to tell. I'm glad you didn't hear me."

After the session, Justin Donnelly reminded himself that even though he had not been able to hear the name the boy alter had unintentionally said aloud, it was very near the surface. It would come out again.

But next week at this time Laurie would be in prison. She'd be lucky if she saw a counselor every few months.

Justin knew that many of his colleagues did not believe in multiple personality disorder.

~ 106

Anne Webster and her husband returned from their trip early on August 26. Moody managed to reach Webster at noon and persuaded her to see him and Sarah immediately. When they arrived in Bronxville, Webster was unexpectedly direct. "I've been thinking a lot about the night Allan died," she said. "You know nobody likes to feel like a fool. I let Karen get away with claiming that she hadn't moved the car. But you know something? I have proof that she did."

Moody's head tilted up. Sarah's lips went dry. "What kind of proof, Mrs. Webster?" she asked.

"I told you that Karen was upset on the drive to the airport. Something I didn't remember to tell you was that she snapped at me when I pointed out that she was very low on gas. Well she didn't get any on the way to the airport and she didn't get any on the way back from the airport and she didn't get any the next morning when I drove down to Clinton with her."

"Do you know if Karen Grant charges her gas, or pays cash?" Moody asked.

Webster smiled grimly. "You can bet if she bought gas that night it went on the company credit card."

"Where would last January's statements be?"

"In the office. Karen will never let me march in and go through the files, but Connie will do it if I ask. I'll give her a call."

She talked at length to her former secretary. When she hung up she said, "You're in luck. Karen's at an outing American Airlines is sponsoring today. Connie will be glad to look up the statements. She's mad clean through. She asked for a raise, and Karen turned her down."

* * *

On the way to New York, Moody warned Sarah, "You know of course that even if we could prove Karen Grant had been in the Clinton area that night there isn't a shred of proof that links her with her husband's death."

"I know," Sarah told him. "But Brendon, there must be some thing tangible we can put our hands on."

Connie Santini had a triumphant smile for them. "January statement from an Exxon station just off Route 78 and four miles from Clinton," she said, "and a copy of the receipt with Karen's signature. Boy, I'm going to quit this job. She's so darn cheap. I didn't take a raise all last year because business wasn't good. Now it's really picking up and she still won't part with an extra cent. I'll tell you this: She spends more money on jewelry than I make in a year."

Santini pointed across the lobby to L. Crown Jeweler. "She shops over there the way some people go to the cosmetics counter. But she's cheap with them too. The very day her husband died she'd bought a bracelet, then lost it. She had me on my hands and knees searching for it. When the call came about Allan she was in Crown's raising hell that the bracelet had a lousy clasp. She'd lost it again. This time for good. Listen, there was nothing wrong with the clasp. She just didn't take the time to fasten it right, but you can be sure she made them replace it."

A bracelet, Sarah thought, *a bracelet!* In Allan Grant's bedroom the day of the plea bargain, Laurie, or rather, the boy alter, had acted out picking up something and shoving it in his pocket. It never occurred to me that the bracelet found with Laurie's blood-stained jeans might not be one of her own, she thought. I never asked to see it.

"Miss Santini, you've been a great help," Moody told her. "Will you be here for a little while?"

"Until five. I don't give her one extra minute."

"That's fine."

A young clerk was behind the counter of L. Crown Jewelers. Impressed by Moody's insinuation that he was from an insurance company and wanted to inquire about a certain lost bracelet, the clerk willingly looked up the records.

"Oh yes, sir. Mrs. Grant purchased a bracelet on January twenty-eighth. It was a new design from our showroom, twisted gold with silver going through it, giving the effect of diamonds. Quite lovely. It cost fifteen hundred dollars. But I don't understand why she'd put in a claim for it. We replaced it for her. She came in the next morning, most upset. She was sure it had fallen off her wrist shortly after she bought it."

"Why was she so sure of that?"

"Because she told us it had slipped off once at her desk before she lost it for good. Frankly, sir, the problem was that it had a new kind of catch, very secure, but not if you don't take the time to fasten it properly."

"Do you have the sales record?" Moody asked.

"Of course, but we did decide to replace it, sir. Mrs. Grant is a good customer."

"By any chance do you have a picture of the bracelet or a similar one?"

"I have both a picture and a bracelet. We've made several dozen of them since January."

"All alike? Was there anything different about that particular one?"

"The catch, sir. After the incident with Mrs. Grant we changed it on the others. We didn't want any repeat problems." He reached under the counter for a notebook. "You see the original catch clasped like this . . . the one we now use snaps this way and has a safety bar."

The clerk was a good artist.

A copy of the January 28 sales slip, a color photo of the bracelet and the signed and labeled sketch in hand, Sarah and Moody went back to the Global Travel Agency. Santini was waiting, her eyes alive with curiosity. She willingly dialed Anne Webster's number, then handed the phone to Moody, who pressed the speaker button.

"Mrs. Webster," he asked, "was there something about a missing bracelet the night you were at Newark airport with Karen Grant?"

"Oh yes. As I told you, Karen was driving the client and me back to New York. Suddenly she said, 'Damn it, I've lost it again.' Then she turned to me and, very upset, demanded to know whether or not I had noticed her bracelet in the airport."

"And had you?"

Webster hesitated. "I told a teeny-weeny fib. Actually I know she was wearing it in the VIP lounge, but after the way she carried on when she thought she'd lost it in the office . . . Well, I didn't want her to explode in front of the client. I said very positively that she hadn't been wearing it at the airport and that it was probably around her desk somewhere. But I did phone the airport that night, just in case someone turned it in. It's really all right. The jeweler replaced it."

Dear God, dear God, Sarah thought.

"Would you recognize it, Mrs. Webster?" Moody asked.

"Certainly. She showed it to Connie and me and told us about it being a new design."

Santini nodded vigorously.

"Mrs. Webster, I'll be back to you shortly. You've been a big help." In spite of yourself, Moody thought as he hung up the phone.

One last detail to put in place. Please, please, Sarah prayed as she dialed the office of the Hunterdon County prosecutor. She was put through to the prosecutor and told him what she needed. "I'll hold on." As she waited she told Moody, "They're sending someone to the evidence room."

They waited in silence for ten minutes, then Moody watched Sarah's face light up like a sunburst and then a rainbow as tears welled from her eyes. "Twisted gold with silver," she said. "Thank you. I need to see you first thing in the morning. Will Judge Armon be in his chambers?"

107

Karen Grant was thoroughly annoyed on Thursday morning to find that Connie Santini was not at her desk. I'm going to fire her, Karen thought as she snapped on lights and listened for messages. Santini had left one. She had an urgent errand but would be in sometime later. What's urgent about anything in *her* life? Karen thought as she opened her desk and took out the first draft of the statement she was planning to deliver in court at Laurie Kenyon's sentencing. It began: "Allan Grant was a husband beyond compare."

Karen should only know where I am right now, Connie Santini thought as she sat with Anne Webster in the small waiting area outside the prosecutor's private office. Sarah Kenyon and Mr. Moody were in talking to the prosecutor. Connie was fascinated by the charged atmosphere of the place. Phones ringing. Young attorneys rushing by, arms loaded with files. One of them looked over her shoulder and called, "Take a message. Can't talk now. I'm due in court."

Sarah Kenyon opened the door and said, "Will you come in now, please. The prosecutor wants to talk to you."

A moment later as she acknowledged the introduction to Prosecutor Levine, Anne Webster glanced down at his desk and noticed the object in a tagged plastic bag. "Oh for heaven's sake, there's Karen's bracelet," she said. "Where did you find it?"

An hour later, Prosecutor Levine and Sarah were in Judge Armon's chambers. "Your Honor," Levine said, "I don't know where to begin, but I'm here with Sarah Kenyon to jointly request an adjournment of Laurie Kenyon's sentencing for two weeks."

The judge's eyebrows raised. "Why?"

"Judge, I've never had anything like this happen before, especially where the defendent pled guilty. We now have reason to seriously question whether Laurie Kenyon committed this homicide. As you know, Miss Kenyon indicated to you that she didn't remember committing the homicide but was satisfied from the state's investigation that she had done so.

"Now some new and quite astonishing evidence has come to light that casts serious doubt on her culpability."

Sarah listened quietly as the prosecutor told the judge about the bracelet, the jewelry salesman's statement, the purchase of gas at the Clinton service station and then gave him the written affidavits of Anne Webster and Connie Santini.

They sat in silence for the three minutes it took Judge Armon to read the affidavits and examine the receipts. When he had finished, he shook his head and said, "Well, I've been on the bench for twenty years and I've never seen anything like this happen. Of course, under the circumstances, I'll adjourn the sentencing."

He looked at Sarah sympathetically as she sat gripping the arms of the chair, the mixture of emotions obvious in her face.

Sarah tried to keep her voice steady as she said, "Judge, on one level I'm obviously ecstatic and on another I'm devastated that I allowed her to plead guilty."

"Don't be so hard on yourself, Sarah," Judge Armon said. "We all know you've turned yourself inside out to defend her."

The prosecutor stood up. "I was going to talk with Mrs. Grant before the sentencing about the statement she wanted to make in court. Instead I think I'm going to have a little talk with her about how her husband died."

"What do you mean the sentencing isn't going to take place on Monday?" Karen asked indignantly. "What kind of snag? Mr. Levine, I think you should realize that this is a terrible ordeal for me. I don't want to have to face that girl again. Just preparing the statement I'm going to make to the judge is upsetting."

"These technicalities come up," Levine said soothingly. "Why don't you come in tomorrow around ten. I want to go over it with you."

Connie Santini arrived in the office at two o'clock fully expecting to have Karen Grant's wrath descend on her. The prosecutor had warned her to say nothing to Karen about her meeting with him. Karen was preoccupied, however, and asked the secretary no questions. "You handle the phones," she told Connie. "Say I'm out. I'm working on my statement. I want that judge to know all I've been through."

The next morning, Karen dressed carefully for her meeting. It might be a little much to wear black today to the courtroom. Instead she chose a dark blue linen and matching pumps. She kept her makeup subdued.

The prosecutor did not keep her waiting. "Come in, Karen. I'm glad to see you."

He was always so pleasant and really a very attractive man. Karen smiled up at him. "I've prepared my statement for the judge. I think it really gets across everything I feel."

"Before we get to that, a couple of things have come up that I want to go over with you. Want to step in here?"

She was surprised that they did not go into his private office. Instead he took her into a smaller room. Several men and a stenotypist were already there. She recognized two of the men as the detectives who had spoken to her in the house the morning Allan's body was found.

There was something different about Prosecutor Levine. His voice was businesslike and remote as he said, "Karen, I'm going to read you your constitutional rights."

"What?"

"You have the right to remain silent. Do you understand that?"

Karen Grant felt the blood drain from her face. "Yes."

"You have a right to an attorney . . . anything you say can be used against you in a court of law . . ."

"Yes, I understand, but what the hell is going on? I'm the widow of the victim."

He continued to read her her rights, to ask if she understood them. Finally he requested, "Will you read and sign the waiver-of-rights form and speak to us?"

"Yes, I will, but I think you're all crazy." Karen Grant's hand shook as she signed the paper.

The questions began. She became oblivious to the video camera, barely aware of the faint clicking of the keys as the stenographer's fingers flew over the keyboard.

"No, of course I didn't leave the airport that night. No. I wasn't parked in a different spot. That old bag Webster is always half-asleep. I sat through that lousy movie with her snoring beside me."

They showed her the charge card receipt for the gas she had purchased at the service station.

"That's a mistake. The date's a mistake. Those people never know what they're doing."

The bracelet.

"They sell plenty of those bracelets. What do you think, I'm the only customer that store has? Anyhow I lost it in the office. Even Anne Webster said I didn't have it on at the airport."

Karen's head started to pound and the prosecutor pointed out that the catch on her bracelet was one of a kind, that Anne Webster's sworn statement was that she *had* seen the bracelet on Karen's wrist in the airport and had called to report it missing.

Time passed as she snapped answers to their questions.

Her relationship with Allan? "It was perfect. We were crazy about each other. Of course he didn't ask me for a divorce on the phone that night."

Edwin Rand? "He's just a friend."

The bracelet? "I don't want to talk about the bracelet anymore. No, I didn't lose it in the bedroom."

The veins in Karen Grant's neck were throbbing. Her eyes were watering. She was twisting a handkerchief in her hands.

The prosecutor and detectives could sense that she was beginning to realize she could not talk her way out of it. She was beginning to feel the net closing around her.

The older detective, Frank Reeves, took the sympathetic approach. "I can understand how it happened. You went home to make up with your husband. He was asleep. You saw Laurie Kenyon's bag on the floor beside the bed. Maybe you thought that Allan had been lying to you after all about being involved with her. You snapped. The knife was there. A second later you realized what you'd done. It must have been a shock when I told you that we'd found the knife in Laurie's room."

As Reeves spoke, Karen's head bowed, her whole body sagged. Her eyes welling with tears, she said bitterly, "When I saw Laurie's bag I thought he had been lying to me. He had told me on the phone that he wanted a divorce, that there was someone else. When you told me she had the knife, I couldn't believe it. I couldn't believe Allan was really dead either. I never meant to kill him."

She looked imploringly into the faces of the prosecutor and detectives. "I really loved him, you know," she said. "He was so generous."

108

"It's been quite a weekend," Justin said to Laurie as she settled herself on the couch.

"I still can't get it through my head," Laurie said. "Do you realize that this is the very hour I expected to be standing in court being sentenced?"

"How do you feel about Karen Grant?"

"I honestly don't know. I guess I'm having trouble believing that I had nothing to do with her husband's death."

"Believe it, Laurie," Justin said gently. He studied her carefully. The euphoria of the swiftly moving events had vanished. The aftershock of all the strain was going to show for a while. "I think it's a great idea for you and Sarah to get away on vacation for a couple of weeks. Do you remember that not long ago you told me you'd give anything to play the golf course at St. Andrews in Scotland? Now you can do it."

"Can I?"

"Of course. Laurie, I'd like to thank the little boy who's taken such good care of you. He was the one who knew you were innocent. Can I talk to him?"

"If you like."

She closed her eyes, paused, sat up as she opened them again. Her lips tightened. Her features softened. Her posture altered. A polite boyish voice said, "All right, Doctor. I'm here now."

"I just wanted to let you know that you've been great," Justin said.

"Not that great. If I hadn't taken that bracelet, Laurie wouldn't have been blamed for everything."

"That's not your fault. You did your best, and you're only nine years old. Laurie is twenty-two and she's really getting strong. I think that soon you and Kate and Leona and Debbie ought to start thinking about joining her completely. I've hardly seen Debbie in weeks. I haven't seen that much of Kate or Leona either. Don't you think it's time to release all the secrets to Laurie and help her to get well?"

Laurie sighed. "Gosh I have a headache today," she said in her normal voice as she settled back on the couch. "Something's different today, Doctor. The others seem to want me to do the talking."

Justin knew it was an important moment, one that must not be wasted. "That's because they want to become part of you, Laurie," he said carefully. "They always have been part of you, you know. Kate is your natural desire to take care of yourself. She's self-preservation. Leona is the woman in you. You've frozen your normal womanly responses so long they had to come out another way."

"In a sex kitten," Laurie suggested with a half smile.

"She is, or was, pretty sexy," Justin agreed. "Debbie is the little girl lost, the child who wanted to go home. You're home now, Laurie. You're safe."

"Am I?"

"You will be if you'll only let that nine-year-old boy put the rest of the puzzle together. He's admitted that one of the names you're forbidden to say is Opal. Let go a little more. Have him surrender his memories to you. Do you know the boy's name?"

"Now I do."

"Tell it to me, Laurie. Nothing will happen, I promise."

She sighed. "I hope not. His name is Lee."

109

The phone would not stop ringing. Congratulations were pouring in. Sarah found herself saying the same thing over and over. "I know. It's a miracle. I don't think it's really sunk in yet."

Bouquets and baskets of flowers were arriving. The most elaborate basket came with the prayers and congratulations of the Reverend Bobby and Carla Hawkins.

"It's big enough to be from the chief mourner at a funeral," Sophie sniffed.

The words sent a clammy shock through Sarah. "Sophie, when you leave, take it with you, please. I don't care what you do with it."

"You're sure you don't need me anymore today?"

"Hey, give yourself a break." Sarah walked over to Sophie, hugged her. "We wouldn't have made it through all this without you. Gregg is coming over. His classes start next week, so he's leaving for Stanford tomorrow. He and Laurie are taking off for the day."

"And you?"

"I'm staying home. I need to collapse."

"No Dr. Donnelly?"

"Not tonight. He's got to drive to Connecticut for some meeting."

"I like him, Sarah."

"So do I."

Sophie was starting out the door when the phone rang. Sarah waved her off. "Don't worry, I'll get it."

It was Justin. There was something in his quick greeting that set off a warning signal to Sarah. "Is anything wrong?" she demanded.

"No, no," he said soothingly. "It's just that Laurie came up with a name today and I'm trying to remember in what context I heard it recently."

"What is it?"

"Lee."

Sarah frowned. "Let's see. Oh, I know. The letter Thomasina Perkins wrote me a couple of weeks ago. I told you about it. She's decided that she's stopped believing in Reverend Hawkins's miracles. In the letter she pointed out that while he was praying over her, he referred to Laurie as 'Lee.' "

"That's it," Justin said. "I noticed it myself the day I watched that program."

"How did Laurie use the name?" Sarah asked.

"It's what her nine-year-old boy alter calls himself. Of course it's probably just coincidence. Sarah, I've got to run. They need me upstairs. Laurie's on her way home. I'll call you later."

Sarah hung up slowly. A thought so frightening, so incredible and still so plausible burned in her mind. She dialed Betsy Lyons at the real estate agency. "Mrs. Lyons, please get out the file on our house. I'll be right over. I need to know the exact dates that the Hawkinses were in our house."

Laurie was on her way home. Gregg would be along any minute. As she ran from the apartment, Sarah remembered to hide the key under the mat for him.

~ 110

Laurie drove cross Ninety-sixth Street, up the West Side Drive, over the George Washington Bridge, west on Route 4, north on Route 17. She knew why she had this terrible sense that her time was running out.

It was forbidden to tell the names. It was forbidden to tell what he had done to her. Her car phone rang. She pushed the ANSWER button.

It was the Reverend Hawkins. "Laurie, Sarah gave me your number. Are you on your way home?"

"Yes. Where is Sarah?"

"Right here. She's had a minor accident but she's all right, dear."

"Accident! What do you mean?"

"She came over to pick up some mail and has twisted her ankle. Can you come directly here?"

"Of course."

"Hurry, dear."

~ 111

The issue of *People* magazine with the Reverend Bobby and Carla Hawkins on the cover arrived in mailboxes all over the country.

In Harrisburg, Thomasina Perkins oohed at the sight of that picture of the Hawkinses and almost forgave them their neglect of her. She opened to the cover story and gasped at the totally different picture of the Hawkinses taken twenty years ago. His gold earring; the powerful hairy arms; the beard. Her stringy, dark, straight hair. They were holding guitars. Memory flooded Thomasina as she read: "Bic and Opal, the would-be rock stars." *Bic.* The name that had haunted her for so many years.

Fifteen minutes after he spoke to Sarah, Justin Donnelly left his office to drive to Connecticut for the seminar he was attending. As he passed his secretary, he noticed the open magazine on her desk. He happened to glance at one of the pictures in the spread, and his blood ran cold. He grabbed the magazine. That heavy tree. The house was gone but the chicken coop in the rear . . . The caption read: "Site of the home from which Reverend Hawkins launched his ministry."

Justin raced back to his office and from Laurie's file grabbed the reconstructed picture and held it next to the one in the magazine. The tree, heavier in this new picture, but with that same gnarled, wide trunk; the edge of the chicken coop in the old picture, exactly the same as the side of the now-visible structure. The stone wall that ran beside the tree.

He raced from the clinic. His car was parked on the street. He'd call Sarah from the car phone. In his mind he could see the television program and the Reverend Bobby Hawkins praying over Thomasina Perkins, praying that she would be able to name the people who had abducted Lee.

In Teaneck, Betty Moody happily settled down to read the new issue of *People* magazine. An unusually relaxed Brendon was taking a couple of days off. His lip curled when he saw the picture of the Hawkinses on the cover. "Can't stand those two," he muttered as he looked over her shoulder. "What did they find to write about them?"

Betty flipped the pages to the cover story. "Sweet, Jesus," Moody muttered as he read: "Bic and *Opal,* the would-be rock stars . . ."

"What's the matter with me?" Brendon shouted. "It was plain as the nose on my face." He dashed for the foyer, stopping only long enough to grab his gun from the drawer.

112

Sarah sat at Lyons's desk and analyzed the Kenyon-Hawkins file. "The first time Carla Hawkins came into this office was after our place went on the market," Sarah commented.

"But I didn't show it to her immediately."

"How did you happen to show it to her?"

"She was going through the book and noticed it."

"Did you ever leave her alone in our house?"

"Never," Lyons bristled.

"Mrs. Lyons, a knife disappeared from our kitchen around the end of January. I see Carla Hawkins was looking at the house several times just before that. It isn't easy to steal a carving knife from a wall bracket unless you have at least a little time alone. Do you remember if you left her in the kitchen by herself?"

Lyons bit her lip. "Yes," she said reluctantly. "She dropped her glove in Laurie's room, and I left her sitting in the kitchen while I retrieved it."

"All right. Something else. Isn't it pretty unusual for people not to bargain on the price of a house?"

"You were lucky, Sarah, to get that price in this market."

"I'm not sure about how much luck is involved. Isn't it highly unusual to offer to close, then allow the former owners to stay on until they decide to move and not even charge them rent?"

"It's extraordinary."

"I'm not surprised. One last observation. Look at these dates. Mrs. Hawkins often came out on Saturday around eleven."

"Yes."

"That was just the time Laurie was in therapy," Sarah said quietly, "and they knew it." The chicken head that had so terrified Laurie. The knife. The picture in her journal. Those people in and out of the house with the boxes that hardly weighed a pound. Laurie's insistence on going back to the clinic the night she came home, right after the Hawkinses had stopped by. And . . . The *pink* house! Sarah thought. Carla Hawkins mentioned it that night I had dinner with them.

"Mrs. Lyons, did you ever tell Mrs. Hawkins that the corner house on our street used to be a garish pink?"

"I didn't know it had been pink."

She grabbed the phone. "I have to call home." Gregg Bennett answered.

"Gregg, I'm glad you're there. Make sure you stay with Laurie."

"She's not here," Gregg said. "I'd hoped she was with you. Sarah, Brendon Moody is here. Justin is on his way out. Sarah, the Hawkinses are the people who abducted Laurie. Justin and Moody are sure of it. Where is Laurie?"

With a certainty that went beyond reason, Sarah knew. "The house," she said. "I'm going to the house."

~ 113

Laurie drove down the familiar street, resisting the impulse to floor the accelerator. There were children playing on the lawn of one of the houses. Years ago Mama hadn't allowed her out front alone because of that boy who drove so fast.

Sarah. A twisted ankle isn't so bad, she tried to tell herself. But it wasn't that. There was something terribly wrong. She knew it. She'd sensed it all day.

She steered the car from the street into the driveway. Already the house seemed different. Mama's blue tieback draperies and scalloped shades had been so pretty. The Hawkinses had replaced them with blinds that, when closed, were totally black on the outside, giving the house a shuttered, unwelcoming look. Now it reminded her of another house, a dark, closed house where terrible things happened.

She hurried across the driveway, along the walk, up the porch steps to the door. An intercom had been installed. She must have been seen, because as she touched the bell she heard a woman say, "The door is unlocked. Come in."

She turned the handle, stepped into the foyer and closed the door behind her. The foyer, usually brightened by the light from the adjoining rooms, was now in semidarkness. Laurie blinked and looked around. There was no sound. "Sarah," she called. "Sarah."

"We're in your old room, waiting for you," a voice responded from a distance.

She began to climb the stairs, at first quickly, then with dragging footsteps.

Perspiration broke out on her forehead. The hand that clung to the railing became soaking wet, leaving a damp trail on the bannister. Her tongue felt thick and dry. Her breathing became quick, short gasps. She was at the top of the stairs, turning down the hallway. The door to her room was closed.

"Sarah!" she called.

"Come in, Lee!" This time the man's voice was impatient, as impatient as it used to be long ago when she didn't want to obey the command to go upstairs with him.

Despairingly she stood outside the bedroom door. She knew Sarah was not there. She had always known that someday they'd be waiting for her. Someday was now.

The door swung inward, opened by Opal. Her eyes were cold and hostile, just as they had been when Laurie first met her; a smile that was not a smile slashed her lips. Opal was wearing a short black skirt and a T-shirt that hugged her breasts. Her long, stringy dark hair, tousled and uncombed, hung limp on her shoulders. Laurie offered no resistance as Opal took her hand and led her across the room to where Bic was sitting in an old rocking chair, his feet bare, his shiny black chinos unbuttoned at the waist, his soiled T-shirt exposing his curly-haired arms. The dull gold earring in his ear swayed as he leaned forward, reaching out for her. He took her hands in his, made her stand before him, a truant child. A scrap of pink material was on his knee. Her bathing suit. The only light was from the night-light in the floor socket that Mama had always left on because Laurie was so afraid of the dark.

The loud thoughts were shrieking in her head.

An angry voice, scolding, *You little fool, you shouldn't have come.*

A child crying, *Don't make me do it.*

A boy's voice yelling, *Run. Run.*

A weary voice saying, *It's time to die for all the bad things we did.*

"Lee," Bic sighed. "You forgot your promise, didn't you? You talked about us to that doctor."

"Yes."

"You know what's going to happen to you?"

"Yes."

"What happened to the chicken?"

"You cut its head off."

"Would you rather punish yourself?"

"Yes."

"Good girl. Do you see the knife?"

He pointed to the corner. She nodded.

"Pick it up and come back to me."

The voices shouted at her as she walked across the room: *Don't do it!*

Get away!

Run!

Get it. Do as he says. We're both tramps and we know it.

Closing her palm around the handle of the knife, she returned to him. She flinched at the vision of the chicken flopping at her feet. It was her turn.

He was so close to her. His breath was hot on her face. She had known that someday she would walk into a room and find him just like this, in the rocking chair.

His arms closed around her. She was on his lap, her legs dangling, his face brushing hers. He began to rock back and forth, back and forth. "You have been my temptation," he whispered. "When you die you will free me. Pray for forgiveness as we sing the beautiful song we always sang together. Then you will get up, kiss me goodbye, walk to the corner, put the knife against your heart and plunge it in. If you disobey, you know what I have to do to you."

His voice was deep but soft as he began, " 'Amazing Grace, how sweet the sound . . .' "

The rocking chair thudded back and forth on the bare floor. "Sing, Lee," he ordered sternly.

" 'That saved a wretch like me . . .' " His hands were caressing her shoulders, her arms, her neck. In a minute it will be all over, she promised herself. Her soprano voice rose clear and sweet. " 'I once was lost, but now am found . . . was blind but now I see.' " Her fingers pressed the blade of the knife against her heart.

We don't have to wait, Leona urged. *Do it now.*

~ 114

Justin drove from New York to New Jersey as fast as he dared, all the while trying to reassure himself that Laurie was safe. She was going directly home and meeting Gregg there. But there had been something about her this morning that troubled him. Resignation. That was the word. Why?

As soon as he'd reached the car he'd tried to phone Sarah to warn her about the Hawkinses, but there was no answer at the condo. Every ten minutes he pressed the redial button.

He had just started north on Route 17 when the phone was answered. Gregg was in the condo. Sarah was out, he told Justin. He expected Laurie any minute.

"Don't let Laurie out of your sight," Justin commanded. "The Hawkinses were her abductors. I'm certain of it."

"Hawkins! *That son of a bitch!*"

Gregg's outrage sharpened Justin's awareness of the enormous suffering Laurie had endured. All these months Hawkins had been circling around her, terrorizing her, trying to drive her into madness. He pressed his foot on the pedal. The car shot forward.

He was turning off Route 17 at the Ridgewood Avenue exit when the car phone rang.

It was Gregg. "I'm with Brendon Moody. Sarah thinks Laurie may be with Hawkins in the old house. We're on the way to it."

"I was only there twice. Give me directions."

As Gregg spat them out, Justin remembered the way. Around the railroad station, past the drugstore, straight on Godwin, left on Lincoln . . .

He didn't dare speed as he passed Graydon Pool. It was crowded, and families with young children were crossing the street, heading toward it.

An image came to Justin of a fragile Laurie confronting the monster who had kidnapped her when she was a four-year-old child in a pink bathing suit.

115

Laurie's Buick was in the driveway. Sarah rushed from her car up the porch steps. She rang the bell repeatedly, then twisted the knob. The door was unlocked. As she pushed it open and ran into the foyer, she heard a door slam somewhere on the second floor.

"Laurie," she called.

Carla Hawkins, her blond hair disheveled, tying a robe as she came down the stairs, said frantically, "Sarah, Laurie came in a few minutes ago carrying a knife. She's threatening to kill herself. Bobby is talking her out of it. You mustn't startle her. Stay here with me."

Sarah pushed her aside and bounded up the stairs. At the top she looked around wildly. Down the hall the door to Laurie's room was closed. Her feet barely touched the floor as she rushed to it, then stopped. From inside she could hear the rise and fall of a man's voice. With painstaking care she opened the door.

Laurie was standing in the corner, staring blankly at Bobby Hawkins. She was holding the blade of a knife against her heart. The tip had already penetrated her flesh, and a trickle of blood was staining her blouse.

Hawkins was wrapped in a floor-length white terry-cloth robe, his hair loose and full. "You must do only what the Lord wants of you," he was saying. "Remember what is expected of you."

He's trying to make her kill herself, Sarah thought. Laurie, in a trancelike state, was unaware of her. Sarah was afraid to make a sudden move toward her. "Laurie," she said softly. "Laurie, look at me." Laurie's hand pushed the blade a fraction deeper.

"All sins must be punished," Hawkins said, his voice a hypnotic singsong. "You must not sin again."

Sarah saw the look of finality that came over Laurie's face. "Laurie, don't," she screamed. "Laurie, *don't!!*"

The voices were shrieking at her.

Lee was yelling, *Stop.*

Debbie was crying in terror.

Kate was shouting, *Wimp. Fool.*

Leona's voice was the loudest. *Get it over with!*

Someone else was crying. Sarah. Sarah, always so strong, always the caretaker, was coming toward her, her hands outstretched, tears streaking her face, begging, "Don't leave me. I love you."

The voices stilled. Laurie flung the knife across the room and stumbled forward to gather Sarah in her arms.

The knife was on the floor. His eyes glittering, his hair disheveled, the robe Opal had wrapped around him at the sound of the doorbell slipping from his shoulders, Bic bent down. His fingers grasped the handle of the knife.

Lee would never be his now. All the years of wanting her, fearing her memories were over. His ministry was over. She had been his temptation and his downfall. Her sister had kept him from her. Let them die together.

Laurie heard the hissing, swishing sound that had haunted her all these years, glimpsed the blade gleaming in the semidarkness, cutting the air in ever-widening circles, powered by the thick hairy arm.

"No," Laurie moaned. With a violent shove, she thrust Sarah away, out of the path of the knife.

Sarah, off balance, stumbled backwards and fell, her head smashing into the side of the rocker.

A terrible smile slashing his face, Bic advanced with measured step toward Laurie, the darting blade blocking her escape. Finally there was no place to go. Pressed against the wall, Laurie looked into the face of her executioner.

~ 116

Brendon Moody floored the accelerator as he drove down Twin Oaks Road. "They're both here," he snapped as he saw the cars in the driveway. Gregg at his heels, he raced to the house. Why was the front door ajar?

There was an unnatural silence about the darkened rooms. "Check this floor," he ordered. "I'm going upstairs."

At the end of the hallway the door was open. Laurie's bedroom. He ran toward it. Some instinct made him draw his gun. He heard a moan as he reached the doorway and took in the nightmarish scene.

Sarah was lying on the floor, dazed, trying to struggle to her feet. Blood trickled from her forehead.

Carla Hawkins stood frozen a few feet from Sarah.

Laurie was backed into a corner of the room, her hands raised to her throat, staring at the wild-eyed figure approaching her, sweeping a knife in ever-widening arcs.

Bic Hawkins raised the knife high in the air, looked down into Laurie's face, inches from his own, and whispered, "Goodbye, Lee."

It was the instant Brendon Moody needed. His bullet found its target, the throat of Laurie's abductor.

Justin rushed into the house as Gregg was racing through the foyer to the staircase. "Upstairs," Gregg shouted. The shot sounded as they reached the landing.

She had always known it would happen this way. The knife entering her throat. Sticky warm blood splashing over her face and arms.

But now the knife was gone. The droplets of blood spattered over her were not her blood. It was Bic, not she, who had slumped and fallen. It was his eyes, not hers, staring up.

Laurie watched motionless as the gleaming, compelling eyes flickered and closed forever.

Justin and Gregg reached the doorway of the bedroom together. Carla Hawkins, kneeling beside the body, was pleading, "Come back, Bic. A miracle. You can perform miracles."

Brendon Moody, his hand at his side, still holding the gun, stood dispassionately observing them.

The three men watched as Sarah struggled to her feet. Laurie walked to her, her hands outstretched. They stood looking at each other for a long minute. Then in a firm voice Laurie said, "It's over, Sarah. It's really over."

~ 117

Two weeks later, Sarah and Justin stood at the security check in Newark Airport and watched Laurie walk down the corridor to the gate for United Airlines flight 19 to San Francisco.

"Being near Gregg, finishing college at UCSF is the best possible choice for her now," Justin assured Sarah as he noticed the worried expression that replaced her bright goodbye smile.

"I know it is. She can play a lot of golf, get her game back, get her degree. Be independent and still have Gregg there for her. They're so good together. She doesn't need me anymore, at least not in the same way."

At the bend in the corridor, Laurie turned, smiled and blew a kiss.

She's different, Sarah thought. Confident, sure of herself. I've never seen her look that way before.

She pressed her fingertips to her lips and returned it.

As Laurie's slender form disappeared around the corner, Sarah felt Justin's arm comfortingly around her shoulders.

"Save the rest of the kisses for me, luv."

About the Author

MARY HIGGINS CLARK is the beloved author of fourteen novels. Her bestsellers include *Moonlight Becomes You; Silent Night; Remember Me; I'll Be Seeing You; A Cry in the Night; Weep No More, My Lady; Stillwatch; The Cradle Will Fall; A Stranger is Watching;* and *Where Are the Children?* Her three collections of short stories are entitled *The Anastasia Syndrome & Other Stories, The Lottery Winner: Alvirah and Willy Stories* and *My Gal Sunday: Henry and Sunday Stories.*

Her books are worldwide bestsellers and she has received the Grand Prix de Literature of France.

She was the 1987 president of the Mystery Writers of America and, in 1988, Chairman of the International Crime Congress held in New York.

Mary Higgins Clark has five children and six grandchildren. She lives in Saddle River, New Jersey.